BY THE AUTHOR OF "CHARLEY WAG"

FANNY WHITE

AND HER FRIEND

JACK RAWLINGS

A Romance of

A YOUNG LADY THIEF AND A BOY BURGLAR

INCLUDING

THEIR ARTFUL DODGES; THEIR STRUGGLES AND ADVENTURES
PRISONS AND PRISON-BREAKINGS; THEIR UPS AND DOWNS
AND THEIR TRICKS UPON TRAVELLERS, ETC., ETC.

With Twenty-one Original Illustrations

LONDON

GEORGE VICKERS, ANGEL COURT, STRAND

CRINOLINE.

The following Prints, Illustrative of Crinoline, are Published, and to be had, beautifully Coloured, of

W. H. J. CARTER, Printseller & Bookseller,

12, REGENT STREET, PALL MALL, LONDON.

Crinoline in Belgravia,	4	6
Crinoline at Cremorne,	4	6
Crinoline in Hyde Park,	4	6
Crinoline at Brompton,	4	6
Crinoline in St. John's Wood,	4	6
Crinoline at the Sea Side,	4	6
The Pretty Horsebreaker	3	6
Our Husbands—Our Fathers,	2	6
Our Wives—Our Mothers,	2	6
Our Grandsons—Our Grandfathers,	2	6
Our Grandaughters—Our Grandmothers,	2	6
The Model Husband,	2	6
The Muddled Husband,	2	6
Crinoline in the Water,	3	6
Crinoline in Japan,	2	6
Crinoline in Danger,	2	6
Crinoline going Out, " Good bye, Tiny dear "	2	6
Cross Readings near Charing Cross	1	6
Crinoline—Fashion gains custom,	2	6
Crinoline.—The Progress	2	6
Crinoline.—The Surprise,	2	6
The Comic Act of Parliament against Crinoline,	0	6
The Social Parliament, by ALBERT SMITH, (full of fun),	0	6
The Philanthropic Divine and the Lady waiting for a 'Bus	2	6
Crinoline on board the Great Eastern Steamer, 4 Beautifully Coloured Plates, each	3	6
Crinoline at the Pic-Nic,	3	6
Crinoline—Too Fast to Last	3	6
Crinoline—At Last too Fast,	3	6
Crinoline—Clearing the Barrier,	2	6
Official Regulations on Female Dress (such fun)	0	6
The Crinoline Cooper,	2	6
Crinoline at the High Style,	2	6
Unexpected ascent of Crinoline,	2	6
The Cat asleep under the Crinoline,	2	6
" What can they be looking at, Topsy ?"	2	6
" It's no use, Tiny,"	2	6
" It is to be done, Tiny; I hope no one is looking,"....	2	6
Crinoline, or Questions unanswered,	2	6
John Bull running down Crinoline,	2	6
Crinoline, a Scene at the West End,	2	6
Crinoline, (A Smack amongst the Rocks)	2	6
Crinoline in the Ball Room,	2	6
A Wedding Present of Crinoline Service,	2	6
The Book of Amusement and Laughter, 30 Plates,	2	6
The Beerometer,	1	0
Musjid, Winner of the Derby, 1859,	9	0
" My Name is Norval," 21 Coloured Plates,	2	6
Doing the Gun Trick, Coloured,	2	6
The Attack by Baron de Vidil on his Son,	1	6
The Murderous Affray between Roberts & Major Murray	2	6
The Great Fire at London Bridge,—coloured	1	6
The Dreadful Railway Accident,	1	6
Fun,—Our Rifle Volunteers, 16 Coloured Plates,	2	6

All sent carefully packed, Post Free, on receipt of Stamps or Post Office Order, by

W. H. J. CARTER,

12, REGENT STREET, PALL MALL,—S.W.

CONTENTS.

LIST OF ILLUSTRATIONS.

FANNY WHITE

AND HER FRIEND

JACK RAWLINGS.

AWFUL POSITION OF A YOUNG LADIES SCHOOL.

CHAPTER I.

SHOWS HOW AN EXTREMELY UNPLEASANT ACCIDENT HAPPENED TO MISS MACSPARTAN'S YOUNG LADIES, AND THE EFFECTS OF THAT ACCIDENT UPON MISS FANNY WHITE; AND ALSO DESCRIBES WHAT A VERY NICE YOUNG GENTLEMAN WAS MASTER JACK RAWLINGS, AND NARRATES THE GREAT SERVICE HE RENDERED TO THE UNFORTUNATE MISS STIGGINS.

"HELP! help! help!"

A piercing shriek! A chorus of twenty-one maidens in dire distress!

Twenty-one maidens of various ages and sizes, the youngest five, the eldest fifty! Twenty-one unprotected spinsters carried away against their will, screaming frantically for the assistance which came not to save them from destruction!

An awful thing would have been such a disaster to befal any twenty-one maiden ladies, but all the more so when these ladies happened to belong to the most select of all select academies—that superintended by Miss MacSpartan, of Virginia House, Bow.

"Help, help, help!" shrieked the twenty-one maidens.

"We shall all be robbed!" cried the rich parlour boarder, who was known to have muffins and marmalade for breakfast every morning, and was believed to sleep at nights with a patchwork coverlet of bank-notes over her, and a bag of sovereigns for her pillow.

"We shall all be murdered!" exclaimed the romantic young lady who took in the *Halfpenny Journal* on the sly

"We shall all be ruined!" groaned the eldest spinster teacher.

"Hold your tongue, Miss Stiggins!" said Miss MacSpartan to the last speaker, in awful tones of reproof, "you don't know what you're talking about."

"Help, help, help!" shrieked all the ladies together, this time louder than ever.

Miss MacSpartan made up her mind to die defending the life and honour of her pupils, and wondered how it would read in the newspapers. Miss Stiggins thought of the young midshipman, whose portrait, together with a pale wisp of yellow hair, she treasured in her writing-desk, and wondered if he felt as she did that moment when he went sinking down, down through the briny waters of the Atlantic.

Crash!

Six of the twenty-one maidens shot violently forward into the laps of half-a-dozen others. Five charming spinsters found themselves suddenly seated in a hay-field. Miss Stiggins was thrown violently against Miss MacSpartan, to the serious derangement of the latter lady's head-dress, which was false, and the former's teeth, which were not her own.

"Pompey! Help! Stop them!" shrieked the lady-principal of Virginia House, incoherently; but Pompey, like a prudent black footman as he was, pretended not to hear, and sat disconsolately in the dust by the roadside rubbing his damaged plush.

And what was it which caused all this disturbance? What had occasioned so many maidens, brought up at an establishment where the comforts of a home were combined with the best instruction (see Miss MacSpartan's advertisement), to lose their centre of gravity?

Only the upsetting of a coach.

And why was the coach upset?

Because Stubbings the driver had had just a trifle more liquor than was good for him.

And how came he to drink too much?

Because he had been kept waiting. And who had kept him?

Who? why, Fanny White!

The midsummer holidays were near at hand, and Miss MacSpartan, according to custom, had arranged the annual treat for her pupils, which in this instance consisted of a picnic in Epping Forest.

She had hired a strange vehicle, which resembled in appearance a stage coach cut in half, and part of a hay waggon inserted in the middle and covered with a black waterproof covering. She had engaged a driver, warranted steady and sober, who now lay on his back in a dry ditch roaring forth scraps of bacchanalian songs, which, if she had only understood them, would have brought her black front with sorrow to the grave. She had provided hampers of provisions, consisting mainly, it must be confessed, of the rejected scraps of the week, covered over with a two-inch layer of flour and water, supposed by the uninitiated to be pastry. She had herself superintended the mixing of the lemonade, and with her own fair hands had packed up no less than two bottles of home-made currant-wine.

The ride from Bow to the forest had been delightful, the day had been lovely, the pie had been found filling, and everyone but Miss Stiggins, who had sat down too carelessly after the cattle had been there, had enjoyed themselves.

But, alas, for Miss MacSpartan, she little knew what cruel Fate had in store for her!

The time came for going home again, and the greater part of the interesting spinsters were gathered under the wings of the lady-principal, but there was one yet missing.

Miss Fanny White was nowhere to be found!

Miss Stiggins suggested she had lost her way, and would drag out a miserable existence amongst the trees of Epping, subsisting on blackberries and roots.

The romantic young lady whispered that she had eloped.

Another pupil drew a dismal picture of Fanny being dragged damp and cold from some slimy pond, with the best part of her boots and embroidery eaten away by tadpoles.

Time dragged on, and the sun went down, and the wind came up, and the twenty maiden ladies gathered closer round their protectress shivering in their summer muslins,

wondering and surmising beneath their breath as to what *could* have become of Fanny.

But, at length, when every one had given her up, Miss Fanny appeared, looking very flushed and rather tumbled. Most likely she had been running and was out of breath, and furze bushes, as everybody know, play the very deuce with muslin frocks and white petticoats.

"Where have you been?" asked Miss MacSpartan.

"In the wood," replied Miss White.

"What have you been doing?" asked Miss MacSpartan.

"Looking for you, ma'am," replied Miss Fanny; and so she had for almost five minutes. As to the other hour and three-quarters we will talk about that presently.

Miss MacSpartan was of the same opinion.

"We'll talk about this presently," said she; "we had better go home now, Miss Stiggins; where's the coachman?"

Now Stubbings, the coachman, had long since got tired of flicking the flies off the horses' tails, and had adjourned to the nearest public-house for "half a pint."

But half pints are very deceptive, and though Stubbings never ordered more than that quantity at a time, yet the pewter measure was so often filled that almost before he knew it his head was heavy and his pocket light.

Miss MacSpartan could not be expected to comprehend the various phases of intoxication. She noticed a peculiarity in the coachman's walk, but that she put down to age; she noticed an indistinctness in his utterance, but that she attributed to his want of education; she noticed that he pressed her hand in helping her into the vehicle, but that she thought was no more than civility, and considering it was many, many years since even a coachman had pressed her hand, perhaps she was right not to take notice of it publicly.

All her young ladies being stowed carefully and tightly in and on the coach, Stubbings mounted the box and started homeward.

The first mile was smooth and satisfactory, the second was rougher and noisier, but when the third commenced the jolting and shaking of the rickety old vehicle first made Miss MacSpartan fear something had gone wrong.

Faster and faster, noisier and noisier! The patriarchal coach shook as if no two pieces could hold together. From one side of the road to the other it staggered and reeled.

Then from the inside came forth the heartrending cries for help; then the twenty-one maiden ladies raised their voices and besought assistance, while their Jehu, shouting and swearing like a whole regiment of troopers, lashed the horses and urged them onward, till driving on to a bank, the crazy vehicle lazily rolled on to one side, tumbling the ladies over, within and without, like so many ninepins.

It certainly was a critical position for twenty-one maidens to be placed in, for Stubbings, being too far gone to rise from the ditch, and the blooming spinsters knowing nothing about cutting the traces, or sitting on the horse's heads, the playful quadrupeds were amusing themselves by kicking the coach to pieces, which perhaps, after all, was the very best thing they could do.

But assistance was at hand, though they knew it not; a strong arm was enlisted in their service, and forced black Pompey to do his duty. The traces were severed, the horses quieted and tied to some neighbouring trees, without their knowledge, for as all the young ladies, struggling pell-mell and any end uppermost inside, were letting off periodical screams of surpassing shrillness, it is not likely that they would be able to hear any other sound, while as for the maidens who had been lodged on the haycocks, they were mostly of tender years, and were still endeavouring to make up their minds whether they should laugh or cry.

Presently, however, those inside became conscious that by some means the horses had been quieted, and then a general attempt was made at the arrangement of skirts and the subduing of obstreperous crinolines.

"This is all your fault, you base girl!" said Miss MacSpartan to Fanny, as she put on her front hind part before.

But just then a sudden crash was heard, which drew forth another piercing scream from all, and through a broken window in what had been the side, but was now the top of the coach, peered a handsome, good-tempered-looking young gentleman's face.

"Can I be of any service? Let me help some of you out," said a voice which accorded well with the face.

Miss MacSpartan was shocked. "*It's a male!*" she cried, and struggled desperately with her disarranged flounces.

Fanny White made bold to reply to the strange young gentleman's question in the affirmative, and in another moment he had tight hold of her hand, and she actually had the audacity to plant her foot, and a very pretty little one it was too, on the revered shoulder of Miss MacSpartan, and suffer herself to be drawn through the broken window.

It was all very well, of course, for the gentleman to assist Fanny from the overturned coach, and very kind and proper, but there certainly did not seem to be any good reason why when she was safely through, he should put his arm round her waist and whisper something in her ear, and why she, instead of being indignant and repulsing him, should whisper in return something else; however, such was the case. And what they whispered we shall perhaps know presently.

A minute afterwards he was back at the coach-window ready to assist all in turn.

One by one the whole of the spinsters were helped from their perilous position.

Miss Stiggins was the last. She sat huddled up in one corner of the ruined vehicle, vainly endeavouring to re-fit the teeth which Miss MacSpartan's Roman nose had dislodged at the first concussion occasioned by the overthrow.

"Now, madam, let me assist you," said the obliging young gentleman—which remark referred not to the teeth, but to her extrication from the coach.

Miss Stiggins shook her head dismally, and looked with terror at the height she would have to clamber, for no friendly shoulder was there to form a stepping-stone to the high-up window.

"Now then, ma'am," said the youth a second time, and Miss Stiggins essayed to mount, but fell back again.

"I can't do it," she cried despairingly.

"Miss Stiggins, I'm ashamed of you!" said Miss Mac-Spartan, reprovingly; and the young ladies, with the exception of Miss Fanny White, gathered round the coach to see their teacher's egress.

And what became of Fanny? We shall see presently.

The handsome young stranger, seeing Miss Stiggins' dilemma, lowered himself into the coach, and entreated the elderly spinster to make use of his shoulder to mount to the upper regions, and at the same time Miss MacSpartan stretched forth her long bony hands to assist her head teacher to *terra firma*.

Miss Stiggins refused to avail herself of the stranger's offer, and obstinately sat in one corner of the vehicle, her false teeth chattering in her head, and deaf alike to the remonstrances and entreaties of her proprietress.

The fact was, in the first place, Miss Stiggins had large ungainly feet; in the second, her boots were patched and unsightly; and in the third, a sudden crack had warned her that the sustaining tape of one of her under-garments had given way; and it was owing to these circumstances she declined the proffered aid of the unknown.

At last, however, summoning up courage to entreat the stranger to close his eyes, she managed to mount upon his back, then Miss MacSpartan caught her thin arms in her skeleton fingers, and hauled with all her strength, and her young helper at the same time suddenly straightening himself, she flew up through the broken window something like a Congreve rocket, and landed shaken and discomposed, but otherwise safely, on the green sward, amidst the laughter of all the pupils of Virginia House, Bow.

Then the strange young gentleman who had arrived so opportunely scrambled out by himself and raised his hat to Miss MacSpartan, and presented her with a small piece of flimsy cardboard, upon which was inscribed, in the minutest letters—

"*Mr. John Rawlings.*"

Then Miss MacSpartan bowed and thanked him for the service he had rendered her in tones of Johnsonian grandeur, and then Mr. John Rawlings put his hand to his heart and bowed in a manner it would have done Lord Chesterfield good to witness, and the pupils of Virginia House gathered round and expressed to each other in whispers their high approbation of the appearance and manners of the strange young gentleman.

"Dear me!" cried Miss MacSpartan, suddenly—the idea for the first time occurring to her—"by what means are we to return to the Academy?"

It was a question not easily answered, and the more imaginative pupils pictured to themselves the delights of camping out for the night under the trees and getting their breakfast the next morning off herbs, roots, and berries.

"If you will allow me, madam," said Mr. Rawlings, "I will mount one of your horses and ride over to Woodford, where I shall doubtless be able to obtain some conveyance for yourself and charming charges."

"The idea, sir, is worthy of you!" replied the lady; "I will thank you much if you will put it into execution."

Mr. Rawlings with another bow hurried into the wood where the horses had been fastened and was soon hidden from view by a leafy screen, but presently the twenty-one spinsters heard the sounds of horse's hoofs galloping along the high road in the direction of Woodford, and disposed themselves in groups awaiting patiently the return of their handsome courier.

Miss MacSpartan sat quietly in the dusk, twiddling her thumbs, and trying to think of some means to help to pass the time, when the idea occurred to her that it was a favourable opportunity to improve the occasion by giving Fanny a severe lecture upon the impropriety of her conduct that afternoon.

"Miss White," she commenced.

But not seeing anything of Miss White, she paused here and turned round at her young ladies; but it was too dark to distinguish faces at any distance.

"Miss White," she repeated; "I desire you will answer me!"

Still no answer.

The rest of the pupils looked blankly into each other's faces, and presently arrived at the conclusion that Fanny White was not there, and expressed their conviction to the lady-principal.

At first she refused to credit them; but when her own eyes convinced her of the truth of their statement, she was completely dumbfounded, but before she could speak general attention was called to Pompey, the black footman, who came running up to the circle of damsels as fast as his legs would carry him, his tongue lolling several inches from his mouth, and his eyes wide open and staring, as if with mingled surprise and fright.

Halting in front of Miss MacSpartan, he attempted to speak, but his haste had been too great, and he stood before her panting and blowing like an over-fed porpoise in crimson and gold, surrounded by twenty curious and inquiring spinsters.

"Oh, Miss! Oh, ma'am!" he gasped at last. "They've bolted!"

CHAPTER II.

MORE ABOUT MR. JACK RAWLINGS—A GOOD DEAL OF MYSTERY, AND A CLOTHES-BASKET.

WHO was Jack Rawlings?

If you had asked his schoolfellows at Mr. K. V. Kanem's Collegiate Establishment, they would have told you the boy who never went home for the holidays.

If you had asked Mr. Jabez Dallett, solicitor, he would have answered, always supposing it to be possible to get an answer from a lawyer without having to pay six-and-eight pence for it, that there were some things best not inquired into; and then he would have shaken his wicked old head, and laid his dirty finger upon his rubicund nose, and tried to look very knowing.

If you had asked Mr. Jack Rawlings himself, he would have sighed, and said, "Goodness knows," and looked rather unhappy for a few seconds, when some merry thought would strike him, and he would look up with a happy smile upon his handsome face, and turn aside the question with ome good-humoured joke.

Mr. K. V. Kanem's collegiate establishment for young gentlemen was, according to rule, situated next door to Miss MacSpartan's select academy for young ladies, and to that gentleman's house, one fine October evening, about ten years previous to the commencement of this story, was brought a pale-faced little urchin six or seven years old.

The gentleman who accompanied him gave his name as Mr. Jabez Dallett, and introduced the boy to Mr. Kanem as Jack Rawlings, the son of one of his clients, who was desirous of having his offspring well educated in England during his absence abroad.

Mr. Kanem asked for references. Mr. Dallett pulled out a greasy leather pocket-book and paid the first quarter's schooling in advance, and Mr. Kanem professed himself perfectly satisfied.

This was all he knew concerning our hero.

Mr. Dallett occasionally wrote to the schoolmaster when he forwarded the quarterly money to ask how the young gentleman was progressing, and received in return the most wonderful accounts of the advances he made in his studies; but neither the solicitor nor any one else ever called to see the boy, and Mr. Kanem's house was the place he looked upon as home.

Year after year he remained there, till from a pale-faced lustrous-eyed little boy he grew to be a handsome good-tempered youth, the head of the school both in doors in his studies, and out of doors in all athletic sports and exercises.

But at a comparatively early age, what Mr. Kanem called his "fatal propensities" began to develope themselves, by which he meant to imply, that his looking through a hole in the playground palings, at Miss MacSpartan's young ladies disporting themselves upon the grass-plat, would by degrees lead him to ruin—perhaps the gallows.

Certain it is that Mr. John Rawlings viewed the softer sex generally with great admiration, but it was not till Miss Fanny White became an inmate of Virginia House that he particularized.

Decidedly he showed his good taste in selecting her for the especial object of his adoration. She was more than pretty, and, what was singular, in height and general appearance she was so like him that anyone would have taken them for brother and sister. They had the same coloured eyes, the same coloured hair, the same pink and white complexion; indeed, had they changed clothes, I doubt much whether either Mr. K. V. Kanem or Miss MacSpartan would either of them have discovered it.

It was perhaps, however, more owing to Fanny's masculine style than anything approaching feminine in the appearance of our heroine.

The acquaintance between the two was made in this wise.

One fine afternoon, Jack Rawlings going to his accustomed peep-hole, to ascertain what Miss MacSpartan's young ladies might be doing, was startled on applying his right eye to the crevice, to find his view limited to the left eye of Fanny White, but being naturally of a bold temperament, and, moreover, calculating that so bright an eye could not be set in a plain face, made bold to address it, and the pretty little rosebud of a mouth connected with the bright optic as boldly replied.

Thus commenced this friendship. Pyramus-and-Thisbe-like, they whispered their vows through a chink, and, at times passed through more substantial tokens of affection in the way of letters intricately folded, and small presents of cheap jewellery, sweetstuff, and plum-cake; and so stood affairs a month before the famous picnic at Epping Forest.

The month, however, brought about strange alterations with regard to Jack Rawlings.

One day he received a message that Mr. Kanem desired to see him in the library, and thither he repaired without delay.

"Mr. Rawlings," commenced his instructor.

"Hullo!" thought our hero, "what's in the wind now? *Mister* Rawlings!"

"Mr. Rawlings, I have this day received information, which induces me to believe, that after the conclusion of the term you will no longer remain a pupil in this establishment."

"He can't have found out about Fanny?" thought Jack; but he merely bowed his head to Mr. Kanem, who continued,

"You will leave here, my young friend, carrying with you the good wishes of all——"

"Where am I going to?" interrupted Jack.

"Home, I suppose."

"Home!"

"Yes; why not?"

"I didn't know I'd got one."

"Don't you know who your parents are?"

"No."

"Have you no friends or relations?"

"No."

"Don't you know Mr. Jabez Dallett?"

"No."

"He has always paid for your schooling; who did you think did that?"

"I never thought about it."

"Dear, dear! this is very remarkable!" said Mr. Kanem,

reflectively, polishing the top of his bald head with a pocket-handkerchief. "Then you don't know where to go when you leave this establishment?"

"I shall go to London," said Jack, without hesitation.

"What to do?"

"I must go and see this old gentleman who has paid for my schooling; perhaps he can tell me something about my affectionate parents."

"Well; perhaps that is the best thing you can do. I will give you his address. Here it is: Mr. Jabez Dallett, Solicitor, No. 44, Otherend-court, Temple."

"Thank you, sir. Perhaps I had better go at once."

"It might be as well."

In half an hour's time John Rawlings was on his road to London for the first time in his life. He had plenty of self-possession, and managed admirably well, and without any particular adventures found his way to Otherend-court, where he was not long in discovering No. 44.

On the door-post was painted, in what had once been white, but was now a yellowish-brown, "First Floor. Mr. Jabez Dallett, Solicitor;" and for this gentleman Master Jack Rawlings inquired, when he had tumbled up the steep flight of stairs which led to the office.

Three dissipated-looking clerks were gathered together discussing something in an undertone, and took not the slightest notice of Jack Rawling's entrance, and even when he inquired for Mr. Dallett, one of the clerks merely turned lazily round, stared at him from top to toe, and then resumed his conversation with his companions.

Jack did not approve of this, and repeated his inquiry in a louder tone.

"I say, Snaggs!" said the man who had stared at him; "I say, Snaggs, he wants the guv'nor!"

"Lor, now, who'd have thought it!" said Mr. Snaggs, derisively.

"Is he in?" asked Jack, rather impatiently.

"I say, Snaggs, is the guv'nor in?"

The trio seemed to consider this a capital joke, and laughed accordingly.

"Snaggs, I want you!" cried a harsh, grating voice from an inner room, and Jack concluded by the way in which the three clerks jumped apart like parched peas, it could belong to none other than Mr. Dallett. Accordingly, when Mr. Snaggs opened the door which hid the head of the firm from the public gaze, our hero followed him in, and remained standing unobserved, while Mr. Dallett, for it was he, gave some orders to his clerk.

When Mr. Snaggs left the room, Jack remained, and met the astonished gaze of Mr. Dallett, who, it will be remembered, had not seen him for something like eleven years.

"Hullo! who the deuce are you?" asked the coarse looking man sitting at the table, his hand grasping at the same time something which looked to Jack very like a life preserver.

"I'm called John Rawlings, but I've come to you to find out my true name."

Mr. Dallett scowled at him for a few seconds from beneath his eyebrows, but when he lifted his face to reply it was covered with smiles and good temper. "What can I do for you, my dear boy?"

"Tell me who my parents are."

"Parents—Dear, dear! Parents I think you said?"

"Yes," said Jack, impatiently; "I suppose I had some."

"Ha, ha, ha! Very good, Mr. Rawlings. Shrewd fellow you are; you wouldn't like to be a lawyer's clerk, would you?"

"Not if I know it," said our hero, with schoolboy earnestness.

"No, of course you wouldn't. Certainly not. What would you like to be?"

"I should like to know who and what my parents are, Mr. Dallett."

"Of course you would. Very natural—very. I'm a great admirer of nature. Ain't you, Mr. Rawlings?"

Jack disregarded the question, and returned to the charge. "Is it true, Mr. Dallett, that you paid for my schooling?"

"No."

"Mr. Kanem told me you did!"

"Well, now, I tell you I didn't. Don't you think I ought to know?"

"Certainly, sir; but how——"

"I sent him the money, if that's what you mean; but as

it was not my own money I sent, I can hardly be said to have paid it. You understand?"

"Whose money was it, then?" asked Jack, eagerly.

"Your own!"

"Mine?"

"Yes."

"You don't happen to have any more of it about you?" said Mr. John Rawlings.

"Yes, I have."

"How much?"

"Fifty pounds!"

Jack rubbed his hands with delight.

"Where did it come from?"

"The same place you did."

"Where was that?"

"Out of a washing-basket!"

"Out of what?"

"A washing-basket!"

"Do you mean to say my mother was a laundress?"

"I know nothing about it, so decline to hazard an opinion."

"Where did the basket come from?"

"I can't say."

"Where did you find it?"

"On my doorstep."

"Well!"

"Well, I heard you squalling inside, but just as I was going to pack you off to the workhouse I saw a note directed to myself, pinned on to the softest part of your body."

"A note! Where is it?"

"Destroyed. It had not any signature, so it doesn't matter. This note contained bank-notes to a considerable amount, and an entreaty that I would see you come to no harm. My first thought was to let you take your chance, but finding a postscript begging me to accept a twenty pound note for my trouble, I changed my mind and the note, sent you off to Mr. Kanem's, and now, considering you old enough to look after yourself, I hand you the balance of the money, the fifty pounds."

"Thank you, sir, but——"

"Good morning, Mr. Rawlings."

"If you would allow me to——"

"Good morning! Take care of yourself."

Our hero left the office. As he did so a smile came over Mr. Dallett's face as he said to himself, "I think such a twister as that is worth an extra pint of porter. Lor, how he took it all in!"

CHAPTER III.

CHIEFLY CONCERNING AN INFURIATED FATHER, AN APOLOGETIC SCHOOLMISTRESS, AND A RUNAWAY SPINSTER; WITH SOME ACCOUNT OF AN EXCITING CHASE AND A GLORIOUS CAPTURE.

POMPEY gasped for breath for some seconds, during which time the twenty-one maiden ladies formed a circle round him, and stared in wonder at his ebony countenance.

"Oh, Missy 'Spartan," stuttered he at length; "oh, golly!"

The lady-principal frowned in a condemnatory way at the exclamation, and Pompey continued,

"Oh, Missy lady, I see 'em go! Young mas'r he whip him up; young Missy she held on by him neck. Ouf! Off they go!"

"Do you mean to imply that Miss Fanny White has gone off on horseback with that young man?"

"Yes, Missy 'Spartan; that's him!"

"Gone off with a young man! and with her arm round——! Oh dear, dear! what a sad thing for Virginia House. The artful little jade! If I only catch her, I'll—I'll——Run, Pompey! Get on the horse. Gallop after them directly; bring them back! And her father coming this very evening to take her home!"

Pompey was not great on horseback; indeed, he looked upon those useful animals as dangerous creatures, nevertheless, at his mistress's command, he determined to make his first attempt at riding.

After a few trivial accidents, such as mounting with his face to the tail, throwing his leg over with such force as to bring him on the ground again upon the other side, and so on, he managed to obtain a seat upon the saddleless back of an old grey mare, and then clinging to the mane to urge her into some semblance of a trot

Miss MacSpartan was metaphorically sitting upon thorns until his return, but when at length he did appear in the distance riding by the side of a post-chaise, hope returned to her virgin heart, and she rehearsed to herself the speech she would make to the offending girl, whom in fancy she saw kneeling at her feet and entreating pardon.

Alas for her fancies! They were doomed to be without the slightest foundation in fact.

Pompey had ridden over to Woodford, but without seeing a trace of the fugitives, but at the inn there he learnt that a young lady and gentleman had arrived there a short time previously, but had left again immediately in a post-chaise for London.

Now Pompey had had, according to his own idea, quite sufficient riding for one day, and decided not to follow the couple any further. The thought however struck him that Miss MacSpartan might wish to return to Virginia House with her pupils, so took upon himself to bring back to the depths of the forest the other post-chaise of the Woodford Inn.

By its aid, and in detachments the twenty spinsters, damp, dejected, crushed, and limp, were conveyed back to the delightful suburb of Bow, the last load bearing Miss MacSpartan and some of the elder pupils.

"Oh, please Miss, an old gentleman by the name of White has been waiting to see you and his daughter this ever so long, and he's a walking up and down the drawing-room carpet like the lions at the S'logical Gardings, and a muttering to hisself like anything!"

These were the first words Miss MacSpartan heard on arriving at her own door, and I think you will allow they were not the very pleasantest she could have wished to greet her.

She hurried to her own room to re-arrange her disordered front, and make herself more presentable.

Mr. White was a stockbroker; Mr. White was large of limb, rosy of countenance, and toddling of gait; his hair was long and quite white, his teeth were short and quite black, his body was round, his head was square, his hands were large, his eyes small, and his general appearance was that of a man well-to-do in the world, with a comfortable balance at his banker's, and several dozen of fine old tawny port stowed away in his cellars.

His rosy face was assuming a purple hue of indignation as he toddled backwards and forwards over about three square feet of carpet, muttering to himself words which would have sent the proprietress of the house into fits had she heard them.

At length Miss MacSpartan appeared, wearing her newest and most fascinating head-dress, and her equally fascinating, but not quite so new, smile.

"Pretty goings on—fine goings on, indeed!" said the old gentleman, continuing his walk, and only answering the deep curtsey of Miss MacSpartan by a heavy lopsided motion of his head and shoulders—a cross between a familiar nod and a respectful bow.

The lady did not exactly know what reply to make, so simpered, and tried to put herself into an attitude.

"This is a fine time of night to bring home your young girls, isn't it?" said Mr. White, stopping before the lady, and looking her full in the face.

"We should have been sooner, sir, but we met with an accident."

"Oh, of course, of course Look at me—I never met with an accident, and I've lived in the world some sixty years!"

Gradually and tremblingly Miss MacSpartan broke the news to the old gentleman, who received the tidings with a burst of passion directed against picnics, schools, forests, and, in short, everything connected with the day and its grand disaster.

Miss MacSpartan pretended not to hear any of the bad words which proceeded from the lips of the infuriated parent, and overwhelmed him with apologies and excuses for her own share in the matter. She made but one practical suggestion, and that was, the chaise being still at the door, that Mr. White should instantly start in pursuit.

"Why the devil didn't you think of that before?" he growled, as he pushed roughly past her, hurried to the street door, and squeezed himself into the post-chaise.

The present of a guinea and a few words to the post-boy were sufficient to make him comprehend what was required of him, and in a few moments the old gentleman was being whirled along in the direction of London at a spanking rate.

Now it so happened that the runaway couple had met with a series of delays, and on arriving in the neighbourhood of Bow, being unwilling to rattle past the doors of Virginia House through fear of discovery, they had made a considerable round, and consequently were but little in advance of their pursuer, who, foaming, fretting, and swearing, was every minute endangering his life by popping his irascible bald head out of the window in the hope of obtaining a glimpse of the chaise of those he was chasing.

At length his perseverance was rewarded, for in the extreme distance he saw a post-chaise, which he made no doubt contained the objects of his pursuit, jogging steadily along.

"Another guinea if you overtake them in five minutes!" shouted the old gentleman, perfectly crimson with passion; and the post-boy dug his spurs into the aged quadrupeds, and urged them to a speed which must have astonished them pretty considerably.

Fortune favoured the post-boy, for the chaise they were endeavouring to overtake appeared, if anything, to slacken its pace as they approached.

"Stop—stop!—you thief—you villain—you ravisher!" screamed Mr. White, leaning the upper half of his body out of the carriage, and shaking his fist at those in advance.

The driver of the other chaise turned round as if in doubt, and then pulled in his horses and waited quietly by the roadside till the other drew up.

"You—you—infernal young scoundrel—you ruffian—you —you——!" cried Miss Fanny's papa, almost inarticulate with rage, as he looked in the chaise and saw, seated by the side of Jack Rawlings, a young lady dressed in the clothes his daughter was accustomed to wear, and with a thick veil drawn over her features "And you, miss! you little brazen hussy! Come home with me!—Get out of that seducer's carriage!—I'll teach you to run away from school!"

"And who the deuce are you, sir?" asked Jack Rawlings, with the greatest coolness in the world.

"Who am I?—who am I? You reprobate, I'm this artful jade's father. And what have you got to say to that?"

"Only that I'm jolly glad you're not mine. I dislike a man who can't keep his temper."

"Take care, sir—have a care—I know you, and you shall suffer for this. I know who you are!"

"The deuce you do! It's more than I do myself," said Jack.

"Come out, hussy," said old White, addressing himself to his daughter.

"Well, my dear," said Jack, speaking to the lady by his side, "if that weak-minded and abusive old party is your guv'nor, perhaps you'd better go with him." And he leant over and whispered a few words in her ear; then, to the further increase of the rage of paterfamilias, a loud kiss echoed through the carriage.

"Come out, you baggage!" and Mr. White, unable to stand it any longer, half dragged his daughter, sobbing bitterly, from the side of Jack Rawlings, and thrust her into the chaise in which he had pursued them.

"Good night, Mr. White!" said Jack, politely raising his hat; "take care of your daughter, she's one in a thousand; she'll make a good wife to anyone thinking of going into the matrimonial line."

The postilion of Jack's chaise bent over the horse and laughed; and Mr. White's daughter pressed her handkerchief to her face, while her shoulders shook with the poignancy of her grief, and choking, half-stifled sobs came from beneath her thick veil.

"Good night, Mr. White!" said Jack, a second time.

The old man growled out a curse.

"The same to you, sir—drive on, post-boy." And the chaises parted, the one containing Jack going on towards London, while Mr. White and his charge were conveyed back to Bow.

It is not to be wondered at that the irascible old father, seeing his daughter whimpering and crying in one corner of the carriage, and remembering the expense and trouble to which he had been put, should not have been in the best of tempers.

First of all he relieved himself by giving vent to a long string of oaths and execrations, and then he proceeded to read his daughter a long moral lecture upon the crime she

had committed, but she sat patiently, never answering a word, and only showing signs of life by the occasional heavings of her shoulders.

"Answer me, miss, directly! How dare you sit there blubbering like a great fool?"

Still no answer.

"Can't you speak, you jade?"

No answer being made to any of his appeals, Mr. White, to his shame be it recorded, so far forgot himself as to raise his hand and strike his daughter a tolerably sharp blow on the ears.

Then came an answer, but neither in the tone nor the words he had anticipated.

"I say, measter; come, none of that now!" said a deep-toned *male* voice, at the same time that a couple of horny fists projected from beneath the shawl, and placed themselves in a pugilistic attitude of defence.

The old man was completely taken aback, and certainly it was rather a surprise for him.

"Who the devil are you, eh?"

"I'm post-boy at the Woodford Inn. Excuse me, measter, but who's the fool now? He, he, he!"

This was too much for old White, for his powers of endurance were decidedly limited, so, seizing the unfortunate post-boy by the back of the neck and a bunch of his petticoat, he opened the chaise-door—they were luckily going up hill, and slowly at the time—and by a vigorous push, and a well-timed kick, sent him flying into the dusty road.

Even then the post-boy was not beaten, for, rising from his low position, and adjusting what portions of dress still remained to him, he called out at the top of his voice—

"I tell you what, old fellow, I'm jiggered if I don't have you up for assaulting an unprotected female!"

And where was Fanny, after all?

Astride one of the horses in a neat postilion's dress, she was directing the chaise which contained Jack Rawlings towards London by the shortest road, and with the greatest speed. And uncommonly pretty she looked perched across the great quadruped, and very well her leathers became her; and Jack felt more and more pleased at what he had done, and did not for a single moment regret the hole this little affair had made in his fifty pounds.

CHAPTER IV.

CONCERNING THE DISINTERESTED OFFER OF THE GENTLEMAN WITH THE DONKEY-CART, AND THE HOUSE WHERE FANNY WHITE AND HER FRIEND JACK RAWLINGS ULTIMATELY OBTAINED SHELTER FOR THE NIGHT.

"JACK!" cried Fanny, turning round, and looking in at the window of the post-chaise, "where am I to drive to? We're just entering London, and I don't know which way to turn."

This was rather a poser, for Jack saw at once that driving to an hotel with Fanny for post-boy must eventually lead to discovery. Suddenly a bright idea struck him.

"Do you see such a thing as a dark lane about here?" asked he of his pretty postilion.

"Yes, there's one just by as black as ink. But what then?"

"Do you think you could manage to upset the chaise?"

"Good gracious, what do you mean?"

"Can you do it?"

"I don't know, but I'll try."

"All right! Don't hurt yourself. You'll find a ditch the softest place to fall in."

Jingling and crashing, Fanny turned the creaking old vehicle sharply round the corner, and in less time than it takes to write these words, the chaise was lying on its side, and Fanny was picking herself out of the ditch, which happened, fortunately, to be tolerably dry.

"That was capitally managed," said Jack, approvingly, struggling through the chaise-window; "now for your traps." And by dint of pulling and hauling the few articles of clothing Fanny had been able to pack up were extracted, and Jack, leaving the plunging horses to their fate, shouldered the packages, and the couple prepared to accomplish the remainder of their journey on foot.

They trudged on merrily enough for some distance, till Jack found the burthen he had undertaken by no means a light one, and hailed with delight a feeble glimmering in the distance reflected on the sign of a public-house.

"That will do for to-night, I think," said he, eyeing it approvingly, as he rapped at the door.

"Hullo!" cried a gruff voice inside. "Who's there?"

"Travellers!"

"How is it outside?"

"Open the door. Look sharp, for we're tired!"

"You're not coming in here. We don't want no tramps."

"Let be!" cried a shrill woman's voice, "I'll see who they are." And the door was opened a few inches, and a stream of light issued full upon the travellers.

"Well, what is it?" asked the shrill voice.

"I and my—my brother—are walking to London, but want a béd here for the night."

"Your *brother*, eh? He's a funny brother, I'm thinking," and a long bony finger pointed at Fanny's postilion dress, which in the upset, without her knowledge, had been considerably torn, and revealed rather more of her form about the shoulders than is customary for ladies, even at public balls, to display.

"Be off, you baggage!" continued the woman; "what do you take this place for? I'd have you know it's as respectable an inn as you'll find this side London. Be off! or I'll set the dogs at you."

There was no help for it, the door was slammed in their faces, and the two runaways resumed their march a trifle less cheerful, it must be confessed, than when they started.

The first thing of course was to repair the dilapidations in Fanny's dress, in which Jack rendered material service, and just as it was completed a noise of wheels was heard, and a loud voice carolling forth a popular street song, made itself far more audible than melodious.

"Here's a chance," thought Jack, as the wheels approached, and proved to be attached to a light donkey-cart, driven by a gentleman of shabby exterior, whose head was surmounted by a rough fur cap, which, as he neared Jack and his companion, he removed in order to scratch his red hair with greater ease to himself.

"Well, my young fly-by-nights, what's up?" said he, with easy familiarity.

"We're dead beat," replied Jack; "can you give us a lift?"

"Where do you come from?"

"Far down country way."

"Ah, so I thought. What will you give us for a lift into London?"

"Half-a-crown."

"Can't be done at the price. But look here, young shaver give us hold of those bundles, and I'll carry them for nothing."

"You're a trump!" said Jack, pitching Fanny's female apparel into the cart; and the pair trudged valiantly along by the side of their packages, conversing with the driver.

They did not, however, proceed far together, for the man suddenly rising from his seat, lashed into his donkey unmercifully, upon which the animal started off at a sharp trot, leaving our adventurers far behind, staring blankly into one another's faces as the sound of the wheels died gradually away in the distance.

"Well, that *was* a green thing for me to do!" said Jack, in tones of disgust. "There are all your Sunday petticoats gone for good, Miss Fanny. I must say though, it has one advantage, you'll be forced to keep on boy's clothes, and you look ten times handsomer than ever in them."

Fanny smiled approvingly as she glanced down at her tight fitting leathers and natty boots, and evidently did not think it very dreadful to be condemned to wear them.

"What are we to do for the night?" asked she, after a pause, during which they had walked over the intermediate distance, and were, at last, actually in the great metropolis.

"That's just the question I was asking myself," answered Jack.

"Don't you know?"

"Can't say I do."

"We can't walk about the streets all night."

"I should think not. Hullo! here's a lot of people!"

The pair had unwittingly turned into the flaring, glaring, riotous, world-famed Haymarket, and found themselves, although it was now very late, amongst a larger concourse of people than they would have expected to find even in the daytime.

As they walked up the busy thoroughfare, and glanced in at the brilliantly illuminated *cafés*, and saw strange scenes new to both of them, they felt they had taken the first step towards "seeing life," the ambition which had actuated them to plan the elopement, and had thus far carried them successfully onward.

Many were the kindly notices taken of the two "handsome boys" by ladies gorgeously attired, and with cheeks the colour of peonies, who were amusing themselves with an evening saunter through the west end. Many were the pressing invitations they received; but that was not precisely what they required, so, with the exception of a little occasional "chaff," they passed on their way quietly enough.

It was all very well while the lamps were alight, and the people about; but when night slowly gave way to morning, and the lights flickered and fluttered before they flared up and expired, and the streets became gradually deserted, then it was that the excitement which had kept up the spirits of our two runaways failed, and worn out and exhausted they were glad to seek the shelter of a deep archway, and seat themselves upon some stone steps in its gloomy recess.

Then it was they made the acquaintance of Mrs. Death, an elderly lady, who unknowingly influenced the whole of their future career.

And this is how it happened.

As they sat together beneath the archway, an old woman dressed in the vilest rags came stumbling along, mumbling with her toothless jaws, and muttering to herself.

As she stood beneath a light they obtained a good view of her. Her whole aspect might have been written in three letters—G I N.

In every feature, in her gait, in her speech, in her dress, appeared that one short word, written in legible characters; and as she stood there before them, without being aware of their presence, they shrank closer into the deep shadow, to avoid being seen by her.

Their fear was well-founded, as they learnt afterwards to their cost.

It was not the frightful appearance alone of this hideous beldame which alarmed them—and that was enough to scare an ordinarily courageous person—it was the habit she had of mumbling with her toothless gums, as if in the act of addressing some personage unseen by them; it was the wild, weird, fantastic way in which she moved, the strange way in which her disordered dress was folded round her. Everything, in short, connected with her showed her dissimilar, in all respects, to the ordinary drunken hags who haunt the public streets after nightfall, prowling about in search of plunder, peering with cat-like eyes into the depths of darkness, and occasionally rousing the inhabitants of quiet streets with strange discordant yellings and hootings, like some unrespectable and intoxicated owl out on the spree.

It was in vain Fanny shrank further and further into the shade, clinging to Jack for protection; it was in vain they whispered plans of escape into each other's ears, the lynx-like eyes of the hag soon pierced the darkness in which they sought to envelope themselves, and then, with tottering steps, she approached the archway, blocking up their only means of egress with her tall, ungainly figure.

"Well, my pretty dears!" said she, in a voice resembling the croaking of frogs in a marsh; "and what are you doing here?"

"The streets are as free to us as you, I suppose?" Jack answered.

"Don't be hard on a poor old 'oman as never did you any harm; but as you say, my bonny boy, the streets are free, so I'll just come and sit down alongside of you." And she suited the action to the words, but so arranged herself that they could not well leave the archway unless she rose to let them pass.

Jack allowed her to seat herself in silence; indeed, much as he disliked her close proximity, he did not exactly see in what way he could resent her intrusion.

"There, my dears! now we are all comfortable," continued the old woman. "Lor! who'd have thought we three could not muster enough money between us to pay for a bed. It's a strange world, aint it?"

"It does not follow we couldn't pay for a bed because we happen to be out here."

"Oh! he's a clever boy, a bonny boy, and will have his bit of fun on a poor old 'oman. As if people slept under dry arches for their amusement! Lor, bless you! I know every arch in London, and there ain't one on 'em as comes up to the twopenny rope! Did you ever sleep under the Blackwall railway?"

"No."

"Well, that's about the best free sleeping-ground in London, to my taste, but the trains wakes you up so precious early. Lor! what with them perlice, and "Societies," and "institooshuns," its no easy matter for a poor body to get a good night's rest. I say, you haven't got a piece of bacca about you?"

"No."

"You're sure of that?"

"Quite certain."

"Or a little sixpence to give a poor woman?"

"No."

"Perhaps the other young gentleman in boots would help an old 'oman?" continued she, pertinaciously turning towards Fanny, who had hitherto remained silent.

The truant school-girl, looking into the black darkness, saw only the sparkling eyes of the hag, the pupils distended like a cat's, glaring, as it seemed, ferociously at her.

"Jack," said she, in a whisper to our hero, "give her half-a-crown and get rid of her. She frightens me dreadfully."

The old woman heard the words, low though they were spoken, and her eyes sparkled doubly at the mention of "half-a-crown." Who could they be, she wondered, huddled up there like poverty-stricken beggars, and yet could talk of silver in that off-hand manner?

She determined to find out more about them!

"Look here," said Jack; "do you know of any place where we can get a bed hereabouts?"

"Not without money."

"Psha! Of course not."

"I do know a place close by."

"Where is it?"

"I'll show you, if you like."

"If you do you shall have the sixpence you were asking for."

The old woman mumbled and gnawed at her gums, grinning with delight.

"It ain't much of a place to look at, but it's a stunner to sleep in."

"All right! Which way?"

"Oh, it's a grand bed they've got!" continued the hag, mumbling more to herself than addressing Jack; "a grand bed! There was a young man, nigh a week ago, as went to sleep in it, and he hasn't woke yet!"

"Are you an Irishwoman?" asked Jack, smiling.

"No country owns me," she answered. "East and West, North and South, it's all the same to me; but my words are true. You'll never sleep sounder than in the bed I'll take you to."

She had risen as she spoke, and prepared to lead the way. Fanny clung frightened to her lover.

"Do not go with her," she cried; "it is dreadful! There is something awful in her manner!"

"Pooh!" said Jack, trying to shake off the alarm he felt; "it's all right enough. Come along. Those stones would give us the ague if we stayed there all night."

"Are you coming?" asked the hag.

"Yes; show the way."

For nearly a quarter of an hour the pair followed the grim hag in silence, threading narrow, noisome courts, blindly following through filthy alleys, with narrow, damp, dirty, plague-stricken houses on either side; then emerging for a moment into broader, better lighted thoroughfares, flitting across the road, and again diving into narrow courts and alleys.

At length their conductor stopped before a dismal house, in a poor, unlighted street.

It had evidently once been a fashionable quarter. The houses were large, but dismantled and dilapidated.

Attached to the railings were here and there the remnants of the old extinguishers used formerly to put out the links of aristocratic visitors, and over the fanlights of the doors were strangely and fantastically carved heads and figures. Scarcely a window in the whole row was whole; in some instances attempts had been made to keep out the wind and rain by pasting paper over the fractures, or filling them up with dirty linen; but in the majority of cases the elements had free entrance, and went whistling and whirling through the deserted rooms.

Before one of these houses, which looked, if possible, more grim, battered, and dirty, than its neighbours, the old hag

stayed her course, and motioning the two to remain silent, she tapped in a peculiar way against the shutters.

A light gleamed for a moment through a crevice, and presently the door opened a few inches.

A word or two from their conductress, however, caused it to open wide, and there in the passage stood, awaiting their entrance, a man whose style of beauty was only inferior to that of their guide.

Fanny shrank back dismayed, and even then they would have retreated had they not been quickly and quietly surrounded by a group of five or six men, whose type of face resembled the English bulldog, and who uncouthly but civilly made signs to them to enter.

The moment they stepped into the passage the door closed behind them as noiselessly as it had opened, and they were left in total darkness.

"If you will follow me," said a man's voice in persuasive tones, "I will lead you to the room where my other visitors are assembled. I must apologize for this cold reception, but my waiters are gone to-bed."

As he spoke a bright stream of light darted from the lantern which he carried, and revealed the length of the passage with its green and mildewed walls, from which the paper hung in shreds and patches.

As fearfully they followed their strange landlord, they became aware of sounds of merriment, proceeding, as it seemed to them, from beneath their feet. Shouting and singing with that total disregard to everything which people who have imbibed as much as is good for them, are apt to indulge in.

Down, down they went by the direction of their host, till they arrived at the bottom of a steep flight of steps, green and slippery with damp, when their course was stayed by a massive door, from the other side of which the sounds of uproarious merriment they had heard above appeared to come.

This door their conductor after a few moment's pause unfastened and threw wide open, giving our hero and heroine admittance to a huge cellar brilliantly lighted, and in which a scene was being enacted which the most graphic pen must needs fail in describing.

Men and women in every conceivable stage of intoxication, fought, wrangled, and made love; some scrambling in confusion on the floor; others lying helpless across beer barrels, still grasping in their hands the half-emptied glass; while all were screaming and shouting at the top of their lungs in a way which would have done credit to the "dangerous ward" in Bedlam.

And this was the introduction of Fanny White and her friend Jack Rawlings to their hotel!

CHAPTER V.

RELATES SOME OF THE ADVENTURES WHICH BEFEL FANNY WHITE AND HER FRIEND JACK RAWLINGS IN THEIR "HOTEL," AND ALSO DESCRIBES HOW THEY MADE UP THEIR MINDS TO GO TO BED.

THEY stared aghast for some moments at the hideous scene of drunkenness and debauchery around them, and would fain have beaten an immediate retreat, but the door had been locked and bolted behind them, so that they had but the choice of remaining in the comparatively quiet corner where they stood on entering, or to advance into the midst of the discordantly shrieking and yelling mob, who surrounded the long deal table placed down the centre of the cellar.

The old hag who had brought them to this scene of vice, stood grinning at their side watching every movement upon their part with her cat-like eyes, and mumbling with her toothless gums as usual.

"What a dreadful place!" whispered Fanny to Jack Rawlings; "let us make our escape before they have noticed us."

Jack indicated to the hag, who was watching them intently.

"Surely we can buy her off," said Fanny, understanding what he meant in a moment.

Jack shook his head.

"Why not?"

"Because if they are sure of all the money we have about us, they will not be content to part with us for half!"

"HUSH, FOR HEAVEN'S SAKE! THERE'S A MAN UP THE CHIMNEY!"

"What do you mean?"

"Can't you guess where we are?"

"No. You do not mean they will rob us. Where are we?"

"In a thieves' kitchen!"

Their old conductress had observed the whispering, though even *her* ears had not been acute enough to catch any of the words spoken, but fearing it might mean mischief, a plot perhaps to escape, she quietly but steadily urged them to advance further into the cellar.

They had scarcely advanced half-a-dozen paces when some of the drunken ruffians at the table caught sight of them, and in an instant the whole of the assemblage who were sober enough to rise started to their feet and seized the first available weapon. The hag pushed roughly past Fanny and our hero and stood in a theatrical attitude before them.

"Mother Death!" vociferated some score of lungs in various accents of pleasure and surprise, and letting fall the weapons they had hastily taken up, they welcomed her with genuine enthusiasm.

A score of lips greeted her, a score of greasy beer-cans were thrust towards her, while Bet Clarke paused in the middle of her combat with Whopping Nan respecting some disputed claim to a watch, and advanced with ease, if not elegance, to greet the new-comer with a rough but hearty salutation.

In the general confusion, Jack and Fanny for the time escaped observation, but it was not for long they were left in peace.

"Here's two pretty boys," said Bet Clarke, chucking Fanny under the chin, "and who may you be, young shaver?"

"Leave 'em alone," cried Mother Death, "they're **my** lambs!"

A shout of laughter greeted this announcement, and one big burly man exclaimed—

"Ah, mother, you allus picks up something good! You're a cunning old hand."

"Don't you make any mess of it this time then."

"Come, don't keep on throwing that job into a fellow's teeth. How the devil he got clear is a wonder to me!"

"Hush! can't you hold your tongue? They're listening."

"All right, mother! Here's your good health! and I say, mates, fill up, and we'll have a toast. Here's good luck to Mother Death's lambs!"

Amidst shouts of hoarse merriment the pewters were raised full and set down empty; but this drinking, when every one's attention was bent upon the liquor, gave Jack the opportunity he desired, and cautiously drawing close to Fanny's side, he whispered in her ear the share he wished her to take in the plot which he had formed in his mind for discovering more concerning their rude entertainers.

Accordingly, when the men after a pause looked round to see what had become of Mother Death's lambs, they saw one—the one in a postilion's dress—fast asleep upon a hard bench, while the other, evidently accustomed to make himself at home, had drawn himself a mug of beer, and having abstracted a pipe from the hand of a man sleeping the sleep of drunkenness on the damp floor, had picked out the softest tub, and with his feet upon the rude planks which served for a table, was making himself as comfortable as circumstances would allow.

"You're a cool hand," said one of the disreputable party, addressing Jack Rawlings.

"Is this the best beer you've got?" asked our hero, tossing off his mugful and holding it out to be refilled.

"Well, I'm blowed! Do you think I'm a waiter?"

"No; you don't look enough like a country curate for that; perhaps you're stable-helper, though."

"I'm as good a man as you any day."

"Really now; I shouldn't have thought it! Then you see I'm just from the country, and don't know much of you London gentlemen."

One or two men who had been talking together eyed Jack rather curiously, as if to make out if he were really the fool he pretended to be, but Jack was up to them, and put on the appearance of a country lout so well that their momentary fears were soon quieted. They withdrew a few steps however from the others, and commenced a conversation in a low tone, quite unconscious that Fanny, with eyes shut and ears open, was eagerly listening to every syllable they uttered.

"You got the worst of that, Joe," chorused his select friends, as Jack made the answer recorded above, and Joe relapsed into sulky silence, while our hero, puffing deliberately at his pipe, surveyed the ugly faces around him with a cool, steady gaze.

"I say, you fellows, what a precious dull lot you are!" suddenly cried Jack, "now, in my part of the country they sing songs and dance when they've got a jolly party like this together."

"Not when the beer's all gone, do they?"

"Oh! if that's what makes you such precious bad company," said Jack, feeling in his pocket and extracting a coin, "you'd better get some more, and make a night of it."

Joe eagerly clutched at the money Jack held out, and, either accidentally or by design, pushed rather roughly against our hero, from whose hand flew the remainder of the money he had held, amongst which were two or three sovereigns.

The eyes of all the assemblage glistened at the sight of the gold; nevertheless, somewhat to Jack's surprise, they suffered him unmolested to pick it up and return it to his pocket.

Fanny, feigning sleep, heard a conversation between two of the ruffians, who seemed to be of a somewhat better stamp than the others, and Mother Death.

"There—there!" cried the hag, as Jack's sovereigns rolled on the floor; "now do you believe me?"

"Perhaps they're duffers."

"Get along with you; you're one yourself."

"Do you think he has any more?"

"Lots of 'em. Did you ever know a chap with only a couple of yellow boys who kept 'em loose in his pocket or let 'em tumble about the ground?"

"Look at Joe! How he's eyeing the shiners! He'll be down on that young chap in a minute!"

"Let him dare lay a finger on him! There isn't one of you who wouldn't curse the day he ever touched one of Mother Death's lambs without her permission."

"Well, mother, how's it to be done?"

"Does the bed-room work?"

"You're not going to try that again?"

"Why not?"

"Only—only——" faltered a burly ruffian.

"Only because you made such an infernal mess of the last job," said Mother Death, scornfully.

"It's all very well you're saying that, but when you bring the devil himself here, and call him one of your 'lambs,' it's a little too much for us."

"You'll have to manage this job a little better, and so I tell you."

"Any way but that."

"They'll sleep in that bed-room to-night."

"Ha! ha! ha!" laughed the other, who had hitherto remained silent; "and where will they wake?"

Fanny heard this conversation with fear and trembling, but she managed to retain her outward composure, and, save a little faster beating of her heart, to lie perfectly motionless on the hard bench unnoticed by the conspirators.

So far Jack's plan had succeeded, but his further idea of making the men intoxicated and then effecting his escape with Fanny, he soon found to be impracticable. He might as well have attempted to make the sea drunk by pouring half-pints of beer into it as hope to overcome such seasoned topers as those who now remained sober, and with a sinking in his heart he confessed to himself that the only chance of escape was from that sleeping-room, which, as he had not yet seen it, was of course a doubtful hope.

Jack, however, had found a champion, though one without much power of assisting him.

Bet Clarke had been taken with our hero's appearance. His smooth red and white cheeks, his handsome eyes, and curling hair, presented so different an appearance to the haggard faces and bloodshot eyes of the majority of her admirers, that she determined if possible to save him from the fate which she knew by experience awaited him and his friend.

"What are you going to do with that boy?" she asked, advancing boldly to Mother Death, and indicating Jack with her finger.

"What's that to you?"

"You mustn't let him come to grief."

"Mustn't, eh? and why not?"

"Because I say so."

"Oh, lor! Here's a game. Here's Bet been and fallen in love with one of my lambs."

The two men greeted the announcement with a hoarse chuckle, and Bet, turning to one of them who happened to be her favoured admirer for the time, exclaimed passionately—

"Bill; you will promise me no harm shall happen to him. I've served you well and never harmed you; let the little fellow go this time."

"What ails you, Bet? A fellow must live."

"I don't know what it is, but there's something in his face which makes me feel different to what I ever felt before when I look at it."

"Now, look here, Bet! Mother Death says he's got a pocket-full of regular Bank shiners, and I'm not a-going to throw away a chance like that."

"I'll get you the money. You shall have every farthing of it, only don't injure him."

"I can get it all myself."

"How? Tell me how!"

"Well, if you must know, these two young gentlemen will sleep in the bedroom to-night."

"No, no; it must not be. I tell you, Bill, it shall not be!"

"Who will prevent it?" asked Mother Death, menacingly.

"I will."

"You?"

"Yes! I give you fair warning."

"Take care. We've short and certain means of silencing troublesome people."

"I don't care for you, Mother Death! I defy you! Was it not enough two years ago that you brought me to this hell, that you seduced me from a good and virtuous calling to bring me to this vicious hole, but, that now I have served your vile purpose, you must taunt and threaten me? Take care for yourself; I will have just and full revenge for all you have made me suffer!" And the girl drew herself up to her full height, her limbs quivering with passion.

"Bet!" cried her paramour, "you've been drinking, or summut. I never see you took this way afore."

"Luckily for you, Bill Monk. Perhaps if you had it would have been the worse for you!"

"What the devil is the matter with you?"

"I mean that you might have been rotting in a prison now, but for me; I mean that in a hundred different ways at various times I have done you service, saved you from prison, from transportation—yes, from the *gallows!*"

"Hold your row, can't you?" said Bill Monk, fiercely.

"I *can*—but what if I *wont?* No, Bill dear, tell me you were only joking; tell me they're not to sleep in that room to-night."

"Whatever Bill says," burst in Mother Death, "I tell you they are. Who are you to come between me and my prey?"

"Of course they will sleep there," growled Bill.

"Then beware for yourself. You have refused the only request I have ever made you, and remember if to-morrow they are missing it is in my power to denounce you as a villain, a thief, a murd——"

She never completed the word, for Bill Monk raised his arm and drove his fist with all his giant's force against her mouth!

The blood spirted forth, and she fell heavily to the ground with a faint cry!

One or two of those nearest to her looked round at the noise, but seeing what it was turned away again. Such scenes were common enough there!

Fanny who had been listening eagerly to the whole of the conversation could hardly restrain herself, indeed it was but the knowledge of her own impotency to revenge the blow, which prevented her from starting to her feet.

Jack turned round with the others, and seeing a woman lying bleeding on the ground, was in a moment at her side, and glaring fiercely round, endeavouring to discover the author of the brutality.

He raised her gently in his arms, and placed her on a bench; as he did so she furtively touched his hand with her lips, and attempted to speak, but faint from the effects of the blow, and loss of blood, she was unable to do so, and Mother Death dreading that she might reveal some of the secrets of the place, bustled round her and succeeded in moving Jack from her side, under the pretence of its being more a woman's place to assist one of her own sex.

A woman! Who would have thought that wicked, cold-blooded, toothless hag, to be of the sex! She was, indeed, to be pitied who once fell into the hard, cold grasp of Mother Death!

Fanny having heard all she was likely to hear, thought it more prudent to awake, and accordingly, yawning to the full extent of her pretty mouth, and stretching her beautifully moulded arms, she rose from the bench upon which she had been reclining, and made her way to Jack's side.

Choosing her opportunity, when no one was near, she recounted to him the whole of the conversation she had heard. It rather disconcerted him, it must be confessed, for he had been looking forward to the bedroom as likely to afford them some means of escape, while from Fanny's narrative, it appeared to be the place in which they were likely to apprehend most danger.

There was but little time to be wasted in reflection, and Jack soon made up his mind how to act.

Approaching Mother Death, who was still leaning over poor Bet Clarke, under the pretence of taking care of her, he requested that he and his brother might be shown their bedroom, as they were tired, and wished to retire for the night.

Mother Death started up with alacrity.

"Bill Monk," said she, "send some one to see the bed is properly aired. My lambs are tired, and want to go to rest."

Bill went off himself upon the errand, but the moment that the old hag's head had been turned to address him, Bet Clarke had seized as a glorious opportunity.

"Don't sleep," said she, in a whisper to our hero; "there is danger!"

Mother Death turned sharply round, but neither of them appeared to have stirred, and she was satisfied. It would have gone hard with Bet had her words been heard by any other than he to whom they were addressed.

Fanny and Jack took their seats silently side by side on a bench. It was a critical moment for them as they sat waiting for their bed to be "properly aired." While they sat waiting there they made a new acquaintance: the acquaintance of one who will figure largely in this story.

A lean, pitiful, half-starved dog came prowling about for any odds and ends it could find to keep its mangy skin upon its bones, and seeing our hero and Fanny sitting almost immoveable, after a few moments' deliberation, made up his mind they were not to be feared, and commenced rummaging about at their feet, and gnawing at a bone, which it would have puzzled anything but a dog to get nourishment from.

Now Jack had a great affection for animals, and put out his hand to encourage the poor beast, but so accustomed had he been to connect hands alone with blows, and feet with kicks, that he slunk away when Jack would have patted him, and retreated behind a beer-barrel.

Our hero, pitying the condition of the poor cur, took a piece of half-raw meat from the table and held it towards the half-starved beast, who, after much sniffing, advanced towards him with his tail between his legs.

"What an ugly brute!" exclaimed Fanny, and, indeed, the appearance of the dog warranted the exclamation.

He was nothing but a mongrel, he had scarcely an inch of tail, his short hair was rough and mangy, while in addition to his other charms, he had lost the sight of one eye, which however looked up blear and glazy when he raised the other. Still there was something about him which showed great intelligence, and as he took the piece of meat from Jack's hand, and wagged the stump of his tail, he cocked up his one bright eye and gave him a knowing look, as much as to say, "I'm a deuced clever dog, but I know better than to make a parade of my attainments before such an ignorant lot."

While he was yet engaged in eating the meat, which he did in a species of sidelong and surreptitious manner, and while Jack and Fanny were watching him, Bill Monk re-entered the cellar. Bet looked at him earnestly, as if desirous of calling his attention, but he did not even glance in her direction, but walked straight to where our hero was sitting.

"Your bed is ready," said he, in a surly tone; then catching sight of the dog, and being in a bad temper, he vented it upon the poor brute by kicking it violently in the ribs, thereby sending it flying, yelping, and howling across the room.

"What did you do that for?" asked Jack, angrily.

"What's that to you? It isn't your dog."

"Only that I consider it a brutal act to treat a dumb animal in that way. I should say you were the man who knocked over that poor girl just now."

"What if I am?"

"I don't know what they say to such an act in London, but where I come from, if a man did such a thing he would be termed a coward and a bully," answered Jack, quietly.

"Oh, that's what you say, is it? Well now, what would you say if I thrashed you into a mummy for your impudence?"

"I should say you were a deuced deal cleverer than I took you for."

"Will you try?"

"With all my heart."

"Come on, then, and be damned to you!"

Bill Monk tore off his coat and placed himself in an attitude; Jack did the same, while an admiring circle crowded round them to see the sport.

It took but a few minutes to show our hero that he could do what he liked with his adversary, for though the latter was a tall, athletic, powerful man, he knew nothing of the science, while Jack was a complete master of it.

Without entering into a minute description of the rounds, let it suffice that Jack danced nimbly round his antagonist, avoiding his ponderous blows, and hitting him sharp taps about the eyes and nose, till Bill Monk began to feel, in the language of the P. R., groggy, and to hit out wildly; then Jack, watching his opportunity, and throwing the whole of his strength into one blow, hit him between the eyes and sent him down like a ninepin.

"Now, I think we'll go to bed," said Jack, coolly putting on his coat again.

CHAPTER VI.

HOW FANNY WHITE AND HER FRIEND JACK RAWLINGS WENT TO BED.

It must be confessed, in spite of the outward coolness of his demeanour, Jack did not feel quite comfortable, not being sure that the ruffians who had formed a ring round them while fighting might not take it into their heads to avenge the fall of their comrade, but the fear was groundless, and under the escort of Mother Death, and accompanied by Fanny, he left the cellar for the bedroom—the room where they had every reason to believe some foul play was intended!

With a hope they would "sleep well," delivered in a tone full of meaning, the old hag left them, and they had opportunity to look round the dismal apartment into which they had been ushered.

It was a large, lofty room, with a huge, fantastically carved mantel-piece, and had evidently been once a handsome chamber, though now fallen into ruin. The paper hung in strips from the wall, showing the discoloured plaster underneath, the rain had stained the ceiling with long green and yellow blotches, and as for the furniture, with the exception of the bed, it was all of the very commonest and cheapest description. The floor was uncarpeted, and as they walked across it, the boards creaked mournfully, as if dismally bewailing their degradation.

The bed seemed strangely out of keeping with the rest of the furniture. It was one of the old-fashioned four-posters, with heavy, dark-coloured curtains, and hangings of the same sombre shade, which imparted to it something of the appearance of a hearse. The top was richly carved, and represented in grotesque confusion skulls and cupids peering out from wreaths of flowers. It was truly a strange bed to find in such a house, but it evidently had been part of it, for the carvings corresponded with those on the mantel-piece.

Jack took all this in at a glance, and conveyed his impressions to Fanny; but they had no time to waste in useless surmises; their object was to escape.

First, to guard against surprise, he and Fanny moved between them a long deal box of great weight against the door, then, arming himself with the poker, he commenced a careful search for any sign of treachery; while Fanny, looking resolute enough, followed close behind him.

The search was productive of no beneficial results; they saw nothing which could lead them to suspect foul play was intended; nevertheless, their desire to escape was rather heightened than decreased by the air of mystery which hung about the apartment.

"We'll see what can be done with the window," said Jack.

It was a queer old-fashioned casement, high up the wall; but, by dint of mounting upon the table, he managed to reach it and look out.

"Can you see anything, Jack?"

"Deuce a bit! It's all dark. Wait a moment, though," he continued, his eyes getting more accustomed to the darkness. "There's a light, and—yes, it must be—there's the river!"

"Can we get out through the window?"

"It will be a good way to drop."

"Never mind that," said Fanny; "better break a leg than stop here to be murdered. And she looked down at her own shapely limbs still invested in the post-boy's tights, and thought of the different ways she and Jack had expected to pass the night.

Jack muttered an ugly oath.

"Goodness! what's the matter?"

"The cursed window wont open!"

It was too true! It had been well and firmly secured with both nails and screws.

"There's another window, Jack. Try that."

"They would scarcely be such fools as to nail up one window and not the other," Jack replied.

Fanny took a high chair, and just managed to reach the window; with one touch the casement flew open.

"Jack—come here—quick! It's all right. It's open."

Jack descended from his perch, and carried the table on his back, like a snail its shell, to the other window, and mounted quickly to it.

A cry of despair escaped from his lips!

The window opened, it is true, but outside were thick iron bars placed only three or four inches apart.

"Can't you file through them?" asked Fanny.

"What with? Even if I had the proper tools it would be the work of hours."

"What are we to do?"

"Stay cooped up here till we see what happens."

"Hush! what was that noise?"

"I heard nothing."

"Yes! There it is again!"

"Where?"

"At the door!"

"I don't hear it."

"Listen!"

A perfect silence ensued.

Then came a sound of whispering outside the door. Jack grasped the poker firmly, and took a few steps towards the entrance to the room.

The whispering was renewed. It was some one calling to him from the outside.

"Who's there?" asked our hero, in a low tone.

"It is I—Bet Clarke, whom you helped just now."

"What do you want?"

"Let me in."

Jack Rawlings remembered the way she had raised his hand to her lips, and misinterpreted her motives, and though under other circumstances he might not have felt so indisposed to receive her as a visitor, still, as matters now stood, he did not feel justified in removing the barricade; besides, Fanny might have objected.

"I can't admit you," he answered. "What is it you want?"

"To thank you, and prove my gratitude?"

"Not to-night, my good girl. Some other time."

"You misunderstand me. No other time will do. Your life is in danger."

"How do you know it?"

"I have no time to explain now. You must escape."

"Yes, that's all very well; but how are we to do it?"

"I'll tell you. There is a secret spring by the side of——"

"What are you doing there, you jade?"

These words were spoken in the rough, coarse tones of Bill Monk, who appeared to have come across the girl as she knelt at the door whispering through the keyhole.

"Nothing—nothing!" Jack heard her reply, in frightened tones.

"I'll teach you to come prowling about the passages. Go down-stairs!"

"Who are you, to command me in that way?"

"I'll show you who I am. You've been talking to that fellow in there."

"I have."

"Which one?"

"The one who thrashed you."

Bill Monk growled forth a frightful oath.

"You'd blow upon me, would you? You'd like to see me swing, would you? Be off! Get down-stairs."

"Not unless you swear to me no harm shall happen to those inside."

"I wont swear anything of the sort."

"Then I wont move."

"You wont?"

"No."

There was a heavy, sickening crash, as of some hard substance hitting more yielding matter, a faint cry, and the sound of the fall of some heavy body outside.

Then all was still.

Jack placed his ear against the door to listen for some sound, but a death-like silence reigned. Fanny, who had advanced quietly, and had heard the latter part of the conversation, strove to peer through a crack in the wood; but all was dark. She could discern nothing.

For several minutes they remained listening intently, but without hearing a sound. Suddenly, Fanny leapt to her feet.

"The water is coming in!" she exclaimed. "I am quite wet!"

"Water!" cried Jack, horror-struck. "It is *blood!*"

From the passage through the crevice between the bottom of the door and the floor flowed in the crimson stream. Sluggishly the ensanguined tide advanced, till, in a hollow in the boards where Fanny had been kneeling, it formed a gory pool.

Bill Monk must have murdered his mistress!

"By Heaven!" exclaimed Jack Rawlings, "if ever I leave this place alive that man shall pay dearly for this night's work!"

He kept his oath.

Their chance of escape seemed well-nigh gone. They went carefully round the gloomy apartment in the hope of discovering the secret spring which Bet Clarke had mentioned. They pressed every knob, they touched each projection, but without any result, and as they looked mournfully into each other's faces, and read there the absence of all hope, the same gloomy despondency alike filled both their hearts. Discouraged and disheartened, despairing of life, they sat down upon the edge of the funereal-looking bed.

"There's nothing more to be done, Fanny darling. We must wait patiently for release or death."

"From what I heard them talking about when I pretended to be asleep, I think some one they entrapped in this way managed to escape."

"I don't see how he could have managed it."

"Neither do I. We've tried every possible place."

"Every one."

Again they fell silent, and for some minutes neither spoke a word, but thought with regret of the happy, joyous career they had anticipated being so suddenly cut short.

Suddenly Fanny's face sparkled with joy, and she leapt to her feet.

"I have it!" she cried, "I know what we can do."

Even her enthusiasm was barely sufficient to arouse Jack from the apathetic state into which he had subsided.

"What is it?" he asked, languidly.

"You lazy fellow. You never tried the chimney!"

In a moment Jack was on his feet and inspecting the huge fireplace. It was one of those ancient, old-fashioned ones, projecting into the room, and large enough for several people to stand inside, and as Jack looked up at the huge orifice allowed for the escape of the smoke, hope returned to his heart, for to one so well accustomed to athletic sports as himself, it seemed no great difficulty to ascend the chimney. Even though, supposing them safely at the top, their escape was problematical. The house might be detached, and with no means of descent from the roof, they might be seen by some of the ruffians, who, under those circumstances would certainly make little difficulty of silencing them in the most effectual way. Nevertheless it was well worth the attempt.

Jack having acknowledged the seeming practicability of escape by the chimney, it only remained to put the idea into execution, so, swinging himself off the ground, he swarmed some little distance up, sending down in his stead an enormous quantity of soot. Fanny waited anxiously below.

"Hullo!" she heard her lover exclaim, in a half-choked voice, but which yet betrayed considerable alarm, and in another moment he came silently down from his sooty elevation.

"Will it do?" asked Fanny. "Shall I be able to manage it?"

"Hush, for Heaven's sake! There's a man hid up the chimney!"

"Only one."

"I only saw one."

"Well, then, I don't see anything very dreadful in that. If you and I can't tackle him between us it's a pity."

"Yes, it's all very fine, but I'm not used to single combat in a chimney, and its rather awkward work, especially if our antagonist happens to be over your head."

"What's to be done, then?"

"Pull him down."

The pair advanced cautiously, and Jack, by getting on a chair, was able to reach the leg of a man which he had discovered when he first attempted the ascent, and with a vigorous pull brought that limb together with the accompanying body to the ground.

It lay there quite motionless! It was in vain Jack addressed it in a variety of tones, commencing with the persuasive and ending with the ferocious.

Not a word could he extract in reply!

Feeling somewhat alarmed—for a vague fear had taken possession of him—he advanced and looked into the face.

It was the cold, glassy stare of a corpse which met his gaze! Surely a more horrible sight could not well be imagined. The man had evidently been dead some days, and what

added to the horror of this disgusting spectacle, rats had in many places torn the flesh from his skull, here and there exposing the bone itself. The features, as far as they could be discerned, were twisted and distorted as if the sufferer had died in the greatest agony.

"This must be the wretched man I heard them talking about," said Fanny, turning from the corpse in disgust; "no wonder they could find no trace of him."

"Yes," answered Jack; "and it is a warning for me, for had he not been there I should have been caught in the same way."

"Do you think he was alive and went up of his own accord?"

"Certainly. He suspected something wrong and tried to make his escape. Doubtless he tried the windows as we have done, but finding escape by them impracticable, determined to attempt to scale the chimney, which narrows like a funnel, and there, without doubt, he stuck fast and perished miserably."

"What an awful fate!" said Fanny, covering her eyes with her hands, to shut out the sickening spectacle.

"Perhaps a better one than is reserved for us!"

"There is not a single chance left us now."

"Not one."

It is impossible to give an idea of the awful death-knell those words appeared to convey to our hero and heroine.

They sat there, side by side, full of life and love, and yet convinced that in a few hours time, at the latest, they would both be senseless corpses, and yet they were powerless to reverse their fate!

With a sudden flare and flicker the candle went out, and thus added one more horror to those from which they were suffering.

The grey morning light was just becoming visible in the east, and a cold, pale reflection was transmitted into the chamber in which they sat.

It gleamed fitfully on the top of the carved bedstead, bringing, as it appeared to them, the death's head into undue prominence; it lit up the carved mantelpiece, and as the light increased, made the shadows so fall that the skulls seemed to wear a mocking, gibing expression.

This was but fancy; but there, stretched upon the floor, was something more horrid, more awful than fancy could suggest.

The first gleam of morning sunlight which penetrated to this gloomy apartment fell full upon the face of the disfigured corpse, imparting to the lips the semblance of a smile.

Awful as the spectacle was, there was a strange kind of fascination about it. Fanny shuddered, and turned away her head; yet still she saw it in her mind's eye; she pressed her fingers firmly over her organs of vision, yet still she knew it was there.

At last, in sheer desperation, and worn out with the fatigue and dreadful excitement, she threw herself upon the bed, drawing the curtains close around her. Jack, after a few minutes' yawning, followed her example. "I will not go to sleep," thought he; "but I may as well rest a little."

Five minutes afterwards he was in as sound a sleep as only falls to the lot of the young.

He was awakened by a hand grasping his arm. In a moment the horror of their dreadful position, which he had forgotten in refreshing sleep, returned to him.

"Hush!" whispered Fanny, laying her hand over his mouth, when he would have spoken. "Do you not hear voices?"

"Yes. Heaven bless you, Fanny dearest, our time has come!"

For the last time, as they then thought, their loving lips met in a long embrace. The whisperings became louder, then ceased altogether, and then, to their horror, they felt the bed on which they lay quickly assuming a perpendicular position.

It was but the work of a moment. Frantically they clung to the bedclothes, and looked with horror at the frightful abyss below them; then gradually they felt their strength giving way, their hold relaxing, till, with a heart-rending cry of despair, they left go and fell.

Down—down! It seemed as if they never would reach the bottom; strange noises sounded in their ears, strange figures floated before their eyes; the falling rapidly through the air deprived them of breath and sense, so that when they reached the bottom, stunned, bruised, and helpless, they lay there, unconscious, and without motion.

This was the way Fanny White and her friend Jack Rawlings passed the first night of their elopement!

CHAPTER VII.

UNDERGROUND LONDON.

"JACK!"

No answer.

"Jack!"

"Hullo!"

"Are you hurt?"

"Well, I'm not quite sure."

"You're not very bad, at any rate."

"No; are you?"

"I'm all right. I tumbled on something soft. I hope it wasn't you, dear."

"How did it all happen? What has happened?"

"Can't say, exactly."

"Where are we?"

"Haven't the least idea."

"How did we get here."

"Shot out of bed, like coals down a cellar."

"I say, don't you find it rather damp?"

"It is moist."

"By Jove, I should think it is!" said our hero, who had advanced a few paces, and got up to his knees in water, as a reward for indulging his exploring propensities."

"How are we to get out?"

"We must discover first where we are. It's so pitch dark I can't see a thing."

Jack, in pursuance of his laudable design, rose again to his feet, and staggered a few steps forward regardless of the wet till he discovered there was a hard wall in front of him, by the simple process of hitting his head against it.

"I tell you what, Fanny, I know where we are."

"Where?"

"In a sewer."

"A sewer?"

"Yes. I've often heard and read of them. They are of great size, and extend for miles and miles under the London streets, possessing innumerable branches, and altogether as complicated as the catacombs."

"That's not a very bright prospect for us, Jack. I don't see how we can hope to escape."

"Sooner or later they flow into the Thames. If we could only find the right direction, and could follow it, we should be right enough."

"That's easy enough to do."

"I can't say I see my way."

"Why, if it falls into the Thames, it must be a gradual descent all the way, so if we only go downwards we shall be sure to get to the mouth in time."

"Bravo, Fanny! I believe you're right. Come, let's get on our way at once."

It was a long, long, weary struggle.

Slowly, and with extreme difficulty, they made their way through the close, dark brick vaults to which Mother Death's gang had consigned them.

Slowly, holding each other firmly by the hand, they advanced along the turbid stream, stumbling across ugly, misshapen objects in their path, shuddering as they did so, and fancying that once those shapeless, undistinguishable masses might have been human forms, full of life, and love, and hope, till ruthlessly shot into their fearful tomb by the base, murdering, plundering gang, with whom Fanny and Jack, thus early in their career, had fallen in.

Suddenly in their precarious course, Jack stopped and burst into a fit of chuckling which ended in real laughter.

"Good gracious! Jack, what is the matter with you?" asked Fanny, in an alarmed tone, and certainly she had some reason to be frightened, for, of all places in the world, a sewer seemed the last to choose to be merry in, especially when the probability of ever escaping from it was, to say the least of it, doubtful.

Nevertheless, in spite of the horror of the gloomy vaults, Jack's laughter reverberated along the arched roof, sounding hollower, and more ghostly, as it died away in the distance.

"What is the matter, Jack?"

"They're sold, regularly sold; upon my life I can't help laughing when I think of it."

"What do you mean?"

"Their object, of course, in shooting us down underground was to obtain our money."

"Well?"

"When I laid down on the bed, I never took off my clothes, and here it is, every farthing of it, in my coat pocket."

Although Fanny did not feel quite merry enough to join in Jack's laughter, she saw at once that they would not be so badly off as she expected, in the event of their escaping; but she was not of so sanguine a temperament as her friend, she already felt her limbs giving way beneath her, as they staggered on their painful course, she dreaded that ere they could reach a place of safety her strength would fail her, and that nothing but a slow, torturing, miserable death, would release her from the foul dungeon.

Jack, on the contrary, thanks to an extraordinary amount of physical strength, and good training in athletic sports, was very hopeful, and trudged manfully on, making light of such accidents as getting up to his waist in foul water, or knocking all the skin off his legs against some projecting masonry.

Still, when hour after hour passed by, and still they toiled through the dark, foul passages, without a single ray of light to guide them in their course, without a single sound of life to cheer them on their way, it must be confessed he felt a little disheartened.

For himself he cared little; he had great confidence in his own strength and powers of endurance, but it was for Fanny he dreaded most, and not without cause.

After many weary hours of painful walking, she felt she could proceed no farther, and sank exhausted upon a projecting stone, Jack supporting her as best he could.

They had no means of reckoning time; already it appeared to them as if they had passed weeks in the vaults, and the events of the previous day seemed quite things of the past.

Within the space of twelve short hours they had lived years.

After a prolonged rest again they started on their career.

Stumbling and staggering along the rough, uneven path, till in the distance they saw a welcome sight.

A sight which brought the blood leaping into their heads; a sight which caused them both involuntarily to utter an expression of thankfulness; a sight which filled their breasts with hope, which made him think escape was nigh at hand.

Glimmering faintly in the far distance they saw—LIGHT!

The real sunlight penetrating into their gloomy dungeon

Hope added strength to their feet; they quickened their pace, and hurried as fast as the obstacles in their course would allow them towards the welcome sight.

Regardless of the hideous objects in their path, heedless of the swarms of fierce rats swimming around them, they waded deep pools of inky water, and climbed heaps of dirt and filth, in their anxiety to reach the wished-for goal.

And for what?

Disappointment!

When they arrived at the spot from whence the light proceeded, they saw it came through a grating far, far above their heads, and quite out of their reach!

The anguish of that moment is not to be described.

Disheartened, sorrowing, crushed in spirit, they rested awhile beneath the grating, through which the sunlight came slanting down, lighting upon them, and tinging them with its golden hue, as if in mockery.

Sadly and longingly they looked upward at the grating, and listened to the sounds of life above. It was evidently a busy thoroughfare, for the noise of vehicles passing was incessant. One after another they rolled by, making a hollow sound, as of distant thunder, echo through the dismal vaults.

In vain Jack cried, with the whole strength of his lungs, for help; in vain Fanny added her shriller tones to his, till the whole dreary passage resounded with their cries.

The sound never arrived in the bustling thoroughfare, or at least if it did, was drowned in the roar of the gay throng, and the ceaseless rattle of carriages, carrying the world upon its errand; shopping, visiting, pleasure seeking, unconscious of the two wretched creatures below them, wellnigh mad with despair at being so near life and freedom, and yet so immeasurably removed from it.

Sadly and despondingly, with hearts sinking, and hope nearly dead, they watched the sunlight fade away, and listened to the sounds of life and happiness gradually becoming fainter, and the roll of vehicles occurring at rarer intervals.

Then, at last, all grew dark, and they could barely even distinguish where the grating was. Night had set in, and wearied and hopeless, they still sat gazing at the black darkness before them, and drawing imaginary pictures of terrible deaths in their gloomy dungeon.

Sadly and silently Jack held out his arms towards Fanny, and enclosed her in a loving embrace. Neither spoke, but the same thought that one or both of them, before the morrow dawned, might be a corpse, was passing through each of their minds.

Exhausted nature must be restored, and strange and incredible as it may seem, both our hero and heroine were speedily overcome with sleep.

When they awoke next morning it was but to a new horror!

By the pale, grey light of dawn struggling through the grating above them, they saw upon the walls, in the water, around them, on every side, a host of moving, black animals. Nearer and nearer the creatures approached them, till one, more adventurous than the rest, leapt upon Fanny's pretty leg, still encased, luckily for her, in the post-boy's leathers, and was speedily followed by the others.

The truth struck them at once.

They were attacked by the rats!

Fortunately several pieces of wood happened to be lying about, and each, seizing a piece, they defended themselves as best they could; but for this lucky chance they must have fallen an easy prey to these ferocious animals. As it was it was as much as they could do to keep them at bay. Jack received several severe bites, but Fanny, protected by the leathers, preserved her shapely calves from injury; nevertheless it was a severe fright to them, and the morning was far advanced before they were entirely free from their ravenous assailants.

When at length they were driven off, though, they congratulated each other upon that escape, still it seemed as if they were but reserving themselves for another and equally horrible death—starvation!

Again in the quiet morning, Jack essayed to make his voice heard in the street and again without success.

Nothing now remained to them but to endeavour to pursue their way to the river, upon the chance of being able then to effect their escape. Again they started on their painful way, pursuing it in silence. Neither had sufficient hope left to cheer the other, and with sinking hearts they saw the light from the grating fading away behind them, and nothing before them but black impenetrable darkness.

While they were yet continuing their way they heard a voice behind them.

It sounded like the regular beat of the piston of a steam engine.

"What can that be?" asked Fanny, faintly.

Before Jack could reply a stream of water came flowing swiftly from behind, carrying with it much of the lighter refuse matter lying about.

"Good heavens!" exclaimed our hero, in terror; "there has been no rain lately. *They are flushing the sewer!*"

Such was indeed the case, and the volume of water increasing rapidly every moment as it rushed riverwards, showed them that in a few minutes its force would be stronger than they could stand against.

There was no time to be lost. A small artery of the main sewer was at hand, which seemed to offer temporary refuge. And into that Jack hastily thrust Fanny, following himself just as the full impetuous tide came sweeping by.

There in comparative safety they watched the torrent sweeping by, carrying with it its mass of filth and impurity, but even where they were, was far from safe, for the water reached where they stood, and every moment mounted higher and higher.

Here it was Fanny's strength failed her!

She strove to rise and proceed farther up the low, narrow passage, but it was beyond her power, and again she sank down with a moan, the first she had uttered, and expressed her inability to proceed.

Jack's course was decided in a moment. He caught her in his arms, and thus encumbered made his way over the slimy obstacles which lay in his path till he was suddenly checked by finding nothing but a wall before him.

Uttering an exclamation of despair, he deposited his lovely burden on the damp ground, and eagerly felt the smooth wet wall on every side.

Not an opening! Not a chance of escape!

The branch into which they had turned extended only a few hundred yards!

Retreat was impossible!

Progress was impossible!

The water mounted higher and higher every moment!

Nothing but a lingering death by drowning was before them!

They saw their fate, and were powerless to avert it!

Again raising Fanny in his arms, he kept her head as far above the reach of the filth-stained liquid, as possible, and encouraged her to hope, with despair in his own heart.

The water already was up over their waists!

Lovingly and tenderly he addressed a few words of affection to his beautiful companion, but he had given way to despair himself.

Slowly but surely, the water mounted higher and higher; already it had reached nearly to Fanny's lovely neck.

A cry of joy broke from Jack's lips!

Fanny, weak as she was, echoed the cry!

There, above them, immediately above their heads, they saw the means of escape. Suddenly, and without warning, a trap-door had been opened, and once again they saw the welcome light of day. Sparkling and dancing through the opening, came the sunlight, gilding even the filthy tide which a moment before had threatened them with destruction.

From the trap-door hung a stout piece of rope, which but simplified their means of escape.

Where it would lead them they knew not, but at any rate they might once more tread the solid ground, once more see the sparkling, brilliant daylight.

Without a moment's hesitation—for there was truly no time to be lost—Jack still bearing Fanny in his arms, seized the rope, and easily, thanks to his athletic exercises, climbed up and laid his lovely burden on the ground.

Then mounting himself, and drawing a long inward breath of satisfaction at the narrow escape they had had, he looked round to discover what manner of place it was to which they had got.

It was a small, low wooden shed, without any attempt at furniture, in which he found himself. A small window threw but a dim light into the remote corners, the stream of sunlight falling as it happened immediately upon the black hole, through which they had ascended from the sewer beneath.

Lying near the trap-door were a number of shapeless forms which puzzled Jack to make out.

He approached nearer.

An insufferable stench arose from them.

Still, nothing daunted, he determined to ascertain what they were. He turned over one with his foot.

It was a dog.

Another and another. They were all dogs who had died evidently in great agony, from the strange shapes into which their bodies were bent in the pangs of death, and the painful expression still remaining in their glazed eyes.

"Fanny—Fanny!" cried our hero; "see here! Where on earth can we have got to?"

Fanny did not answer.

Jack, alarmed, hurried to her side.

Her ashy pale face, and helpless, listless limbs, frightened him in no little degree.

She was senseless!

The exertion she had gone through, the alarm, the excitement, had been too much for her, and at last, now that she was safe, she had no longer been able to preserve her senses.

She had fainted!

"Good Heaven!" exclaimed Jack, "she is dead!" And frantically he rushed to the door to bring the nearest person he could find to her assistance.

It was locked, but in his present state that made little difference to him. With one blow from his powerful shoulders he broke it open, sending the splinters flying in every direction.

Making his exit, he found himself in a small paved yard; behind him was the shed where Fanny lay senseless, before him was the high wall of a large mansion.

One window alone was within his reach, and to that he clambered.

Looking through it, he beheld a large apartment, which at the first glance he believed to be untenanted.

In one corner of the room was placed a furnace, and over

it a huge retort, while all about were scattered crucibles, alembics, glass instruments, bottles containing various coloured fluids, in short, the whole paraphernalia of a working chemist.

When Jack's eyes became more accustomed to the light, he perceived near the furnace in the laboratory a singularly handsome man, though dressed in the commonest suit of fustian, bending over a dog upon the floor, apparently in the last agonies of death. To this animal from time to time he gave small doses of some dark liquid contained in a bottle which he held in his hand.

Jack tapped gently at the window. The chemist however was too deeply absorbed in his experiment to take any notice of our hero's gentle knock.

Suddenly, with one sharp yelp, the unfortunate animal turned over upon its side and expired. The experimentalist carelessly kicked the body on one side.

Again Jack rapped at the window.

This time he was heard.

With a furious glance the occupant of this Chamber of Horrors sprang through a small door near the window through which Jack was looking, seized him by the collar, and, owing to the suddenness of the attack, easily bore him to the ground. Then holding a sharp, glittering poniard within a few inches of his throat, demanded the reason of his presence.

CHAPTER VIII.

STRANGE, MYSTERIOUS, AND HORRIBLE.

WHEN the late Earl of Stonecliffe departed this life, and was borne in a coffin covered with crimson velvet and gilt-headed nails to the family vault of the Stonecliffes, the whole world talked of it.

He had been a famous man had the Earl of Stonecliffe; for a short time he had been prime minister, and had made all manner of Acts of Parliament; for a time he had been a staunch patron of the turf, and had lost more money in that way than he cared to count; but in his old age, believing horseflesh to be vanity, and politics vexation of spirit, he retired into private life and the gout, and died at last at a good old age, as an English nobleman should.

When he departed this life, however, to return to our original sentence, he left his affairs in what is commonly called a deuce of a mess. No less than six claimants started up to the Earldom, and the lawyers licked their lips with delight.

The great Stonecliffe case is still well remembered in the law courts. The difficulty was not to prove whom he married, but whom he married *first*, for in addition to the regularly received Lady Stonecliffe, a publican's daughter in the eastern counties, a Parisian ballet-dancer, and an Italian lady of rank, claimed to have been legally wedded to this scamp of a nobleman.

After several weeks' litigation, with which none but the lawyers employed were satisfied, the case was decided in favour of the lady who had all along been received as his wife.

She had two sons, the eldest of whom became Earl of Stonecliffe, while the other, Lord Manningtree, dragged out a miserable existence as a young nobleman, with nothing but his title to live upon.

Percy Lord Manningtree was universally considered a "charming young man," he was remarkably handsome, and particularly agreeable in conversation. His voice was soft, pleasant, and insinuating, though there were people who declared it was put on, nothing, in fact, but fine acting, and that his real temper was demoniacal, his true mind vicious, wicked, and depraved.

Which was the correct statement, the reader will before long have an opportunity of judging for himself.

Between this nobleman and the Earldom of Stonecliffe was only one life—that of his niece—the present earl's daughter.

The one great peculiarity connected with Lord Manningtree was the extraordinary ardour with which he devoted himself to the study of chemistry.

His brother laughed, and said he was seeking the Philosopher's stone; others considered him slightly out of his mind upon this one point; but to sneers, persuasion, and laughter, he was alike indifferent, and for hours every day would shut himself up in his laboratory, admitting no one,

and refusing point blank to give any account of his proceedings.

It does not require Zadkiel's crystal ball to enable the reader to guess that it was upon this nobleman engaged in his chemical studies that Jack Rawlings intruded.

*　　　*　　　*　　　*　　　*

"How came you here? How dare you play the spy upon me?" asked Lord Manningtree in a voice hoarse with passion of our hero.

Jack saw his only chance was to keep cool.

"I could tell you better," he answered, "if you took your knuckles away from my throat."

The nobleman complied with the limited request, though he did not entirely relinquish his hold.

Jack told him the story of his adventures.

"It's impossible!" said his lordship, when the narration was finished.

"Of course you know best," said Jack, humbly, but with a slight twitching of his lips.

"What proof have you of the truth of your statement? Take care what you say; it may save your life."

"Proof! what do you think of my dress?"

Jack pointed to his trousers, which were saturated with slimy filth and wet.

"Hem! where's your companion?"

"In that shed, and if you want to be of real use, you'd better see if you can't recover him, instead of asking me questions."

Lord Manningtree accompanied Jack to the place indicated, where they found Fanny still insensible.

His lordship did what most people would have done under the circumstances.

He stooped and unfastened her collar and shirt.

As he did so, his eyes rested upon Fanny's beautiful neck and bust.

"You have told me a lie!" said he, turning to Jack, and pointing to the senseless girl.

"Yes," said our hero, coolly; "she isn't my brother, if you mean that."

"Is that the only one?"

"Yes."

"Will you swear it?"

"With the greatest pleasure."

"You've got an honest-looking face, so I'll trust you."

His lordship applied restoratives, and, in a short time, he had the pleasure of seeing the lovely girl show symptoms of returning to consciousness.

While he had been attending to her, however, he had had opportunities of feasting his eyes upon her almost faultless form, and being but mortal, he straightway fell in love with her—at least, what *he* called love—but being likewise prudent, he forbore to give the least inkling of the feeling to Jack, who was standing by watching him, and wondering if it were equally necessary to open the shirt which she wore quite so much.

"Excuse me," said Jack, "but may I ask if these dead dogs are your property?"

Lord Manningtree looked confused for a moment, but quickly recovering himself, answered in the affirmative.

"There has been a great mortality among them, apparently?"

"Yes."

"Have they died recently?"

"Yes."

"Hullo! there's one of them alive," exclaimed Jack, as from the heap came forth a piteous whine, and a slight movement was discernible.

"Alive!"

Lord Manningtree drew forth the poor unfortunate animal and eagerly scrutinised its appearance. Then pulling from his pocket a small case he opened it.

It contained a number of tiny glass bottles, each holding a few drops of liquid.

One of these he selected, withdrew the stopper, and emptied the contents down the trap-door into the sewer.

"That's of no use," he muttered, as he did so.

It was a wretched, mean-looking dog who had thus come to life again, with a short scrubby stump of a tail, and blind of one eye.

"Fanny!" cried Jack, "it's the dog we saw at Mother Death's place.

It was, indeed, no other; and the poor creature seemed to recognise Jack, and crawled towards him, evidently in

VENUS AT HOME.

great pain, and wagged its stump in the feeblest possible way.

"I should like to have the poor brute," said Fanny.

"Would you, indeed?" asked the nobleman.

"It cannot live," said Jack.

"If you would like to have it," said Lord Manningtree, again addressing Fanny, "I could easily make it well."

So saying, he raised the animal from the ground, and dropped a small portion of a crimson fluid, which he took from a bottle in the case before mentioned, down its throat, and replaced it on the ground.

"In a few hours," continued he, "it will have entirely recovered. Now I will detain you no longer, though I hope on some future occasion to see you again."

"You're very kind," said Jack, taking the dog in his arms, and preceding Fanny through a gate which led from the courtyard.

That was just what Lord Manningtree desired.

Stooping over our heroine he whispered a few words in her ear.

What they were, as she did not mention them, even to Jack, we have no means of ascertaining, but they certainly caused her to blush, and look prettier than ever.

The first thing to be done was, of course, to array themselves in rather more becoming and respectable attire.

Jack, at a large ready-made tailor's, procured a suit which fitted him to a nicety, and then proceeded to a fashionable milliner's, and, from written directions given by Fanny, secured for her an equally satisfactory outfit.

Every moment he waited at the milliner's added to his wonder, for, having been hitherto among the uninitiated, he had no idea of the number of curiously-shaped (to male eyes) linen garments it behoves a lady who would follow the fashion to wear.

At length all the required articles were got together and paid for; and Jack, hailing a cab, put in his load, and drove to the hotel at which he had left Fanny.

She, declining his offers of assistance, disappeared into a bed-room; and when she again revealed herself to his astonished eyes he could hardly believe he saw correctly.

That she was beautiful he had known all along, but that she was of such surpassing loveliness he had had no idea.

At Miss MacSpartan's dress had been restricted, and all the little additions to female attractiveness thrown aside as snares of the devil by the august lady-principal; but now, with no one to restrain her, Fanny had given full scope to her natural taste for fine dress.

She knew well how to make the most of her attractions, and when, with a few trifling alterations, the dress had been put on, and fastened over her magnificent bust, which it revealed without displaying, when her beautiful hair had been elegantly arranged, when her pretty feet had been encased in the most perfect fitting silk stockings and dainty slippers, and she appeared without warning before our hero, no wonder he was taken aback, and stared in amazement, as if doubting whether it were indeed his Fanny who stood before him in neither the character of the school-girl, nor the post-boy, but the perfectly beautiful woman.

She soon convinced him she was the same; and as Jack strained her to his heart, covering her face with kisses, she the while feebly protesting against such injuries to her new dress, they certainly looked the handsomest and most loving couple one would wish to see.

Jack ordered dinner, and, indeed, considering it was more than twenty-four hours since either of them had tasted anything, it was quite time he did.

After the meal, as they sat lazily sipping their wine in luxurious ease, which contrasted favourably with their experience in the sewer, Jack proposed they should resolve themselves into a committee of ways and means.

Examining his purse he found nearly half of the stock of money he had received from Jabez Dallet had gone.

"Fanny," said he, "we must do one of two things—either pinch and scrape, and make these few pounds last as long as possible, or else we will go in for pleasure wholesale, and enjoy everything while the gold lasts. Which shall it be?"

"Pleasure!" cried Fanny, without a moment's hesitation. "What would be the use of pinching and scraping? the money would still go."

"Yes, but it would be longer about it."

"Oh, bother! Let us enjoy ourselves, and see life while we can, and then——"

"What then?"

"Trust to something turning up."

"All right, Fanny darling!" cried Jack, joyously; "we'll go in a buster!"

A sneaking, cringing waiter softly opened the door, tapping after he had done so, and begged in his master's name to know if they would sleep there that night.

As it was late and they were both fatigued, Jack answered in the affirmative, and the servile attendant withdrew with a cunning leer upon his lips, as he noticed Fanny's beautiful, voluptuous form, and Jack sitting by her side in an affectionate attitude.

After a short time, Fanny made a movement towards retiring for the night, and Jack, pressing his lips to hers, took his departure to the smoking-room to taste the comforts of a cigar before turning in.

The cigar finished, the punch swallowed, Jack sought and found the waiter, who volunteered to show him his room, the chambermaid not being in the way.

"This way, sir; this room, sir," said he, opening the door and trying hard to peep in. "Good-night, sir!"

"Good-night!"

"Nothing else you want, sir?" continued the pertinacious waiter, going through violent gymnastics, in order to see into the bed-room.

"Nothing."

The door was closed, and the waiter went slowly downstairs, with a reflective expression upon his ugly face.

"Good gracious, Jack! what brought you here?" cried Fanny, as he entered the room; "I thought you'd gone to bed."

"I'm going," answered Jack, taking off his coat.

Fanny tossed back her hair which she had loosened from its bands, and which fell in luxuriant silky tresses over her ivory shoulders and looked doubly bewitching in her deshabille.

"Well, I'm sure!" said she.

*   *   *   *

It was late the following morning when Fanny and our hero made their appearance downstairs, and were met by the obsequious waiter.

Breakfast concluded, Jack on some slight pretence went out.

On his return he flung a small pink ticket into the lap of the charming Fanny.

"What is it, Jack?" she asked; "what have you been getting?"

"A box at the Opera, darling, for to-night."

Fanny clapped her hands with joy, for theatres and operas had been forbidden her by her father, and consequently she longed the more for them.

"What shall we hear?"

"The *Traviata*."

"Charming! It's a little improper, isn't it?"

"Yes, dear; but it's all in Italian."

"What a shame!" said Miss Fanny, in tones of disappointment.

The opera necessitated another visit to the milliner's, for our heroine, owing to the shameful conduct of the gentleman with the donkey cart before related, had no dress but the one she wore, and the postboy's, neither of which, pretty as they both were, were exactly suitable for the first tier of boxes at the Theatre Royal Covent Garden.

Fanny gave the necessary directions respecting her dress, and ordered it to be sent home as soon as possible, but at any rate in time for the amusement of the evening.

She did not then think of the weary work-girls, the heavy aching eyes, the tired fingers, the exhausted frames, that would have to work with redoubled energy to complete the garment in the prescribed time.

She learnt that afterwards, as we shall see.

The dress was sent to the hotel at the appointed time, was tried on, and fitted beautifully. It was cut very low in the body, so as to reveal a good deal of her lovely white neck, and the sleeves were little more than broad ribbon across her shoulders, but then her arms were so perfectly moulded it would have been a shame to cover up more than was absolutely necessary.

The carriage Jack had ordered arrived, and Fanny keeping it waiting a wonderfully short time, took her seat by Jack's side full of expectation; and the loving pair rolled away to Covent Garden.

The opera had already commenced when they arrived, and were ushered to their box, so that their entrance was scarcely noticed, but when the curtain fell upon the first act, and Fanny withdrew her attention from the stage and raising the lorgnettes to her eyes scanned the magnificent house with its tier above tier of boxes, filled with the rank and beauty of England, she became conscious that several opera-glasses were directed to the box in which she sat.

Every moment the number increased, and she felt herself the centre upon which hundreds of male eyes were fixed.

Jack noticed it, and his heart fluttered with pleasure to think that she should meet with such general admiration.

The gentlemen declared unanimously she was the most charming girl they had ever seen, while the ladies, eyeing her in a disparaging manner, said for their part they couldn't see anything in her, but thought she looked bold and impudent.

The curtain arose upon the second act, and called away the attention of those who came to listen to the music from Fanny's box, but the regular frequenters of the Opera, who came to see and be seen, still directed their lorgnettes towards our heroine.

One gentleman in the stalls, a remarkably handsome man, was even more persevering in his attentions than the others, and at length, when the music again ceased, left his seat, and a few moments afterwards stood at the entrance of the box.

It was the gentleman whose study of chemistry Jack had interrupted.

It was Lord Manningtree!

It must be remembered that when Fanny and our hero first saw him he was attired in an ordinary working-man's suit of fustian, and that they were ignorant of his name and rank, consequently when he appeared at the back of their box elaborately dressed, and one of the most distinguished-looking men in the house, it is not strange that for a few moments they doubted if he were the same individual.

Upon that point he soon eased their minds by expressing his hopes that they had experienced no ill effects from their sojourn underground.

Fanny made a suitable reply, and in a few minutes his lordship managed to draw her into conversation.

In the pleasing art of talking amusingly and well about nothing Lord Manningtree was unrivalled, and as Jack saw Fanny becoming more and more engrossed with his lively prattle, more animated in her replies, and more genial in her laughter, he entertained some rather unpleasant thoughts respecting that agreeable nobleman.

He would have given anything to stop the *tête-à-tête*.

Twice he made the attempt, but failed.

Rescue was near at hand.

Again the box-door opened and a young gentleman of very juvenile appearance, the sole aim of whose existence appeared to be to hold a glass in his eye, made his appearance, and stared vacantly round.

Jack looked up astonished.

"Oh, dem it!" said the stranger.

Our hero was puzzled what to reply to this strange salutation, but just as he was about answering somewhat roughly, the uninvited visitor, taking the glass from his eye, and by that means recovering his sight, saw the object of his search sitting by Fanny's side, engaged in earnest conversation.

"I say, Manningtree," drawled he; "it's cruel—positively cruel, leaving me down there all by myself, and you with such a lovely creature—demmit!"

"I couldn't let Lord Manningtree have her all to himself, could I?" continued the languid youth, addressing Jack.

The nobleman looked excessively annoyed at the mention of his title.

Fanny heard it, and rejoiced at the attention paid her by a lord, but even that sank into insignificance when that nobleman said, turning to his friend—

"Permit me to introduce his Grace the Duke of Pulborough."

"Delighted to have the honour—pleasure—demmit!" said his Grace, in answer to Fanny's bow.

It was indeed a triumph for her. The daughter of an obscure merchant, the last-week school-girl, to be sitting in an opera-box with Lord Manningtree beside, the Duke of Pulborough behind her!

I am afraid that in the pleasure and excitement of the moment she almost forgot Jack, who, in a far from enviable state of mind, sat sulkily at the back of the box, scowling at the two members of the aristocracy.

The opera came to an end, and the two noblemen insisted upon seeing Fanny to her carriage, and were rewarded by a glimpse of the prettiest ankle in the world, as she got in, followed by Jack.

"I shall certainly call at your hotel to-morrow," said Lord Manningtree, "to ascertain if you got back safely."

"Oh, yes—of course—so shall I—certainly—oh, yes—demmit!" said the young duke; and the brougham drove off, leaving the two noblemen standing hat in hand upon the pavement as they made their final bow to Fanny.

Jack was sulky and discontented, but Fanny knew certain means of curing him; indeed, ere they had been in their room at the hotel half-an-hour she had brought him round to his original good-tempered frame of mind, and had made him laugh immoderately at her imitation of the young duke's language and manner.

*   *   *   *

Time went swiftly on, and still day after day came some fresh round of amusement for Fanny and our hero.

"What?" cries the reader, "how much longer is that fifty pounds going to last?"

It has been all spent long ago.

"Then they must be terribly in debt?"

They do not owe a single farthing.

"Then how the deuce do they manage it?"

This is the way it was done.

Lord Manningtree, as already stated, conceived a passion for Fanny when he first saw her in the post-boy's dress lying senseless on the ground.

Now, his lordship was comparatively poor, being the younger son, and did not see his way clearly to increase his intimacy with our heroine, till it occurred to him to make use of the young duke.

His Grace was wealthy and wished to be "fast," but only having just broken away from leading-strings had as yet scarcely had an opportunity of indulging his fancies. To him, with smooth tongue, came Lord Manningtree, and artfully suggested to him the renting of a quiet villa at St. John's Wood, and offering it as a residence to our hero, who, of course, would be accompanied by Fanny.

The offer was made, and, after some hesitation, accepted; but while the duke had the satisfaction of being paymaster, Lord Manningtree had the pleasure of using the house as if it were his own.

Fanny led a life of happiness.

Admired wherever she went, sought after by men of fashion, flattered by every one, with a comfortable, well-appointed house, horses and carriages whenever she required them, and tickets for operas and fêtes continually at her disposal, her life was one ceaseless round of gaiety.

Still Lord Manningtree was no nearer the fulfilment of his wishes.

Fanny, in spite of the most brilliant temptations, remained faithful to our hero.

But a crisis was near at hand.

The Duke of Pulborough, after having paid the expenses for some months, came to the conclusion that it was not altogether a satisfactory way of spending his money, and having confided that idea to Lord Manningtree, that nobleman determined upon immediate action.

From time to time he had made tempting offers to Jack. Proposed to get him a commission in an Indian regiment, offered to procure him an appointment at Constantinople, and promised to exert all his influence to get him made consul of Owyhee Islands; but Jack saw the object was but to get him out of the way, and resolutely declined any appointment which would separate him from Fanny.

Now, finding it impossible to remove Jack from Fanny, he determined to attempt the reverse, namely, removing Fanny from our hero by persuading her to elope with him.

This was more easily said than done.

His smooth, silvery speeches had little or no effect upon our heroine.

She was willing to accept his admiration and his presents, but not his love.

He told her of his love.

She laughed at him.

He entreated her to fly with him.

She laughed the louder.

He pressed her for an answer, and she left the room without replying.

She told Jack of the offer she had received.

"You had better accept it," he answered, coolly.

"Accept it! What do you mean?"

With a face full of laughter, Jack bent over her till his lips touched her fragrant hair, and whispered something in her ear.

Fanny did agree to Lord Manningtree's proposals.

The next time he came he found the beauty alone in her boudoir.

Delicately tinted blinds shed a soft light throughout the room: the odour of flowers added to the languor which pervaded the apartment, and there, in the middle, reclined Fanny, upon soft, yielding cushions, in a negligent, voluptuous attitude.

One of her slippers had fallen off, but she had not attempted to replace it, but was carelessly swinging her pretty foot backwards and forwards from the couch, disclosing, as she did so, several inches of her beautifully formed leg, while her morning-dress, open in front, left perhaps somewhat less to the imagination than some prudish people might think correct.

Hesitatingly, and with her countenance suffused with blushes, she agreed to fly with him that night, and the enraptured nobleman, after a lengthened visit, tore himself away, his heart beating violently at the prospect of the speedy consummation of his desires.

At the appointed hour Lord Manningtree was waiting for her.

Slowly and tremblingly she advanced to meet him, her agitation so great that she could scarcely speak.

He addressed her encouragingly, and assisted her to the carriage he had ready waiting.

For some time they drove on in silence.

Lord Manningtree placed his arm round her unresisting waist.

"My darling!" said he; "now nothing shall separate us. I have long dreamt of a lovely angel, a beautiful being to love and be loved by, and now I have found her. Can you guess who I mean, dearest? Do you know her name? It is Fanny."

"You're very kind. I'll tell her of your complimentary remarks, my lord."

It was the voice of Jack Rawlings, and as his lordship leaned forward they were the features of that gentleman he saw, grinning beneath the thick veil, which he had supposed to conceal the face of the lovely Fanny.

CHAPTER IX.

CONTAINS A LITTLE EXPLANATION, A MODERATE AMOUNT OF EXCITEMENT, AND A GREAT DEAL OF WICKEDNESS.

JACK RAWLINGS had for some time been smarting under the conduct of Lord Manningtree. He had never in his heart really approved of the arrangement concerning the house, but gave way on Fanny's account, as she seemed to wish it. Accordingly, when she told him of that nobleman's infamous proposals, the idea at once struck him of having his revenge upon him.

He carried his plan into execution as related in the last chapter.

He had previously arranged with Fanny that under cover of night, and disguised in his clothes, she was to leave the villa at St. John's Wood, and proceed to some lodgings he had taken in one of the southern suburbs of London, and thither he accordingly repaired, after making a most polite speech to the nobleman, thanking him for his disinterested kindness, and more particularly in having given him a lift so far upon his way.

Lord Manningtree swore savagely, but offered no resistance to his alighting, and Jack got out from the carriage, and trudged gaily on, chuckling to himself at what he had done.

Now that Fanny and Jack were again thrown upon their own resources, they saw at once the necessity of obtaining some employment; but that was no easy matter. Fanny wavered between the stage and the work-room, and at last decided in favour of the latter, supposing she could find employment.

It was certainly a great fall from her recent position, but she minded it little, and set about seeking employment with a good heart.

Everybody has heard of Mrs. Herringbone, or if they haven't, are ashamed to confess it.

Mrs. Herringbone was a famous West End milliner and dressmaker—famous in more ways than one; her name had, on several occasions, been brought before the public, and never with any good or moral tale attached to it.

Not knowing her character, it was at her establishment that Fanny first tried for work.

Mrs. Herringbone herself was a tall, thin, lathy woman, with an uncomfortable twitching about her throat, as if she had swallowed her own name and didn't like it. Her bones were sharp and angular, and would have stuck all over her in ungainly knobs and bumps, had not the whole art of dressmaking been called into use in the manufacture of her apparel.

It was indeed a labour to make her at all presentable.

She had to be squeezed in where she was too large, and padded out where she was too small, and when she was once attired for the day, I firmly believe it would have puzzled herself to say which was woman, and which was padding in her own form.

In spite of the smile which was usually on this woman's face, there was something about her countenance coarse and repulsive, which struck Fanny as being far from agreeable the first moment she saw her.

Her address was good, her manner quiet and pleasing; she seemed taken with Fanny's appearance, and, after very few questions, she agreed to take her for a few weeks on trial.

Fanny went back to the lodgings delighted with her success.

Had she only known the crimes of which her employer had been guilty her joy would have been considerably lessened.

Had she been able to read her heart, and see the hellish designs of the woman as she gazed on her beautiful coun-tenance, she would have shrunk from her as from a hideous reptile.

But no outward signs betrayed the foulness of the mind within. Her face was as skilfully disguised as her body.

The moans and despairing shrieks of those she had wronged had long since been silenced in the quiet of the grave. The house which had echoed with the cries of her victims told no tales; its walls could not relate the spectacles it had witnessed.

No—all seemed peaceful and quiet—and Fanny White was preparing to tread the path of degradation and vice, forced forward by the cold, unrelenting hand of Mrs. Herringbone, as many an ill-fated girl had done before her.

With the first day of Fanny's experience at the dressmaking establishment, came the shadow of suspicion that all was not as it should be, with the second came confirmation, with the third actual proof.

A poor wretched girl, faded, wan, and thin, with the hectic glow of consumption on her cheek, was among the fashionable milliner's victims.

She had been ordered rest and quiet.

Surely it was not rest that sitting eighteen hours every day, sewing mechanically on and on till the thread moved before her eyes in a thick confused mass, and her hands trembled, and her brain reeled.

She, taking compassion on Fanny's youth and beauty, took upon herself to warn her of what she might expect.

No better warning could she give than the story of her own life, and these were the words in which she related it:—

"My father was the clergyman of a small village in one of the western counties. I had a happy life till the fiend crossed my path.

"He came in a tempting shape.

"A young and handsome officer quartered in the neighbourhood was our constant guest.

"You can guess my story already.

"It was but one of a thousand similar. You can imagine the real love on my part, the assumed affection on his, the vows, the protestations, the promises of marriage. The story is as old as the hills.

"One ill-fated morning I became a mother!

"My father I had thus far succeeded in blinding, but the secret was no longer to be kept back from him.

"He cursed me!

"He disowned me!

"I cannot bring my tongue to repeat the hard name he called me as he turned me from his door.

"Perhaps I deserved it, though still it seems to me I was more 'sinned against than sinning.'

"I will not weary you with the history of my struggles and temptations, my only object in telling you this much is to warn you of the woman in whose house we are.

"I succeeded in obtaining a situation here as you have done. Fool that I was, I actually rejoiced at it. I little knew for what I had been hired.

"Then I was young and pretty. These sunken cheeks were well-filled then, these lustreless eyes were as brilliant as your own.

"What changed them? Ah, you may well ask that. This woman, our *owner*, she it was who tempted me, she it was who held out golden inducements to me, and extolled the happy life I should lead.

"Do I look happy?

"It is sufficient for me now to tell you I sold myself.

"For a few shining, golden coins I gave myself up to her —and her friends.

"What was it to me that those friends were men of rank, men of title and position, men who made laws for their country's good? What law can they make to restore me that I have lost? What position can they give to compensate for the home that is mine no longer? What can——"

A violent fit of coughing interrupted the flow of her words, and, to Fanny's horror, her mouth filled with blood.

The poor girl had wrought herself up to so great a degree of excitement as she related her simple, and, alas! too common tale, that in her weak state she had ruptured a small blood-vessel.

Mrs. Herringbone was sent for; Doctor Mulberry was sent for; and while one looked disconcerted, and the other preternaturally wise, the same idea was in both their minds —that she had not many hours to live.

That evening, when Fanny left the fashionable milliner's,

and joined Jack, who always waited for her at the corner, she had rather a melancholy expression upon her pretty face, which her lover noticed.

She told him the sad story she had just heard.

"Oh! that sort of thing wont do," said he, indignantly. "You musn't go there any more."

"I can't help it," faltered Fanny.

"The deuce you can't! Why not?"

"Because Mrs. Herringbone made me sign an agreement to stay with her three months."

"Pooh! never mind that. You're quite justified in breaking it."

"But—but——"

"But what?"

"You know the dress I went there in was rather shabby, and—and——"

"Well?"

"Mrs. Herringbone offered to advance me my pay, in order to get some better things."

"And you accepted the offer?"

"Yes."

"You've made a pretty mess of it, then. But never mind, Fanny dear; I'll keep watch, and if anyone offers to insult you they shall feel the weight of my fist, as sure as my name is Jack Rawlings." And our hero certainly meant what he said.

The following morning, when Fanny arrived at her place of employment, the first news which greeted her was that of the death of the poor unfortunate, an outline of whose pitiable story she had heard the previous evening from her own lips.

Found dead in her bed!

That was all they knew of the matter.

No one had heard the last weary sigh of the escaping spirit.

No tender, loving hand moistened the parched and feverish lips, or softly touched the aching brow.

Found dead in her bed—and that was all!

Could the dead rise from their grave to impeach the fashionable milliner?

No. There was not a voice to rise to accuse her of cruelty, of negligence, of *murder!*

Such things are happening every day around us; but what is the word of a poor, overworked, wretchedly paid, badly treated creature against that of a wealthy West-End lady?

It is only when some dreadful case is brought prominently forward, when the spirits of the departed cry aloud from their pauper graves, that the world arouses itself to inspect the miseries of its unfortunate sisters.

This poor, friendless, forlorn girl found no mourners but her companions in misfortune.

They did not pity, they *envied* her!

For some days Fanny worked on in constant dread of the machinations of her fashionable mistress. She could not bear to look upon her, knowing her character as she did, and in her presence averted her eyes with loathing from the painted, smirking, made-up features of Mrs. Herringbone.

Whether this lady noticed her conduct or not, she redoubled her attentions to Fanny. She spoke kindly to her, and granted her indulgences; but whenever our heroine felt more kindly towards her the spirit of the poor girl whose sad story she had heard rose before her, and she repulsed the fashionable woman.

This was not to continue.

The greed of gain had yet to be satisfied.

Mrs. Herringbone asked Fanny to make one of a small supper party.

What could she do?

She asked Jack.

There was no excuse she could make to avoid accepting it. She went.

And this is how Mrs. Herringbone had composed her supper-party.

Having secured Fanny, she asked a few ladies residing in a northern suburb, who, without any visible means of support, managed to keep their horses, carriages, and servants, and drive well-dressed in the Park, the admiration of men, and the envy of wealthier, better educated, and higher positioned women.

The majority of these were only too glad to be patronized by Mrs. Herringbone.

Then having invited one or two of the principal ballet-dancers from the opera, her list of ladies was complete.

For gentlemen she was at no loss.

There were few who would not have gone on their knees to beg for an invitation.

Without mentioning names, let it suffice that some of the wealthiest and noblest men in town were asked to "drop in."

But to one—an old superannuated prime minister—Mrs. Herringbone sent a special note, written by her own lean hand, on pink scented paper.

It was very carefully worded, but gave this dissolute old peer to understand that, if he came, there was "something" specially reserved for him—a delicate tit-bit, too good for the common herd.

How the old premier mumbled with his toothless jaws—for he got the note in the morning, and the wonderful ivories were still recumbent in their case—how he chuckled and rubbed his hands with delight!

He knew Mrs. Herringbone.

He knew the meaning of that daintily worded epistle.

It was a sight to see that old nobleman preparing for conquest.

His stays were pulled in the tightest, his coat padded out to the fullest, his wig was the freshest, his garments the newest, as he put on his hat with a jaunty, rakish air, and tottered into the Park.

And what was the effect of this toilet?

Did he look the buck he imagined himself?

No. It was but a hollow mockery.

It was as if a death's head were peering forth from a fine suit of clothes.

This was the gentleman Mrs. Herringbone had decided upon to be Fanny's beau!

The eventful evening arrived; and our heroine arrayed herself for the party.

Jack swore she never looked so lovely, but as, as a rule, he swore the same thing at least twice a day, perhaps there is not much reliance to be placed on his statement upon this occasion.

Jack saw her safely through London to the door of Mrs. Herringbone's private residence, and left her there with the promise that he would call for her when the party was over.

Even to her he did not reveal the plan he had formed in his own mind.

Dreading some foul play, he determined, while Fanny remained within the house, never to remove out of earshot. And he kept his resolution.

For hours he paced backwards and forwards beneath the lighted windows, from whence at intervals came sounds of merriment, music, and laughter.

He began to think his fears unfounded, yet still he paced on, resisting all temptations to draw him from his post. Sometimes he stayed in his course and looked up wistfully at the windows; but neither the soft-eyed sirens of the night, nor the offer of a gentleman returning from a dinner-party, to "stand him anything he liked to give a name to," could draw him away from the front of the house.

A policeman, after eyeing him suspiciously for a quarter of an hour, and deliberating whether he should march him off to the station-house as a desperate burglar, altered his mind, and endeavoured to fraternize with him; but Jack was in no mood for conversation, and cut the guardian of the peace very short, and that worthy walked away sulkily to rouse the poor homeless wretches from their fitful slumber on the doorsteps.

"Help!"

It was only one word, but spoken in tones of abject distress.

The reply was a merry peal of laughter; still the voice sounded to him like Fanny's.

It came once more.

Just then the door of the house had been opened to give admittance to a boy from the pastrycook's, and Jack, taking advantage of this, rushed into the passage and, despite the resistance of two able-bodied footmen, forced his way upstairs.

Let us now return to Fanny, and discover the causes of those cries.

When she arrived she had been ushered in solemn state into Mrs. Herringbone's best drawing-room, where she found the "select party" already assembled.

The eyes of the old ex-Prime Minister sparkled as he glanced at the "something" procured for his especial benefit, while the other young ladies shrugged their pretty white shoulders disdainfully, and whispered to each other that they didn't think much of her.

The fashionable milliner advanced and greeted her warmly, and led her to the side of the old gentleman, who put on the feeblest, sickliest semblance of a smile, which puckered up his wicked old face till it looked like a walnut-shell, and told her it was the happiest moment of his life.

Before supper everything was conducted with the greatest decorum. Certainly the conversation was a little more free and easy than one would hear in fashionable circles; but, then, Fanny was not *very* prudish herself, and was not disposed to be too critical.

Supper was announced, and Fanny was led to her seat by the ancient lord, and then began the evening's amusement.

Champagne flowed as freely as water; the generous wine exhilarated all, and Fanny felt her spirits rising and her fears sinking.

It was astonishing how attentive people were to her. Her glass was never empty, and Mrs. Herringbone urged her to drink, and laughed at her scruples.

Then it was that Fanny perceived the effect the intoxicating beverage was having upon others.

Mademoiselle Cerise, of the Royal Italian Opera, had been persuaded to favour the company with her new dance, which, as she wore a long dress, necessitated a good deal of pinning up and arrangement of skirts. Then young Lord Owlett volunteered to play the part of the lover in the new ballet. He did it to perfection, said the other guests—rather too well, Fanny thought.

Without specifying the variety of attitudes and employments of the company, it is quite sufficient to state that Fanny saw the character of those by whom she was surrounded, and recognised the truth of the statements of the poor girl who had only that day been laid in her shallow grave.

She rose to go, but was forcibly detained.

She listened with disgust to the conversation around her; and when the old peer increased his familiarities, and young Lord Owlett attempted to place his arm round her, then it was she turned and appealed to Mrs. Herringbone for aid and protection.

A sneering, scornful laugh was her only reply.

Emboldened by her loneliness and unprotected state, the ruffians gathered round her, laughing and mocking her distress, and openly admiring her personal charms.

"Help!"

That was the cry Jack heard in the street.

The detestable wretch who had invited Fanny to what she believed to be her ruin, whispered in her ear—

"Do not resist him. Your fortune will be made if he takes a fancy to you."

Before Fanny could reply in indignant tones to this degrading proposal, Mrs. Herringbone had left the apartment; she was a cautious lady, and knew she could not be held responsi e for what took place in the room during her absence.

Our heroine turned her glance round to see if there were pity for her helpless position in any one face.

No. They all wore the same hard mocking expression—the same callous indifference to her fate.

While Fanny was repelling the ex-lawgiver upon one side, Lord Owlett stole round upon the other unperceived, and bent his head till his lips were within an ace of touching her lovely ivory shoulders.

Then came a sudden uproar.

A table covered with glass was overturned with an awful crash, a frightful blow was struck, and Lord Owlett lay senseless on the floor, the blood gushing from his nostrils, while the old premier was vainly endeavouring to refix the luxuriant head of somebody else's hair he wore which had been disarranged in the scuffle.

Fanny sprung to Jack with an exclamation of delight, and clasped her arms round his neck, while he, his eyes flashing fiercely, glared round as if anxious to settle accounts with the rest of the company.

No one, however, offered to interfere with him until he reached the door, when, according to the orders of Mrs. Herringbone, shrieked over the banisters, one of the tall footmen endeavoured to arrest him.

Jack quietly knocked him over like a ninepin, and pursued his way into the street with Fanny unmolested.

CHAPTER X.

WHICH IS CHIEFLY CANINE.

IT is to be hoped the reader has not forgotten the dog upon which Lord Manningtree effected so wonderful a cure.

The poor animal so strangely rescued was taken home by Jack, and nursed and petted till he returned to his original agility and sprightliness, and then became the constant companion of his walks, and showed his gratitude in the many ways dogs have of doing so.

He was a clever dog.

He was a sensible dog.

He was an accomplished dog.

These attributes were arranged on one side, but then on the other—

He was an ugly dog.

He was an eyeless, tailless dog.

And last, and worst of all, he was undoubtedly a "low" dog. A dog of vulgar and dissipated habits, a dog who was literally continually poking his nose into what did not concern him, and what is more, to his owner's grief, he was a dog of thievish propensities.

It was not that when hungry he helped himself to a dinner from the larder, or that he occasionally made a foray into a butcher's shop, but that it was his custom when unobserved to purloin any article he might see and run off with it; and what was more, no correction could teach him to abandon his roguish habits.

"We must give him some name, Jack," said Fanny, one morning.

"Of course. What shall it be?"

"Oh, there are plenty of names. Spot, or Rough, or Lion."

"My dear Fanny, do let us be original. Let us give him a name which in some way applies to him."

"I can't think of one."

"I have it!"

"Well?"

"On account of his thievish trick we will call him—

' FILCHIT !' "

So Filchit the poor animal was called, and day by day he gave additional proof of his right to the cognomen.

In all the minor branches of doggish cleverness he was an adept. Begging, shamming dead, and such-like tricks were too simple feats for him, and in spite of his want of tail and missing eye, he possessed more than double the sagacity of any other dog with the proper appendage to his hind quarters, and the full complement of eyes.

The only fault Jack found with him was that he was *too* clever, and rather apt to lead him into scrapes by the exhibition of his tricks before a scoffing public.

One day the poor animal got Jack into a far from agreeable position, though it afterwards turned out well; and this is how the affair happened.

Jack had been trying hard to obtain a situation in order to add to the paltry stipend Fanny received from Mrs. Herringbone, but had failed in every attempt he had made. He had both advertised and answered advertisements, but without success, and was walking through some of the back streets in the city, pondering whether a leap from one of the bridges would not be the shortest way to end his troubles, when his notice was attracted to the extraordinary behaviour of his dog.

A short, ungainly man had just emerged from a neighbouring court; he had a hard, calculating face, his features were large and irregular, and altogether he presented a far from pleasing appearance.

His dress, too, was remarkable, he wore a pair of short white trousers—so short they scarcely reached to the top of his half Wellington boots—a frayed and dilapidated coat with brass buttons, and a tie which perhaps a fortnight before had been white. His head was surmounted by a shocking bad hat, and as he limped rather than walked along, his exterior was so remarkable as to attract the attention of "Filchit," who, running a few steps in front of him, turned round and stood up gravely on his hind legs.

No notice being taken of this act, the dog jumped upon

him leaving the mark of his dirty forepaws upon the white trousers.

The man, irritated, raised a heavy stick which he carried and aimed a blow at the animal, and, although he missed him, "Filchit" thought it his duty to bark violently. Jack proceeded to the dog's defence; the gentleman with the white trousers swore, the dog barked and yelped at his boots, and the mob hurrahed.

How it happened was impossible to say, but in some way the gentleman slipped and fell upon the pavement. Filchit sprang upon him, and the mob pressed close round.

Jack choked the animal off, and assisted the stranger to rise, which he did, calling down curses upon the dog and his owner, which were not lessened by the discovery that, in the confusion incident to his fall he had been deprived of a large hunting-watch which he usually carried.

"You rascal! you villain! I'll indict you for robbery with violence—I'll transport you and your infernal dog—ugh!"

"My dear sir, let us be cool, and talk over this matter quietly."

"Cool! It's all very well for you, Mr. Jackanapes, standing there grinning, to talk of being cool. How would you like it yourself, sir, eh? How would you like it?"

"It's annoying, certainly."

"Annoying—well, you are a cool hand."

Jack bowed, and the mob laughed.

This irritated him more than ever.

"Police—police! Where the devil are the police? Here, you fellow, I give this person in charge."

"What for, sir?"

"How dare you ask impertinent questions? Take him away—take him to the station-house. He shall go across the water for this, or my name isn't Joshua Grubb."

The end of it was Jack *was* taken to the station-house, and what is more, kept there till the next morning, when, no one appearing to prosecute a charge against him, he was discharged, after being cautioned by a respectable but feeble-minded old magistrate not to do it again.

But this little adventure was not yet at an end.

Jack determined to seek the residence of Mr. Joshua Grubb, and compel him to apologize for his conduct; not that our hero cared much to receive an apology, but he anticipated some fun in his interview with the man.

By help of the Post Office Directory he discovered that Mr. Joshua Grubb's official residence was No. 32, St. Saw-bones-alley, Thames-street, and thither he repaired without loss of time.

St. Sawbones-alley, as no doubt all men know, is a tiny passage leading from Thames-street to the river.

So narrow was it that it gave Jack the idea that the summer sun had warped the two huge warehouses which stand at its entrance, and made them start apart, and thus leave a narrow chink, which might one day be filled up again, and the whole of its inhabitants shut up like flies in a book, between the brick walls of Messrs. Cotton, Spinner, and Company's warehouse on the one side, and the Brothers Oiley manufactory on the other.

By dint of repeated questioning and severe cross-examination, Jack, after some time, found himself at the entrance, and there a new difficulty awaited him.

The Directory had given the number "32" as that of the house where Mr. Grubb's offices were to be found, but as the whole alley did not contain above eight houses, Jack was rather puzzled, but eventually he made the discovery that the numbering of the houses commenced mysteriously at 29, and was then not long in reaching his destination.

Upon the dingy doorpost of No. 32 was painted, in white letters, "Grubb and Lush, Solicitors—First floor," and to the first floor our hero boldly repaired, arriving there after no more severe accidents than crushing in his hat against a projecting beam, and rasping the skin off his left shin against the stairs.

Mr. Grubb answered the door himself, and in the darkness of the stairs, not recognising Jack Rawlings, invited him into the office in the most civil tones imaginable.

"Hullo! It's you, is it?" said Mr. Grubb, in no very pleasant tones, as he recognised our hero.

"You're quite right, Mr. Grubb. I myself stand before you."

"Hum! Very proper conduct on your part, young man, very proper. You have come here, without doubt, to return me your thanks for not having prosecuted you and that confounded dog."

"Nothing of the sort."

"Oh! then may I ask you to account for your intrusion? An Englishman's house is his castle, and, by Jove! sir, his office is his fortress. What is it you want?"

"An apology."

"The deuce you do! What for?"

"Your shameful behaviour yesterday afternoon."

"My shameful behaviour?"

"Yes."

"Well, I like that! Your beast of a dog knocks me down, you or your associates rob me of a valuable watch——"

"Take care what you say. Defamation of character is no joke, Mr. Grubb."

"Well! what the devil brings you here?"

"When I entered only to demand an apology—now I have altered my mind. I want compensation for having passed the night in a prison cell by your directions."

Mr. Grubb began to bluster and swear, but Jack stopped him.

"Do not force me to go to law," said he; "you ought to know I can recover large damages for false imprisonment."

Mr. Grubb began to feel uncomfortable.

"What are you, young man?" he asked, in milder tones than he had yet used.

"At present I am out of employ."

"The very thing, my dear young friend, the very thing."

Jack thought the old man had gone suddenly mad, as he advanced towards him, holding out his hand.

"The very thing—your fortune's made," and he seized Jack's hand, and worked it up and down as if he were an enthusiastic milkman working the cow with the iron tail.

"What's the very thing?" asked Jack, freeing himself from the grasp of Mr. Grubb.

"Come and be my clerk!"

Jack did not feel quite so overjoyed at this offer as Mr. Grubb appeared to expect, but nevertheless it struck him that it might have its advantages.

"Capital business! Thousands of pounds passing through my hands daily."

"Then you want security?" said Jack, doubtingly.

"No—no. I think we can dispense with that, for unless you have a strong partiality for wafers, or can manage to realize a fortune out of old almanacks, there is little fear of my being a loser by you."

"Then as to terms?"

"Well, I think I may fairly offer you a pound a week under existing circumstances. No thanks, young man—I can afford it."

This munificent offer did not strike Jack as being very enormous, nevertheless, after a short deliberation, he determined to accept it, and accordingly, the following morning, he was regularly installed as clerk to the firm of "Grubb and Lush."

It was not long before he learnt further particulars respecting his employer, for Mr. Grubb was the sole member of the firm, Mr. Lush being a myth, his name appearing upon the door-post only as an additional stamp of respectability, which stamp, to tell the truth, the place sorely needed.

Mr. Grubb, although he called himself a solicitor, was in reality a money-lender, and not an over-respectable one either; but Jack was not very particular, and as long as he got his weekly twenty shillings, and was not expected to do any dirty work, he was content to remain in the position which chance, by means of the dog Filchit, had so strangely thrown in his way.

CHAPTER XI.

RELATES SOME FURTHER PARTICULARS CONCERNING THE NOBLE FAMILY OF STONECLIFFE, AND SHOWS LORD MANNINGTREE IN THE LIGHT OF AN AMIABLE AND AFFECTIONATE UNCLE.

THE Earl of Stonecliffe's town-house was one of the sights of the metropolis.

He was a wealthy man, and his mansion was furnished throughout in a most magnificent manner. His picture-gallery, his drawing-room, his study, all in their way were gems, and there is little wonder that people viewing all his treasures should look upon him with envious eyes, and break the tenth commandment, by coveting and desiring their neighbour's house.

The Earl of Stonecliffe was giving a grand dinner-party.

The windows of his mansion blazed with innumerable lights, while outside a crowd of admiring youths clung to the area-railings, in the vain hope that they might see something which would initiate them into the mysteries of the manners and customs of the English aristocracy.

As each successive carriage drew up, the street-boys, after their manner, pushed and elbowed one another to obtain a glimpse of the occupants, and chaffed and jeered to the horror and indignation of the family-butler, at the noble lords and ladies as they alighted.

Inside the house, which resembled a palace in its magnificence, all was one blaze of light. The brilliant chandeliers were reflected back from looking-glasses, and glittered on a thousand articles of value which lay about on tables and cheffoniers.

The air was heavy with the odour of green-house plants. The rustle of costly dresses, intermingled with the ceaseless flow of conversation, rose occasionally above the sounds of a small but perfect band of music, which, concealed from sight, played softly a selection of the best music.

This was the entertainment to which the Earl of Stonecliffe had invited his guests.

In and out among the brilliant company, moving with an easy, graceful motion, Lady Gertrude went hither and thither, carrying happiness and sunshine in whatever direction she bent her steps.

Happy and beautiful, innocent and lovely, she made her way through the crowded rooms unconscious of what was about to befal her.

Many of the guests remarked the unwonted pallor which had spread over her lovely cheeks, but when questioned she had but one answer.

She was suffering from slight indisposition, she said, a bad headache, but that was all.

The Earl of Stonecliffe eyed her uneasily, as if alarmed at her appearance; which alarm was not lessened when suddenly she sat down, and raised her hand to her throbbing brow, while an expression of great pain spread over her beautiful face.

Luckily the guests were too much occupied with their various pursuits to notice her, and, in a few moments, she recovered herself sufficiently again to mingle with them; but there was now an air of languor and fatigue in her movements, and she could hardly force herself to speak in answer to the numerous inquiries she received on every side.

The hour appointed for dinner arrived, but yet it was not announced.

Lord Stonecliffe, one of the most punctual of men, fidgeted uneasily, and glanced every moment at the clock.

One of the expected guests had not arrived, and the earl was anxiously awaiting him before giving the word to proceed to the dining-hall.

The missing one was his brother, Percy, Lord Manningtree.

Suddenly, unannounced, his lordship was amongst them.

There was, perhaps, nothing so very extraordinary in this, although the visitors started and whispered to each other at his sudden presence; but, then, it must be remembered, that Lord Manningtree had made for himself a far from enviable reputation by his mysteriousness and dabbling in occult sciences.

Anyhow, there he stood amongst them as handsome and saturnine in appearance as ever.

He was dressed entirely in black, without a single ornament or order upon his person.

His aristocratic lips, set off by a silky, black moustache, curled satirically as he noticed the sensation his sudden appearance had created, but to all save one he gave the same greeting of a cold grave bow.

The one exception was Lady Gertrude!

His face assumed some semblance of cordiality as he grasped her outstretched hand and inquired anxiously after her health, for he could not but remark the paleness and trembling in the countenance and form of his niece.

The Earl of Stonecliffe greeted him warmly, and the party being now complete, the dinner was announced, and the aristocratic assemblage proceeded to the hall where the sumptuous repast had been laid.

Nothing would be gained by cataloguing the various dishes which were handed round, nor the choice wines with which the elegantly-cut glasses were filled, suffice it that the whole entertainment was well worthy of the nobleman who gave it, and the princely fortune which he possessed.

The conversation never flagged, and of all present, Lord Manningtree was the pleasantest and most amusing.

Yet it was hard for his listeners to tell whether he was in earnest when he spoke, for the cold, hard smile played about his lips, while he gave utterance to the most approved sentiments and seemed to belie his words.

Chance or his own management had placed him next to the Lady Gertrude, and upon her he lavished all his wit and cleverness.

It was his custom to do so always.

She appreciated it and enjoyed his company more than that of any other person she met in the hollow world of society.

Surely there was no harm in her admiring her father's brother!

True it is, he was some seventeen years the junior of the Earl of Stonecliffe, but still he was her uncle, and certain it is she only looked upon him in the light of that relation.

Lord Manningtree had the power of fascinating all with whom he conversed, that is to say, when he exerted himself to do so, and it would indeed have been strange had this young and innocent girl been able to resist him, the more especially when he came by her side naturally as a near relation.

The dinner proceeded merrily. There was none of the stiff formal grandeur about the Earl of Stonecliffe which casts a gloom over entertainments, however good the viands, however rare the wines. He was amongst people of his own class, and could enjoy their society and they his, without detracting from his dignity.

Again during dinner Lady Gertrude felt the sudden faintness come over her, her brain seemed to whirl round, and she clutched the table for support, while the agony she was suffering was apparent by the expression of her beautiful eyes.

It lasted but a moment!

Lord Manningtree alone witnessed it!

Hastily filling a glass with water he gave it to her.

She eagerly drained it to the bottom.

"Are you better, Gertrude?" he asked, in soft gentle tones, of the suffering girl.

"Much. In a few moments I shall be quite well."

He wisely left her to recover quietly, and forbore further questioning.

Later in the evening when the roses had again returned to her cheeks, and something of the old, sparkling gaiety to her deep blue eyes, he filled her glass with a rich rare wine of a famous vintage.

Then filling his own glass he addressed her in a low tone so as to be unheard by the other guests.

"Gertrude, it has gone out of fashion to drink toasts, and even for two people to take wine together, but you would not refuse *me*. I drink to your health and happiness."

He raised his glass to his lips as he spoke and poured the generous wine down his throat.

"Your health and happiness in return," said Lady Gertrude, smiling, as she likewise drank the wine he had given her.

A moment afterwards a great change came over her face.

It was the old expression of pain intensified a hundredfold.

This time it was seen by all.

The company rose simultaneously, while the Earl of Stonecliffe hastened to his daughter's side.

She had risen from her seat and strove to speak, but her tongue refused to move.

Her lovely face became perfectly livid, and her eyes seemed starting from her head, as, with a sudden shriek, she fell back senseless.

Lord Manningtree, who had been standing by her side apparently unmoved, twirling his black moustache, stretched forth his arm as she fell, and supported her fainting frame.

As he moved to carry her to another apartment his elbow either accidentally or by design knocked the glass from which she had drunk the wine to the ground, where it smashed into numberless pieces.

Those of the party who disliked Lord Manningtree, and he had several enemies, afterwards declared there was a dark frown of devil's triumph on his face as he bore the senseless girl to the door.

SELF MURDER!

The happiness and merriment of the party were at an end.

The guests could not get rid of the memory of that pale, distorted face, and the Earl of Stonecliffe was indeed in no fit state longer to entertain his visitors.

Gertrude was his pride, his hope, his happiness. She was all he had remaining to remind him of his wife, whose loss he sincerely deplored, and now his darling lay stretched senseless on a couch in the room above—dying!

Yes, there was no denying the fact.

The physicians who had been summoned, looked grave, and shook their heads sorrowfully, and after an hour's dreadful suspense for her well-nigh distracted father, they told him to prepare for the worst.

All the visitors, with the exception of Lord Manningtree, had taken their departure.

He, in virtue of his relationship, had remained.

There, standing at the head of the couch, his elbow resting in the palm of one hand, while with the other he still twirled his moustache, he looked down with the same cold immovable smile at the white, death-like face beneath him.

He heard the physicians conversing together, and although to all outward appearance he paid no attention to their words, in reality he listened eagerly.

"A most remarkable case," said one.

"It is indeed strange."

"Can you account for this sudden attack? I frankly confess I have never met with a similar case in the whole course of my experience."

"I have."

"Indeed!"

"Yes—once only. That was when I was called in to see a lady who subsequently died, and whose disease gave rise to the famous 'Horsleydown poisoning case.'"

"Poison!"

"Hush! Do not speak so loud."

"Surely you do not suspect she has been murdered?"

"I keep my suspicions to myself, whatever they may be."

Lord Manningtree interrupted the conversation at this point.

"May we hope, doctor?" he asked. "Cannot your skill avail to save the poor girl from the grave?"

"I can do no more, my lord. Nature, the great restorer, must take its course. In half an hour's time I may be better able to inform you."

Lord Manningtree buried his face in his pocket-handkerchief.

He was not a man of much emotion, nevertheless, he could not witness poor Gertrude in the state she now was unmoved.

"Lord Manningtree," said the doctor, after some time had elapsed, "there is *no hope*."

"None!" said the second doctor.

"Are you certain? Do not say she cannot live while yet a chance remains to save her."

"No such chance exists, my lord."

"Good heavens! Is she——"

"She is dead!"

The room appeared to whirl round as Lord Manningtree heard these words, but he quickly recovered himself, and hurriedly left the chamber of death.

"Dead—dead!" he exclaimed, as he sprung into the street. "Dead! One obstacle removed from my course. Gertrude dead!"

And this was the way Lord Manningtree's sorrow for the death of his niece, Lady Gertrude, expressed itself.

CHAPTER XII.

CONTAINS SOME ADDITIONAL FACTS RESPECTING MR. JOSHUA GRUBB AND HIS CLIENTS, AND ALSO RELATES HOW, AND WHY, JACK RAWLINGS TOOK A COLD BATH.

THE office of Messrs. Grubb and Lush, of which Jack had usually sole possession, was not what would be considered a lively place—indeed, it was recorded that a young merchant who had taken the place at one time, a week afterwards hung himself to the centre beam, taking care to commit the rash act the day before quarter-day.

Whether this were the fact or not, it is very certain that he could not have stopped there long without desiring to do so, for of all dismal, dirty, dreary, dusty, dingy, damp, disgusting holes, the office of Messrs Grubb and Lush was surely the worst.

It had one smoke-grimed, filthy window, which afforded a miserable prospect of a squalid court, where dirty, half-naked children played and quarrelled in the gutter from morning till night, and where more than half-drunken hags repaired to settle their differences.

This certainly afforded a little amusement and excitement to our hero, but after a time he found fights, oaths, and torrents of Billingsgate abuse palled upon him, and was neither so interesting nor instructive as might be desired.

It was hard work for him to pass away the hours between nine and five in this dreary hole.

Mr. Grubb had no work for him to do, but kept him for the same reason he had added the name of Lush to his own on the doorpost—to give an air of respectability to the concern.

Here it was that Jack Rawlings spent eight hours of his existence daily; while Fanny was toiling at Mrs. Herringbone's establishment at the other end of London.

After the row at her supper-party, narrated in a former chapter, Fanny had determined to throw up her engagement at any cost.

Jack waited upon the fashionable milliner, and announced that intention; whereupon Mrs. Herringbone produced Fanny's written agreement with her, and at the same time made a great to-do about the money she had advanced our heroine.

Jack threatened to expose her.

She said she didn't care.

He threatened to punish her for her hateful conduct.

She held up the memorandum of the amount Fanny was indebted to her, and swore that, unless she came and worked it out, she would have her arrested for debt.

In short, Mrs. Herringbone proved herself a little too strong even for Jack.

There was no help for it.

Fanny was forced to return to her employment.

Then it was this detestable wretch took her devilish revenge upon Fanny, whose only fault was the resistance she had made on the occasion of the memorable supper-party.

Night after night was she, upon some paltry excuse, kept at her work long after the others had left.

Slaving and toiling, sometimes till the early morning light forced its way through the windows and illuminated her pale, haggard face, but whatsoever hour it was she left, Jack was sure to be there waiting to meet her, and conduct her home, if but for a few hours of happiness, before they again resumed their daily occupations.

To return to St. Sawbone's alley.

Jack Rawlings was naturally of an inquisitive turn of mind.

Fanny declared he wanted to know *too* much.

Be that as it may, his curiosity was aroused by his employer and his mysterious method of conducting business. He had been three weeks in the office without three people calling, yet continually he heard voices talking with Mr. Grubb in his private office; and as Jack knew they did not pass through the room in which he sat to get there, he arrived at the very natural conclusion that there was some other entrance to the house which at present was unknown to him.

Having nothing better to employ his time than cutting quill pens into toothpicks and speculating upon the subject, he was not long in conceiving the idea of exploring Mr. Grubb's private office, into which he had not hitherto ventured.

The following day, his employer being absent, he put this plan into execution.

It was getting late in the day when Mr. Grubb went out, telling Jack he should not return again that evening.

He could not have had a better opportunity.

Giving his employer time to get out of the house, he waited anxiously listening till the sound of his footsteps died away, and quiet reigned supreme in St. Sawbone's Alley.

Then he opened the small door of communication, and stepped into Mr. Grubb's private office.

There was not much there to distinguish it from other rooms—at least, not at the first glance—but Jack was not contented with eyeing it superficially, he examined it closely.

In one corner of the apartment was an iron safe of enormous dimensions, and against the wall near to it stood a good-sized bookcase, filled with law-books, which, however, did not seem to be often disturbed, judging from the collection of dust upon them.

Then for the matter of that everything was more or less covered with dust, which gave him the impression that the contents of the apartment had departed this life, and were slowly mouldering away to their original state.

However, what puzzled him the most was, that there certainly was no other visible entrance to the room besides that through the outer office.

He could not believe his eyes, for he was as positive that he had heard voices talking in that apartment, as he was that his eyes could not discover the means by which they had obtained an entrance.

The room was furnished shabbily enough with a quantity of second-hand office furniture, and as Jack glanced carelessly at the table before which Mr. Grubb's well-worn chair was placed, he saw that the key had been left in one of the drawers.

The temptation was too much for him—he could not help opening it and looking in.

And this is what he saw.

Lying there, side by side, in loving proximity were a couple of heavily loaded life-preservers and a revolver capped and charged.

While Jack was looking at these, and wondering at the mystery attached to Mr. Grubb, he heard that gentleman's voice, as it seemed to him, within a few inches of his ear.

It came from the bookcase.

Hastily returning the pistol to its place, Jack sprang to a small cupboard and crept in just as the shelves of law-books revolved upon a centre, and gave entrance to Mr. Joshua Grubb and a stranger.

Jack shut himself in, and held the door. He could not see the stranger, but he heard his voice.

It sounded familiar to him, although he, for the moment, failed to recognise it.

It was Lord Manningtree.

"More money!" said Mr. Grubb, addressing his lordship. "Impossible!"

"I tell you I must have it."

"What security have I? One young and healthy life stands between you and the property."

"Not a healthy life," said Lord Manningtree.

"How do you know?"

"Because by this time to-morrow the obstacle to my succession will be removed!"

"Removed?"

"Yes."

"Is she ill?"

"She will be."

"Will she die?"

"Really you ask too much, Mr. Grubb."

"Take care, my lord; you are playing a rash game. Think of what may happen."

Lord Manningtree's answer was a fierce oath.

This took place on the afternoon preceding the earl's dinner-party.

As Jack pursued his way homewards pondering over the mystery of Mr. Grubb's office, and wondering what Fanny would say to it all, he arrived at the foot of Blackfriars-bridge.

It was getting dusk, and our hero quickened his pace, as he knew Fanny would be anxiously expecting him.

Flitting before him was one of those dark shadows which abound in the great metropolis.

The shadow of a lost woman!

In her arms the shadow held a child, which ever and anon sent forth a shrill wail as the cold east-wind chilled its puny form.

Then the woman—its mother without doubt—wrapt her own miserable rags the tighter round the shivering infant and pressed it the closer to her bosom as she hurried along.

Hesitating, she paused, and in a low voice broken with sobs implored charity of a passer-by.

"Be off—go to the workhouse!" was the reply, in rough, surly tones.

The shadow bearing the semblance of a woman drew a long weary sigh, and kissed her infant.

Had Jack been a little closer to her he might have heard her soliloquy—

"Poor thing," she murmured to herself, "thou shalt not live to a life of want, of misery, of shame, as I have! The ears of the world are closed to the tales of woe, of such unfortunates as I. It has no mercy! Cruel, cruel! where is there rest for us, my darling?" and again she kissed the baby, and looked longingly at the dark waters eddying beneath the bridge.

"There, there is rest at least," thought she.

Jack had loitered behind, watching the poor woman with much interest.

He pitied her, and dreaded what her motive might be for being on the bridge.

Still she watched the turbid waters flowing rapidly beneath her till her brain grew confused, and her eyes dizzy.

Still Jack, keeping behind, watched her movements.

One more long, loving kiss.

One more fond look.

The poor creature mounted the parapet of the bridge.

Jack rushed forward to detain her.

He was too late.

One wild, despairing shriek echoed through the sharp, keen air, and the woman, pressing her infant tightly to her bosom, plunged into the water beneath.

With the death-cry ringing in his ears, Jack peered eagerly over into the darkness.

He detected something floating with the tide.

No boats were near.

A crowd of idlers had collected in a moment, and strove to penetrate the gloom, shrieking forth confused directions.

Before any one could perceive his intention, or interfere to stop the rash act, Jack had torn off his coat and precipitated himself into the stream beneath.

A cry of horror escaped from the bystanders as they saw him dart through the air and cleave the dark waters.

Then all was lost!

Not a sound, not a sign, came to the eager listeners above, that any of the three beings who five minutes before had been full of life and strength were in the land of the living.

Down, down he went through the deep waters with the impetus the height from which he had jumped gave him.

Down, down, till he thought he must touch the bottom.

Then striking out vigorously, he again regained the surface and looked around him. The lights on the bridge were only just discernible in the evening haze.

He had been caught by the current, and carried far, far away from the spot at which he had first touched the rapid river.

* * * * *

Before him he saw some object still floating on the foul waters.

Exerting his utmost strength he struck out manfully, and just as it sank he reached the spot.

Down, down again he dived till the water bubbled and surged around his head, filling his mouth and ears, and almost depriving him of breath.

But he was rewarded for his exertions!

Immediately before him as he dived he saw the sinking woman and her child.

One more stroke of his muscular arms and he was near enough to stretch forth his hand and clutch the floating drapery.

To his horror, as he rose to regain the surface, the weight attached to the shawl he held seemed tightened, and, looking down, he saw the body of the poor unfortunate again sinking through the turbid waters.

He was too much exhausted to dive again, and the poor luckless woman must needs meet the fate she had sought.

Still, however, Jack grasped the shawl, for wrapped in its folds was the poor infant the woman had not hesitated to consign to a watery grave.

When Jack regained the surface the lights on the shore seemed faint and hazy in the distance.

The tide had carried him into the centre of the stream, and swept him far, far away from the spot where he first made his plunge into the murky waters.

Strong as he was his strength was fast failing. Madly he struck out, hoping to reach the bank; but a few seconds convinced him the attempt was useless.

"Help! help!" he shouted.

For some moments he waited in the most anxious and painful suspense for an answer.

But it came not.

He heard only the tide rushing with force against some barges moored in the distance.

If he only could reach them! he thought. But wishing was of little avail.

He struck out again, but, encumbered as he was, he had the horror of being carried by them at the distance of a few yards only.

Despair took possession of his mind, and with a hurried thought of Fanny, and a hastily muttered prayer for her welfare, he resigned himself to his fate.

Still, however, he mechanically retained his hold of the shawl in which the infant was wrapped, and, as a last resource, lay upon his back and suffered the tide to carry him whither it would.

But help was nearer than he thought.

He had given himself up for lost, and paid no attention to a splashing noise, till a cold, wet nose touched his hand as he floated down the river.

With a cry of joy he hailed it.

It was a dog.

It was Filchit.

The sensible animal seemed at once to understand what was required of him, and only acknowledged his master's caress with a grateful whine.

Jack in a moment saw his opportunity of escape, and partly supporting himself by the faithful beast with his disengaged hand, he exerted himself to paddle to the shore.

Even with Filchit's aid the task was a hard one, but, at length, exhausted and fatigued, Jack reached the bank.

Filchit scrambled out after him, and wagged his stump with redoubled energy at seeing his master safe again on dry land, and fawned upon him, looking up into his face, and whining, and displaying his joy in a thousand doggish ways.

The frequenters of the Jolly Billy-boy were in no little degree alarmed at the sight of a stranger, with the wet streaming from all parts of his person, and tightly clutching something wrapped in a shawl in his arms, appearing suddenly in the small sanded floored parlour in which they were assembled discussing the affairs of the nation, and making ridiculously microscopic bets upon the forthcoming Limehouse regatta.

Jack forced his way into the room, and, without a word, seized the nearest tumbler, which contained a steaming liquid composed of about equal parts of brandy and water, and tossed it off at a draught.

Then he condescended to explain and hurriedly to narrate his adventures to the astounded listeners in the bar-parlour of the Jolly Billy-boy.

A doctor was sent for to attend to the infant, who showed no signs of life; and it was then, when Jack unwrapped the shawl from the poor little senseless baby, that he for the first time discovered a packet of letters and other papers neatly folded in one corner.

Hastily thrusting these into his coat-pocket, and resisting all the entreaties of the landlord, at all events, to wait till his clothes were dried, and leaving the child he had rescued from a watery grave to the tender mercies of Mrs. Potts, the landlady of the Jolly Billy-boy, he hailed a passing cab, jumped into it, and in a few seconds was bowling merrily along the road on his way to the house where Fanny was anxiously expecting him, wondering what accident could have detained him, and prevented his coming to meet her as usual when she left Mrs. Herringbone's.

When the cab drew up before the door she feared something dreadful had happened to her lover, but her mind was speedily set at ease by seeing him leap uninjured from the cab and enter the house.

She flew to meet him.

She extended her beautiful arms; but for the first time Jack did not respond, for he feared an embrace from one in his moist condition might rather damp her ardour, but when an hour later he had retired to bed, as the most fitting place to recover from his ducking, he gave Fanny a spirited account of his adventures, laughing at her fears, and making no mention of the dreadful moments when he forbore to hope, and gave himself up as lost.

Filchit was properly rewarded with a large bone, for being, as aforesaid, a dog of vagrant habits and low tastes, he eschewed delicacies, and preferred to regale himself on such hard and unsavoury morsels as only a dog could extract nourishment from.

And this was the end of Jack Rawlings' cold bath.

CHAPTER XIII.

TREATS OF THE ARTS AS THEY WERE NOURISHED AT THE GRAND ABYSSINIAN MUSIC-HALL.

THE reader must suppose several weeks to elapse between the conclusion of the last chapter and the commencement of the present one.

Jack Rawlings is a hero, but yet he managed to pass over a considerable number of days without any striking adventure befalling him.

He still went regularly every morning to the office of Messrs. Grubb and Lush, and remained there doing nothing till the evening; but just at present he had more reasons than one for being dissatisfied with his employer. The one great reason, however, was that, do all he could, he had been unable to extract a single farthing in the way of salary from his mysterious master, which, to a gentleman in his position, was rather a trying circumstance; for, as well as being without money himself, Fanny's engagement with the detestable Mrs. Herringbone had come to an end, and, although she had tried to procure employment in a variety of ways, she had only met with a succession of repulses.

"Fanny," said Jack, suddenly, to our heroine, one evening, after they had been discussing their affairs, and got rather dismal over them; "Fanny, I've got an idea!"

"Good gracious, Jack! how you startle one."

"I have, though, in reality."

"What is it?"

"Why shouldn't you get an engagement at one of the music-halls?"

"You must be dreaming, Jack. They'd never take me."

"Why not?"

"I can't sing—at least, not much."

"Pshaw! Never mind."

"I can't dance."

"That's of no consequence."

"I should be afraid to learn the tight-rope."

"Certainly."

"Well, Jack; you are the most provoking fellow in the world. What, on earth, is it I am to do?"

"Can't you guess?"

"No."

"Try."

"Don't tease me. I haven't the least idea."

"Don't you know of anything else for which people frequent music-halls?"

"No."

"Did you never hear of people flocking to see some performer who in her profession was excelled by many of whom no notice was taken?"

"Well, you tiresome fellow, tell me why they do so?"

"For the sake of feasting their eyes on beauty."

"And you think I am pretty enough to succeed in that line?" asked Fanny, coquettishly.

Jack's admiring glance was sufficient answer as to his opinion on the subject.

"But what should I have to do?"

"Learn one or two 'patter' songs, dress yourself well, and take care to display a few inches, more or less, of those charming ankles of yours; and I'd lay a wager you prove an attraction such as no manager in his senses would neglect to engage."

It was agreed between them that it was well worth the trial, and accordingly, the following morning, Fanny arrayed herself carefully in her best attire, making herself, if possible, more bewitching than ever, and proceeded to make a round of visits to the proprietors and managers of metropolitan music-halls.

She found, however, they were in nowiso so willing to engage her as Jack in his sanguine dreams had expected.

One gave a surly negative; another a courteous apology; a third had as many ladies in his company as he could afford. Thus repulsed, Fanny determined to make one more attempt only, and that was at the Grand Abyssinian Music-Hall, Whitechapel; so, hailing a cab, she proceeded thither.

The manager, director, and proprietor of the Grand Abyssinian was a portly, well-to-do personage, who had risen to his present position from being pot-boy at a neighbouring tavern, where he was known as Solomons; but, on entering his present line of business, he considered it too common, and altered it to Eugene Montmorency, under which euphonious title he appeared upon all the gigantic "posters" in the neighbourhood.

From this gentleman Fanny likewise got an answer in the negative, but as luck directed it, several things combined to induce him to alter his decision.

In the first place it had been raining, and the pavement was wet and muddy.

In the second Fanny wore her best dress.

In the third Mr. Montmorency had a great admiration for pretty faces, and was drawn to the window of his private residence to see our heroine depart.

These were the causes. The result was that, firstly, Fanny, to avoid contamination from the dirty pavement, raised her dress considerably on leaving the house; secondly, that by so doing she displayed a good deal of her well-turned leg; and thirdly, that Mr. Montmorency rang the bell furiously, and despatched one of his myrmidons to bring the lady back.

"My dear young lady," said the proprietor of the great Abyssinian, when Fanny, looking very much surprised, again made her appearance in his parlour—"my dear young lady, what on earth induced you in seeking an engagement to make no mention of your chief charm?"

Fanny looked puzzled, for she had no idea to what he referred.

Mr. Montmorency pointed downwards to her pretty boots.

Fanny comprehended in a moment, and when she again left the manager's house it was under the engagement to appear nightly as a character singer and dancer at the Abyssinian Music Hall at a tolerably satisfactory salary.

"You see," said Mr. Montmorency to his principal assistant, when announcing the engagement of the new "star," "you see legs is legs, and clerks and such like find 'em pleasant to look at, especially when there's a pretty face atop of 'em, and I tell you what, sir, she's a regular stunner, and we'll have the posters out, announcing her first appearance. Oh! she's a screamer." And the manager rubbed his hands and chuckled with delight, while the present principal singer, who was henceforth only to take the second place, could hardly keep her paint on, so warm did she become in abusing the "bold-faced upstart" who was about to usurp her place.

Fanny, delighted with her success, hurried home to relate her good fortune to Jack, who listened with delight to her account of her interview with the great man.

Then for the next few evenings what fun the house rehearsals were!

How pretty Fanny looked, and with what pleasant emphasis she sung the song written for her by a seedily-attired youth, retained by Mr. Montmorency as poet laureate to his Music Hall.

But the triumph of all was when the fancy dress came home.

Certainly, as Fanny remarked, it was rather short in the skirt, and low in the body, but she had not any scruples about wearing it, and Jack, as soon as he saw her attired in it, proceeded straightway to fall in love with her a second time.

The night of her first appearance in public as Mademoiselle le Blanc arrived, and Fanny, accompanied by Jack, made her way to the "Grand Abyssinian."

Behind the scenes she met with but a cool reception. She was looked upon as an interloper, and the ex-chief lady before alluded to addressed her in tones and words which were supposed to contain biting sarcasm, but to Fanny they only appeared as slightly defective in grammar.

From the audience our heroine met with a most flattering welcome.

They were not art critics, and did not notice that occasionally her voice was a trifle out of tune, or if they did, did not care for it; for, with the exception of two gentlemen, friends of the deposed dancer, who tried to rouse the multitude to hiss, and otherwise express their disapproval, and were, in consequence, summarily ejected, the applause was unanimous, and the manager was perfectly justified in announcing in the bills that Mademoiselle le Blanc had proved a "decided success;" and thus it was that Fanny commenced a new and prosperous career, which, however, she afterwards found was not entirely a bed of roses; but of that in its proper place.

*　　*　　*　　*

The reader will doubtless remember that Jack, on the evening he jumped into the Thames to rescue the poor woman, who had thought death to be the only relief from her sufferings, though he had failed in saving her life, had nevertheless succeeded in bringing the unfortunate infant which she had held at her bosom to the shore.

This child he gave into the charge of the buxom landlady of the Jolly Billy-boy, and to that comfortable but unaristocratic public-house he repaired daily, to inquire into its chances of recovery.

These visits led to the first approach to a quarrel which Fanny and her lover had ever had.

She insisted that Jack must possess more interest than he chose to own in the poor little child, and refused to believe his solemn vows to the contrary, till at last our hero, wearied by the display of causeless jealousy, fairly lost his temper.

But the cloud soon blew over. Fanny agreed to believe anything and everything, and they acted up to the old saying of "kiss and be friends," and carefully avoided the renewal of the subject.

Still something must be done for the motherless infant; he could not consign the poor thing to the tender mercies of a Board of Guardians and the parish beadle.

His deliberations ended by his entering into an arrangement with Mrs. Potts to look after the little thing, and bring it up as her own child in consideration for a small weekly stipend which Jack agreed to furnish.

For some days the packet of papers wrapped in the shawl with the child totally escaped his memory, but when he recollected them he at once set about searching for them, in the hope that they might throw some light upon the child's parentage.

His search was in vain.

Strange as it may appear, the papers were nowhere to be found.

Either he had not in his hurry put them in his coat-pocket, as he thought, or else some one had abstracted them.

If the latter, who could it have been?

So the child was put out to nurse, and Fanny obtained an engagement at the Abyssinian Music Hall, and Jack continued his official life under the able tuition of Mr. Grubb, which three circumstances are surely enough for this chapter.

CHAPTER XIV.

WHICH IN A VERY SHORT SPACE MANAGES TO TOUCH UPON A VARIETY OF TOPICS, BESIDES INTRODUCING SOME NEW BUT DISREPUTABLE CHARACTERS TO THE READER'S POLITE CONSIDERATION.

IT has already been stated that Fanny's public life was not altogether a bed of roses, which may be readily understood when it is remembered how many different persons she had to please.

First and foremost came Mr. Montgomery the manager, but Fanny had managed in a perfectly excusable manner to start a lively but innocent flirtation with him, and consequently had him at all events upon her side.

Next came the British public as represented by those ladies and gentlemen who could afford to pay the sum of threepence for admission to the Grand Abyssinian, and these she could generally manage to conciliate, for she soon noticed that whatever and however she sang, provided only her petticoats were short enough and her attitudes sufficiently striking, she was sure to be rapturously applauded.

With the gentlemen, in short, Fanny was an universal favourite, but the ladies were either more difficult to please or had different tastes to the lords of the creation, or were jealous, for certain it is that Fanny, from some cause or another, got pretty liberally abused by those of her own sex.

"Bold" and "improper" were the mildest of the adjectives tacked on to her name; "brazen," "abandoned," "depraved," were epithets showered upon her by the tongues of the wives of the pork butchers and pawnbrokers situated near the Grand Abyssinian. Indeed—if the truth were as these ladies declared it—Fanny's special mission at the Music Hall was to tempt the aforesaid pork butchers and pawnbrokers from the paths of virtue.

However, this abuse only afforded our heroine and her lover amusement, and many were the merry laughs they had over the comic scenes in real life, which they saw acted in the "Body of the Hall" at the Grand Abyssinian.

It was a source of great gratification to Jack that the Music Hall where Fanny had obtained her engagement was situated at the eastern part of the metropolis.

He had not really any fear that she would be persuaded to leave him, nevertheless he was just as well pleased that she should not be thrown into the way of any sparkling, fascinating young gentleman with plenty of money and soft speeches, and he knew there were not many in the Abyssinian Music Hall sufficiently tempting to induce her to accept their offers.

"Mademoiselle's le Blanc's Benefit!"

"Be sure to come early!"

"Unprecedented attraction!"

These were the words printed in red and blue letters at least a yard high, on gigantic posters and stuck on all dead walls and available places in the neighbourhood of the Grand Abyssinian Music Hall.

It was the literal fact.

Fanny had been so successful and had put so much money into the pocket of Mr. Montmorency, that that gentleman one day in the heat of the moment, and helped by a couple of extra glasses of hot rum-and-water, actually proposed to her that she should have a "benefit-night," a thing none of her predecessors had ever dreamed of, and our heroine was not slow to accept the generous offer.

We will pass over the interval between the announcement and the arrival of the grand night; and on the occasion of Mademoiselle le Blanc's benefit let us take our seat in the front row to watch not only the "inimitable performance of the talented troupe of artistes," but likewise. the movements of two suspicious-looking and seedy individuals who have taken their position by a pillar which in a measure hides them from view, and in the shadow of which they carry on an earnest conversation.

The magnificent orchestra of the "Abyssinian" strikes up and plays a selection of operatic airs, so tortured and altered that it would puzzle the composer himself to say whether they were his own or not.

The two mysterious visitors do not seem to care much for music, and under the shelter of the noise made by the trombone and big drum continue their conversation.

The overture is concluded and lightly tripping down the stage comes the heroine of the evening.

Mademoiselle le Blanc!

Silence reigns in a moment as she gracefully acknowledges the greeting she receives from the audience.

The two, alone, still continue their all-engrossing conversation.

"Hush!"

"Silence!"

"Turn 'em out!"

Shout several pair of powerful lungs, making twenty times more noise than the two talkers.

One of the mysterious gentlemen growls and holds his tongue, and mutters to the other that the "niggers" come next, and they can go on with their conversation during the choruses.

The other nods his head, and growls out a running accompaniment of curses to Fanny's song.

Our heroine had a new song, and a new dress for the occasion of her benefit, and succeeded in working up her audience to a high pitch of pleasurable excitement.

She was attired as a Highlander.

The short kilt and bare knees, the handsome plaid, the short stockings, the bonnet with the badge of the clan in front. In short, the whole attire suited her admirably.

She came forward and sang her song, which, by-the-bye, had nothing to do with the North Britons, and was rapturously encored; then she sang another, and that was encored; then she varied the proceedings with a dance, and if the song was "rapturously" encored, goodness only knows what adjective to apply to the applause which followed the dance.

The audience seemed to think they could remain there all night to see her stand upon the tips of the toes of one foot, the other leg being stuck out at right angles, and whirl round and round like a teetotum, and never stopped to inquire whether this was in keeping with the character of the staid and sober chieftain she represented.

It will be readily understood that Fanny got sooner tired of this amusement than the audience, so after having been re-called five or six times, she refused to come any more, and the threepenny-paying public were forced to content themselves with the "Massachusetts Warblers," and a selection of popular negro melodies.

It was evident the two talkative strangers had not come to the Hall for the sake of the music; they smoked incessantly, and drank raw spirit, so nearly raw as to call forth the astonishment even of the waiter who supplied them, but beyond this did not appear to pay the slightest attention to what was going on around them.

Shortly after midnight the performance for the benefit of Mademoiselle le Blanc came to an end.

She and Jack walked quietly home together; some of the audience followed their example, while others, it is to be feared, loitered idly by the way, and possibly got entrapped by some of the roaring lionesses walking about seeking whom they might devour.

The two shabby men set off at a great pace towards the city.

Arrived there they took a northerly direction, and about an hour and a half after the closing the doors of the "Grand Abyssinian" for the night, they had left London behind them, and were walking along through one of the quiet suburbs.

Their destination seemed peculiar, for they turned down a short road which led to the cemetery alone.

Stopping before they reached the iron railings, one of them from a hole beneath a hedge extracted a spade and pickaxe. Then again they proceeded silently on their way.

Looking carefully round to make sure they were unperceived they cautiously and silently proceeded to mount the iron railings, clamber over them, and drop noiselessly among the shrubs planted by the wall.

There could be no doubt as to their hideous errand.

They belonged to that class of men who nightly ransack the graves to procure a living by the sale of corpses to doctors and others interested in the study of anatomy, and unable to obtain subjects upon which to experiment save by stealth.

They were body-snatchers!

After a lapse of some little time the pair again appeared, and clambered back from the cemetery, but this time they were somewhat encumbered.

The first got over safely, then the other handed him "something" wrapped in long white drapery.

Something stiff and stark, that had only the day before been laid, as it was supposed, peacefully in the grave only to be disturbed at the Judgment-day.

A low whistle, and a light cart drove rapidly round the corner.

Into this the men put their ghastly burden, following it themselves, and in another minute were driving rapidly back to the great metropolis.

CHAPTER XV.

IN WHICH LORD MANNINGTREE SEES A GHOST.

LORD MANNINGTREE's laboratory was not a lively place to enter at any time, but when the shades of night were falling it was doubly horrible.

It would be no shame to any one, however bold and courageous, to feel a little trepidation at entering this strange apartment, for, independently of the usual paraphernalia, such as retorts, crucibles, and alembics, which lay scattered about, puzzling the uninitiated by their strange weird forms, there were other objects horrible and frightful in themselves without the adjuncts which surrounded them.

It was not alone the row of dark grinning skulls upon a low shelf—it was not the whole skeleton only partially concealed by the half-drawn curtain, but besides these there were around the room a series of jars arranged, each containing some hideous preparation of the human form, and upon a long wooden table in the centre of the apartment, upon the particular occasion I would introduce the reader to this den of horrors, lay stretched the stiff, stark corpse of a man prepared for dissection, and only partly hid by the cloth thrown over it.

A strange light, of a bluish tinge, proceeded from the furnace, and danced and quivered upon the various dreadful objects around, one moment imparting a fiendish, sneering expression to an Indian's skull, the next lighting up the ghastly features of the dead man, or fitfully glancing over the array of bottles and their horrible contents.

The laboratory was unoccupied by any living being.

It need, indeed, be one endowed with strong nerves and accustomed to such sights who could bear to be alone in this gloomy chamber, with no other companionship than that torn from the grave.

There is a sound of approaching footsteps, and of voices in discussion.

The key turns in the lock; and Lord Manningtree, accompanied by an individual we have met before, enter the laboratory; and the nobleman relocks the door.

Lord Manningtree's companion upon this occasion was no other than Mr. Grubb, Jack's employer, who advanced boldly, almost undismayed by the spectacle before him.

It was not his first visit to this strange place; nevertheless, in spite of the bold, firm step with which he walked, it was evident from his countenance that, though tolerably familiar with the scene, he was not over-well disposed towards it.

Lord Manningtree routed out a couple of seats from a heap of lumber in one corner, and produced a large meerschaum pipe, with a long cherry-wood stem, then, supplying himself with tobacco, which he took from a jar made from a small skull, he lighted his pipe, and puffed away for some moments in silence.

Mr. Grubb fidgeted with his feet, altered his position every minute, and gave other unmistakeable signs of being ill at ease, which his host either did not or would not perceive.

It was certainly a strange apartment in which to entertain a visitor.

"Well, my lord," said Mr. Grubb, rather uneasily; "what is it you want with me in this dismal hole?"

"Don't you smoke, Grubb?" asked his lordship, paying no manner of attention to the question just addressed to him.

"No," growled Grubb, sulkily enough, as if he were one of the bears in the Zoological Gardens, and had climbed to the top of the poll, and failed to receive the expected bun.

"What a pity," remarked his lordship. "You lose a great pleasure." And again he puffed away in silence, watching the blue wreaths of smoke curl gracefully round and vanish into air.

"If that's all you've got to say I shall be off."

Lord Manningtree laughed, and twirled his moustache, looking like a fashionable Mephistopheles.

"Are you going to pay me what you've borrowed?"

"Haven't the least intention of doing so."

"Then I tell you what—I'll have it one way or another. I'll send men to take possession of your property."

"What property?—the corpses?" and Lord Manningtree pointed to the body on the table with a laugh.

Mr. Grubb had not before perceived what was beneath the sheet.

He shuddered now as he glanced at it.

"You're quite welcome to it," said his lordship; "perhaps you'd like to take it home with you"—and he turned down the sheet lower, thus revealing the ghastly, distorted features.

"No—I don't like joking on such subjects—cover it up again," said Grubb, fidgeting uneasily in his chair.

The nobleman did as requested, and resumed his seat with a faint, triumphant smile playing about his lips.

"You haven't such a thing as brandy, or any spirit down here, have you?"

"Plenty, my dear Grubb."

"Perhaps you'd give me a drop?" said the pettifogger, whose courage was fast oozing away.

"Certainly, with the greatest pleasure."

Lord Manningtree took down a jar from one of the shelves containing some hideous preparation preserved in spirit.

"There you are, my dear Grubb. Never mind that trifle inside—it wont hurt you."

Grubb turned faint as he saw the contents of the jar, and then placed it as far from him as he could.

"Excuse me," said Lord Manningtree; "I have forgotten something. I will be back directly"—and he unlocked the door.

"For goodness' sake, do not leave me in this frightful place alone."

"Why not?"

"I shall go mad."

"Nonsense! You'll find it very comfortable. There's a skeleton to talk to when you get tired of this gentleman"—and he playfully indicated whom he meant by poking the corpse in the ribs with his finger sparkling with brilliant precious stones.

"I wont stop here alone!" and the frightened lawyer endeavoured to assume a bullying tone, but failing singularly, his loud tones dying away into a little feeble cry for help.

"Oh, very well! if you don't like it, I'll remain," said his lordship, obligingly; "and we'll proceed to business."

"With all my heart," said the poor little man, glad of any excuse to call away his attention from the ghastly objects around him; "but hadn't we better have a light?"

"There's light enough for what we want," said Lord Manningtree, and, as he spoke, a brighter flame than usual sprang from the furnace, making the ghostly occupants of this den of horrors look doubly frightful by its bluish gleam.

"Mr. Grubb," said the noblemen, in his blandest and most insinuating voice, "what terms are you inclined to propose?"

"None. I'll have the money, or I'll blow upon you."

"No, surely, my dear Grubb, you wouldn't do that?"

"I will, though."

"Reflect well, and see what accusation you could bring against me."

"Murder!"

Lord Manningtree started, and his cheek blanched, but in the uncertain light it passed unnoticed.

"Ha, ha, ha! That's a good joke, Grubb. What a wag you are!"

"Ha, ha, ha! I'm glad your lordship thinks so."

"That's right. But look here, Grubb; perhaps you wouldn't mind explaining this particular witticism?"

"Not in the least."

"You're very funny, you know, but a trifle obscure."

"You remember the night of the Earl of Stonecliffe's dinner-party?"

"Certainly."

"You remember Lady Gertrude's sudden illness, and subsequent death?"

"These are painful memories, Mr. Grubb."

"Possibly. But they are very necessary ones."

"Go on."

"Lady Gertrude, my lord, died from the effects of poison!"

Lord Manningtree started from his seat with an oath.

Had Mr. Grubb known his intention he would hardly have remained so quiet, but prudential reasons restrained his lordship from committing the crime which had entered his head of effectually ridding himself of his visitor, and he again resumed his seat.

"Nonsense!" he said; "it can't be true."

"I have proofs of what I say."

"Do you know the murderer?"

"I do."

"Tell me his name. If your statement is correct, I will never rest till I have brought him to the scaffold."

"Take care what you say, my lord."

"What is the poisoner's name?"

"Percy, Lord Manningtree!"

For a few moments there was a complete silence, during which the money-lending, rascally attorney strove to peer through the darkness and discern the thoughts passing in his companion's mind.

"Ha, ha, ha!" said his lordship. "I said you were a wag, Grubb; you ought to write for *Punch*, you ought, 'pon my honour."

Mr. Grubb was not prepared with a suitable answer, for he was not a skilful general, and had risked his entire chance of victory on his one deadly shot.

Had Lord Manningtree answered him by a furious burst of passion, Grubb would have been ready for him, had he been terror-struck and abjectly begged him to conceal the crime, Grubb was quite ready to make terms with him for keeping the secret, but to be rewarded only with a hearty roar of laughter was a little too much too bear; the idea which had occupied his thoughts day and night for many weeks ridiculed was more than he could bear, to say nothing of the sudden dispersion of his golden dreams by the hearty guffaw of the young nobleman.

Still, though discomfited Grubb's conviction remained the same.

He still believed that Lady Gertrude met her untimely death by means of poison, and that Lord Manningtree was instrumental in the matter.

"Your lordship seems to think it very funny," said Grubb, when he recovered from his temporary confusion.

"Yes—a devilish good joke."

"May I ask the reason?"

"Certainly. I'm laughing at your presumption."

"My presumption?"

"Yes; and your silliness."

"It isn't so good a joke as I thought. Perhaps your lordship will not object to tell me, in what way I presume, and also in what way I am silly?"

"You presume in thinking that you can dictate to me; you are silly in imagining for a moment that the word of a low, underbred, pettifogging, money-lending attorney can weigh down that of a nobleman, brother of the wealthiest peer of the realm."

"You would not like to be accused of murder?"

"Certainly not."

"Suppose I tell you that unless you agree to what I propose, I shall denounce you!"

"If I thought that to be your intention you would never leave this place alive," answered Lord Manningtree, in cool, hard tones, which made Mr. Grubb feel exceedingly uncomfortable.

"Why should you care if you are innocent?" he asked.

"Because it is not a pleasant position in which to be placed—besides, juries do sometimes make mistakes."

"My lord, listen to me. I have a scheme to propose, which will benefit us both and secure my silence."

"What is it?"

"Lady Gertrude is dead—of that there is no doubt—we will not go into the question of the means by which she met her end."

"Go on."

"Between your lordship and the richest earldom in the kingdom there is only one life."

"Of course, I know all this."

"Unquestionably. I am merely reminding you of a few necessary circumstances."

"Well?"

"If the Earl of Stonecliffe dies before the year is out you will become possessed of the title and vast estates."

"That will be the case whenever he dies."

"Not necessarily. The Earl is not an old man; what more natural than that he should marry again, what more natural that he should beget children, who would become his heirs?"

"It is possible, but not probable."

"Excuse me, nothing is more likely."

"I don't see what you have to do with my brother's affairs. What is it you wish me to do?"

"The Earl of Stonecliffe may die before the year—even before the present month has passed away."

"He *may*. But he has always been considered very healthy."

"So was Lady Gertrude, my lord, yet she died."

"What do you mean?"

Lord Manningtree knew full well the point at which Mr. Grubb was aiming, but he determined to pretend ignorance to the last.

"I mean the same means which removed your niece from your path may get rid of your brother."

"Poison!"

"Thank you, Lord Manningtree. I see you are of the same opinion as myself, respecting the cause of Lady Gertrude's death."

The young nobleman perceived in a moment the fatal mistake he had made, and knew that with a man like Grubb it was useless to endeavour to retrieve his error.

This last speech of the little attorney's, who was congratulating himself inwardly upon his cleverness, decided his fate.

His doom was sealed!

"I have been studying poisons lately," said Lord Manningtree, rising and knocking the ashes out of his pipe.

"Indeed, my lord! Don't you find it rather unhealthy?"

"Not at all. I have plenty of safeguards."

"I'm delighted to hear it. So valuable a life as your lordship's is worth preserving."

"What! for the hangman?"

"Don't joke on such subjects. I feel a cold shiver all down my back."

Lord Manningtree, making the excuse of attending to his furnace, went for a few seconds behind a screen.

Hastily throwing some spirit into a small porcelain dish, he lit it, and emptied upon the flame part of the contents of a small phial which he extracted from a leather case which he took from his pocket.

Then hurriedly seizing a queerly-shaped mask, he hurried back to his companion.

"Look here, Grubb. This is the way I guard against the poisons."

His lordship put on the mask, which entirely covered his face, leaving only the glass-covered apparatus to see through and a small hole through which to breathe.

"Lor!" said Grubb, amazed.

"You see," continued his lordship, "my countenance is hidden and free from the effects of any poisonous fumes."

"Yes; but how do you breathe?"

"Through this small hole."

"Then, in the event of the atmosphere being poisoned, you would inhale it."

"Not at all."

"Why not?"

"Because inside this mask, and fitting tightly to my mouth, is a small frame filled with sponge. This sponge is soaked in a particular liquid which purifies the air as it passes through."

"Lor! does it, now!" said Grubb, who had no appreciation for the wonders of art, principally, no doubt, because he failed to understand them.

"Yes. It's a wonderful contrivance!"

"Is it comfortable to wear?"

"Yes, pretty well."

It certainly was worthy of remark, that Lord Manningtree appeared to find it so comfortable that he evinced no inclination to take it off, but resumed his seat still wearing his strange head-dress, which made him look more like the diver at the Polytechnic than the fashionable young nobleman he was.

"What a strange smell there is!" said Grubb, sniffing suspiciously."

"It's only some of my chemicals. You'd soon get used to that."

"You haven't told me yet what you think of my proposition."

"Do I understand you right? Your idea is that the Earl of Stonecliffe should be got rid of by poison, that I should inherit his property, and that you should have your share?"

"Precisely. Is it a bargain?"

"You fool!"

"Eh! what?"

"You fool!"

"You don't mean to be personal, I hope, my lord."

"Do you think that if such a plan ever entered my head I should trust *you* to share it with me. Blockhead, you have shown me your hand and I have profited by it."

Grubb turned pale, and a feeling of faintness and nausea seized him.

"What do you mean? What have you been doing?"

"You will soon find out."

"You refuse to accept me as your partner in this enterprise?"

"I do!"

"Then beware, Lord Manningtree, for I will—I denounce you as a murderer!"

"Pooh! no one will believe you."

"Suppose I have witnesses?"

"Which you have not."

"At all hazard, I will brand you with a stain which shall last you through life. Percy Lord Manningtree shall appear at the prisoner's bar on the charge of having wilfully taken away the life of Lady Gertrude by means of poison!"

"Percy Lord Manningtree will do nothing of the kind."

"You defy me?"

"Yes; I laugh at you!"

Grubb put his hand to his forehead. It seemed as if a heavy leaden weight were pressing upon his brow, so suffocating had the atmosphere become.

"You do not know what you are braving."

"I do, perfectly well."

"And you still hold to your resolution?"

"Certainly."

"Why?"

"*Because you have not five more minutes to live!*"

A ghastly pallor crept over the attorney's features as he heard these words spoken in calm, deliberate tones.

He strove to move, but his limbs were paralysed.

He strove to speak, but his tongue refused to perform its office, and for a few moments he could do nothing but glare wildly with distended eyeballs at the tall, upright figure of the nobleman standing before him, his head still enveloped in the ugly, but life-preserving mask.

With sudden energy, partly recovering the use of his limbs, he threw himself upon the ground before Lord Manningtree's feet.

"You do not mean it? Say, you do not mean it!" he cried, in an agony of despair.

"The words I have spoken are the truth!"

"Oh! save me! save me! Spare my life! I did not mean what I said! I feel the fumes of poison choking me! Spare me!" and the abject wretch grovelled on the ground before the other's feet.

"It is too late!"

"No—no—not too late!" You cannot mean me to die thus suddenly. Give me a day—an hour—only to talk with you! I will do anything you wish, only spare me this dreadful agony."

"It is no more than you had planned for my brother to endure!" said his lordship, calmly and coldly, and without betraying the slightest symptoms of relenting.

"I did not mean it!—I swear I did not mean it!"

"Do not die with a false oath on your lips!"

"Oh, spare me!"

"It is too late. Your doom is sealed. In your death is my only safety. You have but two minutes more!"

"Devil! you, too, shall die with me!"

Grubb, with sudden energy, sprang to his feet and clutched Lord Manningtree by the throat firmly with one hand, while, with the other, he strove to tear from his face the mask which rendered the poisoned air powerless to hurt him.

FILCHIT PERFORMS A DEED OF DARING.

The young nobleman, though surprised by the suddenness of the attack, was not unprepared.

He closed with him, and strove to unloose the fingers which clung with wonderful tenacity in painful proximity to his windpipe.

For a few moments the issue of the struggle seemed doubtful; but the wretched attorney was no match for the athletic young man, and, after the space of but very few seconds, Lord Manningtree succeeded in freeing himself from his antagonist.

With one vigorous exercise of strength, he flung Grubb upon the ground, where he lay senseless, only occasionally indicating, by a heavy in-drawn breath, that life still remained in his miserable frame.

Lord Manningtree coolly unlocked a cupboard, and extracting therefrom a volume of a racy and exciting French novel, threw himself again into his chair, and speedily became deep in the work of fiction, and apparently totally unconscious of the dreadfu reality which lay stretched at his feet.

When his lordship had concluded one chapter, he slightly altered his position, and in doing so, knocked his foot with some violence against the prostrate man.

A faint groan escaped from his lips, which had assumed a purple hue, and about which hung a thick foam.

Lord Manningtree scarcely glanced at his victim, but commenced a new chapter.

After the lapse of about a quarter of an hour his lordship shut up his book, first carefully placing a marker at the page where he had left off, and returned it to the cupboard.

Then he proceeded to examine the body of the attorney.

One glance sufficed.

He was dead!

The murderer deliberately unlocked the door, through which he had rushed upon Jack when he emerged from the sewer, and proceeding to the shed, he raised the trap, disclosing the black abyss beneath; then returning for the body of the attorney, he flung it, without hesitation, through the opening into the sewer.

He heard the body splash into the filthy waters, and then closed the trap with a smile of sardonic triumph upon his face.

The laboratory was still full of the poisonous fumes, so the noble owner left the door wide open to allow the fresh night-breeze to sweep in and cleanse it thoroughly.

For the convenience of being in close proximity to his jealously-guarded apartment, and yet wishing to avoid the life-destroying atmosphere, he wheeled his chair outside into the yard, took off the hideous mask which had hidden his face, and quietly lit his meerschaum, determined to enjoy a comfortable smoke, and cogitate over the past, the present, and the future.

The night was pitch dark, not a single star had condescended to appear; but for that his lordship cared not, as he sat there coolly and sedately puffing forth volumes of smoke from his huge pipe.

His pipe and his thoughts lasted him for upwards of an hour, at the end of which time, feeling tired, he resolved to secure his laboratory for the night and retire to rest.

With this intention he re-entered the Den of Horrors, now entirely freed from its poisonous vapours, but he had not taken three steps into the interior before he stopped in his course and gazed fixedly with distended eyeballs at *something* before him.

It was the form of a woman.

A form draped in the long, hideous white garments of the grave, and with the band still fastened beneath the jaw.

A form of surpassing beauty.

A form with a delicately moulded, aristocratic face which his lordship knew only too well.

"It is Gertrude's spirit!" he exclaimed, in hoarse, terrified tones, and then with a shriek he sank senseless on the floor.

CHAPTER XVI.

THE FIRST STEP IN THE PATH OF CRIME.

THE inhabitants of St. Sawbones-alley were at first rather shy of Jack Rawlings, but after a time, seeing him appear regularly every day, noticing that he was very good-looking, and remarking that he was comparatively harmless, they began to consider him as one of themselves.

Sarah Jane, the red-haired daughter of the coal and vegetable purveyor, went so far as to watch for his arrival every morning, and robbed her father's oil lamp of the greater part of its contents to grease her fiery locks and present as far as possible an enchanting appearance to our hero.

The agonies that poor young woman went through in order to attract Jack were something awful.

The lamp-oil was a trifle to what she did.

Hearing small waists were aristocratic, she systematically tied several yards of string round her body, and noticing that one morning Jack stared with every symptom of admiration at the ankles of a pretty girl crossing the top of the alley, she made a point of displaying her own hoofs and thick legs on every available occasion, when our hero happened to be in sight, but all to no purpose.

Jack resisted the blandishments of this siren, and passed her day by day, as she herself pathetically expressed it to her bosom friend, "without so much as a wink!"

A fresh cause of surprise occurred to Mr. Rawlings, which, although it was a deep mystery to him will not cause the reader any great surprise.

For a whole week Mr. Grubb never came near the office! Jack could not imagine what had become of him, and expected him to turn up every minute.

How was he to know the ghastly, half-decomposed body which for four days floated backwards and forwards in the sewer with the tide was that of his late master?

How was he to identify the body picked up floating among the weeds in the Essex marshes as that of Mr. Grubb?

The bunch of keys and two farthings in his pocket could never lead the energetical and indefatigable police to suppose it was the eccentric money-lender's corpse streaked out in the dead-house, waiting to be claimed.

To all but *one* Grubb's disappearance was an inscrutable mystery.

Lord Manningtree might have been able to throw a light upon the matter, but who would think of applying to *him?*"

What was a rascally money-lender the less in the world to the brother of the Earl of Stonecliffe?"

So Jack wondered at the disappearance, and the body was buried in a pauper's grave, and the fashionable Lord Manningtree went to the Opera and the Haymarket afterwards, and the world went round none the less smoothly by reason of the breaking up of the firm of Messrs. Grubb and Lush.

Jack, after the lapse of a second week from the date of Grubb's disappearance, got rather tired of the monotony of sticking wafers on the office ceiling, balancing the ruler, and staring out of window at the red-faced, red-haired Sarah Jane opposite, so after a little deliberation he determined to endeavour to discover some clue to his master's whereabouts.

He little thought of looking for him in a deal coffin some three feet underground!

The first drawer he broke open in his search contained nothing but old letters, but one of these was directed to him at a little street in Camden Town.

This Jack concluded to be his private residence, and thither he repaired without loss of time.

It was a close, narrow street, where the houses looked as if they were ashamed of themselves for having grown so tall, and were apparently considering whether they could mend the matter by toppling over into the street, and it was at one of the shabbiest and dirtiest of them that Jack, guided by the letter, stopped in front of, and rung the bell.

A slovenly, slipshod girl, who looked as if a Turkish bath would do her a world of good—provided, at least, she was not *all* dirt, in which case she would melt away altogether—answered the bell: after some considerable delay, which appeared to have been occasioned by her endeavouring to struggle into her gown, as she came to the door fastening it, and looking red and hurried.

She almost tumbled over the mat when she saw Jack standing on the step, for it was seldom any one well dressed or respectable-looking stopped in that street.

"Does Mr. Grubb live here?" asked our hero, blandly.

"Lor-a-mussy!" cried the damsel.

Jack repeated his question.

"Missus—missus!" shrieked the slave; "ere's another on 'em."

"Hold 'im tight till I come," shouted another voice, over the banisters.

Jack, amazed, and wondering what the deuce it all meant, stared in astonishment at the servant girl, who stared at him in return with open mouth and eyes.

In a few moments a huge, amazonian-looking woman came down the stairs, and along the passage, till she stood in the doorway, which she completely blocked up, and placed her arms akimbo, scowling at our hero with an air of defiance.

"Have you come to pay the rent?" she asked, defiantly.

"My good woman——"

"Don't good woman me! I want none of your blarney, and unless you hand over one pound four and tuppence, and pay for the broken tea-cup, I'll denounce the whole lot of yer as swindling, runaway, blackguardly, treacherous, ill-mannered, bad-tempered, money-lending, money-stealing pickpockets. Be off with you! I'd abuse you, only I've had a good eddikation, and know better."

"I assure you, madam——"

"I want none of your assurances—I want my money."

"I hope you may get it," said Jack, politely.

"Drat your impudence! Where's my one pound four and tuppence?" And the virago held her fist in close proximity to Jack's nose.

"Mr. Grubb will pay you, I dare say."

"If I only knew where he was I'd make him."

"You don't know, then?"

"I'll tell you what, young man; if I did, I'd forget my good manners and give him such a trouncing as he never had before in his life, and when you next sees him you may tell him he'd better not let me catch sight of his ugly face again. That's all."

"Thank you, ma'am, for the information you have given me," said Jack, as he walked rapidly away, with the infuriated landlady yelling "One pound four and tuppence" after him as long as he remained in sight.

When he turned the corner and disappeared, she boxed the slave of all work's ears for standing in the way, and then hit her a punch in the back for stumbling over the pail standing in the passage, and retired to her own room to growl to herself, while Jack pursued his way back to St. Sawbones-alley, still more puzzled than when he started on his voyage of discovery.

It has already been stated that Jack had not received a single penny of his stipulated salary from Mr. Grubb, and now that that gentleman had taken his departure without warning, and as there seemed no probability of his return, our hero determined to act upon an idea which had, more than once, crossed his mind.

It was an idea that at first had caused a shudder to run through his frame.

It was an idea that at the first glance seemed to border upon crime.

It was an idea he shrank from, but which, after a time, seemed to be less and less culpable.

At last it seemed to him that, so far from being a crime, it was the proper thing to do.

Why should not he have his rights?

He determined to help himself to the money due to him for his services as clerk to the renowned firm of Grubb and Lush.

No sooner had he definitely arrived at this conclusion than he determined to act upon it.

It was in vain that evening that Sarah Jane watched for his exit from the office from her father's coal-shed.

It was in vain that Fanny waited till the last minute for him to take her to the "Grand Abyssinian."

He was otherwise engaged.

Taking the poker, which was the only convenient weapon he could lay his hands upon, he entered his employer's private room, and proceeded systematically to work to force open all the drawers and examine the contents.

The locks were old, the wood was rotten, and it required but little exertion to force them.

One alone resisted his efforts.

"Here," thought he, "is the cash!" for hitherto those he had opened had contained nothing but bundles of old papers and legal documents, and he began to fear his search was useless.

With one vigorous wrench the lock of the small drawer flew off, and Jack bent over it eagerly to scrutinize its contents.

What was that little parcel wrapped up so carefully in silver paper, and put away in one corner?

What could it be?

With hands trembling with anxiety he unfastened the paper.

From it there dropped three things.

The first was a long silken tress of hair, the colour of which was dark as the raven's wing!

The second was a lady's glove which had once been white, but was now of a dingy yellow colour from age, everywhere except upon two fingers, and a few spots on the back of the hand which were of a much darker hue.

The colour was not to be mistaken.

It was the stain of blood!

The third thing which fell from the packet was a folded piece of dingy paper much worn, as if by repeated unfolding and of a pale yellow coffee colour from age.

That too was spotted with blood!

It was a marriage certificate!

Jack was amazed at finding such relics in the keeping of the old money-lender, and was about to throw them away in disgust, but the thought occurred to him that they might be of some value; accordingly wrapping them up carefully again, he placed them securely in his waistcoat pocket, and resumed his search.

After a lengthened hunt he was rewarded by coming across a good-sized cash-box, which on being shaken, emitted the unmistakeable jingle of gold.

Taking the poker, he strove to break the lock, but for some time it resisted all his efforts, but at length with a mighty blow he forced it open, and sovereigns flew about the room!

Not in twos and threes, but in scores!

Jack Rawlings contemplated the golden treasure for some minutes, glutting his eyes with the sight of the glittering coin!

It was a moment of anxious deliberation with him!

When he first commenced the search for his master's gold he eased his conscience by saying he was only about to take what was rightly his due, but now that money to a hundred times the value of what was justly his, lay scattered before him.

Its owner was not forthcoming!

Why should he not take it all?

The tempter stood at his elbow, and whispered in his ear. He started from his seat, hurriedly crammed his pockets with the treasure, and then removing everything from the office which could lead to his detection, he hurried into St. Sawbones-alley, and made the best of his way home.

For days Sarah Jane waited disconsolate in the coal-shed for his arrival, but he never appeared again, and she, after a time getting over the disappointment, formed an alliance with a highly respectable chimney-sweep, and brought up a numerous progeny of small sweeps and potato merchants, who gambolled in the gutter, and spread themselves over the pavement, after the manner of their kind.

When Jack got home he discovered it was past the time at which he should have started to bring Fanny home from the "Grand Abyssinian," nevertheless he determined to start for the Hall, on the chance of meeting her in order the sooner to tell her what he had done, and to hear what she would say to it.

He had not proceeded far when a sight met his eyes which caused him to start back, and burst forth in a very strong reprehensible manner.

He saw Fanny advancing towards him, leaning on the arm of a young and handsome man.

CHAPTER XVII.

THE YOUNG MAN FROM THE COUNTRY.

HARRY BELVOIR was a handsome, bold-eyed, merry young man, who had seen some eighteen or nineteen summers.

Both his parents had died before he had even learnt to call them by their names, and he had been handed over to the sole guardianship of his uncle Pigley.

Now Uncle Pigley was not a very agreeable or good-tempered old man.

Uncle Pigley was cross, harsh, fat, and unmarried, but to make up for never having taken unto himself a wife, he lived on terms of suspicious familiarity with the elderly cook of his establishment.

This may have been only the village scandal, but it is very certain that one day after Master Harry had called the greasy superintendent of the pots and kettles an "old ——" (I shouldn't like to write the word), his uncle's manner towards him changed very materially, inasmuch as his language got coarser, and his manners more unbearable, and Master Harry led what is commonly called a "sad life of it."

Scowls and growls were the most cordial welcome he ever received from his most affectionate guardian, curses and blows were not at all unfrequent, till Harry finding one day he was nearly as tall, and much more muscular than his uncle, shot out a few expletives in answer to a violent explosion on the part of the old man, which completely electrified him, and, figuratively speaking, knocked him all of a heap.

Harry formed a sudden resolve.

"Uncle," said he, in soothing tones, "I want to go to London."

"You're a fool."

"Perhaps I am, uncle; nevertheless I want to go."

"Go to the devil for all I care."

"You're very kind."

"Ugh!"

"You've always looked after me very affectionately."

"Humph!"

"But now I want to see a little life, uncle; so if you'll give me some money, I'll go up to town."

Uncle Pigley swore a huge oath, but after a furious and stormy debate Master Harry had five-and-twenty sovereigns counted out into his hand, and was dismissed with a curse to find his way to London as best he could.

He did not find it a very difficult matter to make his way from Leicestershire to the great metropolis, but when he at length arrived under the shadow of St. Paul's, a sense of loneliness came over him at finding himself among such crowds of people without a single soul to speak to.

Being a complete stranger, and not knowing which way to turn, after gazing up at England's great cathedral till he got a crick in his neck, he bent his steps eastward, through busy, bustling Cheapside, till he got to the Mansion House, where he stayed again to inspect the residence of the Lord Mayor.

Then on he trudged, although it was nearly dark, but all ways were the same to him, till the streets got narrower and dirtier, and the trim, sparkling, well-lighted shops were replaced by open stalls, lit by huge flaring gas jets, which flickered and roared as he passed.

Still on he went, wondering at the swarms of people who hovered around the stalls, as if attracted by the incessant hoarse shouts of " Buy—buy—buy !" until he came to what he thought must be the residence of some powerful noble-man, so brilliant were the lights, and so gorgeous the decora-tions; but when he got nearer he perceived over the doorway, in flaming letters of gas, the words—

"ABYSSINIAN MUSIC HALL,"

while at the entrance a placard announced the pleasing fact that a host of talent appeared nightly, and that the admit-tance was only threepence.

Harry Belvoir did not deliberate long.

He was tired, thirsty, and longing to be amused, and he entered to satisfy his desires.

The Hall of Harmony was brilliantly illuminated when he entered, and three male individuals in seedy black coats and dirty white ties were assisting two old and scraggy ladies to murder an operatic chorus.

Harry didn't think much of that, neither was he particu-larly enchanted with the performance of the cat-like cousins of the Cannibal Islands, which appeared to him to consist entirely of two men in tights trying how nearly they could break their necks.

In short, Harry Belvoir thought the Grand Abyssinian Music Hall neither more nor less than a "do," in point of amusement, and being tired, he turned his back to the stage, lit a cigar, and dropped off into a sound sleep before he had time to know it.

With a start produced by a sudden and prolonged noise he awoke.

Jerking his head up, he tried to look as if he had not been asleep, he stared hard at the stage, with an assumed wide-awake expression peculiar to people under his circum-stances.

As soon as he looked at the stage, however, he perfectly recovered from his sleepiness.

There, dancing, twirling, and spinning before him, was an object with the most beautiful face and symmetrical legs he had ever witnessed.

He appealed to some one sitting near him, and asked the name of the enchantress.

"Mademoiselle Le Blanc !"

As long as she remained upon the stage he could not take his eyes from her—he followed every movement, feasting his eyes upon her beautiful and voluptuous form, and scowling fiercely when he remembered that, for the small sum of threepence, every one was entitled to a similar privilege to that he was now enjoying.

"What hair ! what features ! what ankles !" he exclaimed to himself; for, be it here remarked, the Leicestershire dairy-maids and such like, with whom he had associated, were neither remarkable for beauty of person nor symmetry of limb.

When Fanny concluded her performance and disappeared through a side-door, kissing her hand, it seemed to Harry as if the lights in the Hall had been suddenly lowered; and, after an unavailing attempt to attend to the comic "nigger" duet, which followed next in the programme, he rushed from the Hall, and made his way to the stage entrance, where he waited in the hope of again catching a glimpse of the fair charmer.

He was not disappointed.

By an extraordinary chance it happened to be the very night upon which Jack was rummaging out Grubb's drawers, and was, consequently, unable to fetch Fanny from the Hall, as was his usual custom.

Although our heroine had not seen Jack behind the scenes, she fully expected to find him waiting for her at the door enjoying his evening smoke, and consequently lingered for a few moments on making her exit.

But no Jack was to be seen !

This can be satisfactorily accounted for by the fact that our hero—hero, though he is—had not yet discovered the secret of being in two places at the same time.

Instead of Jack, she saw leaning against a lamp-post and

regarding her fixedly, a handsome, dark-eyed, dark-haired youth, with just the inclination of a moustache shading his upper lip.

She was tolerably well used to be looked at, and by this time was well able to protect herself from insult, so she did not take much notice of Mr. Harry Belvoir, but stepped to the kerb for the purpose of hailing a cab.

There was not one in sight.

While she was yet waiting in expectation, and while Harry Belvoir was yet watching her, a man, bearing the outward semblance of a gentleman, accosted her.

It was evident by his speech and gait that he had been imbibing pretty freely, yet he was sober enough to know what he was about.

Harry's eyes flashed fire as he saw this man address his idol with familiarity.

She answered him curtly.

He was not to be repulsed.

With a savage laugh he placed one arm round her slender waist.

Fanny's blood boiled with passion at this indignity, and, exerting all her strength, she hit him across the face with her full force.

He was staggered, but still persisted in his efforts to retain his hold of his lovely burden.

Fanny shrieked.

Her assailant laughed.

Harry Belvoir stepped behind him and in a moment the drunken wretch was tripped up and lay helpless on the pavement, staring vacantly at the stars and growling un-meaning oaths of revenge.

Harry took off his hat to Fanny with much politeness.

She thanked him warmly for his exertions in her behalf. Then blushing and stammering he offered to escort her home.

She readily accepted the offer, for now her worldly know-ledge had increased considerably since she left Miss Mac-Spartans select establishment, and she was enabled to take the measure pretty accurately of any man with whom she conversed.

"Warranted harmless," was her verdict upon Harry, before she had been five minutes in his company.

Without any hesitation she took his arm, and the pair walked off together.

Harry prattled on incessantly, and paid our fair heroine many outrageous compliments in the course of conversation, but she took them goodnaturedly, knowing that he uttered them in good faith.

I fear it was something like an oath that Jack Rawlings muttered when he met Fanny close to home, on the arm of a young and handsome stranger, and I fear, moreover, he took rather a different view of the matter to the other two, but as the mischief was done he put the best face upon the matter he could assume, and asked Harry Belvoir in to supper.

How the young Leicestershire gentleman's heart beat at the invitation ! but when Fanny absolutely pressed his arm with her pretty hand and said, "do come," he scarcely knew whether he were standing on his head or his heels.

It is needless to say he did accept the invitation, and it will not excite a great deal of surprise that when Fanny took it into her pretty little head to flirt with him the whole evening, Jack retired to a sofa as cross as two sticks and altogether in an evil temper.

Bedrooms are privileged places, otherwise I might be tempted to relate the scene which occurred when Fanny and our hero retired for the night, but as before the storm began Fanny had arranged her beautiful hair in a delicate coquettish little cap and Jack had assumed a voluminous white garment of a queer shape, I feel it would be intrusive, to say the least of it, to remain longer in the apartments, so must leave the quarrel and reconciliation to the imagination of our readers.

*   *   *   *   *

Harry Belvoir took up his residence in the same house with our hero and the charming danseuse.

This proceeding was looked upon by Jack with unfeigned disgust.

It was in vain he reasoned with himself, and declared himself convinced of Fanny's constancy ; do what he would he could not take kindly to the young stranger, and caught himself scowling at him at least a dozen times a day.

Fanny, on the contrary, appeared to delight in his company, and more for the sake of teasing than anything else, whenever Jack abused, she praised.

But Harry Belvoir did not long remain the country innocent he was on his first arrival in London.

A young and good-looking man with money to spend and no one to restrain him, is not likely to be long in a large city without being put up to a thing or two; it is not therefore to be wondered at that Master Harry in a very short space of time altered his feelings towards our heroine, and instead of regarding her as a species of idol to be looked at and worshipped from afar, he began to consider her precisely what she was—a particularly beautiful and fascinating girl!

Fanny did not remark any change in his manner, but still looked upon him as a handsome boy as free from vice as any male of nineteen could be.

Fanny flirting, Jack jealous, and Harry happy! So stands the story at the end of the seventeenth chapter.

CHAPTER XVIII.

RELATES A REMARKABLE ADVENTURE WHICH BEFEL JACK RAWLINGS, AND THE WAY IN WHICH HE MADE THE ACQUAINTANCE OF MISS MATILDA SPRIGGS.

IT was a close, sultry evening, and Jack had not felt equal to the exertion of accompanying Fanny to the "Grand Abyssinian," he had therefore contented himself with putting her into a cab and promising he would fetch her from the Hall of Harmony.

It was a promise he was destined to break.

As before said, it was a close, sultry evening. Jack lay for awhile on a sofa at the open window of their lodgings, lazily watching the people passing by, and contemplating reflectively the fragrant blue smoke which curled from his cigar.

Even these amusements became tedious after a time, and he longed for more active employment.

The sun had set and still the thermometer marked eighty-two. There was not the faintest breath of wind to cool the atmosphere, nevertheless, tired of remaining indoors, he determined to take a quiet stroll, so tired was he of endeavouring to find coolness and ease in the low ceilinged room and hard horse-hair sofa of the lodging-house.

When he got out of doors matters were not much improved. He looked at his watch and found it still wanted a couple of hours to the time at which it would be necessary to start for the Abyssinian.

How could he pass those weary one hundred and twenty minutes?

He could not eat ices all the time. It was too far to walk to the swimming-baths.

What *could* he do?

The Baby!

He had not been for nearly a fortnight to the Jolly Billy-boy, to inquire after the luckless infant he had rescued from a watery grave.

He would pay a visit to Mrs. Potts!

Pleased with the idea of having something to do, he whistled for Filchit, who came bounding along the pavement like a cricket-ball hit for a "fiver," and started for the water-side publichouse.

Strolling leisurely along, the never failing cigar in his mouth, he arrived, without any noticeable adventure, at the Jolly Billy-boy.

Not so Filchit!

That unrespectable and vagrant dog had not been taken out for some days, and accordingly testified his joy in a variety of ways more forcible than pleasant.

First he rushed madly into a ready-made baby linen-warehouse, and so frightened a young woman cheapening small caps, that her tribute to the population had the print of a dog's head on its left shoulder to its dying day.

Next he plunged into a butcher's shop, boldly snatching a piece of meat from the block, and bolted out again, hotly pursued by the butcher, his myrmidons, and some score of tagrag and bobtail shouting and yelling at his heels.

In endeavouring to make his escape, he ran between the legs of an old woman standing in front of a crockery stall, and upset her into the midst of the fragile wares, her head firmly fixed in a water-jug, and her hands and feet scattering destruction among the plates and dishes.

The butcher, in his haste, tumbled over her, the others over him, and for the next five minutes no whole body was to be distinguished in the struggling mass, which appeared all legs and arms, like a parcel of windmills gone out of their minds, and bent upon having a lark.

Thanks to this confusion, Filchit escaped without further difficulty, and just as Jack reached the Jolly Billy-boy overtook him, looking very penitent and demure, at the same time licking his chops for the remnant of the flavour of the stolen meat.

That was not the only mouthful Filchit had that evening.

Jack entered the waterside publichouse, and was cordially welcomed by Mrs. Potts, who gave him most wonderful accounts of the way her little charge was progressing, and forthwith woke the youngster from a sound sleep, and brought him to our hero for inspection.

To his shame be it spoken, Jack could never, for the life of him, see the difference between one baby and another.

They all had plump cheeks and wide, staring eyes; they were all more or less bald; they all had the same kicking, struggling legs and arms; and most dreadful of all, they all cried and shrieked in the same shrill, discordant tone.

"Bless its little 'art! He begins to take notice—he do!" said Mrs. Potts, affectionately.

The "taking notice" in this instance being that the small infant made a sudden grab at Jack's watch-chain, and being repulsed, clutched his hair with astounding energy for one of such tender years.

"Ah!" said Jack, sententiously; "you'd better take him away, Mrs. Potts."

"*Him*, sir! It's a *her!*"

"Good gracious! you don't say so," said Jack, surprised, for he had never hitherto asked the sex of the baby, feeling sure it was a boy.

"I do say so, sir; and the sweetest, lovingest, dearest little pet as ever was," and Mrs. Potts further testified her satisfaction by tossing the baby into the air and repeating a species of chuckling sound, which words cannot express, and which no male ever yet succeeded in imitating.

"By the way, Mrs. Potts," said Jack, "I may as well pay you a week or two in advance, as I don't know when I shall be down in these parts again."

Mrs. Potts curtseyed.

"Can you change me a note?"

"I think I can, sir."

Mrs. Potts took the bank-note and hurried into the bar, where her husband, at that very moment, was drawing a pot of "threepenny" for a couple of as unpleasant ruffians as one would wish *not* to see on a dark night in a lonely lane.

The worthy, motherly landlady, without noticing the customers, at once explained her errand to her better half, who leisurely counted out the requisite number of sovereigns, and placed the bank-note in a greasy leather purse.

The two ruffians winked at each other, and nudged a third, who had just entered.

Jack, leaving a sovereign with the landlady of the Jolly Billy-boy, took his departure.

No sooner had he got into the street than the three ruffians sauntered coolly out after him.

Jack whistled to Filchit, who followed close at his heels.

The three followed our hero, keeping as much in the shade as possible.

No one perceiving their movements could have doubted their intentions; but Jack remained in ignorance of his followers.

Once, it is true, Filchit made a decided stop, and growled savagely, but our hero, looking round, and seeing no cause for alarm, pursued his way.

By degrees the gang of villains advanced nearer and nearer to their unsuspecting victim.

Gradually they approached him—one on each side of the way, the third in the middle of the road.

Jack heard their footsteps and turned round—but it was too late!

Already one of the gang had seized him, and was compressing his windpipe in a way that certainly meant mischief, while another, in front, was coolly helping himself to the contents of his pockets.

Jack was powerless.

He could neither exert himself nor call for assistance.

He felt his senses gradually departing.

He gasped painfully for breath.

In another moment he would have been senseless had not an ally come to his assistance.

The help so sorely needed came in the shape of—

THE DOG FILCHIT!

With a savage growl he sprang upon the hinder part of Jack's principal assailant, and fixed his teeth firmly in the ruffian, so that it was some weeks before he could sit down with any comfort.

Owing to the suddenness and fierceness of the attack the villain was forced to relinquish his hold of our hero's throat. Jack was not slow to take advantage of the opportunity thus offered. With a tremendous left-hander, delivered sharply from the shoulder, with that unerring precision which had rendered him famous at Mr. Kanem's, he felled the man who had been rifling his pockets to the ground: and then, considering discretion the better part of valour, not knowing how many more of the ruffians there might be at hand, he took to his heels, and ran whistling to Filchit to follow his example.

Now when a man has been knocked over by another he does not, as a rule, feel particularly friendly towards the individual who caused him to kiss mother earth.

The ruffian whom Jack had so served was no exception to this rule, and as soon as he saw our hero running from the battle-field, he started in pursuit, together with one of his companions. Filchit's teeth had incapacitated the other for rapid locomotion.

Jack, turning, saw that he was pursued, and increased his speed, hoping soon to reach some lighted thoroughfare where his assailants would not dare molest him.

In his haste he took the wrong turning.

He heard an exulting shout behind him, but did not at first understand the cause.

In a few moments it became apparent.

The street down which he had turned was no thorough-fare.

He was fairly trapped.

The end by which he had entered was blocked by his pursuers, who had now swelled to some dozen or more.

Before him was the high brickwall of a large stable.

"Help!" he shouted.

The answer was only a cheer of derision.

His pursuers knew the inhabitants of the street they were in would side with *them*.

There was no help there for Jack.

No help!—Yes. By a miraculous chance our hero found means of escape.

Some bricklayers had been at work at one of the houses, and had left their ladder still leaning against the wall.

With cat-like agility Jack reached the house-top in a moment.

This proceeding on his part baulked his pursuers, who gave a savage yell as he stood on the coping-stone and made them a polite bow; but after a few seconds of deliberation three of them advanced and commenced to ascend.

Jack waited till they were about half-way up, and then hurled the ladder from its resting-place on the roof into the street below.

Without waiting to see the effects, he clambered over the sloping slates and among the battered chimney-pots, hoping to find a place where he could let himself down into the street again, but in vain.

At length his course over the house-tops was stayed by a narrow passage, which divided the street from which he had ascended from a larger, wider, and much more aristocratic one.

The leap he would have to make to gain the roof of these other houses would have been nothing under ordinary circumstances, but jumping from sloping slates upon sloping slates, with the prospect of a fall of sixty or seventy feet, was in no way encouraging.

However, he determined to make the attempt.

Obtaining as firm a footing as he could manage, he swayed his body two or three times backwards and forwards, and then made the spring.

He alighted on the opposite side, but, as ill-luck would have it, the slate on which his feet first rested was loose, and no sooner had he touched it, and before he could regain his balance, than it slid rapidly with him to the edge.

There was no coping-stone to stop him.

Instinctively, he threw himself forward upon his face, but it was too late; and with a cry of agony he slipped over the edge.

Madly and wildly he stretched forth his hands to grasp anything which might stay his fall.

His fingers encountered a water-pipe. This he clutched with the energy of a dying man, and slid down it some few yards, then lost his hold, and fell heavily.

Not to the ground, however. Had he done that his name would not have been printed upon our title-page.

No, luckily for him, the leaden top of the cistern was between him and the ground where he fell, and on to that he plumped with a sound which must have rather astonished the young tadpoles inside.

Stunned and motionless he lay for nearly an hour, only betraying life was not extinct by low moanings of pain; for a man doesn't drop twenty feet without feeling the effects of it.

After some time he began to recover consciousness. He sat up, and rubbed his eyes with the back of his hand, and tried to remember how he got where he was.

Slowly it all returned to him, and, at the same time, the knowledge that the sooner he got from his present unpleasant position, the better.

A small window opened from the house on to the cistern-top. This he tried, and to his joy found unfastened.

Raising the sash as quietly as possible, he obtained an entrance into the house, but now the difficulty was how to get out of it without being discovered by the inhabitants.

The room he was now in was evidently a lumber-room, a species of warehouse for all broken and useless furniture, huge trunks, and battered boxes. There he had nothing to dread, but still he could not remain there for ever.

Cautiously he opened the door, and listened for any sounds which might guide him in his course.

All was still.

The chirping of the crickets, and the ticking of a large, solemn-faced clock, were the only sounds which met his listening ear.

Taking off his boots he strove noiselessly to descend the stairs. It was late, and he could only hope the family had all retired to bed.

Light of foot as he was, he could not prevent the boards creaking every now and then, but at length, without any mischance, he reached the first landing, and paused to take breath.

Suddenly, to his horror, he perceived a light below advancing steadily upwards; scarcely knowing the best thing to do, he opened a door at random, and rushed in hoping to hide till the light had passed.

Master Jack in hopping out of the frying-pan had stepped comfortably and quietly into the fire.

The room he had entered was well lighted, and by the side of the dressing-table sat a lady wrapped in a loose dressing-gown intently perusing a rather dirty novel.

This lady was no other than Miss Matilda Spriggs.

Miss Matilda Spriggs was a lady who had been younger, but this was a fact she studiously ignored, or as day by day went by and increased her age, she assumed more and more girlish manners, and strove to pass herself off as a young, an artless maiden.

The tip of Miss Matilda Spriggs's nose was red, the colour of Miss Spriggs's eyes was the lightest green, and altogether she gave one the idea of having had all her colour washed out at an early age, and at the same time a good deal of starch put in.

In spite of all this, however, Miss Matilda was intensely romantic. She had never had a lover, but would have given her ears for one, but being denied such a luxury, she contented herself with borrowing well-thumbed romances from the circulating library, and identifying herself with all the heroines therein described.

When Jack invaded the sanctity of her bedroom, she gave a little shriek.

"My dear madam," he commenced, "let me entreat you——"

"Murder!" interrupted the maiden.

"I implore you——"

"Thieves!"

"Let me explain that——"

"Fire!"

"My dear young lady——"

That was more effectual; Miss Matilda Spriggs softened at "young lady."

"I assure you," continued Jack, "I am here with no evil designs. Do I look like a robber?"

Miss Matilda Spriggs looked up at our hero and could not help acknowledging that he looked much more like a handsome young gentleman.

"Explain your presence," said she.

Jack told her the whole of his story.

Truth is stranger than fiction, and Miss Spriggs, though well read in romance, could at first barely credit the truth of his statement, but his open, cheerful manner, and above all his handsome face, soon convinced her; and so much done, she thought it a fitting opportunity to assume her girlish manners and to try to commence a mild flirtation.

Jack saw how the land lay, and for the sake of the fun warmly entered into the scheme.

Miss Spriggs giggled, and was ashamed of her attire.

Jack swore she couldn't look more lovely in any garb than in that she now wore—which perhaps was not very far from the truth.

At last Miss Spriggs's modesty was shocked by discovering that it was long past midnight, and she talking to a strange gentleman in her bedroom! She insisted upon showing Jack out, making him promise he would not look at her ankles as she went downstairs, and that he would come and see her when she was more becomingly attired.

Jack promised everything, gallantly kissed her hand first and her lips afterwards, and once more emerged into the fresh air, and hurried home as fast as his legs would carry him.

CHAPTER XIX.

GIVES SOME ACCOUNT OF MRS. O'FLANNAGAN'S MYSTERIOUS LODGER.

"BEDAD! Mrs. Murphy, you may well say that. She's the rummiest customer I've had this ever so long!"

Mrs. O'Flannagan was the speaker, and Mrs. O'Flannagan was a tallbones, hard featured woman without a perceptible curve in her body.

From the tips of her shoulders to the bottom of her petticoat was one continuous straight line. Waist she had none, while as for as her side view she looked more like a plank stuck up on end than a woman.

Mrs. O'Flannagan lived in Tweezer's-alley, which is a turning out of Great Pincers-street, but if you look for it on the map of London, I doubt whether you will even find it marked, so small and insignificant is it.

Perhaps the less said about the view from the house windows in Tweezers-alley the better. The front view was entirely confined to the opposite edifices, and at the back all air was blocked out by the offices of the Jordan Society for the diffusion of flannel petticoats to the female Hottentots.

"But you let her the rooms!" said Mrs. Murphy, continuing the conversation.

"Indeed, and I did, for it was myself that could see she was a trueborn lady, every inch of her, and one as had known better days."

"Poor thing!"

"It's yourself as has a kind heart, Mrs. Murphy, and you may well pity her."

"What's she done since she's been here?"

"It's crying she's been, but the last time I went to her door she spoke up cheerfuller like and seemed more spirited."

"Hush, here she is!"

"By jaber's, your right!"

The subject of this conversation suddenly appeared descending the stairs, and Mrs. O'Flannagan and her friend Mrs. Murphy started apart like parched peas, to give her egress.

She merely acknowledged their presence by a stately bend of her head as she walked by them.

Her appearance was sufficiently remarkable to attract attention.

She was tall and commanding in her figure, her hair was of that brilliant golden hue so loved by artists, while her eyes were of a deep blue, but with a soft, melancholy expression, which ill became her youth and beauty.

She was attired in the deepest mourning, and before she emerged into the street she hid her features with an extra thick crape veil, which would have prevented her nearest friend from recognising her.

Slowly and laboriously, as one unaccustomed to walking, she pursued her way towards the fashionable quarter of the town, unheeded by the busy throng who hurried past her bent upon a thousand different errands.

What was her object in threading her way through the dirty crowded streets?

What was the secret which appeared to press so heavily upon her smooth, white forehead?

That it was some fixed purpose which brought her to the West End was evident from the decision with which she pursued her way.

That it was something painful to her was shown by her continually raising her handkerchief to her eyes.

Unknown, uncared for, muffled so that recognition was impossible, she paused before the threshold of the Earl of Stonecliffe's mansion.

The mansion which but a short time back echoed with the sounds of merriment, but which was now hushed and still, and bore upon its front death's gloomy seal.

What was her errand there?

*　　*　　*　　*　　*

It is necessary that we should go back a little in the course of our story to my Lord Manningtree, whom we left lying prostrate and senseless on the floor of his laboratory.

How long he remained so he knew not; but when he recovered consciousness the sun was high in the heavens, and the noise in the busy street told him day had far advanced.

For a moment he failed to remember the events of the previous night, but in a short time the hideous truths came swarming across his mind like some diabolical phantasmagoria.

He saw again the beseeching upturned face of the wretched attorney, he heard his pathetic tones imploring for life, and in his mind's eye saw the dying expression of mute agony on his countenance.

Then what came next?

Lord Manningtree shuddered, and strove to drive back the awful recollection—but it would come.

He shut his eyes.

It only appeared with the greater distinctness.

He strove to convince himself it was a dream.

He failed.

Ever before him arose that one dreadful figure—that form in the awful garments of the grave.

That form which bore the semblance of his niece, Lady Gertrude—the very image of her, yet unlike, for while the features were the same, the expression was hard and severe—cold and unrelenting, as if the dead could not forgive.

It was too dreadful!

That afternoon Lord Manningtree appeared as usual in the Park.

Those who spoke to him remarked that, imperturbable as he usually was, it was evident something had happened to disturb the equanimity of his mind.

Gloomily he viewed the passing throng—bitterly he made remarks on such as he knew.

As he leant against the railings, with a troubled expression upon his classically handsome face, gnawing angrily at his black moustache, he looked the image of what one would suppose the Evil One to be!

And not inappropriately.

Percy Lord Manningtree had more of the devil than of the human in his nature!

As he stood there, his moustache curling upwards, giving an extra sardonic expression to his face, more than one fair lady, in acknowledging his salutation, shuddered as his eye rested upon her.

Agreeable, handsome, and amusing, Lord Manningtree was more feared than liked, though, in his presence, no one appeared to remember the dark tales current respecting him.

He had now some deep plot in his mind! A plot which he hardly trusted himself to think of in detail. A plot of crime and wickedness. A plot of sin and shame. Everything was to be sacrificed to an inordinate affection for wealth and position.

Suddenly Lord Manningtree turned and walked rapidly away from the spot where he had been standing long enough to attract general attention.

With rapid strides he proceeded in the direction of his brother's mansion.

With firm, determined steps he threaded the busy thoroughfares, passing unheeded the greetings of his acquaintances, until he stood before the Earl of Stonecliffe's residence.

"This may be mine," he muttered, half aloud. "It *may*? It *shall*! Have I not gone so far as to make further hesitation puerile? Who will dare assail me in the character of Earl of Stonecliffe? What whisper of calumny against the richest earl in the kingdom will reach my ears? None! The die is cast. Favour me, Fortune, for Percy Lord Manningtree stakes everything—life, wealth, reputation, honour—on this final throw!"

A poorly-dressed woman had approached close to him ere he finished his half-spoken thoughts.

She was clothed entirely in black, and over her face hung a veil so thick that the keenest eye would have failed to recognise her features through it.

Lord Manningtree started when he discovered her close proximity.

He turned and faced her!

Unshrinking and resolute she stood before him.

"What is it? I have no money for beggars!" said he, impatiently.

"I scorn you and your money," answered the woman, in sweet yet sad tones, "I loathe and hate you, Lord Manningtree!"

"Ha! you know me!"

"Too well."

"What do you mean? Begone! or I give you in charge."

"Beware! You are about to add another crime to the long list already chronicled against you—murder will out!"

Lord Manningtree raised his hand as if to strike the woman standing unflinchingly before him, but the sound of approaching footsteps caused him to pause.

In a moment she had gone!

Vanished into the shades of evening, which were rapidly falling.

It was with less firmness upon his brow than he had hitherto worn that his lordship knocked at the door of his brother's mansion.

"Could it be," he thought, "that his crimes were really known? Had he been watched—were spies even then upon his track?"

He laughed at the idea as soon as formed.

No. The woman was but some wretched impostor, who strove, by mystery and vague threats, to extract money from him.

The Earl of Stonecliffe had been weak and ailing ever since his daughter's death.

Lady Gertrude had been his all in all—his life, his happiness.

Death had robbed him of his treasure, and since then he had felt but little interest in anything.

Great politician as he was, his seat in the House of Lords, night after night, remained vacant. His club knew him no more; his stall at the opera remained unoccupied.

He was an altered man.

A grief-stricken, heart-broken man.

His title, his wealth, his position availed him not one jot.

Death respected not the titled lady; wealth would not bring him back his darling Gertrude; position aided him not in softening the poignancy of his first anguish.

This was the crushed, suffering man that Lord Manningtree envied!

The earl welcomed his brother warmly. He had ever felt a strange affection for him, and throughout his life had looked upon him with admiration.

He was proud of possessing so handsome, so strange, so mysterious a brother!

Heaven knows there was little enough to be proud of.

The room into which Lord Manningtree was shown was a strange one.

It had originally been intended for a smoking-room, but being considered too good for that purpose, had become a sort of idle, lounging-room, were, however, none but favoured guests were admitted.

It was decorated and ornamented after the style of one of the chambers in the Palace of the Alhambra, for the earl, when young, had made a lengthy tour in Spain, and had returned to his native land full of the beauties of that most gorgeous and magnificent building, and with the determination of constructing an exact model of one of the chambers which had most pleased him.

The result was the apartment in which Lord Manningtree discovered him.

The beautifully-shaped horse-shoe arches, the delicate imagery on the walls, the harmonious blending of many vivid colours, contrasted pleasingly with the pure white of other portions, and presented altogether an appearance almost fairy-like, and which instinctively reminded one of the *Arabian Nights*, not from any definite connexion so much as from the general Eastern magnificence and luxury.

Here, in a deep recess, reclining upon soft crimson cushions, lay the Earl of Stonecliffe. Behind him was a heavy curtain of the same rich colour, which served to conceal the plain wall, as well as to give a grand splendour to the appearance of the chamber.

Everything was in perfect keeping with the character of the room. No unsightly furniture disfigured the apartment or marred the illusion. The only seats were the soft, silken-covered cushions, the only tables the two carved stools upon which to rest a book or a coffee-cup.

The first glance showed Lord Manningtree that his brother was really ill. The events of the last few months had marked additional furrows in his face, and streaked his hair with silver, while the pallor of his cheeks and the languor of his frame showed how severely his daughter's death had told upon him.

Should he wait and let nature take her course?

That was the momentous question Lord Manningtree asked himself as he contemplated the Earl of Stonecliffe's worn and haggard appearance.

"No—no—no!" a thousand devils seemed to whisper in his ear, as he deliberated.

The conversation between the two brothers was warm and affectionate. Sincere on the part of the elder, false and assumed on that of the younger.

Lying hypocrisy and deceit were his stock in trade, and he used them liberally.

He lamented with the earl the untimely decease of the Lady Gertrude. He spoke well and apparently with deep feeling on the subject, but every word, every gesture was a spoken or an acted falsehood.

"I would have given my life for hers!" said Lord Manningtree, with every appearance of earnestness and truth.

Was it fancy or reality?

As he uttered these words it seemed to him that a sound as of a deep sigh floated through the room.

He started violently.

He raised himself from the cushions on which he was reclining and stared around.

There was not any one to be seen!

Could it have been only his guilty imagination?

He could account for it in no other way.

"Percy," said the earl, "there is a cup of coffee just behind you on a ledge, can you reach it for me?"

The devil was at Lord Manningtree's elbow whispering in his ear again, "Only one life between you and wealth. Only one life!"

His lordship took from his pocket a delicate glass bottle containing some liquid, and moved to fulfil his brother's request.

The hand containing the bottle was over the cup!

In another moment the contents would have been emptied into it!

The cup fell to the ground and was smashed into a thousand atoms, and the liquor spread itself over the paved floor.

Lord Manningtree, with a wild cry, placed his hand to his forehead and rushed into the centre of the apartment, where a fragrant fountain leapt into the air, and fell into a marble basin, diffusing coolness throughout the chamber.

What was it caused this action on his part?

What was it that made this frigid, imperturbable man so far forget his character?

Why at the last moment had he suffered himself to be baulked in his intention?

It was because he saw something which might have startled a stronger, less guilty man than he.

It was something he had seen in his laboratory the night Grubb had visited him.

It was but a woman's face.

But that face was the face of Lady Gertrude!

Not bright and cheerful as in life, but fixed and stony as when she slept her last sleep on the couch, after the earl's dinner party.

"A LITTLE ROW WITH CABBY."

This it was which caused Lord Manningtree to start back in alarm!

This it was which caused him to drop the cup and baulked him in his criminal intentions.

*　　*　　*　　*　　*　　*

When the old Irishwoman's mysterious lodger returned to the house after a lengthened absence, she hurried past that good lady, pale and agitated, and retreated to the privacy of her own room.

Once there, she locked the door, threw off her bonnet and cloak, and buried her head in her hands.

Only for a few seconds did she preserve this attitude.

Suddenly rising from the seat into which she had thrown herself, she stood erect, with an expression of defiance on her pale but lovely face.

As she stood there, she looked like a beautiful statue, so perfect was her form, so complete her immobility.

Then a dark smile came over her countenance, and she clenched her tiny hand in a way that boded no good to him she threatened in her mind.

Raising one arm, the perfect moulding of which would have sent an artist into raptures, she spoke.

There was no one present to hear her.

It was but to her ownself she addressed the words.

"I swear," said she, " that my whole life shall be spent in baulking and unmasking him. The pleasure of my wretched existence shall be to thwart him at every turn. If I fail or turn aside a single moment in this the purpose of my life, may my limbs wither, my body decay as *he* would have had them !"

Who did she refer to in this solemn vow ?

Was it possible her hatred was directed against Percy Lord Manningtree ?

We shall see.

CHAPTER XX.

JACK RAWLINGS HAS A SERIOUS LOSS, A QUARREL, AND A BIT OF DISSIPATION.

" THE devil!"

It was Jack Rawlings who spoke those words, with an earnestness and emphasis worthy of a better cause.

Fanny let the novel she was reading fall to the ground, as she started to her feet surprised.

"The devil!" repeated Jack, turning over all the papers in an open desk before him.

"Good gracious, Jack! What *is* the matter?"

Jack made no reply.

With an agitated manner he continued fumbling about the desk.

"Jack! why don't you tell me what's the matter?"

"I've lost something."

"Lost?"

"Yes."

"What?"

"Money!"

"Is that all?"

"Quite enough, too, I think."

"I thought something serious had happened."

"Hang it, Fanny! don't you call that serious?"

"No."

"Well, you take it coolly."

"What would be the use of going into hysterics about it?"

"Without doing that, you might show some little interest in finding it."

"Poor Jack! now don't get savage. Shall I go down on my knees on the floor to hunt for his little sixpence?"

Jack growled out an ugly word, which was very sad conduct upon his part, but then he had some provocation, it must be confessed.

"Don't swear, Jack, there's a good boy!"

This made our hero a little more angry than before, and his reply to Fanny was not couched in the mildest of language.

"Is it a fourpenny piece, or a sixpence, you've lost, dear?" asked Fanny, mischievously.

"I've lost more gold than you ever saw in your life!"

"You don't say so!"

"I have said so."

"What's to be done?"

Jack made no immediate reply; he was busily engaged in examining the lock of his desk.

Suddenly he started to his feet.

"By Heaven, I've been robbed!"

"Nonsense!"

"I tell you I have. Look here! There is a bit chipped out of the desk by the lock!"

"That was done before."

"How do you know?"

"I saw it yesterday."

"That I'm sure you didn't. I tell you what, I'm——"

"Hush! There's some one at the door."

There was indeed a gentle tap at the door, and in reply to Jack's surlily growled forth permission to enter, Harry Belvoir made his appearance.

"Good morning!" said he gaily, as he entered with a jaunty air, and took off his hat and gloves, thus evincing a decided intention of stopping some time.

Mr. Harry Belvoir appeared in most gorgeous array.

A fashionably-cut coat, a white waistcoat, a hot-house flower in his button-hole, primrose-coloured gloves, and the remainder of his attire in accordance.

Jack growled out something about "conceited puppy," as he took his seat by Fanny's side, and engaged her in a lively conversation.

Jack sat gloomily without speaking a word, but the impatient movement of his foot betrayed how annoyed he was by the visit of the young swell.

"Uncle Pigley has been behaving dutifully," said Harry Belvoir, "and has sent me a princely remittance."

"That accounts for your wonderfully grand appearance," said Fanny, with a smile.

"Yes; and for something else as well," replied the young man, producing from his pocket a good-sized morocco case. "Will you oblige me by accepting this?" he continued, handing it to her.

An exclamation of delight broke from Fanny's lips as she opened the case.

There was good cause for it!

The present she had just received consisted of a most beautiful bracelet.

A bracelet a countess might have been proud to wear.

Diamonds and emeralds tastefully arranged sparkled and glistened in the sunlight—the eyes of the recipient scarcely less so!

With many thanks she took it from its resting-place and essayed to clasp it round her perfect arm.

"Permit me," said Mr. Belvoir, and his fingers fastened the costly present and lingered long round the white slender wrist, and seemed reluctant to leave it.

Jack chafed and fumed till his blood was near boiling point, but by a great effort he restrained his passion, and appeared outwardly tolerably calm and decidedly sulky.

At last, to his great relief, Fanny's visitor took his departure.

"Look, Jack! Isn't this a beautiful bracelet?" said Fanny, when the door closed behind Harry Belvoir.

"Very pretty!" said Jack without looking at it.

"Now do turn round you great, sulky old man."

Fanny, as she said this, placed herself in a graceful attitude, and assumed a bewitching smile, which would have told even upon St. Anthony had he beheld it.

Jack was but mortal, and knew he should yield if he glanced, so kept his back resolutely turned towards the lovely girl.

"What's the good of such tawdry rubbish?" said he; "it isn't worth a hundredth part of that I have had stolen!"

"That I'm sure it is!"

Jack turned and examined it.

"By Jove!" he exclaimed, "they're real stones! Where did that young shaver get money for this?"

"His Uncle Pigley."

"Damn Uncle Pigley! I believe my sovereigns paid for this!"

"Jack, are you mad? Do you know what you are saying?"

"Perfectly. I believe that he broke open my desk and robbed me of my money!"

"Anything else?"

"Yes. I think it more than probable that you assisted him, and that that bauble is your share of the plunder."

Poor Fanny was completely staggered by this accusation.

Her first impulse was to avail herself of woman's refuge—tears—but a second's deliberation convinced her that the mad charge caused by jealousy would best be met by calm, cool words.

She tried her best; but the loss of the money, and the irritation of Harry Belvoir's visit, had sunk Jack's gentleness into the savage anger of the bear.

Every soothing word Fanny uttered he but considered additional proof of her guilt.

In the heat of passion he called her by a hard name.

It was one which no woman would submit to tamely.

It roused her.

She turned upon him with the fury of a lioness.

She reproached him.

He retorted.

She scolded.

He rose, put on his hat, and left the house, banging the door after him.

One other thing he did.

He whistled for Filchit, and because the dog waited to examine a bone, sent him howling down the street with a blow from his cane.

After this little ebullition, the balmy air and a fragrant Havannah, Jack soothed down a little, and by the time he had walked as far as the Regent's Park, he had tolerably well recovered his temper.

Fanny did not recover herself quite so rapidly.

For the first time since their elopement she felt anger against her lover.

Had Harry Belvoir paid a second visit while she was in that state, Jack might have had real cause for jealousy!

When our hero arrived in the neighbourhood of the Regent's Park he felt rather at a loss to know how to dispose of himself.

Primrose Hill presented few attractions, the nursery-maids in the long walk less; Hampstead was too far, the Colosseum too slow.

Listlessly he rambled on till he reached the entrance to the Zoological Gardens.

He had never been there, and in the idle carelessness of the moment, caring little whither he went, he paid his shilling, and entered the world-renowned Gardens.

It was not for the purpose of looking at any other beasts but those of his own species that he entered; so without troubling himself as to which direction he took, he proceeded to an open part of the grounds, and flung himself at full length upon a bench, nearly opposite the cages where the lions and tigers pace drearily backwards and forwards the livelong day in about twice their own length.

Jack had not been reclining many minutes on this bench before he became aware that he was the object of inspection of the occupant of a neighbouring seat.

The individual who was regarding him so intently was a short, middle-aged man, dressed in a light gray suit.

But for one thing his appearance would have been ordinary enough.

What made him remarkable were his eyes.

They were not large, nor were they particularly handsome, but their brilliancy was something out of the common. They twinkled and glistened in the sunlight with an arch expression of merriment provocative of laughter, and as he gazed at our hero, Jack felt an almost irresistible inclination to rise from his seat and address him.

Indeed, he was on the point of doing so, when a loud savage roar from one of the beasts attracted his attention in a different direction.

It was the animals' feeding time, and from all parts of the gardens elegantly dressed ladies and children flocked to see the beasts ravenously tearing huge pieces of raw meat, growling and snarling over it the while.

This pleasing sight had no particular attraction for Jack, neither apparently had it for the gentleman in gray, who still retained his seat, his eyes winking rapidly at our hero as if to challenge him to speak.

A more than ordinarily savage growl proceeded from one of the cages.

"Help!"

A piercing shriek coming from the same cage startled the assembled company.

Another and another, each more heart-rending than the preceding, followed in rapid succession.

Everyone, including the little man in gray and our hero, flocked to the cage from whence the cries proceeded.

It was empty!

"There ain't been nothing in this 'ere cage since the old lion died," said one of the keepers.

As if to contradict the statement, an angry growl proceeded from the inner part hidden from sight.

A faint moan as of a man in agony followed it.

The keepers hung back. They were afraid to enter the cage!

The moans became fainter and fainter.

The excitement of the assembled multitude was intense.

Jack found himself next to the little man in gray.

"How dreadful!" he exclaimed.

"What is dreadful?" asked he, of the twinkling eyes.

"Some poor creature has certainly been drawn into the den by an infuriated beast, and is expiring in great agony."

"Ha, ha, ha!" laughed the little man, quietly, in a strange way, which appeared to shake his whole frame.

"It is no laughing matter," said Jack, indignantly.

As if to disprove his statement, a sudden peal of laughter burst forth from the inner cage.

"Haw, haw, haw! haw, haw, haw, haw!"

This hearty guffaw alarmed the people gathered round, if anything, more than the previous moans; but the idea instantly occurred to the keepers that some trick had been played upon them.

The door of the cage was quickly unlocked, and two of them sprang in.

With straining eyeballs those outside watched them disappear into the interior.

In breathless silence they waited for their reappearance.

When they at length emerged from the inner den their faces wore a puzzled expression.

They whispered to one another, and made no answer to the inquiries addressed to them.

"What is it?" asked Jack.

"What did you find inside?" said the little man.

"Nothing at all!" replied the keeper, surlily.

"Nonsense!"

"Impossible!"

"Ridiculous!"

These were the words chorused by those waiting in suspense.

"You'd better see for yourselves, then," said the keeper.

All those near the front crowded to avail themselves of the permission.

All returned with disappointment written upon their faces.

The den was perfectly empty!

Jack was one of those who entered.

When he came back, the little gray man met him with an extra roguish twinkle in his eyes.

"Well," said he, "what did you see?"

"Nothing."

He gave the same low inward chuckle he had done before.

"It's very strange!" said Jack.

"Not at all!"

"What do you mean?"

"It is easily accounted for."

"I should like to know how."

"So would a great many others."

"Could you explain it?"

"Perhaps I could, if I were so disposed."

"I don't understand it," said Jack.

"Very possibly not. Neither do you understand many other very simple things."

"I don't call this simple."

"Look here! Do you know whose this is?"

The little man opened his hand, and showed Jack his own watch.

"It's my watch!" exclaimed Jack, surprised.

"Precisely," said the other, returning it to him. "Now, I dare say, you don't understand how I got possession of that?"

"That is much more easily accounted for. I suppose you abstracted it from my pocket."

"A very wise conclusion," said he, ironically. "Do you think you could take mine in the same way?"

"I'm not a pickpocket!" said Jack.

"I'm delighted to hear it," retorted the other, gravely.

"I should like to know what you mean about this mystery being easily explained."

"So you shall, Mister Rawlings."

"You know me?"

"So it appears."

"May I ask who you are?"

"Certainly, sir—certainly. My name is Gimp—Jim Gimp—at your service."

"I never heard your name before that I can recollect."

"Very possibly not—I may say, nothing more likely—for considering I have a name for every day of the week, and some dozen to spare, it would be odd if you should have chanced to have met me under the name of Gimp."

"Have I ever seen you before?"

"Yes, at Bow—before you ran off with——"

"Hush! Under what name did I make your acquaintance?"

"You saw me, sir, professionally. This is my business card—"

As Jack read the words on the pasteboard a light gradually dawned upon him.

"Do you mean to tell me," said he, "that all that disturbance we had here just now was nothing but the effects of ventriloquism?"

"That is the fact."

"That you produced the sound of the lion's roar, and the man's moaning?"

"I do."

"And that at so great a distance you could make your voice appear to come from that cage?"

"Yes."

"It seems almost incredible."

"It is a fact. I have retired from my profession, except upon particular occasions; but I like to make a trial of my ventriloquial powers occasionally."

"I should think so. What fun you must have."

"Yes, pretty well. I've played some capital tricks at times."

"In what way?"

"Well, look here, Mr. Rawlings, I'm going to have a good lark this evening, I expect. If you like to come with me, I shall be very glad of your company."

"I shall be delighted. Where are you going?"

"There's a grand masquerade at one of the theatres to-night. It will be great fun, I expect."

"First rate, I should think. Is it expensive?"

"Oh! I'll get you a ticket. Be at the stage-door at ten o'clock to-night, and I will pass you in, and get you some sort of dress to wear."

"Thank you."

"Don't mention it."

"Good-bye for the present."

"Good-day, Mr. Rawlings."

"Of all queer freaks for a man to meet with in the Regent's Park Zoological Gardens this is the queerest," said our hero, to himself, as he strolled out to get some dinner to prepare for the evening's dissipation.

CHAPTER XXI.

THE MASQUERADE AND ITS CONSEQUENCES.

AT the appointed hour of ten o'clock Jack was at the stage-door of the theatre.

He had not to wait long for his new-formed acquaintance.

A cab came dashing along, and drew up sharply at the door, and Mr. Gimp alighted therefrom, and greeted our hero cordially.

With a familiar nod, the ventriloquist passed the stern-looking door-keeper, merely alluding to Jack as "a friend of mine;" and in another minute our hero found himself in a strange demoniacal-looking place.

Huge beams and posts crossed and intersected each other in every direction.

Ropes, chains, windlasses, and different species of machinery lay in every direction, while above their heads a constant noise as of distant thunder made speech a labour.

"Where the deuce are we?" said Jack.

"Under the stage," replied his conductor.

"What's the cause of that infernal row?"

"The people dancing overhead."

Jack was conducted by Mr. Gimp to a small, dark, close room occupied solely by a gentleman with an unmistakeable Hebrew cast of countenance, who was sitting disconsolate among a pile of dresses of every description.

"My friend and I want dresses for to-night."

"Happy to oblige you, Mishter Gimp. What shtyle of coshtume?"

"What will you be?" Gimp asked Jack.

"I'm not particular—anything."

"Charlesh the Shecond, an Italian brigand, a monk, a nobleman of the reign of Louish the Fourteenth? Shay the word."

"I'll have a monk's dress," said Mr. Gimp.

"Would your young friend like a female dress? He's fair. He'd make a very pretty girl."

Jack negatived this decidedly.

After some little delay he was provided with a nondescript costume supposed to represent a courtier of the time of the Stuarts.

He looked remarkably well in it.

A wig of light-coloured hair hung down in curls upon his collar, and the slightly effeminate expression of his face was entirely done away with by the glossy brown moustache he assumed for the occasion.

It was really a handsome dress, and vastly superior to the generality of masquerade attire.

Jack, as he surveyed himself in the glass, had no reason to be dissatisfied in any way with his personal appearance, for, in truth, he looked as handsome a cavalier as ever graced the brilliant rollicking court of the second Charles, or made smooth flowing verses in praise of his loosely attired, free spoken, ringleted mistresses.

This strangely assorted pair, the monk and the cavalier, entered the vast arena where thousands of people in fancy costumes, more or less satisfactory, were disporting themselves in the giddy waltz.

The brilliantly-lighted theatre, the gay dresses, the enlivening music, all had an inspiriting effect upon Jack, while as for the monk, beneath whose cowl the merry eyes twinkled and glistened more than ever, he beat time to the music with his sandalled feet, and nodded his head to and fro in a way which reflected little credit upon his gown.

It was barely eleven o'clock, and as yet the majority of visitors had not arrived, nevertheless there was a fair sprinkling of shepherds and shepherdesses trying with all their might to look innocent.

Lords and ladies endeavouring to "behave themselves as sich" and to hide from the spectators that they were but lawyers' clerks and milliners' apprentices.

Soldiers who stumbled over their wooden swords at every step, sailors who were sea-sick in going to Gravesend, lawyers who had never approached nearer the bench than to carry their master's blue bag thither, and brigands who would have gone into fits at the sound of a pistol-shot, formed the majority of the male masquers.

Amongst the ladies there was perhaps even a greater variety of attire, though dresses which permitted short skirts appeared to be the favourites.

Empresses whose grammar was defective conversed in a free and easy style with milkmaids well known in the neighbourhood of Oxenden-street, and Titania, in short petticoats, was exchanging repartees of a doubtful tendency with a "nigger" melodist, as black as lamp-black and oil could make him.

Among the whole crowd a tall figure continually passed hither and thither, speaking to no one, and making no reply to the bantering remarks addressed to him.

He wore a long black domino which came nearly to his feet, and his features were concealed by a half-mask.

The only relief to his sombre appearance was a magnificent and massive gold chain, which hung round his neck, and the glittering links of which appeared with advantage upon the samite domino which he wore.

He attracted universal attention, but seemed to be totally unaware of the excitement he caused.

Wherever he went he seemed to cast a gloomy shadow, and the spriteliest conversations and the most telling jokes were suspended till he had passed out of hearing.

He seemed like a withering blight passing amongst the merry-makers.

Hither and thither he went with noiseless, cat-like tread, approaching each separate group of masquers, but mixing with none.

He was a mystery!

Jack had not long to stand alone with Jim Gimp.

The syrens of the dance quickly assailed him, and one dressed in the stage costume of a peasant, which, as everybody knows, is as unlike the real thing as the manners and customs of the representative are the innocence of the country girl, carried our hero off in triumph, and almost before he knew what she was about, had whirled him into the midst of the giddy throng, and was twirling him round like a great top.

Jack soon warmed into it.

A few moments before he had been almost regretting Fanny was not there. Now in his excitement she was forgotten, and he laughed and shouted and danced with the best of them.

He whirled his little peasant partner round till her short dress stood out at a wonderful angle, he slapped Jim Gimp on the back whenever the intricacies of the dance brought them into proximity, and when at length, exhausted and breathless, they pushed their way to the refreshment-room, Jack, totally disregarding the fact that the ten guineas he had in his pocket was all he possessed in the world, gave most reckless orders for champagne.

Cool and effervescent, it slipped gratefully down their parched throats.

Then Mr. Gimp, whose partner was a young lady, elegantly attired (if that term is applicable) as a heathen goddess, insisted upon ordering more wine, until the whole party got to an extreme pitch of merriment, and again plunged into the dance with renewed energy.

Twirling rapidly across the stage with his partner, Jack came into violent contact with a troubadour, from him shot off to a French marquise of the old *regimé*, and cannoned from her against a fat and pompous man, who had inserted his legs into tights, which proved the correctness of their name by causing him such exquisite pain when he moved, that although he saw our hero and his partner coming, he was totally unable to get out of the way, and accordingly received the whole force of the collision.

With a crash and a far from pious exclamation he fell to the ground—his tights splitting with a loud crack as he did so.

To save himself he caught hold of the skirt of Jack's partner, which came off in his hands, not, however, until she had lost her balance.

She clung to Jack—Jack seized a gentleman appropriately attired as the devil, by the tail.

The tail came out, and all three rolled upon the ground together.

No pity for such accidents as these.

A roar of laughter greeted the disaster, in which all joined with the exception of the poor devil whose tail had been pulled out.

He stood with that appendage in his hand, eyeing it ruefully, and wondering how much Mr. May would charge him for the damage done to the costume.

Jack was first on his feet, and offered his hand to assist the others to rise.

His late partner, however, was unable to do so. The wine she had drunk was taking effect, and she could do no more than express her undying attachment to Jack, and shed copious tears of affection.

The obese old gentleman whose tights had split preferred to sit upon the floor rather than rise and display the havoc occasioned by the fall, so Jack, after assisting this pair to shuffle along the floor out of the dancers, surrendered the little peasant-girl to the care of the stout gentleman, and went in search of Jim Gimp.

When he discovered his new-found friend, that gentleman was fast approaching more than natural hilarity.

He had discarded the heathen goddess, and had instead for his partner a young lady in a strangely inconsistent garb, being a curious compound between the dress of the middle ages, a circus dancer, and the present fashion; but as the great object of showing a well-turned leg and pretty foot was gained, no one cavilled at its incongruity.

Jack's arrival was hailed with a shout by Mr. Gimp, who was on the point of conducting his partner to supper, and that young lady at once offered, in a good-natured way, to introduce Jack to a particular friend of hers.

The particular friend happening to be very pretty, our hero made no objection; and the four, arm-in-arm, proceeded to the supper-tables.

Surely there never was such a supper!

Not with reference to the eatables and drinkables, although they were of the best quality, but for uproarious fun and frantic laughter.

The sparkling champagne produced laughter.

Laughter begat noisy merriment.

Noisy merriment became irrepressible.

Mr. Gimp volunteered a song, but being unable to recollect the words, sang the first line over half-a-dozen times, and would have gone on much longer had he not been forcibly removed by a couple of waiters.

The two young ladies followed him, and signalled Jack to do the same; but he, having still preserved his senses, and having no wish to appear in his courtier's suit at a police-court, thought it more prudent to remain.

The masqueraders were beginning to disperse. Outside it was broad daylight, and the pleasure-seeking throng were beginning to yawn and think it was time to be getting home. It certainly was time!

Scarcely one there was sober. Jack was, perhaps, as good as any of them, but even he was beginning to be uncertain as to the number of gas-lights, and rather undecided as to the direction in which he was walking.

He had just made up his mind to leave when his attention was attracted by a female figure, gracefully draped, and wearing a mask, who, by her movements and general appearance, seemed vastly superior to the majority of those young ladies who were present.

She had a commanding presence, and passed by without noticing the rude jests of the semi-drunken men collected in knots upon the now half-deserted stage.

She walked straight to the spot where Jack was standing. She approached him!

He was looking in a different direction.

She stood at his side!

She laid her hand upon his arm!

He turned and faced her!

"You do not find pleasure in this debauchery?" she said, in soft, sweet tones.

"It's very good fun."

"Still, it is not satisfying. It is not with such as these," said the strange lady, waving her hand disdainfully towards the masquers—"it is not with such as these you should associate."

"You're very kind," said Jack, regularly puzzled by her manner and her words, which were evidently those of a real lady.

"I have much I wish to say to you."

"It's rather late," said our hero, yawning.

"I know it."

"What is it you would say to me?"

"I cannot tell you now—not in this place."

"May I ask your name?"

"That you will never know."

"Why not?"

"Do not ask me."

"What is it you require of me?"

"Will you meet me to-morrow?"

"With the greatest pleasure."

"In Richmond Park."

"At what time?"

"Between four and five in the afternoon."

"I will remember."

The lady looked doubtingly at him, as if fearful to trust his memory.

Perhaps she was right, for, without being absolutely intoxicated, he was in that state that he would probably have but a very confused recollection of the night's adventures on the morrow.

"I will write it down," said she.

Taking off her glove for that purpose, Jack saw the most beautifully white hand he had ever beheld, and noticed, moreover, that her fingers were loaded with valuable rings.

Hastily writing a few words on a card, she gave it to Jack, who thrust it into his pocket, and offered her his arm.

She refused it, turned from him, and in a moment was lost to sight.

Jack, whose curiosity was thoroughly aroused, hastened to the door hoping to obtain another glimpse of the mysterious lady.

Drawn up before the door was a handsome, well-appointed brougham.

Just as Jack reached the door he saw the lady with whom he had been conversing, handed into the carriage by a tall man, who raised his hat politely as the brougham drove off at a rapid rate.

"Whose carriage was that?" asked Jack of a sleepy policeman, standing by.

"Don't know, I'm sure," said that functionary, opening his hand and looking at a half-sovereign which he had evidently just received.

Jack put a sovereign in his palm.

"You're sure you don't know?"

"Well, sir, I shouldn't like to swear it, but if that there carriage don't contain the Lady Alice Brandon I'm only fit for a rural beat!"

"Impossible!"

"In course, if you says it's impossible, it are," answered the guardian of the peace, with a reckless disregard to his Lindley Murray, and he pocketed the sovereign and walked away.

Jack turned towards the gentleman who had handed her into the brougham.

He was still standing on the same spot, with his eyes fixed upon the ground.

It was the same individual who had appeared in the commencement of the evening habited in a black domino, and had created so disagreeable a sensation by his solemn gloominess.

His mask was removed now.

Jack recognised him.

It was Percy, Lord Manningtree!

Meditatively our hero put off his courtier's suit and resumed his own garments, being careful to transfer the card he had received from the lady to his own pocket; then hailing a cab, he jumped into it and was driven home.

The cocks were crowing and industrious maids-of-all-work were cleaning the door steps as he arrived before his lodgings, and after paying the cabman double his fare, but half what he asked, he let himself in with as little noise as possible, and crept upstairs to the sitting-room, not daring to venture further in the dark and his present state.

Hastily throwing off the greater part of his clothing and wrapping himself in a large railway rug, he curled himself down upon the sofa, and in five minutes from the time he entered the house was in as sound a sleep as he could have desired.

CHAPTER XXII.

A WOMAN'S REVENGE.

WHEN Fanny awoke the morning after the masquerade and found Jack's place by her side still vacant, she began to have some feelings of regret and alarm.

She had gone off to the Gregorian Music Hall at night, full of indignation against her lover, but firmly persuaded he would be, as usual, waiting to meet her and conduct her home after the performance.

But no Jack appeared.

Still indignant, she retired to rest, having no doubt in her own mind that before long he would return home; but when she awoke in the morning, and still there was no trace of him, a vague feeling of fright took possession of her.

She hurriedly dressed herself and descended to the sitting-room.

There, on the sofa, she beheld the truant, Master Jack, in a sound slumber and snoring most unromantically!

Her first impulse was to wake him.

She resisted it after a moment's deliberation.

She let him sleep on undisturbed.

While she was lacing her boots a sudden idea occurred to her.

She would try to discover where he passed the night, previous to his return home.

Actuated by this motive, she instituted a rigid search in his pockets which would have done credit to a custom-house official.

These are the articles her search brought to light:—

A piece of half-smoked cigar.

A bunch of keys.

A photographic portrait of a French ballet-dancer.

Two champagne corks.

Part of a torn masquerade dress.

A half mask.

Seven half-pence.

An empty purse.

A crumpled card with some words pencilled upon it!

The former articles had quite sufficiently aroused Fanny's indignation, but this last wrought her to the highest pitch.

It was bad enough his going to the masquerade without her, but his daring to make an appointment with some "Jezabel" (so Fanny styled her) was unpardonable.

The writing on the card was very pretty and elegant.

The words were few—

"Richmond Park, near the White Lodge, between 4 and 5 o'clock. Do not fail to come!"

That was all!

Not a name, nor even a single initial to give a clue to the writer!

Fanny felt what jealousy was like, for the green-eyed monster had attacked her, and she did not even know the name of her rival.

Jack still slumbered, unconscious of the discovery Fanny had made.

His clothes lay littered about the room.

Our heroine, seeing them there, conceived a plot.

She would, she thought, disguise herself in his clothes, and keep the appointment on his behalf!

It was a bold idea; but she proceeded at once to put it into execution.

Locking the door, she quickly divested herself of her own apparel and donned his.

It has already been mentioned that they were wonderfully alike; and when she had assumed his dress, except that she looked a trifle more feminine, no one would have discovered the difference.

Her great difficulty was with the waistcoat. Do what she would, she could not make it meet; but her woman's ingenuity quickly discovered a way of letting it out behind, and a quarter of an hour after the idea first struck her she stood before the looking-glass as jaunty and pretty a youth as one would wish to see.

Placing a cigar in her mouth, and assuming something of a swagger, she walked into the street, first having removed every trace of her presence from the room, and made her way to the Waterloo Railway Station, *en route* for Richmond!

It was not nearly the time for which the appointment had been fixed; but Fanny feared to remain in London, dreading she might be addressed by some of Jack's friends, in mistake for him, and also fearing that he himself might wake, and hurry to the station to intercept her.

Accordingly she took her seat in a first class carriage, and was quickly whirled down to Richmond.

As she walked through the town, on her way to the park, she had to run the gauntlet of a ladies' school, all the pupils of which looked with admiration at her pretty face—not knowing her sex—from beneath their eyelashes as she passed.

Indeed Miss Carvsed, the daughter of an eminent London butcher, expressed her willingness to die for him,—meaning Fanny; but finding on her return to the select academy a copy of ardent verses wrapped round a bottle of medicine, and addressed to her by the chemist's sentimental assistant, she forgot Fanny, and determined to live for the sake of the youthful apothecary.

Leaving Fanny to enjoy herself in the sylvan groves of Richmond Park, we must return to Jack, whom we left in a sound sleep on the sofa in the sitting-room.

Everything has an end; and our hero, tired as he was, at last awoke, and immediately rolled off the hard sofa upon which he had been sleeping.

Raising himself from the floor, he rubbed his eyes and stared around him in the way peculiar to gentlemen suddenly awakened, and with no decided recollection of how or when they went to sleep.

Gradually the adventures of the preceding night returned to him, one by one.

In due course he remembered the mysterious lady, and the appointment he had made to meet her in Richmond Park.

In default of anything better to do, he lay on his back, stared hard at the chandelier, and began to wonder.

He wondered who she was, and what she wanted with him. He wondered where Fanny was, and what she had thought of his absence. He wondered what o'clock it was, and if he hadn't better get up.

A church clock striking two decided him on that point, and throwing off the railway rug, he stood in light and airy costume on the hearthrug.

"The devil!"

"Confound it!!"

"Dash it!!!"

"What the deuce did I do with my trousers?"

"Where the dickens is my coat?"

It was certainly an awkward predicament in which to be placed. He dared not, for some time, venture in the Hottentot costume of a railway rug out of the room.

He dared not ring the bell and summon the slave.

His only hope lay in Fanny. He hoped she would enter and assist him in his trouble. But Fanny didn't come, and he heard the clock strike three, and he had to be at Richmond by four o'clock.

At length he summoned up courage to make a bolt upstairs to the bedroom, where he speedily invested himself in another suit of clothes, rushed downstairs, hailed the first Hansom, jumped into it, and promised the Jehu double fare if he caught the train.

Plunging, tearing, and galloping, they went through the crowded streets, and arrived at the platform just as the bell was ringing.

Jack put his hand in his waistcoat-pocket to pay the man. There was no money there!

Rapidly he felt in all his pockets with a like result.

The cabman became insolent, a mob of grinning porters and street-boys collected, Jack fumed and swore, the cabman refused to let him go, the whistle sounded, the train steamed away from the platform before his eyes, and our hero, to put an end to the altercation, was compelled ignobly to seek the nearest pawnbroker's, and deposit his ring there for a few shillings, in order to pay the importunate cabman.

There was no other train for more than an hour, so Jack was forced reluctantly to abandon the idea of keeping his appointment with the unknown lady, still, however, he resolved to go down by the next train, on the chance of finding her still waiting at the trysting-place in Richmond Park.

Fanny amused herself easily in the Park and in strolling about Richmond Hill till the time arrived for the meeting, when she directed her steps to that part of the Park bordering upon the enclosure of the White Lodge.

On re-entering the Park, not knowing in which direction the part she sought lay, she inquired of one of the Park-keepers.

That individual stared her fiercely in the face for some moments before he gave her the required information.

He suspected from the tone of her voice that she was of a different sex to that which her dress implied, and his suspicions were heightened by observing the extreme delicacy and smallness of her features, as well as her minute hands and feet.

He directed her as to the path she was to take, but himself followed at some little distance behind out of curiosity.

Fanny had not to wait long at the trysting-place before a handsomely attired lady appeared, and advanced towards her.

She was closely veiled, and our heroine was unable to distinguish her features, but saw enough to convince her that her rival (as she imagined her) was young, and doubtless beautiful.

As they approached within speaking distance the Park-keeper appeared upon the scene.

"Wait!" whispered the veiled lady, as she passed by Fanny without turning towards her, or otherwise showing she was conscience of her presence.

The Park-keeper sat down upon a bench, and whistled a popular tune.

The veiled lady strolled about, and appeared to have no particular object in doing so.

"Follow me at a distance," again whispered she, as her walk brought her near Fanny.

Our heroine did as she was bid, and her guide led her to a more secluded spot.

The Park-keeper followed. He was of a curious turn of mind, and he wished to see what it all meant.

The veiled lady had waited for Fanny, and when the latter approached her was about to speak, when, through the trees, she saw the uniform of the Park-keeper, with the owner inside, coming straight towards them.

"Be silent!" whispered she; "we are watched! Meet me here again this day month. I will take good care we are not then interrupted."

Before Fanny could reply the lady had vanished amongst the trees, and in her stead the Park-keeper stood before her.

"Do you know her ladyship, sir?" asked he.

"What do you mean, fellow?"

"Oh, yes! What do I mean? You know well enough."

"I shall report you for your insolence!"

"Certainly, sir, if you like; but I meant no offence. You see, it isn't the first time Lady Alice has made these sort of appointments."

"Lady Alice! What do you mean?"

"Lor bless you, sir! Do you mean to say you don't know who that lady was who was here just now?"

"I have no idea!"

"Lor!—to think of that now."

"Who was she?"

"I shouldn't like to mention names."

Fanny slipped some money into his nowise reluctant palm.

"Who did you say she was?"

"Lor! I thought everybody about here knew Lady Alice Brandon!"

"Lady—Alice—Brandon!" repeated Fanny to herself, as she made her way down into the town again. "Lady!—oh, the artful huzzy!"

The train which whirled Fanny back again to London passed another on the down line.

That one contained Jack Rawlings!

Fanny was just in time for her performance at the Abyssinian; and on her way there she mentally registered a vow that she would go that day month again to the Park, and unmask Lady Alice Brandon.

Alas! she little knew how much would happen to her before that time arrived.

The perils and dangers to which she was shortly to be exposed she little recked of. She dreamt not that events would shortly come to pass which would materially alter, not her own alone, but her lover's future life.

She saw not the threatening clouds gathering around her. As yet the title of Lord Crokerton was but to her an empty name—alas! she little thought how she would live to curse the owner of it!

Jack, of course, did not meet the lady in the Park, and, calling down all manner of unpleasant things upon the heads of those who had hindered him from keeping the appointment, he returned sulkily enough to London, with just the wherewithal in his pocket to purchase a glass of beer, upon which he walked home, lit his pipe, and smoked furiously for some time, till the soothing weed had its effect upon him. His temper became calmer and his manner softer as he sat still smoking and wondering why Fanny had not returned home.

CHAPTER XXIII.

THE MYSTERIES OF A MUSIC HALL.

No one, surely, with eyes in his head could have lived in London and yet remained in ignorance of the existence of the Great Abyssinian Music Hall.

Why, the thing would have been impossible.

Did it not appeal to you from the advertising columns of all the penny papers? Did it not stare you out of countenance from every available dead wall in the metropolis, in every conceivable combination of glaring reds and greens and yellows? Did it not peep up at you from the feet of lamp-posts, and strive to catch your eye in every size and shape at every turning—in every nook and corner?

There was no mistake about the Abyssinian! It went the entire animal in everything.

It advertised most. It came out strongest in size and colour. The bill-posters could not get a bill printed large enough to suit the taste of the spirited proprietor, who was himself a great and greasy man, wearing huge waistcoats of rich velvet, and a pound weight of watchguard.

A child of Israel was this, who had tried many trades, and made a pot of money—who had begun life as Solomon, and passed through the Court with a first-class certificate—who had started again as Sloman, and been burnt out with a heavy insurance—who had got through another little mess very satisfactorily as Abraham, and turned up again as Braham—who had made a good thing of it at Paris as Monsieur de Porky, and was now making a very fine thing indeed at the Abyssinian with another alias.

He had begun life, as I told you before, as a potboy, and had worked his way up steadily, from shirt-sleeves and an apron, to the gorgeous purple velvet waistcoat and the glossy white silk hat for which, in the Abyssinian days of glory, he was celebrated down Houndsditch way and all about Whitechapel.

He had built the Hall himself, and it stood upon the site of a "good dry skittle-ground," to which, as the police reports of the period will inform you, young men from the country frequently accompanied gentlemen of property to decide wagers relating to the throwing of heavy weights.

It was at the bar of this public-house, in those days, that bets respecting the spelling of words were so frequently decided, by reference to a dictionary the worthy landlord kept close at hand, by the side of the nutmeg and lemons on a shelf behind the bar.

There was at that time a select harmonic every Monday and Saturday on the first floor, at which our old friend Airy Blossom, the Warbling Tomtit, took the chair, and filled it to overflowing.

Upon other nights in the week there was sometimes a

select dancing party, at which the flowers of the east, not to mention the aristocracy of the Isle of Dogs, did largely congregate.

Again, on other nights, still more select company attended canine congresses, or a little sparring for the "Ben" of Conky Ike, or the Infant Goliah, or any other member of the fancy at that time high in public-house favour.

There was not a little trouble with these select meetings from time to time, and the sitting magistrate at the nearest police-office had our friend Boniface down in his black book before long; and only the very hardest swearing, at five shillings a head, got the license renewed when the time was up.

But after a while, when enough money had been made otherwise, the spirited proprietor built his hall, and began to make his fortune in good earnest.

Standing in the centre of an over-populated neighbourhood, a hideous locality peopled by the vilest and most vicious, the dirtiest, most squalid, poorest, and most depraved, the Hall, with its glare of gas and acres of plate-glass, seemed like a glimpse of heaven.

The twopences were always forthcoming somehow or other, and the body of the Hall was always crowded. The choicest children of Israel filled the stalls, and you might any night have found there the most showy jewellery and the dirtiest finger-nails in London.

A host of talent was of course engaged.

The world-famed Blackney came with brougham and pair. The inimitable double-voiced vocalist was also there, with a penny pipe and a hair-comb and paper.

The widely-renowned and incomparable Sam Leatherlungs danced his deathless double-shuffle every evening, and peppered the pomatumed head of the chairman with the cloud of dust he kicked up during the performance.

Billycock the monoloquist talked himself hoarse; and Billygoat, the original Jumping-Jack, jumped himself out of countenance.

Also came the bewitching Mrs. Bouncer, in scarlet boots and ravishingly-embroidered underclothing; and the fascinating Miss Cheek, whose songs were so taking, if, perhaps, a trifle immodest, but whose symmetry was, it must be confessed, as faulty as her grammar.

All these good ladies and gentlemen brought a considerable quantity of grist to the Abyssinian mill, but decidedly the greatest success of all was Miss Fanny White, with which we have to do; and with a humble apology to the reader for this long description, we will go back to that young lady, and recount what a dreadful scrape she got into, and how she and the spirited proprietor fell out.

It fell out in this wise.

There lived and flourished, half-a-dozen years ago, a horribly wicked and monstrously thin old nobleman, who disgraced the peerage, not to say humanity generally, by his awful goings on.

This dreadful old man, whose name was Lord Crokerton, was close upon seventy years of age, and was as miserable a fragment of humanity as you could well wish to see; but he nevertheless was a great rake, and, I am ashamed to say, for their sakes, a huge favourite with the ladies.

He was, at the same time, a great legislator; and now that he is gathered to his fathers (down below), his wise sayings and doings will long be remembered.

When he departed this life, his biography occupied a prominent place in the newspapers.

They made verses about him; and at the music halls the mention of his name brought down thunders of applause:

"Lord Crokerton, the great and good, all glory to his name,
  'Tis writ in deathless letters on the blazing scroll of fame.
                    Singing tol de rol, &c."

There was very little doubt about Lord Crokerton for all that. He was a horrible old rascal. A detestable old scamp whose memory will be execrated as long as any of his miserable victims remain upon earth with breath enough to curse him.

When he was not legislating his lordship was generally scouring London in search of some new intrigue. One evening he looked in at the Abyssinian and saw Miss Fanny White.

Miss Fanny was dancing her celebrated dances, and was dressed, or perhaps we ought more properly to say undressed, in the most bewitching style, and she created a great sensation in the old gentleman's highly susceptible heart.

"Who's that new gal you've got hold of, Ike?" cried his lordship to the spirited proprietor, who happened to be sitting in one of his own stalls, smoking a shilling cigar and drinking brandy and water.

"Fine girl, isn't she, my lud?" said the publican, who knew the peer very well, and was on terms of familiarity in consequence of some little business connected with a poor French ballet-dancer, which we need not enter into.

"Fine girl!" screamed Crokerton, smacking his spindle leg in ecstasy. "She's de-lic-i-ous! Introduce me."

"I'm afraid it can't be worked, my lud."

"Why not?"

"It wont wash!"

"Why not, I say?"

"Previous engagement."

"Hang engagements. Aint I made of money?"

"There's no doubt of that, my lud."

"Is there any woman alive incorruptible?"

"Not many where your ludship's concerned."

"Of course not."

"Except this one."

"This one—rubbish! Look here, Ike; I know your game, you hook-nosed sinner. I've had dealings with you before."

"And always found me on the square, my lud."

"Curse you! you've cheated me over every transaction."

"Oh! my lud, them words for you——"

"There, shut up, please. I can't bear virtue out of a melodrama. Let's talk sensibly."

"Certainly, if we can."

"If we can, as you say. What do you mean to begin with?"

"Mean?"

"Yes; do you want me to pay you for the introduction?"

"My lud, I wouldn't take a halfpenny from you. I should only be too happy to serve you."

"Yes, of course you would."

"Only——"

"Only——"

"Only in this case it's no good. It's not the least ha'porth of good, and you're throwing your time away."

"How's that?"

"She's engaged, as I say, and she would not be unfaithful to her young man."

"Young man, indeed; what is the wretch? Some of your pothouse pipers here, I suppose? Is it the chairman, or, ha, ha! is it you? Yes, by the Lord Harry, I've hit it. It's you!"

"Egad, my lud! I wont deceive you, I wish it was, but my nose is quite out of joint in that quarter."

"Think it would be, so much of it too."

"You're full of your fun, my lud, al'ays was. But as I was saying, I've no chance there. I gave her a good broad hint last pay-day. If doubling her present salary was any object to her I would have come that expense."

"And she did not see it. By Jove! I don't wonder either. I confess if I were a lady I should not let you make love to me under twenty pounds a minute."

The spirited proprietor winced a little, and gulped his grog.

"Anyhow," said he, "let that be as it may, you'll find she wont have you, even at that price."

"Will you introduce me?"

"Yes."

"When?"

"Now, if you like."

"Be it so. Let's go at once."

They went accordingly. The way lay through a low doorway and under the platform, across a couple of damp cellars, the floor of which was the bare earth, up a crazy staircase, and so behind the scenes, where the professional ladies and gentlemen were congregated, rather warm and greasy for want of air and space, waiting for their turns.

Miss Fanny, however, was not there. She had left the Hall immediately after her last call, and gone away in a cab with her friend, Jack Rawlings.

His lordship, having cursed his fate and the lady, the Music Hall proprietor and its domestic arrangements, took himself off, saying he would come another night.

He was not long in keeping his word. Next night, indeed, he turned up in Whitechapel, with his best wig on, and carrying a huge bouquet, which he sent, (I mean the bouquet, not the wig) to the object of his affections.

Now it so happened that it was Miss Fanny's birthday,

LORD CROKERTON AND FANNY IN THE LONELY HOUSE AT FULHAM.

and Master Jack, scapegrace that he was, had forgotten it. What was more natural then, than that when the bouquet came she should think that he had sent it, and that it was a little delicate attention upon his part.

She was just going on for her first turn when the bouquet arrived, and she had only just time to kiss and smell it, before she ran up the stairs and skipped on to the platform.

All through her song and dance you may be sure she was looking about eagerly among the audience for her young lover.

But she could not see him anywhere.

"Most likely he's gone behind, and is waiting for me there," thought she.

She sang her songs, therefore, and danced her dances, and retired precipitately. She had taken the bouquet on to the platform with her, thinking that it would please Master Jack. She kissed it and took it away with her, and you can easily imagine the delight of that naughty old nobleman at the sight thereof.

He sat in the middle of the stalls and gloated his horrible old eyes upon the fair form before him.

He followed with greedy gaze the graceful movements of the young girl, by turns full of passionate energy and voluptuous languor.

At times she appeared to float sylph-like through the air, her soft, gauzy, half-transparent garments clinging to her symmetrical limbs, faultless in their well proportioned accuracy.

Then rousing herself suddenly, and as though with a mighty effort shaking off the lethargy which enthralled her, she darted wildly into the dance, and her nimble feet seemed to twinkle like the spokes of a revolving wheel, and then again as suddenly subsiding into the same soft, seductive languishing, her half-closed eyes, full of sleepy, pent-up passion, lavished lascivious glances upon the occupants of the stalls, and among them the delighted nobleman, who foresaw his conquest to be now a positive certainty, and in anticipation revelled in the wild delights of lawless desire.

But presently, after the dance was terminated, and she had left the stage—after the lapse of about a quarter of an hour, and just as he was rising from his seat, with the intention of betaking himself by the underground route he had over-night travelled to the singers' dressing-rooms, one of the young gentlemen who formed part of the chorus touched his arm, and with something of a grin, handed back to him his bouquet.

Lord Crokerton opened his eyes to the utmost, and tared at it.

"What's this for ?" cried he.

The boy grinned more than ever.

"The lady sent it you, sir."

"Sent it back ?"

"With her compliments, sir."

"What's she mean by that ?"

But the young gentleman in the chorus did not know what it meant, or, at any rate, did not appear to be willing to impart any information.

He seemed to know something about it, though, for the young imp grinned from ear to ear—a huge grin, more like a gash in his face than a natural parting of the lips.

His lordship tried to keep his countenance, so that the youth might not enjoy himself too much at his expense, and he sat down and went on with the sherry-cobbler he had been drinking, and which he had left unfinished.

The boy retreated, but only to peep round a distant corner and grin more horribly than ever.

His lordship waited with what patience he could muster until the boy's objectionable head was at length withdrawn, and then he turned his attention to the bouquet.

He carefully parted the flowers and peeped in.

Then drew from it a folded paper, unfolded it, and uttered an ejaculation of disgust.

When Fanny had had time to examine the bouquet, after she came off the platform, she was not long in discovering that there was a note inside.

She drew it forth eagerly, and looked at the direction.

It was directed to her, but the handwriting was unknown to her.

She was very much astonished. Who was it from ? She had supposed that it was from Master Jack, but these were not his heavy down strokes.

As, of course, the best way to find out who it was from was to open the paper and read, she opened it and discovered —a ten pound note!

With it a very nicely worded, studiously polite epistle, which, nevertheless, brought the blushes to her cheeks, and caused her eyes to flash with rage and shame. It was his lordship's handiwork.

He proposed an interview, which he had every confidence in being kept. It must be confessed that he was considerably staggered when the bouquet came back to him, and more so still when inside it he discovered the very carefully composed note, which he supposed would have effectually achieved the conquest of the pretty dancer.

When the spirited proprietor came into the stalls some time afterwards, he found his lordship moodily chewing the end of the straw, through which he had imbibed the cobbler.

"Well, my lud !"

"That girl's a fool !"

"What girl !"

"You know well enough."

"Oh! ah! to be sure. What, have you spoken to her ?"

"No; but I wrote."

"Got an answer ?"

"Got the letter returned."

"Just as I said."

"Is it ? However, you'll see before I've done. I'm not beaten yet, mind."

"I know your ludship's persevering."

"I seldom set my mind on achieving an object which, in the end, I do not succeed."

"True, my lud."

"Consequently that girl shall be mine, or by——"

"Don't swear, my lud, but look here."

"Well."

"Will you make a bet about it ?"

"Certainly."

"Dozen of champagne you don't succeed this time !"

"Done."

"You'll lose."

"Shall I ? Stop, though."

"You want to cry off."

"Not I, only I want to make two stipulations."

"Certainly."

"The first is that you don't interfere."

"'Pon my honour."

"Never mind your honour. The second is——"

"That I help you ?"

"God forbid ! The second is, that the champagne doesn't come out of your cellar. I don't see the fun of working hard only to get poisoned in the end."

With that his lordship rose, and made his way towards the door. On his way he met with Mrs. Bouncer, the serio-comic lady, with whom, in days gone by, before she was quite so fat and coarse, his lordship had had some little love passages of a tender nature.

Her his lordship thought fit to take into his confidence to a certain extent, and when Mrs. Bouncer found that mischief was meant to her fair rival, she willingly lent all the aid in her power.

"And that is only a little information," said his lordship, interrupting the lady's profuse offers of assistance.

"What time does she leave ?"

"Her second time is at ten."

"Does any one come to fetch her ?"

"Sometimes her lover, or brother, or whatever he is."

"Sometimes she goes alone ?"

"Yes."

"Does she walk ?"

"When she is alone she generally rides, I believe."

"Not got a carriage of her own, I suppose ?"

"Oh, no ! She goes in a cab."

"That's all I want to know. Good night."

Lord Crokerton, with this information, abruptly departed, and made the best of his way home.

Arrived there, and in his dining-room, his lordship rang for his valet.

Mr. Simperton answered the summons, and stood politely attentive.

"Got a job for you," said Lord Crokerton.

Simperton inwardly winced and outwardly smiled.

"You've acted many characters at different times," said his lordship.

"And I trust, my lord, retained a good one of my own."

"Hold your tongue, fellow ! I say, you dress up well. You make a good blackguard."

"With a good deal of disguise, my lord."

"I want you to dress yourself as a cabman."

"Yes, my lord."

"You must also hire a cab."

"Yes, my lord."

"Then I'll tell you what to do next."

*   *   *   *   *   *

Pretty Fanny went home in a pet. She and her friend, Jack Rawlings, had a few words about one thing and another—though, mind you, not one allusion did the young lady make to Master Jack's neglect and forgetfulness.

Women, in like circumstances, seldom do. They brood over those sort of injuries, say nothing, but never forget them.

About a fortnight afterwards, when Jack had forgotten all about it, Miss Fanny renewed the subject, and gave him a bit of her mind very properly.

In the meantime, something very awful had to happen, and we must not anticipate.

The night after that upon which Lord Crokerton made his present of the bouquet there was a violent thunderstorm.

Jack had promised to come for his sweetheart at ten o'clock, but he did not keep his promise.

Fanny waited for him more than an hour, expecting every moment that he would arrive. At last, wearied and worn out, and not a little angry at Jack's unaccountable neglect, she determined to go home alone.

One of the chorus boys offered to go for a cab, but she declined the civility.

"I daresay there is one at the door," she said.

She went to the door of the Hall to look for one. No sooner did she make her appearance, than a four-wheeler drove towards her.

"Cab, miss ?"

"Yes."

The man jumped down from his box, though with a certain degree of clumsiness, as if he had not been all his life accustomed to getting off and on a cab-box; then opened the door, and assisted her to enter the vehicle.

She gave her address, which he hardly waited for, before he climbed back to his place; and the cab drove away at a brisk pace.

Fanny leant back, and now that she was free from observation, burst into tears.

She was very much vexed at Jack's neglectful conduct. What did it mean? Was he beginning to get tired of her? Had she not been a fool to run away with him? How would it all end?

She asked herself these questions, but could find no satisfactory answer for any of them. She rocked herself to and fro, and cried harder than ever, and as though her heart would break.

All at once though, when she was quite worn out and exhausted with weeping, it suddenly occurred to her that she had been a very long while getting home.

She wiped her eyes, and looked out of the window.

She could not recognize the streets through which she was passing.

The cab was going at a great rate.

What did it mean? The man had made a mistake.

She rubbed the glass with her handkerchief, and peered anxiously out, expecting every moment to come to some building which she would recognise, but failed to do so.

The cab seemed to go faster and faster!

She must stop the driver.

She felt for the check-string, but there was none!

She tried to let down one of the windows behind the driver's back, but they would not open.

She next attempted to open the windows in the doors, but was again unsuccessful.

The cab was getting over the ground at a terrific speed. The man must have been running a race with some other vehicle.

But this would never do. She must stop the cab.

She began to drum against the glass, and to call out at the top of her voice.

She hammered and called in vain!

The man drove on, if anything, faster.

He took not the slightest notice of the noise she made.

He must have been as deaf as a post.

She tried the doors, but could not open them from the inside.

This state of affairs, however, could never last. She must stop the cab.

How?

There was only one way: she must break the glass.

No sooner said than done.

Smash!

The driver jerked round his head.

The cab stopped suddenly.

The man got down, and approached the door.

"Did you want anything?—what's the matter?"

"Matter? Where are you taking me?"

"Home! It's all right."

"Stop! I want to get out!"

"You're not there yet."

"Let me get out, I say!"

"Sit quiet, or it will be the worse for you."

"Let me get out! Help! help!"

She rose up, and strove to push through the doorway, but the cabman clutched her by the wrist.

Quick as thought, then, he plunged his hand into his breast-pocket, and drew forth a tiny phial.

Holding her by the wrist, he gave her a sudden jerk towards him.

At the same moment applied the phial to her nostrils.

In spite of herself, she was forced to inhale a long breath.

But as she did so, a giddiness seized her—a violent pain shot through her throbbing temples.

She gasped for air—the objects around her swam confusedly before her fast glazing eyes.

In another moment she was perfectly insensible—rigid and motionless in a deathlike swoon.

CHAPTER XXIV.

THE LONELY HOUSE AT FULHAM.

UPON the Middlesex side of Hammersmith Bridge, about half a mile nearer Charing-cross, lies a wild tract of country, mostly covered by nursery-gardens and meagre grass land, with here and there an old-fashioned house standing alone, damp, and gloomy in its flat patch of private ground, wherein the unruly growth of weeds seems effectually to have overcome and subdued all floricultural endeavours.

It was here, standing perfectly isolated, many hundreds of yards removed from any other habitation, and only approachable by a narrow lane, lined upon either side by hedgerows, was a house called Yew-tree Lodge, the property of Lord Crokerton.

It was a dreary enough looking building, and was surrounded by so high a wall that only a glimpse of the upper part, beginning from the second floor windows, could be obtained from the road.

It was said to be haunted, and occasionally, at dead of night, strange sounds had been heard to issue therefrom, and sometimes a piercing shriek had awakened the sleeping echoes, and filled such listeners as lay awake and heard it, with a shuddering terror.

When, a year ago, the old building was razed to the ground, two skeletons were found bricked into one of the walls—two skeletons locked in what seemed to be a deadly struggle.

One of the rooms—and this was the one which attracted most attention—was very curiously constructed.

It was, in all respects, a double room.

There were double walls, with a space between, a double floor, a double ceiling, a double door, and no window.

This apartment was, when closed, completely air-tight, and wholly impervious to sound.

The loudest and most piercing shrieks could not have penetrated beyond its precincts.

For what purpose had such a room been built it was impossible to say, although many tales of violence and atrocity where miserable women were the victims were freely circulated.

The room had been in existence in the time of Lord Crokerton's father, a nobleman who during his life had achieved a most unenviable notoriety for profligacy and licentiousness. The son had followed in the father's footsteps; and many sins lay heavy upon his wicked soul, when at length, after a wearying and painful illness, he lay gasping upon his death-bed in the family mansion in Piccadilly.

In the meantime, however, with sincere apologies for this digression, let us return to poor Fanny, who had fallen so easily into the trap laid for her destruction.

The swoon which had succeeded the application of the tiny phial to her nostrils endured for more than an hour.

She began to recover her consciousness to some extent, when at length the cab came to a standstill before the gate of the old house in Fulham.

She dreamily opened her eyes, with a weary sigh, and strove to raise herself from the recumbent position into which she had fallen.

But the effects of the powerful narcotic which had been so artfully administered to her were not yet sufficiently dissipated.

She vainly strove to rise, but found that all her strength had deserted her.

She tried to cry out, but her tongue refused to utter a sound.

Even if this had not been the case, however, and the power of speech had not deserted her, her cries for help would have been in vain in such a wild and unpeopled locality.

She cast a despairing glance around upon the dreary waste of land stretching as far as her eyes could reach, and relieved only by the faintest speck of light, seen far, far away in the extreme distance, and coming probably from some mean hovel where dwelt a labourer and his family, miserably poor, callous and hardened, most likely upon whom a cry for help would not, in all probability, have much effect. It was not at all likely that any assistance would be afforded her from such a quarter, let her shriek as loud as she might.

The valet, who had acted as cabman, descended from the box and rang the bell hanging by the side of the huge wooden gates. The person whom it was intended to summon, however, appeared to be rather hard of hearing, for he was obliged to ring several times before he got any answer.

Then suddenly, and without any warning footstep upon

the other side to indicate her approach, the gate was flung open, and a very ugly old woman made her appearance, carrying a candle in her hand, which she shaded in such a manner that its rays were all concentrated upon her own hideous countenance.

"Who's there?" cried the old woman, in a shrill, querulous tone.

"Who's there?" repeated the valet, with some contempt in his tone, which, however, was not a very loud one, and, as it appeared, quite inaudible to the person to whom it was addressed. "You've got no ears, I suppose, you old superannuated female kangaroo."

"Oh, it's you, is it, Mr. S.? I hope I haven't kept you waiting."

"Not a moment—you stupid old pig," replied the gentleman, beginning his sentence in a bawl and ending in a whisper.

"I thought you hadn't been long. I was listening for you."

"Listening, you call it, old dunderhead. Ah, you aint half as deaf as you used to be."

"I never was deaf."

"No, not regularly deaf," replied the valet, screaming at the top of his voice, "only a little—hard—of—hearing."

While this brief conversation had been going on, the valet had drawn the cab into the yard and closed the gates behind it.

When he had done so, he opened the cab door, and offered Fanny his arm to alight.

But she drew back, with a look of disgust.

"Don't be afraid, miss; no one will hurt you."

The old woman held up the candle, and peered into the interior of the cab with an expression of fiendish delight which filled the shrinking girl's heart with terror.

"What a pretty young lady!" said the old woman.

"Why have I been brought here?" cried Fanny, in great alarm. "Who's house is this?"

"Oh, it's a very pretty house," said the valet, "and you will be well taken care of."

"Don't be afraid, my dear," put in the old woman; "you are among friends."

But Fanny was not quite so sure of this. The appearance of the old woman was not in her favour. The valet was closely shaven and very villainous. The spot was very lonely. The house wore an ill-favoured appearance which boded the friendless girl no good.

There would have been very little use in screaming for help, as I have said, before entering the house gates. The gates closed, all hope of help was left without.

She would fain have resisted her removal from the cab; but what good were her weak efforts against the united strength of the two wretches into whose hands she had unhappily fallen?

The valet motioned to her to alight, and at the same time, encircling her wrist with his strong fingers, gave her a persuasive jerk, which almost dislocated her arm, and obliged her to step forward towards the ground.

Taking her arm then in his, and still keeping a strong hold upon her wrist, he led her towards the house, the door of which the old woman had left open.

They proceeded up a long passage, and entered a dark wainscotted room.

Here, having placed her upon a sofa, he left her with the old woman and retired down the passage.

When he had gone a few yards, the old woman followed him, and Fanny heard a brief dialogue which they held together, and which was necessarily conducted in a very loud tone, owing to the female's hardness of hearing.

"Is he coming?" the old woman asked.

"He will be here in about an hour's time, I should think," replied the other.

"He knows she is here, I suppose?"

"Yes; I sent to him directly I caught her."

"Very well, then I shall expect him."

"Of course. He's sure to come. Bless you, he is more anxious about this one than any other I have ever known him to be after. It has cost a pretty penny already, I can tell you."

"He is not one, though, to spare money when the fancy takes him."

"That would be my way if I was a man of property."

"There is no accounting for tastes," said the old woman; "for my part, I can't think how men can be such fools as to run after bits of chits of girls."

"That's what you say," said the valet, and went away laughing.

Presently, Fanny, still listening, heard the sound of wheels and a slamming to of the gates.

After this the house was for a time perfectly still—no sound of the old woman's movements breaking the deathlike silence.

Miss Fanny sat upon the sofa, a prey to reflections that were anything but agreeable.

Into whose hands had she fallen? For what purpose had she been thus kidnapped?

Alas! it was impossible to hide from herself the atrocity intended.

That some well-meditated and deep-laid scheme, of which she was the unhappy victim, had been successfully carried into effect, there could be no doubt; and her thoughts reverted to the present of the bouquet, and to the glimpses which she had obtained over the shoulder of the chorus-boy, of the wicked-looking old man in the stalls at the music-hall.

It was through the instrumentality of this person that she had been brought here! and, although ignorant of his name and rank, she could not doubt but that he was possessed of considerable wealth, and that he would lavish large sums of money upon the accomplishment of his lawless desires; consequently, it was to be supposed that the servants in his pay would serve him well, and would not be likely to be easily—that is to say, cheaply—corrupted.

The question was now, what was to be done? When she turned the matter over in her mind, she was inclined to think that it was the wisest course which she could possibly have pursued—to submit quietly, and appear to make no resistance.

By adopting this plan she would disarm suspicion, and induce her captors, to some extent, to relinquish their vigilance.

The first question was, who was in the house besides the old woman? If there was nobody else, it would not be so difficult, perhaps, for Fanny to overcome her, and effect her escape.

She was by no means so weak and fragile a flower as not to be able to defend herself.

The effects of the narcotic had almost gone by this time. She still had a headache, and felt slightly giddy; but her strength was rapidly returning, and she felt ready for any effort.

Meanwhile, what had become of the old woman?

Not a sound was to be heard in the house, in which reigned the silence of the tomb.

When she had gone away, she had left the door open. This surely promised well. It looked careless.

Fanny thought she might as well peep out into the passage, and see how the land lay.

The old woman had left a candle burning upon the table. Fanny took this in her hand, and took a step towards the door.

It was only a step though; for the sight which met her eyes brought her to a sudden standstill.

It was the long thin fingers of a hand round the side of the door, drawing it slowly to.

Very slowly—very noiselessly. There was, somehow, something very horrible in this mysterious movement, which filled her with an almost indescribable dread and terror.

When, however, she could summon courage to overcome this feeling, she made a sudden spring forward, and endeavoured to tear the door open.

But before she could do so, the fingers were withdrawn, and the door closed with a snap.

She turned round the handle, hoping to be able to pull it open again; but it was locked. She knocked at it loudly, and called at the top of her voice, but received no reply.

When, desisting from her efforts, she stood silently listening, the unbroken stillness of the house appeared to be even greater than before.

She was quite at a loss now what steps to take. How could she take any steps without making some noise?—and it was very evident that she was watched.

Even if the old woman did not hear her, she would probably see her, for she must be waiting outside, in the passage.

The only way to escape, if escape were possible, must be by the window. Fanny took up the candle, and looked round.

There was no window.

She was in the double room, of which mention has been made.

There was no means of leaving the apartment except it was by, the door through which she had entered, and the chance in this direction was but a very poor one.

She went back and pulled at the handle, then she knocked loudly, then again she raised her voice and loudly called for help.

All in vain. No one heard her—no one heeded her.

She was caught in a trap. She was powerless, and at the mercy of her captors, who might offer any violence to her with impunity, as far as the interference of the outward world was concerned.

There was nothing for her to do, though, but wait and see what step her enemies would take.

She must wait an hour. The valet had said that in an hour's time the person by whose orders she had been brought thither would make his appearance. Until then it was probable that she would be left undisturbed.

The time passed with tedious slowness, every moment appearing to be drawn out to an unnatural length.

She sat where she had hitherto been sitting, and wearily counted hundreds to pass away the time.

Would the hour never pass away? Surely an hour must have passed ere this!

Ah! a noise at the door. He had come.

But no; it turned out to be the old woman, who entered with a decanter of wine and a couple of glasses.

"I have brought you some refreshment, my dear," said the old woman; "you're not tired of waiting, are you?"

"Waiting for what?" asked Fanny. "I am tired of remaining here. Why am I being kept at all?"

"Oh! that's all right," replied the old woman, who seemed to guess at the meaning of the words, which had not been uttered in a tone sufficiently loud to penetrate her wooden head; "that's all right. You will be very happy if you don't act like a silly."

"What's your master's name?" cried Fanny, raising her voice.

But the old woman replied only with a cunning grin and a shake of her head.

"Try a little of this beautiful port wine," said she, filling two glasses, and handing one to the young girl.

But the thought that it was drugged instantaneously flashed through Fanny's mind.

She must not drink it; but, still, if she could pretend to do so, and, without creating suspicion or being discovered, throw the contents of the glass away——

An idea occurred to her—

"I cannot drink it without something to eat. I feel so faint."

"Certainly, my dear. What would you like?"

"Have you a biscuit?"

"I'll get you one directly."

She then left the room, closing the door behind her, and, quick as thought, Fanny changed the wine glasses.

Rapid as were her movements, however, she had scarcely time to do so before the old woman returned again. It would seem that she had hurried back, fearful lest the victim might do what she had done.

When she came into the room again, Fanny could not help noticing that the old woman glanced eagerly towards the glasses.

When she had gone away she had left Fanny with a glass in her hand. She had a glass in her hand still, and it was difficult to tell whether or not it was the same.

The old woman, therefore, stared hard at her and the wine, and handing her a biscuit, sat down and helped herself to the disengaged glass.

"Drink it up, my dear," said the hag, with a horrible grin, which she intended for a coaxing smile. "Drink it up; it wont hurt you."

Fanny, however, munched her biscuit instead.

The old woman swallowed the contents of her own glass, and again urged her companion to drink.

After a little more persuasion, she did so, and replaced the glass upon the table.

"How do you feel now, my dear?" asked the old woman.

"Very well, ma'am, thank you."

"That's well."

There was rather a long pause after this. Fanny sat silently nibbling her biscuit. The old woman kept her eyes fixed upon her.

At last she said again—

"How do you feel now?"

"Very well, ma'am, thank you," replied Fanny again.

"That's well."

Another pause ensued, considerably longer in its duration than the first.

The old woman kept her eyes upon Fanny. Fanny, in her turn, watched her companion narrowly.

Presently the old woman sighed, and passed her hand across her forehead.

Fanny still watched her, but made no remark.

"It's very hot," said the old woman.

And again she wiped her face, upon which great drops of perspiration rolled like beads.

Fanny could not refrain from an outward chuckle of delight.

She was not slow in attributing her companion's uneasiness to the proper cause.

The wine *had* been drugged, and the old woman had partaken of the contents of the glass intended for the young girl.

Before very many minutes had elapsed, the old woman heaved a heavy sigh, and again pressed her hand upon her head.

"This room is so close," she muttered; "very hot—stifling hot—intolerably hot!"

As she spoke, she tore her dress open at the neck, and sat panting for air.

Her face was alternately as red as blood and as pale as ashes.

The perspiration stood upon her forehead, and from time to time she wiped it away upon her sleeve, or wiped her mouth, the lips of which were dry and parched.

Suddenly, however, she seemed to recollect herself, after she had been for some time nodding helplessly in the chair, rolling her head from side to side like an intoxicated mandarin. Suddenly she seemed to awaken to a dim consciousness of what she was doing and what she ought to do, and drew herself up stiff and upright on her chair.

"How do you feel now?" she asked.

It was evident that as yet she had no suspicion that she had herself fallen a victim to the devilish scheme by which she would have effected the poor girl's ruin.

Fanny made no answer to the question; and the old woman, after mumbling incoherently for a few moments, sank back, in a state of semi-collapse, from which she did not again recover.

A few ineffectual struggles she made from time to time, in the hope of once more pulling herself together and getting into an upright posture; but it was all in vain.

Consciousness had entirely deserted her.

At length she sank down, a shapeless mass, and sliding slowly from the seat of the chair, squatted on the floor, in that particularly helpless and impotent condition which is ordinarily described as "all of a heap."

Fanny sat watching her for some minutes, without offering any assistance—without indeed, moving a step towards the spot where she had fallen, fearing that she might by some chance arouse the old woman from her stupor.

After a while, though, she made a step forward, and laid her hand upon her shoulder.

She appeared to be unconscious of it. The drug now held her entirely under its stupifying influence.

Fanny, however, wished to make quite sure of the fact, and she took the old woman by the shoulder and shook her violently to and fro.

Without effect. She was as though she had been dead drunk.

Under these circumstances, then, the time had arrived when she should make an attempt to escape.

Leaving the old woman sprawling upon the floor, Fanny took the candle, and set about her project.

To the door, of course, was her attention first directed. She turned the handle and opened it without any trouble; but the triumphant smile, which her success thus far had called forth, suddenly died away when she discovered at about a yard's distance another door of solid oak, to which upon the inside was no handle or any other means of opening it.

Fanny pushed at it, and tried to drag it towards her by inserting her nails behind a ledge in the carving, but all in vain.

The door remained as fast as ever. It was clear that the means of opening it must be either a secret, known to the old woman and her agents alone, or else that the door could only be opened from the outside.

In either case, Fanny could not very easily perceive how she was to benefit by this mode of egress.

She returned to the old woman, and having twisted her about with very little ceremony, emptied her pockets of their contents.

They contained, among a large quantity of rubbish, a bunch of keys, and a letter, sealed with a coronet, and directed to Mrs. Green, Yew Tree Lodge, Fulham.

It ran as follows:—

"S. may bring some one to-night. Panelled room. Take care. No noise. Draught.

"C."

Fanny read the letter twice, deciphering the handwriting only with extreme difficulty. The meaning was, however, plain enough. She was the person alluded to.

A sleeping draught was to be administered to her. She was to be brought into a panelled room—the room, in fact, in which she now found herself—where escape was impossible, where no living soul could see or hear the fiendish outrages committed upon her.

Where her shrieks would reach no human ears save those of the monsters whose clutches she had fallen into, where her prayers for mercy would avail her naught, where her shame and ruin could be safely effected, and where afterwards cold-blooded murder might succeed outrage and dishonour.

She took up the candle again, and proceeded round the room, carefully examining the walls.

They were hung, at intervals, with oil paintings of a shameful character—the subjects of which would have been sufficient to convince her, had other evidence been wanting, into what a den of infamy she had fallen.

At last, in one corner of the room, she came to something which at first she took only for a ledge of wood.

Upon looking at it, however, with greater care, she found that it was a door.

She was inclined to utter a joyful exclamation at the sight; but having pulled it open, her rejoicing was at an end, upon finding only a large dark cupboard, quite empty.

The discovery, as far as a means of escape was concerned, appeared to be quite useless; but, upon reflection, she saw a way by which it might be turned to some account.

She would put the old woman into it.

No harm could come of getting her into a place of security, in case she should presently recover from her state of torpor. In all probability, the person by whose directions Fanny had been kidnapped would very soon arrive. It would, then, be better to make it appear as though they had gone on according to his directions.

If it should so happen that the old woman was the only inmate of the lonely house—a state of things which Fanny saw some reason to believe to be the case—by getting her out of the way, did her master possess a means of entering the house, penetrating into the panelled room, without her assistance, he would not know what had become of her, and would, perhaps, suppose that for some reason or other she had left the house.

Decidedly, this then was the best course to pursue. There was, in fact, no other course left open to her. She could do nothing until Crokerton arrived; and until he arrived, if she had to contend with him alone, she would be uncertain as to what sort of antagonist he would turn out to be.

With some little difficulty—for the fair Green was no small weight, Fanny dragged her across the room, and bundled her, neck and crop, into the cupboard.

Then she fastened the door, by means of a bolt upon the outside, and panted for breath.

Scarcely had she done so, however, when she fancied she heard a slight noise at the room door.

She had only just time to throw herself full length upon the sofa, and close her eyes, as though she were asleep, when Lord Crokerton entered the apartment.

CHAPTER XXV.

THE PROFLIGATE LORD AND HIS VICTIM.

LIKE a thief in the night—like a satyr stealing into the leafy bower where slumbered some unconscious wood-nymph —like one of the hoary elders invading the chaste sanctity of Susannah's bath, did this sinful old wretch creep into the panelled room, in which he hoped to find his stupified victim, defenceless and at his power.

There she lay—her eyes closed, her gentle bosom heaving as if in peaceful slumber.

Had the wine had a proper effect?

Had the potion been administered?

Was she drugged?

He noiselessly approached the couch, and taking the candle in his hand, shaded his eyes as he gazed down upon the fair form of the young girl.

She was very beautiful. Her long, soft eyelashes drooped over her peachy cheeks; her rich, red, pouting lips, slightly parted, displayed her tiny milk-white teeth.

The soft clinging material of which her dress was composed, showed off to the greatest advantage the voluptuous contour of the form it hid from his greedy eyes.

He looked down at her, long and earnestly, and would have stooped to press upon her full, moist mouth a Tarquin-like kiss, when suddenly she opened her eyes, and rising upon her elbow, looked the nobleman steadily and sternly in the face.

Lord Crokerton, not easily abashed at most times, was upon this occasion considerably taken aback.

The suddenness of the girl's movement, and the fixedness of her regard, entirely unnerved him, and he had not a word to say for himself.

Like a thief, he had been creeping towards her. Safe he had thought himself to be from all intrusion or interruption; and now, in the moment of shameful detection, he cringed and cowered like a lashed hound.

He put the candle down upon the table, and tried to smile and appear at his ease.

He cut, however, such a paltry and pitiable figure that Fanny, whose sense of the ludicrous, it must be confessed, was considerably stronger than her virtue, burst out laughing.

"Well, old gentleman!" said she, "what do you want?"

His lordship, seized with a sudden bashfulness, such as he had not known for the last sixty years, scratched his wig in the silliest manner possible, and giggled so that his mouth, full of false teeth, got all awry.

He recovered himself, though, after a while; and thinking it best to carry her by storm, plumped down upon his knees, and began to make violent love to her.

At which Miss Fanny laughed, long and loudly.

But his lordship was not to be easily daunted. He pleaded his cause much better than the most fervent youth could have done.

He told her that he had never loved anybody half as much—that, if she would be his, he would settle a most magnificent allowance upon her.

To show that he was in earnest, and meant what he said, he drew forth a fat pocket-book, from which he took quite a handful of rustling, flimsy paper, and placed note after note in the pretty little hand, which, however, was large enough to grip them all.

But, in spite of his passionate pleadings, Miss Fanny did nothing but laugh.

At length, growing desperate with the delay, he would have taken her in his arms.

But Fanny twisted like an eel out of his grasp.

Then, as he strove once more to seize her, she doubled up that pretty fist of hers—the one with the notes in—and dealt my Lord Crokerton such a terrific right-hander on the nose, that it spread him out flat upon the floor, where he lay, bleeding and gasping, a sight pitiful to behold.

He certainly must have been a desperate old man to wish, after this, to renew his love-making.

But he did.

Scrambling up, more dead than alive, he resumed the conflict.

But, alas! he knew not what a Tartar he had caught.

One—two—followed in awfully quick succession.

One—two! Sayers himself, though he might have hit a little harder, could not very well have done the business with a finer show of science.

It is all very well, of course, to make heroines of delicate, lackadaisical young females—coy, young namby-pamby maidens, in whose mouths butter would melt with difficulty —and who could only flutter and scream, and wrestle weakly with their ravisher, but in the end to become a victim to his violence.

I can't help it if you don't like her; but Fanny was not one of this sort.

She was a spanking, bouncing young wench—beautiful

enough, in all conscience, to excite the desires of the most cold-blooded; but she was, withal, as strong as a young bull.

Voluptuous, graceful, pliant, and muscular.

She could love and languish; but, when her blood was up, she could scratch and bite.

She would make love one moment, and, the next, fight like a little she-devil, as she was.

One—two—delivered with precision, brought poor old Lord Crokerton to the ground again.

His wig was knocked off.

His false teeth jumped like a frog out of his mouth.

Then he lay flat upon his back, spread out like a plaster, rolling his eyes, and groaning.

Fanny leant over him.

"Do you want any more?" said she.

His lordship gasped "murder," and made a motion with his hands, as though to ward off another "one—two," if any were coming.

"You were never a very handsome old man," said the young lady, "but this hasn't improved you."

"Go away! murderess," gasped the old man.

"Don't say that. I haven't quite killed you, though such a horrid old wretch as you are well deserve it."

"I shall never be myself again."

"Be some one else, then. You cannot change for the worse."

"Oh dear! oh dear! my poor nose is broken."

"It was always too long."

"You shall suffer for this, you hussy."

"You've suffered enough already."

"I'll have the law on you."

"Ha! ha! ha! I'm not afraid."

"We'll see that."

"Yes, we will. It will all come out at the police-court— only I shall speak first."

"You daren't do it."

"We'll see what I dare do. What a talk there'll be about it! All the penny illustrated newspapers will have a portrait of the hoary-headed old villain and the virtuous maiden. Wont that be fun?"

The old gentleman groaned dismally. He felt that what she said was not far from the truth.

He was not aware that she was ignorant of his real name, and he supposed that, if she chose, she could very easily expose him. It would be best to conciliate her, if he only knew how.

And yet he would dearly have liked to have had his revenge for the shameful way in which she had ill-treated him, if he could only have hit upon a plan for so doing.

If he could only think—but he could not think. Thought had been pretty well knocked out of him.

An old man at Lord Crokerton's time of life does not receive the punishment he had had and get over it easily.

Miss Fanny had put on her bonnet again, which some time back she had laid aside, and was getting ready to depart.

"Open the door, if you please," said she, "I want to go."

The old man, however, did not seem to hear or understand what was said to him.

He was sitting upon the floor, propped up, with his back against the wall, and his chin resting on his breast.

Fanny spoke to him in a louder voice, and yet he took no notice of her.

She paused a moment in the occupation of fastening her bonnet-strings, and looked at him attentively.

Then drew near to him, laid her hands upon his shoulder, and shook him gently.

Still he remained silent.

She shook him a little harder, and he rolled over and lay motionless upon his side.

A sudden terror seized upon her. Was he dead?

She ran to the table, and filled a glass of wine from the decanter, a few drops of which she poured into his mouth.

The old man heaved a sigh and opened his eyes.

"Give me air," he gasped; "I'm suffocating."

"I don't know how to open the door."

"Knock at it loudly."

"I have been doing so."

"Not loud enough, though. She's very deaf."

"Who is?"

"My housekeeper."

"The old woman?"

"Yes."

"But, can't you open it yourself?"

"No, I cannot."

"Cannot you give me instructions?"

"No, it cannot be opened from the inside. The old woman must open it. Be quick, I shall die if I don't get some air."

And as he spoke, in faint, weak voice, his head again dropped down upon his breast.

Fanny again poured some wine into his mouth.

"Speak," she cried. "Try and hold up a little longer. Is there no way of getting out of this hateful room?"

"None, except by the assistance of the old woman."

"Then we are lost."

"Why?"

"Because she is here."

"Where?"

"In a swoon, in the cupboard."

The old man groaned.

"There's no hope for us, then. The room is air-tight. We shall die as surely as though we were buried beneath the earth. Yes, we are in our tomb."

His voice seemed to grow fainter as he spoke.

A deadly pallor had stolen over his wasted face.

He lay perfectly motionless, screwed up in an attitude which was grotesquely ghastly.

Fanny rose from the floor, where she had been kneeling by his side, and crossed the room to the cupboard, where she had left the old woman, and about whose fate she had, for some time past, felt no small amount of anxiety.

She lay there in exactly the same position as that in which Fanny had left her. Her face was red and swollen; her mouth open; her tongue lolling out; her eyes, half open, looked glazed and bloodshot.

Fanny uttered a shriek at the sight of her, and staggered back, half stupified with horror.

Was she the only one left alive? And for how long?

Was this fatal room to be, as Crokerton had predicted, *their living tomb?*

CHAPTER XXVI.

EXTRAORDINARY BEHAVIOUR OF THE DOG FILCHIT.

THE room grew every moment hotter and hotter.

She gasped for air.

She was suffocating.

An intolerable thirst tormented her, which there were no means of allaying. To drink any more of the filthy wine would only make it worse. What was to be done?

Fanny White was not the sort of young lady, as I have said before, to be very easily overcome. She would not say die without a struggle. But what was the good of a struggle under these circumstances?

She took up the candle again, and commenced a circumspection of the inside of the door.

She had done so before. She had not the faintest hope of finding anything to reward her for the trouble; but, then, what would you have? It is very hard to sit down, with one's hands in one's lap, and wait for death.

It is very hard, in the full enjoyment of youth and ruddy health, to make one's mind up that the game of life is played out, and that there is nothing for it but to face the destroyer.

She, therefore, still hoped on against hope. She took the candle in her hand, and searched; bent upon leaving no stone unturned which might lead to a discovery.

She held the candle a good deal on one side, so that she might scrutinize every crack and crevice.

Suddenly, though, the candle slipped from its socket.

It fell to the ground.

The light was extinguished.

She stood for a moment in the pitch darkness, and her state of mind it would be difficult to describe, so varied were the conflicting emotions which agitated her brain.

But when, after the first confusion and bewilderment, the full horror of the situation burst upon her, she lost all command over herself; for a few moments her reason seemed entirely to have deserted her, and, in frantic terror and frenzied desperation, she battered madly at the door, flinging herself against it and shrieking loudly for help.

All at once the door flew open, and she almost fell forward into the passage.

She rushed out and gasped the fresh air.

Then stood struck dumb with astonishment and delight at her miraculous escape.

How had it been effected?

But she was not doomed very long to remain in uncertainty.

A well-known yelp met her ear.

A well-known moist nose pressed against her hand.

The celebrated dog Filchit was frisking round her, wagging his wisp of a tail and barking rapturously.

What was he doing there? How on earth could she account for his presence?

In the distance, at the other end of the passage, Fanny saw a faint light.

She walked quickly in that direction, and found that it was a candle which the old woman had left burning upon the kitchen-table. Taking it in her hand, she returned to the double-room, accompanied by her four-footed friend.

She paused upon the way, however, to listen, supposing that she should hear some movement in the house—the footsteps of the person who had accompanied Master Filchit.

She could hear nothing, though. The dog had come by himself.

But how about the door! Had he opened that unaided?

She went back to the room carrying the candle, her first anxiety being to see how fared her late companions. To her great joy, the old lord showed some signs of recovery now air had been admitted into the room.

She did not go near the old woman, though, for she was afraid to look upon her face again, and, besides, she wanted to get safe away before anybody arrived to question her egress from the house.

Before going she could not, however, resist the desire to ascertain how it was that Master Filchit had opened the door, and she examined the outside.

The door without was covered with various devices carved in the oak of which it was composed, and when shut, it was next to impossible to detect any opening or anything in the shape of a handle.

How then could Filchit have got the door open? It must have been that he jumped up against it, and accidentally touched some spring.

Fanny held the candle close to the wood, and passed it over the greater part without being able to discover any clue to the enigma.

"How did you do it, Filch?" said she, at length appealing in desperation to the dog himself.

At which Master F. wagged his tail and looked uncommonly knowing.

"How did you do it, I say?"

Then Filchit barked sharply twice, and jumped up against the door, catching his fore-paw in a brown painted iron-ring which moved a lock with a loud click.

That was how he had done it, he seemed to say. He must have followed the cab from London, found his way somehow or other in some sly corner into the house, and having watched about and discovered the manner in which Lord Crokerton had opened the door, presently when he heard Fanny's cries for help, and heard her beating against the panel, he began to jump up against the lock, and finally succeeded in liberating his mistress.

Miss Fanny caught him up in her arms and kissed him rapturously. Then having wasted as much time as she thought she could do safely, for any moment, for all she knew, some others of Lord Crokerton's servants might make their appearance, she made the best of her way to the outer door.

It was not now a very difficult matter to make her escape. In a few moments more she was standing out in the lane, Filchit still in her arms.

She had not the remotest idea in what direction she ought to turn, but the first consideration was to get as far as possible away from the house, out of which she had just made her escape.

She found it far from an agreeable walk down the dark lane, the road of which was in such a dilapidated condition, full of deep ruts and unexpected ditches, that it was quite a break-neck journey.

She wandered on and on, thinking she would never any more come within the limits of civilization.

All round her upon every side was pitchy darkness. Not the faintest glimmer of light could she perceive to cheer her onwards, and at times she came to a standstill, so hopeless did the prospect before her appear, and asked herself whether it was possible that she could have turned in the wrong direction, and was all the while walking away from London.

She had met nobody during her walk, or she would have inquired the way.

At last she heard footsteps approaching, and she quickened her pace to meet the person whoever it was.

But suddenly the thought occurred to her, suppose it was some rustic savage, some loafing bricklayer's labourer—some ruffianly tramp!

To what frightful treatment might she not be subjected? to murder, or worse?

The spot was awfully lonely—a narrow lane with high hedges—on either side fields spreading out to an unseen distance in the darkness.

Fortunately there was a gap in the hedge by the roadside.

Without hesitating a moment to reflect about the matter, and with an agility which few other women would have been capable of, Fanny forced her way through into the field, and stood perfectly still listening.

Then she heard the sound of voices.

There were two men. They approached nearer, talking as they came.

"What was that, Bill?"

"What?"

"That rustling row with the bushes."

"I didn't hear anything."

"Ah, a rabbit most likely."

"Wish we'd been in time to knock it on the head; we might have had a bellyfull for once in a way."

"Time we did, Bill."

"You're right there. For that matter I'd like to catch anything a knock on the head, if there was anything to be got by it."

"Wish we could drop across some one."

"By the Lord, I'd split anyone's skull for a fourpenny bit."

"It's a nice quiet place too; there aint the least fear of any cursed bobby dropping down on you while you were at the job."

"We might shove the body over into the ditch, all nice and comfortable."

"Shove it down into this night soil, and it wouldn't be found perhaps for a day or two."

"Wish we'd the chance."

They walked slowly on, pursuing this horrible dialogue until their voices were no longer audible to the terrified listener.

She waited there for full five minutes after they were gone, fearing to move hand or foot lest the two ruffians might by some chance retrace their steps and come back and find her.

At last when she thought they had gone far enough to allow her to come out in safety, she made her way through the gap and ran down the lane.

On and on she hurried, quite reckless of the pools of water through which she plunged, and the ruts into which she stumbled.

At length, far ahead, she saw a row of lights. It was the high-road.

She struggled onwards now with a lighter heart, and in course of time reached the end of the long lane.

She found herself in a highway which turned out to be the Richmond-road, and here she presently came across an empty cab going towards London.

She made a bargain, and away she went, thanking Heaven that at last she had nearly come to the end of her troubles.

Nearly.

Not yet awhile, though.

She was dead beat when at last she arrived at her lodgings, and not in the very best of tempers.

She opened the door with a latch-key which she carried and groped her way up-stairs.

She had quite made up her mind about one thing, and that was that she would give Mr. Jack a little bit of her mind.

She came up the stairs biting her lips—boiling over.

She flung open the door.

The room was dark and deserted.

"He's never had the impudence to go to bed and leave me," thought Miss Fanny.

THE LANDLADY OF THE "PRIVATE HOTEL" THREATENS JACK RAWLINGS.

She flung open the bed-room door with a great deal of unnecessary noise. It was dark.

"Jack."

No reply.

"Jack, I say."

No reply yet.

"Can't you answer, stupid?"

And she stamped her heels as she spoke, for at times, like all young ladies of spirit, she could be very peppery when her blood was up, and Jack had to take care upon these occasions that he did not get his ears boxed.

As she could get no answer, she struck a match and lit a candle, when she was very much astonished to find that the bed was empty.

She looked all round the room, and could see no sign of her lover. After a moment's reflection, she came to the conclusion that he must have gone out in search of her, and this idea certainly mollified her a little.

"Perhaps he has left me a letter," she thought, and she went in search of some scrap of paper.

Sure enough, then, on the table in the sitting-room there lay a note.

Fanny went and looked at it.

Then flushed suddenly crimson.

Then snatched it up and tore it open.

It was rather a suspicious-looking note, mind you.

It was on pink paper, in the first place.

In the second place, it was folded cocked-hat wise.

In the third place, it was written in a lady's hand.

"Who's it from?" said Fanny, in a greater rage than ever; "what's he mean by having letters? Who, I sh ould like to know, has had the impudence to write to him?"

The fact was very easily ascertained when the letter was torn open. It ran thus:—

"In great haste I write these few lines to ask you to meet me again to-morrow at the same place. I shall not sleep a wink all night for thinking of you, and the dear pretty things you said to me,

"ALICE BRANDON."

"Oh !!!" cried Fanny, in a kind of screech, and her throat was so full of something or other that it very nearly choked her. "Oh! the wretch! oh! the minx! She should never sleep again except once, if I caught hold of her. Oh! that Jack! and to think of what I've suffered to-night for his sake, and the offers I've refused. Men are all alike. They're monsters! They're liars! They're fools! And Jack's a worse fool than any of them, and this minx with her rubbishing pothooks and her horrible spelling. No, I think it is spelt well, for a wonder, but there are no stops. And the horrible scent it smells of! Oh! oh!! oh!!! How I should like to have the scratching of her for a quarter of an hour!"

She was in a furious rage, and stamped and screamed and almost had hysterics, but changed her mind, and at last came to a desperate determination.

Which was—

That she would leave Jack Rawlings for ever.

"I used to like him a little," said she, "but I don't now. I'm tired of him. I hate him. I don't think I ever really cared for him."

CHAPTER XXVII.

THE "HELL" IN WINDMILL STREET.

SHE was quite determined to run away, but she did not exactly intend to begin the world empty-handed.

There was no money to take away from the lodgings, and there were no articles of any value, but she had in her pocket a roll of notes which Lord Crokerton had given her.

Upon reflection she thought that it would be best to assume male attire. She therefore got out a suit of Jack's clothes, which fitted her to a nicety, and having put them on, secured the notes about her person, and lighting a cigar, she walked downstairs and out of the house.

Master Filchit was very desirous of being of the party, but she preferred to leave him for the present with Jack, and therefore drove him back into the house.

She walked along through the dark, deserted streets without any particular adventure befalling her, until she arrived at Leicester-square.

Here the idea occurred to her that she would like some refreshment.

But there was more difficulty in so doing than would easily be supposed; for how was she to get change?

Five-pound notes are capital things in their way, but they are not better than waste paper to others.

Whatever would a crossing-sweeper do with one of these flimsy pieces of bank paper supposing the bank happened to be closed for the day, and he wanted to buy a pint of beer?

In some poor neighbourhoods the shopkeepers will have nothing to say to half-a-sovereign if tendered to them by an unknown customer.

Fanny thought it extremely unlikely that she would be able to change all her notes, even if she changed one, and she certainly ought to lose no time.

Next day the numbers might be stopped at the bank.

While she was turning the matter over in her mind, she had been walking on towards the Haymarket and now paused in the crowd which is every night to be found at the corner of Windmill-street.

She was yet uncertain where she should go for supper, and to avoid the importunities of such of the gaily-dressed ladies flaunting upon the pavement as were attracted by Fanny's interesting appearance, she turned up by the side of the baker's shop, and came to a halt a little further up the street.

She paused close to two men who were engaged in earnest conversation, and who, having their backs towards her, did not notice her approach, or lower their voices.

"What are you about, then, to-night?" one asked.

"Oh!" the other replied, "I'm on the same lag as I have been all the week. I shall nab my customer before I've done, that's certain; but it's slow work. In the meantime I should like something else to turn up."

"So should I. I only wish I'd got the office to break into this gambling-house, for instance."

"Ah! that would be business."

"I should rather think it would, and a good pot to be made too."

"How so?"

"Because we should nab half-a-dozen swells of the first water."

"Do any swells go there?"

"Bless you, yes! There's generally a lord or two in the room mixed up with the legs."

"I thought the swells had given up going to those sort of places."

"Then you were never more mistaken in your life. Not that I mean to say that there's much of the old Crockford game going on. That's all knocked on the head now, but there's a good deal of quiet elbow-shaking yet."

"And if we broke in we might get hold of one of them, you think?"

"I should rather hope so, if we worked the oracle properly."

"And a tidy little sum might be pocketed for hushing up——"

"Hush! Some one will hear you."

And the two policemen in plain clothes, for such they were, beat a retreat, and left Fanny wondering.

Where could the gambling-house of which they had spoken be situated.

She felt very curious about it, but there appeared to be no way of satisfying her curiosity.

She had always longed to go into one of these London "hells," of which she had read so much in novels and romances pretending to give pictures of London life.

If lords went in they could not be such unsafe places. Suppose she could get in; but how?

If she could only manage it, she thought she might easily change her notes for gold.

Who could say, she might break the bank and win thousands. The heroes of the romances she had eagerly devoured often came away with their pockets bursting with the proceeds of a night's gambling.

How she would like to try it!

While thus thinking, upon the opposite side of the way came strolling up in a glossy white hat, a gentleman with whom she was tolerably well acquainted.

It was her fellow-lodger, Mr. Harry Belvoir.

He came strolling up the street smoking his cigar, very carelessly, his hands stuck into the hip pockets of his shooting coat, his glossy hat a good deal on one side.

When he arrived directly opposite to her he began to cross over, and Fanny in a great fright shrank back into a dark corner, supposing that he must have caught sight of her.

Such, however, proved not to be the case.

He was staring very hard in her direction, but it was not at her.

He was staring at a shop, the shutters of which were closed but the doors of which stood ajar.

At this door he was about to knock when two fashionably-dressed young men came swaggering up and rattling their walking-canes against the door, laughing loudly as they did so.

But the summons, if such it was, was unheeded, for the door instead was suddenly slammed to.

The young men rattled their canes upon the panel louder than before.

But nobody took any notice of them.

"Nobody at home, I suppose?" cried one.

Then they hammered again.

"It's no go, Jack," said the other; "we'd better slope." And so saying, they retired.

Hardly had they gone, however, when a brougham drew up a few yards off, from which a quietly dressed, but evidently wealthy, aristocratic man descended.

He, having dismissed his carriage, cautiously approached the door, and rubbed his thumb upon it in a peculiar manner.

Immediately afterwards the door was opened.

Then as quickly closed again, allowing no glimpse of the interior to be obtained from the street without.

Very shortly afterwards another gentleman approached, and was in like fashion admitted.

Then Mr. Belvoir, who had been lighting a cigar, drew near to the mysterious portal.

As he laid his hand upon it, Fanny laid hers upon his arm.

"Hullo!" he cried.

"Hallo!"

"What do you want?"

"To go in with you."

"Go in where?"

"Into the 'hell.'"

"What 'hell?' What do you mean?"

"You know; it's all right."

"I know nothing, young gentleman, except that it's time such as you were in bed."

"Don't you know me, Mr. Harry?"

"How should I?"

"You ought to."

"Eh!"

"You ought to, I say, if you weren't a gay deceiver."

"Why, hang me, you don't mean——?"

"Don't I, though?"

"It's not——"

"Isn't it?"

"Mam'selle——"

"Exactly."

"Le Blanc?"

"Without a doubt."

"But what on earth has brought you out here, and in this attire?"

"The fact is, I want to see the inside of a gambling-house. Jack wouldn't bring me, so I've come in his clothes."

"And beautiful you look."

"Yes, to be sure. Will you take me in with you?"

"Wont you be afraid to go?"

"Why?"

"Gambling-houses are dreadful places."

"So I've heard. That's why I want to come, if you will take care of me."

"Well, I'll do my best."

"Come along, then."

And as she spoke, Miss Fanny rubbed her thumb up the door, as she had seen the gentlemen do.

The door was immediately opened, and she and her friend entered the shop.

A man with a cab, who seemed to be enormously muscular and strong, closed the door behind them, and leading the way across the shop, knocked at another door at the back.

This being opened from within, another man, apparently of the prize-fighting profession, made his appearance, stared at them very hard, and passed them through the third door, when they found themselves at the foot of a narrow staircase.

Up this they made their way into a room on the second floor, which was brightly lighted with billiard lamps.

Here they found assembled about a score of men, all well dressed, though it was far from difficult to see that the social position of some of them was not of a very exacted character.

The Jewish tribe predominated, and there was much costly jewellery displayed upon vests of vast magnificence.

There were, however, some evident swells present, and all were seated round a large table, which occupied the centre of the room, playing at *rouge et noir.*

"You will have to stake something," whispered Belvoir to Fanny. "I will pay for you."

"I have some money," said she; "will they change me a note?"

"Do you want change?" said a man at the end of the table; "I can oblige you."

"If you please," said Fanny, and pushed the roll of notes over to him, "forty pounds."

Harry Belvoir stared in amazement.

The men round the table glanced up eagerly, and whispered to one another.

"You shouldn't have shown all that money," whispered Harry, "among these thieves."

"Thieves!"

"Ay, they're no better, some of them."

"I shall be robbed, then. Give me back my money."

And she leant across the table to the man who was turning over the notes.

"All right, sir; I'm just taking the numbers," said he, and he appeared to feel in his pocket, as though for the change.

But at that moment a bell rang loudly, and a loud cry upon the stairs of "police" caused every one to spring to their feet.

Suddenly the gas was turned out.

Next moment all was confusion.

A general rush was made for the door, and Fanny was thrown violently to the ground.

Half stunned, she managed to scramble to her feet, and assisted by Belvoir, beat a retreat by a window leading on to a housetop.

Here, having crawled like cats for some twenty yards along a paparet, they got through an attic window into an empty house, ran downstairs, and out into the street.

"Thank God! we're safe," cried Belvoir.

"But how about my money?" said Fanny.

"That's gone for good, I'm afraid."

"I shall never get it back?"

"Not likely."

Fanny burst into tears.

CHAPTER XXVIII.

THE EARL OF STONECLIFFE BREATHES HIS LAST, AND LORD MANNINGTREE STEPS INTO HIS SHOES.

THE Earl of Stonecliffe was dangerously ill.

His brother, Lord Manningtree, assumed, if anything, a still more sombre cast of countenance, as he moved about amongst his acquaintances, shaking his head dismally when the earl's illness was mentioned.

He was a man of few words, but those he did utter upon the subject expressed much sorrow, and left his hearers with the impression that, whatever might be his faults, indifference to his brother was not one of them.

They did not know his powers of acting.

When Lord Manningtree was alone, when sitting in complete solitude in his den of horrors; when hidden from human gaze, then was the time to see him in his true character.

But few living beings had ever fully understood his diabolical nature, and they had only found it out when in the agonies of death.

Lady Gertrude, in her last pangs, caught sight of the handsome but devilish face, illumined with fiendish joy; but was she not numbered with the dead?

Joshua Grubb knew it when he lay writhing at his feet in the agonies of death, and he did not live to tell the tale.

No. To the world Lord Manningtree was a heartless cynic, mayhap; but the darker traits in his character were not yet exposed.

As he sat, one gloomy afternoon, in his laboratory, calculating within himself the chances of his speedily entering into possession of the vast Stonecliffe estates, there came a knock at the door.

A trifle, surely; but it found him unprepared, and he started, as if caught in some act of wickedness.

The knocking was repeated.

He did not answer.

He was not willing to be disturbed.

Louder than before sounded the blows upon the door, and the handle was tried.

His lordship smiled sardonically at the failure of the intruder to obtain an entrance.

"My lord—my lord!"

It was the voice of his valet, and he knew that unless something important had happened he would not venture to disturb him.

"What is it?" he asked.

"Can I speak with you a moment, my lord?"

"Certainly."

"Will your lordship unfasten the door?"

"Why should I?"

"What I have to say is only for your lordship's ears."

"Speak, fellow. I hear you, however low your utterance."

"Your lordship's brother——"

"Ha! What of him?"

"He is unfortunately——"

"Dead!" interrupted Lord Manningtree, eagerly.

"No, my lord—not dead—but dying."

Lord Manningtree had acted wisely in not giving his valet entrance, for had he done so the servant could not have failed to notice the expression of joy and malignant triumph which swept over the heir's countenance.

"How do you know this?" he asked, quietly.

"One of the Earl's servants has just been here to tell your lordship."

"Well!"

"I thought your lordship would naturally like to know at once—and—and——"

"And what?"

"I hope when your lordship is Earl of Stonecliffe you will not turn me away, your lordship."

"How can you speak of such things?" said he, in tones of quiet reproof. "My brother yet lives, and I should be the last person in the world to calculate upon his decease."

"I beg your lordship's pardon."

"It is granted."

"Can I do anything for your lordship?"

"No."

"Not go to the Earl's house with any message?"

"I will go myself immediately."

In pursuance of this design, Lord Manningtree doffed the common fustian suit he generally wore when at work in his den, and assumed the attire of a gentleman, and ere half an hour had elapsed from the time he received tidings of the serious turn his brother's illness had taken, he was standing before his house.

When he entered he was at once shown to the room in which the Earl lay confined to his bed.

When he glanced at his face he could hardly believe his eyes, so great was the alteration a few days had made.

As the wealthy peer lay back upon the pillow, his face hardly less white, he looked like one risen from the dead.

There was a ghastly expression upon his thin, pale, aristocratic face, athwart which every now and then a twinge of excessive agony passed, and almost every moment a low moan of pain escaped his lips.

No one who saw him could doubt that his days upon earth were numbered.

"This is very kind of you, Percy," said the Earl, in a voice so faint that Lord Manningtree was forced to partly guess the words by the movement of his lips.

"My dear brother, surely you did not doubt that I should come to your side the very moment I heard how ill you were?"

"I knew you would."

Lord Manningtree silently pressed his brother's hand.

"Thanks, Percy. You would hardly think this hand had no longer power to move," said he, with reference to his long, white, emaciated fingers, which lay on the coverlet.

"My dear brother, how dreadful it is to see you reduced to this state. It will be long before we see you about again."

"Very long."

"When do you suppose?"

"Never!"

"Tush! do not take so gloomy a view of the matter. There is nothing serious the matter with you."

The Earl shook his head feebly.

"Do not despond."

"I do not. I hope, ere many hours have dragged by, to have rejoined my darling Gertrude."

Lord Manningtree's face immediately assumed an expression of grief, which, if not real, was a most wonderful piece of acting.

"What time is it, Percy?"

"About half-past three."

"Half-past three?"

"Yes."

"No more?"

"Hardly so much."

The Earl of Stonecliffe gave vent to a deep sigh.

"What is the matter? why do you ask?"

"Do you not know what it is I suffer from?"

"No."

"Has no one told you?"

"No; what is it?"

"A fierce internal fever! A fever which scorches me like fire, which parches all the moisture of my body, and eats and eats away at my brain till I feel as if I must go mad."

"Dreadful!"

"It is indeed."

"Do you suffer much now?"

"No words can give you the slightest idea of the agony."

"Do you do nothing to alleviate your sufferings?"

"Yes."

"What?"

"That mixture gives me immediate relief. Without it, I should die."

"Shall I give you some?"

"Not yet."

"Why not?"

"I dare not touch it till four o'clock."

"But if it alleviates your pain why not take it at once?"

"The doctor ordered me to take it every two hours; if I take it oftener it will kill me."

"My poor brother! Does it really do you good?"

"I think so. Indeed, the doctor declares there is a possibility of my recovery, with great care and strict attention to his directions."

The fiendish smile leaped over Lord Manningtree's countenance as he muttered to himself—

"That you never shall!"

"Is it not nearly four o'clock?"

"It wants a quarter."

"I must try to sleep, Percy; but promise me the moment the clock indicates the hour you will awake me."

"Certainly, if you wish it."

"Thank you. Remember, Percy, when I am gone, that I never believed a word of the evil whispered against you. I always knew you to be a kind, affectionate brother."

"You were not mistaken."

"No. Your kindness to my poor Gertrude showed you were not the bad man your enemies would have led me to believe you were."

Again Lord Manningtree pressed his brother's hot feverish hand, and again the same look of devilish triumph flitted over his dark, handsome features.

Worn out by the fatigue of talking, and overpowered by the weakness consequent upon his illness, it was not long before the Earl of Stonecliffe fell into a species of sleep.

Sleep! It seemed a mockery to call it by that name.

It was a fitful, uneasy, unrefreshing slumber.

Repose there was none.

The hideous images which floated before the wandering mind of the dying nobleman were more frightful than can be imagined by those who do not know what delirium brought on by fever is.

After a pause, during which the Earl lay in a state of semi-unconsciousness, his younger brother rose noiselessly from his seat.

His first action was to remove the life-giving medicine away from the Earl's reach when he awoke.

His next was to carefully knot up the bell-rope, which hung ready to the sick man's hand, to a height which in his weak state it would be quite impossible for him to reach.

This much done, his lordship proceeded to the bookshelves, took down a racy French novel, ensconced himself comfortably in a luxurious arm-chair, and speedily became immersed in the contents of the volume.

As the clock struck four, the Earl of Stonecliffe awoke and glanced eagerly in the direction where the bottle of refreshing medicine was usually placed.

It was not there!

His bloodshot eyes roamed round the room till they rested upon his younger brother, whose interest in the book before him was most remarkable.

"Percy."

No answer.

"Percy."

"Well!"

"Is it not four o'clock?"

"Yes."

"It is time for my draught."

"Indeed!"

"Percy?"

"What is it?"

"Why do you not bring it me?"

Lord Manningtree turned over a page of the novel and commenced a fresh chapter.

"I shall die without it! My throat is parched and dry! For Heaven's sake be quick."

Lord Manningtree showed no signs of moving.

"Quick! Quick! I shall die!"

"Yes," said his loving brother, half aloud, "and I shall be Earl of Stonecliffe!"

"What do you mean? I do not understand you!"

His lordship laughed a low laugh, as no doubt did his tutor the devil, when he saw the scheme of his most promising pupil.

"Percy! Would you see me die for want of your aid? Quick! Give me the draught."

"I have no object in keeping you alive!"

The Earl of Stonecliffe failed for the moment to understand the full meaning of these cold, diabolical words, although the fact that his brother either could not or would not bestir himself to save his life forced itself upon his mind, and he sank back exhausted, with a low, wailing cry.

Then remembering the bell, his hand moved slowly and feebly along the wall feeling for it.

But it did not meet his touch.

He felt only the smooth wall!

Again and again he tried, and each time without success.

Raising his eyes to discover the cause, he saw it knotted up far out of reach above his head.

Imagine his despair.

Dying for want of that which was within his sight.

Seeing one who could have helped him had he been so minded.

Knowing that were the bell-rope but a few inches lower down, he could obtain that which would preserve his life.

Seeing and knowing all this, but yet utterly and completely helpless!

The thirst in his throat increased.

His mouth felt like a furnace.

The very breath he drew in went scorching and burning through his lungs.

A raging fire seemed to be destroying his vitals.

With all this, he saw but a few yards beyond his reach that which would have afforded him instant relief.

He tried one more appeal to his brother.

"Percy! Percy! Unless you would for everlasting suffer the pangs I now endure, ease me of my dreadful agony!"

"You will soon be easier."

"Not unless you bring me the medicine. Oh, Percy, have pity on me!"

"There is one thing which will cure your suffering completely."

"Give it me, for mercy's sake! What is it?"

"I do not give it you. It comes of itself. It is now drawing near you rapidly."

"What do you mean?"

"DEATH!"

"Percy! Percy! Is this a time for joking? Help me or I die!"

Lord Manningtree answered never a word!

To this and all succeeding supplications he turned a deaf ear.

Ensconced in the comfortable easy-chair, he read on as if there were nothing out of the common in the room with him.

Viewing him as he sat placid and serene, it was next to impossible to believe that in very truth the last act of a dismal tragedy was being played within a few yards of where he reclined, supremely indifferent.

A fellow-creature was vainly struggling against the mighty conqueror, Death.

The sufferer was his own brother!

Half-a-dozen steps on his part might have preserved the life which was ebbing fast!

Yet he moved not!

Without stirring he listened with demoniacal calmness to the entreaties of the Earl of Stonecliffe.

Without moving a muscle of his face he heard the sobs and groans of his brother.

The raging thirst increased every moment and the Earl was well-nigh driven mad by the torture of the fever which consumed him.

He strove to call for assistance, but his parched lips clove to the roof of his mouth, and only a feeble inarticulate murmur proceeded from his feverish lips.

Angrily he gnawed at the blankets which covered him.

Even the minute amount of moisture which he thus extracted seemed to afford him relief, still it was but momentary.

His long thin fingers feebly clutched at the coverlet, and strove to drag it towards him.

Even this was beyond his powers!

Greedily his eyes strained to the utmost, glared at the bottle the contents of which would restore him.

Lord Manningtree remained perfectly unmoved, only raising his eyes to his brother when a groan of agony louder than usual caused him to fear some one might be attracted to the room by the sound.

Fainter and fainter grew the moans, till the earl, silent and helpless, lay gazing vacantly upwards, clutching the counterpane nervously the while.

His senses had deserted him.

He was unconscious.

After a lapse of some minutes, Lord Manningtree rose deliberately from his seat, replaced the book he had been reading, and advanced to his brother's bed-side.

Eagerly he laid his hand upon the earl's heart.

It had ceased to beat!

The pulse was not perceptible!

Hurriedly he snatched a small looking-glass and held it for a few seconds over the face of his brother.

When he withdrew it, it was undimmed!

With a sigh of relief he replaced it.

His end was accomplished.

His crimes had met with the reward he desired.

His brother was dead, and he no longer was the portionless Lord Manningtree, but the wealthy Earl of Stonecliffe.

Even his elation did not prevent his taking all the necessary steps to prevent any suspicion of foul play resting upon him.

With calm, steady hand he smoothed and adjusted the bed-clothes, then replaced the table and the medicine close to the bedside and unknotted the bell-rope.

Then he gave one careful glance round the room to make sure there was nothing which could lead to his detection.

Throwing open the room door he pulled lustily at the rope till the bell pealed and reverberated through the whole house.

"Help! help!" he cried, with the whole strength of his lungs, and presently all the servants, accompanied by the doctor, who had just arrived, appeared at the entrance to the chamber of death.

"My poor brother has fainted! Quick! Restore him or he may never wake!"

The doctor made his way to the bedside.

One glance was sufficient.

"It is too late, my lord!"

"Too late?"

"Yes."

"What is too late?"

"My presence here, my lord! Your poor brother will never breathe again."

"Dead!" cried Lord Manningtree, with well feigned amazement and horror.

The doctor bowed his head in token of acquiescence.

"No! Surely he cannot be dead! It was but a few minutes since he was speaking to me."

"Nevertheless, my lord, such is the case!"

"Are you sure it is not merely a trance?"

"Quite sure, my lord."

"Positive?"

"I am not in the habit of having my professional word doubted."

"Do not be offended. Make allowance for me, I entreat you. This shock—this dreadfully sudden shock, has made me forget my self-possession."

And so it appeared; for Lord Manningtree, the immovable, the cold, the cynical, actually shed tears of grief for the loss of his brother.

It was late in the evening when he left the house of grief, and with wobegone aspect sought his own home.

How mean and shabby everything looked there.

Articles which contented him well as Lord Manningtree, only seemed fit to be burnt by the Earl of Stonecliffe!

He had arrived at the summit of his ambition! A wonderful career of pleasure and dissipation seemed open before him, and in his mind he speedily disposed of much of the vast wealth which his brother had acquired during the time he enjoyed the title.

The following day he received a letter, the envelope alone of which caused him great delight, for it was directed in the writing of the family solicitor to "The Earl of Stonecliffe!"

CHAPTER XXIX.

ON THE TRACK.

WHEN Jack Rawlings started to discover what had become of Fanny, he had no idea which direction to take.

He knew she must have left the Abyssinian long before, but still in the hopes of obtaining some tidings of her there, he started for the Music Hall.

It was a little past midnight when he reached the doors, and the spectators were dispersing.

Hastily pushing his way in, he made for the dressing-room, which he found deserted save by Miss Patty Herman and the comic singer, who were enjoying a sociable pot of porter together, and running down the others of the company.

It so happened that Fanny White was the subject of discussion and depreciation when our hero hurriedly entered.

He would not have been particularly pleased if he had heard the disparaging remarks made concerning her.

Her charms were said to be the result of padding and paint.

Her voice was likened to a crow's.

Her dancing to the clumsy evolutions of a bear on a hot iron.

And her morals were stated to be of the lowest possible description.

When Jack entered the room they became suddenly silent, and there was an awkward pause, till Jack asked abruptly if they knew what had become of his wife (for it was thus he designated our heroine to others).

"Dear me! Hasn't she reached home yet?

"No."

"Well, I *am* surprised! She left here two hours ago."

"The deuce she did!"

"I hope nothing has happened to her."

This speech certainly came under the head of white lie, for nothing would have given Miss Herman greater pleasure than to know that she would no more have to play second fiddle to Fanny.

"Happened! What could happen to her?" asked Jack, angrily.

"Bless me, Mr. Rawlings, how you do snap one up! I didn't say anything had happened."

"Can you tell me anything about her?" said Jack, addressing the comic singer.

"Nothing, except——"

"Except what?"

"Only that—however, it's no business of mine, so perhaps I'd better hold my tongue."

"You'd better speak out unless you want your ugly head knocked against the wall."

"Lor, Mister Rawlings!" said the young lady, with a faint shriek.

"Mr. Rawlings, but for the presence of this fair blossom of the softer sex I should feel it incumbent on me to give you a thrashing," said the comic gentleman.

"Nonsense! Tell me what you know, or take the consequences."

"I know nothing."

"By Jove! I believe that's about the truth."

"But——"

"Well?"

"I suspect——"

"What?"

"You wont be angry if I tell you?"

"No."

"Nor fly in a passion?"

"No—no!"

"Nor swear, nor anything of that sort?"

"Of course not. Go on."

"Well, it's my opinion that Miss Le Blanc has——"

"Why don't you speak?"

"I hardly like to say it."

"Don't be a fool!"

"Well, I think she has eloped with Lord Crokerton!"

"You infernal liar!" roared Jack in a rage, rushing at him, and seizing him by the throat.

"Mr. Rawlings," said the singer, in half-choked accents, "Mr. Rawlings, pray remember there is a lady present."

Jack let go his hold.

"Now," said he, "tell me what reasons you have for thinking this, or by the Lord Harry! I'll break every bone in your body."

"Reasons?"

"Yes. I speak plain enough, don't I?"

"In the first place, Lord Crokerton, a night or two back, sent her a large bouquet."

"Psha!"

"In the second place, that bouquet contained a note."

"Pish! How do you know that?"

"I saw her take it out myself."

"Well! Did she read it?"

"I can't say. It was my turn to go on, and I left her with it in her hand."

"Go on."

"When she went on next, she took the flowers with her. She pressed them to her bosom, and all that sort of thing."

"Well?"

"The next thing I saw was the young lady carefully put a note between the flowers, and send the bouquet by one of the boys to Lord Crokerton, who was sitting in the stalls."

"Of course. It was his own letter she returned."

"Ha, ha! You think so, do you?"

"Of course. Don't you?"

"I only relate facts, I don't give my opinion."

"So this is all your reason for believing she has gone off with that helpless, decrepit, worn-out, abandoned old profligate?"

"No, it isn't."

"What more is there, then?"

"Lord Crokerton was here again to-night."

"Well?"

"As soon as Miss Le Blanc had finished her performance he left."

"What of that?"

"I offered to escort the young lady to a cab."

"Well?"

"She declined my offer."

"I don't wonder at it."

"That is all I have to tell you, sir."

"Ha, ha, ha! A fine cock-and-a-bull story. Excuse me, but I can't help laughing."

"Of course, you can laugh if you like, but it doesn't seem any laughing matter to me."

"Perhaps not."

"Of course, you can believe it or not, as you think fit."

"Oh, of course! Thank you. Good evening. I've no doubt I shall find her at home when I get back. Good evening."

In spite of the merry way in which Jack endeavoured to laugh off the suspicion, he could not but dread that there might be some foundation for it.

He strove to overcome the feeling which was fast taking possession of him, that Fanny was unfaithful; but he greatly feared that even if she had not eloped with the wicked old lord, that he had perhaps used force to compel her to comply with his desires.

Such, we know, was indeed the case.

Fanny had been abducted by Lord Crokerton, but thanks to her nerve and the dog Filchit, she had been enabled to escape from the den of infamy into which he had lured her, and, as well, to carry off with her some considerable spoil.

Jack, despairing of doing anything more to discover her whereabouts that night, returned home, savage and disconsolate.

There he was to learn that which would rouse his anger and despair to the highest pitch.

He let himself in and proceeded to the sitting-room.

In the dim light afforded by a gas-lamp outside the house, he thought he detected something like an envelope lying on the table.

Hastily striking a match, he lit a candle and seized the letter.

He did not doubt that it was from Fanny, accounting for her absence.

Eagerly he scrutinized the handwriting of the direction.

It was not Fanny's.

Who could it be from?

He turned it over to break the seal, when he discovered some one had been beforehand with him.

It was the letter which Lady Alice Brandon had written him, which Fanny on her return had opened, and which led to her again leaving the house in a fit of jealousy.

For some little while he was unable to understand exactly what had happened.

He read the letter through, and wondered who the deuce had opened it, yet still he failed to comprehend Fanny's absence.

Shortly the truth dawned upon him.

Looking around the small apartment where he and Fanny had spent so many happy hours in loving dalliance, and where they had over and over again, sitting side by side, his arm twining around her slender waist, declared that come what would they would never desert each other, and sealed the promise with a burning kiss—

Looking round this apartment, he perceived, strewn upon the floor, the whole of the garments which Fanny had worn in the morning.

The handsome silk dress, the embroidered petticoat, the dainty stockings, all were there together, with many others which it would have puzzled Jack to give a name to.

What did it all mean?

What had happened?

He glanced round the room as if half expecting to see Fanny in the costume of Mother Eve waiting to greet him.

It was inexplicable.

At present it was an unfathomable mystery.

He passed his hand across his brow to assure himself that he was awake and in his right senses.

Then, quick as thought, he ascended the stairs and entered the bedroom.

Fanny was not there.

He looked about him, and his eye rested on the closet where he kept his own attire.

The door stood ajar.

He threw it open, and discovered that a whole suit of clothes was missing.

Further search convinced him that a change of all the articles of a gentleman's toilet had been abstracted from the drawers.

The truth struck him in a moment.

Fanny, enraged with jealousy by Lady Alice Brandon's letter, had determined to absent herself from home, but fearing to venture into the streets at so late an hour in the dress appertaining to her sex, had purloined a suit of his attire in which to seek some shelter for the night.

He was overwhelmed by the thought that she had in truth deserted him.

He cursed his own folly in having agreed to the meeting with Lady Alice.

"But," said he, "thank Heaven! the matter is so easily explained."

His idea was immediately to start in pursuit of his runaway love, explain everything, and implore her to return and live with him again, assuring her that her jealousy was unfounded, and the letter only the result of a mad frolic at a masquerade.

It was easy to say "seek her out," but it was no such easy matter to set about it.

The wilderness of the great metropolis was a wide field for the search, but he did not despond.

He felt sure in the end that he would be successful; still now, at first starting, he knew not what direction to take.

Even from the door of the house he could not tell whether he should turn to the right or the left.

What was he to do?

How prosecute the search in the darkness of night without a single clue to guide him?

For some minutes he sat, his head buried in his hands, pondering over the difficult task before him.

With a sudden cry of joy he sprang to his feet.

Happiness beamed upon his handsome face, and joy was in his heart, for he had discovered a sure and certain method by which to track Fanny step by step upon her way.

The dog Filchit.

He would put him on the scent, knowing, sooner or later, that his brute nature would lead him to the spot which Fanny had chosen for her retirement.

"Filchit—Filchit!" he called.

The dog came tearing from his bed in the kitchen at the sound of his master's voice, and fawned upon him, wagging his stump of a tail with extraordinary power, while a twinkle in his eye seemed to say, "I know what you want, and I'll do all I can for you."

He was a sensible dog was Filchit!

Jack showed him some of the clothes that Fanny had worn, and shortly had the pleasure of seeing that he fully understood what was required of him.

With nose close to the ground he went down the stairs and out into the street.

Our hero, snatching up a good stout stick and his hat, followed, and overtook him before he had proceeded half the length of the street.

On, on, past the twinkling gas-lights; on, on, past the drowsy policeman, yawning at the street corners, who turned and looked after Jack, as, regardless of everything but the dog before him, he threaded the deserted streets.

The clocks were striking two when Filchit halted before a house with a gas lamp over the entrance, and looked up inquiringly into his master's face.

"Hullo!" thought Jack, "she can't have gone in here. Whose house can it be?"

A policeman happened to be slowly pacing along on the opposite side of the way.

Jack crossed and accosted him.

"Can you tell me whose house that is?" he asked, pointing to the one before which Filchit had stopped, and about the door of which he was now sniffing sagaciously.

"None o' yer chaff!" said the guardian of the peace.

"Don't you know?"

"Yes, and so do you."

"I shouldn't ask if I did."

"Look here, young gent; unless you wants to spend the night in the lock-up I'd advise you not to poke yer fun at me;" and the peeler marched off sulkily into the next street.

Despite the lateness of the hour, lights were still burning brightly in the rooms on the first floor of the house.

Jack stood and deliberated.

He had a great mind to knock and question whoever answered the door.

He feared, however, that Filchit might have made some mistake.

In that case how could he account for his conduct.

While he still stood deliberating the door was flung open suddenly, and a man leapt forth into the street, treading on Filchit's tail, and causing him to howl with pain, and then knocking up against our hero with such violence as almost to upset him.

"I beg your pardon, sir—Hullo!"

"Hullo!"

"What, you here? Who'd have thought of stumbling against you at this time in the morning."

It was Jim Gimp, his face betokening unusual hilarity, partly owing, no doubt, to his free use of the bottle.

"Are you going in, Jack?"

"I wanted to, but I didn't know how to manage it."

"Oh, it's easy enough. I'll take you in."

"Does a friend of yours live there?"

"What?"

"Isn't it a private house?"

"Eh? Oh, lor! Bless his poor, innocent little heart! A private house! Ha, ha, ha, ha!"

"What the deuce is it, then?" asked Jack, with no little trepidation, for he feared Fanny might have been lured into a house of ill repute.

"What the deuce is it, then?"

"You're not in league with the police?"

"No. I have a most praiseworthy abhorrence of them."

"Well, then, I don't mind telling you."

"Well?"

"That house is a 'hell'?"

"A 'hell!'"

"Yes. A gambling-house!"

"What the devil can Fanny have been doing there?" Jack asked himself.

Before he had time, however, to frame any question by which to ascertain whether any one had been present corresponding in appearance to our heroine, Jim Gimp started off, relating his own adventures, and in so doing unknowingly gave Jack the information he desired.

He told how two good-looking, well-dressed youths had entered late in the evening.

How they had sat down at the table where the highest play was going on.

He narrated the extraordinary run of good luck they had had at first; all of which is already known to the reader.

Then came the reaction.

Jim Gimp related how they, after being within an ace of breaking the bank, began steadily to lose, until they left the place penniless.

Jack had no difficulty in recognising Fanny from the description Gimp gave.

But who was it with her?

By dint of questioning he obtained from the ventriloquist a tolerably exact description of her companion.

There could be no doubt about it.

His worst fears were realized.

His jealousy was not without cause!

He felt certain, from Gimp's description, that the second youth was Harry Belvoir.

Such, we know, was indeed the case!

Filchit, in the mean time, had recovered the scent, and was endeavouring, by every means in his power, to call his master's attention.

Jack, when he made the discovery as to Fanny's companion, growled forth an oath, much to the astonishment of Jim Gimp, for he, never having for a single moment suspected either of the youths to be of a different sex to that indicated by their dress, was at a loss to account for our hero's evident interest.

"How long is it since they left?"

"Hardly half-an-hour—but I say——"

"Good night," said Jack, hurrying after the dog, much to the animal's delight.

"I say, can't I do anything for you?" asked Jim Gimp, staying our hero's course, and holding him by the coat-tail.

"Nothing, thank you."

"But——"

"Good night!" repeated Jack, struggling to disengage himself from the other's hold.

"I wish you'd——"

"Confound you! Don't you see I'm in a hurry."

Jack wrenched his coat from the grasp of the ventriloquist, and ran the whole length of the street at full speed in pursuit of Filchit, who was already some distance ahead.

"Well, I *am* blowed!" muttered Jim Gimp, as, unable to penetrate the mystery, he pursued his homeward way, pondering over the extraordinary behaviour of Mr. Jack Rawlings.

Jack hurried on, following his dumb guide till the dog stopped in front of a seedy disreputable coffee house.

He knocked without hesitation (for the door was closed).

After some little delay a yawning slip-shod girl, holding a flaring tallow candle in her hand, made her appearance.

Jack poured forth a whole volume of questions without giving her time to answer one.

Her first idea was that "the gent was drunk," but receiving the present of half-a-crown, came to the conclusion that he was nothing of the sort, and agreed to answer his questions.

From her, Jack learned that two young gentlemen answering to the description he gave, had endeavoured to procure beds there, but as they were already full (the beds, not the gentlemen), they were forced to turn them away.

Again onwards!

Again on the track!

Morning was far advanced, yet still forward.

On—on!

Jack swore to himself that he would never rest till he had tracked them to earth.

"I will find out where they are and bring Fanny back," said he. "As for that damned scoundrel," he continued, alluding to Harry Belvoir, "I'll——"

What he intended to do he did not say, but he clenched the stick he carried, and shook it violently in a way that boded evil to any individual across whose head and back it might descend.

Still Filchit jogged steadily onwards with nose bent to the ground.

They had been proceeding along Oxford-street for some time but now the dog turned up the Edgware-road, and after going some little way diverged suddenly to the left and led our hero through a perfect labyrinth of slums and back streets.

Jack had no idea where he was, nor in what direction he was proceeding.

He trusted implicitly to Filchit.

His confidence was not misplaced!

By-and-bye he caught sight of the Great Western Hotel, and so knew something of his whereabouts, but Filchit still jogged on with his shambling, lop-sided motion, wagging his stump of a tail and occasionally looking back to make sure Jack was following.

Again the dog paused before a low, shabby-looking house, upon the door of which he read the words, "Private Hotel."

All seemed quiet, but when Jack knocked at the door it was answered so immediately as to lead to the belief that nocturnal visitors were not very rare.

Jack described the appearance of Fanny and Harry Belvoir, and inquired if they were there.

The servant stammered forth an answer in the affirmative.

"No, no! They're not here, they left an hour ago," screamed a hideous beldame, whom Jack rightly guessed to be the landlady, over the banisters.

"That wont do," said our hero. "I know better than that."

So saying, he coolly stepped into the passage, followed by Filchit.

The landlady, in an enormous nightcap and a still more enormous passion, came down the stairs and stormed at Jack to her heart's content, but he seeing it was useless to attempt to stem the torrent, sat down quietly in the hall-chair and waited till the outburst had in some degree subsided.

"My dear madam," said he, quietly, with the greatest politeness, "allow me to observe that you have wasted a great deal of breath upon me to no effect. Beware how you attempt to deceive an *officer of justice!*"

The shot told.

"An officer of justice?" repeated the old woman.

"Yes. Now show me the room in which they are."

"They are not here, indeed," said the beldame, but in a much fainter voice than before.

"Nonsense. You have contradicted yourself half-a-dozen times already."

"No, I haven't."

"You have. First you said they had never been here, then you said they left an hour ago; you also stated you had refused them admission. Come now, this sort of thing wont do. Tell me in what room they are, and here is half a sovereign for you."

The old hag was not proof against the gold; she eagerly clutched the proffered coin.

"They're in the front room on the first floor," said she.

"Is there another room adjoining?"

"Yes."

"Any communication between the two apartments?"

"Yes; a small door."

"Is it locked?"

"Yes."

"On their side?"

"No, the other."

"Capital. Could not be better. Show me the way to it!"

Jack was conducted to the room he wished, the dog Filchit following close to his heels.

"Now for a scene!" said Jack.

CHAPTER XXX.

WHAT JACK RAWLINGS DID IN THE SHABBY HOUSE IN PADDINGTON.

WHEN our hero was ushered into the room adjoining that into which the landlady had informed him Fanny and Harry Belvoir had been shown, he was some moments before he could distinctly make out the bearings of the apartment.

He impressed caution and silence upon the yawning, slip-shod maid-of-all-work.

He refused all offer of a light, fearing it might betray his presence.

Alone he groped his way across the room, and felt the wall carefully for the door of communication.

It was some time before he found it.

When he did so, his hand came in violent contact with some portion of the lock, and a loud clattering noise was the result.

Tremblingly he waited, fearing the disturbance might lead to a discovery sooner than he wished.

Holding his breath, he listened intently.

"I'm sure some one must be there."

In an instant he recognised the voice.

It was Fanny's!

Jack mumbled some inarticulate words, which, however, had a savage meaning.

"Nonsense," said a male voice—that of Harry Belvoir— "all the people went to bed an hour ago."

"I think I shall follow their example."

Jack ground his teeth together.

"By all means. Let us go to bed."

"Is your room near mine?"

"Quite close."

"SPEAK, MAN! HOW DID YOU GET HERE?" ASKED MRS. CARVSED.

"Indeed!"

"So near, in fact, that it might be called the same."

"What do you mean?"

"Surely, Fanny, you comprehend?"

Whether Miss Fanny comprehended or not, she assumed a tone of great innocence as she answered—

"I assure you I do not."

"Fanny—Fanny! you must know I adore you. You cannot be ignorant that ever since I left the country and came to reside in London I have been day by day falling over head and ears in love with you!"

"Ha, ha, ha! what *would* Uncle Pigley say?"

"Damn Uncle Pigley!"

"Oh! Mr. Belvoir—what shocking language!"

"Oh, never mind that. Don't interrupt a fellow."

"I beg your pardon. You were making such a pretty speech. You were saying that——"

"That I adored you!"

"Precisely."

"That my affection increased every moment!"

"Exactly."

"And that—that——"

"Well?"

"That I couldn't live without you!"

"Good gracious! You don't say so?"

"Fanny, for pity's sake, don't make fun of me!"

"Most decidedly not. I feel flattered."

"As I was saying——"

"Well—what?"

"I—I——"

"Pray go on."

"I wish you——"

"Dear—dear! How slow you are in coming to the point."

Jack shook his fist savagely at the closed door, in the direction in which he conceived Fanny to be.

"Jack Rawlings is unworthy of you," continued Harry Belvoir.

Now Fanny, although she was very irate with our hero,

and fully disposed to find any amount of fault with him herself, did not feel disposed to listen complacently to any disparaging remarks respecting him from a third person.

Her design, however, at present, was to draw Harry Belvoir on for her own amusement.

"Unworthy of me?"

"Yes."

"In what way?"

"Every way."

"Dear me!"

"Surely, you must know it?"

"Know what?"

"That he you live with is a low, common fellow, without money, position, or parents."

"Thank you, Mr. Belvoir," muttered Jack; "I owe you one for that."

"He hasn't more money than you."

"Less."

"His position, certainly, is not much superior to your own."

"I should think not!"

"And as for relations, he hasn't got an Uncle Pigley."

"Conf——"

"Now, don't use bad language."

"Why will you wander from the subject? Tell me, will you grant my request?"

"That depends upon what it is."

"Cannot you guess?"

"No."

"I want you to accept me in the stead of that young good-for-nothing fellow, Jack Rawlings."

"Curse his impudence!" growled Jack.

Fanny burst forth into a merry peal of uncontrolled laughter.

Harry Belvoir looked confused.

"Ha, ha, ha!" laughed Fanny.

"What the deuce are you laughing at?"

"You."

"Me?"

"Yes. Ha, ha, ha, ha!"

"I don't see anything to laugh at."

"I do."

"What?"

"The idea of the little school-boy having got so forward as to conceive such a thing!"

"I do not see anything so strange in it."

"You're too young, Harry—much too young."

"Whatever my age may be, I'm strong enough to compel you to yield to me."

Jack noiselessly unlocked the door, and prepared for a rush.

Fanny began to feel a little frightened.

She had only intended to play a little comedy, and was unprepared for the serious turn that matters had taken.

Harry Belvoir advanced towards her.

He addressed her by endearing names.

Fanny, frightened, drew away from him.

He placed his arms round her waist.

She screamed.

With a cry of rage, Jack burst through the door, waving his stick above his head.

It was totally dark!

Fanny did not recognise her lover.

She considered it was but part of a diabolical plot on the part of Harry Belvoir to gain his vile end.

She did not know it was rescue and succour.

With a wild scream she rushed out of the room, downstairs, and into the street; while the would-be beau, guessing who the intruder must be, without hesitation flung open the window, and dropped to the ground below.

Jack cursed and swore at being thus foiled in his revenge upon Fanny's assailant; nor was his anger lessened on discovering that Fanny, too, had escaped.

And where was Filchit?

He, as well, had disappeared!

Under these disastrous circumstances, Jack turned his steps homeward, and arrived at his lodgings with the milk.

Feeling exhausted, but not sleepy, he applied himself to the spirit bottles and tobacco; the consequence of which was, that in less than an hour, he had smoked and drank himself into a helpless state of stupor; and when the servant came to tidy the room, she found him lying on his back on the hearth-rug, snoring like a whole herd of swine.

*   *   *   *   *

To return to Fanny and Harry Belvoir.

It would be tedious and unprofitable to follow regularly the arguments which Harry Belvoir used to convince Fanny that he was blameless in the fright she had had.

At last she was convinced.

Then she herself proposed that they two should live together, occupying separate rooms.

Her object in doing this was twofold.

In the first place, she wanted a protector; for experience had shown her that, with her great personal charms, she could not venture about London alone.

In the second, she was without money, and thought it advisable to find some one who would be able to supply her with the necessaries of life.

After a day or two of this strange mode of living, Harry Belvoir confessed that the few shillings he had remaining after his losses in the gambling-house were all spent.

How were they to get more?

That was the question which occupied them for many hours.

Every way but one was discussed.

That one was in both their minds, but neither liked to be the first to express it.

At length, Harry Belvoir broke the ice.

"I don't see how we can get money, unless we help ourselves to some of that of other people."

"Do you mean——?"

"Burglary!"

The few scruples Fanny possessed were speedily overcome, and, before long, it was agreed that they two should make an attempt at systematic robbery as soon as an opportunity presented itself.

Harry was not long in finding one.

The intended victim was Miss Tabitha Greenway.

Miss Tabitha Greenway was a rich old maid, with a peculiar prejudice against banks and securities of all kinds.

Banks, she thought, were always breaking, and securities proving insecure.

Stocks were vanity, and Railway Companies vexation of spirit, according to her notion; and she accordingly trusted to the strength of her own iron safe, and deposited all her worldly wealth within it.

Plate, gold, and jewels, were all locked up there; and, if report said truly, that iron safe contained property to the amount of several thousand pounds.

It seemed a tempting job to our heroine and her companion.

There was another peculiarity about Miss Tabitha Greenway which deserves especial notice, for it had a great influence upon those of our characters whose fate we are more particularly following.

Miss Tabitha Greenway was extremely romantic.

Not a sensation novel was there which she did not read, not a thrilling melodrama which she did not witness.

Her bedroom was ornamented with the portraits of handsome young men with jet black eyes and moustaches, to which she pointed at times with a sigh, when talking sentiment with friends; although she and they both well knew that never in her life had she had a lover, and that those dashing portraits had all been bought at prices varying from sixpence to half-a-crown at different brokers' shops.

Upon her book-shelves stood a volume containing Lord Byron's works; and in a small closet, kept as religiously closed as her iron safe, she was believed to keep such works, in both French and English, as are not generally supposed to be perused by the softer sex.

Now Miss Tabitha Greenway had a great ambition.

An ambition which not unfrequently attacks ladies of a certain age, when they are given to the perusal of works of a light tendency.

An ambition which, though really harmless, might, had she been a few years younger, have led to serious results.

She sadly wanted a lover!

Not such a lover, my dear young lady reader, as you in the innocence of your heart imagine.

Not one who would take her to balls and theatres.

Not one who would make her presents of Covent-garden bouquets.

Not one who would profess unlimited affection.

No! That was not what she required.

What she wanted was a gentleman—young and good-looking, if possible—who would play the part of a character often met with in romances, but rarely in real life.

She wanted that sort of love which in reality is next to an impossibility, and which is dignified by the name of "Platonic affection."

This was Miss Tabitha Greenway's ardent wish.

We shall see in the end whether it was gratified.

CHAPTER XXXI.

HOW MISS TABITHA GREENWAY LOST HER MONEY AND FOUND A LOVER.

THE night fixed by Harry Belvoir for his first burglary in company with our heroine was as good a night for the job as any thief could have desired.

Dark, tempestuous, and stormy.

The wind came twirling and sweeping round the corner, knocking about many an old gentleman's umbrella, and playing the very deuce with the ladies' petticoats.

All but a few poor, wretched, homeless outcasts remained indoors, and gathered round the fire, thanking their stars that they had not to stir out; while the policemen had all taken shelter in their favourite areas, and were enjoying cold meat and the smiles of the cook in the cleanest part of the coal-cellar.

It was not without some trepidation that Fanny donned the male attire Harry had bought (on trust) for this very expedition.

She certainly never looked handsomer than when in man's dress.

Her appearance was of course effeminate, but nevertheless she made the most charming boy that it is possible to imagine.

Soon after midnight, the pair sallied forth into the dripping and deserted streets.

Save but for the rattle and splash of some cab hurrying upon its way, the great metropolis might have been the city of the dead.

Through the mist and rain, through the fog and chilly night air, over the sloppy pavement, across the muddy gutters, they pursued their way to Jonquil-terrace, where Miss Tabitha Greenway resided.

Arrived before the house, Harry Belvoir, not yet being expert in the profession he had adopted, paused and deliberated as to the best course they should adopt.

While they were yet lingering undecided, a dripping cab drove up to the door, and as soon as it was opened, Miss Tabitha herself sprang from the vehicle, displaying a pair of legs which might have rivalled bed-posts in thickness, and rushed into her residence.

This necessitated a change in the plans of the midnight burglars, for they knew they could not attempt to enter the house under an hour's time.

To stay in the streets was impossible, for the weather was so bad, and the rain descended so violently, that no one in their senses could dream of remaining exposed to it.

The public-houses were all closed, and they were forced at last to take shelter under an archway, and wait patiently till the time came at which they could safely make the attempt to enter the house.

While they were waiting there, a young girl, plainly and neatly dressed, came hurrying by.

By the light of the gas-lamp, Fanny recognised her.

She was one of those poor unfortunates employed in Mrs. Herringbone's millinery department.

Moreover, she was one of those to whom Fanny had taken a great fancy, on account of her kind, good-hearted manner.

The girl paused before the archway.

She wavered.

She hesitated.

Apparently, she was deliberating whether to take shelter there.

The sight, however, of two figures in male attire decided her not to do so.

She pursued her way.

Scarcely had she proceeded half-a-dozen yards, when Harry and Fanny, who, in default of anything better to do, watched her movements, saw two men in the garb of gentlemen spring to her side.

"Ha, ha! my little darling! Caught at last!"

"Yes; fairly trapped——demmit!" said the second.

"You must pay the penalty, my pretty one."

The girl answered not a word, but struggled to free herself from the grasp of her tormentors.

"How the bird flutters! It's no use, my dear."

"Unhand me, or I call for assistance."

"Call, by all means, little one, and see who will come."

"Oh, yes! call——demmit!"

"Let me go," said the poor milliner, the tears starting into her eyes.

"You must give me, then, a kiss from those pretty lips."

"Never."

"Don't be so demnition cruel."

The first ruffian strove to obtain the favour he sought, by means of brute force.

"Help!" shrieked the girl.

"I must seal that charming mouth." And again the miscreant bent his bloated face and coarse, sensual-looking lips to hers.

"Help! Will no one help me?"

It is impossible to describe the agonizing tones of entreaty in which these words were spoken.

"By Jove! I will!" cried Harry Belvoir, springing forward.

"Who the deuce is this fellow?" said the cowardly villain who played the most prominent part in the disgraceful attack upon the poor helpless girl.

"I'll show you who I am," said Harry.

He endeavoured to force him to leave go his hold upon the pretty seamstress.

He partially succeeded.

In return, he received a violent blow between the eyes, which made him see more lamps in the street than ever the commissioners dreamt of placing there.

He could not put up with this.

His anger was roused.

The blow aroused the demon within him.

With a bound, like that of an infuriated tiger, he threw himself upon the scoundrel.

He was prepared for him.

He met his advance with a stinging blow upon the temple.

Harry Belvoir had met with his match.

They were both good boxers, and there, in the middle of the road, they set-to.

The assailant's companion, finding the coast clear as he thought, fancied it a good opportunity to ingratiate himself with the poor girl who had originated the fight.

She strove to escape him.

In vain!

Despite her cries, the ruffian succeeded in placing his arm round her, and was bearing her away in triumph, when unexpected succour arrived.

She needed it sorely.

The help she received came from her old work-room companion.

It was indeed Fanny who rushed to her assistance.

Suddenly facing the poor girl's second assailant, she placed herself in as near an approach to an attitude as she could copy from remembrance of some sporting pictures Jack had.

"Oh!—I say!—demmit!"

This was the sapient but slightly incomprehensible remark of the gentleman.

Fanny's reply was forcible.

Extending her left arm, with all her whole force, and throwing the weight of her body into the blow, she caught the ruffian on the tip of his aristocratic nose, and felled him to the wet, sloppy pavement.

He went down as if he had been shot.

His head came in contact with the kerb-stone.

He lay there, helpless, bruised, and insensible.

"Not so bad for a beginner," muttered Fanny, half aloud.

The poor girl was profuse in her thanks to her rescuer.

Fanny sent her off, without listening to them, and without revealing her name and sex.

Then she turned to see how Harry Belvoir was getting on.

He too, although he had a tough antagonist to deal with, had, after a protracted struggle, obtained the advantage.

His adversary was winded.

He struck out wildly.

Every one of Harry Belvoir's blows went home.

One more well directed one sent the unmanly coward to join his companion on the pavement.

Harry Belvoir and Fanny together dragged the fallen foes to the archway, and propped them up against the wall;

and then, thinking they had allowed sufficient time to elapse, again bent their steps towards Jonquil-terrace, and again came to a stand before the door of the house occupied by Miss Tabitha Greenway.

All was silent.

No lights were visible.

The whole neighbourhood seemed buried in sleep.

Silently and cautiously using his centre bit and skeleton keys, in a truly workmanlike manner, Harry succeeded in his task.

The door opened noiselessly.

They entered!

The passage was dark as pitch.

They could not see an inch before them.

Harry Belvoir, however, was prepared for this, and produced a dark lantern, which he had brought with him.

A long ray of light went dancing and quivering along the passage, resting principally upon the locks and handles of the doors.

After two or three unsuccessful attempts, they discovered the room in which the strong iron safe was placed.

Harry Belvoir, with the knowledge of so much wealth only divided from him by an iron plate, set to work with renewed energy,

Alas! Disappointment was the sole result!

He tried all he knew, but in vain.

Picklocks and skeleton keys were alike powerless to open the doors of the massive safe!

It was with a growl, and the use of sundry strong adjectives, that he flung his implements upon the floor.

"It's no use after all!" said he, despondingly.

"Try again!" suggested Fanny.

"It's no good. The cursed thing resists all my efforts."

"Is there no other way?"

"None!"

"There must be."

"I don't know of it, if there is."

"I do."

"What is it?"

"Why not open it the proper way?"

"What the deuce are you talking about?"

"Open it with the proper key!"

"Pooh! That's absurd!"

"Not at all."

"Where is the key to come from?"

"I'll get it."

"How can you?"

"Trust me for that. It must be somewhere in her bed-room."

"Confound the old cat."

"I'll search everywhere for it."

"If you fail?"

"I shan't."

"It's very dangerous."

"Not very."

"Take care you don't get discovered."

"Trust me for that."

Fanny, taking the lantern in one hand and her boots in the other, crept silently up the stairs.

Doubtful which room was the one she sought, she opened a door at a venture.

Luckily, she was right in her choice.

With noiseless tread, she entered the sleeping apartment of Miss Tabitha Greenway.

Now it so happened that Miss Greenway had that night been to the theatre, and had witnessed a new and startling melodrama in five acts, with the appropriate tremulous music and the proper quantity of bigamies, murders, rescues, abductions, and coloured fires.

The hero of the piece was a stranger upon the London boards, and as in his character he had made up uncommonly well, this romantic young lady deemed it correct to foster a platonic attachment for this individual.

On her retiring to bed, however, instead of going to sleep as a well-conducted lady should, she had taken down the volume of Lord Byron's works containing "Don Juan," and had perused some of its most vivid lines.

Having done this much, she crossed her eyes to reflect.

Reflection at two o'clock in the morning, when accompanied by closed eyes, is apt to produce sleep; and it was not long before Miss Tabitha sank into a state of slumber, in which the hero of the play, Don Juan, and herself appeared before her mind as playing im-

portant parts, all quite in accordance with their respective characters.

From this slumber she suddenly awoke!

A slight noise startled her!

She opened her eyes!

She looked straight before her!

There, not four yards from her bed-side, stood a handsome young man!

The reality tallied so well with her dream, that it required some moments for her to convince herself that she was awake.

Snatching off her night cap, and letting her thin wisps of yellow hair float in disorder about her scraggy shoulders, she screamed!

It was not a particularly loud or shrill scream; nevertheless it caused Fanny to utter an exclamation more in accordance with her disguise than with her sex.

"Fire, thieves, murder!" shouted Miss Tabitha Greenway, fear getting the upper hand of romance.

"Hush, for Heaven's sake!" cried Fanny.

"Fire!"

"I can explain all!"

"Thieves!"

"Listen to me!"

"Murder!"

"Don't make such an infernal din!"

Fanny was losing her temper.

"Fire, thieves, murder!" again shrieked Miss Tabitha, with the full power of her lungs.

Harry Belvoir thought discretion the better part of valour.

He was not constitutionally brave; and as he did not see in what way he could benefit our heroine by remaining in the house, he quietly decamped, leaving her to settle the matter as best she could.

Miss Greenway's shrieks eventually aroused a sleepy policeman at the street corner, who, with heavy strides, advanced to the house from whence they proceeded.

Fanny had lost her opportunity of escape.

She was, as yet, a novice, and was too much flustered by the discovery that the lady was awake to attempt escape at the time.

The sound of the policeman ascending the stairs recalled her to her senses.

But it was too late!

In a moment she decided upon the course she would adopt.

The boots which she carried in her hand she flung hastily beneath the bed, and with a demeanour outwardly calm, but in reality quite the reverse, she awaited the entrance of the guardian of the peace,

He was accompanied by Sally!

Now Sally was Miss Tabitha's maid-of-all-work, and a fine life she led of it.

Sally was red-haired, nervous, and subject to toothache.

The first did not add to her personal charms.

The second caused her to make her appearance with her best Sunday-going crinoline put on outside her night-dress.

The third had kept her awake, and had made her tie up her face with a dirty cotton pocket-handkerchief.

"Fire, thieves, murder!" screamed Miss Tabitha, with renewed energy at the arrival of these reinforcements.

"Now what's all this here row about?" asked the policeman, peremptorily.

"Fire!" said Miss Tabitha, wildly, covering her head with the counterpane, and speaking from beneath the clothes.

"Nonsense!" said the policeman.

Sally looked at Fanny, and sniggered.

"Look here, young man, and be careful what you go to say," continued the policeman, addressing our heroine, and copying the bullying tone of the presiding magistrate in Arrow-street, as well as he could. "What's your business here? Eh?"

"No business," said Fanny, coolly.

"What brings you here, then?"

"Pleasure."

"What do you mean?"

"Ask Miss Greenway."

"What does he mean, mum?"

The answer from beneath two blankets and a counterpane was unintelligible.

"Unless you can explain your presence here, young man, I'll march you off to quod, as sure as eggs is eggs!"

"I've no objection to explain, if the lady doesn't mind."

"Speak, man!" said Miss Tabitha, obliged to put out the tip of her nose to avoid suffocation.

"Well, then, I came in at Miss Tabitha's own invitation!"

"My gracious!" cried Sally.

"The devil you did!" said the policeman.

"The base deceiver!" said Miss Tabitha.

"She asked me up here herself!" said Fanny; "begged and entreated me to come."

"Well, I never!" cried the astonished maid-of-all-work.

"It's all very rum!" observed the policeman.

"I heard him talking to her in the hall," remarked Sally, "but I never thought she'd 'a been and asked him into her bedroom!"

"Speak! Recollect your'e upon your oath, Sally. Confess all you know," cried Fanny, boldly.

"Please, sir, then, I heard you and missus, cos for why, I was lying awake with the toothache, which is a rampageous pain, and she says, says she, 'Come in,' and then I heard you come in."

"Well, and what then?"

"I heard missus say, 'Come along, it 'll do you good, and me too.'"

"Sally, I give you a month's warning from to-day, for your wicked falsehoods."

"It's only the truth I'm speaking."

"Go on."

"Please, that's all."

"Quite enough, I think."

"Have you anything to say to this, mum?" asked the policeman.

"Say! Yes. I'd been to the theatre, and when I came home I asked the cabman in, and gave him a glass of spirits, and that's the simple truth."

"Look here," said Fanny to the policeman, "you just look under the bed, and see what you'll find."

"None of your larks, young man."

"Look!"

"What for?"

"See for yourself."

The policeman raised the hangings of the bed, in spite of the screams and protestations of Miss Tabitha.

He discovered Fanny's boots!

"This sort of thing wont do," said he.

"Bless us! What next?" exclaimed Sally.

"What do you say to that, mum?"

"Oh, let the young man go, if he'll promise never to say a word about it," said Miss Greenway, terrified by the circumstantial evidence, and fearing an exposure.

"Of course I shall not mention the occurrence," said Fanny, politely.

"Sally," continued the affrighted lady, "I'll double your wages if you'll stay with me and hold your tongue."

"And I'm not given to gossiping, mum; but if you'll throw in the baker's boy as wishes to keep company along o' me, but followers ain't allowed, I'll do it with pleasure, mum."

"Have all the baker's boys, if you like."

"I think I've done my duty, mum," said the policeman, apologetically rubbing the back of his hand across his mouth, and winking at Sally.

"Oh yes—certainly; and if you'll call to-morrow, you shall be amply rewarded."

"Thank you, mum. Good night!"

"Good night, Mr. Policeman."

"Farewell, Miss Greenway," said Fanny, with a wonderful amount of impudence.

In a few minutes, she was out in the empty, deserted streets, thanking her stars for her lucky escape from what might have proved a serious accident.

Her anger, however, at the desertion of Harry Belvoir knew no bounds.

"Jack would never have left me when I was in a mess," said she.

CHAPTER XXXII.

DESCRIBES THE MISTAKE JACK MADE ABOUT AN OLD GENTLEMAN'S SNUFF-BOX, AND THE TROUBLE HE GOT INTO ABOUT IT.

JACK RAWLINGS, as may be imagined, was not in the best of tempers at failing, after all, to track Fanny; for, try as much as he would, all his efforts were unavailing.

After a while he resigned himself, however, to a state of bachelorhood, and put up with such stray comfort as he could find in the streets of the metropolis after nightfall.

Day after day dragged wearily on, and Jack gave up all hope of finding Fanny.

Day after day he strolled purposelessly about the streets, accompanied by his dog Filchit, in the vain expectation that something might turn up.

At last, in a manner most unexpected, something did turn up.

Jack Rawlings was fond of his morning-pipe; and one day, being out of tobacco, he went into a large shop, near the top of Oxford-street, to replenish his exhausted pouch.

An elderly man, evidently a church dignitary, was in the shop, having his gold snuff-box filled.

Jack could not help casting envious glances towards the precious metal.

The old gentleman had a square head, a red face, and funny little tufts of white hair sprouting out from beneath his looped-up hat.

The old gentleman was commanding in address, and dictatorial in his mode of speech; and, most of all, the old gentleman was choleric in temper.

His snuff-box filled, he left the shop; and Jack gave his modest order for an ounce of birds'-eye.

Filchit seemed particularly sprightly.

He frisked about.

He wagged his tail.

He jumped up, and put his dirty paws on our hero's best pair of trousers; and in other ways misconducted himself.

Jack was at a loss to account for this unwonted liveliness.

He discovered the cause afterwards.

Just as Jack was leaving the shop, the old gentleman returned, fussing and fuming.

"I left my snuff-box behind," said he.

The shopman looked everywhere for it, but could not see it.

"I don't think it's here, sir."

"Bless my heart! Don't tell me!" replied the clerical dignitary, angrily.

"I cannot see it, sir."

"Have you seen it, young man?" asked the elderly parson of Jack.

"No; I have not," replied our hero, civilly.

"Not seen it! Bless me! Snuff-boxes don't walk away by themselves—especially when they're made of gold."

The shopman looked frightened, and Jack defiant.

"I only know I've not seen it," he said.

"One of you must have it," said the clergyman, fuming with rage.

"You don't mean to accuse me, I hope?" said Jack. "I wouldn't take the thing!"

"I don't know that."

"Well, look here, old gentleman; if you can't keep a civil tongue in your head, I wont help you to look for it."

"Who wants your help, young Jackanapes?"

"And if I find it, I'll see you blowed before I return it you."

The church dignitary turned purple with rage, and but for his cloth would doubtless have sworn.

Jack left the shop, followed by Filchit.

He had not gone more than half the length of the street before a dog came running up to Filchit, after the manner of his kind.

Filchit, contrary to his usual practice, took not the slightest notice, and continued on his way.

The other dog, emboldened, took the additional liberty of inflicting a slight bite on the hind leg of the dog Filchit.

That was more than canine flesh and blood could stand; and Filchit turned round savagely, and pursued his adversary.

Opening his mouth to attack his antagonist, something fell from it!

It was a snuff-box!

The very identical gold snuff-box which the old gentleman had lost!

Jack hurried forward to pick it up from the pavement.

He had formed no fixed idea as to whether he would seek out its owner and return it to him, or whether he would put it in his own pocket and say nothing about it.

He stooped to pick it up.

Before he could do so, however, he was seized from behind.

Seized securely by the collar of his coat!

"You young rascal! you profligate young thief! you villain! you reprobate! I've got you now."

"It looks like it," said Jack.

"What have you to say for yourself, you young gallow's bird! you burglar! you rascal! you scoundrel! eh? What have you to say for yourself now? Caught in the act, you young imp! you ruffian!"

"When you've quite done, I don't mind telling you."

"Why don't you speak, you confounded rascal?"

"I'm going to."

"Don't stand jabbering there, you thief."

"I am no thief!"

"Ha, ha, ha! I like that! Police!"

Wonderful to be related, a policeman actually came at his call, and seized Jack on the other side.

"I give this fellow in charge for robbery," said the parson.

"All right, sir," said the policeman, tightening his hold.

"I didn't steal the snuff-box," said Jack.

"I'll be ——"

The policeman, fearing to hear a clerical dignitary commit himself by the use of profane language, coughed violently, and drowned the conclusion of the sentence.

The end of the matter was that Jack was marched off to the station-house by the policeman, followed by a crowd of jeering boys, rejoicing in seeing some one with a good coat on "took up."

It was in vain that Jack protested his innocence.

In vain he related the way in which he discovered Filchit had been the thief.

He was only laughed at!

No one believed the story.

No one knew the school in which the tailless dog had been brought up, and the lessons in thieving he had had instilled into him when a mere puppy.

So the dog was left to go his own way, and Jack was marched off to Arrow-street.

It is by no means a pleasant or lively thing to pass a night in a police-cell, and so Jack found when locked up with a drunken tailor and a brutal wife-beater for eighteen hours.

However, he had a wonderful capacity for sleep, under any circumstances; and picking out the softest corner of the cell, he soon fell into a profound slumber.

The following morning Jack's case was one of the first called on.

He told his story; but was disbelieved, and ultimately fully committed for trial.

That afternoon he was removed to Newgate in the solemn funereal prison van, which seemed but a hearse to him.

As he entered the massive doors, and surveyed the thick stone walls, hope died within him.

Escape from the metropolitan prison seemed impossible.

Our hero saw nothing before him but to drag out a miserable existence for the next six or eight months in a House of Correction, or some similar diabolical invention, separated from Fanny, and debarred from tobacco.

But Fortune was about to favour him; and it was not doomed to be many weeks before he again clasped Fanny in his arms.

Both of them fully repented their lovers' quarrel, and our heroine had grown so disgusted with the behaviour of Harry Belvoir that she determined never again to speak to him; while, as for Jack, if he could have had his way, Harry Belvoir's regular features would have been so disfigured that Uncle Pigley would have disowned him at once and for ever.

As it was, Fanny, disguised in man's clothes, was wandering about London in search of lodgings, and Jack was confined within the gloomy walls of Newgate.

CHAPTER XXXIII.

RELATES THE WONDERFUL WAY IN WHICH JACK RAWLINGS ESCAPED FROM NEWGATE.

JACK RAWLINGS had not been long in Newgate before he formed the acquaintance of one or two gentlemen eminent in their profession, but whose business was looked upon by a parental government as neither in accordance with social nor moral laws, and who were unfortunately "in trouble," on account of different trifles, varying from manslaughter to "wipe snatching."

Jack, being naturally of a sociable temperament, soon chose one or two from among these gentlemen with whom to be familiar, and in spite of warders and watchfulness,

contrived to hold conversations with them, in which prospects of escape or acquittal formed a great subject for speculation.

It was not long before Jack discovered that one of the warders, named Jack Horley, was a "right screw;"* but at present he was without means to obtain assistance from this individual, being entirely without money.

It was not long, however, before this want was supplied.

Supplied in a manner as strange as unexpected.

"I say, guv'nor, I've summat for you," said he to our hero one day.

"Something for me?"

"Yes."

"What is it?"

"A cross stiff."

"A what?"

"A cross stiff."

"What the deuce do you mean?"

"Come, now, don't sham so jolly innocent."

"I don't know what you mean."

"Gammon."

"I don't, indeed."

"Walker!"

"Tell me—there's a good fellow."

"What are you going to stand?"

"I don't possess a single penny."

"Come, that's a little too good. Do you mean to say you really don't know what I've got for you?"

"How the devil should I?"

"Don't you?"

"No."

The warder looked cautiously round, and listened at the entrance to the cell for any sound down the long passages.

All was silent as the grave.

He advanced towards our hero.

He took off his hat.

From the lining he extracted a bulky letter, which, after a moment's deliberation, he handed to Jack.

"A letter!" cried he. "Why didn't you say so before?"

"You knew well enough."

"I didn't."

"Well, only to think of a prig being so jolly green as not to know a 'cross-stiff' meant a smuggled letter!" muttered the warder.

Jack took no notice of the remark.

He broke open the envelope.

"I say, guv'nor, you'll recollect I had a deal o' bother about that letter," said the warder.

"Oh, yes," said Jack.

The warder cast a lingering look at our hero as he took his departure, rather doubting whether he would ever receive any pecuniary recompense.

No sooner had his gaoler left, than Jack tore from the envelope a roll of bank-notes, and gazed at them, scarcely able to believe his eyes.

Who could have sent them?

Who was there in the whole world, with the exception of Fanny, who cared a single straw whether he were in prison or not?

Could she have sent them?

No.

That was very unlikely.

Who, then, was it?

A small scrap of paper fell from amongst the notes.

Hoping it might give some clue to the name of his benefactor, Jack hastily picked it up.

Four words in a feminine handwriting were upon it.

Four words which rather increased his mystification, for they showed clearly that Fanny was not the sender.

Four words which set him wondering for the rest of the day.

The four words were simply these:—

"From a sincere friend."

Jack did not know that he possessed such a thing; but felt uncommonly glad that so useful a person should have turned up at the very moment he was most wanted.

Concealing the notes, according to the best of his ability, in various parts of his dress, he went to sleep that night with a lighter heart than he had known since first he entered Newgate's gloomy portals.

He now had money; and what would not money do?

The thick walls seemed to melt, the iron-hasped doors to

* Open to bribery.

fly open, the massive locks to drop off, before a little magic roll of paper which he held in his hand.

The paper was covered with a wavy watermark, and was printed and stamped for "The Governor and Company of the Bank of England."

The following morning, when the expectant warder entered Jack's cell, his greatest hopes were more than realized.

Our hero held out a white, crisp five pound note to him, and begged him to accept it.

The warder having declared he was first "blowed" and then "blessed," held it up to the light, bit one corner, and rubbed it between his dirty palms to assure himself it was really good.

"You're too much of a gent to be in prison," said he, in the warmth of his heart, to Jack, as he banged the cell-door and strode down the passage.

"That's all very fine," thought our hero; "but still I don't see my way to get out."

But the warder had his plans.

An opportunity of escape was not so far distant as it appeared.

Two days after Jack had made the present to his gaoler, that worthy entered his cell, with a look of deeper meaning than usual on his vacant face.

He looked cautiously round, to make sure there was no chance of his being overheard.

"I say, mister," said he, in a hoarse whisper, to our hero.

"Hullo!" replied Jack.

"I've got a question to ask you."

"Out with it, then."

"A deal depends on your answer."

"Well, what is it?"

"You don't happen to be a whitewasher by trade?"

"A whitewasher?"

"Yes."

"Ha, ha, ha! What the deuce do you mean?"

"Are you one?"

"No."

"You're quite sure of that?"

"Yes."

Jack answered decidedly; yet he could not but feel that there was more in the man's question than at first appeared.

"You couldn't take a big brush in your hand, and dip it in a pail, and splash away at a ceiling, could you?"

"Well, I think I could manage that."

"Will you try?"

"If it will give you any particular pleasure."

"Look here, mister. Some people are born fools, and others gets to be fools in the course of nature. I don't know which is your case, but it's certain one on 'em is."

"Thank you," said Jack.

"Now, then, are you a whitewasher?"

Jack was again about to answer in the negative, when it struck him that the warder must have some hidden design in his pertinacious reiteration of that one question.

"You just said you could do the brush and pail business," continued the goaler.

"Oh, yes."

"Well then, for the third and last time of asking—are you a whitewasher?"

"Yes," replied Jack, boldly.

"Oh! that's right," said his questioner, in tones of evident satisfaction; and forthwith strode from the cell, without a word of further explanation.

For the whole of that afternoon Jack puzzled his brains to no purpose in trying to guess the meaning of the strange behaviour on the part of the gaoler.

The following day cleared up the mystery.

Early in the morning the warder appeared at the cell-door, accompanied by another individual.

"This is the gent as can do it," said the gaoler, addressing his companion, and at the same time winking at Jack.

"Oh! So you are a whitewasher by trade, are you?"

The eyes of the gaoler sparkled and blinked like those of an owl in the sunshine, as he directed a series of rapid telegraphic winks at our hero.

"That's the profession I was brought up to, sir," said Jack—wondering, at the same time, what it could all mean.

"That's all right."

"Can I do anything for you in that line?" asked our hero.

"Well, yes. I don't see the point of your sitting here, eating your head off, when you can be of use."

"Certainly not."

"Well, there is a ceiling that wants doing up a bit, and I think you'd better turn your hand to it."

"With pleasure."

"That's right."

"When shall I begin?"

"At once."

Then turning to the warder—

"I say, Horley, just show this young whipper-snapper the room."

Horley pulled his hair, and signalled Jack to follow him.

"You see, mister," said he, as they tramped along the passage, "either I or one of my mates will have to keep an eye on you; 'cos for why, there's a skylight in the room, through which you might pop out and make your escape as easy as anything."

Jack Rawlings perceived at once the plan which the gaoler had formed for him, and determined to avail himself of it as soon as an opportunity offered.

Our hero was conducted to a goodly-sized room—lighted, as Horley had informed him, by a large skylight.

There he found all the paraphernalia of the trade of which he had professed himself a member.

Horley assisted him to don the white garments, and helped him to place the ladders and planks which were to enable him to approach within reach of the ceiling.

One end of the plank was so placed as to be immediately under one corner of the skylight!

"Now, then, mister, you'd better get to work."

Jack dipped his huge brush in the pail, and plentifully bespattered the ceiling, the floor, himself, and even Jack Horley, who was standing beneath.

"A little of that stuff goes a great way," said the gaoler, wiping away the whitewash which had fallen on his upturned face.

For some little time Jack continued his occupation in silence.

Horley still remained in the apartment, and while he was present our hero did not dare to make any attempt at escape.

Before long, however, Horley was called away; but Jack was not left to himself, for another gaoler took the place of watcher, and amused himself by making unpleasant remarks to Jack.

"Not the last time you'll be on a scaffold, I expect," said he.

"I hope not," said Jack, cheerfully.

"Perhaps the next one will be outside, instead of inside Newgate."

"What, Exeter Hall?" asked Jack, with an air of innocence.

The warder growled out an unintelligible reply, and Jack Rawlings chuckled within himself at having shut him up.

"Bill—Bill!" shouted a voice outside.

"What's the row?" asked the man who was watching Jack.

"Come here."

"I can't."

"Why not?"

"'Cos I've something to do."

"What's that?"

"Watching a cove whitewashing."

"Never mind him—come here."

"What for?"

"You've left the door of one of your cells open."

The warder was not proof against this.

The prospect of dismissal for neglect of duty made him start from his seat and rush down the gloomy passage, his keys jingling in his hands as he went.

No sooner had he disappeared than our hero heard the lusty voice of Jack Horley roaring out a fragment of an old ballad:—

"The brave prisoner leapt through the window and all,
A handful of straw broke the force of his fall;
And long ere the watchers returned from the ball,
He had sped far away, and was quite out of call.
          Singing—Tooral di toddle de ray."

Jack accepted the words as a hint to himself, and, in a moment, rushed to the end of the plank, caught hold of the ledge which supported the skylight, and by a slight muscular exertion swung himself up, threw his legs over, and stood upon the roof of Newgate.

Here a new difficulty presented itself.

It was broad daylight, and the streets were thronged with passengers.

He could not dare to walk across the roof, for he could not do so without ensuring observation.

After a few moments, he came to a bold resolve.

It was liberty he was struggling for, and it was worth the attempt; for if he failed, he was but where he was before.

He knew that if he were seen by any one in the street, trying to hide behind projections, or slink quietly along unperceived, that they would imagine him at once to be an escaped prisoner. He therefore decided to walk boldly along, as if he had a right to be on the roof of the great metropolitan prison.

His workman's dress favoured this design; and he proceeded to put it into immediate execution, for he well knew that but a few minutes could elapse before his escape was discovered.

Boldly and undaunted he walked along, upright, and courting observation; even, in one instance, going so far as to shout an answer to the chaffing remark of a facetious omnibus driver.

Arrived at the termination of the prison-roof, he discovered that before he could reach the tops of the adjoining houses he must scale a formidable-looking cheveaux de frise, and drop some seven or eight feet upon sloping slates.

He had no time for deliberation, but at once set about making the attempt.

He found, to his great joy, that the cheveaux de frise had become rusty from the action of the weather, and refused to turn; it, therefore, was by no means so difficult an object to surmount as it at first appeared.

A few seconds saw him on the other side, hanging by his hands to the coping, and preparing to drop on to the roof of the adjoining house.

He let go his hold, and alighted on his feet. As ill luck would have it, the slate upon which he descended was loose, and gave way with his weight.

He lost his balance, and fell.

A sharp projecting stone came between his eyes, and covered his face with blood; while his ankle twisted beneath him, causing him the most exquisite pain.

As he lay bruised and stunned, he heard shouts from the roof of the prison, which showed him his escape had been discovered, and that the gaolers were on his track.

This nerved him to a fresh effort.

He rose to his feet, and in spite of the pain his foot gave him, managed to hobble along the roof, looking for an open trap-door through which he might make his descent into a house.

It was some little time before he discovered one; but, at length, his search was crowned with success.

He discovered a trap-door in the roof, which had been left open; and through it he went, and to his great delight, found himself in the upper story of the house occupied by Mr. Carvsed, the eminent meat salesman.

Once in the house, the difficulty was to reach the street unperceived; but our hero, trusting in his usual good luck, determined to walk boldly down the stairs, hoping Fortune would favour him, and that he would meet no one on the way.

He had descended the first flight, and was congratulating himself upon having proceeded so far in safety, when the door of a bedroom suddenly opened, and Jack Rawlings stood face to face with Mrs. Carvsed!

It was an awkward meeting!

The wife of the meat salesman was a fat, red-faced, jolly-looking woman, with as strong a mind as a woman need have; still it is not surprising that thus suddenly coming across Jack Rawlings, she should utter a shrill scream.

It is to be borne in mind that our hero's appearance was not, at this time, particularly prepossessing.

He was attired in white.

His clothes had been tattered and torn in his escape.

His face was covered with blood from the wound in his forehead.

He limped as he walked; and altogether he presented somewhat of the appearance of one of Pepper's ghosts, who had broken away and gone out on the loose.

As aforesaid, it is not surprising that at the sight of this gaunt apparition Mrs. Carvsed should utter a shrill scream.

Jack made her a polite bow.

She stared.

He made her another.

"Speak, man! How did you get here?" she asked.

"Through the trap-door, ma'am."

The coolness of the answer took her completely by surprise; and before she could make any reply, Jack's ready invention supplied him with a story, by means of which he hoped to escape from the dilemma in which he found himself.

"I am a plasterer by trade, ma'am."

Mrs. Carvsed glanced at his dress, and saw it was covered with the splashes of whitewash.

She saw no reason to disbelieve his statement.

Jack continued:—

"I was engaged on a job a few houses off; and wishing to alter the position of the ladder, I endeavoured to do so, but it was too heavy for me. I overbalanced myself, and fell with great violence, as you may see."

"Poor fellow!" said Mrs. Carvsed, in a sympathising tone.

"If you would allow me to rest a few moments, and wash my face and hands," continued our hero, "I should be very much obliged to you."

"Mr. Carvsed isn't at home," said his better half.

"Hurrah!" thought Jack; "if I can't talk over the old lady it's a pity!"

"But," continued the meat salesman's wife, "I see no reason why I should not comply with your request."

"Thank you, ma'am," said Jack, civilly, with another low bow.

Under the application of soap and water and a rough towel, Jack soon assumed his own natural expression; and when he again appeared before the astonished eyes of Mrs. Carvsed, she could hardly believe that the handsome young man she saw before her was in verity the gaunt, miserable, bleeding object who had frightened her so much when she had emerged from the bed-room.

"What are you going to do, young man?"

"I think I shall walk to the nearest hospital, ma'am."

"You can't walk through the streets that figure!"

Certainly there was some truth in her statement; for a young man in a white dress stained with blood would be rather likely to attract attention in a public thoroughfare.

Mrs. Carvsed ran down stairs with an agility quite surprising when her fat was taken into consideration, and quickly reappeared, bearing a warm, comfortable great coat on her arm.

"You look honest, young man; so if you'll promise to return it, I'll lend you my husband's winter wrapper."

"I'm very much obliged to you, ma'am."

"Perhaps you'd like a glass of something? You look quite faint."

Jack thought perhaps he would.

Mrs. Carvsed took him into a comfortable little snuggery, and put before him a steaming glass of hot brandy and water.

She declared first she couldn't touch a drop herself.

Then that it must be the smallest drop in the world.

The end of the matter was that she took her seat at the little table opposite our hero, and supplied herself with a similar beverage to that Jack was sucking down like a fish; and our hero, exercising his powers of fascination, so pleased and amused Mrs. Carvsed that she remained there chatting and talking for more than a couple of hours, when suddenly recollecting that her husband would be home in twenty minutes, she pushed Jack out of the house the back way, with her blessing and half-a-crown to take a cab.

Jack Rawlings drew a long breath of relief when he found himself in the street—free.

The great coat formed a capital disguise; and with a light heart and very little fear of being recognised, he lit his cigar and walked rapidly through the London streets.

But where was he to go to?

Where was Fanny?

These two questions he was unable to answer to his own satisfaction; but he determined to proceed to his old lodgings, in the hope of finding her still there, or at all events obtaining some tidings of her whereabouts.

We shall see how he succeeded.

FANNY DASHES THE PORTER AGAINST HER FATHER'S GATE.

CHAPTER XXXIV.

RETURNS TO OUR HEROINE, AND RELATES THE STEPS
SHE TOOK TO DISCOVER THE WHEREABOUTS OF JACK
RAWLINGS.

AFTER Fanny's miraculous escape from the clutches of the
law, she left the house of Miss Tabitha Greenway with
thankfulness in her heart, and a profound contempt for
Harry Belvoir, who had so basely deserted her in the hour
of need.

Come what might, she determined nothing should induce
her, under any circumstances, to speak to him again, unless
it were to give him what is commonly called a piece of her
mind.

Her thoughts naturally enough reverted to Jack, and she
resolved to pocket her pride, to return to him and confess
that for once in her life she had been jealous without cause.

She knew well enough how glad he would be to receive
her.

She knew that a hearty welcome was waiting for her.

It was just getting daylight as she reached the modest
row of houses where they had lived so happily together for
so many months, but she remembering that she was still
disguised in male attire, deemed it more prudent not to
knock at the door, as such a proceeding would have involved
an unpleasant explanation with the servant.

Slowly she paced before the house, looking longingly at the
window of the room where she supposed Jack to be calmly
sleeping.

Alas! as the reader already knows, such was not the case.

Our hero was just then snoring on a wretched pallet-bed
within the gloomy walls of Newgate.

Fanny, secure in her disguise, walked backwards and
forwards before the house, wondering how soon the inhabitants would awake.

At last, feeling tired, she seated herself upon a doorstep.

Now, when it is remembered that Fanny had not had a wink of sleep all that night, and that, moreover, she had gone through a great deal and endured much fatigue, it is not perhaps a very remarkable occurrence that she should fall off into a deep slumber five minutes after she sat down.

At any rate such was the case.

A noise of shouting and hammering at last awoke her.

She glanced immediately at the window of the room in which she and Jack had spent so many happy hours.

It was wide open.

Through it she saw several people in the apartment, while a confused murmur of voices proceeded from it.

What could have happened?

Her heart beat violently, and her breath came fast.

Her lovely bosom heaved convulsively, and she shuddered as a sickening dread came over her.

Before the door of the house stood a knot of men talking together.

She addressed one of them.

A burly, ill-tempered looking individual he was, with an enormous double chin, over which was a hideous gap, supposed by people learned in anatomy to represent his mouth.

Assuming something of a swagger and masculine manner, she spoke to him.

"I say, my good man, what's all this disturbance about?"

"Sale," said the man, surlily.

"A sale?"

"Yes. Don't I speak plain?"

"You look so, anyhow."

"None of your sauce, young whippersnapper, or I may knock your nose into your mouth for you."

"Better knock it into your own—it might make it smaller."

The man turned away with a curse, and Fanny looked round for some one whose appearance looked more communicative.

She could not have fixed upon a better personage than the brisk, dapper little man whom next she addressed.

"Is there a sale going on in that house?"

"Not to say going on, sir, but will be."

"Whose property?"

"A party by the name of Rawlings, I believe, sir."

"Rawlings!" said Fanny, maintaining her composure admirably; "I once knew a man of that name. What is this one like—do you know?"

"Oh, he's a good-looking young fellow enough, but a sad scamp, sir; an awful young rascal."

"The deuce he is."

"Yes, indeed, sir."

"In what way?"

"Well, sir, petticoats. Ever since the time of Adam, sir, petticoats has been the undoing of man—though I fancy Eve wasn't much troubled with the garments in question."

"This Mr. Rawlings was rather fond of the ladies, eh?"

"Well, sir, it mayn't be quite fair to speak in the plural, but there certainly was a most scrumptious young woman lived with him that folks said wasn't his wife."

"Indeed! how very remarkable!" said Fanny, as she entered the house and proceeded to the room where the sale had just commenced.

Fanny White being missing, having, as we know, gone off, in a moment of anger, with Harry Belvoir, and Jack Rawlings being forcibly detained through the kindness of her Majesty's government, the owners of the house where they had lodged became alarmed about their prospects of rent, and seeing no prospect of the return of their lodgers, determined to sell their effects.

Fanny was just in time to see the first lot put up.

It was rather trying to her to witness her own property, as well as many articles which Jack valued very much, sold by auction.

Yet how to prevent it?

She determined to make an attempt, at all events, and to trust to her usual good fortune to carry her safely through.

All her own apparel, together with such articles as she knew Jack would like to retain, she bid for.

Recklessly she bid; for as she had not the means of payment, it mattered little to her whether she said five pounds or fifty.

The auctioneer was enchanted at finding the things go off so well, and our heroine, with mingled feelings of pleasure and dismay, saw lot after lot knocked down to her, and the articles piled up in a corner of the room ready to be removed.

The sale was finished, and the auctioneer requested to be allowed to speak to her.

"The majority of the articles are your property, sir," said he.

"I believe so," answered Fanny, with much sincerity.

"Before you remove them it is customary to deposit half the money, and to leave name and address."

"Oh certainly—certainly," replied our heroine, "a capital arrangement," which, considering she did not possess five pounds in the world, was a tolerably bold thing to say.

Just then the auctioneer happened to stoop, and in so doing disclosed the end of a banker's cheque-book sticking out from his pocket.

Fanny determined to possess herself of it.

But how was it to be done?

"I don't think all the boxes I purchased are there," said Fanny, pointing to the huge pile.

"They are indeed, sir, I assure you."

"I'll ask the man," she continued.

Instead of questioning him, she sent him off, no wise unwilling, to the public-house.

"I don't see the first lot I purchased," she said, coming back to the auctioneer.

"That's it, sir; the bottom one of all."

"Nonsense; that's the second."

"The first, I assure you."

"The second."

"It isn't, indeed."

"Well, all I can say is you wont get a farthing from me unless you show me the first lot."

The auctioneer sighed.

The thermometer stood at something frightful in the shade, and the box she insisted on seeing was undermost of all.

Still, so good a customer was not to be offended.

He called for the man, but that worthy being busily engaged guzzling at the public-house half-a-dozen houses distant, did not respond, and the auctioneer was forced to disencumber himself of his coat, and set to work with a will to remove the heavy packages.

This was what Fanny had planned.

This was the opportunity she sought.

While the man, mentally cursing, was busily employed, she abstracted the cheque-book from the pocket of his coat, tore out half-a-dozen pieces of grey paper, stamped and headed "London and County Bank," and returned the book to the place from whence she took it.

At length the box was pulled out from the heap, and Fanny expressed herself perfectly satisfied, apologizing at the same time for the trouble she had given the unfortunate man.

He did his best to look pleased as he made a civil reply, but it was a dead failure.

"You say it is customary to deposit half the amount," said Fanny.

"Such is the invariable custom."

"If I give you a cheque for the full sum, you will have no objection to my removing the things at once?"

"Most certainly not."

"I will do so."

First, however, our heroine, who had a wonderful aptitude for business, hailed the first empty cab that passed, and had all the packages piled upon the roof and crammed inside.

"Now, sir, I'll give you the cheque."

The auctioneer bowed.

"You've no objection to one on the London and County?"

"Oh, no! In fact, they are my own bankers."

"Indeed; what a remarkable coincidence!" said our heroine, with the most innocent air possible to be imagined.

She took from her pocket the blank cheques she had abstracted, and selected one of the grey slips of paper and proceeded to fill it in leisurely enough.

The signature puzzled her for a moment, but having no time for deliberation, she wrote the name which came uppermost in her mind, and handed the valueless document to the auctioneer.

He received it with profuse acknowledgments, signed a receipt, and put the cheque securely away into his pocket-book.

His politeness carried him so far, that he actually descended the stairs with Fanny, and saw her safe into the cab.

"Where shall I tell the man to drive to, sir?" he asked.

Our heroine had not the least idea, but with admirable presence of mind answered, " No. 9, Grosvenor-street."

The vehicle drove off at a rapid rate, and the auctioneer was left hat in hand, bowing his respectful adieux, and wondering what the deuce could have brought the young swell so far from his own fashionable region to attend a third-rate sale of clothing and personal property in the suburbs.

At last, he settled in his own mind that the young gentleman must have been in love with "that devilish fine gal that lived with Rawlings;" and feeling quite confident that such was the case, and having no misgivings, he went quietly home, had a snug little dinner, and continued perfectly happy till the cheque with which he had been paid was returned to him with " No effects" printed across it.

To say that the unhappy auctioneer stormed would give no adequate idea of the state of mind to which he was reduced, and certainly his pleasure was not increased by discovering the cheque was one abstracted from his own book, and that, in addition, there were four or five others missing.

"Thank heaven! I know the young thief's address," he muttered.

He jumped into the first hansom he met, and was rattled at a good pace to Grosvenor-street.

Arrived at number nine, he knocked a long ponderous rat-tat-tat at the door.

It is needless to say his inquiries for Fanny did not meet with success.

Indeed, much to the contrary.

The powdered menial who answered the door treated him with undisguised contempt.

He persisted in his inquiries.

The flunkey threatened to give him in charge.

He grew indignant,

The footman became furious, and at last he was content to slink away abashed and take refuge in the cab.

His revenge fell upon the poor driver—for he paid him only his exact fare, despite all threats and remonstrances.

I very much fear his wife had a bad time of it that evening, and believe that but for this disastrous occurrence, his youngest boy, Wight Reginald, would have sat up till nine o'clock, as usual, instead of being sent supperless to bed at half-past six.

But to return to Fanny.

By the time she had ridden a mile or two, she began to feel comparatively safe; so stopping the cab, she informed the driver she had altered her mind, and instead of going to her father's house in Grosvenor-street, she would be driven to the north of London, where she wished to obtain lodgings.

The cabman suspected something wrong, but seeing a large fare before him, with the prospect of an additional *douceur* for holding his tongue, said nothing, but did as he was told.

Fanny was entirely ignorant of the geography of the northern portion of the metropolis, and left it entirely to the option of the driver whither she should be taken.

He, rightly imagining that concealment was her great object, took her to a quiet little street, where lodgings were to be had, and where, provided the week's rent was punctually paid in advance, no questions were asked; and there he deposited his fare, together with all her boxes and parcels, and received in return a sum sufficiently large to satisfy even him, and to cause him to remain dumb in spite of the tempting offers of the advertisements in the daily papers—"To the Cabman who took a young gentleman &c., to pay a visit to Messrs. Staff and Whirl, Solicitors, Gray's-Inn."

The street where Fanny sought and obtained lodgings rejoiced in the euphonious name of Little Swinchin-street.

Now Little Swinchin-street was a thoroughfare but little known to the public in general; for it led from an unfinished road, where nobody ever went, to a half-built terrace, where nobody in their right mind would ever want to go to; but the police unfortunately had given Little Swinchin-street a bad name, and, to say the truth, it deserved it.

In the first place, at the corner of the street was a dreary, dismal, desolate-looking public-house. In vain the landlord offered the best stout "three-pence in your own jugs."

The neighbourhood was either shamefully destitute of jugs, or else the inhabitants failed to appreciate the liquor.

Nevertheless, the landlord presented an uncommonly well-to-do appearance, and on Sundays drove out in a gorgeous dog-cart, which was the envy of many much more respectable licensed victuallers.

The way it was managed was a mystery.

The landlord himself was reserved upon the subject; but there were many vague reports about skittles, ratting, cock-fighting, and other noble amusements carried on in his back premises, to which the public-house was only a blind.

But this was only one house of the street.

An air of mystery seemed to pervade the majority of the others.

The day was generally far advanced before the blinds were drawn up—sometimes, indeed, not at all.

About noon, fashionably-attired young gentlemen were occasionally seen to leave these habitations, looking rather sleepy about the eyes and dissolute about the dress.

Then, again, later still in the day, charming young ladies, with cheeks as blooming as rouge could make them, and dresses that looked as if they had been cut out of a book of fashions, would walk quietly down the street and disappear round the corner.

The few respectable inhabitants of the street, who went to bed early, and altogether kept primitive hours, were totally unable to say what time it was when the aforementioned young ladies returned home, except on special occasions—such as a fancy ball at the Holborn, or an extra night at the Argyll—when they returned with a tendency to sing comic songs of a doubtful character, which awoke the echoes of the night.

Fanny, of course, was unaware of the nature of the street in which she had taken up her abode, and, for the first day or two, remained in happy ignorance.

Her first thought, as soon as she was safely housed, was to get rid of her male attire.

But how to do so without creating suspicion?

She did not see her way at all clearly, but, nevertheless, trusted to her usual good fortune; and making up her coat and unmentionables into a neat parcel, she put on a dress suited to her sex, and descended the stairs.

Her landlady honoured her with a steady gaze for some minutes, but made no remark—unless, indeed, a grunt of approval may be considered as such.

When Fanny had made all necessary arrangements, it was too late in the day again to set forth in search of Jack; so ordering tea, she threw herself upon the hard horse-hair sofa, and abandoned herself entirely to the thoughts of her lover, and regrets at having been induced to leave him.

Other thoughts, now that she was left to herself, intruded themselves upon her brain.

Thoughts of home!

Thoughts of her father and her sister Agatha.

It was rather late to begin to have virtuous remembrances, but nevertheless, when she reviewed her past life she was by no means altogether satisfied with it.

It was well enough as a romance, but as a reality, a little of it went a great way.

However, she resolved first to discover Jack, and then hold council with him as to what was best to be done.

She even went so far as to think that he might be induced to marry her, and that they then might settle down in a quiet, prosy, hum-drum every-day life.

Thus thinking, weary and exhausted, she fell asleep.

CHAPTER XXXV.

CONTINUES THE RELATION OF FANNY'S SEARCH AFTER JACK, AND EXPOSES SOME OF THE SNARES TO WHICH AN UNPROTECTED GIRL IS SOMETIMES EXPOSED.

THE morning following that on which Fanny had taken up her abode in Little Swinchin-street, our heroine was up and dressed long before any one else in the house was astir.

Finding it impossible to arouse the sleeping ones, and her anxiety to find Jack momentarily increasing, she set forth alone and breakfastless in quest of her lover.

She knew not in which direction to bend her steps.

Chance led her towards the Strand, and as she paced its weary length, her heart sank within her as she thought how small the chance was of her ever again meeting him she sought.

With her eyes bent upon the ground, she was making her way eastward, when she saw something which made her utter a sudden exclamation of joy.

It was not Jack she saw thus unexpectedly.

It was not even any of his human friends.

It was a dog.

It was FILCHIT!

There could be no doubt about it; there was the tailless dog standing straight before her, regarding her fixedly.

As soon as he saw her, he jumped up and fawned upon her, betraying his joy in a thousand doggish ways.

But who was with him?

The dog surely was not wandering about the crowded streets by himself.

She looked round and saw, leaning against a lamp-post a little way down a by-street, a merry, jolly-looking little fat man, with a rogueish twinkle in his eyes, dressed in a complete suit of grey.

Filchit was evidently on good terms with this little man, for he ran up to him wagging his stump and frisking about right merrily. Then he ran back to Fanny, and said as plainly as a dog could speak—

"Allow me to introduce you to each other."

Fanny took the hint, thinking the stranger might be able to give her some tidings of Jack, and advanced towards him.

He took off his hat politely at her approach.

"I beg your pardon, sir," said Fanny, "but can you give me any tidings of the owner of that dog?"

"Not that I know of, ma'am: but as I have no idea who he belongs to, that is not so surprising."

Fanny sighed.

"The fact is, I happened to go into a police-court to hear the examination of a friend of mine, and when I came out I found this poor animal sitting on the steps. I patted him, and he seemed to take it as an invitation, for he rose up, followed me, and has been with me ever since."

"How very strange!"

"Yes; and what makes it more odd, is that poor Jack Rawlings——"

"Jack Rawlings!"

"Yes, ma'am. Do you know him?"

"It is he I am in search of! That is his dog!"

"The deuce it is. Then I beg your pardon, for I am sorry to say I *can* tell you where he is."

"Where—where? Tell me quickly. Let me go there, or I may miss him."

"No, I think you will find him at home. He is staying with some kind friends who never like to lose sight of him."

"Friends!" cried Fanny, jealously.

"In fact, I am sorry to say, that owing to some slight misunderstanding with a clerical gentleman, respecting a snuff-box, and the obtuseness of the Metropolitan Police, poor Jack Rawlings is at present in prison."

"In prison?"

"Yes."

"How dreadful!"

"It isn't what would be called pleasant."

"Oh, what will he think of me?"

"Think you're a deuced pretty girl," muttered the stranger to himself.

"Are you a friend of his, sir?"

"Well, after a fashion. My name is Gimp. Jim Gimp. Perhaps you've heard him speak of me?"

But Fanny hadn't.

"What prison is he in?"

"Newgate."

Fanny shuddered.

"He will think I have deserted him, that I no longer care for him, when he finds I don't go to him when he is in trouble. I must see him at once."

"Will you accept my escort?"

Fanny looked into the merry, laughter-provoking face of the ventriloquist, and saw she had nothing to fear from him, so she accepted his proffered arm, and the pair made the best of their way to the Old Bailey.

They arrived before the massive portals of Newgate about an hour after his escape had been discovered.

The savage old Cerberus growled forth a whole string of adjectives, which would not repay the trouble of printing, at mention of Jack's name, and proved very uncommunicative, only persisting in his statement that he could not be seen.

Several of the warders came forward, but they only echoed the words of the gatekeeper in tones more or less uncivil.

Jim Gimp, however, took a fine revenge.

Seeing them all clustered round him, he threw his voice to the further end of a long corridor.

"Help—help—murder!" he shrieked in despairing tones, and had the satisfaction of seeing the whole body rush off pell-mell to ascertain the cause of those heartrending cries.

In the confusion he drew Fanny away, and the pair proceeded sorrowfully on their way.

They had not gone any great distance, however, before they heard some one panting and running behind them.

Turning, they faced Jack Horley.

Our hero's munificent present to him had made such an impression upon him that he was resolved to assist him in every way in his power, and had accordingly pursued Jim Gimp to inform him of the escape of Jack Rawlings from Newgate.

He gave them all the particulars with which he was acquainted, and then hurried back as fast as his legs would carry him.

It was a great relief to Fanny to know that her lover was free, but yet the absence of all clue by which to find him made her, if anything, more miserable even than she had been on hearing of his incarceration.

There was nothing more to be done.

Thanking Jim Gimp warmly for his kindness, and refusing his offer to escort her home, she made the best of her way back to Little Swinchin-street, accompanied by Filchit.

She retired to rest early, and next morning awoke with a racking headache and pains in all her limbs; indeed, so very poorly did she feel that she gave up all idea of going out to prosecute her search for Jack that day.

In the afternoon she had a visit from her landlady.

Mrs. Gander was as repulsive-looking a woman as could well be imagined.

Her features were large and coarse and of a Jewish type, while her large full lower lip and heavy double chin scarcely added to her personal charms.

From what has already been said respecting the manners and customs of the inhabitants of Little Swinchin-street, the reader will easily understand that letting lodgings was not the sole source from which Mrs. Gander derived her money.

The moment this wicked old woman set eyes on Fanny in her feminine attire, she formed a plan for compelling her to comply with her disgusting designs.

But Fanny was not so easily to be caught.

She had lived long enough in London and seen enough of life to be upon her guard; and although she pretended not to comprehend the hints her landlady dropped in the course of conversation, she in reality understood quite enough to make her regret she had ever entered her house, and to cause her to form a resolution of leaving it the first thing next morning.

Mrs. Gander left her lodger's room tolerably well satisfied with the result of her mission.

She believed Fanny to be much more innocent than she really was, and arranged her plans accordingly.

When Fanny retired to her bed-room, she noticed, with some alarm, that the key had been abstracted, but, not thinking her landlady would dare proceed to open violence, she contented herself with calling Filchit into the apartment and barricading the door with a small washing-stand.

This done, she undressed herself, and was soon buried in a sweet refreshing slumber.

An hour after midnight she was awakened by a thundering crash.

Fanny, as in duty bound, screamed.

Somebody swore.

Fanny cried "Help!" and stretched her lungs more than she had ever done since she used to sing "Christopher's Curse" at the Grand Abyssinian.

The intruder, however, paid little attention to her shrieks, and as for the inhabitants of the house, they knew well enough what the cries meant, for they had heard them before, perhaps uttered them themselves.

"But what does it matter to us?" said they; so they turned round in bed, and went to sleep again.

By the dim light of an apology for a moon struggling through the clouds, Fanny could only discern that the intruder into her apartment was of the opposite sex.

Unhesitatingly the ruffian moved to her bedside.

There was just sufficient light for him to see the lovely

face and exquisite shape showing through the light covering.

Inflamed by the sight, he endeavoured to place his arm round the shrinking figure, but Fanny knew a trick worth two of that.

When he thought to grasp her lovely rounded form he found only the bolster in his arms.

Fanny had slipped out on the opposite side of the bed with a celerity only equalled by that of a harlequin.

The intruder flung the bolster from him with a curse.

Then he looked round.

There stood Fanny, her long night-dress making her look like the " Woman in White," on the opposite side of the bed.

" Now don't be coy, my dear," said he; " you must give in sooner or later."

" Advance a step nearer at your peril."

" Ha, ha, ha!"

" If you dare to touch me, I'll mark you in a way you'll never forget."

" We'll see that, my angel," was the laughing reply, as he bounded over the bed and caught Fanny in his arms.

Then ensued a terrific struggle.

In a few moments Fanny's night-dress was torn to pieces, and she looked a trifle more like Mother Eve i n the matter of costume than is generally considered proper; but she paid no heed to this, for her blood was thoroughly roused, and she determined to punish the impertinent intruder before she let him go.

Filchit, who had viewed the whole proceedings with his head on one side and a look of deep interest, at this moment gave vent to a low growl.

Fanny had forgotten his presence, but the moment she heard his growl she determined to make him come to her assistance.

" Filchit!—seize him, Filchit!—seize him, good dog!"

Filchit needed no second bidding.

The assaulter had taken off his coat when he entered the room, and, as his back was turned towards the dog, he presented a fair field for a bite.

Filchit availed himself of it in a moment, sprang at the violator, and seized him with a powerful grip.

In an instant it had the desired effect.

The man loosened his hold of Fanny, and she, ashamed of her scant drapery, leaped into bed again, convinced that she was not likely again to be assaulted by the unprincipled ruffian.

In that she was right.

Howling dismally, Filchit still holding fast, he careered round and round the room, making as much noise as a legion of swine.

The uproar was too great to pass unnoticed.

Mrs. Gander, accompanied by four or five curious and affrighted damsels, entered the room, and a pretty scene it was, truly, which met their gaze.

Fanny lay panting in bed, crimson with indignation; while the ruffianly intruder was rushing wildly about the room, putting everything in confusion, and howling with pain, with Filchit hanging firmly on to his hinder quarters by his teeth.

CHAPTER XXXVI.

CONTAINS A SHORT ACCOUNT OF THE STRANGE PLACE AND THE EXTRAORDINARY WAY IN WHICH JACK AND FANNY MET AFTER THEIR LONG SEPARATION.

AFTER the events related in the last chapter, it was, of course, impossible for Fanny any longer to remain an inmate of Mrs. Gander's house.

But there was a trifling difficulty attached to her leaving; namely, that the woman claimed a week's rent, and Fanny had not the wherewithal to meet the demand.

This caused her great uneasiness.

She was determined not to pass another night beneath that roof; but without money, and without luggage, nameless and friendless, where could she go?

What hotel or lodging-house of a reputable character would admit her?

Mrs. Gander refused to allow her to remove her boxes till the rent was paid, but at the same time threw out unmistakeable hints that, if she were so disposed, she might earn large sums of money and lead a happy life of gaiety.

Fanny understood her.

She knew full well the vicious, depraved character of her landlady, and the wicked villanous manner in which she got her money.

She shrank back from her proposals.

She answered her with the indignation and anger which should ever meet such devilish suggestions, and then, to recover her equanimity and to reflect upon the course she should adopt, she put on her bonnet and went for a walk in the Park.

Feeling herself rather exhausted after proceeding some distance, she sat down upon one of the benches.

She had not been there long, before two rough-looking men threw themselves upon the grass at no great distance from her, and commenced a conversation.

They were so placed that, owing to a clump of trees, they could not see the close proximity of our heroine, which fact was fully shown by the freedom with which they discussed a variety of nefarious projects.

Their conversation was intermixed with slang and interlarded with oaths; but Fanny was able to gather from it that they were arranging for a burglary.

The victim was to be an unfortunate lodger in a certain Mrs. MacSpringer's boarding-house.

He was known to have a large sum about him in banknotes, and this it was that the robbers proposed to seize.

The following night was the one appointed for the attempt; and Fanny heard in detail how an entrance was to be effected the back way, and the plan of the house, and the room where the innocent victim slept.

She formed a sudden resolution.

" They mean to rob him to-morrow night—why should not I do it to-night?" thus ran her thoughts. " I know all their plans, why should not I carry them out?—I want money, and see no other way to get it."

Actuated by this motive, she paid a visit to a pawnbroker's, and leaving behind all the under clothing she could dispense with, with the money thus obtained she purchased a second-hand, musty, dirty boy's suit of corduroy, and then, making her way in the evening to the most retired spot she could find, donned the male attire, and, as soon as it was sufficiently late, made her way to Mrs. MacSpringer's lodging-house.

She found everything there exactly as she had heard it described, and a little after midnight she managed to obtain an entrance into the house.

This done, she crept silently upstairs, and reached the door of the room which, from the description she had overheard, was that occupied by the wealthy lodger.

She tried the door.

It was unlocked, and she entered.

The owner of the bank-notes, little dreaming of harm, was fast asleep in bed, snoring most unmelodiously.

Fanny looked around the room, but could see no desk or box likely to contain the property.

It must be under the sleeper's pillow.

Still he snored on in one long dreary tone; and Fanny, emboldened, advanced to the bedside, and placed her hand cautiously beneath the pillow.

Now, having one's hair pulled is by no means pleasant, but when one is awakened out of a sound slumber by a sudden twinge of one's flowing locks, and then, opening one's eyes, one perceives a youth attired in corduroy standing over one, it certainly is, by no means, what would be called pleasant.

The sleeper, to my mind, was therefore perfectly justified, under the above mentioned circumstances, in starting up in bed, and calling out an exclamation which is best not written.

But before he could take any further steps his eyes opened wider than they had ever been before.

" Fanny!" he cried, in accents of the greatest surprise.

" Jack!" she answered, if anything more surprised than he.

Thus it was our hero and heroine met after their long separation.

It took some time for mutual explanation, and it is almost needless to say that neither Jack nor Fanny had very much sleep that night.

There were endless questions to ask, innumerable adventures to relate, and morning was far advanced before their weary eyes told them it would be as well to have an hour or two of repose before commencing the fatigues of the day.

Mrs. MacSpringer was inexpressibly shocked, when Jack came down to breakfast, to see him bring with him a young and lovely girl (for Jack had sent out for a proper dress for our heroine), and gave her decided opinion that she wasn't going to have such carryings on in *her* house, and hinted that our hero had better look out for other lodgings, to which Jack replied it was the very thing he meant to do.

As soon after breakfast as possible, Fanny, accompanied by our hero, chartered a fly, and drove off to Little Swinchin-street, where, by dint of a good amount of bullying, they got all Fanny's things from the avaricious grasp of Mrs. Gander.

Jack, happy in the possession of the large sum of money which had been sent him anonymously when in Newgate, took good lodgings in the neighbourhood of the British Museum, and he and Fanny once more entered upon a happy, loving life together.

Still this was not to last.

Fanny, much as she loved Jack, was seized with an irresistible craving after home.

She longed once more to see her father, but she feared to present herself before his enraged eyes.

Then she began to get jealous of Jack.

He continually went out for hours at a time without telling her his object, leaving her alone with her reflections.

This in itself constituted a grievance; and, as Fanny was not wholly bad by nature, it is only reasonable that she should at times feel a pining after those she had left at home.

This feeling increased day by day, but the result did not come for some days.

But that deserves a separate chapter.

CHAPTER XXXVII.

SOME STRANGE ADVENTURES BEFAL MISS FANNY IN CONNEXION WITH A CERTAIN REVEREND GENTLEMAN VERY POPULAR AMONG FASHIONABLE CHURCH-GOERS.

SINCE Fanny had left Virginia House she had been unable to indulge her passion for the romantic to its full extent.

Her own series of startling adventures would have been the very thing for her—in print. As it was, the reality and the danger attending her pranks had somewhat destroyed the illusion.

The theory was glorious, the practice so-so. Theory was to practice like Jove's tipple to the dustman's "heavy."

Already she had reviewed her flight from Miss Mac-Spartan's model establishment in a hundred different lights. It was deliciously jolly, and Jack was a handsome and thoroughly good fellow. And as her thoughts turned upon Jack, she registered mental ladylike vows never to leave him.

Now, on the other side, was her conduct exactly reputable? Had her doings been quite respectable? And what must her father and sister think of her?

Boldly as she struggled with the blues, putting her present mode of life in its most favourable aspect, her thoughts would return to her father and sister. On the former's account she felt strangely uneasy—a mixture of odd feelings she could not understand.

Had she been a young lady addicted to presentiments, she must have been greatly alarmed; as it was, there was nothing definite in her fears—for such they were—and she strove to repress them, and silence all self-reproach on the subject by mentally voting herself a noodle and homesick.

In this state of her feelings, she was one day amusing herself with the "agony column" of the *Times*, making, in her vivid imagination, whole histories of blighted hopes, forlorn hearts, and faithless swains out of the flowery advertisements, when her eye lighted upon the following:—

"FRANCES WHITE.—For God's sake return home to your poor, ill-used father, who is upon the point of death, and you alone the cause of all his sufferings. Lose no time in coming to his bedside, where you will find your once-sister, AGATHA."

Who can say with what bitter heart-burnings and self-reproaches Fanny White read this appalling advertisement? She accused herself of being her father's murderess, and cast the paper containing the fatal intelligence from her in horror. It seemed like a silent accuser risen up to denounce her as a parricide.

In the first burst of grief and despair she would most certainly have laid violent hands upon herself, had the means

been within her reach. Happily, the thought never crossed her, or Father Thames, the suicide's friend, might have counted one victim the more.

As she grew calmer she began to think how she could repair, at least in part, the mischief she had caused.

She picked up the paper to see if she had omitted anything, and found, to her dismay, that it was a week old.

"Good heavens!" she exclaimed, "then he's already——"

A rising sensation at the throat choked her utterance, and she could not, even to herself, pronounce the fatal word.

Her heart was full to bursting, and she dashed herself on the ground, moaning in bitter anguish. At length a flood of tears relieved her throbbing head, and she arose refreshed, and if not comforted, at least much calmer.

"I'll go at once," she said, as she wiped away the traces of grief from her beautiful but now pallid cheek. "It may not even now be—too—too late!"

A visible shudder ran through her frame as the ominous "too late" escaped her. Recovering herself, however, she began some hasty preparations for her journey, which she completed with such alacrity that in a few minutes she was ready to depart.

"Poor Jack!" she murmured, as she was leaving the room.

She paused a moment on the threshold—advanced a few paces, and stood still, as if uncertain how to proceed.

"No," she exclaimed, "I can't leave him without one word of explanation. I have been the cause of his imprudence as much as he of mine."

Saying this, she seated herself at the table and wrote the following:—

"DEAR JACK—

"By the time you receive this, I shall be far away. I shall always love you the same; it is, therefore, only by giving you up for ever that I hope to atone for the misery I have caused to my (father scratched out) many kind friends. Good-bye, dear Jack! God bless you!—Your loving FANNY."

She kissed this brief farewell over and over again, blotting it sadly with her tears. She then cut off a lock of her golden hair, laid it on the letter, and, unable to trust herself further, rushed from the room.

Darting along the streets almost at a run, endeavouring to drown the sad thoughts that would present themselves by the quickness of her movements, Fanny soon arrived at the corner of Piccadilly.

Here she inquired at the booking-office about the Kingston coach, and was told that it had left about half-an-hour, and that there would not be another that day.

What was to be done? Was there no other conveyance handy? None, was the dreadful reply, and poor Fanny White turned away in despair.

At this instant a dashing drag pulled up at the booking-office, and a clerical looking-gentleman jumped out, and ran past Fanny into the office.

"You have a hamper here for the Rev. Hugh Bell, I believe?"

"The Cedars, Kingston?"

"Yes."

"Here it is, sir. Three-and six to pay, please."

Fanny looked round at the word "Kingston," and evidently attracted the booking clerk's attention, for he said to the gentleman in a stage whisper—

"This young lady's for Kingston, sir. Just missed the coach."

"What then?"

"Nothing, sir, only the young lady seems very much grieved, and I thought, if you'd no objection, that——"

"Oh! I see."

The clerical gentleman walked up to Fanny, and bowed with a peculiar grace and weight, which seemed rather to belong to the laity than to the cloth.

"I hear, miss, that you have been unfortunate enough to miss the coach. If you will do me the honour to accept a seat in my drag, I'm sure you will be very welcome, and I shall have the pleasure of landing you at Kingston some time before that lumbering old springless coach arrives."

"Oh, sir," replied Fanny, "you are very kind, but——"

"You will not refuse me, I beg. Allow me."

Saying which, he took her hand and helped her into the chaise.

"Rattle away, Watkins," said the Rev. Hugh Bell to the coachman, as he jumped in and seated himself opposite Fanny.

They passed some four or five minutes in silence, during which Fanny, having got over the great difficulty, had turned her thoughts to the object of her journey, and all unconscious of the presence of the reverend gentleman, was soliloquising half aloud, while an expression of grief once more appeared on her handsome countenance.

Her travelling companion, seeing that she was in distress, considerately forbore breaking in upon her meditations, until a big tear rolled down poor Fanny's cheek, and then the divine thought it high time to speak.

"Are you a resident of Kingston, may I ask?"

"Yes—no—yes—that is, I was some time since."

"Indeed! Might I ask your name?"

"Certainly. White—Frances White."

The Reverend Hugh Bell seemed rather struck with this.

"Related to Mr. Jobson White, of 'The Rookery?'"

Fanny blushed deeply, as she replied—

"I am his daughter, sir."

"Oh! indeed. I'm very proud to make your acquaintance, Miss White."

Then followed an awkward pause in the conversation.

"Good heavens!" murmured Fanny to herself, "he knows all about it. I have, no doubt, become a bye-word in Kingston, and shall dread to be seen in the town. Another disgrace on which I did not count."

Her companion, on his side, appeared to be in deep meditation, and as he from time to time glanced furtively across at her, pretending to look in another direction if his eye met hers, it was evident that our heroine was the subject of his musings, and tended to confirm the unhappy girl's suspicions.

This silence had continued for some minutes, when it was broken by the Reverend Hugh Bell saying, in a low earnest voice—

"Miss White—you'll excuse my remarking——"

Fanny turned pale.

"My remarking that I am acquainted with your father—that, in fact, he is my personal friend, and that I knew of your—your—ahem! absence from home, and the grief it has caused him, and——"

"You do, sir?" said Fanny, bursting into tears. "Do you know if he still—still lives?"

"I was with him last night, Miss Frances, until a late hour, administering some spiritual consolation to him—and he was dangerously bad."

"Very dangerously?"

"It was thought probable that he would not last the night out. But let us hope. Good heavens! Miss White, are you ill?"

Fanny sank all of a lump down on the seat, and a jerk of the chaise, at the moment the Reverend Hugh Bell stooped forward to catch her, precipitated the fainting girl into his arms.

The worthy divine's face flushed and his eyes brightened as he held the plump, symmetrical form of the unconscious Fanny in his embrace, and he glanced nervously on each side of the road.

They had already passed Hammersmith, and there was no one about; so the Reverend Hugh Bell gently raised his lovely burden, and bending his head down, pressed his lips to hers, at the same time squeezing her fair form with fervour.

The earnestness of the embrace aroused poor Fanny, for without opening her eyes she murmured—

"Jack, dear Jack?"

"Who the devil's Jack," said the reverend gentleman.

This brought Fanny to her senses, and she blushed as she begged his pardon, and endeavoured to extricate herself from her awkward position, which was rather a difficult operation, so loth did the gallant churchman appear to part with her.

Twice she essayed to rise, but each time fell back, the Reverend Hugh accidentally pushing her as he put out his arm to aid her.

"Will you allow me to get up?" said Fanny, in rather a loud tone.

"Certainly, Miss White," said the Reverend Hugh, quickly. "Will you take my hand?"

"Thank you," said Fanny, rather coldly, as she seated herself and arranged her skirts.

"I trust you are better, Miss White," said the Reverend Hugh, somewhat flustered.

"Thank you—yes."

"It was a matter of some difficulty for you to get up,

Miss White—you had fallen so awkwardly into my arms—if, indeed, you could do anything awkwardly."

Fanny was but half satisfied, so she remained silent.

"Will you, please, make my best respects at the 'Rookery,' both to your poor father and Miss Agatha?"

Fanny bowed.

"I must be mistaken," she mused. "It would be so strangely at variance with his previous behaviour—and a clergyman, too. Besides, knowing my father, he would never presume upon what has passed—No!"

The subject of her thoughts was getting uneasy at her silence.

"I trust the faintness has passed, Miss White."

"Perfectly, I thank you. We cannot be far from Kingston now, Mr. Bell?"

"About half-an-hour will bring us there. But I was not aware that you knew my name."

"I heard it mentioned at the booking-office."

"Indeed! You must feel very anxious, no doubt, Miss White, to be with your father."

"I do," said Fanny, with a deep-drawn sigh; "and at the same time I dread to meet his eye."

"Dread?"

"Yes. You know my poor father and I did not agree latterly."

This was the mildest form she had the moral courage to put her conduct into to a stranger.

"And I wish I had some one to go first—to prepare the way, as it were."

"I should be most happy," began the Reverend Hugh Bell, "if——"

"If you only would, Mr. Bell," interrupted Fanny, leaning forward eagerly, and placing her hand entreatingly on his arm, "I should owe you an eternal debt of gratitude."

The Reverend Hugh Bell took her hand in his, and squeezed it gently.

"I should be most happy, Miss White, if I thought you would be benefited by my interference."

As he said this he moved over to her side, still retaining her hand in his, at the same time excusing himself by saying—

"I hope I do not incommode you, Miss White, but I should not wish my coachman to hear anything. Servants are so talkative."

"You are very considerate, Mr. Bell," said Fanny. "But should you object to—to——"

"Certainly not," said the Reverend Hugh, "only I consider such scenes should be confined alone to members of the family."

"Alas! that's true," said Fanny, her head drooping forward on her bosom.

Her *compagnon du voyage* gave her hand a sympathetic squeeze, and his arm gradually stole round her waist.

Fanny allowed it to remain unnoticed for a minute or two, but returning to herself, she was about to address some question to the gentleman, when she discovered the extraordinary lengths that his sympathy was leading him, and endeavoured to disengage herself; but the susceptible ecclesiastic held her firmly.

"Let me go, sir!" exclaimed Fanny, indignantly. "How dare you!"

"My dear Miss White, I assure you——"

"Unhand me instantly!" said Fanny, struggling violently. "What have I done that you should presume to insult me so?"

"Insult you! Nay, Miss White, I swear—"

"You shall suffer for this, sir!" exclaimed our heroine, as he drew her towards him, and, in spite of her struggles, imprinted a kiss on her cheek.

"You'll have the whole county down upon us, Miss White," said the Reverend Hugh Bell, getting somewhat alarmed at her high tones.

Fanny had disdained to scream, or she might have settled it at once. As it was, she managed, by a vigorous jerk, to disengage herself, and darted over to the other seat.

"Stop, coachman; I'll get out here."

The Reverend Hugh caught her by the dress, and endeavoured to draw her towards him; but Fanny, whose blood was now thoroughly aroused, delivered him a round-handed blow in the face, that caused him to stagger back, and the blood spurted from his nose and messed his reverend face.

At the same instant the coachman, in obedience to Fanny's summons, pulled up, and she jumped out.

She ran along, scarcely knowing how far she was from

Kingston, and only thinking of avoiding the Reverend
Hugh Bell and his loathsome caresses.

"If I ever have a chance," she said, "I'll have ample
revenge on that insolent parson. He'd better look to it the
next time we meet."

She began to look about her, and was somewhat alarmed
to find that she did not recognise the locality. In her per-
plexity she came to a standstill, and it was with considerable
relief she saw a man coming towards her.

"How far is it to Kingston, pray?"

"Not five minutes' walk, miss; but you're coming away
from it. You must turn back, and take the first turning on
the left."

"I've just passed there."

"Ah! you've got out of the main road. You can see
the town from that turning."

"Thank you."

She quickly retraced her steps, and in a few minutes she
stood at the lodge leading to her father's house.

With a trembling hand and a sickening sensation at
the heart she rang the bell. A strange porter opened
the gate, and in rather an off-hand manner asked her
business.

"I am going to see Mr. White."

"No you aint."

"What do you mean?"

"Now, it's no use a making a disturbance; I've got orders
to admit nobody."

"Do you know who I am, you insolent fellow?"

"No, and I don't care!"

And with this he endeavoured to close the gate, but
Fanny pushed resolutely against it and endeavoured to force
her way in.

The man caught her by the arm and endeavoured to force
her back by brutally twisting it round. Fanny, however,
slipped from his clutch, and suddenly seizing him with both
hands by the throat, dashed him against the gate.

"For the future, fellow," she said, stalking majestically on,
"learn to treat your mistress with respect."

"Mistress?"

"I am your master's youngest daughter."

"Oh! I'm very sorry, I'm sure, miss," said the man,
shaking himself together, and advancing towards her with
a cringing step, "but Miss Agatha gave me very particular
orders to admit no one."

"What! literally *no one?*"

"Them was her words, miss."

"But she surely told you——"

"Nothing, miss, but that no one was to be admitted—
pertikerlarly females!"

"Good heavens!" thought Fanny, as she passed on
towards the house, "can it be possible that my own sister is
so turned against me, or has she a particular object in keeping me from my poor father?"

She rang the bell. It tinkled out a low, mournful death-
knell that struck dismally on her ear. The knocker had
likewise been muffled, and everything seemed to denote the
almost immediate presence of death.

The door was opened by one of the servants, who, in spite
of the thick veil she wore, instantly recognised our heroine.

"Good heavens! Miss Fanny!"

"Ah! Horrocks. How is my f——, your master?"

The man made no reply.

"He's not——" gasped Fanny.

"No, Miss Fanny. *Not yet.*"

"Is he lying in his own room?"

"Yes, Miss Fanny."

Without waiting for more, Fanny ran lightly upstairs.

A thick Turkey carpet had been laid down on the landing to
deaden the sound. A door stood ajar on the left, and a faint
cough from within announced it to be the sick-chamber.

Fanny paused on the threshold and placed her hand to
her heart, endeavouring to summon up courage to enter.
Her hand touched the door-handle, but she withdrew it
affrighted, thereby causing it to emit the faintest possible
chink.

Slight as the noise was, it evidently caught the invalid's ear.

"That's her, Aggy!" exclaimed a peevish voice; "I knew
she would come!"

"Don't distress yourself on her account, dear father; she
can have no good feeling left—the wanton!"

"Silence!" almost shrieked the old man; "how dare you
speak thus of your own flesh and blood?"

"I speak thus warmly on your account, dear father."

"Judge not, lest ye be judged!" broke in the sufferer, with
awful solemnity:

The unhappy listener leant against the doorway for
support, and raised her hand to her throbbing head.

"There again! What's that?" exclaimed the old man,
who had caught the faint rustle of Fanny's garments.

His daughter was now convinced that there was some one
without, and walking on tiptoe across the room, she noiselessly opened the door, and the two sisters stood face to face.

CHAPTER XXXVIII.

MORE RESPECTING THE INHABITANTS OF TWEEZER'S
ALLEY, WITH ESPECIAL REFERENCE TO PHIL DAVENANT.

MR. PHILIP DAVENANT was of good family.

That is to say, his mother's second cousin had married an
Irish nobleman, and he had several relations occupying
tolerably good positions in the world.

Somehow, however, they were not inclined to do very
much for him, or perhaps it would be more correct to say
they were tired of holding out a helping hand to one who
it seemed was doomed never to rise in the social scale.

They called him a spendthrift—and in that they were perfectly right, for Phil Davenant had no more notion of saving
and economy than he had of flying.

He was one of those merry, careless, good-hearted fellows
who, as long as they have a shilling in their pockets, are
willing to share it with any one in need.

When Mr. Philip had money to spend, he spent it in a
jovial manner—whistling and singing the while, without a
thought of the morrow.

When Mr. Philip had no money (which was of much
more frequent occurrence), he whistled and sung just as
merrily, as he buttoned his coat high up in the neck to hide
the want of linen, and inked his sock so that the crack in his
boot might be less perceptible.

There is little wonder, perhaps, that his relations got tired
of assisting such a reckless character; and there was no one
who acknowledged his faults with greater readiness than
Phil. Nevertheless, he took no steps to improve, and continued living from hand to mouth in the best way he could.

Had Phil Davenant been called upon to state his profession, it would have been rather a puzzling job.

He was naturally clever, and could turn his hand to
almost anything.

He had been clerk in a bank, scene-shifter at a trans-
pontine theatre, actor of "supers'" parts, newspaper
reporter, comic singer at a "free-and-easy," and half-a-score
other occupations.

From one cause or another, he had given them all up, one
after the other, and was now earning a precarious livelihood
as messenger in a money-lender's office in the daytime, and
check-taker at one of the theatres at night.

It will readily be understood that neither of these
employments proved very lucrative—but what did that
matter to Phil?

As long as he had his bread and cheese in the middle of
the day, and his pint of stout and pipe at night, he went
about shouting out merry songs in a fine mellow voice, and
slapping his acquaintances on the back with a violence
which made them wince again.

Perhaps, Phil Davenant's great weakness was admiration
for the softer sex.

He was not dissolute or depraved, still he could not help
falling in love with every pretty face he saw; and, to tell the
truth, there were several pretty faces that could not help
returning the compliment.

Phil Davenant was by no means bad-looking, and when
he was got up for a Sunday walk with the then idol of his
heart, cut rather a dashing appearance.

Who was to know the time he had expended in folding
and tying that gorgeous scarf so that neither the frayed ends
nor the dirty portion should be visible?

Who was to know how often the coat had been turned,
and that the well-cut trousers had not been made for him?
While as for his jewellery, without a microscopic examination, one would have been led to believe he carried fifty
pounds' worth about him at least, in rings, scarf-pins, and
watch-chains.

However, in spite of all his fine appearance, Mr. Phil
Davenant had to screw and pinch occasionally; and it was

JACK RAWLINGS IS INVITED TO PAY A VISIT BEHIND THE SCENES.

impossible that on the salary he received from his two employers he could live in very grand style.

To tell the truth, this gentleman lodged in Tweezer's-alley, and Mrs. O'Flannagan was his landlady.

Now it is to be hoped the reader has neither forgotten Mrs. O'Flannagan nor the mysterious lady who took up her abode in that worthy dame's house, for she has by no means played her part yet in this story; and, strange as it may seem, this very Mr. Phil Davenant is about to become implicated in it.

And this is how it came about.

Phil had returned from the theatre after the conclusion of his duties, and was sitting in the barely-furnished room which answered the purposes of dining-hall, sitting-room, and sleeping apartment to him. He had just finished his second pipe, and was deliberating whether he would drink the remainder of his porter then, or leave it a little longer, when the door of the apartment opened, and a stranger stood before him.

The stranger was a young woman of remarkable beauty. She was tall, and of a commanding appearance. Her beautiful blue eyes wore a look of extreme melancholy, while a mouth as lovely as a rosebud was compressed firmly, as if no power on earth could ever stamp a smile upon those lips.

Her hair rippled in golden waves above a high, white forehead, and altogether Phil Davenant thought he had never in his life seen so lovely a creature, and straightway fell in love with her, and resolved to forget Mademoiselle Henri, his last flame, a dancer at the theatre where he was employed.

Phil Davenant started to his feet when this lovely apparition entered the room.

From the description he had received, he recognised her at once as his mysterious fellow-lodger.

He made no doubt that, being strange in the house, she had mistaken his room for her own.

He said as much.

"I have made no mistake," said his visitor, in sweet, plaintive tones; "I merely wished to have some conversation with you."

Phil stared in amazement. There was something in the lady's manner which entirely prevented his attributing the same motive to her for entering his apartment at so late an hour, that he might have given to Mademoiselle Henri, had she made her appearance there.

"It is rather late," stammered he, at length, in reply.

"I know it. I selected this hour to visit you, as I wished to prevent the possibility of our conversation being overheard."

Phil offered his visitor the solitary chair which his apartment boasted.

She declined it, but advanced further into the room, closing the door carefully behind her.

Now Phil Davenant possessed a vast amount of that very useful quality called "cheek," but, for once in his life, he was completely taken aback.

It was a mystery he was totally unable to fathom, and he could do nothing but stare at his visitor in blank amazement, and wonder what the deuce it all meant.

There was something in her air and manner, which told him as plainly as possible that such speeches and flatteries as he would have used ordinarily would, in this case, be entirely out of place.

"Is there anything I can do for you, madam?" he asked, at length.

"Yes."

"I am sure any service I can render you I shall be only too happy."

"You can do me a very great service."

"Give it a name, ma'am."

"It is a request I have to make which will sound very odd coming from my lips, but that you should grant it, is necessary to the furtherance of my plans."

"What is it?"

"Marry me!"

"Mar—ry—you!" gasped Phil.

"Yes."

"Marry!"

"That is the service I wish you to render me."

"The deuce!"

"I see I surprise you."

"You do, indeed."

"My proposition needs explanation?"

"I think it does."

"Will you give me your attention for a short time?"

"Certainly."

"To begin, then—I am alone in the world."

"So I suppose."

"I have a great object in life—an object before which everything must give way—an object which has transformed me to what I am, has taken from me all woman's nature, and made me almost a fiend."

Phil Davenant began to think she was a lunatic, and felt rather uneasy.

She seemed to read this thought, and answered it.

"No," said she, "I am not mad—not yet—though Heaven knows I have gone through enough to deprive me of my senses; but at present I am as sane as yourself. Listen while I plead some justification for the request I have made you. As I told you, I have one great object alone for which to live——"

"May I venture to inquire what that is?"

"I cannot tell you."

"Then may I ask in what way my marriage with you will further your end."

"I am about to explain. I am alone in the world—I once was called beautiful——"

"Indeed you are so still."

"Thank you, sir; but I am not inclined for compliments. I was about to observe that the life of a young and unprotected woman in the great metropolis is fraught with danger. What I need is a protector—not a husband."

Phil bowed. He did not as yet see the exact point at which his fair visitor was aiming.

"To put it in a few words, the proposal I wish to make to you is this:—I wish you to allow me the use of your name, and to be able to turn to you (in public only) as my husband. In return for this, I will pay all expenses of lodging and so on, and whenever I may require you to assist me in any way I will pay you a stipulated sum for your services."

"Bless my heart!" said Phil; "I never had such a proposal made to me in my life!"

"I suppose not. Is it a bargain?"

"You wish for a husband in name only?"

"Precisely."

"It is very strange."

"Do you agree?"

Phil rubbed his chin reflectively.

"What answer do you make?"

"Will you give me time to deliberate?"

"Five minutes."

"You will not require me to go against the law in any way?"

"No."

"Nor to commit any crime?"

"No—no."

"Well, then, it's a bargain."

"You agree?"

"I do."

"Thank you—thank you. You have relieved my mind of a great weight."

"When shall the ceremony take place?"

"No ceremony is necessary."

"Not necessary?"

"No. It is only the name of wife I require, and that you can give me."

"With pleasure."

"Thank you again, a thousand times."

In her gratitude the fair girl took Phil's hand in hers and pressed it warmly.

Phil Davenant, emboldened by this, advanced nearer.

"Let me at least seal the marriage-contract on those lips," said he.

In an instant the whole appearance of his visitor changed. Her eyes seemed to flash fire, as, drawing herself up to her full height, she replied—

"Not a step nearer, sir—not a single step, or you shall form a nearer acquaintance with this!" and she took from the bosom of her dress a sharp-pointed glittering stiletto.

Phil started back.

The lady continued, more calmly, "There is no reason why we should not remain good friends, and that will surely be pleasanter; but remember the slightest attempt at familiarity on your part will turn me into your enemy. You understand me?"

"Perfectly."

"You agree to all my terms?"

"I do."

"Then for the present, adieu. To-morrow I will tell you what I wish you to do first."

"Good night, madam."

She replied with a stately bend of the head, and left the apartment.

Phil threw himself into his solitary chair with a vacant, bewildered expression upon his face, and stared for some time at the ceiling in silence.

"Well, of all the rummy goes I ever heard of," soliloquized he, "this beats them. Ha, ha! Phil Davenant passing off as a married man! I wonder what the little Henri will say to it. Well, it is a queer start."

Upon the strength of this, Mr. Phil filled and lit his pipe, and smoked reflectively for some time, till the gray dawn made its appearance struggling through the dirt-encrusted window of his attic, when, remembering he must be at the office in a few hours, he knocked out the ashes from his pipe and tumbled into bed for a short snooze before beginning a fresh day.

And how did the fair young girl pass the night?

All through the long long dreary hours she paced up and down the narrow bed-room she had occupied, muttering incoherently to herself; but ever and anon one word rose clear and distinct above the others, pronounced with the emphasis of concentrated hatred, and that word was—

"REVENGE!"

CHAPTER XXXIX.

SHOWS HOW OUR HERO SOUGHT TO CONSOLE HIMSELF FOR THE LOSS OF HIS LADY-LOVE.

WHEN Jack Rawlings discovered, instead of the fair and lovely girl, a letter addressed to himself in tremulous handwriting, his heart misgave him, for he felt something had gone wrong.

With many doubts and fears he broke the seal, and read the words Fanny had written him before starting for Kingston.

Now Jack was occasionally rather hasty in jumping at conclusions, and no sooner had he read the epistle than he settled in his own mind that our heroine was faithless, and, as he himself expressed it, had gone off with that brute of a Harry Belvoir or some other infernal scamp.

Now, although we know that in this instance his opinion had no foundation, still he was in some measure justified in arriving at this conclusion; but far be it from me to attempt to extenuate Jack in the course he adopted to show how little he cared for the loss of the fair one.

The truth is he did care very much, but his pride would not allow him to confess it.

During the whole of the daytime he lolled about indoors, smoking a great deal more than was good for him, and abusing in good round terms the female sex in general, and Miss Fanny White in particular.

As the evening drew on Master Jack became more and more restless, and at last, unable any longer to remain alone with his own gloomy thoughts, he put on his hat and went forth into the gas-lit streets, and whistled to the dog Filchit to follow him.

Caring little whither he went, he turned his steps westward and arrived before very long in front of the door of one of the minor theatres.

Now it so chanced that at this theatre there happened to be a great attraction.

A new burlesque had been produced, in which all the male characters were personated by ladies, and as it happened that all the parts were equally good, it only remained for the dear creatures to outshine each other in the matter of dress, and the consequence was that a general curtailment of skirts had taken place.

Now Jack had ever had an eye for a well-shaped calf; indeed, but for what he had seen, through the hole in the palings of Mr. Kanem's establishment, of Fanny's extremities, the whole course of his life might have been different; so he was not long in making up his mind to enter the dramatic establishment, before the portal of which he had lingered to peruse the play-bill.

Leaving Filchit outside to amuse himself as best he might, he paid his admission, and in a very few minutes found himself reclining in a comfortable orchestra stall, waiting for the green baize to rise.

The overture commenced and ended, the curtain rose, and the burlesque commenced.

Now this particular burlesque differed but little from others of the same species.

There was the usual amount of jokes and bad puns, the proper complement of funny songs, and a sufficient number of comic dances to make a merry, lively, sparkling piece, and Jack was well pleased and laughed heartily.

Now it so happened that in one particular scene there was a grand pantomimic procession.

It struck Jack that one of the ugliest masks gave him a nod of recognition as he sat in the centre of the front row of the stalls.

Had it only been once, our hero would have thought nothing of it, but again and again the same thing occurred, and he racked his brain in vain endeavours to guess who of his acquaintance could be concealed beneath that hideous mask.

At the conclusion of the scene a dirty little imp of a boy suddenly appeared in the stalls, and pushed his way to the spot where Jack was sitting.

Arrived before our hero, he handed him a scrap of paper curiously folded.

Jack unfastened it, and found scrawled in pencil in the inside—

"DEAR JACK—

"Follow bearer, and he will bring you to me—prime fun going on.

"Ever yours,
"JIM GIMP."

The mystery then was explained.

The nodding mask was, without doubt, the ex-ventriloquist.

Jack at once left his seat, and was led by his impish conductor through a low doorway and up a steep ladder "behind the scenes."

Leaning against a wing was the grotesque mask, but as Jack approached, it assumed an erect attitude, and held out a hand which appeared strangely out of proportion with the gigantic head.

"How are you, Jack? Glad to see you all right out of the stone-jug."

"I know your voice, although I can't see your face."

Mr. Gimp, by vast exertions, struggled out of the huge mask, and revealed his merry, good-tempered face bedewed with perspiration.

"But," resumed Jack, "how is it you've come to this? You're not hard up?"

"Hard up! not a bit of it; but some of the most scrumptious girls you ever saw are engaged in the ballet."

"Well!"

"How innocent we are."

"What do you mean?"

"Don't you see, by engaging myself as a 'super,' I not only earn a shilling a night, but am able to improve the occasion by increasing my acquaintance with those angels in gauze and silk-stockings you see over there."

Jack looked in the direction indicated, and saw two "angels"—one engaged in drinking porter out of the pewter, and the other in endeavouring to raise her right leg to a level with her head.

"Still at your old tricks, Jim?" said our hero, laughingly.

"Yes."

"What a fellow you are!"

Apparently, Mr. Gimp seemed to take this as a great compliment, for he smiled blandly and strove to look modest.

"Is the missis here?" asked the ventriloquist.

"No."

Jack answered so shortly, and in so surly a tone, as to show his friend something had gone wrong in that quarter, but he continued—

"That's famous! I thought I didn't see her. You're game for a lark, I suppose?"

"I should think so."

"All right. I'm going to have a snug little supper up in my rooms, and you must come."

"With pleasure."

"Do you know Letty Burton?"

"No."

"I'll introduce you."

"Thanks."

Letty Burton proved to be the young lady practising the saltatory movement before mentioned; but she desisted from her gymnastic efforts as soon as she saw Gimp desired her presence, and came bounding towards him.

Jack was formally introduced; and his friend then discovering he had to go on, struggled into his mask again, and rushed upon the stage as one of the noble duke's retainers.

Jack was left alone with Letty Burton—and no bad thing was that either.

At least, so Jack thought.

Letty Burton was a splendidly handsome girl, with dark flashing eyes, which yet had the power of melting into the most voluptuous softness. Her luxuriant black hair was gathered in thick braids behind a small but well-shaped head; while as for her figure it was perfect.

Many were the amorous lawyer's clerks, and would-be Lotharios who, night after night, came into the pit at half-price to feast their eyes upon her charms; and it was rumoured that a certain nobleman had more than once made liberal offers to her.

Be that as it may, it was currently reported that to noblemen and clerks alike, this young girl turned a deaf ear.

Yet she was not by any means strait-laced, neither were her morals of the highest order. Indeed, I doubt much whether any careful mother would have deemed her a desirable companion for her son. She was willing to go any reasonable lengths, but always stopped short just in time.

At last, the burlesque came to an end, and the small supper-party met by agreement in one corner of the green-room.

There were three other ladies besides Letty, and one or two gentlemen—in fact, altogether as merry an assemblage as a man could wish to make one of; and as, laughing and joking, they made their way to the stage-door, on their road to Jim Gimp's lodging, many of the uninvited looked after them with longing eyes.

"I say, Jack," said Jim, "I feel in wonderfully good spirits—I'm game for any mortal thing."

"So am I," rejoined our hero.

Just then they emerged into the street, and Jack accidentally pushed against a passer-by.

Turning to apologize, he found himself face to face with Harry Belvoir.

Their greeting was not over-cordial, as may be imagined.

Jack hurried after Jim Gimp and seized him by the arm, pointing at the same time after his supposed rival.

"You see that fellow, Jim ?"

"Tall fellow—swell—new hat on ?—yes."

"I've got a grudge against him."

"The deuce you have !"

"Yes. Do you think we could play him some trick ?"

"Of course we can. I'll ask him to join us."

"I don't see much trick in that."

"Trust me. I'll engage before this time to-morrow he will repent most thoroughly of having accepted the invitation."

Jack was not quite convinced, but allowed his friend to have his own way; and Jim, in pursuance of his plan, hurried after Harry Belvoir, accosted him, and, without any great difficulty, persuaded him to join the party.

They were now eight in number—four ladies and four gentlemen.

They hailed a couple of four-wheeled cabs, and the party were soon safely stowed away in them, though not without a great deal of laughing and joking, and compression of ladies' skirts, and little shrieks and gentle remonstrances from the fair damsels at discovering strange arms round their pretty little waists.

The cabs rolled away with their lively freight, and I am sadly afraid that as Master Jack sat with his arm encircling Letty Burton, the remembrance of Fanny White faded gradually from his mind, and he gave up himself entirely to the happiness of the time being.

And thus they went on merrily enough, till the cabs pulled up with a jerk before the hospitable mansion of J. Gimp, Esq., and the whole party alighted.

CHAPTER XL.

A SUPPER, A KISS, AND A SHOWER-BATH.

MR. GIMP'S supper, as might be expected, was not very costly and grand.

The viands were substantial, and there were plenty of them; and as the guests had all good appetites that was a great thing.

But after all it was not so much the eating and drinking the guests cared for, although they did ample justice to the food, as for the merry, sociable, laughing, talking, joking time, when the punch had been brewed and the wine-bottles uncorked.

Then it was that Mr. Gimp hoped nobody objected to smoking, and produced an enormous meerschaum-bowl which he filled with the fragrant weed; and finding that nobody did object, the other gentlemen produced pipes and cigars.

Then Jack suggested to Letty that she should try a cigarette, which he manufactured expressly for her; and after that, the other gentlemen took the hint, and before long such a fume of tobacco rose on every side, that the room never afterwards got quite free from the odour.

Then comic songs were sung and jokes made, which sent the whole company into hysterical shrieks of laughter, although they would scarcely bear repeating.

Harry Belvoir enjoyed himself as much as any one present, and Jack could not help fearing that Jim Gimp had forgotten the promise he had made.

But he had not.

He had been engaged, for some time past, in a whispered conversation with a pretty little light-haired girl, and had not escaped a quantity of rather pointed chaff in consequence.

We shall shortly see the result of that conversation,

The heat of the room and the fumes of tobacco produced thirst, and bottle after bottle disappeared, till the company grew decidedly merry, a trifle affectionate, and a little noisy.

Then the young lady who had fallen to Harry Belvoir's share accidentally mentioned that she had brought a fancy dress with her, and immediately there arose a clamour that she should appear in it, and after a good deal of persuasion and sundry glasses of wine, she consented to do so, and for the purpose of complying with this request retired into Jim Gimp's bed-room.

The place she vacated at Harry Belvoir's side was immediately usurped by the pretty little fair-haired girl; and Harry, having arrived at that state to which a free mixture of liquors is apt to bring an unseasoned youth, hardly noticed the change, and was perfectly content so long as he had a companion.

To say that any of the company were as sober as judges are proverbially supposed to be, might be bordering upon an untruth, but as yet none of them were in an advanced stage.

Jack, who had prudently confined himself to one beverage, had only got so far as to consider Letty Burton the nicest girl in the world, to the complete exclusion of Fanny; while she, for the first time in her life (if report spoke truly) had found a man for whom she could really care.

Had our heroine known how soon her lover would supply her place, she would have deliberated longer ere she departed for Kingston; but not being gifted with the power of second sight, she remained in happy ignorance of the manner in which he passed the first evening after she left him.

She would not have been best pleased either, had she seen the way in which Jack pressed his lips to those of the dark-eyed beauty who sat by his side; nor would she have hesitated to apply some hard names to the lovely girl who raised her lustrous eyes to those of our hero.

Surely, in this case, ignorance was bliss.

The party went on right merrily.

They had divided into couples, and each pair was occupied in the manner that pleased them best; laughing, joking, singing, smoking, drinking, and altogether making such an uproar, that the lodger on the floor below knocked against the ceiling, and holloaed himself hoarse in his endeavours to obtain silence; while the landlady called over the banisters that she would thank Mr. Gimp to pay the rent and be off.

But to neither of these polite speeches did any of the party pay the least attention.

Jack was making fast progress in the affections of Letty Burton, who had already agreed to go with him to a nice little *tête-à-tête* dinner at the Star and Garter, on the following Friday.

Harry Belvoir's first companion had made her appearance in the fancy dress, and had been enthusiastically applauded; but her beau was too busily engaged with the fair-haired girl to pay much attention to her re-entrance.

It must be confessed that the auburn-haired young lady seemed very much taken with Master Harry, and it did not create much surprise when she disappeared into the inner room, and was followed, after a short interval, by Uncle Pigley's nephew.

Jim Gimp saw them go, and chuckled and coughed with delight, but refused to allow any of the company to participate in his merriment : but catching Jack's eye, he gave him a knowing wink, and whispered—

"Now for the little game."

The fair-haired girl emerged before very long from the inner room, hardly able to speak for laughing; and then she and Jim Gimp had a long conversation together, during which sundry sounds of a mysterious character were heard issuing from the bed-room.

Jim Gimp rose to his feet.

"A speech ! a speech !" was the cry.

"Just so, ladies and gentlemen. I have delayed until this late period producing something which I feel sure will amuse you. If you feel inclined for a good laugh, follow me."

The whole party rose with as much steadiness as they could manage, and Jim led the way into the bed-room.

No sooner, however, did his fingers touch the handle of the door, than a terrific sound of falling water was heard, mingled with piteous cries for help.

The light streamed fully into the inner room, as a drenched figure darted from what appeared to be a cupboard, but was, in reality, a shower-bath.

The figure was that of Harry Belvoir !

Denuded of his coat and waistcoat, with the water dripping from the ends of his hair, and the few garments he had on in a state of complete sop, he looked more like a drowned rat than a young gentleman.

With a bewildered air Master Harry stared around him; but recovering partly from the shrieks of laughter and jeers which beset him on every side, he turned fiercely round, and asked the company collectively what the devil they meant.

This **only** produced fresh merriment; but Jim Gimp

stood forth with a face as grave as an undertaker at a funeral.

"Mr. Belvoir, I must ask you to explain your conduct."

"My conduct?"

"Yes, sir."

"Certainly, Mr. Belvoir. You were asked here by Mr. Gimp, at my solicitation," said Jack, "and then you behave yourself in this shameful way. It's disgraceful!"

"Disgraceful!" chorused the young ladies, led by the light-haired one.

Harry Belvoir was in a glorious state of obfuscation.

He had considered a practical joke had been played upon him (which indeed it had), but owing to the grave faces and reproachful language of the company, for they had all taken their cue from the giver of the entertainment, he began to have a confused idea that he had done something very dreadful.

"Mr. Belvoir, you ought to be ashamed of yourself," said Jim Gimp.

"Yes, that you ought," chorused the young ladies again.

"Such conduct will be your ruin, young man!" said Jack, gravely.

"And he never even apologizes for appearing before ladies in his shirt-sleeves," remarked Letty Burton.

Harry Belvoir, thus assailed on every side, looked helplessly round, shivering in his wet things.

"Now don't move from that spot," said Jim, sternly. "Your conduct is quite bad enough, without making puddles all over a gentleman's bed-room."

"But look here," began Master Harry, in piteous tones.

"We are looking," rejoined the others, simultaneously.

"I'm dripping wet."

"You don't say so."

"Lend me some dry things to put on."

"I've only one suit in the world," said Mr. Gimp, "and I'm wearing that."

"But what am I to do?"

"Go home."

"Where is my coat?"

"I haven't got it."

Harry Belvoir, cold and shivering, got thoroughly angry.

"I tell you what," said he, "this is some infernal foolery on your part, Mr. Rawlings. I'll pay you out for it some day."

"All right, my dear boy! Don't lose your temper."

"Temper be——"

The ladies gave a little shriek of horror.

"This language before ladies is not to be allowed, Mr. Belvoir."

"Turn him out," suggested one young lady.

"Yes—turn him out—out with him—turn him out," resounded on every side.

Oaths, prayers, and entreaties were alike useless, and at three o'clock in the morning Harry Belvoir found himself in a deserted street, with nothing on but a shirt and a pair of trousers, neither of which had a dry stitch in them.

The remainder of the party went back to the room, after ejecting this young gentleman, and enjoyed more laughter at his expense, and remained there enjoying themselves till one by one they dropped off to sleep, in a variety of attitudes, more easy perhaps than elegant; and thus ended Mr. Jim Gimp's supper-party, and Mr. Harry Belvoir's discomfiture.

CHAPTER XLI.

ADMIRAL RATTLIN FORMS A RESOLUTION, AND MINNIE MEETS WITH AN ACCIDENT.

AWAY, far away from busy, bustling, smoky, noisy London; away from scenes of vice and crime; away from sin and wickedness, to the quiet and peace of the country.

For a while part of our scene is changed from the smoke-grimed bricks and mortar of the great metropolis to the green trees and shady lanes of the quiet little country village of Easthorpe.

No railway has penetrated yet to this remote corner, and should any of the readers of these pages form the rash resolution of endeavouring to reach that secluded spot, I can only tell them that they must take the train to Bristol, and then inquire their best way of proceeding.

But with the actual village of Easthorpe we have little to do.

It possessed some two-dozen houses, a tiny church, over-grown with ivy, a good, old-fashioned inn, and a pump; but did not differ essentially from hundreds of other west country villages.

Near Easthorpe was a large, handsome mansion, which lifted itself up from among the fine trees which surrounded it with an air of dignity, which seemed to say, "you wont find another house like me for twenty miles round."

This was indeed the case.

When any chance traveller straying that way caught sight of the old-fashioned chimneys and gable-ends of the old mansion, rising above the aged oaks, or when any pedestrian stayed his course to look up the long avenue, through the curiously wrought iron gates, to the front entrance, and inquired to whom the magnificent place belonged, he received for answer—

"The Earl of Stonecliffe."

Should his curiosity carry him farther, and should he ask to whom the rich pasture-land stretching far away to the distant hills, belonged, still the answer was the same—

"The Earl of Stonecliffe."

The covers filled with game, the large cornfields, the wooded hills?

Still the same reply—

"The Earl of Stonecliffe."

For miles and miles around, farther than the eye could reach, the land was the Stonecliffe property.

The inn in the village was the "Stonecliffe Arms;" the church contains monuments of Stonecliffes from time immemorial; the pump had been erected by the tenth Earl; the schools built by the thirteenth; and now all this valuable property, together with Stonecliffe Castle, in Yorkshire, a small estate in Sussex, and the London house, were the property of the nobleman whom we have known under the title of Lord Manningtree!

Passing, however, by Easthorpe House, and progressing towards the village, the chimneys of another residence rose above some trees, upon the opposite side of the road.

This house was the property of Admiral Rattlin, an old sailor, who, having served his country till he lost a leg, had retired upon a wooden stump and his half-pay, to his native village, where he had built himself a house, which he named, after England's greatest commander, "Nelson Retreat."

It was a strange style of residence, for the admiral had been, in a great measure, his own architect, and had built a strange, low, rambling house, which, however, was uncommonly comfortable, and thither he had retired with his two daughters, Olivia and Minnie, to pass the remainder of his days in peace and quietness.

He was a bluff, loud-voiced old man, with a wonderful memory for stories calculated to raise a blush on the face of his female listeners; but the old fellow meant no harm, and was, in everything, the very soul of honour.

Miss Olivia, his eldest daughter, was one of the prim and precise school.

She was no longer young. She dressed usually in sombre colours, affected the society of clergymen, and professed to be inexpressibly shocked at many of her father's expressions.

Minnie, the younger, was in many respects the reverse of her staid and severe sister.

She was only eighteen—and as lovely a girl as one would wish to see.

Light and airy in all her movements, she flitted about from place to place like a fairy carrying sunshine and happiness wherever she went.

She was certainly her father's favourite, for he was apt to lose his patience with the demure Miss Olivia; who carried her ideas of propriety so far as to object to wearing low-necked dresses (she was very scraggy), and was known to have once made a round of half a mile to avoid getting over a stile into a field where some men were at work.

One fine October morning, the admiral and his two daughters were sitting at breakfast when the subject of the new Earl of Stonecliffe was broached.

"He's coming down here to-day to stay at the 'house,'" observed Minnie.

"So I hear," rejoined the admiral, between two bites from a piece of toast.

"You'll call upon him, of course, papa?"

Miss Olivia gave a small shriek.

"What's the matter, 'Livy?'" asked her father.

"The idea of Minnie mentioning such a thing," said the eldest. "Call upon him, indeed!"

"Why not?"

"You must have heard the dreadful stories about him."

"What stories?"

"About his sin and wickedness, and his gloom, and his unholy studies in chemistry."

"Ha! ha! Livy. Why, what does that matter to me?—he wont make me sell my soul to the old gentleman."

"I don't know that, father; but it is not so much for you, or for myself, I speak, as for the young and artless Minnie."

"I'm very much obliged to you," retorted the younger sister.

"What is it you're aiming at?" asked the admiral. "If his lordship did go on a little wild—if he did live with a ballet-dancer, and so on——"

Olivia shrieked.

"How can you talk in that way, father?"

"What's the harm! I tell you what, Miss Livy, all that false sentiment about not calling things by their right names is an infernal mistake."

"I'm sorry you think so, sir. If I could only persuade you to sit under the Reverend Mr. Gorbell, it would be better for you."

"Perhaps my father wouldn't care to have the Reverend Mr. Gorbell's arm round his waist."

"What do you mean?" asked Olivia, crimsoning.

"Oh, I daresay!" continued Minnie. "I may have been mistaken. It certainly was not the conduct of one of the elect."

"Haw! haw! haw!" laughed the admiral, half-choking himself with his egg. "Fairly caught, Livy—trapped beautifully."

"I am surprised, father, you should encourage my sister in these scandalous and immodest speeches."

"It seems to me, my dear, rather more immodest for you to suffer the reverend gentleman to clasp you to his sanctified heart than for Minnie to mention it."

Olivia sighed a deep sigh.

"You are all going on the downward path."

"Thank you, my dear."

"I'm truly sorry for you. Go and call on this man of Belial—go and sell your youngest daughter to the evil spirit, if you like, but don't ask me to speak to the Earl of Stonecliffe."

"I have no intention of doing so; but I shall certainly go myself."

And so the conversation ended.

Breakfast concluded, the admiral started on his daily tour round the garden, stumping along the gravel-walk and making little round marks wherever his wooden leg came down.

Olivia had an appointment at the school with the Reverend Mr. Gorbell, and Minnie was left to her own devices.

It was a lovely morning, and she determined to go for a walk.

She put on her cloak and hat, and started in the direction of Easthorpe House; but soon left the high-road, clambered over a stile, revealing, had there only been any one to see it, a good deal of white stocking and shapely leg, and struck across the fields.

She had not proceeded any great distance before she entered a large meadow, in which several bulls were grazing; but being a brave girl, she thought nothing of them till she was half-way across, when her attention was attracted by the singular behaviour of one of the animals.

A young bull was standing in the path tossing his head in a threatening manner, and pawing the ground uneasily with his fore-feet.

Minnie began to feel a little frightened, but pursued her way.

The bull roared out a savage bellow.

Minnie stopped.

The animal advanced towards her.

She turned and fled.

The bull followed.

With the greatest alarm, Minnie found the savage beast was gaining rapidly upon her, and that she could not hope to reach the boundary of the field without being overtaken.

Fear to her feet lent wings, and she raced over the ground as fast as her pretty little feet would carry her.

She heard the savage snortings of the enraged animal close behind her—she almost felt his breath.

Still she raced onward.

Every moment she expected to feel herself cast into the air.

Suddenly, a sharp crack as of a rifle was heard.

The bull gave a bellow of pain.

Minnie was too frightened to turn, but still ran on.

She reached the stile.

Totally regardless of the display she might make, she clambered up it only too thankful at her escape.

Her foot slipped, and she lost her balance.

With a shriek, she fell forward.

Something arrested her fall, however—and that something was a man!

A tall, handsome man he was, with a thick black moustache and piercing eyes.

"I beg your pardon, sir."

Minnie blushed and stammered as she said this, for she had literally fallen into the stranger's arms, and he seemed in no hurry to relinquish his lovely burden.

"Beg my pardon! What for?"

"I thought—that is, I was afraid—that—that I had inconvenienced you."

"Not in the least, I assure you."

"I was frightened, and I didn't exactly see where I was going."

"That bull will never frighten anyone again."

Minnie, in the excitement of the moment, had forgotten all about the bull, but now looked back into the field.

There, some fifty yards from the stile, lay the savage beast—dead.

Minnie looked inquiringly at her dark companion.

He answered her mute appeal with the greatest calmness.

"Yes. That is my doing. I saw you were in danger, and having my rifle with me, I put a ball behind his shoulder."

"You killed him?"

"So it appears."

"But you will get into sad disgrace?"

"You think so?"

"Certainly."

"Why?"

"For shooting it."

"I will take my chance of that."

"It's lucky no one saw you."

"Who does it belong to?"

"The Earl of Stonecliffe, I suppose. It is his field."

"Indeed!"

The handsome stranger had released Minnie from his arms, but still held her hand in his.

She suddenly remembered that, but for his timely aid, she might have been gored by the infuriated animal, for the fact was, the events of the last few minutes had so bewildered her that she scarcely knew what she was doing.

"Thank you—thank you very much," said she, warmly.

"For what?"

"For the service you have rendered me."

"Nonsense! It was good practice for me. I was a good two hundred yards distant."

Minnie gave him a glance of admiration.

"I think I must be going home, now," said she, taking her hand from his.

"Allow me to accompany you—at all events through the fields."

"Thank you, but—"

But what Minnie never said, for the stranger taking up his rifle, was already walking at her side.

Through the three or four fields which they had to cross before reaching the high road, he walked by her, entertaining her with numerous anecdotes, till when they reached the spot where they were to part, she felt quite sorry their walk had terminated.

"Good-bye," said he, holding out his hand.

"Good-bye, and thank you very, very much for your timely aid," she rejoined.

While he still held her hand in his the sound of wheels announced the approach of some vehicle.

The stranger vaulted over the stile just as a low pony-carriage came driving rapidly along the road.

His appearance was so sudden as to cause the animal to shy across the road, and nearly upset the driver, who was indeed no other than Admiral Rattlin.

"You blundering, boobyish blockhead, can't you see where you are coming to?" roared the admiral. "If I had you on board ship I warrant I'd teach you better manners."

"I beg your pardon, sir," said the stranger, in a civil tone which contrasted favourably with the old admiral's outburst; "I beg your pardon, but I had no idea you were so near."

"Damn it, sir——"

"Hush! don't make use of such language before a lady."

"A lady?"

"Yes."

The admiral turned his head and saw Minnie, who by this time surmounted the stile.

"Papa!" she cried.

"My daughter!"

"Your daughter!" echoed the stranger.

"Now, look here," said the admiral, rather mystified and very angry, "none of your hanky-panky tricks here. Just tell me what the devil all this means?"

"What is it you wish to know, sir?"

"I want to know what the dickens you mean by frightening me and my pony? and how the deuce it is you come to be gallivanting about the country with my daughter?"

"In the first place, sir, I didn't know this young lady *was* your daughter."

"What's that to do with it? You knew she was somebody's daughter, didn't you—eh?"

"Papa——"

"Hold your tongue."

"But, papa, I want to speak to you."

"Well, what is it?"

"This gentleman has done me a great service."

"The deuce he has!"

"He has saved my life."

"What business had you to go where it wanted saving?"

"It was an accident, papa, and but for this gentleman I should have been tossed by a bull."

"Tossed, eh? Well, sir," continued the admiral, turning to the stranger, "so you saved Minnie's life, did you?"

"I am afraid, sir, your daughter rates my services too highly. I did no more than any one in my place would have done."

"Well, let's hear all about it."

From the two the admiral got a full account of the adventure, although strange as it may appear, neither of them recollected to mention the second episode at the stile.

The bluff, peppery old sailor altered his manner the moment he heard that his daughter had been exposed to real danger, and rescued by the courage and coolness of the handsome stranger.

"I beg your pardon, sir; I do, indeed," said he. "Pray excuse the words of a cross-tempered old salt. You've rendered us a great service, and I'm very much obliged to you. Come and take pot-luck at the 'Retreat'—no excuses—jump up behind—come along! Jump in, Minnie."

Away the pony chaise went again with its additional load, Minnie and the stranger chatting pleasantly together, while the admiral let off a string of adjectives and various expressions at the quadruped which drew them, which, however well they might have been suited to the deck of a man-of-war in the olden time, would hardly look well in print.

Arrived at the house, they found Olivia had brought the Reverend Mr. Gorbell in to dinner, consequently they had rather a large party.

"Father, have you been to call on that sinful nobleman?" asked Olivia.

"Yes, my dear."

"What did he say?"

"What did he look like?"

The two sisters asked these questions simultaneously.

"I didn't see him, so I can't say."

"I'm afraid the young man is a brazen pot," said the Reverend Mr. Gorbell, solemnly.

"And what may that be?" asked the admiral.

The reverend gentleman shook his head, as much as to say he wouldn't define the term, but that it was something very dreadful.

"I'm afraid he's a lost sheep," sighed Olivia.

"So he is," said the Reverend, with a groan.

"Dinner, dinner!" shouted the admiral; "come along, Mr. Gorbell. Will you take Olivia, Mr.—Mr.—Bless my heart! I never asked you your name," he continued, addressing the handsome stranger.

"I am usually called the Earl of Stonecliffe," said he, with a quiet smile.

————

CHAPTER XLII.

IN WHICH A LADY AND GENTLEMAN TAKE UP THEIR RESIDENCE AT THE "STONECLIFFE ARMS."

IT is necessary that we should return to Mr. Phil Davenant, and see how he prospered after accepting the extraordinary proposal of his beautiful fellow-lodger.

The morning after the interview described in a preceding chapter, he woke with a confused idea of what had occurred, but he was hardly dressed before a knock at the door told him of the arrival of a visitor.

The lovely visitor of the previous night entered the room.

"I have come, Mr. Davenant," said she, "to ask if you repent of your decision."

"I certainly do not," said he.

"It is well. Are you prepared at once to leave London?"

"Scarcely. Why do you ask?"

"Because you must do it."

"But my situation?"

"You must give it up."

"My appointment at the theatre?"

"You must choose between my proposal and your present position."

"You wish me to give up everything for an uncertainty?"

"No. I guarantee you shall be no loser."

"What is it you require me to do?"

"I told you last night. To travel with me wherever I may go, and give me the protection of a husband and the name of a wife."

"May I ask your name?"

"Mrs. Davenant."

Phil was rather taken aback at this.

"Yes; but I mean before you—that is to say, before we were mar—"

"You want to become acquainted with my real name?"

"Yes."

"That I cannot tell you."

"Why not?"

"Because I have particular reasons for keeping it a secret."

"Indeed."

"Yes. When you find occasion to address me before strangers you may call me Laura. Usually I shall pass simply as Mrs. Davenant."

"Then I will go at once to resign my situation."

"Do so."

Phil took up his hat to depart.

"Stay one moment," said the lady.

Phil paused at the door.

"This," continued she, giving him a bank-note for a considerable amount—"this will show you I am in earnest."

Phil was profuse in his thanks.

"On your way back here go to a fashionable tailor, and procure two suits of mourning—the best that can be had. Get everything you may think necessary for a gentleman's outfit—bring me the bills, and I will pay them."

"Thank you. You are very generous."

"Generous! But that you can serve me you might starve in the street ere I held out a helping hand to you. I generous!"

"That takes the gilt off the gingerbread," Phil muttered to himself as he left the room.

That night many heads were turned to look after the beautiful girl, who, leaning upon a gentleman's arm, walked the length of the platform of the Great Western Railway, and finally took their seats in a first-class compartment.

"Who are they?" was the question asked by many a one, struck by the symmetry of figure of the youthful lady with the thick crape veil drawn over her features.

But no one was able to answer the question. The guard only knew they were going to Bristol; but one cunning traveller caught sight of their luggage, upon which "Mrs. Davenant, passenger to Bristol," was inscribed.

The train bore them whirling through the rich country, dashing through tunnels and over embankments to Bristol, and there, at a late hour, deposited our two travellers.

They proceeded at once to the best hotel.

"I am sorry," said the lady to Phil, "to have to ask you to begin helping me at once, but will you ascertain if the theatre is open, and also if the performance is likely to be concluded by this time."

Phil speedily obtained the required information from the waiter.

The theatre was open, and as the performance that evening was for some one's benefit, it was hardly likely to conclude before midnight.

"Then, Mr. Davenant, I must trouble you further. Will you proceed at once to the theatre, and ascertain for me the name of the leading actress, and the hour at which morning rehearsal will be over to-morrow? Do this with caution."

Phil departed on his errand, and Laura (for we will call her by the name she gave herself) threw herself upon the hard horsehair sofa, with a weary sigh.

"There is much to be done," said she. "Many days of weary watching and waiting—many nights of restless anguish; but the time will come—and sooner than give up my designs I will go through fire and water to accomplish them."

When the chambermaid came to speak upon the subject of bed-rooms, she was decidedly puzzled at Laura's desire to occupy a separate room. It was a thing she did not at all comprehend, and she said as much to the waiter, who declared, if he were the husband, he'd be blowed if he'd stand it; but for all that she did as Mrs. Davenant had ordered.

Phil came back with the information.

He had discovered an old friend in the person of the under scene-painter, and had easily obtained from him the particulars he desired.

Mrs. St. Aubyn was the principal actress, and the morning rehearsal would conclude about half-past twelve.

After a luxurious supper, this strange couple retired to their separate rooms for the night—the lady to ponder over plans of revenge, and the gentleman to rack his brains to discover some clue to the mystery in which he had become involved, until he fell asleep.

"Have you any commands for me to-day?" asked Phil of Laura, the next morning after breakfast.

"No; I have things to attend to in the town myself, but I will not in any way interfere with your amusements. Meet me in the ladies' waiting-room at the railway-station, punctually at three o'clock, and remember whatever you may hear or see to be careful not to express surprise."

Phil bowed and left the room.

"Of all the strange adventures that ever happened to a fellow," muttered Phil, as he lit his morning pipe, "this is by far the strangest. I don't half like it now, but it doesn't seem a bad sort of life. She's a splendid girl; but a regular tartar."

So saying, he strolled listlessly away to spend his time in idling about till three o'clock.

*   *   *   *   *

It was half-past twelve o'clock, and the rehearsal of the new melodrama had just concluded at the Theatre Royal, Bristol.

The ladies were putting on their bonnets as they discussed the latest scandal; and the manager was flying about in a passion and perspiration, swearing the thing would prove a complete failure unless they put a little more life into it.

The eminent tragedian, Mr. Gulp, was drinking half-and-half with a scene-shifter, and Mrs. St. Aubyn was just leaving to go home to an early dinner, when a dirty little imp rushed frantically up to her.

"Please, marm, here's a lady here as wants to speak with you."

"What is her name?"

"She wouldn't say—said as how you'd be none the wiser if she did."

"What does she want?"

"Don't know, marm."

"Some poor creature, doubtless, who wants an engagement," thought Mrs. St. Aubyn, whose real name, by-the-bye, was Carter.

"Tell her to walk this way," she added, with an air of the greatest condescension.

In a few minutes, Mrs. Davenant appeared upon the stage.

The leading tragedian gave a theatrical start as he caught sight of the beautiful young girl, and Mrs. St. Aubyn registered a mental vow that if she could prevent it, she would never allow so dangerous a rival to play on the same stage with her.

"You wished to speak with me, young woman," said she, patronisingly.

"In private, if you please."

"May I ask the nature of your business with me?"

"I will explain when we are alone."

Mrs. St. Aubyn led the way into the wretched little cupboard which served for a dressing-room, followed by Mrs. Davenant.

*   *   *   *   *

A little before three o'clock Phil was waiting on the platform of the railway-station.

He had already looked several times into the waiting-room, but it was untenanted.

"What the deuce am I likely to see to surprise me?" he thought, as he paced backwards and forwards, his mind recurring to the strict injunctions he had received to betray no surprise at anything.

The clock struck three.

Before the last stroke had sounded, he was on the threshold of the waiting-room.

Laura was not there.

There was only one lady in the room, and she was older, and in every respect different in appearance to her of whom he was in search.

Her hair was jet-black, and her complexion was a deep olive colour.

Undecided what to do, Phil remained for a few moments at the door.

The dark lady advanced with rapid steps towards him, and laid her hand upon his arm.

"Hush!" she whispered, "I see you do not recognise me."

"Why—what—oh, the deuce! You're not——"

"Hush!"

"It's all very well," thought Phil, "to tell a fellow not to be frightened or surprised at anything, but when a lot of pantomime tricks come to be played off in real life, it's likely to throw a fellow off his balance."

"I am still Laura Davenant," whispered the lady. "What alterations I have made in my appearance were necessary for the furtherance of my plans."

"Exactly."

Phil felt obliged to say something.

"Give me your arm."

He did as he was told.

"Now take me to the front entrance. You will see there a carriage with two horses. Hand me into it, and then get in yourself."

"Where are we going?"

"The driver has his instructions."

All happened exactly as Mrs. Davenant had arranged, and the moment they were both seated, the driver flourished his whip, and they rattled away at a fine pace.

For miles and miles through the country, where autumn had tinged the leaves with russet, they drove on and on.

The lady, fully occupied with her own thoughts, returned no answer to the observations Phil addressed to her; so, after a short time, he made himself comfortable in his corner and went to sleep.

When he awoke, they were driving rapidly by a gentleman's park, where, in the distance above the trees, rose the chimneys of a noble mansion.

"Hullo! whose place is that?" asked Phil, yawning.

"It is the Earl of Stonecliffe's."

Phil actually started from his seat at the tone in which those words were spoken.

In the bitter inflexion of the voice was concentrated hatred and passion.

"I shouldn't care about meeting this young lady if I were the earl," was Mr. Phil Davenant's mental comment.

Still the carriage drove on rapidly into the little village of Easthorpe, and pulled up sharply before the door of the "Stonecliffe Arms."

"We stop here to-night," said Laura; "make all necessary arrangements."

The landlord was desponding at first, and feared he could not accommodate the lady and gentleman; but after consulting his pretty, rosy-cheeked daughter, became more hopeful, and said he'd do his best.

And thus it was that two strangers took up their abode at Easthorpe.

For the first few days, excitement was intense in the village respecting them; and stories, attributing frightful crimes to them, were current. But after a week or two, when they found no detective came to apprehend Laura for murder, and no outraged husband to shoot Phil for seduc-

"HELP! HELP! LET ME OUT—I WILL NOT STAY HERE!" SHRIEKED FANNY WHITE.

tion, they came to the conclusion that it was all right, and paid little or no attention to the movements of this singular couple who became domiciled at the "Stonecliffe Arms."

CHAPTER XLIII.

RELATES THE PLEASANT TRICK PLAYED BY MASTER JACK RAWLINGS UPON THE HONOURABLE MR. PERCY VERE.

THE waking in the morning after the debauch in Jim Gimp's rooms was rather a sad affair.

Every one had had too much wine, and too little sleep; and all were, more or less, cross, and out of sorts, as they aroused themselves from their uneasy slumbers, only to gaze around them upon the ruins of the feast.

Broken wine-bottles, shattered tumblers, fragments of dress, and cigar ends, lay littered about in disgraceful confusion; and in the midst of the chaotic mass sat Jim Gimp upon one corner of the table enjoying his morning pipe.

"Hullo! you lot!" said he, as he saw symptoms of waking among his guests. "Ain't you going to get up to-day? It's past eleven o'clock a good deal."

Mr. Gimp looked none the worse for his previous night's debauch.

His countenance was jovial, merry, and rubicund as ever, and as he puffed out huge volumes of smoke from his capacious mouth, he looked jolly enough to make his guests ill with envy.

It must be confessed the ladies did not present a very ravishing appearance when they awoke, for sleeping on the floor in a crinoline does not add to the grace and beauty of a dress, any more than tossing restlessly on a sofa-cushion improves the smoothness of the hair.

Lotty, indeed, acting upon our hero's advice, had disencumbered herself of her hoops, and they now swung slowly to and fro in the morning breeze, like a huge parrot's cage, calling for many rude and objectionable remarks from the gentlemen.

By-and-bye, all the party being sufficiently aroused, some pretence at breakfast was made.

Strong coffee and red herrings were in great demand, but in spite of the efforts of all the party, and the declaration that they were "all right," they all bore a stamp of "seediness" about them which was painful to behold.

With the exception of their dress, Jack and Lotty were in the freshest condition. Indeed, they went so far as to discuss various plans for spending the day together.

Jack, whose money was not yet exhausted, made the dark-eyed beauty munificent offers, and at last, in utter oblivion of Fanny White, it was agreed that this pair should proceed to Richmond, for a dinner at the "Star and Garter."

No such vulgar travelling as railroads was dreamt of.

Jack had money in his pocket, and determined to spend it like a prince.

He hired a very smart dog-cart for the day, and with the charming Lotty by his side, trotted down to Richmond in grand style.

Arrived at the "Star and Garter," the horse put up, and the dinner ordered, there remained about an hour before the sumptuous repast would be ready, so to wile away the time our hero, and his new love, set out for a stroll along the river bank.

Having proceeded some distance towards Teddington, Lotty professed to be rather tired, and the youthful pair seated themselves upon one of the benches placed along the towing-path.

They had not been there many minutes, before a tall and distinguished-looking man, apparently a foreigner, took his seat beside them, much to their disgust.

He was an aristocratic-looking man, with a profusion of black beard and moustache, and glittering white teeth, which he showed whenever he spoke.

His dress was neat and good, and what jewellery he wore was evidently of the best quality.

He either did not observe, or else was indifferent, to the plainly perceptible disgust of Jack and Lotty at his presence, and commenced a conversation in slightly broken English, with our hero, who answered him shortly enough.

But he was not a bit disconcerted, and continued talking with unbroken fluency.

While they still sat on the bench, a lady, simply but elegantly dressed, passed by.

As she did so, Jack had some confused recollection of having seen her face before, but racked his brain in vain endeavours to remember when and where.

She had not gone far, ere she turned and retraced her steps.

This time, however, she did not pass the bench, but came straight up to Jack.

"Mr. Rawlings, I think?" said she, in a sweet low voice.

"That is my name."

"You do not recollect me?"

"I was just puzzling my brains, by trying to remember where I had seen you before."

She gave a deep sigh.

"Can I speak with you for a few minutes?"

"Certainly."

"Alone?"

Jack glanced at Lotty, who had listened to this short conversation with jealous ears, but the love of adventure in him was too strong to keep him by her side, and he rose with an apology to the dark-eyed girl, and followed the mysterious stranger to a clump of trees a little way off.

"Do you remember the night of the masquerade?" she said.

"Yes."

"And the lady who spoke to you there?"

"Yes—but, you are not——?"

"I am!"

"Who?"

"That lady!"

"Lady Alice Brandon!"

"You know me?"

"Yes."

"Well! It must have been told sooner or later."

"You wished to speak with me?"

"Yes."

"What would you say?"

"First—will you answer me one or two questions?"

"With pleasure."

"Who is that dark-eyed girl, who was sitting by your side?"

"A friend of mine."

"And that foreign-looking man?"

"I don't know."

"He is not a friend of yours?"

"No, thank goodness!"

"Do you love that black-haired girl?"

Jack was rather taken aback by the abruptness of this question, but managed to stammer an answer in the negative.

"Then listen to what I have to say. It may sound strange coming from a woman's lips, but still I cannot conceal from you that——"

"Jack, it's time to go back to the hotel."

Lotty had stolen upon them unperceived, thinking the conference had lasted quite long enough; and now took possession of Jack's arm, looking a whole armoury of daggers at her rival.

It was perfectly useless hoping to get rid of Lotty, and Lady Alice seeing this, held out her small delicate hand, and bade Jack adieu; not, however, before she had whispered in his ear, appointing a place of meeting for the following day.

Now, Lotty had been highly enraged at our hero's coolness in leaving her, and in order to wreak her revenge had flirted violently with the stranger while Jack had been away.

"Jack," said she, "that gentleman—Mr. Vane—has kindly consented to dine with us."

"The deuce he has! I think he might have waited till he was asked!"

"Now, don't be angry, there's a good fellow. You don't know what a nice man he is!"

The foreigner advanced, and extracted from an ivory card-case a small highly-glazed card, upon which was printed in minute characters—

"*The Honourable Percy Vane.*"

and handed it to Jack, who bowed stiffly enough.

"An English name, I perceive," said our hero.

"Yes, I am an Englishman."

"I thought from your conversation you were a foreigner."

"Oh, no! But I have resided much time abroad."

"There's something odd about this," thought Jack. "I'll keep my eye on the gentleman."

During the walk back to the "Star and Garter," Jack maintained a gloomy silence, but Mr. Vane fully made up for it, by talking incessantly the whole way in a most amusing manner.

Lotty professed herself delighted with him.

This did not add much to Jack's pleasure.

The dinner passed off slowly enough, and it was not until they were sitting quietly sipping their wine that the Honourable Mr. Vane proposed, in the most natural way in the world, that they should amuse themselves by a game at cards.

Then it was that the idea struck Jack that this distinguished-looking individual was nothing more nor less than an adventurer, or a fashionable swindler.

Now, Jack was no mean opponent at games of skill, and he determined, if his surmises should prove correct, to turn the tables upon Mr. Percy Vane.

With alacrity he accepted the offer, and when the aristocratic gentleman suggested they should remove to his lodgings at Twickenham, our hero did not hesitate to comply with his proposition.

The three started without loss of time, though it must be confessed Lotty would have preferred spending the rest of the evening alone with Jack, but that was not to be so; resigning herself to her fate, she accompanied them over Richmond Bridge to the lodgings of the Honourable Percy Vane, which, considering his name, were rather shabby, to say the least of them.

It evidently afforded the aristocratic gentleman no little pain to find he had met with his match, and that play as he would he was unable to get the better of our hero, whose courage and spirits rose with the heap of gold on his side of the table.

But Jack's fortune was too good to last.

Luck changed, and Mr. Vane seemed in a fair way of winning back all he had lost.

Our hero, while he had won, had not cared much to scrutinize his opponent's play, but now that the tables were reversed he watched him more closely.

Lotty, who had been sitting on a sofa lazily turning over the leaves of a handsomely-bound book, had got tired of that amusement, and was also from her seat watching Percy Vane, who was winning trick after trick, in a most surprising manner.

Suddenly she started forward, but instantly recovered her composure.

"What is it, Lotty?" asked Jack.

"Nothing."

Though she answered "nothing," our hero felt convinced this was not the exact truth, and suddenly their eyes meeting, her brilliant black orbs said, as plainly as eyes could speak—

"Be careful of that man."

Jack watched his opponent closely, but for some time was unable to detect him in the act of cheating, till, through a foolish blunder, the Honourable Percy Vane suffered a card to drop from his sleeve.

Jack saw it plainly enough, but took no immediate notice of it.

He determined to bide his time.

The Honourable Percy Vane proposed some refreshment.

Jack professed to be very thirsty.

His host produced wine from a cupboard, and Jack strolled to the fireplace.

Now, over the fireplace was a looking-glass, which enabled our hero to see plainly what was going on in the room, although his back was turned.

The door of the open cupboard hid Percy Vane from Lotty, but thanks to the reflection in the glass, Jack perceived his noble entertainer put a few drops of some dark-coloured fluid into two of the wine-glasses, before placing them on the table.

"Very well, Mr. Vane!" he muttered to himself. "We will see who is the cleverest. I very much think I can beat you with your own weapons!"

Unconscious that he had been watched, the honourable gentleman placed the two doctored glasses on the table, and immediately filled them with wine.

"Let us drink to our better acquaintance," said he, filling a third glass for himself.

"I know you quite well enough!" muttered Jack.

Our hero turned sharply round and brought his elbow into contact with a large china chimney ornament, which fell to the ground, and was dashed into twenty pieces.

"'Pon my life I'm very sorry!" said Jack. "I can't think how I did it!"

So saying, he stooped and began to gather together the pieces.

"Pray don't trouble yourself," said his host.

But Jack continued to pick up the broken china, so the Honourable Percy Vane was forced to stoop and help him.

The opportunity which Jack sought presented itself, and he availed himself of it in a moment.

With wonderful dexterity, and lightning-like rapidity, which would have made Herr Frikell turn pale with envy, he shifted the wine-glasses, so that one of the doctored ones should take the place of that which the Honourable Mr. Percy Vane had reserved for himself.

The next moment he was again bending over the fragments of the broken vase.

The pieces gathered together, their host returned to the table, and took the glass of doctored wine in one hand; at the same time sweeping all the money he had won from our hero into a capacious pocket-book.

"It is rather late, my friend," said he, addressing Jack, "or I would be happy to give you your revenge. Any other time I shall be most happy."

"You are very kind."

"I drink to your better luck," he added, and emptied the contents of the wine-glass down his throat.

Jack pledged him as he followed his example.

Lotty raised her glass to her lips, and a dread fell upon Jack.

He knew not how to prevent her imbibing the liquor which would deprive her of her senses.

He was forced to act quickly.

Shifting his position, he managed to give her elbow a sharp blow.

The result was, the wine instead of trickling down her pretty white throat was spilled over her new silk dress.

Now it is not pleasant to any lady's feelings to see a purple stain down the front of a new silk dress; and I very much fear Miss Lotty so far forgot herself as to call our hero an "awkward muff."

Jack expressed the most vehement distress at the accident, and endeavoured, with his pocket handkerchief, to wipe off the vinous fluid.

This necessarily brought him in close proximity to the dark-eyed beauty.

"I did it on purpose," he whispered in her ear. "The wine was doctored!"

Luckily Miss Lotty was not of a very nervous temperament, and received this news with great outward calmness, but took good care to resist all the pressing solicitations of Mr. Vane to be allowed to refill her glass.

It was not long before the effects of the drug began to show themselves upon their host.

But as yet he suspected nothing.

He had planned to rob our hero while under the influence of the narcotic, and was waiting patiently for it to take effect.

He felt a sense of drowsiness stealing over him, but he attributed it to natural causes, and struggled manfully against it.

At length, no longer able to withstand it, he closed his eyes, and in a few moments was buried in a deep lethargic slumber.

In a few words, Jack explained the state of the case to his lovely companion.

Then approaching the sleeping man, he extracted from his pocket the book in which he had placed his roguish winnings, and then, accompanied by Lotty, descended the stairs, and they made the best of their way back to the "Star and Garter."

That establishment, however, was closed for the night, and when at length after much trouble they succeeded in arousing the slumbering waiter, it was only to hear that the stables were locked up, and they could not have the horse till the following morning.

What was to be done?

Jack conversed in a low tone with the dark-eyed girl, and the result of this whispered conference was that Jack asked the waiter if he and "his wife" could have a bed there for the night.

Being stimulated in his answer by the present of half-a-crown, he became slightly energetic, and after a short delay, Jack and Lotty were ushered into a large, handsome room, and left alone for the night.

The first thing Jack did was to examine the contents of the pocket-book.

It contained a quantity of rubbish in the way of "flash" bank-notes and "duffing" sovereigns, and from a mass of papers fell a "ticket-of-leave," which left no room for doubt that the convict Ebenezer Chalk and the Honourable Percy Vane were one and the same person; but beyond Jack's own money it contained but few articles of real value.

The pocket-book inspected and refastened, Jack took—but it would be intrusion to pry into all our hero's movements, so we will for the present wish him good night, and pleasant dreams.

CHAPTER XLIV.

RETURNS TO OUR HEROINE, AND GIVES SOME ACCOUNT OF THE SISTERLY BEHAVIOUR OF THE ELDER MISS WHITE.

THE two sisters were face to face!

The one erect, hard, cold, defiant.

The other eager and suppliant.

"So you have returned at last, Miss Frances!" said her dear sister, in no pleasant tone of voice.

"Yes—yes—I only saw the advertisement to-day. Where is my father? Let me see him!"

"It is impossible."

"Impossible?"

"Yes."

"Why?"

"I'm sure I hear Fanny's voice. Why don't you bring her to me?" murmured the dying man, in a querulous tone.

"Yes—yes—father, I am here!" cried Fanny, eagerly striving to make her way past the gaunt young woman, who barred her entrance.

"On my own responsibility I decline to allow you to enter."

"For what reason?"

"You brazen, bold-faced, impudent hussey," replied the elder sister, her anger getting the better of her caution.

"You painted, padded woman of Babylon!—you child of wrath!—you vessel of vice!—How dare you ask me such a question?"

"Have you quite finished?" asked Fanny.

"Finished? I would talk to you for hours, if I thought by so doing I could do you good. But no, you are an outcast; a *creature!*—Ugh! Leave the house!"

"Not until I have seen my father."

Fanny perceived that her sister's design was to prevent her having an interview with her father, but determined to thwart her in this.

The elder Miss White, by the use of strong language, hoped to extract an outburst of passion from our heroine such as would warrant her in having her turned out of the house.

But Miss Fanny was not to be disposed of so easily.

She answered her sister with the greatest outward serenity, although it must be confessed her tongue itched to give her a bit of her mind.

"You will not admit me into my father's room?"

"No."

"Then I shall go in without permission from you."

"You will do nothing of the sort."

"Father—father!" cried our heroine, raising her voice. "It is I!—Fanny!—am I to be turned away from the door of your room?"

"No—no!—let her in! Do you hear? Let me see her before I die!"

In his eagerness, the old man raised himself in his bed, and spoke in louder tones than he had used for some days; but the exertion was too much for him, and he fell back on his pillow exhausted.

"You have killed your father!" said Miss White, in tones of the deepest reproach.

"It is not true! How dare you say so?"

"Such anger is most unseemly, Miss Frances, in the chamber of death."

"Let me in! let me in! I say. You have no right to keep me from my father."

Miss White's only reply was to enter the room herself, and before Fanny could follow her to slam the door in her face and lock it.

For two long hours Fanny waited in the dreary passage outside the chamber-door.

Waiting for news of her dying father.

Waiting for an opportunity of once more seeing his face alive.

At the end of that time, the door opened slowly.

Fanny started eagerly forward.

"You may enter," said her sister.

Our heroine was too much pleased to notice the tone of spite and triumph in which those three words were spoken.

Eagerly she hastened into the chamber.

There, on the bed, was the father she had not seen for so long.

His thin, pale, pinched features looked like wax, and appeared preternaturally white in the gloom of that October evening.

"Father—father—speak to me—say that you forgive me."

The old man answered never a word.

"Oh, why will you not speak to me?"

Still the same silence.

Afar off stood our heroine's sister, with a smile of triumph on her hard, cruel face.

Fanny advanced, and took one of the thin hands, which lay outstretched upon the coverlet, in her own.

It was icy cold.

The truth struck her in an instant.

Her father was dead!

With a piercing shriek, she flung herself upon her knees at the bedside, and covered the inanimate hand with kisses.

Her sister still smiled the bitter smile of triumph.

Fanny was hardly conscious of her presence.

She only knew that she had been kept from her father's side while he was dying.

She only knew that he had been as ready to pardon her as she was to beseech forgiveness, and that but for the cruelty of her elder sister, she might have been made happy.

But what was her reason?

Why should Miss White have desired so much to keep her from her father?

She could not understand it.

Her sister touched her on the shoulder as she knelt by the side of the corpse.

"Are you content?" she asked. "Are you satisfied now that you have witnessed the effect of your own wickedness?"

Fanny stared vacantly at her for some seconds.

"The law cannot touch you," continued her elder sister, "but you are, nevertheless, as much an assassin as if, with a sharp weapon, you had taken the life of this poor old man!"

"It is untrue!" cried Fanny, springing to her feet. "It is you who have murdered him! It is you who have caused him pain and anguish—by keeping me from him on his death-bed!"

"If you cannot command yourself better, Miss Frances, you must leave the house."

"I have no wish to stay in it."

"Then go."

"So I will, but——"

"But what?"

"Not yet."

"When?"

"I shall stay for the funeral."

"You shall not!"

"We will see."

"I will have you turned out, if you refuse to go quietly."

"You dare not."

"I will."

"I defy you. The house is as much mine as yours, until the reading of the will."

"You *shall* go."

"I will *not!*"

"You shall be compelled."

"I know the law well enough to be sure that you cannot use force—and, without it here I shall remain."

Miss White was forced to acknowledge herself beaten, and gave way with a very ill grace.

"Why should she be so very anxious to get rid of me?" thought Fanny. "There is something more in this than I know of—I must keep watch."

She did watch patiently, but without discovering anything till the day before the funeral.

Dr. Chickweed, who had attended Mr. White during his illness, was a very young man.

In appearance he looked even younger than his age.

He was very tall and very thin, with huge, ungainly limbs which, as he walked, swayed about as if they belonged to any one rather than himself.

His hair was long and of a pale straw colour—and to add to his beauty, he was in the habit of saturating his wisps of hair with bear's grease, and flattening them down upon his low, receding forehead.

To give himself an air of wisdom, which, in sooth, he sadly wanted, he was accustomed to wear a pair of green spectacles—through which he had the greatest difficulty in seeing.

He dressed always in black—in a suit of clothes which appeared to have been made for a man twice his size; but certainly his tailor must have had awful difficulties to contend with in making allowance for the strange angles and knobs in his ungainly body.

This was the man to whom the care of the body of Fanny's father had been entrusted, and who, every day since the death, had called to inquire after the health of Miss White.

Once or twice Fanny had met him in the passage, and had noticed, with disgust, that he had leered at her frightfully from beneath his green spectacles.

She little thought then how important a part he was about to play in her life.

The day before the funeral, Fanny was sitting reading quietly in her own room, when the sound of voices—one of them, her sister's—attracted her attention.

She rose softly and went into the passage, and looked over the banisters.

Immediately below her was a landing, upon which was placed a sofa.

On this sofa sat Dr. Chickweed, and on that gentleman's knee, with her arm round his neck, sat Miss White!

Fanny could hardly refrain from laughing at this strange and unexpected sight, and as she had no wish to play the spy, was about to retire quietly again into her own room when the mention of her own name attracted her attention.

" You're sure your sister Fanny was to have it ?"

This was the speech our heroine heard from the lips of Dr. Chickweed.

She determined to wait to hear more.

" Quite sure," said her elder sister, in reply to the inquiry of her medical lover.

" But it must be prevented in some way."

" Undoubtedly."

" But how ?"

" That's the question."

" I think it is to be done—yes—I think we can manage it."

"Tell me how, Socrates."

Dr. Chickweed's christian name was Socrates.

" Well, it's a bold game to play," said the doctor.

" But it's for a large stake."

" Yes," murmured Dr. Chickweed, thoughtfully. " A large stake, but a great risk !"

" You're not afraid ?"

" Oh, no !"

" Why do you hesitate, then ?"

" Do you know what it is I am thinking of ?"

" No. How should I ?"

" It would deprive Miss Fanny of her liberty."

" The artful minx, she deserves to lose it."

" And might result in serious consequences."

" It would do her good to be confined——"

" Is she at all that way ?"

" Nonsense, Socrates ! You know what I mean."

" Oh, you mean shut up."

" Yes. It would stop her rambling propensities. She wouldn't be able then to go running about after young men and dress indelicately."

" We'll put a stop to all that."

" It's the best thing we can do."

" I think so."

" Do you know she actually was bold-faced and impudent enough to have a lover before I had, though I am—ahem—quite a year older."

Miss White was thirty if she was a day.

" But you have one now !" said Dr. Chickweed, as he bent over her and gave her an oily kiss.

Miss White tried to blush but failed in the attempt.

" What is it you propose, Socrates ?"

" Marriage !"

" For her ?"

" No, my angel, for you."

" Pshaw ! I want to know how she is to be disposed of ?"

" Tell me exactly what the will says ?"

" How should I know ?"

" You told me you had managed to find and read it."

" Well, for goodness sake don't talk so loud."

" What did it say ?"

" It said that if Fanny returned home before my father's death, she was to inherit the bulk of the property."

" Nonsense !"

" It did, indeed."

" Well ?"

" She has returned home——"

" But she will not have a farthing of the property."

" Who will prevent it ?"

" The law."

" How ?"

" A lunatic cannot possess property."

" A lunatic !"

". Yes."

" But Fanny is as sane as I am."

" Hush !"

" What do you mean ?"

" That sane or insane, I intend in three days' time to have her fast in a private madhouse !"

It must be confessed, Miss White was a little taken aback by this confession, and she had disagreeable ideas as to the illegality of the proceeding.

" It will be a great risk, Socrates."

" Not if we manage it properly."

" How will you set about it ?"

" Oh, it will be no difficult matter. I and a friend of mine will sign the necessary certificate. You, as her nearest relative, will take the lead in the matter."

" But will any respectable keeper of a lunatic asylum receive her without further proof ?"

" I don't know about any respectable one doing so, but an acquaintance of mine in the country will be only too glad to number her among his patients."

" I hardly like the business."

" It isn't pleasant, but still our immediate union depends upon obtaining the money."

Miss White sighed.

A bird in the hand she thought worth any number in the bush, and she believed she had secured the yellow-haired doctor for a husband.

" Do you agree to the plan ? Shall it be as I have arranged ?"

" You will marry me at once ?"

" Immediately, my darling."

" It would be a kindness to prevent the poor girl returning to her sinful courses and depraved associates."

" A great kindness !"

" The best thing we could do for her would be to put her out of the reach of temptation."

" The very best thing."

" Well, then, I think——"

" What?"

" I think that——"

" You will agree to my plans."

" I will."

" Delightful creature !"

Another oily kiss.

" Lor ! Socrates, how you do tumble one about !"

It may be easily fancied that Fanny's sensations at overhearing this conversation, were not particularly pleasant.

She did not know how to act.

She heard the whole plan of the demoniacal arrangement, by which she was to be deprived of the money which by her father's will was hers.

What should she do ?

If she were to leave the house immediately they would, without doubt, manage to evade the law and deprive her of her rights !

If she remained, she was liable to be seized at any moment and sent to a madhouse.

What could she do ?

In despair, she leant her head forward upon the banisters. A comb fell from her hair.

Down it went, till the sharp points caught Dr. Chickweed on the nose, and brought the water into his eyes, as he was about to repeat his embrace of Miss White for the sixth time.

" The devil !" said the doctor.

" Oh, my !" said Miss White.

They had raised their eyes simultaneously to see from whom the comb had fallen, and just caught a glimpse of a skirt and an ankle.

The glimpse was quite sufficient.

The skirt and the ankle they knew to belong to Fanny.

" The devil !" repeated the doctor, scratching his yellow locks.

" What's to be done ?" asked the lady.

" I wonder how much she has heard."

" We must find out."

" How can we ?"

" I don't know."

" We must do something."

" What ?"

" Suppose she has heard everything ?"

" Well !"

" She will get the start of us."

" In what way ?"

" She will be prepared, and instead of our obtaining the fortune, she will get it, and we shall be put in prison."

" Oh, my gracious !"

" She must not leave the house !" said the doctor, firmly, after a pause of some moments.

" Who will prevent it ?"

" We must."

" How ?"

" We must lock her into her room for to-day."

Miss White and her lover went up the stairs.

Fanny heard them coming, and having little doubt they wanted to seize her at once, set to work to barricade the door.

It was a lost move upon her part.

The key of the room door was on the outside, and with a beating heart, Fanny heard it grate in the lock, and knew that she was a prisoner.

She ran to the window.

Escape from it was impossible.

It was a great height from the ground, and no friendly tree or water-pipe was near to aid her in the descent.

With a weary sigh she turned back and sat down upon a sofa to indulge in her gloomy reflections.

She knew there were people continually passing within sound of her voice, and she thought of shouting to them to come to her rescue.

But she refrained in time.

It was the very thing of all others her sister and the doctor wished her to do, as then they could publicly state her to be insane, and call the passers-by to listen to her mad shriekings.

But Fanny thought of this, and remained silent.

She was in the lion's den, and it behoved her to act with caution.

She knew she had nothing to hope from her sister.

Her only chance was to work upon the apparently susceptible heart of the yellow-haired doctor.

But would she have the chance of doing so?

She feared not.

Altogether it was a dismal prospect for her.

She repented already of having deserted Jack, and would have given anything to be once more folded in his arms.

But this was not to be for some time yet.

The day went drearily on, and our unfortunate heroine remained a close prisoner.

Night came, but no one had been near her.

At last worn out and weary, hoping sleep would come to her relief, she cast off her things and threw herself upon the bed.

For many hours she tossed restlessly upon the hot pillow listening to the distant church clock, which only told her how slowly time dragged on, till at last, from sheer exhaustion, she fell into a troubled slumber, in which all the terrors she feared presented themselves before her mind with ten times multiplied horrors.

CHAPTER XLV.

THE MADHOUSE.

THE first thing which met our heroine's gaze when she awoke the following morning, feverish and unrefreshed, was the form of the yellow-haired, green-spectacled Dr. Chickweed.

Behind him, half frightened at what had been done, was Miss White.

"How dare you come into my room, sir?" asked Fanny, indignantly, of the doctor.

"Hush, my dear young lady; pray don't excite yourself."

"What do you mean?"

"You see she is still in the same deplorable state," said the doctor, turning to Miss White.

"What deplorable state?" asked Fanny. And then for the first time became conscious that another gentleman was in the room.

A tall, benevolent-looking gentleman he was, with long, flowing white hair, and a benign expression of countenance.

Fanny recognised in him a Dr. Baker, who for many years had resided some little distance from Kingston.

She resolved to appeal to him.

"Dr. Baker," she cried, "you know me?"

"Yes, my dear—yes—keep quiet, there's a good girl—keep quiet."

"Why should I keep quiet? It is all a conspiracy; that sandy-haired man and my sister have been plotting my ruin!"

"Hush, my dear. You'll get ill if you excite yourself so much."

Fanny, in her eagerness and excitement, strove to rise from the bed, but found to her horror that broad leather straps had been fastened across it, which effectually prevented her from moving.

"What does this mean? Why am I confined in this way?"

"Don't excite yourself, there's a dear," said Dr. Baker.

"No, pray don't," said Dr. Chickweed.

"Keep quiet for my sake," said her sister.

But Fanny was thoroughly roused.

"Listen to me, Dr. Baker," said she. "I overheard those two last night plotting to get my father's money by putting me into a lunatic asylum."

"This is the strange delusion you mentioned to me," said Dr. Baker to the sallow Chickweed.

"Yes. Dear me, it's very sad. To think of her not knowing her best friends."

"Jack! Jack! come and rescue me," called Fanny, half beside herself with impotent rage.

"Who is Jack?" asked Dr. Baker, suspiciously.

"Some low rascal, I believe, whose acquaintance she made when she was away from home."

"Dear—dear. This is very sad!" said the goodnatured doctor, fully taken in by the specious lies of Socrates Chickweed, M.D.

"It is," said that gentleman, mournfully.

"Very!" said Miss White, applying her handkerchief to her eyes.

"Dr. Baker—you surely don't believe I am mad," cried Fanny.

"Dear me, if she gets so violent we must send for a strait-waistcoat."

"She had better be removed at once," said Dr. Chickweed.

"I'll go to-day to see the gentleman you mentioned as likely to take care of her," said Miss White.

"I won't go," screamed Fanny; "it's an infamous conspiracy. I'll denounce you; I heard all you said yesterday."

"I suppose you have no objection, Dr. Baker, to sign the certificate for this poor young lady's detention in an asylum."

"No—no—none at all. It's the best place for her. It's a sad thing; very sad."

Dr. Chickweed produced the necessary document, and Dr. Baker affixed his signature to it.

Fanny was in a dreadful state.

She saw her complete powerlessness.

She knew that every word she spoke would be but considered additional proof of her insanity.

She buried her head in the pillows of the bed and relieved herself by a burst of tears.

"That will do her good—poor thing!" said Dr. Baker, as he left the room.

Dr. Chickweed and her sister followed him, and our heroine was alone with her thoughts.

What could she do?

She was helpless!

The story of the conspiracy she had overheard was too wild and improbable to convince any one previously prejudiced against the belief that she was in her right senses.

Then at last a dreadful feeling came over her.

A feeling which chilled her blood, and sent a cold shiver through her frame.

Could it be the thought that after all they were really right, and that, in truth, she *was* mad?

Was the conversation written on her memory but the delusion of insanity?

She felt her brain reel at the thought.

She strove to raise her hands to her aching brow, but the strap prevented her doing so.

She felt that it would not be long ere she, indeed, would lose her senses if she were kept in this awful agony.

With no companion but her own sad thoughts, she lay helpless in bed for many long hours.

At length a servant whom she had known from childhood entered the room, bearing some food upon a tray.

Fanny rejoiced at this lucky chance.

"Lucy—Lucy," she exclaimed, "come here. I want to speak to you."

But Lucy only looked frightened, and did not approach nearer.

"Lucy, surely you do not believe I am mad."

"The doctor says you are, miss."

"But I say I am not. I ought to know."

"But you're not a doctor, miss."

"Dr. Chickweed is a scoundrel, Lucy, and wants to rob me."

"Oh, don't, miss, please don't; he said you'd go on like that, and that when you did you was dangerous."

"I tell you he is a villain. Oh, if I only had my hands free!" and Fanny struggled vainly with her bonds.

This so frightened the poor waiting-maid, that, setting down the tray, she rushed from the room.

Now, if the truth must be told, Fanny was beginning to feel uncommonly hungry, and the sight of the viands so near her, and which she was powerless to reach, did not add to her happiness.

Either by design or accident several more hours were allowed to elapse before any one came near her.

Then it was her sister who entered the room.

"Do you want to starve me?" cried Fanny, angrily.

"Now don't be violent, there's a dear," said her sister, coolly.

"Violent! It is enough to make any one violent, such treatment as this; but I know your fiendish plans. You shall suffer for it some day."

Miss White turned a shade or two paler, but answered calmly—

"I'm so sorry you suffer, Fanny dear. What can I do for you?"

"Unfasten these straps, and give me something to eat."

"I cannot unfasten the straps, but I will feed you, dear."

"Don't trouble yourself," replied our heroine, fiercely.

"It is no trouble, Fanny; or rather, I should say, in your sad state it is a melancholy pleasure to be of service to you."

"My sad state! You know as well as possible there is nothing the matter with me."

"Poor Fanny!"

"You and your vile lover plotted all this; I overheard you."

"Hush! Try and forget these strange delusions, dear."

It may be easily imagined how these answers irritated Fanny; how her blood boiled within her at each speech of her sister's.

But she was quite helpless.

She knew her sister did not believe her insane, and it was unspeakable torture to hear her talk as if she were.

Ultimately she was forced by the pangs of hunger to submit to be fed by her elder sister, who accompanied each spoonful with an expression of sympathy or pity.

Fanny registered a mental vow that if she ever got the opportunity, she and her villanous lover should be made to pay the full penalty for their wickedness.

There had doubtless been some narcotic mixed with the nourishment Fanny had taken, for no sooner had she finished eating than a sense of drowsiness came over her, and before long she fell into a sound slumber.

When next she recovered her senses she felt the sensation of rapid motion.

Opening her eyes, she discovered that she was in a railway carriage.

On each side of her sat a man.

It was night, but by the flickering light of the oil-lamp she saw they both had low, brutal-looking features.

For some moments she sat regarding them without their being conscious that she had awoke from her long slumber.

At length she moved.

"Come, none of that," said one of the men roughly, laying his hand upon her arm.

"Take your hand away," she said, indignantly. "What do you mean by it?"

The man laughed a low, coarse laugh, but took no further notice of her.

"Do you not hear what I say?"

"Oh, yes! I hear."

"Where are you taking me?"

"You'll find out when you get there."

"Help, help!" she called, not thinking she was in a carriage going over the ground at the rate of forty miles an hour.

"Shut up. We don't want any of your noise."

But Fanny was not to be so easily silenced.

She called loudly for assistance, despite all the efforts of her custodians to make her hold her tongue.

At length she became silent.

She had formed a plan of escape.

A plan, wild and rash.

A plan which, to carry into execution, would be almost certain death.

She determined that if she could catch her watchers off their guard she would leap from the door as the train went rushing and whirling on its way.

For this purpose she feigned sleep.

The two men, after congratulating themselves on her once more becoming peaceable, composed themselves in their respective corners, and before long their hard breathing told our heroine they were slumbering.

Fortune seemed to favour her.

Holding her breath, she made her way to the door of the carriage.

She put her arm outside, and felt the cold night air blowing upon it as she turned back the handle.

Still the door did not open!

It was locked!

Despair took possession of her.

Then she thought she would clamber through the window.

There were no bars to prevent her doing so.

She had already raised one shapely leg, and in a few moments more, in her desire for freedom, she would have been cut to pieces beneath the wheels; but luckily for her one of her watchers happened to awake.

With a loud oath he seized her by the waist, and called to his companion.

Together they pulled her back into the carriage.

In a moment something was slipped over her head. Her arms were pinioned to her side, and she was again a prisoner.

"That's spoilt your little game, young woman," said one of the men.

"She's a reg'lar dangerous one," said the other.

"You don't believe I'm mad?" cried Fanny.

"Oh, no! Not at all!" replied the man, with a cunning wink.

"Most decidedly not," added the other, with a hoarse laugh.

Fanny saw it was useless to attempt to convince them of her sanity, and resigned herself to her fate, and sank back into her seat, wondering much within herself whither they were taking her, and what chances she had of escape.

It was a bad prospect for her, and so she confessed to herself with a sigh.

Presently the train slackened speed, as they neared a station.

Hope revived within our heroine's heart.

"At all events I shall see people to whom I can tell my story," she thought; "or even if not, I shall see the name of the station, and discover what part of England I am in."

Alas for her hopes!

It was too dark to distinguish the name of the station from where she sat, and her custodians would not permit her to approach the window.

The train stopped.

"Now then. You must get out here!" said one of the men, roughly.

Fanny rose with alacrity, but she was not suffered to alight so easily.

The door had first to be unlocked, and then her two watchers got out first, and signed to her to follow.

She determined to make one appeal to the people loitering about before she suffered herself to be marched off by the two men.

"Help! help!" she cried. "Do not let them take me away!"

Two sleepy porters and a benevolent-looking old man came to her, attracted by her cries, while those passengers by the night train who were not asleep looked curiously from the windows of the carriages.

"Hullo! What's all this about?" asked the benevolent-looking old gentleman; "what are you doing with this lady?"

The bearing of Fanny's custodians altered considerably, on being thus addressed, and the elder of the two, touching his hat respectfully, whispered something in the ear of the old gentleman.

"Oh, indeed! Poor thing! How very sad!" replied he to the whispered communication.

"It is not true—don't believe it," shrieked Fanny, in despair. "I am not mad!"

"Poor thing! There then, go along quietly, there's a good girl!" said the old gentleman, soothingly, as he took up his carpet-bag and went his way.

"Good Heaven!" exclaimed Fanny, passionately; "will no one ever believe me? Am I to pass the rest of my life as a lunatic?"

The two porters looked after her compassionately.

"Poor girl! She's a bonny lass, too," said one.

"It's a sad pity!" replied his companion.

And so our heroine was taken on her way by the two men, pitied by all, but believed to be out of her mind.

It was dreadful agony to her—almost more than she could bear.

She shuddered as she looked forward to a lifetime to be spent immured in a hideous prison, with no companions and no hope!

A vehicle was waiting for them outside the station.

Fanny and one of her guardians got inside, while the other mounted the box, and drove away at a rapid rate.

She looked eagerly from the window, in the hope of being able to ascertain where she was.

But in vain.

At first their way led through the narrow, deserted streets of a small town, but before long they struck out into the open country.

As Fanny caught sight of the fields and hedges, in the obscure light of early morning, she sighed as she thought of the time which might elapse before she again would see them.

On—on still they drove at a rapid pace—now ascending a steep hill, and then rattling quickly over the smooth, level road.

The cold grey dawn of morning was dispersing the thick black night clouds as the carriage stopped before a huge gate in a high brick wall.

All around looked flat and desolate.

The morning mists were rising from the land around them, lending a dim obscurity to the scene, and casting an additional gloom over it, while afar off, a pale ray of light struggled with the thick cloud bank.

It was some time before the gate was opened; but at length it moved upon its hinges, and the carriage drove slowly in.

The gate closed again behind them with a dismal clang.

It sent a cold shudder through the frame of our heroine, who felt that now indeed all communication with the outer world was shut off, and that she was in truth a prisoner!

The carriage drove slowly up a broad gravel road through a large garden.

The very garden had a sad, disheartening effect.

It was so prim, so cold, so stiff, so precise.

The flower-beds all trimmed to a precise pattern, the lawn mown with such scrupulous neatness—all seemed to her so hard and immoveable, that her spirits sank even lower than before.

The house itself was almost like a prison.

It was of red brick, and rose straight, stiff, and stately from the ground.

The lower windows were all barred, and, as the door was opened to give admittance to our heroine, she saw with a pang of despair the multitude of locks and bolts which guarded the entrance to her prison.

"Now then, look sharp—step in!" said one of the men.

Fanny obeyed mechanically, scarcely knowing what she was doing.

The door closed behind her with a sonorous bang; and with a sad heart she heard the clatter of the fastening of the numerous chains and bolts.

Her two watchers put themselves on either side of her, and thus accompanied, she was made to walk the length of a dark vaulted passage.

The sound of their feet echoed dismally through the place as with a regular tramp they led her to confinement.

Suddenly they paused, threw open the door of a small cell, pushed her roughly in, slammed the door again, and hurried back along the passage, laughing heartily as they went, no doubt, Fanny thought, at having at length caged their bird.

Fanny stumbled as she entered the cell, and fell forward.

Luckily, a low pallet had broken the force of her fall; but she lay there scarcely conscious, but dismally bemoaning her sad fate.

The daylight increased.

Little by little our heroine began to distinguish the various articles (and they were few enough) which were placed in her cell.

Besides the bed on which she lay, there was a hard wooden chair screwed to the floor, and a small table secured in the like way.

Light was admitted through a small aperture high up in the wall, much higher than she could reach.

Even this small apology for a window—through which a young child could scarcely have crawled—was guarded by two thick iron bars.

Again Fanny's heart sank.

Deep despondency took possession of her.

How was she ever to escape?

What would be her lot if she were doomed to remain there long?

She shuddered as she thought of it.

She felt sure that a few weeks' solitary confinement in this dismal cell would drive her mad in reality.

At length sleep came to her relief for a while, and, worn out with fatigue, she sank upon the hard pallet, and slumbered.

When she awoke, the sun was struggling through the little window, and fighting valiantly with the rusty iron bars.

For the first few minutes, Fanny was unable to recal the events of the last few days, and looked round bewildered at the cold stone walls.

Then it all came to her.

Her memory returned!

With a piercing shriek, which went echoing the whole length of the vaulted passage till it died away in a low dismal wail, she seized the lock of the cell door in her pretty white hands, and rattled it to and fro, calling all the while for help.

Those delicate hands were cut and bleeding, but she heeded it not.

"Help! help!" she shrieked. "Let me out—I will not stay here—help!"

Only the echo of her own voice answered, shouting mockingly, "Help!"

At length some one came slowly down the passage and paused before the cell where Fanny was confined.

"Lie still, can't you?" the visitor growled, in something the same tone as he would have employed to a cur.

"Let me out!" cried Fanny.

"Oh yes—of course—that's very likely. Anything else you'd like."

"Let me see the master of this den."

"Come—that's a little more reasonable. What do you want to see him for?"

"I want to know by what right he detains me here."

"Oh! that's it, is it?"

"Yes."

"Well, look here; you just keep quiet while I go to find him."

"Oh, yes!" cried Fanny, eagerly, unconscious that her tormentor was but laughing at her.

"You keep quiet till he comes, my dear," continued the man, adding to himself as he stumped along the passage, "and then we shan't have much trouble with you."

Our heroine did as she was told, and remained quiet.

She threw herself again upon the bed to await the arrival of the master; but with woman's coquetry, remembering she might make an unfavourable impression upon him in her present disordered and untidy state, she hastily made as good a toilet as she could, and then began listening with breathless suspense for the sound of a footstep echoing through the passage.

But it came not.

Despair again took possession of her.

She felt she was in reality becoming deprived of reason.

Again she flew at the door, as if by her puny efforts to force it from its hinges.

Again she shook it, till those exquisite white arms were stained with blood.

Alas, 'twas useless!

The strong iron bars seemed to mock her misery.

The stone walls frowned menacingly upon her.

She shrieked and screamed.

She sank exhausted upon the floor, and bitterly sobbed out an acknowledgment of her own helplessness.

But suddenly a strange sound smote upon her ear.

A sound fraught with such mysterious horror, as froze her blood and left her breathless and trembling with dread apprehension.

It was the sound of piercing shrieks, mingled with wild laughter.

Laughter that could have come only from a maniac.

Shrieks which could only have been wrung in fearful agony from a tortured soul.

Fanny listened intently.

The sound as suddenly ceased.

She waited for a long while, but all was silent.

FANNY WHITE ROBS THE FARMER UPON THE QUEEN'S HIGHWAY.

Then again it broke forth with renewed violence.

Again the fearful cry broke the death-like stillness.

Then came the loud banging of doors, and men's angry voices.

Then silence.

Fanny once more began to batter at the door, and cry aloud for help.

CHAPTER XLVI.

RELATES HOW PHIL DAVENANT INVITED THE EARL OF STONECLIFFE TO SUPPER.

PHIL DAVENANT found his new life far from disagreeable. It was a grand change for him, from the hurry-scurry of the money-lender's office, and the close, stifling atmosphere of the check-taker's box.

Now he was a gentleman; he could get up when he liked, go out when he liked, and do whatever pleased him best.

For some days he idled about Easthorpe, talking to the country girls, and strolling about the lovely lanes and fields; but go where he would, do what he would, the thoughts would ever come uppermost in his mind—

"Who is this woman? What are her plans? How am I aiding her?"

"Mr. Davenant," said Laura, one morning after breakfast, "I have something I wish you to do for me."

"I am at your service."

"You have seen the Earl of Stonecliffe?"

"Yes—noble-looking swell, with a black moustache."

"That is he!" said Laura, with a shudder.

"Well?"

"You must make his acquaintance."

"The Earl of Stonecliffe's!"

"Yes."

"How can I?"

"You must find some way."

"I'll do my best."

"But that is not all."

"What more can I do?"

"You must bring him here."

"*Here!*"

"Yes."

"To this dingy little inn?"

"Yes."

"He'll never come."

"He *must!*"

"Of course, if you wish it, I will do my best."

"That's right; you shall be rewarded."

"When shall I set about it?"

"At once."

"To-day?"

"Immediately."

Phil Davenant put on his hat and went out.

He had no very clear notion as to how he was to set about making the earl's acquaintance, but he trusted to his usual good fortune, and went on his way whistling merrily.

Chance made him bend his steps in the direction of "Nelson Retreat," where it will be remembered Admiral Rattlin resided with his two daughters.

Now, it so happened that the admiral was walking, as was his wont, round and round his garden, when Phil arrived at the hedge which divided it from the road; and hearing the strange sound of the stumping of the wooden leg, looked over, impelled by curiosity, to see from whom the sound proceeded.

The old sailor went on his way unconscious that he was watched.

A weed upon one of the flower-beds attracted his attention, and as he was the personification of neatness, he was dreadfully shocked, and growled out a few strong terms of abuse against the neglectful gardener.

The weed, unfortunately, was just too far from the walk for him to reach it with his stick, without stepping upon the bed; but the idea of leaving it there was repugnant to his feelings, so, without reflecting upon the consequences, he placed his wooden-pin upon the mould.

The result may easily be imagined.

The soft earth gave way with the admiral's weight, and the wooden leg sank several inches into the soil.

The old sailor gave a yell of surprise on finding his leg suddenly become half a foot shorter, and struggled to extricate it.

But he was a ponderous man, and each effort but planted him the firmer in his own soil.

Now, unfortunately, the admiral was not blessed with a very good temper, and instead of setting to work patiently to set himself free, he struggled frantically and swore furiously.

Thoroughly enraged, he walked with his sound foot round and round, striving in vain to lift his timber limb from the soil in which it was imbedded.

Round and round he trotted, swearing lustily, and playing the very mischief with the flowers—but the leg only sunk the deeper.

Still he twirled round like a fat old teetotum, till, becoming giddy, he lost his balance, and fell flat on his back in the middle of a bed of tulips.

The treacherous leg snapped short off in the fall; and consequently all his efforts to rise were unavailing, and at length he gave up the attempt in despair, and lay flat on his back like a profane old porpoise, shouting for help.

Phil had witnessed the whole scene, crouched down behind the hedge, in order to laugh unrestrainedly; but seeing that matters were becoming serious, he composed his countenance as well as he could, jumped over the hedge, and hurried to assist the old admiral.

It was no joke to lift him, but Phil was muscular, and, with some little difficulty, managed to raise him.

But then the matter was not settled, for the old sailor was by far too fat and unwieldy to hop to his house, like an elderly cock-sparrow.

Phil, seeing the state of the case, helped him along, and, at last, had the satisfaction of seeing him quietly seated in a chair in his own house.

Then it was that Admiral Rattlin recovered himself sufficiently to discharge a volley of oaths and abuse at everybody and everything.

Phil waited for some minutes, but coming to the conclusion that the old sailor's language was neither amusing nor instructive, he was about quietly to leave the house, when the admiral roared after him, in a voice of thunder—

"Hi! Stop! Where the devil are you going?"

"Into the village," replied Phil, quietly.

"What 'the deuce do you mean by trying to get away before I've thanked you?"

Mr. Davenant did not know what reply to make to the question, so held his tongue.

"Look here," continued the admiral; "we're going to have a dinner to-day, and you'd better join us. My eldest daughter has asked a parson, because he can drawl and look sanctimonious; my youngest daughter has asked a lord, because he saved her from a cow. I have to pay for the dinner, and I'll be hanged if I aint fairly entitled to ask the man who picked me out of the tulip-bed!"

"You're very kind, but——"

"Nonsense; no 'buts'—you must stay."

"My wife——" faltered Phil, fearing to neglect the object he had in view.

"Your wife? Oh, never mind. Tell her you dined with the Earl of Stonecliffe, that'll stop her tongue."

"The Earl of Stonecliffe?"

"Yes. Do you know him?"

"No—yes—that is, I have seen him."

"Well, will you stop?"

"With the greatest pleasure," answered Phil, highly delighted at the chance Fortune had placed in his way of making the nobleman's acquaintance.

Phil did stay to dinner, and did meet both the earl and the Reverend Mr. Gorbell.

It would be tedious, neither is it necessary, to describe the admiral's dinner-party. How the parson said grace, how the nobleman flirted with Minnie, and how Phil kept his eyes and ears well open. Neither is it worth while to relate the various anecdotes which the old sailor, under the influence of his second bottle of port, narrated to his guests.

Suffice it that the dinner went off very satisfactorily, and that Phil, in pursuance of Laura's directions, made himself as agreeable as possible to the earl, and succeeded well in ingratiating himself with his lordship.

They parted for the night, and Phil returned to the inn, well satisfied with what he had done, to narrate his success thus far to the lady whom he called his wife.

Laura applauded him, and at the same time reminded him that as yet but half his task was done, for that he had still to persuade the Earl of Stonecliffe to enter the village inn to be introduced to her.

It is hardly necessary to follow Phil step by step in the measures he took to bring about the desired result.

He lingered about the park, he strolled through the preserves, he professed an ardent love of painting, in order to gain admission to the nobleman's house, where there was a fine picture-gallery; and all for the one purpose of becoming sufficiently intimate with the earl to warrant him in asking the nobleman to visit him.

At last the opportunity offered itself.

Phil had been walking with the Earl of Stonecliffe and talking much of his wife.

Their way lay through the village, and as they passed the inn, Phil exclaimed suddenly—

"Come in and see her, my lord."

The earl was taken aback by the suddenness of the proposal, and was about to stammer an excuse.

But to this Phil Davenant determined not to listen, and accordingly plunged vehemently into assurances of the pleasure it would afford his wife to make his acquaintance.

Pleasure! He little knew the mark at which Laura was aiming!

The Earl of Stonecliffe, taken completely by surprise, made but a feeble remonstrance, and at length followed Phil up the dark, narrow stairs which led to the sitting-room.

The apartment was untenanted.

Phil, making an excuse, left the nobleman alone for a few seconds, while he hurried to the door of Laura's bedroom, and announced to her, in an eager whisper, that he she wished to see was then seated in the parlour.

This much done, he went back to the earl with profuse apologies, and kept him in conversation till the door opened, and Laura stood in the entrance.

Phil Davenant saw that, for some reason best known to herself, she had taken great pains to make herself appear as attractive as possible.

She had succeeded well, and though still disguised with

dark hair and olive complexion, looked almost as beautiful a brunette as she did when Phil first saw her with her lovely golden hair clustering around her white brow.

Not only was it in her appearance that she strove to fascinate the earl.

By her lively and agreeable conversation she did her best to please him, and so well did she succeed that when the dinner-hour arrived it required but little persuasion to induce his lordship to remain.

A merry, happy, jovial party they had that evening, laughing and talking with the freedom of old acquaintances.

The Earl of Stonecliffe had by no means lost the admiration for a pretty face and a lively manner which he possessed when Lord Manningtree, and he was well pleased to form the acquaintance of so beautiful and fascinating a woman.

Still there were moments when a vague dread came over him.

When a feeling of awe fell upon him.

There were certain moments when gestures and expressions of this handsome woman seemed to remind him of something which had been.

Then for a minute or more the laugh would die away upon his lips, and he would become gloomy and abstracted.

At length the evening came to an end.

The earl felt he could stay no longer, so took his departure, reluctantly enough it must be confessed.

Phil saw him safely down the perilous, break-neck stairs, and then returned to Laura.

He had been astonished at her behaviour the whole evening.

He was at a loss to account for it.

He could not imagine the reason which had made her alter her nature so completely for those few hours.

He little knew how great the strain had been to her, but he partly guessed it when, returning to the room, he found her stretched upon the sofa, her whole frame convulsed with hysterical sobs.

It was not long before she retired to rest, leaving Phil to puzzle his brains over the strange events in which he was forced to participate.

Let us return to the Earl of Stonecliffe.

A strange uneasiness took possession of him as soon as he had left the inn.

An uneasiness which prevented him from going home, but forced him to linger about the spot.

Quickly he paced backwards and forwards before the door of the "Stonecliffe Arms," occasionally pausing, undecided, as if hesitating what course he should pursue.

After reflection he decided.

Leaving the road, he jumped over the hedge into the inn garden, and made for the back of the house.

A light was burning in the window of an upper room, and as the earl watched, the shadow of the figure of a woman was thrown upon the blind, the upper half of which was alone drawn down.

The earl looked about him, and found, lying near the spot where he stood, a long ladder.

He reared it against the wall, so that the top reached to within a few feet of the window where he had seen the shadow of Laura Davenant.

Quietly and cautiously he mounted.

He reached the top, and gazed in at the window.

For a moment he was unable to perceive the occupant of the apartment.

Then, as his eyes became more accustomed to the light, he distinguished her.

He pressed his face close to the glass.

Suddenly he uttered an exclamation of surprise.

A damp perspiration bedewed his forehead, and he turned from the window.

Impelled by curiosity, he again glanced through.

That which he saw inside left no further room for doubt.

With a loud oath, he sprang to the ground, hastily restored the ladder to its original position, and hastened through the wood back to his own house, with rage and despair written on his face.

Yet that he had seen had been more strange and inexplicable than horrible.

He had but seen Mrs. Davenant, in the privacy of her own apartment, remove those splendid braids of black hair from her head and pass a cloth over her face.

But those actions had sufficed to change her whole appearance.

Bright golden locks hung in clusters about a pale, fair face, and that face one that the Earl of Stonecliffe had good reason to remember.

The face he had seen in the pale light in his laboratory, the face he had seen when he attempted to poison his brother's coffee—the face of the girl he had murdered—the face of Lady Gertrude!

CHAPTER XLVII.

THE HORRORS OF THE PRIVATE MADHOUSE—FANNY'S PUNISHMENT AND ESCAPE.

"HELP! help!"

It was in vain she cried.

Her shrieks went dismally echoing along the gloomy corridor, but were answered alone by the demoniacal howl of some wretched maniac aroused from his haunted slumber by her piteous cries.

At length our heroine heard steps approaching.

She listened eagerly, and with a beating heart.

The footsteps came nearer and nearer, and at length paused before her cell.

Her heart beat violently with the hope that she might be able to explain everything, be able to convince the doctor that she was perfectly sane, and be once more at liberty.

The door turned slowly upon its hinges, and opened sufficiently to give entrance to a tall, thin man, of rather prepossessing appearance.

He was no other than Dr. Savage, the owner of the private lunatic-asylum in which Fanny was confined.

He was, as aforesaid, a tall, thin man. His features were regularly cut, and would have been handsome but that the whole effect of his face was marred by his eyes.

Yet they were handsome eyes.

Eyes of a cold grey, which seemed to pierce through you when he bent them upon you.

Hard, determined, relentless eyes they were, which, when you looked in them, revealed not a single soft expression.

You could tell from those eyes that there was no pity to be expected from their owner.

Our heroine's heart sank within her as she looked into that cold, hard face, and noticed those cruel eyes fixed sternly upon her.

"What is it you want?" asked Dr. Savage, sharply. "I heard you were inquiring for me."

"I wanted to explain to you," faltered Fanny, "that—that——"

"Well?"

"That you have made a mistake—that I am not mad, and that you have no right to confine me here."

"Is that all?" said the doctor, turning to leave the cell.

"Oh! do not go away! Listen to me. If you know anything of insanity, I can convince you I am in my right senses."

"I have the medical certificate, and your sister's written authority for confining you."

"It is a plot!—it is all a vile, wicked plot to obtain my money."

"I am told that is the foolish mania which possesses you."

"It is no mania—it is the truth—I swear it!"

"I cannot help it." And again the doctor was about to quit the cell, when Fanny flung herself upon her knees at his feet, and seized his hand imploringly.

"Do not keep me here! Have you no pity? Do you wish really to drive me mad?"

Dr. Savage made no reply, but roughly freed himself from her grasp.

Despair lent her strength, and, rising to her feet, she flung herself upon the madhouse-keeper.

"You shall never leave this cell unless you promise to liberate me."

With a sharp twist of his arm, he forced Fanny backwards, and with slight exertion held her firmly on the bed.

"Now, listen to me," said he, hissing the words slowly through his teeth. "You have had your say, now attend to mine."

Fanny struggled to escape his grasp, but it was a grip of iron, and she merely shifted his hand a little as he continued, calmly—

"Whether you are mad or not does not signify to me in the least. I have authority to keep you here; and as long as the stipulated sum of money is paid, I mean to do so. If it is not——"

"What then?"

"I will turn you out to starve and rot on the road."

"Anything better than being here."

"You think so, do you? Well, now, attend. I have not yet said all I wish. Here you are, and here you will remain, so I advise you to behave yourself quietly and well. If you do so, you will find the place comfortable enough; but if you do not, it will be made a very hell upon earth to you. Do you understand?"

"Yes."

"Then remember before you give way to any foolish outbursts of passion."

There was little doubt that this advice was good, and that Fanny would have done well to follow it; but just then the extent of the injury inflicted upon her was so strong in her, and her anger had risen to such a pitch, that she was disposed to be anything rather than quiet.

No sooner did Doctor Savage slightly relax his hold upon her than she flew at him like an enraged tigress.

The action was unexpected, and for the moment she overpowered him.

But she had not the means of inflicting any serious punishment upon him, and he soon managed to liberate one of his arms, take a small silver whistle from his pocket, and sound it.

In a few moments two men rushed into the cell, freed the doctor from Fanny's grip, and bound her hand and foot.

Then they looked inquiringly at the doctor.

"Cold," said he.

Though unintelligible to our heroine, the two men seemed perfectly to understand what was meant by this single word, and Fanny, powerless to help herself, was carried through the vaulted passage to another room.

There she was rapidly divested of her clothing, and then, bound as she was, placed in a small, upright box, something like a soldier's sentry-box, only more lofty.

Almost before she had time to wonder what would happen next there was a loud, rushing sound.

A sense of numbness came over her.

Her senses well-nigh deserted her.

Icy cold water was falling from a height upon her, pricking her as it fell like so many pins.

She shivered violently, she shrieked loudly; but a fiendish laugh from the men who were inflicting this diabolical torture upon her was the sole response.

The water fell in never-ceasing streams.

Her limbs became paralyzed.

She could not move hand or foot.

She felt her brain reel, her senses deserted her, and she remembered no more till she found herself lying again in her cell, with a small rug thrown over her, with violent cramps and aching pains in every joint of her body.

And this was the way in which Doctor Savage brought his patients to a becoming state of subjection.

But Fanny White had a spirit of her own, and, though cowed for the time, determined to wait her opportunity.

It was a long score she had to settle with her sister and Doctor Socrates Chickweed, but it was to be still longer before an opportunity occurred of paying it off.

Fanny, after she recovered from the shock of the cold-water bath, was unable altogether to restrain the rage which filled her mind whenever she thought of the villany which confined her in this dismal den.

Her anger showed itself in a thousand impotent ways; but for all of them she received some punishment.

Doctor Savage displayed a diabolical cleverness in inventing tortures for his refractory patients; and on those days when our unfortunate heroine was not the victim, she was safe to be told that some of her wretched fellow-prisoners were undergoing them by the piercing shrieks and dismal cries which ran along the arched corridor.

Hitherto, besides the man whose special duty it was to look after her, she had seen none of the inmates of the house, with the exception of Dr. Savage.

For every small offence came a great punishment.

The cold bath.

Half-starvation.

The strait waistcoat.

And last and worst of all, the dark cell.

A dreadful place was that dark cell! Far, far under-

ground, the loudest cries from it failed to penetrate to the fresh air above.

A gloomy hole it was, deep in the bowels of the earth, with green, slimy bricks arching it overhead, and pools of thick, stagnant water on the ground.

Not that this could be seen—at all events not at first—for the place was dark as night; but it was when the eyes became accustomed to the murkiness that hideous creeping things were seen crawling about the wall, and noxious reptiles lay upon the ground.

Then, too, there were rats!

Fierce, wild, angry rats, that required constant watching to keep them at bay.

There was a story, whispered only among the gaolers, that once Doctor Savage had placed a poor sick girl in this den of horrors, for some imaginary fault.

The following morning she was not to be found.

Only a few blood-stained bones, to which fragments of flesh were still attached.

But Fanny did not know this.

Still, when she was ordered by the madhouse-keeper to the dark cell, she shuddered instinctively with a vague terror of the horrible place to which she was to be removed.

The first hour down in that dismal subterranean cell was dreadful.

She shut her eyes, to hide the dreadful creeping things from her sight, but still the recollection of them haunted her mind.

She felt her brain becoming confused and her memory going.

A horrible suspicion crossed her mind.

A suspicion which drove every bit of colour from her face, and for the moment actually stopped the beatings of her heart.

The suspicion which thrilled her to the bone was founded upon her own feelings.

She felt she was in reality going mad!

She felt that her senses were deserting her, and that she was about to become the wretched lunatic she was said to be!

"Death rather than that!" she exclaimed, passionately. "I will escape or die in the attempt. Let me once get clear of this devilish place, and I will never enter it again alive!"

The force of this resolution recovered her for the time, and made her forget the hideous things by which she was surrounded.

"Escape!" that was her one cry, her one thought.

Regardless of the slushy pools and slimy matter which covered the ground in this hideous cellar, she crept forward upon her hands and knees to discover, if possible, where it terminated.

She crawled on and on, her hands coming in contact every moment with some cold, slippery toad, or other noxious creature; but her mind was so fully bent upon effecting her escape that she paid but little attention to the disgusting objects by which she was surrounded.

Still she crept on.

The brickwork of the cell was at an end, and she was in a small, low passage, roughly hewn out of the chalk.

Where would it lead?

Hope revived in her bosom as she caught a glimpse afar off of daylight.

Faint and pale it was, indeed, still it was the precious light of day.

The passage gradually widened, and she saw before her a spacious cavern.

She hurried forward to reach it.

Alas, her hopes were doomed again to be disappointed!

Her course was stopped by a large pool of water, which extended to a great width, and the depth of which she was unable to ascertain.

Baring her beautiful arms to the shoulder, she plunged them into the icy water, but without feeling any bottom.

Her attempt at escape—at all events for the present—was frustrated.

She could do nothing but turn back.

Still, though disappointed, she was not disheartened.

She determined that sooner or later she would reach the cavern, hoping thereby to escape from the hateful thraldom of imprisonment.

How long she remained by the direction of Dr. Savage in the dark cell she did not know, having no means of computing time, but when she was released the hours seemed to have passed with marvellous rapidity, so occupied had she been in forming plans of escape.

Dr. Savage chuckled to himself when he was told that Fanny had become more quiet and subdued.

"I thought I should break her at last," he hissed. "Not one of them can stand against my treatment," and he smiled approvingly.

But Fanny only bided her time.

She was waiting till everything was ready to attempt her escape.

Small in quantity as were the victuals doled out to her, still day by day she managed to lay aside part of them, not knowing how long she might have to remain in the cave without sustenance.

By degrees she tore up some of her clothing and bed-furniture, and plaited it into a rough but strong rope.

This she concealed by keeping it twisted round her body during the day, working at it only when every one had retired to rest.

But still the great problem of the manner in which she would be able to get across the water remained a mystery.

She determined to trust herself entirely to Fate, and accordingly, having made all the arrangements in her power to facilitate her escape, she proceeded to take steps to be removed to the dark cell.

This was at no time a difficult matter, and the order was given for her confinement there.

It was strange with what different feelings she heard this time the sentence passed upon her.

Before she had looked to the removal to the black, gloomy underground chamber as the greatest torture that could be inflicted upon her, now she looked forward to it with delight.

She heard the words spoken, the command given with ill-concealed satisfaction; and when she found herself once more thrust into the damp, dirty, dingy prison, she could hardly refrain from shouting aloud, in the gladness of her heart, for she looked upon it as freedom!

As soon as sufficient time had elapsed for our heroine to make sure she would not be disturbed, she commenced operations.

It did not take her long to reach the water.

It was a hazardous undertaking, plunging blindly forward in the dark into a pool, the depth of which she was unable to ascertain, but she preferred infinitely to do so to remaining behind to be exposed to the cruel tortures of Dr. Savage.

Luckily for her she found lying near the water an old wormeaten, battered plank.

This she hoped would help to support her, should the water prove beyond her depth.

Divesting herself of the greater portion of her clothing, she rolled it up as tightly as possible and flung it across the pool; then, plank in hand, she stepped boldly into the icy-cold water.

It rose above her waist before she had taken half-a-dozen steps, but it was freedom or death, and she persevered.

The ground shelved very abruptly, and, after another step or two, she determined to risk no more by wading, but to endeavour to paddle across.

Trusting herself almost entirely to the plank, she lifted her pretty little feet from the ground, and with her disengaged hand, strove to paddle across.

It was no great distance, and a practised swimmer would have made nothing of it, but as the art of moving in water had not been one of the accomplishments taught at Miss MacSpartan's select establishment, she was unable to reach the opposite side with the ease and rapidity with which Jack would have done so.

Holding on to the plank firmly, with grim tenacity, she managed easily to keep herself afloat; but the weak motion of her disengaged arm did little towards propelling her across.

Still, it was with the greatest satisfaction she observed the distance to the opposite side gradually lessening.

Yet she still had some way to go.

Her strength was failing her.

The diet and cruel treatment of Dr. Savage had made her considerably weaker than when she first arrived at the lunatic-asylum.

The coldness of the water numbed her limbs, and rendered her incapable of much exertion.

The motion of her arms became fainter and weaker.

A dread that her power was insufficient to carry her to the opposite side seized her.

Still, had the chance presented itself of returning to the care of the mad-doctor, she would have preferred persevering in her attempt to escape, even though that attempt were certain death.

Weary and exhausted, she at length was unable to continue her exertions.

Still clinging to the plank, as the only chance of rescue, she again let her feet drop.

They touched the ground!

She could scarcely believe her senses.

It seemed too good to be true.

Yet it was the fact.

There was no doubt about the matter.

Her delicate little feet rested on the hard, firm sand.

She still was a long distance from the dry land; but what did that matter to her now?

She had nothing to do, but to walk steadily on.

This she did, cautiously feeling her way with the plank.

Every step she took the water came less high.

On she went, till it only reached her knees, then her ankles, till, at last, her feet shone through the clear liquid, and the broad pool lay between her and the hateful, dark cell of Dr. Savage's private lunatic-asylum.

The feeling of thankfulness which came over her on finding herself so far safe may be more easily imagined than described.

Though the dangers and difficulties of her escape were by no means over, still the first step was satisfactorily accomplished, and that was a great thing.

She was forced to remain some time upon the opposite bank, to recruit her exhausted energies.

She had no means of calculating time; and as she lay upon the ground, she feared every moment that those coming to release her from the dark cell would become acquainted with her escape, and would institute a search for her.

But, luckily, Dr. Savage had determined that she should have a good spell of it this time, for he had made up his mind to "break her rebellious spirit," as he called it, and no one visited the noisome cellar where she was supposed still to be until hours after she had effected her escape.

After a long rest Fanny rose and donned her clothes, and then set about making her way towards the light.

Every step she took it became brighter and brighter.

Her heart rose within her with the joy of hope.

She saw before her the light of day; and as far as she could see, there was nothing to prevent her, ere long, from standing once more in the fresh, open country, her own mistress once again.

She was walking in a large, lofty cavern, cut out of the solid chalk; the ground was tolerably level, and she was enabled to proceed with tolerable rapidity towards the light.

At last she reached it.

With an irrepressible cry of joy, she looked up, and saw overhead the clear blue sky.

Still, she was not yet free.

The cavern in which she had been walking, had evidently been excavated for the sake of the chalk, and entrance to it had been obtained by the shaft up which she now gazed at the brilliant heavens.

But how was she to get up the shaft?

She could see the remains of an old windlass at the top, but that had plainly been long out of use—indeed, the whole aspect of the place showed it had been long deserted.

The sides, though not smooth, were too precipitous to scale; but with the light of day before her, and the dark cavern behind, the attempt was not to be abandoned at the very moment of apparent success.

Slowly she toiled and climbed up the sides of the shaft.

It was large and wide, and the action of the weather had in many places caused the chalk to slip away, leaving blocks and fissures which afforded her safe footing.

Altogether it was not, by any means, so formidable an undertaking as it had at first appeared.

She had mounted some distance, and was, indeed, only a few yards from the top, when she saw with horror that the short distance which separated her from freedom was quite inaccessible.

For the first time since she had crossed the pool, despair took possession of her.

As she looked up at the smooth chalk, which the rain had covered with a slippery, slimy, green weed, she was forced to acknowledge that to endeavour to climb it would be certain destruction.

The action of the weather had worn the chalk perfectly smooth, and there were no projecting lumps to aid her ascent.

What could she do?

True, she had the rope she had manufactured in her cell with so much difficulty.

But how was she to secure it?

She was standing upon a broad ledge formed by the slipping away of a large quantity of chalk.

Where she was she was perfectly safe, but to be so near freedom, and yet so far from it, was intolerable.

Her eye caught sight of a small tree, growing close to the top of the shaft, and hanging partly over the mouth.

She felt that she was saved!

She took the rope she had made from round her waist, and formed a slip-knot at one end. Then, weighting it with a piece of chalk, she exerted all her strength to cast it over the projecting branch of the tree.

Three times she failed.

The fourth she succeeded.

The rope passed well on to the bough.

She pulled it, and the slip-knot secured it firmly in its place.

The great question now was whether, after all her trouble, the rope were strong enough to support her.

She tried it in every way, and was convinced it would.

Then, with a beating heart, but a steady head, she commenced her ascent.

Holding the rope tightly in her little hands, she planted her feet firmly against the slippery chalk, and then, hand over hand, after great exertions, she gained the surface!

The danger over, and our heroine safely landed, she gave way.

The remembrance of the perils she had gone through, and the dangers from which she had escaped, took all her power from her; and now that all was over, and that there was no need for further exertion, her limbs trembled violently beneath her. Her brain seemed to swim round, and she was forced to sit down upon the edge of the shaft to recover herself.

When she had sufficiently regained her composure, she proceeded to look around, in order to ascertain, if possible, in what part of the country she was.

But there was no clue to guide her.

Nothing but a large, dreary tract of land intersected by low stone walls.

She could form no notion of her whereabouts.

She again sat down to reflect upon what steps she should take.

It was impossible, she settled in her own mind, that she should roam about the country alone, and in woman's dress.

That would, without doubt, lead to her immediate detection, for Dr. Savage, on hearing of her escape, would certainly send messengers in every direction to apprehend her.

The first thing was to get a suit of male attire.

But how was she to do it?

"I will get all the articles of man's dress," said she—"honestly, if I can, but I *must* have them, in one way or another!"

CHAPTER XLVIII.

HOW FANNY WHITE ACTED UPON HER DETERMINATION —WHAT SHE SAID AND WHAT SHE DID—WITH AN ACCOUNT OF A ROBBERY UPON THE QUEEN'S HIGHWAY.

OUR heroine saw at once that if she wished to escape detection it would be useless for her to venture abroad in the open daylight.

She accordingly remained where she was until the sun had set, and the country was covered with the darkness of night.

Then it was she rose, with an air of determination, and, despite the fatigue she had undergone in making her escape, trudged bravely across the fields, till she struck upon a narrow country lane.

This lane she followed, hoping it would lead to some quiet village where she might obtain the articles of clothing she needed.

But Fortune gave her the opportunity without the risk.

She was quietly plodding on her way, making, in her own mind, a story to tell to the shopkeeper, in order to obtain possession of the goods, when she heard the noise of wheels behind her, and looking back, saw a gig jogging steadily along.

Her first dread was that it might be one of Doctor Savage's messengers in search of her, and she drew back into the shadow of some trees, to suffer the vehicle to pass, hoping that she might remain unnoticed.

But such was not to be the case.

"Hullo, little un. Why art hiding away there? Shall I give 'e a lift into town?"

There was light enough for Fanny to distinguish that the driver was a jolly farmer-looking man, and his speech told her in a moment that he had been imbibing more than was good for him.

Our heroine deliberated in her mind whether she should accept his offer or not, and decided that no harm could come of it.

"Thank you," she answered; "I shall be very much obliged."

"Then jump up, my lass."

Fanny did as she was told.

"Thou'st a neat ankle, and art a comely wench, sure-ly," said the farmer, as he tried to put his arm round her waist.

But this Fanny was by no means inclined to permit.

"Come, lass, be sociable like. It's a long ten-mile drive we've got before us."

"Is it as far as that?"

"Every bit. You don't belong to these parts, little un."

"No."

"Where dost hail from?"

"London."

"Deary me. You baint trudged all the way on foot?"

"No. I came by train."

"Ah! Did ye now?"

The farmer, though a little intoxicated, did his best to make himself pleasant company; but every now and then his head would droop forward upon his breast, and he would sink into a sort of half-slumber.

Seeing him in this state first gave Fanny the idea which she carried into effect.

"This is a lonely road," observed she, as they turned into a lane, where the branches of the trees met overhead, completely obscuring what little light there was left in the sky.

"It is that, my lass."

"We are not near any village, I suppose?"

"There's not such a thing as a house under a matter o' four mile."

"Are there any robbers about?"

"I never heard on 'em."

"You've never been attacked?"

"No, my lass."

"You are not afraid?"

"Afeard! Not a bit. I'd like to see 'em try it on. Look here!"

The farmer produced from a side pocket a large horse-pistol.

"Just look a' that. It's loaded chock full, and the first man that tries to stop me would get a couple o' bullets through his head, he would."

"May I look at it?"

"Yes, sure."

Fanny took the weapon into her hands.

She had determined to play a risky game, but it was "nothing venture nothing have" with her.

"I'll trouble you to get down here," said our heroine, quietly.

"Get down?"

"Yes."

"What for?"

"Because I tell you."

The farmer gazed at her with an expression of half-drunken astonishment.

"Haw, haw, haw!" he laughed; "what a jolly wench you are! Haw, haw! I like a joke."

"This is no joke, as you'll find," said Fanny. "Get down this moment, or——" and she pointed the weapon threateningly at his head.

The farmer, though able to converse, had his brain in a queer, muddled state, which prevented him from fully taking in the sense of Fanny's request; however, in a heavy, lumbering way, he tumbled out of the gig, followed by Fanny, who first possessed herself of the rug and great-coat lying on the seat.

By dint of threats, accompanied by the cocking of the pistol, the farmer was induced to divest himself of his coat and trousers, which our heroine secured.

Then taking off one of her petticoats, she tied it over the farmer's head, helped him again into the gig, started him on his way, and retraced her steps, almost before the intoxicated agriculturist fully realized what had happened to him.

Had he been a shade more sober our heroine, without doubt, would have come off second best; but Fortune seemed to favour her, for he had arrived at that maudlin state of imbecility in which a command is sure to meet with obedience; and Fanny, with the garments packed under her arm, got over a gate, and struck across the fields, being afraid to continue in the road, for fear of falling in with any of the emissaries of Dr. Savage, whom she judged rightly to be on the look-out for her.

It was a sad time the farmer had of it that evening.

When he arrived at home, the greeting he received from his wife was not of the most affectionate description.

He had promised to be in by nine o'clock, and it was midnight when he arrived.

He endeavoured to plead an excuse, and his voice betrayed intoxication, and that called down vials of wrath upon his head.

But when he descended from the gig, and made his appearance in the light attire to which Fanny had reduced him, his wife's indignation knew no bounds; but the crowning point of all was the discovery of the petticoat!

In vain he told his story.

It was condemned as a pack of lies; and I can only earnestly hope that none of my male readers may ever have such a curtain lecture as was administered to the farmer that night before he went to sleep by his affectionate spouse.

But to return to our heroine.

She struck across the fields with no fixed design.

Her sole object was to get to a spot where she could effect the change of attire.

The moon had risen, and was shining brightly, and by its aid Fanny tripped lightly over the furrows and clambered over the gates, till she came suddenly upon a good-sized house, to which were attached numerous outbuildings.

Into one of these she crept, and by the light of the moon proceeded to examine the garments.

She could not help laughing as she saw their great size, for the farmer had been a stoutish, burly man.

Nevertheless, they were better than none.

Fanny instituted a rigid search in the pockets.

She could scarcely believe in her good fortune!

Wrapped up neatly in a canvas bag were more sovereigns than she had time to count, while in another pocket she discovered an old-fashioned housewife.

This latter was invaluable to her, and she set to work at once to reduce the size of the coat in order that it might have some little pretension to fitting.

She was not a tailoress, but her practice with her needle at Mrs. Herringbone's had taught her sufficient to make the requisite alterations.

At length the job was completed, and Fanny, in a few moments, was again in male attire—and uncommonly pretty she looked in it.

Rolling up the articles of woman's clothing which she had discarded, together with the fragments of the cloth she had cut from the coat, she took them to a river which ran close by, and, weighting them with a heavy stone, flung them in.

This act did her more good than she could have believed, for, the stone falling from them, the garments floated.

They were seen by some of the messengers who were in search of their owner.

They were recognised and identified as hers.

They made no doubt that she had committed suicide in a moment of insanity.

The search after her was abandoned.

Dr. Savage used some rather strong language at having lost a patient, but soon got over it on undertaking the care of a youth of eighteen, with a large head and weak eyes, who was heir to vast property, and whom, in consequence, his relations were eager to prove unable to look after it.

Fanny returned to a barn, curled herself up in the straw, and went to sleep.

She did not awake till one of the farm-labourers, finding her there, prodded her quietly with a pitch-fork as a hint that she'd better move.

Staggering to her feet, and rubbing her eyes, she was at a loss to comprehend at first what had happened, but it soon returned to her remembrance, and she hastily quitted the barn, made for the high road, and started off at a brisk pace to walk till she arrived at a town or village where she could get some breakfast, and perhaps remain for a day or two, for now that she came to walk she found herself stiff and tired from the exertions of the previous day.

Besides, it was some time since she had worn male attire, and the old farmer's garments did not fit quite easy at first.

At length, after ascending a steep hill, she saw in the vale below a good-sized market-town.

She hailed the sight with pleasure; but she had a great dread of discovery.

She knew neither the name of the town nor the county.

The day of the week, the month, the year even, she was unacquainted with; and she feared that if any unlucky chance were to reveal her ignorance, she would be looked upon with suspicion.

However, she walked boldly on, the bag of gold in one pocket, and the farmer's pistol in the other, and soon entered the town.

She selected a quiet-looking little inn with the sign of the "Horns," went in and ordered breakfast, and before the waiter could bring it, fell fast asleep, with her head on her arms, on the little, beer-stained table of the dingy inn.

Thus far she was safe, but how much longer would she continue so? What plans should she pursue?

All this was a matter for subsequent deliberation.

CHAPTER XLIX.

OF THE CONVERSATION FANNY OVERHEARD IN HER BED-ROOM AT THE "HORNS," AND OF THE RESOLUTION SHE FORMED.

FANNY WHITE, heroine though she is, cannot be expected to be altogether free from the weaknesses of humanity, consequently it will create no surprise to hear that, thoroughly fatigued and worn out by the excitement and hard work she had gone through during the last four-and-twenty hours, no sooner did she lay her head upon her arms, in the dirty parlour of the dingy inn, than she fell fast asleep.

How long she slumbered she had no idea, but when she awoke the shades of night had fallen.

The refreshments she had ordered stood by her side; the beer flat, the meat flabby, and the bread stale.

But hunger is the best sauce, and she set to with a will and speedily demolished the viands, bad as they were.

Thus fortified, she held council with herself.

What was to be done?

Should she remain at the "Horns" for the night?

In that case it rather increased the probability of her capture.

Should she make her way to London and endeavour to find Jack once more?

This plan had numberless objections.

At last her own sense of weariness got the better of prudence, and she determined to remain where she was for the night.

Ringing the bell, she announced her intention to the waiter, in as masculine a tone as she could assume.

Now, as ill-luck would have it, the waiter was not a white-neckclothed individual with a dirty napkin, but a strapping country lass, with cheeks like peonies and coal-black eyes.

This young lady, by a diligent perusal of romances, had arrived at the conclusion that, sooner or later, she would marry an earl, and being of a susceptible and imaginative temperament, no sooner set eyes on Fanny than she determined our hero was a peer of the realm in disguise.

Several things conspired to produce this impression in her mind.

Not the least was, that a wandering Gipsy fortune-teller had prophesied that the nobleman in question would be short in stature, and of light complexion.

Fanny, with her woman's tact, saw at once how matters stood, and determined to turn the affair to her own advantage.

But she was not at all prepared for so extravagant a show of affection as this young waitress was disposed to lavish upon her.

At length, to escape her importunities, she announced her intention of retiring to rest.

But the damsel must needs accompany her to her room, and remain so long instituting inquiries as to whether everything was satisfactory, at the same time throwing out unmistakeable hints, that our heroine lost all patience, and might have been driven to extremities but for the opportune arrival of fresh visitors.

The loud and continued ringing of the bell drew the amorous waiting-maid away, and Fanny, barricading the door to guard against any surprise, threw off her clothes and jumped into bed.

Her head had hardly touched the pillow before she was sound asleep.

Now for a few words respecting the general arrangement of the "Horns" inn.

An enterprising builder had conceived the gigantic notion of erecting a handsome street, and had got so far as to erect the four walls of one house, and dig the foundation of two others, when his funds failed.

Times were hard, and workmen objected to work without pay, so the enterprising builder went through the bankruptcy court, and the skeleton of the houses was advertised for sale.

It was purchased by a London builder, who conceived the noble idea of turning it into an inn, which was done.

But this necessitated some alteration of plans; the principal one of which, however, we need only mention.

The best bed-room on the first floor being considered much too large for any of its probable occupants, was divided into two by a thin lath-and-plaster partition.

It was one half of this room that our heroine occupied, the head of the bed being next the partition.

It will be readily understood by those who have had the happiness of living in a room divided in this way, that every sound in one compartment is heard distinctly in the other.

So much for the explanation of the internal architecture of the "Horns."

Fanny had been some time asleep, when she awoke with a sudden start.

Her slumber had been troubled with unpleasant dreams, in which the madhouse-keeper played a conspicuous part.

The first words she heard on opening her eyes were—

"Dr. Savage!"

So strange did it seem to her that she rubbed her eyes and stared round her with a bewildered expression, almost doubting which was dream and which was reality.

Again, close to her ear, she heard the hated name.

After listening for a few moments the mystery was explained.

Some one occupied the other half of the room, and their bed (for there were two voices) was placed against the opposite side of the partition, so that every sound was distinctly audible.

Fanny listened intently.

"Dr. Savage?" asked a woman's voice.

"Hush! Don't mention names."

Both the voices seemed familiar to her, but for a little while she could not recollect to whom they belonged.

"Why not, Socrates?"

It was the female voice again.

The mention of the name told our heroine at once who the occupants of the next chamber were.

There could be no doubt that her sister Agatha, and the sandy-pated Dr. Chickweed (now her husband) were enjoying a little private conversation before closing their eyes for the night.

What could bring them there?

Had they heard of her escape?

Had they come to assist in apprehending her?

She listened more intently than ever.

"It seems to me, Socrates," said Mrs. Chickweed, "that since we were married you have used me very badly."

"Used you badly?"

"Yes."

"In what way?"

"Every way."

"Don't be a fool."

"It's all very well, Dr. Chickweed, but remember I can take away Fanny from the madhouse whenever I like."

"Thank heaven!" exclaimed Fanny, mentally; "they do not yet know of my escape."

"Yes; but you don't like," rejoined the yellow-haired doctor.

"I don't know that."

"Come, now, be sensible, there's a good girl."

"It's all very fine your trying to get over me that way."

"We'll go to-morrow evening and call on Dr. Savage."

"Well?"

"And ask him about the young lady."

"What for?"

"To inquire into the state of her mind."

"Nonsense!"

"What is nonsense?"

"Your saying that."

"Why?"

"You know, as well as I do, that she is as sane as I am."

"I don't know anything of the sort."

"You don't?"

"No."

"What do you mean?"

"I mean it doesn't follow that because she was sane when we sent her to the asylum that she should be so now."

"Explain."

"Don't you understand?"

"I shouldn't ask if I did."

"Well, then, you must know that some of Dr. Savage's patients, who have entered his asylum with nothing the matter with them, have in a few months become raging and dangerous lunatics."

"How is that?"

"Oh, it is by no means difficult."

"How is it done?"

"Cold baths—solitary confinement—bullyings—whippings—tickling the soles of the feet, and so on!"

"And is this the course that has been pursued with my sister?"

"I hope so."

"You planned all this beforehand, then?"

"Yes."

Dr. Chickweed answered quietly, and with an air of satisfaction.

Fanny's rage knew no bounds.

She had suspected this to be the case, and now had confirmation of her suspicions from the lips of the villain himself.

"Wait till I get a chance of paying you out for this," she muttered.

"Then you propose going to see Dr. Savage to-morrow?"

"Yes."

"When?"

"As soon as it is dusk."

"Why not before?"

"I do not wish my visit known."

Fanny, in her anxiety to hear more, altered her position in the bed, causing it to shake against the partition.

"What was that?" asked Mrs. Chickweed, in alarm.

"What?"

"That noise."

"Rats," said the doctor.

"Nonsense. Some one has overheard us."

"Impossible."

"It's all very well to say impossible, but if our conversation has been heard by any one, it may not be pleasant."

"I have a bottle of medicine with me that would silence the most talkative tongue."

"What is it?"

"Prussic acid!"

"Prussic acid?"

"Yes; and I will use it, too, if need be. Better another man die than I."

"Don't go on like that. Let us go to sleep."

"With all my heart."

Before long the sound of two noses snoring in horrid discord told our heroine that her affectionate sister and conscientious brother-in-law were buried in slumber.

Fanny lay awake some time reflecting upon the course she should pursue, till, worn out, she too fell asleep.

But not before she had sketched out for herself the rough outline of a plan by which she hoped to have full and ample revenge upon her loving relations.

What that plan was we shall shortly discover.

The next morning she made her way into the dingy little room which did duty for a parlour, and, seating herself in the most out-of-the-way corner, waited for the appearance of the occupants of the bed-room next to hers.

FANNY WHITE AND "BLACK PRINCE" ARRIVE AT THE TOWN OF STOKUM-SLUSHY.

She had to wait some time, but at length they appeared.

Dr. Chickweed had his yellow hair parted in the middle and flattened down on his temples, with the full force of two hard brushes and a pot of pomatum, and his better half looked decidedly as if she had been making free with the vinegar-cruet.

Something certainly had happened to sour her temper; and as Fanny looked at the poor man owned by her sister, she felt a feeling akin to pity, which almost induced her to abandon her plan of revenge.

His woe-begone aspect at the sharp answers of his wife showed that the punishment for the crimes he had committed had already commenced.

Fanny, from her retired corner, watched them unobserved herself.

She was determined not to lose sight of them till she had had revenge.

Her breakfast stood unheeded at her side as she watched.

The attentions of the waitress were unnoticed as she watched.

For the whole day Fanny never let them from her sight.

More than once she was nearly discovered.

Indeed, suddenly turning a sharp corner she came face to face with Dr. Chickweed.

But he did not recognise her.

The male attire formed a wonderfully good disguise; besides, the doctor thought her to be safely immured in one of Dr. Savage's cells.

With a mutual apology they passed on.

Had Socrates Chickweed, M.D., known who it was who had pushed against him he would hardly have felt so easy in his mind as he did.

As soon as it was dusk the gentleman ordered a carriage, and his wife, putting on her bonnet, got in, while he gave directions to the coachman.

Fanny crept as close as she dared, and listened intently, but was unable to hear the instructions.

But again Fortune favoured her.

"Where to?" asked the stable-helper of the driver.

"The Asylum."

"The madhouse?"

"Yes."

"Savage's?"

"Of course. There aint any other as I knows on."

"And that's one too many."

"Drive on!" roared Dr. Chickweed, from the window, and the carriage lumbered slowly out of the inn-yard.

Fanny walked quickly up to the stable-helper.

"I say, my man."

"Hullo!"

"Do you want to earn a couple of sovereigns?"

"I aint a fool, and I should be if I didn't."

"Well, then, saddle me a horse as quick as you can."

"I daresn't."

"Why not?"

"Master never let's 'osses out to strangers."

"Not on special occasions?" asked Fanny, slipping some silver into his hand.

"Well, you're a gen'leman. Any one can see that with half an eye."

"Will you do it?"

"No larks?"

"No."

"All right."

"Look sharp, then; I want to overtake the carriage that left here."

"Overtake the carriage! Ho, ho, ho!"

"What are you grinning at?"

"Why, you might stop and have dinner, three courses, sweets, and a bottle o' port, and there be time enough to overtake it."

"How's that?"

"Why, it never was but a plunging, lumbering concern. The horse as draws it is lame, one of the axles is only fastened up with a bit o' rope, and the concern hasn't any springs to speak of, let alone the driver being dead drunk."

"How are the roads?"

"D—— bad!"

"Hurrah! I'll overtake them."

"I should just think you would."

During this conversation the man had been busily employed in saddling a good-looking bay mare which Fanny had selected from the stable as the most promising.

Examining the farmer's pistol, which she still retained, she put it carefully in the breast pocket of her coat, mounted the mare, and in another moment was dashing rapidly along the lane, in pursuit of the carriage containing her affectionate sister and her loving spouse.

CHAPTER L.

THE MURDER IN THE TEMPLE.

In following the fortunes of our heroine we have almost lost sight of Jack Rawlings, whom we left with Letty Burton at the Richmond Hotel.

The morning after the adventure in which the Hon. Percy Vane had appeared to so little advantage, our hero drove his new love back to London.

When he arrived at his lodgings he found his landlady in a state bordering on insanity.

"What is it, old lady?"

He asked the question in sheer desperation, for the loquacious dame had so much to say, and wandered so far from the point, that it was no easy matter to discover what had happened.

"Oh, sir, he came here this ever-so-many times, and he says, says he, 'I *must* see Mr. Rawlings,' he says, "'cos,' says he, 'it's a matter of life and death.'"

"But who was it?"

"He wouldn't give ne'er a name, 'cos, he says, it didn't matter."

"Is he coming again?"

"No, sir; and if you'd seen him here, sir, a matter of six times in an hour and forty minutes, you'd have said something tremendous was going to happen."

"But what was it he wanted?"

"I don't know, sir; but he said it was very special, and

very immediate, and you was to have it the moment you came in."

"It? Have what?"

"The letter."

"What letter?"

"Lor'! To think of that now!"

"What do you mean?"

"I've been a talking on, and never told you he'd writ a note and left it up in your room!"

"Confound you! Why did you not say so before?"

Jack pushed his way past the old lady, and rushed up stairs, where he found an envelope, sealed with a huge seal and directed in an unknown handwriting to—

John Rawlings, Esq.

He tore it hastily open!

There were but a few words inside.

They were as follows:—

"If you wish to hear something which will give you parents, wealth, and position, come to me without a moment's delay.

"J. D."

"Who the deuce can J. D. be?" said Jack.

He examined the writing closely, but failed to recognise it.

There was no date, no clue of any sort by which to identify the writer.

Suddenly he bethought himself of the seal.

It was very large, but he had fractured it in opening the letter, and all he could read was—

JA   TT,
        tor,
HEREND   RT.

For some time he puzzled over this without being able to form any idea as to what the inscription had been.

At last it struck him!

It could be nothing but—

JABEZ DALLETT,
Solicitor,
4, OTHEREND COURT.

Jabez Dallett, it will be remembered, was the lawyer to whom Mr. Kanem had referred our hero for particulars respecting his parentage, but so coldly had that gentleman received him, and so little had he been led to expect from him, that, in the bustle of his adventurous life, he had quite forgotten the existence of such a person.

However, the offer of information was not to despised.

Jack, with the letter in his hand, rushed madly from the house.

He hailed the first cab he saw, plunged into it, told the man to drive to the Temple, and was borne off at a rapid rate to the learned seat of law.

It was getting dusk when Jack reached Otherend-court, but he had little difficulty in finding Mr. Dallett's office, and, for the second time in his life, ascended the dark, dirty, dingy stairs.

As he entered the house he had noticed a man standing a little way from the door, partly hid by the deep shade of a projecting wall.

He had noticed him, but that was all.

He paid no attention to the skulking figure.

Had he looked behind him as he ascended the stairs he would have seen that figure close behind him, creeping stealthily and noiselessly up the stairs after him.

But his mind was too much bent upon the coming interview, and its possible results, to think much of any other subject.

He knocked at the office-door.

"Who's there?" asked a sharp voice.

"Mr. Rawlings."

"Is any one with you?"

"No."

"You're sure of that?"

"Quite."

There was a pause of some minutes, then came the rattling of chains and bolts, and the door was slowly opened a few inches.

" Come in."

Jack pushed at the door till it opened sufficiently to give him entrance.

No sooner was he inside than the door was slammed to and the fastenings again put up.

Not a single ray of light penetrated into the apartment, and Jack was unable to form the least idea of where he was.

In a few moments there was the blue glare of a match, and then a candle was lighted.

By its dismal gleam our hero discovered that he was in the outer office into which he had entered when he first visited Mr. Dallett.

It was the same room; but how strangely altered!

When he had been there before everything was spick and span; now, all was in disorder.

The desks and books were inch thick with dust.

The clerks' stools were thrown down and broken.

The ink was dried in the bottles, and the papers were dirty and wormeaten.

But if the alteration in the room was great, that in the owner was still greater.

From the prim, sharp, business man, the neat, shrewd lawyer, he had altered to the old, sickly, careworn, broken-down man.

His face was innocent of soap and razor.

A ragged grey beard hung from his chin, his eyes were deep sunk in their sockets, and every moment he glanced round him with the nervous, frightened air of a man who dreads detection.

Jack could hardly believe his eyes.

There was about the whole affair an air of so much mystery that he had failed to form any idea of what it all meant, and could only stare at the strange figure cowering before him, and wait for an explanation.

" Are you John Rawlings?" asked the lawyer.

" I am."

" How am I to know that?" he continued, suspiciously.

" Why should you doubt it?"

" Don't ask. I doubt everything and everybody."

" What is it you have to say to me?"

" Hush, hush! Don't speak so loud. We may be overheard!"

" What does all this mystery mean?"

" You will learn before long. Are you quite sure there is no one listening?"

" Yes."

It will be remembered the figure which slunk stealthily up the stairs behind Jack had not been perceived by him.

" Then listen to me."

" I'm all attention."

" You remember coming here to see me just before you left Mr. Kanem's establishment?"

" Perfectly."

" And asking me concerning your parentage?"

" Yes. You said you did not know."

" I told you a lie."

" I thought so at the time."

" When you came to see me on that occasion I was a prosperous, well-to-do man, but it was not all legal business upon which I throve."

" What then?"

" I had a secret, and traded upon it."

" A secret?"

" Yes. The secret of your birth."

" Of my birth?"

" Yes."

" Go on."

" For many years I was paid well for keeping you out of the way."

" Then are you not now?"

" If I were I shouldn't be such a fool as to give up a comfortable annuity for the sake of benefiting you."

" Do you know my father?"

" Never saw him in my life."

" My mother?"

" No."

" Well, for Heaven's sake get on."

" Let me tell the story in my own way."

" All right."

" Well, as I was telling you, it was to the interest of a certain great man to keep your existence a secret. He and I were the only ones who knew that you lived, and my silence was purchased at a large price."

" Well?"

" This great man died."

" And your pension stopped?"

" Precisely. But it was equally important that the great man's heir should purchase the secret. I went to him."

" And he refused?"

" He did. He laughed at me, and fairly told me he didn't care a straw about it. I persisted, and endeavoured to terrify him, but found that I had got hold of the wrong sort of gentleman for that."

" Who was it? What was his name?"

" You will know in good time. He called me hard names; I retorted, and he swore an oath that he would ruin me. I did not care at the time. I thought it only a vague threat; but his words came true."

" How do you mean?"

" Bit by bit my business left me; my managing clerk absconded with the cash-box. In short, everything went wrong, and I became what you now see me."

" Then do I understand you aright that your object in bringing me here is to reveal to me a secret, my knowledge of which will injure the man who has ruined you?"

" Exactly."

" Why did you not tell me it before?"

" I have had a long job to track you from place to place —but I—I—had another reason."

" What was it?"

" Hush! Hush! Draw your chair close to mine—quite close—and I will whisper it to you."

Wondering what this portended, our hero complied with the old man's request.

" When he threatened me with ruin I threatened him with the secret, upon which he said—' Jabez Dallett, mark me. Remain quiet, and I will only ruin you; but remember, one word from you on the subject of the secret to any living soul will be your death-warrant!' "

" Did he mean murder?"

" He did. I saw it in his eye—I saw that my doom was sealed from that time."

" Yet you are not afraid of your fate?"

" Fool! Do you not see if I die, or am killed before speaking, the secret will be buried with me, but if I reveal it first I will have revenge? Yes, when my old bones are rotting away in a pauper's grave you will be rolling in wealth, and he—he will be fighting and clutching at the gold—at the name—at the position, all of which must slip through his fingers and fall into your lap."

Jabez Dallett got quite excited over his long speech, and rubbed his knees with his long bony hands, and cawed out a feeble chuckle.

" Do you mean to say," said Jack, " that I am entitled to some money?"

" Money?"

" Yes."

" A fortune—the wealth of the Indies—a title—everything that man can desire!"

" How?"

" By your birth."

" Tell me who my parents are."

" Yes—yes——"

" Well?"

" Are you sure no one is listening?"

" Yes. Who can there be?"

" I don't know. I am nervous and frightened. If *he* should be there."

" Who do you mean?"

" The man I dread—the man who has ruined me—the man who has sworn to have my life!"

" Nonsense! Where can he be?"

" I don't know. I suppose it is all an old man's foolish fancy."

" Never mind; there's no one here besides ourselves."

" Well, then, your father was the Earl——for Heaven's sake go to the door!"

" What's the matter?"

" The noise! Did you not hear it? There is some one there!"

" I heard nothing," cried Jack, impatiently; " go on!"

" Before I tell you more you must take a solemn oath."

" What is it?"

" It is this. You must swear that come what may you will never falter in the object before you."

" But what is the object?"

" The ruin of the present possessor of *your* property."

"In what way?"

"He must be turned out to die a beggar in the gutter—you must take every farthing from him."

"Trust me for that."

"You swear."

"I do."

"Well, then,——"

"My father was——"

"Your father was one of the noblest in the land—he was the Earl——"

Before Jabez Dallett could mention the name a terrific blow was dealt upon the outer door.

The solicitor started from his seat, shivering violently.

"Go to the door—open it—see who is there!" cried Dallett, the perspiration standing in great drops on his brow.

Jack removed the chains and bolts with as much haste as possible, and flung the door wide open.

There was no one there.

Jack re-fastened the door and returned to the old man, who could hardly speak for fright.

"There was no one there," said he; "now tell me."

"No—no—I cannot tell you now—not to-night. Not now. Come to me to-morrow—in the daylight—then you shall hear all."

"At least, tell me my father's name."

"Not now—no—I cannot speak it now. To-morrow morning."

Jack strove in vain to alter the old man's decision.

His entreaties and expostulations were alike useless.

He could only extract from him that he should hear all particulars the first thing on the following morning.

At length, he reluctantly took his departure, the old man coming to the banisters to light him downstairs.

Neither of them saw the dark figure which slipped so quickly and quietly into the room when the door was opened and their backs were turned.

Jack, full of wonder, returned to his lodgings, and Jabez Dallett, with a nervous glance behind him, re-entered his gloomy abode.

* * * * *

There were not many people in Otherend-court that evening, and of the few who were there none heard the one piercing death-shriek that went up into the night-air.

The cabs rattled by through Fleet-street, the merry-makers and roysterers staggered upon their homeward way, all unconscious of the dreadful tragedy that was being enacted so close to them.

The death-cry was unheard save by one, and he was too hardened to mind it.

A wretched old man lay stretched upon a floor, the blood flowing from a deep gash in his throat, dyeing and matting his long unkempt white beard.

His eyes were fixed with a glassy stare upon the ceiling.

His lips were parted with the cry of his death-agony, but the eyes were sightless, and the lips immoveable.

Jabez Dallett was dead!

CHAPTER LI.

FANNY TAKES TO THE ROAD.

It was some little time before our heroine became accustomed to the motion of the horse.

She had been accustomed to equestrian exercise from her earliest days; but then it is a very different thing to ride on a side-saddle with a flowing skirt to sitting astride the animal and bending over his neck as you urge him to full speed.

At length, Fanny caught sight of the old lumbering coach toiling up a steep hill, and as her object was not to reveal herself till after the worthy pair had paid their visit to Dr. Savage, she drew rein, slackened speed, and walked her steed leisurely up hill.

For the whole of the distance she loitered behind the carriage, marking well the position of the roads and fields on each side of her.

At last they came in sight of the gloomy mansion of Dr. Savage.

Fanny could not repress a shudder as she once more saw the dismal portals which had closed behind her with so ominous a clang the night of her arrival at the lunatic asylum.

She almost wondered at her own courage in being able to approach the dreadful place.

But then she had a purpose!

A purpose which laughed at and defied all obstacles.

A purpose, before which dangers and difficulties melted away like smoke.

And that purpose was—revenge!

I know, my dear reader, that it is very shocking to bear malice, and that a desire to "pay any one out" is most unchristianlike.

Yet Fanny had good reason.

Surely she had been tried enough, tortured enough, ill-treated enough, to make any course justifiable.

At least, so she argued, and as she is my heroine, I cannot presume to differ from her.

The carriage containing Dr. and Mrs. Chickweed speedily obtained admittance through the iron-bound gates into the prim garden, and Fanny reined in her horse and waited patiently for their reappearance.

She had not to wait very long before the gates opened and the carriage came out.

Far distant as she was our heroine heard distinctly the very bad language the doctor made use of as he directed the coachman to drive back to the "Horns."

Fanny could not help smiling and chuckling to herself as she fancied the blank look of despair upon their faces when informed by Dr. Savage of her escape.

The carriage started off at a good speed, for the aged quadruped which drew it knew his head was turned homeward.

Fanny followed at a little distance.

They were approaching the most lonely part of the road.

A steep hill led down into a little valley, through which ran a pretty silvery stream, which was crossed by a ramshackle wooden bridge.

There was no house or cottage within sight.

The road was arched over by trees, which rendered it perfectly dark, and the wind moaning dismally among their tops made it if anything more gloomy than it was naturally.

The carriage containing the doctor and his newly-married wife reached the brow of the hill leading down into the hollow.

Fanny paused and drew from her pocket a fragment of black lace, the remnant of some of her former finery.

This she fastened in such a way inside her hat that it fell over her face, entirely concealing her features.

This done, she put spurs to her steed and soon regained her original position with reference to the carriage.

There was just sufficient light for her to see that it was conducting itself in a way by no means becoming to a vehicle.

It swayed violently from side to side.

It lurched and toppled in a most ominous manner.

The driver was evidently too far gone in intoxication to have any idea what he was about, and yelled and flourished his whip in a way which would have frightened any animal capable of feeling alarm.

When the vehicle reached the bottom of the hill the poor brute that had been condemned to draw it gave way.

It staggered, recovered itself momentarily, and then fell heavily over on its side.

The axle of the carriage, startled out of its sense of propriety by this accident, snapped asunder, the vehicle turned over, the driver was shot off his perch into a dry ditch, and Dr. and Mrs. Chickweed struggled in vain to free themselves.

Fanny rode rapidly down the hill when she perceived the accident.

On reaching the carriage and looking inside, she could scarcely refrain from laughing.

The doctor, in his struggles, had in some way managed to get his head through the hoops of his wife's crinoline, and all his exertions were unavailing to free himself, and there he remained, looking like an ugly old Cochinchina fowl in a hen-coop.

Mrs. Chickweed certainly did not appear to advantage, revealing as she did a great deal of flannel petticoat and rather more than is generally considered proper of the thinnest shanks of legs that can be imagined.

Her shrill voice rose in angry tone above the growling of her husband's oaths.

He responded only by making renewed efforts to escape from the thraldom of the hoops.

It was upon this scene of struggling, bustling, screaming, swearing, confusion, that our heroine looked in.

Dr. Chickweed first caught sight of the black face peering in at the carriage window.

"The devil!" said he, in an alarmed tone.

"Precisely!" replied Fanny, in a feigned voice, and with a polite bow.

"Let me out—let me out!" screamed Mrs. Chickweed.

"Take this infernal thing away from my neck!" yelled the doctor.

"We wont go home till morning," sang the inebriated driver, sitting bolt upright in the dry ditch.

Fanny had fastened the horse to a neighbouring tree, and now proceeded to unwind some stout rope which did duty for harness.

"Can I help you?" said she, again appearing at the carriage window.

"Curse you, yes!" was Dr. Chickweed's civil answer.

Fanny wrenched open the door, and assisted him to alight, but no sooner had his feet touched the ground, than the rope was round his wrists, and a handkerchief stuffed into his mouth.

So unexpected was the attack upon the doctor that he was unable to offer any resistance, and our heroine the next moment tripped him up by a common trick, and then he lay bound and helpless, staring vacantly at the trees overhead.

Without the slightest remorse she served her sister in the same way.

"Not so bad that for a beginner!" said she, smiling complacently.

But the business was not yet completed.

By dint of threats and the farmer's pistol, she brought Dr. Socrates to a thin tree, to which, with plenty of rope, she fastened him tightly, and then fetching his charming wife, served her in the same way.

It certainly was a ludicrous spectacle, this worthy couple bound hand and foot and tied fast to a couple of trees, with their mouths kept wide open by a couple of pocket-handkerchiefs.

Fanny, when she had completed the job, was so pleased with her own handiwork, that she sat down on the parapet of the bridge, and roared with laughter.

As soon as she had sufficiently recovered her composure she examined the priming of her pistol, cocked it, and walked up to Dr. Chickweed, who was quaking with fear.

By dint of threats and bullyings, in all of which the pistol played a prominent part, our heroine extracted from the two unfortunates all the money and articles of value they had about them.

Then leaving them still tied to the trees, staring vacantly at each other without the power of speech or motion, she remounted her horse, jumped over the hedge, and galloped away over the fields as fast as the animal would carry her.

And this was Fanny's first highway robbery!

"'Pon my life," said she to herself, "it must be very jolly. I've a good mind to take to the road altogether."

Dr. Chickweed and his wife remained tied to their respective trees for the remainder of the night, for the road was an unfrequented one, and no passengers came by.

Cold and shivering they remained, unable either to move or speak; and when at length a labourer going to his work discovered their position and liberated them, they were so benumbed with cold as to be scarcely able to stir their limbs.

The old horse which had drawn them thus far was dead, and, although the driver was after a long search discovered and aroused, he was unable to suggest anything better than that the lady and gentleman should walk back to the inn.

With much grumbling they did so, and arrived, weary, hungry, and footsore, at the "Horns," with the story to relate of a drunken driver, a dead horse, and a smashed carriage.

But this was not all.

The landlord could have borne with all this, but that his visitors were penniless.

Fanny had eased them of all their money, and the end of the matter was that they were literally detained in pawn by the landlord of the "Horns" until Socrates Chickweed had written to London and got a fresh supply of cash.

Fanny was partly avenged.

After committing the robbery as already related, she put the bay mare at the hedge, and alighted safely on the other side, and then rode on and on over the fields, till she struck upon a broad turnpike road, which she followed leisurely.

All night long she continued on her way, wishing to put as great a distance as possible between herself and her sister.

As the grey light of morning appeared over the hill-tops, our heroine perceived she was nearing a large town.

Fearful that the horse she rode might be recognised, and suspicion attached to herself, she dismounted, and turned him into a neighbouring field, which, with a crack of her whip, she sent him galloping across, to find his way home as best he might.

Then on foot she pursued her way.

She had not gone far before, at the junction of two roads, she fell in with a couple of countrymen, and from them she learnt that the town before her was called Chalkborough.

She also learnt that a great cattle-fair was to be held there that day.

This discovery she hailed with delight, knowing that in the crowd of strangers who would certainly be present it would be comparatively easy to escape notice.

They entered Chalkborough just as the day's work was commencing.

The sleepy shop-boys were taking down the shutters, and yawning ostlers stood waiting in inn-yards to put up the horses of early arrivals.

Fanny's first care was to rid herself of the two countrymen who had accompanied her thus far.

This done, she made a round of visits to the different outfitters in the town, and from each one obtained some article of the dress she required.

At length all was purchased.

It was still early, and our heroine walked rapidly a little way out of the town till she arrived at a quiet and retired spot, where she effected the change in her attire.

When she again made her appearance in the streets of Chalkborough, walking with something of a swagger, more than one female head turned to look at the handsome youth who strolled jauntily along, tapping his riding-boot with his whip, and whistling merrily to himself.

Certainly Fanny looked remarkably well in her new disguise.

Her head was surmounted by a knowing-looking little hat, her upper lip was decorated with a small light moustache, while the cords, and long riding-boots reaching to her knees, set off her symmetrical limbs to advantage.

A smart cut-away coat completed her dress.

Her hands, neatly gloved, held a pretty riding-whip, and in her pocket, hidden from sight, lurked a formidable six-shooter revolver.

Boldly she walked into one of the first hotels in the town, ordered breakfast, slanged the waiter, and kissed the chamber-maid; then, having completed her repast, lit a cigar, and strolled leisurely to the field where the cattle-fair was being held.

The object which took her there was to purchase a horse.

To attempt highway robbery on foot she saw would be but to be caught and confined in prison, so she had wisely resolved to buy a first-rate animal.

She had not been long in the fair when her attention was drawn to the very animal she desired.

She was no mean judge of horseflesh, and the first glance sufficed to show her the beauties of the coal-black quadruped before her.

Further inspection showed him to be bad tempered, but Fanny, confident in her own powers of horsemanship, cared little for that, and after a good deal of haggling, paid down two-thirds of the sum originally demanded, mounted the horse, and rode slowly through the crowd and out into the open country.

"I must give him some name," thought Fanny, with reference to her recent purchase. "I will call him BLACK PRINCE."

And so the horse came to be called Black Prince, and our heroine rode steadily on, caring little whither she went, deliberating in her own mind as to what would be the safest course for her to pursue.

Before long, she came to a large, wide-spreading, open common, and there she determined to try the capabilities of her new purchase.

In every respect he exceeded her expectations.

He went like the wind, taking her over the ground with his long stride with marvellous rapidity.

"Of one thing I may be sure," said Fanny, as she regained the road and settled down into a steady trot—"of one thing I may be sure, and that is, that in a fair stern chase it will be but little chance my pursuers will have."

Late in the afternoon she reached the town of Humpton, and riding up to the best inn, dismounted and made herself comfortable for the night.

CHAPTER LII.

THE BLOOD STAIN ON THE CEILING.

THE morning after the interview related in a former chapter between our hero and Jabez Dallett, Jack rose early, and after a hasty breakfast made his way again to Otherend-court.

He had had but little sleep during the night.

Excitement and expectation almost prevented him from closing his eyes.

He recalled to his memory each word spoken by the old solicitor, and tried to string them together into something like a connected form.

But he failed in his endeavour.

That he was of good, if not noble birth, Dallett's words left no doubt.

But who was his father?

That was a question which bothered our hero as it has scores of other people, holding even tolerably good positions in the world.

It is, indeed, a wise child that knows his own father, but if Jack's reputation of cleverness had to be founded on that knowledge, he was certainly one of the dullest blockheads upon the face of the earth.

Nevertheless, the mystery was about to be revealed.

It was with a heart beating high with expectation that he put on his hat, and walked quickly through the crowded streets towards the Temple.

It did not take him long to reach Otherend-court.

He mounted the steep stairs two at a time.

He reached the door upon which was inscribed, in dirty white paint—

"*Mr. Jabez Dallett.*"

He knocked.

There was no response.

After a pause, he again applied his knuckles to the panels. Still no reply.

Yet he fancied he heard the sound of some one moving steathily about the room.

He knocked a third time.

"Confound the lazy old man!" he muttered. "He's not out of bed yet, I suppose."

Jack waited with the utmost patience for nearly half-an-hour, only rapping at the door at intervals, but always without receiving any reply.

"Perhaps he has gone out," thought Jack, and he slowly descended the stairs, and went out himself into the court.

He lit a cigar, and paced rapidly backwards and forwards, waiting the solicitor's arrival.

It would have been a capital opportunity for him to study the manners, customs, and personal appearance of lawyers' clerks, had he been so disposed.

But he was not.

His thoughts were all bent in one direction.

The secret he was about to hear took up the whole of his attention.

His cigar lasted no time, for he chewed the end, and smoked with nervous rapidity, and, at last, when the weed went out, he threw it from him angrily, and again ascended the stairs to knock long and loudly against the door of the office of Mr. Jabez Dallett.

Knock as he would, no responsive sound came from the interior.

The blows he dealt the oak door echoed drearily through the old house.

They brought the old gentleman who lived in the second floor to peer over the banisters.

They brought the spruce young articled clerk from the ground floor to look up wonderingly.

They even brought the deaf old housekeeper from her home in the cellars, to see what was the matter.

In short, they brought everybody but the man they were meant to bring.

At last, Jack with one savage kick, which shook the door on its hinges, made his way down stairs again to the office of Messrs. Bruce and Dockett to inquire whether anything was known there of Mr. Jabez Dallett.

Mr. Bruce had not come, and Mr. Dockett had gone out, so Jack appealed to the articled clerk, who tilted up his stool, and stared with an air of immeasurable superiority at our hero.

"Do you know anything of Mr. Dallett here?" asked Jack.

"Rather!"

"Where is he?"

"Isn't he in his office?"

"That's just what I want to know."

"Have you tried?"

"Yes."

"It was you, then, making that infernal row at his door just now."

"It was."

"And you couldn't get in?"

"No."

"Ha, ha, ha! I should have been very much surprised if you could!"

"Why?"

"Because for the last month or two he has refused admittance to every one."

"What was that for?"

"Don't you know?"

"I shouldn't ask if I did."

"Lor! Don't be so touchy. I thought everyone knew old Dallett was——"

"Well!"

"Mad!"

"Mad?"

"Yes; mad as a March hare. Going about with all manner of funny notions. Prattling about some wonderful earl or another, and swearing every one was plotting to kill him."

"Poor old fellow!"

"Old idiot! He ought to be looked-up. If he's got any friends, they ought to take care of him. Put him in an asylum, or something."

"Is no dependence to be placed on what he says?"

"Not an atom. He hasn't the least idea of what he is talking about."

"You can't tell me how to gain admittance to his room?"

"No. It's immediately over the one we are in now, and I often hear him stumping about talking to himself."

"You haven't heard him this morning?"

"No."

"Thank you. I'm sorry to have troubled you."

"Don't mention it."

"Good morning."

"Good—Hi!—hoy! What the deuce is this? Come back—I say, come back!"

Jack, who had reached the door, turned and retraced his steps.

The articled clerk stood trembling, and pale with fright.

He could not speak, but pointed with his finger to a large dark round spot upon the parchment lying on his desk.

"What is it?" asked Jack.

He stooped over the parchment to examine the stain.

There could be no mistake about it.

It was blood.

While he yet bent over it, a second appeared.

A third and fourth followed in rapid succession.

Jack looked up, and saw the white ceiling above them was stained and discoloured, and it was from thence that the tell-tale drops fell.

"Good Heaven!" he cried, excitedly," "old Dallett has been murdered!"

The articled clerk snatched up the office poker, and Jack seized the iron bar which fastened the shutters at night, and the pair ran quickly up the stairs.

For a long time the door resisted all their efforts.

All the other occupants of the house, attracted by the noise, came rushing to the little landing on the first floor, to inquire what had happened.

"Murder!"

The word had an awful sound as it was whispered from one to another.

A few ventured into the office of Messrs. Bruce and Dockett, to see the blood-stain on the ceiling, but they did not care to remain long, watching the crimson fluid as it fell—drip—drip—slowly and regularly into the basin which some one had placed to receive it.

Not only was it those in the house who were attracted to the first floor of No. 4, Otherend-court.

With incredible rapidity the tidings spread that a brutal murder had been committed.

No sooner did this news reach Harrow-street, than a detachment of police started for the Temple, with determination written on their manly brows.

No sooner did the news reach Long's-gardens, than a young gentleman of shabby exterior put on his seedy coat, which, for economy's sake, he always kept on a peg when indoors, and hurried, as fast as his legs would carry him, to Otherend-court, in order to be able to write an account of the murder for the evening edition of the "Penny Plasterer," for which he hoped to be remunerated at the rate of three-halfpence a line.

No sooner were the evening papers published than a variety of placards appeared in the streets, announcing—

"DREADFUL MURDER IN THE TEMPLE!

SHOCKING BRUTALITY!!

APPREHENSION OF THE SUPPOSED MURDERER."

The first paragraph was correct, the last was untrue.

The door leading into Jabez Dallett's office at last gave way, and those nearest surged in.

Then a sight met their eyes which stayed them in their course.

They had entered, expecting to see something horrible, yet when that something met their view they shrunk back from the sight.

Stretched upon the floor lay the body of Jabez Dallett.

He was quite dead.

A hideous wound extended across his throat, from ear to ear.

His white beard was matted with blood and gore.

His hands were clenched violently in the agonies of death.

His face was distorted with pain.

Jack knelt down by his side, and placed his hand upon his heart.

Before he did so he knew that he was dead.

Ere our hero rose again to his feet, however, he noticed something which had hitherto escaped his observation.

Clenched tightly in the hand of the murdered man was a fragment of linen.

Jack extracted it from his grasp.

He examined it closely.

It was not a large piece, yet there was sufficient to show him that it had formed part of a shirt, and that no ordinary one.

It was of fine texture, and showed traces of embroidery, though only a small portion of the pattern was discernible.

It appeared to be part of the dress shirt of a gentleman.

Jack determined to keep it.

It was the only clue by which he was ever likely to discover the secret he was to have learnt from Jabez Dallett.

Who was the murderer?

That was the question asked on every side.

The police arrived, and made a minute inspection of the premises, and took possession of a dilapidated tea-caddy, in the earnest desire to do something.

It was altogether a mystery.

The watch of the murdered man still remained in his pocket, though all the boxes and drawers in the apartment had been broken open, apparently with the idea of plunder.

The police came to the conclusion that some desperate burglar had entered the premises, and meeting with resistance from the old man, had murdered him.

The public agreed in this conclusion.

All accepted it for truth, with one exception.

That exception was Jack Rawlings.

He had his own ideas upon the matter, but prudently kept them to himself.

At the inquest he made no mention of the fragment of embroidered shirt, for he had no desire to thwart his own ends by giving publicity to his suppositions.

From time to time short paragraphs appeared in the daily newspapers, giving the public to understand that the officers were on the track of the murderer, and that he would shortly be brought to justice; but nothing ever came of it, and by and bye the murder was forgotten, or only remembered, to be classed with the inexplicable mysteries which are, alas, of such frequent occurrence.

Our hero, as may easily be imagined, felt great disappointment at failing to learn what it was the solicitor had had to tell him.

He searched diligently among his papers, but failed to discover any document which could throw any light upon his parentage.

His sole hope was in the fragment of linen he possessed.

On that rested the possibility of bringing the murderer to justice, and discovering the secret which would give him wealth and position.

For some days he loitered about the London streets, with the vague hope of meeting some one with a torn shirt front, but of course without any result.

He acknowledged to himself with a sigh, that the only chance of making the discovery would be to wait patiently, to bide his time, in the expectation that sooner or later the man he sought would be thrown in his way.

It was some time before he could get the hideous spectacle of the blood-stained corpse out of his mind.

It was constantly recurring to him in his dreams and annoying him in his waking moments.

In sooth, Master Jack had much to worry him.

He was grieved and vexed at Fanny's abrupt departure, though he tried to persuade himself he did not care.

He made inquiries in every direction to ascertain what had become of her, but without success; and at last, so gloomy and taciturn did he become, that Jim Gimp was at a loss to imagine what had worked so strange a change in him, and Lotty Burton almost ceased to care to associate with him.

But Jack had yet another trouble.

His money was coming to an end, and he did not know in what direction to look for a fresh supply.

Rousing himself, he laid out a programme which he determined strictly to follow.

Firstly, he would obtain a supply of money.

Secondly, he would discover Fanny.

Thirdly, with her to aid him, he would seek out the murderer of Jabez Dallett, in the hope it might lead to that further knowledge which he so much desired.

The first, and all important resolution of getting money, without which the others could not be carried out, presented no small difficulty, but Jack was not one to be easily deterred, so dressing himself carefully, he sallied forth into the London streets, in the hope that fortune would favour him, and that something would "turn up."

CHAPTER LIII.

HOW THE MAYOR OF STOKUM-SLUSHY WENT TO AN EVENING PARTY AND HOW HE CAME HOME AGAIN.

THE Mayor of Stokum-Slushy was a very great man.

He was great in every sense of the word, inasmuch as his position in the little town gave him authority, and the quantity and quality of his dinners gave him rotundity of form.

It was a sight worth seeing when the mayor took part in a procession.

He was overwhelmed with a sense of his own superiority, and overburdened with the enormous amount of flesh he had to carry about with him wherever he went.

In case any of my readers should be disposed to sneer at the town of Stokum-Slushy, let me inform them it is of no mean importance.

At all events, the inhabitants consider it one of the first towns in the British Isles, and not a flourishing tradesman in it but looks at the mayoralty with longing eyes.

The duties of the mayor of Stokum-Slushy are not clearly defined, but it is a well-known fact that a good deal of eating and drinking is connected with all such offices, to say nothing of the crimson robe trimmed with fur, and the massive gold chain.

It was into the town of Stokum-Slushy that Fanny White rode one fine afternoon, mounted on the back of "Black Prince."

According to her custom, she made her way to the best hotel, and dismounted.

The obsequious waiter ran smiling from the door to meet her.

The bowing and scraping ostler took her horse.

The grinning stable-boy got in everybody's way and touched his cap.

Fanny ordered a good dinner, and then, always mindful of her steed, as every horseman or women should, he strolled into the stable to see "Black Prince" enjoy his feed.

Now it so happened that the ostler was a communicative man, and he and Fanny soon entered into conversation.

After the proper amount of small talk upon general subjects, he became almost confidential.

"Look here, sir," said he, in a loud whisper, laying his hand on our heroine's shoulder. "Look here, sir. I can see with half an eye you're a regular gent, so I'll show you something."

"What is it?" asked Fanny.

"It's a thing, I rather think, you've never seen the like of before."

The ostler, with a good deal of ceremony, opened the door of a coach-house, and pointed inside with an air of triumph.

"There!" said he.

Fanny looked in the direction indicated, and perceived one of the most remarkable vehicles it had ever been her lot to come across.

It was a large, roomy, old fashioned coach, partaking somewhat of the nature of a carriage, but more of a market cart.

There was some attempt at gilding about it, and on the panels were painted, in the brightest colours, some wonderful devices, which by a great stretch of the imagination might be supposed to represent coats of arms.

"There!" said the ostler. "Did you ever see anything like *that* before?"

"Never!" said Fanny, emphatically.

"I should think not." And here it should be observed, the ostler's idea of the world was bounded by the limits of his own parish, and that his belief in everything connected with Stokum-Slushy was enormous.

"What is it?" asked Fanny, innocently.

"What is it!" repeated the ostler, in tones expressive of pity at our heroine's ignorance. "Why it's the mayor's state coach."

"Indeed," said Fanny, scarcely able to repress a smile.

"Yes; and I tell you what, we're going to send it out to-night."

"Where to?"

"Why, you see, Lord Mawley is going to give a party, he is; and our Mayor is a going to it, *he* is."

"Indeed! Does Lord Mawley live far from here?"

"Do you want to post it, sir?"

"No. Why do you ask?"

"'Cos if you want to know as a customer, we calls it over ten mile, but if you asks for information, it's just about eight."

"What sort of a road is it?"

"Well, it ain't what you'd call a good road."

"Is it lonely?"

"Yes, sir."

The reader will guess Fanny's object in making these inquiries.

She thought a mayor would probably be worth plundering, and that she might manage to intercept him on his return from Lord Mawley's party.

She obtained all the information she desired from the loquacious ostler, tossed him half-a-crown, and returned to the coffee-room of the inn to enjoy the dinner she had ordered.

The mayor, in the meantime, was in a great state of bustle and excitement.

He had never before been asked to Mawley Court, nor, to tell the truth, would he have been asked now, only there was the prospect of an election for Stokum-Slushy before long, and Lord Mawley was desirous his eldest son should be returned, so wished to conciliate the townspeople.

The mayoress, too, had been invited, and so flustered was she at the unexpected honour, that she could hardly keep her false curls on for excitement.

Then her eldest daughter had been asked as well, and she was fluttering about, her heart palpitating with joy at the thought that her crimson cheeks and plump well-developed form might captivate some "scion of a noble house."

Altogether, when the "state-carriage," came to the door, and the three got in and drove away, followed by the envious glances of all the unasked inhabitants of Stokum-Slushy, they were as jolly a trio as one would wish to see.

The mayor was resplendent in his robes of office; the mayoress was brilliant with old-fashioned jewellery, and her daughter ditto from the natural colour of her complexion.

After a long drive, Mawley Court was reached. The ladies descended and shook out their skirts; the mayor got out majestically, as became his dignity, though perhaps the effect was in some degree spoilt by his having to squeeze sideways through the door, on account of his huge dimensions.

With the party we have nothing to do, beyond chronicling that it was a complete success.

The rooms were hot and stuffy, the dancers were crowded, the ices were liquid, and the lemonade warm, but every one had come with the full intention of enjoying themselves, and all went well.

Lord Mawley took the Mayoress into supper, and the mayor got into a quiet corner, with a game pie before him and a bottle of wine under his chair, and was quite as happy in his way as his wife in hers.

While all the dancing, and feasting, and flirting, and merrymaking had been going on, Fanny had had "Black Prince" saddled, had paid her bill, given a handsome gratuity to the waiter, and had ridden slowly away.

She had learnt much respecting the road to Mawley Court from the communicative ostler, but had determined to ride over it, and inspect it for herself.

About half-way between the Court and the town was a bleak, bare, desolate common, called Hangman's Heath, from an old legend attached to it that a highwayman had formerly been hung in chains upon a small knoll in the centre.

It was a dreary, dismal place, far removed from all habitations.

It was the place of all others for a robbery.

A dank, green pool, covered with slimy weeds, bordered on the road, and in this pool it was that a miller's daughter, who had trusted and been deceived, plunged, with the offspring of her shame, one dark murky night.

Ever since then the common had been said to be haunted, and but few of the inhabitants of Stokum-Slushy were bold enough to venture thither after nightfall.

This was another advantage to Fanny.

She had left the town long before the hour at which Lord Mawley's party might be expected to conclude, but this she had done to avoid suspicion.

She well knew that a mayor was not to be attacked and robbed with impunity.

She knew that it was a very hazardous enterprise in which she was about to engage, but she determined to risk it.

It was as much a love of adventure and deeds of daring which led her into it as anything else.

The time passed slowly enough as she waited on the dreary heath.

At last Lord Mawley's party came to an end.

The last dance was finished.

The last glass of wine drank.

The last shawl put on, and the final adieux uttered.

The mayor and his wife and daughter re-entered the "state carriage."

The noble host returned to his own fireside from hand-skaking in the hall, and Fanny, hearing the sound of wheels slowly approaching, examined her revolver, and walked "Black Prince" from the clump of trees where she had been resting into the road, and there awaited the coming of the Mayor of Stokum-Slushy.

"Stand!" cried Fanny, when the carriage came within a few yards of the spot where she had taken up her position.

No attention was paid to this summons.

The reason was that no one heard it.

In fact, all were buried in sleep.

The two horses, with closed eyes, were jogging steadily and mechanically towards their stable.

The post-boy had fallen forward upon the animal he bestrode, and was enjoying an uneasy slumber.

The effects of the supper were shown upon the mayor by his having subsided into the most comfortable corner, where he reclined, with mouth wide open, snoring like a whole herd of swine.

FANNY WHITE IS PURSUED BY THE DETECTIVES.

The massive head of his better half had fallen upon her capacious bosom, and she too added to the chorus.

The young lady, curled up in a small space, slumbered as soundly, though not as loudly, as her parents, dreaming of the last waltz, and the close embrace of that *dear* young officer with the pretty moustache.

"Stand!"

Fanny called out the word again.

Again no notice was taken of it.

To tell the truth, our heroine was rather puzzled how to act.

Had resistance been offered or fright shown, she was prepared to awe them with her revolver.

Had the coach stopped, she was prepared to ease them of their gold and jewels.

But the coach still came jogging quietly along.

Fanny, holding her pistol ready for use, rode forward, to meet the mayor's "state carriage."

Peeping inside, she became aware of the real state of the case, and could hardly refrain from bursting into a roar of laughter 'at the sight of the mayor's family slumbering so soundly, little dreaming of the danger which threatened them.

"This is highway robbery made easy," thought Fanny, smiling to herself, as she trotted "Black Prince" to the horses' heads.

She seized them, and they, no ways unwilling, came to a dead stop.

So suddenly did they halt, that the postilion, whose nose had been down upon the neck of the animal upon which he was mounted, was brought upright with such a jerk, that a slight push from Fanny sent him rolling into the road.

Before he could rise, indeed, before he had even the most confused idea of what had happened, the cold muzzle of the revolver touched his forehead.

"Speak one word and you are a dead man," said Fanny.

The postilion was sufficiently awake to comprehend that

discretion would be the better part of valour, so he quickly rolled himself over on his side and held his tongue.

"What are we stopping for?" yawned the mayoress, waking up, and stretching herself so vigorously as to catch her husband a sharp blow on the bridge of his purple nose.

"Hullo! Are we at home?" he growled.

"La! oh! oh!" cried his daughter, who, putting her head out of the window to see what was the matter, had found herself face to face with Fanny.

"I must beg you to hold your tongue, miss," said our heroine politely, putting in her head at the carriage window.

"Hullo! Who the devil are you?" bellowed the mayor.

"My name is of no consequence."

"Do you know who I am, scoundrel?"

"Perfectly. The Mayor of Stokum-Slushy."

"And you dare insult me and my family in this way?"

"Oh, no, Mister Mayor. I wouldn't insult either you or your lovely wife and daughter on any account."

The two ladies thought the highwayman was the nicest young man in the world, and so polite.

"But I must trouble you to alight."

"I'm blowed if I will," said the mayor, sturdily.

Even that great man's crimson face paled, however, on hearing the ominous click of the pistol lock, and a moment afterwards perceiving the smooth, shining barrel of the revolver pointed straight at his head.

The mayoress shrieked dismally till Fanny silenced her.

Then, opening the door of the carriage, our heroine assisted the two ladies, and subsequently the mayor, to alight, covering them the while with her pistol.

"I must trouble you to hand me over all the gold and jewels you happen to have about you," said Fanny.

The mayor attempted remonstrance.

Fanny was firm.

Even the gold chain of mayoralty had to be surrendered.

The mayoress sighed as she parted with all her valuables; but she did not like the look of Miss Fanny, as she stood before her, pistol in hand.

As for the mayor's daughter, she fell in love with the handsome highwayman.

The following day she wrote letters to sixteen of her bosom friends, recounting the romantic adventure which had befallen her.

The most glowing description these letters contained of the wonderful young man, his lovely eyes, his splendid hair, &c. &c., all of which account her sixteen bosom friends read with feelings of envy, and devoutly wished they could fall in with the handsome young highwayman.

The mayor and his family, despoiled of their worldly wealth, were assisted by Fanny into their carriage again.

Our heroine gathered together the spoil and mounted "Black Prince."

Then waving an adieu to the great man and pitching a sovereign to the postilion, she put spurs to her noble steed, who responded eagerly, and in ten minutes' time she was several miles away from the scene of her adventure.

And this is a full, true, and particular account of how the Mayor of Stokum-Slushy went to an evening party and how he came home again.

———

CHAPTER LIV.

HOW JACK WENT INTO THE CITY, AND WHAT HAPPENED TO HIM THERE.

OUR hero, as mentioned in a former chapter, had settled in his own mind that the first thing to which he must bend his energies was the getting of money; for without that requisite he knew well it would be hopeless for him to expect to find out either his mistress or the secret of his parentage.

But it is one thing for a man to say "I will obtain gold," and another thing for him to do it.

Jack had no notion in what way to set about getting a sufficient quantity of the coin of the realm to start him upon his travels; but having a vague idea that money was usually to be had in the city, he bent his steps eastward, in the hope of gaining his ends in one way or another—how he had no definite notion.

For the greater part of the day he wandered idly enough about the bustling streets, looking into the windows of the print-shops and staring at the girls getting into omnibuses; but still when the afternoon came he seemed to have arrived no nearer to the purpose for which he had come eastward than he was when he left home.

Tired and exhausted, he made his way to the Royal Exchange, and rested himself there till a magnificent beadle warned him away just before "'Change" time.

He had no idea in what direction to bend his steps, and turned from right to left, exactly as his fancy prompted him.

After an hour of trudging over the hard pavement he found himself in Lombard-street just as it was beginning to get dusk.

Before one of the banks he paused, to allow an old white-haired, furrowed, crabbed-looking man to cross the pavement.

But this was exactly what the old gentleman did not appear at all inclined to do, for he stood on the top step, scowling fiercely at Jack.

On looking again at him our hero saw that he held in his hands a large canvas-bag, which, judging from his uneasiness, and the house from which he was emerging, Jack concluded to be filled with the coin of the realm.

"What a glorious haul that would be if it contains sovereigns!" thought Jack.

He determined to watch; for although the chances of his obtaining possession of the bag seemed small, still he did not think it altogether hopeless.

Jack lit a cigar, and loitered about, keeping an eye on the old man.

The gentleman with the money-bag, after deliberating with himself, seemed to make up his mind to take a cab.

He hailed the first four-wheeler which passed.

Jack sauntered near, in order, if possible, to hear the address given.

"What will you take me to Paddington for?" asked the old man.

"Five bob!"

"Nonsense. I'll give you two."

"You're a funny old man to want to ride in a cab."

"Cab! You don't call that thing a cab, do you? It's a fever-box."

"None of that now."

"How much did you charge the last corpse you took to the hospital? You didn't get your fare, I suppose, and want to get it out o' me?"

The cabman tried to drive away.

"Stop!" shouted the old man. "I hailed you, and you must take me."

"I'm d——d if I do."

"Then I'll summons you."

"What for?"

"For refusing a fare."

"Come, now, I ain't a-going to take you to Paddington for two bob."

"Take me as far as you can on the way then."

"All right."

"Stay; I'll engage you for an hour. That'll be the cheapest."

The old man opened the cab door, and as he put the bag inside Jack heard a musical chink.

The man followed, banged to the door, and the cab moved slowly away.

It was a time-fare, however, and the driver was not at all disposed to hurry his horse, and Jack found no difficulty in keeping pace with it.

Presently the vehicle pulled up short before a publichouse, and the driver dismounted.

"Hi! Hullo!" shouted the inside. "What are you doing? Go on!"

"I can't."

"You can't?"

"No."

"Why not?"

"'Cos the harness is broke."

"I tell you you must, or I wont pay you a farthing."

"All right, guv'nor."

"Hi! stop, you infernal scoundrel, I'll summons you—I'll give you two months— I'll—I'll——"

"Don't you fret yourself, guv'nor, and don't get in a passion, 'cos at your time o' life it's dangerous."

It was the cabman's turn now.

"You impudent thief, drive to the police-court."

"I knew'd a man once as got quite vicious and excited, as might be you, and he fell down dead in a 'plectic fit," said the cabman, grinning from ear to ear.

"Let me out—let me out—do you hear?"

"Oh yes; I ain't deaf, and you've got good lungs."

"Then why the devil don't you do it."

"Not if I knows it; leastways, not till you've paid me the two bob for the hour."

"You don't think I'm going to pay you for bringing me through two streets?"

"You can sit the hour out if you like, guv'nor. If you want me you'll find me in the publichouse."

The old man fumed and swore, but the driver paid no manner of attention to him, but entered the ginshop and related the story of his fare with great glee.

The old man appeared at first about to jump out and follow the truant driver; but on second thoughts he feared to leave the money-bag in the cab, and yet dared not take it with him into the publichouse.

"I'll pay him out yet," muttered he. "It is lucky I'm in no hurry. I'll sit here for the hour, so that he can't get another fare, and then I wont pay him a farthing;" and he rubbed his knees and chuckled as he thought what a fine revenge that would be.

Jack followed the driver into the publichouse.

He listened to it and applauded it, offering at its conclusion to stand the cabman whatever he liked.

The cabman liked "just a little drop o' gin," and he had it. Then he liked just a little drop more, and he had that, till at last the little drops became a considerable quantity, and he arrived at that state in which a person is supposed to be unable to see a hole through a ladder.

This was just what Jack wanted.

It was now quite dark, in addition to which one of those thick yellow fogs, for which the English metropolis is so famous, had spread itself through the streets.

Jack left the publichouse and walked straight to the cab. The driver had left his cape on the box, and in this our hero enveloped himself.

The old man inside failed to perceive the change, and laughed with delight at having wearied out the cabman.

The vehicle started off at a rapid rate.

"Ha! ha! ha!" chuckled the inside passenger, hugging his money-bag. "I've got the best of you after all, Master Cabby, and I'll get my ride for the two shillings."

So saying, he pulled the stump of a dirty clay pipe from his pocket, stuffed it with coarse, rank tobacco, which he carried loose in his waistcoat, lit it, and puffed out volumes of smoke in his delight, till suddenly remembering smoking so quickly was a great waste, he took to puffing slowly and deliberately, as was his usual custom.

He was an awful old miser was that white-haired man with the bag of gold.

He might have tossed sovereigns on the floor and rolled in them had he been so disposed.

He might have dined off gold, have slept on gold, have dressed in gold, had he chosen so do to, but his delight was different; his only pleasure was to pinch, and scrape, and save, and to add sovereign to sovereign.

He hated and distrusted banks, and kept the whole of his money concealed in the cellar of the wretched little cottage in which he lived, with a faded, aged, old housekeeper, every whit as penurious and disagreeable as her master; and it was thither he was returning, or thought he was returning, when seated in the cab puffing his pipe, with our hero on the box lashing the old rib-showing animal into some semblance of a trot.

On and on he drove.

The old miser looked at his pinchbeck watch and chuckled as he found the hour for which he had engaged the cab had expired.

"I wont pay him another halfpenny—not a halfpenny," he muttered, rubbing his hands. "He may go on driving as long as he likes, but I'll only give him the two shillings—or wait a moment—I've got a bad half-crown somewhere, he shall have that, and I'll make him give me sixpence change. He! he! he! a ride and a sixpence for a bad half-crown. Capital!"

Yet it seemed to him that going at the rate at which they were now progressing, they ought long since to have reached Paddington.

He let down the window and put his head out.

The fog was not so thick here, and he could see a little around him.

What he did see failed to assure him.

On one side of the road were fields, on the other at intervals carcasses of unfinished houses.

He knew of no such place through which he should pass on his way from the city to Paddington.

The road was evidently not the high road, for it was full of ruts and holes, and the cab jumped and jolted about amongst them as if it were possessed.

But still they drove on.

Again the miser put his head out of the window.

"Hi, cabby! Stop! I say, where are you taking me?"

"It's all right," said Jack.

"What have you brought me here for?"

"The roads is up," replied our hero, in an assumed tone.

"Where are we?"

"You'll see in a minute. It's all right."

With this explanation he was forced to be contented, but in his mind he was far from easy.

Nervously he clutched his bag of gold, as the suspicion entered his head that robbery was intended.

He had almost made up his mind to leap from the cab while it was in motion at all hazards.

He had even gone so far as to put his hand out of the window to open the door when the vehicle pulled up with a jerk, which sent him forward with a bump against the opposite seat, and materially injuring his thin bony nose.

The driver dismounted, came to the cab door, and flung it wide open.

"Hullo!" asked the miser, "what does this mean?"

"Can't take you any further for two shillings."

"Where are we?"

"Oh, go across the fields and you'll get to Paddington—in time."

"Nonsense!" and the old man began to feel alarmed. "I'll give you another sixpence to drive me to the Royal Oak," and as he said this, he thought with a cunning leer of the bad half-crown.

"I wont take you a step further," said Jack; "not for sixpence, nor yet for a bag of gold."

The miser thought the words were spoken with ominous significance, and he clutched the treasure and pressed it tightly to his breast.

"Come, old gent, jump out," said Jack.

But the "old gent" didn't seem to see it, and preferred to retain his seat.

"Now then, guv'nor, you've had a good two bob's worth—out with you."

"I'm not going to get out in this lonely place without even knowing where I am."

"Well, then, hand out that bag."

"What bag?" was the trembling answer.

"That canvas bag. Now, none of your tricks. Hand it out!"

"I wont!" exclaimed the miser, in almost a shriek. "You shall take my life first."

"That wouldn't be nearly so useful," said Jack; "in fact, rather the reverse, and might lead to unpleasant results."

"Police! Help!" shouted the occupier of the cab.

"Now, don't make a noise, because it isn't a bit of use, and it may frighten the cats."

But the old man still continued to shout, so Jack jumped inside the cab and seized him by the throat, holding him sufficiently tight to make him feel very uncomfortable, without doing him any serious harm.

While he held his throat with one hand, with the other he took possession of the bag of gold, notwithstanding the struggles of its owner.

Having at last succeeded in emptying the shining sovereigns into his own pockets, he considerately returned the bag to the old man; and partly that he might not lose it and partly that he might not shout too loud, he rolled it up and thrust it into his mouth.

This done, he tied his hands firmly together and wished him good evening.

No sooner was all this done—and it is to be borne in mind that the action did not take a tenth part of the time occupied by the description—Jack bounced over a hedge into a field, and set off as fast as his legs would carry him, though he was as ignorant as the old miser as to what part of the country he was in.

Before he had taken half-a-dozen steps, a heavy hand was laid upon his shoulder!

He started violently!

He made no doubt the officers of justice had hold of him!

Looking round he perceived a policeman!

Yes, there in the unmistakeable blue livery, was one of Sir Robert Peel's public servants!

Jack deliberated in his mind for a second.

Should he fight and make a run for it, or should he try by cunning to evade the officer?

"Halves!" said the policeman.

"What do you mean?"

"Come, none of your gammon! I saw you rob the old gent, and unless you give me a fair share of the plunder, I'll peach!"

Jack saw the sort of gentleman with whom he had to deal.

"All right," said he.

"That's well. I thought you looked a sensible fellow. Halves, mind you!"

"Come," said our hero, who by this time had his arm free. "It isn't much, so I'll fight you whether you have all or none."

"No, no. Fair play."

"If you mean by fair play, that you're to have half the swag and I'm to have all the risk, I don't see the fun of it."

"You refuse to give me my share?"

"I do."

"Then I apprehend you in the name of the law," said the constable, valiantly.

Jack waited till he was close to him, and then quietly knocked him down.

Bending over him to see that he was not likely for a while to interfere with him, he saw something sticking out from his pockets.

They were handcuffs!

In a moment he had slipped them neatly over the policeman's wrists and had snapped them securely.

Then, once more at liberty, he turned his steps towards the red glare in the sky which denoted the busy metropolis, and reached home very late, dreadfully fatigued, but the richer by a couple of hundred pounds.

CHAPTER LV.

OF THE MISFORTUNE WHICH BEFEL FANNY WHITE AND HER HORSE, "BLACK PRINCE."

AFTER plundering the mayor and his family, as related in a former chapter, Fanny White put spurs to her noble steed and rode rapidly away from the scene of the robbery.

She was well aware that mayors were not to be plundered with impunity; and that the officers of justice would soon be upon her track.

But for that she cared little.

As long as she had the power of planning, and her horse, "Black Prince," she cared little who might be chasing her.

Without apprehension she rode on and on.

She was but imperfectly acquainted with the geography of the country, and had been afraid to make too many inquiries for fear of exciting suspicion.

Still she rode on.

The cold grey dawn gave place to a brighter and a warmer light, and as the sun rose, she saw in the far distance the glimmer of its rays upon the ocean.

A thick pall of murky smoke spread itself out a little to her right.

It denoted some large town, but what it could be she had no idea.

Still she rode on.

It was broad daylight when she entered the town.

She soon discovered that she had arrived at the maritime metropolis of Great Britain.

She was in Liverpool.

At once she determined upon the course she would pursue.

Riding slowly along she looked out on every side for a respectable livery-stable.

She was not long in discovering one suited to her mind.

She dismounted; summoned the ostler; swaggered about a good deal; talked large: and, finally, entrusted "Black Prince" to his care.

She agreed to pay rather more than the usual sum for his maintenance, in order that extra care might be taken of him, and that he might be ready for her at any hour of the day or night.

The reason she determined upon separating herself from him for the present was, the fear that so remarkably fine an animal might draw attention to her, and, perhaps, lead to detection.

The horse disposed of, her next step was to purchase a large portmanteau.

Then hailing a cab she drove to a large outfitting warehouse, and purchased several fashionable suits of clothes which she had packed neatly into the portmanteau.

Then she bade the driver take her to the Lime Street Railway Station, and then paying him his fare she dismissed him.

But Fanny had no intention of proceeding to London.

She did not doubt but that a detective was in waiting at all the metropolitan stations with a full description of her appearance, hoping to apprehend her for highway robbery.

But our heroine was not to be so easily caught.

She merely waited till the down train from London came in, and then coolly walking round from the departure to the arrival platform, mingled with the passengers to appear as one of them.

Then hailing another cab, and having her portmanteau put on the roof, she directed the man to drive to the Adelphi Hotel.

Bowing waiters opened the cab-door, and our heroine was soon comfortably seated in the coffee-room with a substantial breakfast spread before her.

To this she did ample justice.

The meal concluded she made her way to the smoking-room, selected the most comfortable easy-chair, lit a cigar, and—went to sleep.

And no wonder, considering it was thirty hours since she had been in bed, and in that time she had committed a robbery, and ridden about forty miles.

When she awoke she became conscious that she was the object of scrutiny to a sanctified-looking waiter who, under pretence of arranging the room, was prying curiously about.

The truth was, the attitude in which our heroine had been reposing had been a trifle too unstudied, and the negligent way in which she had allowed her arms to hang revealed the outline of a form which, however beautiful in a lovely woman, appears strange and unsuited to the opposite sex.

The waiter gave a little sharp dry cough when Fanny awoke.

"Hullo! Have I been asleep?" she asked, yawning.

"Yessir."

"No wonder either, considering I was travelling for eight and forty hours without stopping."

"Indeed, sir."

"Yes. I have just come from the Continent."

"Yessir."

"I can have a bed here to-night, of course?"

"Yessir."

"I may wish to remain here a few days—a week, perhaps."

"Yessir."

"See that I have everything as comfortable as possible. I'm not used to roughing it."

"Yessir. *What* name did you say, sir?"

This was a subject which Fanny with all her foresight had quite forgotten, but she knew it would not do to hesitate.

"Edgar Delaine," said our heroine.

"Any relation to the Marquis of Porchester, sir," asked the curious waiter.

"I'm his son," answered Fanny, abruptly.

"Oh, my lord, I beg your lordship's pardon. I didn't know, my lord, I'm sure," and the obsequious waiter very nearly overbalanced himself, he bowed so low.

His suspicions all vanished like smoke before the magic title.

Fanny had every reason to be well pleased with the effect produced by her bold assertion.

She had had no idea of passing herself off as a member of the nobility, but had mentioned the first name which rose to her lips.

Still there was the fear of detection.

Should she be able to play the part?

That was the question.

There was much depending upon it.

She had gone too far to retract.

She nerved herself for it, and determined that nothing but the arrival of the *real* Lord Delaine should disconcert her.

When night came, Fanny took the opportunity, when she was alone and free from all fear of interruption, of inspecting the spoils she had obtained from the mayor and his family.

The jewels were, without doubt, of great value, as was also

the gold chain of office, but still they were not like ready-money, and of that our heroine had but little.

How to dispose of the jewels.

That was the question.

Fanny knew enough of police arrangements to feel sure that any attempt upon her part to offer them for sale would be almost equivalent to handing herself over to justice.

Still there was much danger in keeping them about her person.

Were she to be apprehended with the mayor's property upon her, nothing could prevent her conviction, although she hoped, in case of her being brought before a magistrate without the valuables, that she would be able to brazen it out.

At length she hit upon the following plan.

She packed the jewels and the gold chain into a neat little parcel, and by the first train the next morning sent it off to London, addressed—

JOHN RAWLINGS, Esq.,

KING'S-CROSS STATION.

To be left till called for.

In this way she hoped to rid herself of the valuable property, the possession of which might lead to such unpleasant results, though she still would be able to regain it the first convenient opportunity.

This done, however, she found she had very little money—scarcely five pounds. And as she had been living in rather grand style at the Adelphi, she felt sure that her bill there would swallow up every farthing she possessed.

She determined to attempt another robbery.

In pursuance of this plan, she called at the livery stable where she had left "Black Prince," and left word that she should require her horse at ten o'clock; then returning to her hotel, in the course of conversation informed the waiter that she was going out that evening, and should not be back till late.

This done, and her dinner eaten, she devoted the remainder of the time till ten o'clock in thoroughly cleaning and reloading her revolver.

As the hour at which she had appointed to be at the stable struck, she left the hotel.

Twenty minutes later, she was once more astride her bonny steed, and trotting gaily along through the suburbs of Liverpool.

Remembering that she had much time to spare before she dared attempt to stay any of the passengers on the Queen's highway, and also that it would be well to reserve her horse's strength, in case of pursuit, she suffered the trot to lapse into a walk.

Many were the heads which turned to take a second glance at the handsome young horseman who sat his steed so bravely. But Fanny had no desire to court observation, and chose the most unfrequented roads.

The clocks had just struck eleven, and our heroine was in a narrow lane, so dark she could hardly see a yard ahead.

The night was black as pitch, and any struggling rays of light which might have shone were effectually prevented from reaching the lane by the thick canopy of trees which overshadowed it.

So dark was it, that although she heard the sound of horse's hoofs coming towards her, she could see no sign of anyone approaching.

She deliberated with herself.

Should she stop the approaching horseman?

Was it not yet too early?

Was she not still too near the town?

These prudential thoughts, however, did not deter her, and she resolved to make the attempt.

Backing "Black Prince" as close to the hedge as possible, and drawing her pistol, she awaited her victim.

He came.

Unconscious of the snare, he advanced quietly along, the reins hanging loosely on his horse's neck.

When he was parallel with her, Fanny advanced.

She laid one hand upon the reins, while with the other she presented the smooth, shining barrel of her pistol at the traveller's head.

"I am sorry to inconvenience you," said she; "but I must trouble you for any money you have about you."

The gentleman thus attacked was taken completely by surprise.

His first idea was to fly, but Fanny's hand held the reins. Then he thought of resistance.

But he did not like the look of the revolver.

"Look sharp!" said our heroine. "I've no time to lose."

It was too dark for Fanny to see the smile of satisfaction which came suddenly over the man's face.

Had she perceived it she might have known it portended no good.

"I've very little money," said the gentleman.

"I'm sorry to hear it," replied Fanny; "still I must trouble you for what you have."

"My purse is almost empty."

"I'll take it, for all that."

"And I have no valuables, except my watch. Let me keep that, I beg? It is worth ten times more to me than it can be to any other person."

"Oh, keep your ticker!" said our heroine, angrily; "only hand me over your money."

The gentleman put his hand first in one pocket, then in the other, but still without producing his purse.

Fanny lost all patience; still, strange to say, it never occurred to her that it might be but a trick to gain time.

"Now, shell out the shiners!" said Fanny; "or——" And she cocked the revolver.

"Or what?"

"Or I shall have to use force."

"All right!" was the reply, as the traveller again pretended to search his pockets.

"I'm afraid I've lost my purse," said he at length.

"Come, no nonsense. That sort of game wont do. Are you going to hand over the money?"

"No—I'm not!"

"You're not?"

"No."

"Then I shall take it."

"You can do as you like about that; only take my advice."

"What is it?"

"Listen."

Fanny listened, and discovered at once the cause of the sudden boldness upon the part of the man she had reckoned upon robbing.

The tramp of galloping horses was momentarily approaching nearer and nearer.

"The deuce!" cried Fanny, alarmed.

"They are my friends," shouted the traveller, triumphantly. "Surrender, in the Queen's name!" and he grasped at our heroine's bridle.

"Stand off," she cried; "or you are a dead man!"

So saying she again presented the pistol at his head.

She could tell by the sound that the horsemen were now quite close to her.

"Help!" shouted the man she had attacked. "Help! I've caught a highwayman. Come along."

"Tally-ho," replied a cheerful voice, "that's a new kind of fox—forward."

Fanny saw she had not a moment to lose if she wished to escape imprisonment.

She fired a couple of barrels of her revolver in the direction of the advancing foe, hit the man who held her bridle over the head with the butt end, put spurs to "Black Prince," and galloped off as hard as she could go.

The others followed in hot pursuit.

Her revolver had evidently done no harm.

She heard them racing behind her.

She heard them shouting to each other.

Still she rode on, digging the spurs into the sides of her noble horse, who seemed to know what was required of him, and to have made up his mind to do his best.

Those in pursuit evidently knew the country well, and shouted directions to each other about short cuts across the fields.

Our heroine, fearing to be entrapped, determined to take to the fields herself, and over the hedge she went in gallant style.

No sooner was she out in the open than a cheery voice giving the view halloo told her she was seen.

Over the hedge, one after the other, came six horsemen in pursuit.

She saw their dark forms for an instant standing out against the sky as she took the leap.

It was a steeple-chase in which the prize, if won by Fanny, was freedom.

"Black Prince" outstripped the other horses in speed, but

the pursuers had the great advantage of being thoroughly acquainted with the country, and, aided by this knowledge, they rapidly gained upon our heroine, who almost gave herself up for lost.

Forward !

On—on they rode, spurring the earth from beneath their horses' hoofs.

Now, with a cry of encouragement, leaping a formidable gate, or ugly hedge !

Then tearing madly across the smooth meadow-land !

Forward !

Shouting, whooping, hallooing, the six huntsmen spurred after Fanny White, who, bending forward on her horse's neck, urged him to his greatest speed.

He responded gallantly. He bounded over the ground at a terrific pace, covering a large space with his enormous stride.

Still they gained upon her, for although they were left far behind in an open field, when it came to the leaps, they knew what spots in the hedge to take, while Fanny had to look out for a suitable place for herself.

And thus they rode on their mad hunt, and Fanny felt a feeling uncommonly like despair when she saw how hopeless it was to attempt to distance them !

At the bottom of the field in which our heroine was now riding, rose a high, thick hedge, in itself no ordinary jump for a horse ; as she neared it she saw upon the opposite side that a small river ran, which, though not formidable in itself, became so when coupled with the hedge.

Shouts from behind called on her to surrender.

They never dreamt she would attempt the leap !

But she determined to chance it !

" Stop !" cried they all, for they thought she did not perceive the danger.

But she heeded them not !

Just before reaching the hedge she slackened her speed.

A cry of triumph from behind !

They thought she was about to yield.

They little knew the indomitable will, the firmness of nerve and the amount of pluck our heroine possessed.

She pulled in " Black Prince," who, in his reckless haste, would have rushed blindly at the obstacle.

She put him at the fence.

Just as he rose she dug the spurs deep into his foam-flaked sides, and uttered a loud cheer.

Her pursuers pulled up and watched her.

The brave horse rose gallantly at her call, cleared the hedge and the stream beyond it, and with a magnificent bound, landed her safely in the field.

" Bravo ! well jumped !" shouted the huntsman who had led the pursuit, but who could not restrain his admiration for our herine's horsemanship.

Fanny stopped in her course, and took off her hat to the six men, and made them a sweeping bow.

" Do you want to sell your horse ?" bellowed one ; " I'll give you five hundred guineas for him."

Fanny shook her head, and with a merry laugh cantered gaily away. She did not hurry herself now, for she knew there was an effectual barrier between her and her pursuers.

After riding on for more than an hour she saw a pretty little villa standing in its own grounds close before her.

As she had no wish to be questioned, she turned " Black Prince's" head, and was making away from it when the noble horse which had borne her so bravely in the chase stumbled, and, before she could recover him, fell.

But this was not the worst of the matter.

So little was Fanny prepared for such conduct on his part that she was thrown over his head with considerable force into the garden belonging to the aforementioned villa.

There she lay through the weary hours of the night, stunned, bruised, and helpless, with " Black Prince" in a scarcely better plight upon the other side of the hedge.

CHAPTER LVI.

RELATES HOW JACK RAWLINGS WALKED DOWN THE HAYMARKET A LITTLE AFTER MIDNIGHT.

OUR hero, after having discomfited the policeman, as already related, bent his steps towards the metropolis.

He felt tolerably safe, for he did not see what possible clue there could be to his discovery when once he mingled in the crowd of London.

It was eleven o'clock when he reached the Edgware-road. He was tired, but had no wish to take a cab and give the driver the chance of assisting the police in identifying him, so he walked steadily on.

Down Regent-street he went, resisting all the blandishments of the French ladies, with such *very* bright-red cheeks, such enormous crinolines, and such irreproachable boots, who would willingly have linked their arms in his.

But there was an attraction for Master Jack greater than the aforesaid damsels—an attraction which he could not resist—and that was, the display of clean tables and bustling waiters at the far-famed oyster-shop at the top of the Haymarket.

When it is remembered that our hero had not had anything to eat for several hours, and when it is further stated that the shellfish in question were great favourites of his, it will not seem so remarkable that he should pause on his homeward way and turn into the town-renowned supper-rooms.

Oysters, devilled kidneys, and stout are uncommonly good things in their way ; and so our hero thought as he sat at his little table swallowing these delicacies, and keeping his eyes open as usual.

He had not been long in the place before a tall, gentlemanly, good-looking fellow staggered in.

He was neither riotous nor noisy ; but it was plain to see, from his gait and speech, that he had already had more liquor than was good for him.

" Couple of bottles of champagne," he cried, tossing down some gold. " Here, girls, who'll have some ?"

It is needless to say that there were several volunteers.

One charming young lady, with a very bewitching smile, to say nothing of a pair of blue boots and pink silk stockings, became so affected by the stranger's kindness (or the gentleman's champagne), that she wept tears of gratitude ; while a second (a more seasoned toper) expressed her thankfulness in song.

The words were not exactly such as the charming Lady Rodolfa would warble in a drawing-room, nevertheless, they appeared to give general satisfaction to her auditors, who applauded vehemently.

The party altogether became very merry—not to say boisterous ; and at last the waiters were compelled to eject the gentleman and the vociferous lady, as they were becoming objectionable in their personal remarks.

" He's a regular wild one," said a gentleman sitting opposite Jack.

" He seems so," replied our hero.

" Lor', bless your eyes, the things he's done, and the money he's spent—oh, lor', it's dreadful !"

" Is he well known about here ?"

" Well known ?"

" Yes."

" Why, where were you raised ? Do you mean to say you don't know who he is ?"

" I never saw him before."

" What, you a young man about town and never seen *him !* Oh, lor' !"

" Who is he ?"

" You're shamming."

" No, 'pon my honour."

" Why, it's young Lord Delaine."

" What ! the Marquis of Porchester's son ?"

" Yes."

" I've heard of him."

" I should think you had. Why, his face is as well known down the Haymarket as the face of St. Paul's clock on Ludgate-hill."

" He'll come to grief to-night, I expect."

" He generally does."

The man with whom Jack had been talking rose to depart, and our hero finished his meal in silence.

When he left the supper-rooms he deliberated as to which road he should take, but eventually decided on taking " just one turn down the Haymarket."

We all know what that generally leads to ; but in this instance Jack was proof against temptation.

When about halfway down, our hero met Lord Delaine, escorted by a couple of blooming damsels, who, with dresses wonderfully curtailed, left much less to the imagination than is generally considered correct.

Now, it so happened that Jack was acquainted with the ladies in question.

Stay, lady reader, do not condemn him—he had never spoken a word to either in his life.

It was only by repute he knew them.

Jim Gimp had once pointed them out, and cautioned him to beware of them, as they had an unpleasant knack of appropriating the property of inebriated gentlemen and turning them into the street with nothing on but their shirt.

Jack was idle.

He had no Fanny waiting for him at home.

He wanted something to amuse him, so determined to follow this trio at a distance, and see how the matter ended.

Nothing shall induce me to disclose the name of the street into which he followed and finally housed them.

Actions for libel are unpleasant, so I prefer to state merely that it was a shabby and a dirty street.

That it was a street in which all the houses looked half deserted.

A street in which the window-blinds were kept carefully pulled down during the daytime.

A street from whence dismal, dissipated, half-drunken men staggered to the cabstand at unearthly hours in the morning, and from whence howls of drunken joy were heard proceeding at times when respectable inhabitants should have been in bed.

Having said thus much, I think I have described it sufficiently.

Jack watched the three enter the house; and having done thus much, he lit a cigar, leant up against a lamp-post, and waited to see what would happen next.

He stayed at his post some time, till his feet got cramped, and himself disgusted at being there on such a fool's errand.

He was just turning to leave when a bustle and scrimmage inside the house told him what he expected had occurred.

A loud shriek!

Several oaths!

The sound of blows.

Jack crossed over the way.

"If there's going to be a fight," he thought, "I'm ready. I'll join the weakest."

In preparation he tucked up the sleeves of his coat, and clenched his fists.

The noise came nearer to the door, at which he was listening intently.

With a sudden blow it gave way.

It opened, and Lord Delaine, in his shirt and trousers, waving a poker above his head, rushed into the street.

He was followed by three awful bull-headed looking ruffians.

Lord Delaine got his back against a wall, and defended himself with the formidable weapon.

"To the rescue!" shouted Jack, as he leapt suddenly upon them, felling one of the ruffians to the ground, and ranging himself by the side of the young lord.

Thus reinforced his lordship dealt vigorous blows with the poker, and the engagement became general.

Women in every variety of un-dress thronged round the combatants.

Windows were thrown up and heads put forth to see the row, while a confused jargon of French and English swore and applauded on every side.

A weak, light-haired policeman came to the top of the street and looked down, but from prudential motives, declined to venture near the fight till he had procured assistance. So Lord Delaine and Jack were left to fight their way out from the crowd of male and female ruffians as best they could.

They did at last manage it.

How, they scarcely knew themselves, but at last the two found themselves, cut, bruised, and bleeding, standing side by side in the now deserted Haymarket.

"I don't know how to repay you," said Lord Delaine to Jack; "but for you I should have come off badly."

"Don't mention it. I enjoyed the fun."

"That's more than some of them did," said his lordship, looking at the poker which he still held, but which was so twisted and bent by the force of his blows that it looked more like a large corkscrew.

"You did good service with that."

"Yes; I'm muscular when I'm roused. But what is the good of standing talking here? Come with me to my hotel for the night, and we'll talk it over in the morning."

"You're very kind, but——"

"Nonsense, no excuses. Come along; I've taken a fancy to you."

The end of the matter was that Lord Delaine and Jack got into a cab, and were driven to the hotel where his lordship was staying.

After a tumbler of brandy and soda-water neither of them felt much inclined to sit up, so both tumbled off to bed with the agreement to meet at a twelve o'clock breakfast.

Refreshed by their sleep and a cold bath the two young men made their appearance a little before one, and did full justice to the meal set before them.

After Lord Delaine had again thanked Jack for coming to his rescue, and had heard from him the account of how he came to be on the spot, he said—

"I've a proposal to make to you."

"What is it?"

"I'm sick of town life, and I want to get out of the way of it."

"Rather natural after last night."

"I'm thinking of going on a yachting trip. If you've nothing better to do, I wish you'd join me."

"I should be most happy, but I fear the expense——"

"Bother the expense. I've got my own yacht, and it's not likely I'm going to let you pay for your food while I entertain you."

"It would be very jolly," said Jack.

"Will you come?"

"If you really mean it, I shall be most happy."

"That's right. We must have some girls with us though."

Jack sighed as he thought how Fanny would have enjoyed the trip, but it so happened that he did not in the least know where she was.

"Not any of your flaring painted ones you know," continued his lordship; "but something nice, quiet, and pretty. Respectable, but not too particular."

"I know one, the very thing," said Jack, thinking of Letty Burton.

"That's right, and I think I can get another at Liverpool."

"Liverpool?"

"Yes. Didn't I tell you I've got my yacht in the Mersey?"

"No; you didn't say where she was."

"Well, I tell you what; we'll dine quietly here to-day, and then to-morrow run down to Liverpool, and get everything ready."

"As your lordship pleases."

"You'll see about asking this girl you were speaking of."

"Trust me for that," said Jack, laughing.

Our hero was well pleased at the promised trip.

Not only would it be a great pleasure, but likewise, in case the police should have any clue to him, it would be the best way in the world to escape them.

Jack speedily got all his things ready, and found out Letty Burton.

It was no difficult matter to persuade her to come, and the following morning she drove to the hotel, and was introduced to Lord Delaine, who straightway fell in love with her handsome face and splendid eyes.

After a substantial repast, the three proceeded to the railway station and took tickets for Liverpool.

The timely present of half-a-crown secured them a compartment to themselves, and as the train bore them rushing and whirling through the air, their merry laughter showed what a happy party they were.

Arrived at Liverpool, Lord Delaine announced it as his opinion that they had better remain at an hotel till he had seen the yacht was quite ready for their reception.

"What hotel shall we go to?" asked Jack.

"Oh, the Adelphi."

And thither they drove.

Now, it will be remembered that Fanny was staying at the Adelphi, and had assumed the name and title of Lord Delaine.

Arrived at the hotel the waiter ushered the party into a small uncomfortable sitting-room.

"Hullo! What the deuce does this mean?" asked his lordship; "can't I have that front room I had when I was here before?"

"Very sorry, sir; the front room is engaged."

"Engaged?"

"Yessir."

"Who has it?"

"Lord Delaine, sir."

"Who?"

"Lord Delaine, sir; the son of the Marquis of Porchester."

"Lord Delaine."

"Yessir."

"Hang it, man—I am Lord Delaine. Don't give me any of your impudence!"

It is time, however, that we should return to our heroine, whom we left in rather a critical position, stretched stunned and motionless on a flower-bed.

CHAPTER LVII.

MISS HORTENSIA CHICKORY DISCOVERS A STRANGE FLOWER IN HER TULIP-BED.

MR. SETH CHICKORY was a retired grocer.

He had made a fortune by adulteration, and had retired to the country to enjoy the fruit of his labours.

He was an uncouth, uneducated man, though good-hearted and hospitable.

He was a widower, and his house was kept by his sole surviving daughter, Hortensia.

She was not absolutely a pretty girl, though she possessed a certain boldness which made her rather admired by young men in general.

She had been spoilt at a "finishing school," whither her father had sent her, and where she had learnt nothing but that she had better have been ignorant of, for from a tolerably well-conducted quiet girl, she had become a fast young lady, whose whole thoughts turned upon love and lovers.

A steady perusal of French novels procured at school on the sly, had made her morals of the loosest; and though she had not yet fallen from the paths of virtue, it was from no fault of hers.

Miss Hortensia was fond of flowers. At least she said she was, and used to spend great part of her time in tending the plants in her father's garden.

One fine morning going early to look at her tulips, which she hoped to bring to great perfection, she was horrified at discovering the tops of the finest broken off.

Curious to discover the cause, she approached the bed, and there saw, lying among her pet flowers, a remarkably handsome young man with the blood oozing from a wound in his forehead, and his dress torn and stained.

Miss Hortensia Chickory shrieked, but it must be confessed not very loud.

But the young man did not move!

She began to feel frightened.

Was she about to become the heroine of a romance?

The stranger's handsome countenance was death-like in its pallor, and it was only by his laboured breathing that she knew he was alive.

She hastened back to the house, summoned the servants, and had the wounded one brought into the house and laid upon her own bed.

After a short time, as she watched by his side, thinking what an irresistible lover he would be, she had the satisfaction of seeing him open his eyes.

"Where am I?" said he, or rather she (for every reader of course is perfectly aware that the wounded stranger is none other than our heroine).

"Where am I?"

"Where you will be well taken care of," said Hortensia, in her honeyest tone.

"'Orty-'orty—where are yer, my gal?" sung out a cheerful vulgar voice, and in another moment a man whose appearance exactly accorded with the voice, entered the room.

"What's all this 'ere?" he asked, in surprise, in seeing some one habited in a man's dress stretched upon his daughter's bed.

Miss Hortensia told him of the way in which she had discovered our heroine.

"It's rum," said the retired grocer, "very rum!"

"I hope I don't inconvenience you," said Fanny, in a faint voice.

"Not at all, young man."

"Where am I?"

"In the family mansion of Seth Chickory, Esquire."

"How did I get here?"

"My darter; she found you a growing in a toolip bed."

"Can I do anything for you?" asked Hortensia. "Do you fancy anything would do you good?"

"Where is my horse?"

"Your horse!"

"What a swell! He's got a 'oss!" muttered Mr. Chickory.

"He stumbled and threw me, just by your garden," continued Fanny.

"'Ow did you 'appen to be there, young man? The road is on the other side of the 'ouse."

"I had been pursued by robbers."

"By robbers?"

"Yes."

"How romantic!" cried Hostensia, clasping her hands.

"When you're a bit better, young man, if you'll come and pick a bit o' breakfast along o' me, I shall be most 'appy."

"Thank you. You're very kind," rejoined Fanny.

The old grocer stumped out of the room, and Hortensia proceeded to bathe our heroine's forehead and smooth her hair with great tenderness.

I wonder if she would have done it had she known her sex?

I fear not.

"Had you much difficulty in making your escape?" asked the grocer's daughter.

"Yes," cried Fanny; "six of them, armed to the teeth, attacked me, and but for my splendid horse I should by this time have been a corpse."

"Heavens!" cried Hortensia, squeezing Fanny's hand very tight, and then trying to look as if she had not meant to do it.

After a plentiful application of cold water, Fanny felt sufficiently strong to rise to her feet; and though pale from loss of blood, and exhausted, she managed, by leaning on the arm of Miss Hortensia Chickory, to reach the breakfast parlour.

The old grocer received her very cordially, and appeared quite disappointed when he found she would not eat of every dish on the table.

Breakfast concluded, Fanny could not be restrained from going to the stable to see the horse which had carried her so well, for Mr. Chickory had sent his groom to look after him.

"Black Prince," though cut a little about the knees, was not seriously hurt.

The ex-grocer's groom happened to understand horses thoroughly, and Fanny had no hesitation in committing the valuable animal to his care.

Not only did Mr. Chickory agree to look after her horse, but he likewise begged she would take up her abode at his house, at all events till she had quite recovered from the effects of her accident, and this, after a becoming amount of hesitation, our heroine agreed to do.

Hortensia was highly delighted at this arrangement, and only wished her tulips might be broken regularly once a week, provided the accident always brought a handsome young gentleman to stay in the house.

Fanny could not fail to perceive the unmistakeable advances her host's daughter made her at every conceivable opportunity.

She was rather puzzled in what way to take them, for she feared that if she in any way responded the matter might go greater lengths than she desired.

Still she saw that she must assume a certain warmth in her manner towards Hortensia.

That young lady, believing Fanny to be of the opposite sex to herself, followed her about everywhere, always, of course, declaring it was chance which threw them so much together.

Fanny was willing to go all reasonable lengths.

She returned Hortensia's kisses with interest, and pressed her hand as much as the most ardent lover could desire.

But this state of things could not last for ever.

Matters were shortly to be brought to a crisis.

One day, old Chickory being out, Fanny betook herself to a snug little room on the ground floor, which was but little used, hoping there to be able to enjoy an hour's quiet reflection upon the course it would be best for her to pursue.

But the apartment was already occupied.

Miss Hortensia was sitting there reading.

Perhaps she never appeared to better advantage than she did that morning.

MINNIE RATTLIN SURPRISES HER SISTER AND THE REV. MR. GORBELL IN THE ARBOUR.

Her hair was becomingly arranged, and her dress suited her well, though perhaps it was a little more open in front than it need have been.

Her whole attitude was negligent in the extreme.

She was reclining in a large easy-chair.

Her legs were crossed, and her crinoline was expansive.

The consequence was, that a large amount of worked stocking, covering a well-shaped leg, was displayed to view.

To tell the truth, the young lady had carefully studied this attitude, in order to subdue the heart of the handsome stranger; consequently she was not a little disappointed at the cool way in which our heroine regarded the display.

Hortensia and Fanny had a long conversation in that little room.

What it was about I cannot pretend to say; I only know that it ended in the grocer's daughter flying into a great passion and leaving the apartment, banging the door after her with sufficient force to shake the whole house.

When she had gone, Fanny, no longer able to contain herself, burst into a fit of laughter which lasted for some minutes.

That day the dinner passed off more dismally than any of the preceding ones, and, in spite of all Fanny could do to make herself pleasant, it was but a dull affair.

Mr. Chickory fidgeted uneasily in his chair, and seemed to have something on his mind.

Hortensia scowled gloomily, and did not speak.

Fanny was the only one at her ease.

As soon as the cloth was removed, Hortensia rose and left the room.

The retired grocer filled his glass, and then, with many hums and haws, broke the ice and spoke—

"I'm very sorry, sir, to 'ave to say anything rude, but I should just like to know what your intentions is."

"My intentions?"

"Yes."

"On what matter?"

"My darter.　She's a good girl, and 'ad a proper amount

of schooling, and if so be as you wish to make her your wife——."

"My *wife*?"

"Yes."

"It's quite impossible."

"Then look here, mister. I tells you to your face you're a villain."

"Allow me to explain."

"You're a rascally seducer."

"Draw it mild," said Fanny.

"My darter tells me you've been a going on and a leading her to believe as how you loved her."

"Well?"

"But it aint well if you don't. Howsumdever, let that pass. But she comes and she tells me that, this very day, while I was out, you said things to her which you didn't ought to have said, and you tried to do things with her which you didn't ought to try to do."

"Then she says what is not true," replied Fanny.

"Come, mister, none o' that! Don't you go for to call my darter a liar!"

"If she made those statements to you she is something very nearly approaching one."

"What do you mean?"

"I mean that if anything improper was said during our interview to-day hers were the lips which uttered it."

"Do you call it gentlemanly conduct? Do you think 'cos you're a swell you can blacken my gal's good name? Do you call it manly conduct?"

"No, I don't," said Fanny.

"I'm glad of it."

"I call it womanly conduct," continued our heroine.

"What do you mean?" asked the grocer.

"I mean, Mr. Chickory, that I am a woman!"

"A—a—a what?"

"A woman!"

"I don't believe it. It's a trick—it's a lie!"

"I can soon convince you, though I trust you will spare me doing so;" and Fanny spoke in her natural, soft woman's voice.

"Yes—yes; I see it all now," said the grocer.

"You believe me, Mr. Chickory?"

"Yes—yes," sobbed the old man, burying his face in his hands. "To think my darter should turn out so bad. Lying to her old father, and being no better than—— Oh, dear! oh, dear!" and the grocer rocked himself to and fro in his chair, in anguish at discovering the true character of the child upon whom he had prided himself.

"You will agree with me, Mr. Chickory," continued Fanny, as soon as the old man became a little calm, "that the sooner I leave your house the better. I thank you very much indeed for your kind hospitality."

Fanny left the room, went round to the stable, had "Black Prince" saddled, and then, recompensing the groom, rode off slowly towards Liverpool, where she arrived at a late hour of the night.

Leaving her horse as before, she repaired to the Adelphi Hotel, and again entered its portals, to the great delight of the waiter, who began to think his lordship had gone off without paying his bills.

This, it should be stated, was the night previous to the day upon which the true Lord Delaine, accompanied by Jack and Letty Burton, left London for Liverpool.

Fanny, unconscious that the real owner of the title she had assumed was even then planning a visit to the town—even to the very hotel in the smoking-room of which she now sat enjoying her cigar—gave herself airs, and attracted great attention from the cringing waiters, who "my lorded" her to her heart's content.

The cigar finished she went to bed, little dreaming what the morrow would bring forth.

The want of money was even greater with her now than it was before.

She had gained nothing by her last exploit.

The jewels of the mayor and his wife were in London, and her stock of money had diminished to a couple of sovereigns.

What could she do?

The only course open to her appeared to be to get away quietly from the hotel without paying the bill, and go up to London by an early train, and endeavour to dispose of her jewels.

Still, this plan had many drawbacks, and while she still deliberated she fell fast asleep.

CHAPTER LVIII.

HOW THE TWO LORDS WERE BROUGHT FACE TO FACE, AND HOW FANNY WHITE AND HER FRIEND JACK RAWLINGS ACTED IN ACCORDANCE WITH THE OLD ADAGE OF "KISS AND BE FRIENDS."

FANNY WHITE, still attired in gentleman's clothes, and still passing under the name of Lord Delaine, sat quietly in the private room she had taken at the Adelphi, sipping her claret, thinking over her pecuniary difficulties, and forming innumerable plans for bettering her worldly position.

Suddenly, and without warning, the door of the room was thrown open, and the sober-looking waiter stood in the entrance.

"This is Lord Delaine, sir—my lord, I mean," said he, addressing some individual in the passage.

"The deuce it is!" said a cheery voice. "Let's have a look at the impostor."

"There'll be a row," thought Fanny. "I'm in for it now, that's certain."

A tall, handsome, good-looking man appeared in the doorway—no other, in fact, than the true Lord Delaine.

"You can go," said he to the waiter, who still lingered, anxious to hear the end of the affair.

Thus bidden, he had no course but to retire, which he did reluctantly enough, though only to catch a violent cold by listening at the keyhole.

"I understand you call yourself Lord Delaine," said the true son of the Marquis of Porchester.

Fanny bowed.

She saw nothing for it but to attempt to brazen it out.

"May I ask by what right you assume that name and title?"

"You are at perfect liberty to ask any questions you like, but——"

"But what?"

"But I shall decline to answer them unless you inform me by what right you interrogate me."

"What right? Ha, ha! That's good."

"Perhaps you will not object to inform me who you may be?"

"Certainly not."

"Well?"

"*I* am Lord Delaine; and I denounce you as an infamous cheat, a liar, and a swindler."

"How dare you address such language to me?" replied our heroine, boldly, though with a sinking heart, for she felt that she was discovered. "How dare you couple such epithets with my name? You know, I suppose, the consequence of using such words?"

"The consequences may be either that you may bring an action against me for defamation of character, or that you may send me a challenge."

"Precisely."

"Well, I don't care much."

"You will be made to care."

"I differ from you."

"Why?"

"Because *you* will not do the first, and I most assuredly will not do the second."

"You will be compelled."

"We shall see."

"Very well."

"A friend of mine will wait upon you."

"A friend of yours will do nothing of the sort."

"You must fight me, or retract your insulting expressions."

"I shall do neither the one nor the other."

"Then ——"

"Now don't talk nonsense, but listen to me. I am Lord Edgar Delaine, son of the Marquis of Porchester."

"That may——"

"Silence! Hear what I have to say. I am generally considered by my friends to be a good-natured, easy-going sort of fellow——"

"But I——"

"Wait a moment, I have a proposition to make. You are an impostor, that is certain. If you have assumed my name for swindling purposes, I will expose you and have you kicked out of the hotel; if you have done it to obtain a false position, I shall pity you for a fool; and if you have done it for a lark, I will join in a laugh with you, for no one loves a bit of fun better than I do. Come, make a clean breast of it."

Fanny deliberated. She saw that her present position was untenable, and she had a great mind to tell as much of her story to Lord Delaine as would exculpate without criminating herself.

"Bear in mind," said his lordship, "that I have no intention of prosecuting you, for I have not the time to spare to do so."

"You could hardly do so were you so inclined," replied Fanny.

"Well, then, tell me your story."

Our heroine came to the conclusion that that would be the best course for her to pursue.

Accordingly, she told Lord Delaine the simple truth. She told him how she had entered the hotel without any intention of assuming his or any other nobleman's name; how, being suddenly called upon to give her name, she had uttered that which rose first to her lips, and how she had adopted it ever since.

"Then, what is your real name?"

"I beg your lordship's pardon, but had I not been desirous of concealing it I should not have assumed yours."

"Very true. Still I should like to know it. I give you my word not to repeat it."

Again Fanny deliberated.

She thought that if she were to reveal her sex, she would probably excite more sympathy in the mind of the young nobleman than if she allowed him to think she was attired in her proper dress.

"Well, what is your name?"

"Fanny White, my lord," she answered, quietly.

"What?"

"Fanny White."

"Fanny?"

"Yes."

"Why, you don't mean to say that you are a woman?"

"Such is the fact."

"The devil!"

Fanny could not help smiling at the surprise her revelation had produced.

"Well, I must say I think you're about the pluckiest girl I ever came across, and I've known one or two who didn't stick at trifles."

"Which of the three courses that your lordship proposed are you going to carry into execution? Am I to be kicked from the hotel? do you pity me for a fool? or are you going to laugh with me."

"Neither. I'm going to admire you."

Fanny smiled. She saw she had done right in revealing her sex.

"You are a jolly girl, and no mistake. By Jove! I should like to see you in crinoline and calico!"

"I am afraid that can hardly be managed."

"Why not?"

"I do not possess the requisite articles of dress."

"I tell you what, Miss Fanny; after what has occurred, the two rival Lords Delaine can hardly stop in the same hotel."

"Certainly not."

"Well, then, if you don't mind going to another, I will have all the proper attire sent there for you; and then, perhaps, in your own proper character, you will not mind joining myself and a couple of friends at a sociable dinner this evening."

"I should have much pleasure, but——"

"Where is the difficulty?"

"I fear I cannot leave this hotel."

"Why not?"

"It would be perhaps more correct to say, I should not be allowed to go."

"For what reason."

"I owe a bill here, which I cannot pay until—until the arrival of remittances from town."

"Never mind. I'll square it for you."

"You are very kind, but——"

"Nonsense! no excuses, no thanks. You see, you did wisely to make a clean breast of it."

"I do, indeed."

"Well, then, you get ready to be off. My servant will go down Bold-street and order everything feminine you may require, and at seven o'clock I shall expect to see you again."

So saying, Lord Delaine left the room.

Fanny gave a great sigh of relief.

It was a narrow escape she had had; and but for the almost foolish good-nature and love of adventure of the man whose title she had assumed, she might have passed the night in the Liverpool gaol.

As it was, things could not have happened better, and our heroine determined to use all her powers of fascination that evening to please the young nobleman who had done so much for her. Perhaps, too, she had an idea that under certain circumstances he might be induced to do more.

Lord Delaine told the waiter a wonderful story about the gentleman upstairs, who was a foreigner, with an Italian title similar to his own.

The waiter was not deceived, but the present of a sovereign made him hold his tongue.

Fanny's bill was paid, and she took her departure to another hotel, where she found all the articles of female toilet awaiting her, and she spent the rest of the afternoon trying, fitting, and altering her dress, in order to present as charming an appearance as possible at the dinner to which Lord Delaine had invited her.

Jack and Letty were both eager to know the result of the interview between the true and the false lord.

Lord Delaine speedily gratified their curiosity, and told them the whole story, only concealing Fanny's name, in accordance with his promise to her.

Dinner was laid for four, in the room so lately occupied by our heroine. There were already three waiting the arrival of Fanny White, who would complete the party.

Lord Delaine employed his time in dilating largely upon the extreme beauty of his fair namesake; but his lordship was not a close observer, and Jack failed to discover from his description that it was his long-lost love that he was about to meet.

They had not to wait long. The door of the room was thrown open and Fanny entered.

If Lord Delaine had admired her beauty before, he was completely overwhelmed with it now.

She had never appeared to so great an advantage, for his lordship, in sending his servant to order her dress, had told him not to spare expense, and Fanny was consequently arrayed to perfection. Her light hair had been carefully and elaborately dressed; and though she had been compelled, on her assumption of male character, to cut off the majority of her luxuriant tresses, still so well had the hair-dresser done his work, that the loss was hardly perceptible.

His lordship was delighted, and welcomed our heroine with great warmth of manner—so much so, in fact, as slightly to annoy Letty Burton, who whispered to Jack that Fanny's was not the style of beauty she admired.

"Enter, Lord Delaine the Second," said the Marquis of Porchester's son, as the door closed behind Fanny. "Allow me to introduce you," he continued. "Miss Letty Burton—my particular frend——"

"Jack!"

"Fanny!"

"Hullo!" exclaimed his lordship; "I should think you had met before!"

Fanny, heedless of the lookers-on, and of her dress, had rushed into our hero's arms.

"You don't know how glad I am to see you again," said she, holding up her pretty, smiling face to be kissed.

Jack was not slow to respond to the silent invitation, and Letty Burton turned away in disgust, to be followed and consoled by Lord Delaine.

In spite of this unexpected scene the dinner went off very pleasantly.

Lord Delaine recovered his good temper, which had been rather ruffled at first on finding Fanny deserted him for his friend; and by the time Letty had drunk her second glass of sparkling hock, she had nearly forgotten her jealousy.

As for Fanny and Jack, they were completely happy.

Laughing, joking, relating adventures, sipping wine, and smoking cigarettes, the quartette managed to pass a very pleasant evening.

It must be confessed Fanny felt a little disappointed when she heard that the visit to Liverpool was but a flying one, and that they were off for a cruise in two days' time; and, indeed, to tell the truth, our heroine did not much like her lover being exposed to the fascinations of "that creature," as she called Letty Burton.

But Lord Delaine soon put her at her ease, and made her

supremely happy, by inviting her to make the fourth in the yachting party.

It need hardly be said that she joyfully accepted the invitation.

Her spirits rose considerably.

She was no longer the poor, nameless, friendless creature, leading a precarious life, and in hourly dread of Dr. Savage.

She felt now that she could defy him.

It was a late hour before they parted for the night, and when Fanny left, Jack accompanied her to the hotel at which she was staying.

I am not quite sure whether he came back to the Adelphi that night.

The *Firefly* was the name of Lord Delaine's yacht.

She was a pretty little thing, cutter-rigged, of no very great tonnage, but a good sea-boat. She was a fast sailer, and the cabins were fitted up in the most luxurious style conceivable. They were small, but everything that could give additional comfort was there, and when his lordship took his guests on board for the first time, they were loud in their praises.

Indeed, they could not well have been other than delighted. Everything was perfect, and they all looked forward to the cruise with the greatest pleasure.

One day more was spent pleasantly enough, in maritime London, and then all was ready for their embarkation.

The wine and provisions were on board—the few things wanted had been purchased, and the crew stood by the anchor, only waiting for the master and his three friends to come on board to start upon their way.

It was a lovely evening when the *Firefly* left her moorings and glided slowly and gracefully down the Mersey towards the open sea.

Lord Delaine insisted upon his guests drinking success to the voyage in some first-rate champagne; and truth compels me to state they were not reluctant to do so, and thus under most auspicious circumstances commenced their voyage.

The following morning broke clear and beautiful, and as they scudded gaily along before the breeze, with a bright blue sky overhead, they all felt as happy as possible, till the motion of the yacht produced the effect upon them it is apt to, and for some hours both Fanny and Letty were prostrated by sea-sickness, but they soon got over it; and all went merry as a marriage-bell, with the exception, perhaps, that our heroine was a little put out, and made slightly jealous by observing Jack's attention to Letty, and noticing the eager way in which he glanced at that young lady's ankles whenever she ascended the short ladder which led from the cabin to the deck.

But altogether the whole party agreed in pronouncing the excursion "jolly;" and Lord Delaine had every reason thus far for being satisfied with the success of the trip.

Leaving them to pursue their voyage, it is time we should return to some other of our characters, whom we have somewhat neglected of late.

CHAPTER LIX.
THE NURSERY OF CRIME.

THE "Dodger's Delight" was a low public-house.

There was no denying the fact.

Look at it what way you would, it could be called nothing else.

It made no pretensions to splendour. It was not a flaring, glaring gin-palace, with a great deal of gas and looking-glass and with huge vats standing in the bar marked with fabulous quantities.

Neither was it a quiet respectable-looking inn, with notices of Exeter Hall meetings stuck up in the bar.

Much less was it one of those nondescript houses of entertainment called family hotels.

The landlord himself spoke of it vaguely as a beershop. The frequenters usually referred to it in some ambiguous way; and as for the police, they had it down in their black books, and always called it "Jerry Bight's."

It had a low, sneaking, underhand, disreputable appearance, and chance customers were a rarity. Scarcely any one was ever seen in the bar, though many entered the swing-doors.

What became of them afterwards was a mystery to the uninitiated.

Exercising the author's privilege—of going everywhere unquestioned—we will enter the "Dodger's Delight."

A mean, shabby bar it has.

The handles by which the beer is drawn look worn out and rusty, as if never used.

The two biscuits in a dirty basket appear to have been there for centuries.

The walls are filthy and undecorated—save by a few notices of dogs lost and bank-notes stolen.

Mr. Jerry Bight, the landlord, sits grumpily in his bar, smoking a long clay pipe, and nodding condescendingly to those who enter and pass quickly across the dirty floor and through a dingy baize-covered swing-door.

Jerry Bight had once been a fighting man, but his name did not stand particularly well with the members of the P. R.

On more than one occasion Mr. Jerry was believed to have sold a fight, and although he was once matched for the championship, somehow or another the combat never took place.

Whether it was that he had never intended to fight, whether he got alarmed at the last moment and feared to meet his antagonist, or whether the money for the stakes was not forthcoming, was never rightly known; but certainly the fight did *not* take place, and Jerry fell into such bad odour with his sporting friends, that he did not care to go near them.

Ejected from the ring, Jerry turned his attention to the "public" line.

He found, in a little back-street on the Surrey-side of the water, a queer old dilapidated house which had been fitted up for the sale of wine, beer, and spirituous liquors.

The former landlord, after two months' trial of the premises, got into such a desponding state, that he hanged himself one fine morning in his own bar.

But this did not deter Jerry, for he had his own particular reasons for desiring to choose an out-of-the-way spot; and he accordingly took the place, named it the "Dodger's Delight," laid in a good stock of malt liquor, and sat down patiently in his bar awaiting customers.

He was certainly more fortunate than his predecessor, who was reported to have only drawn one pint of ale in the course of a week—and that one upon trust.

Many individuals of both sexes nightly entered the doors of the "Dodger's Delight," but the odd part of the matter was that, as already stated, although they were seen to enter, they were but rarely observed to leave, and the bar of the public-house was invariably deserted.

Had you gained the confidence of a policeman, and asked him to explain the apparent mystery, he would have told you that the "Dodger's Delight" was a thieves' house-of-call, and had you pressed him still further, he would, perhaps, have taken you into the interior and shown you a strange sight.

And this is what you might have seen.

After entering the bar and exchanging salutations with Jerry Bight, you would have gone through the dingy baize-covered door, and then, had you been alone, would most probably have tumbled down a steep flight of stone steps; but having so able a guide as Inspector X, he informs you of your danger, and with his help you descend the worn, slippery steps.

Another swing-door has to be passed, and then you find yourself in a glare of light, and before you a long vaulted cellar filled with a collection of as disreputable-looking vagabonds as you can well imagine. Of all sizes and all ages, they sit, stand, and lounge about the place, shouting, joking, singing, and laughing, as if such things as magistrates and policemen were not.

It is to this nursery of crime that I would introduce you.

It is midnight, and the noise and feasting are in full swing.

Some of the less hardened topers had already given way before the potency of Jerry Bight's liquors, but the majority were in full force, though, perhaps, a trifle noisy.

Mother Death was there, Black Jack was there, indeed a fine sprinkling of all the London thieves and blackguards were assembled in the cellar of the "Dodger's Delight."

The fun was at its height, the cans were circulating freely, and everyone was doing his best to enjoy himself, when suddenly amongst them there appeared a tall man dressed entirely in black, with his face completely concealed by a low slouched hat.

"A spy—a spy!" cried a dozen voices, with appropriate adjectives.

Those nearest the intruder rushed towards him.

He stood immovable.

It was not till one approached close to him that he stretched forth his hand, and then it was to seize him by the throat, and hurl him backwards with terrific force.

With a howl of rage at their comrade's fall, the others rushed upon him.

He stepped back a pace, and drew a revolver from his breast.

The sight of the weapon caused his assailants to pause.

"Fools!" said he, in a deep bass voice; "you don't know what you do."

"Oh, don't we though!" answered a ruffian, advancing, with an oath.

The stranger threw off his hat, and revealed the handsome features of the Earl of Stonecliffe!

All started back in surprise.

His appearance was evidently unexpected, but they appeared to know him well.

"I beg your pardon," growled Squinting; Bill "but how was I to know as it was your honour?"

"Never mind."

"You see, with that there cap on, a body couldn't see your face."

"That's just what I wore it for. You don't suppose I'm such a fool as to want every one to know of my visit to the 'Dodger's Delight.'"

"What brings your honour here?"

"Business."

"Can we help you?"

"Yes, or I should not have come."

"What is it?"

"I'll tell you presently. I must have a talk with Mother Death first."

"Mother Death, you're wanted!" shouted one of the ruffians; and after the cry had been several times repeated, the old hag made her appearance.

She looked even more disgusting and repulsive than when first we saw her.

The shrivelled skin fitted so tightly over her bones that her head looked exactly like a skull.

The toothless jaws muttered and mumbled incoherently, as usual, and her deep-set eyes glared fiercely at the earl as she advanced towards him.

"What is it?" she asked, abruptly.

"Hush! don't speak so loud."

"What do you want with me?"

"I've got a job on hand."

"Oh, what a clever boy he is, so handsome and so wicked! What crime is it now?"

"A truce to foolery—I want your assistance."

"And you shall have it. When did you ever come to me in vain?"

"Never."

"Mother Death is of some use to you yet—oh, yes," mumbled the old woman, rubbing her skinny hands together, and chuckling diabolically.

"Then you will do me a service?"

"What is it?"

"Will you do it?"

"Yes; if—if it isn't any hanging matter."

"Ha, ha, ha! Of course it isn't; I could do that without your assistance."

"Of course you could."

"But why have you grown so particular all of a sudden?"

"I'm an old woman—I'm getting very old, and I see strange things o' nights. Creeping, crawling things come about me, and the devil himself sometimes sits upon my chest, grinning at me, and he says, 'You can't escape me, do what you will,' and he laughs, and mocks, and seizes my heart with red-hot pincers. You don't know what I suffer when I'm alone in my bed-room."

"Would you not like to have a companion at night—some one to talk to when these dreadful things appear to you?"

"What do you mean?"

"I mean that if you could get some one to occupy the same room with you it would be pleasanter."

"I've tried to, but none of them will do it. They're all afraid of me. They think I've sold myself to the devil, and wont come nearer me than they can help."

"But suppose I find some one who will share your room?"

"What are you driving at? You have some deep-laid scheme in your head."

"I have."

"What is it?"

"I want you to look after a young girl for me."

"A young girl?"

"Yes; a charming young creature."

"Pretty?"

"Beautiful!"

"You used not at one time to care about getting rid of such."

"Perhaps not."

"What am I to do with this one?"

"Keep her closely, watch her strictly, suffer her to speak to no one but yourself, and, above all, hold your own tongue."

"Who is she?"

"Never mind."

"What is her name?"

"You are too curious."

"I may be curious, but I keep secrets none the less well for being intrusted with the whole instead of part."

"I cannot tell you this."

"Do as you like."

"Such is my intention."

"Tell me, then, at least, in what light I am to look upon this lovely angel."

"What do you mean?"

"Am I to pet her?"

"You *pet*?"

It certainly did seem strange to hear the hideous, bleareyed, toothless old hag talk of petting, and the earl was perfectly warranted in his exclamation; nevertheless Mother Death did not altogether seem to relish it.

"Well, well," she continued, "you must have your own way; but I should like to know whether your object is to make the beautiful damsel fall in love with you."

"Pshaw! Do you think I should come to you to aid me in that?"

"Then you fear her—she knows some secret of yours."

The Earl of Stonecliffe started, and brought his fist down heavily on a table.

"Yes, she does!" said he, with an oath.

"Then you want her well guarded?"

"Yes."

"And you will pay well?"

"Of course."

"When will she come?"

"I do not know exactly. Be ready to receive her any day, and at any time."

"It shall be done."

"Stay. You must look a little more respectable, or you will frighten her. Take this, and buy a black dress—you can keep the change."

The Earl of Stonecliffe tossed her a heavy purse as he spoke, through the meshes of which gold sparkled and glittered.

Mother Death seized it eagerly, and devoured it with greedy eyes before she hid it in the bosom of her dress.

"Mind you keep her securely."

"You may be sure of that."

"If she escapes, it will be my ruin and your death."

"But——"

"But what?"

"If she is so dangerous when she is at liberty, is there not a more certain method of making her keep silence?"

"How do you mean?"

The hag sunk her voice to the lowest whisper—

"People don't talk from their graves!"

"Some do. I tell you poison cannot harm her, steel cannot hurt her."

"You have tried?"

"I have."

"Well!"

"She has risen from her grave to torment me—curse her!" growled the earl.

"When she is once under my care she will trouble you no more," replied the hag, with a hideous leer.

"Good. Now send Black Jack to me—I want to talk to him."

"About this?"

"Never mind what about—send him here."

Mother Death, mumbling to herself, as was her custom, shuffled away from the place, and mixed with the throng who caroused around the long deal table.

At first there had been some curiosity evinced by them about the object of the earl's visit, for he was well known to the majority of them, and they were well aware that his visits to the "Dodger's Delight" generally gave some among them a job, which was certain to be well paid for.

They had suspended their conversation for some moments and gazed at their noble visitor and Mother Death, but their speech was in too low a tone for them to overhear it, and after a time they returned to their various amusements.

A successful robbery had been committed the night before, and the burglars had brought the spoil to the cellar for division.

They had quarrelled, as a matter of course, over their respective shares, but after all had been settled, cards and dice were produced, and a large party sat down to gamble away the booty which had been obtained at the risk of their necks.

Such a scene of passion and blasphemy may be more easily imagined than described.

The oaths and rage of the losers, the semi-drunken delight of the winners, were alike horrible.

The Earl of Stonecliffe, as we know, was not very particular, but the scene before his eyes was almost too much even for him, and he was glad to turn from it to discourse with Black Jack.

Black Jack was one of the leaders of the band of law-breakers who nightly assembled at Jerry Bight's.

He was a tall, burly man, possessed of vast muscular power, and, though a criminal of the worst stamp, had some pretensions to good looks.

His real name was not known.

He had come upon them unexpectedly, but his deeds of strength and daring soon raised him in the esteem of the ruffians with whom he associated.

Owing to the darkness of his complexion and the colour of his luxuriant beard, he had obtained the name of "Black Jack," and, as such, was known far and wide.

Hitherto he had always managed to keep clear of the police; for although he was well known to them, both by sight and repute, they had never yet been able to catch him in any felonious act.

Such was the man who now stood by the side of the Earl of Stonecliffe, listening to the instructions that nobleman was giving him.

Mother Death prowled about, edging as near to these two as she dared, in the hope of overhearing something of their conversation; but in this she was disappointed. It was conducted in too low a tone for anything but a few unconnected words to reach her ears.

"Be sure you come by the early train," said the Earl to Black Jack, as he turned to leave the cellar.

That was all Mother Death heard which could afford her the least clue to the strange business in which she was called upon to take a part.

"Here, my lads," said the Earl, pausing by the swing-door, "here is something for you to drink success to me."

He tossed a couple of sovereigns on the ground, and then rapidly left the "Dodger's Delight," regained the public thoroughfare, hailed a Hansom cab, and was driven away from the disreputable neighbourhood to which he had paid so mysterious a visit.

There is honour among thieves, and the two sovereigns presented to the company by the young nobleman were fairly spent in liquor for the benefit of all.

Black Jack alone did not partake of it.

He sat apart, meditative and gloomy, and long before the carouse was at an end rose and left the cellar.

CHAPTER LX.

THE REVEREND MR. GORBELL MAKES LOVE, MINNIE RATTLIN MAKES TEA, AND PHIL DAVENANT MAKES A DISTURBANCE.

ADMIRAL RATTLIN is as jolly as is consistent with his crippled state.

It is so long since we heard anything of this elderly naval hero that I am sure my readers will be glad to hear this fact.

Very little has been doing lately at Nelson's Retreat.

Olivia has been going to meetings and lecturing her younger sister.

Minnie has been growing prettier every day, and flirting occasionally with the Earl of Stonecliffe.

It is needless to say that this amusement, harmless as it was, called down the gravest reproofs from Olivia, who professed to consider the whole male sex objects to be avoided.

However, events were about to occur which would prevent her expressing those sentiments again.

One fine evening, just after sunset, Minnie went into the garden to water her flowers.

She had nearly finished when, in turning quickly round, a thorn on a rosebush caught her dress, and tore it very considerably.

Minnie stooped to gather it together and pin it up, so as to make it present a respectable appearance.

She was screened from observation by a group of large shrubs, so did not take any particular pains as to the manner in which she raised her skirts, and consequently displayed a large amount of well-shaped leg.

Her horror was great on hearing her own name pronounced, as it seemed to her, in her very ear.

She hastily let her dress fall over her shapely limbs, and turned quickly round.

There was no one visible.

Surely she was to be excused for feeling some alarm.

She peered through the shrubs, blushing as she did so, but no one was to be seen.

Who could have pronounced her name?

She determined to quit the spot.

She was on the point of doing so, when again she heard the word "Minnie" spoken quite close to her.

This time she recognised the voice.

It was that of the Reverend Mr. Gorbell.

But where was he?

Had he the power to render himself invisible?

Suddenly, the admiral's youngest daughter remembered that the back of a small summer-house was immediately behind a clump of laurels near her.

She made no doubt the reverend gentleman was seated there.

But who was with him?

It was not likely that he would sit in an arbour by himself, to indulge in a soliloquy respecting her.

Minnie was curious.

The temptation was too great to be resisted; so she carefully pushed aside the intervening boughs, made her way to the back of the summer-house, and—listened.

Far be it from me to defend the course pursued by Miss Minnie Rattlin.

I know she was very wrong in endeavouring to overhear conversation never intended for her ears; but still, as an impartial chronicler, I am obliged to record the fact.

It happened that there was a hole in the boards at the back of the arbour, caused by the falling out of a knot, and to that Minnie applied one of her merry, sparkling eyes.

It was very naughty and very shameful of her, no doubt, to play the spy; but she was naturally curious, and the mention of her own name had made her long to know in what way she was the subject of conversation.

Looking through this chance hole in the boards, she was very nearly revealing her presence by a fit of laughing.

There, sitting in the summer-house, close by the side of the Reverend Mr. Gorbell, was her staid, solemn, sedate, prim sister Olivia.

Mr. Gorbell, never very attractive in his personal appearance, now in Minnie's eyes appeared ten times worse than she had ever seen him before, as with a smirk upon his face, which was meant to be very engaging, he looked and leered at Miss Olivia Rattlin.

"I'm afraid she is a vessel of vice," said the reverend gentleman.

"Alas! yes," sighed Olivia.

"How sad it is she should go astray, following the seductions of a wicked nobleman, instead of sitting under me and listening to my discourses!"

"What a canting humbug he is!" thought Minnie, for she knew that the remarks applied to her.

Mr. Gorbell continued beating time to his words with a little pudgy hand.

"To think that Miss Minnie should be so black a sheep—to think that the good example of her dear sister should have no effect upon her—to think——"

"You needn't squeeze my hand so tight," said Olivia; for the parson, in his earnestness, had suffered his fingers to rest upon Miss Rattlin's.

"Excuse me, dear Miss Olivia, but my sorrow at seeing a lamb going astray makes me forget all the manners and customs of the world."

"Hypocrite!" muttered Minnie between her teeth.

"I was observing," continued the parson, removing his hand,—"I was observing, that if I could be of any service to Miss Minnie, nothing would give me greater satisfaction. I should consider it no hardship to sit alone with her for hours, provided I could promote her spiritual welfare by so doing."

"You needn't do that!" said Olivia, rather sharply, not seeming to relish the idea.

"Of course not. My dear Miss Olivia, if she will not listen to *your* voice, how could *I* hope to succeed?"

For some moments the pair remained silent; and Minnie, was about to withdraw from her post of observation, when she saw Mr. Gorbell quietly, and as if by accident, slide his hand into her sister's lap.

Now, if the truth must be told, Olivia had only objected to the pressure of his fingers because she thought it was the proper thing to do, for in reality she was rather pleased at what she considered a delicate attention.

When he had removed his hand at her words, she had felt rather disappointed; and now that it was again near her, she hesitated as to whether she should notice it or not.

At length she spoke.

"Mr. Gorbell, do you know where your hand is?"

She thought this a somewhat milder way of putting it.

"Yes, my dear young lady, yes," replied he, rubbing his hand upon the dress with some degree of force. "I was admiring the beautiful texture of the silk. Is it not wonderful to think that it should be the produce of a little worm? It is almost miraculous—wonderful!"

Mr. Gorbell turned up the whites of his eyes as he said this, but did not remove his hand.

"The ways of nature are *all* wonderful," he continued. "The production of silk from the worm, the production of children from——"

"Oh!" cried Olivia, covering her face with her hands, "don't——"

"Don't what, my dear young lady?"

"Don't talk to me in that way."

"Be sure, dear miss, no word would escape my lips which could shock you in the remotest degree."

Again there was a long silence.

By some means, however, best known to the lady herself, Olivia's hand dropped till it came very near that of the Rev. Mr. Gorbell's.

That gentleman's glided stealthily along till it touched it. He seized Olivia's fingers in triumph, and carried them to his greasy lips.

"Oh, don't," said Miss Olivia, offering a feeble—*very* feeble resistance.

He knew what that meant, and accordingly repeated the operation.

"Use is second nature," and Miss Rattlin ceased to object.

Minnie, still spying, could scarcely restrain herself from bursting into a merry peal of laughter.

Emboldened by the passiveness of Olivia's resistance, Mr. Gorbell evidently resolved to proceed a step further, and salute the lips of the blushing spinster.

Minnie guessed what he was after and determined to have some fun.

Her watering-pot was still full, the roof of the arbour was only formed by twigs and creepers.

Noiselessly she mounted upon an old roller which lay next the woodwork, and just as the Rev. Mr. Gorbell was about to enfold her sister in a chaste embrace, she emptied the whole contents of her watering-can upon the creepers, directly over the spot where the pair were seated.

"The devil!" cried the clergyman, leaping from his seat, very nearly drowned.

"Oh! oh! oh!" cried Olivia, in an ascending scale of shrillness.

"What was it?" asked the reverend gentleman; "it couldn't have been a waterspout."

"Don't be a fool!" answered the lady.

"What dreadful language!"

"What shameful behaviour!"

"Whose? Mine?"

"Yours! No. That artful little minx's—that pert, conceited, spying, lying, mischievous jade of a sister of mine."

"Oh, what shocking expressions! Remember, my dear young lady, that this is not the language of the elect!"

"Bother the elect! They never had their new silk dresses spotted with rain-water."

"Such expressions, Miss Olivia, are not——"

"Go to Bath!"

"I think I've been," said Mr. Gorbell, ruefully surveying his damp garments.

"None but a brute would make a joke of this affair!"

The fact was Olivia was thoroughly put out, and scarcely knew what she said. She was decidedly savage, or, as the Yankees would express it, her "dander was riz."

"After all," said Mr. Gorbell, soothingly, "you don't know it was your sister who did it."

"Who else could it have been, Mr. Gorbell? just tell me that. If you are going to take the part of that little hussey, I shall at once resign my sitting in your chapel and withdraw——"

"My dear Miss Olivia——"

"Don't 'dear' me. You ought to know better, you wicked old sinner."

"But I assure you——"

"I don't want to hear a word. Why don't you wipe my dress, instead of standing jabbering there?"

Minnie's practical joke had shown the reverend gentleman Miss Olivia in a character he had never dreamt of her possessing. So far, it had done good.

He acted upon this broad hint, and went down upon his knees, extracted his best bandana from his pocket, and did his best to remove the wet, which completely covered one side of her dress.

"I'm not fit to go in to dinner," said Mr. Gorbell, as he surveyed his own piteous plight; "what shall I do?"

Olivia did not vouchsafe him an answer, but swept by him out of the arbour and towards the house.

After a moment's hesitation, her clerical admirer followed. He came to the conclusion that one of Admiral Rattlin's good dinners was not a thing to be lightly surrendered.

Immediately after emptying the watering-pot, Minnie turned and ran to the house.

She hurriedly changed her dress and brushed her hair, and then went downstairs to await the arrival of her sister and Mr. Gorbell, and to enjoy their discomfiture.

No sooner did she see them near the house than she ran into the passage to meet them.

"Good gracious, Livy!" said she, with well-feigned astonishment, "has it been raining?"

"No, it hasn't," replied her elder sister, sulkily.

"But you are quite wet, dear! Good gracious, Mr. Gorbell, and you too. Have you been rescuing my sister from the duck-pond?"

"The fact is, Miss Minnie," replied the clerical gentleman, "we have met with an accident."

"Goodness me! What was that?"

"You know very well," said Olivia, in a tone that was meant to be severe.

"*Did* she get wet and lose her temper?" said Minnie, laughing. "Poor thing! she shall have a glass of brandy, and put her feet in hot water, before she goes to bed."

"You are very funny, Miss Minnie, I daresay; but it isn't the way to talk to your elder sister."

"There, there—was she savage? Never mind, Livy dear. Go and change your things, or you may catch cold, and that would be a pity, for your nose always *does* get so red then!"

"Be quiet, miss."

"Certainly, dear, if you wish it. But what can we do for poor Mr. Gorbell?"

"Never mind me," said that gentleman faintly, shivering with cold.

"I'm afraid your trousers are quite sopped, Mr. Gorbell, and papa having only one leg, I'm afraid his wouldn't be of much service. Livy, dear, *you* haven't got anything you could lend Mr. Gorbell to put on while his trousers are being dried?"

"Minnie, I'm surprised at you."

"Are you, dear?"

"Your conduct and your speech are most indelicate."

"Not so indelicate, dear, as your standing on the top of the stairs with your dress looped up."

This last shot told, and Olivia, who had no reason to be proud of her ankles, beat a hasty retreat; whereupon Minnie summoned her father to assist Mr. Gorbell, and then threw herself into an arm-chair and laughed for ten minutes without stopping.

At length the necessary changes of attire were made, and Olivia came down from her room, looking as cross as two sticks; and Mr. Gorbell made his appearance in a suit of the admiral's, with his white tie draggled and crumpled, and with a general appearance of discomfort.

Olivia looked daggers all dinner time at her younger sister, but I very much fear Minnie was not much disconcerted thereat.

A good dinner and plenty of wine restored Mr. Gorbell to his usual spirits—which, by the way, were always of the dismalest; and even Olivia thawed a little, though she had registered a vow in her own mind, that one day, sooner or later, she would pay her sister out for this trick.

After dinner they returned to the drawing-room, the tea was brought in, and Minnie proceeded to make it.

Mr. Gorbell was politely handing her the kettle, when a sudden loud knock at the door made him start so as to spill plenty of the boiling fluid over his own shoes, and cause him to howl with pain.

But he was not the only one who was startled.

All expressed their surprise, and the old admiral, awakened from his after-dinner nap, roared out to know what the devil was the matter.

The door of the room was thrown violently open, and a young man without a hat rushed frantically in.

"My wife—my wife!—Have you seen anything of her? Do you know where she is?"

"Confound it, sir!" cried the old sailor, "I don't know you or your wife. What the deuce do you mean by coming here and making this uproar?"

"I beg your pardon, Admiral Rattlin, my name is Davenant—Phil Davenant; but I suppose you do not recognise me?"

"Yes, I do. You're the young chap that came to my assistance when I smashed my timber leg. Can I do anything for you in return?"

"Tell me—where is my wife?"

"Have you lost her?"

"Yes."

"Come here, my dear boy, and let me shake hands with you. I congratulate you—I do, upon my word."

"A truce to this, sir. Can you tell me where to find her?"

"You don't mean to tell me you're going to look for her?"

"Of course I am. Do you know where she is?"

"Not I. I've nothing to do with other men's wives, though once upon a time I——well, I'll tell you the story some time, when my daughters are out of the way."

Phil Davenant turned to leave the room as abruptly as he had entered.

"Wait a moment?" sang out the admiral.

"What is it?" asked Phil, pausing.

"Don't be a fool."

"What do you mean?"

"If your wife's run away, let her run. You'll do no good by cutting after her."

Phil banged the door, and was out of the house almost before the admiral had finished his sentence.

After a short conversation about the strange disturbance made by Mr. Philip Davenant, it began to be rather dull, so Mr. Gorbell departed for his own home.

The admiral and his daughters went to bed, and Phil Davenant scoured the country, asking every one he saw if they knew anything of his wife.

CHAPTER LXI.

THE ABDUCTION OF LAURA DAVENANT.

It was quite true.

Laura had disappeared in a most unaccountable manner, and Phil was half frantic in consequence.

He had been for an evening stroll, and on his return found his wife was not in her room.

Where could she be?

She never ventured out alone, especially after dusk, except into the inn garden.

But she was not there.

A little boy who did duty as boots and stable helper at the "Stonecliffe Arms" deposed that he had seen her leave the inn and enter the garden, but that was all that Phil could learn.

She was not in the garden now, but it seemed incredible that she could have been taken away by force without her

having given an alarm, which would have been heard by many.

For a moment Phil thought it possible that he had been made a victim of, and that she had gone off leaving him to pay the bill; but a momentary glance round her bed-room convinced him that such was not the case.

Lying upon the dressing-table were several jewels, and in a casket, which had been left open, Phil saw sufficient sovereigns to pay the bill twenty times over.

He could not understand it at all.

He was still more puzzled when, on making a further inspection of the room, he found that even the light shawl she usually wore when she went out was in its place, and that, in short, nothing was missing but Laura herself.

From what he had often heard her say, he knew she had many enemies in the neighbourhood.

But who were they?

He had no idea.

Acting upon the impulse of the moment, he ran off to Nelson Retreat, in the hope of learning some news of his missing wife; but it was a vain hope as we have already seen.

When he left Admiral Rattlin's, he started off walking rapidly along the road, asking every one he met whether they had seen anything of a lady at all answering Laura's description.

Leaving Phil Davenant to search for his lost wife, we must go back a little in our story, in order to recount how the lady in question came to be missing.

It was very seldom that Mrs. Davenant (as she was called) ventured out in the daytime.

When the shades of night were falling, she occasionally took a few turns up and down the inn-garden; and this she had done on the evening of her disappearance.

Now the inn-garden was adjacent to the road, only being separated from it by a high hedge, and Laura had not been walking long upon one side of this hedge, before the Earl of Stonecliffe appeared upon the other.

He raised his hat and made her a polite bow, which she returned, and though still divided by the hedge, they for some time kept up a conversation across the leafy barrier.

The earl, however, made no allusion to the discovery which, it will be remembered, he made by peeping through the bed-room window, that Laura's face and Laura's hair were of a different hue naturally to that they appeared to the public generally.

Doubtless he thought it rude to make remarks about a lady's toilet to her face.

Be that as it may, he strove his utmost to be pleasing and agreeable, and that was a matter in which his lordship never failed.

Oddly enough he led the conversation to his own rights to the title and estates.

Laura listened more eagerly to that than to anything else.

"It's very strange," said the earl, "but ever since the first time I saw you I have felt irresistibly led to make a certain communication to you."

"Indeed! What is it?"

"It is respecting my right to these vast estates."

"Surely you are the rightful owner?"

"I'm not so sure of that."

"What do you mean?"

"It is that I wish to talk to you about. I think you can help me."

"Indeed!"

"Will you do so?"

"I think you are mistaken, my lord. I surely cannot be of assistance to you."

"Will you listen to what I have to say?"

"Certainly."

"Then I must ask you to grant me a great favour."

"What is that?"

"Will you mind stepping through the gate into the road for a few minutes?"

"Why should I do that?"

"Because I have no wish that what I am about to tell you should be known to all Easthorpe, and at the distance you are now from me I am compelled to speak loud."

Laura deliberated.

Her thoughts rose somewhat thus—

"It is quite impossible that he can have recognised me. He would not talk thus if he had any idea who I really am.

MOTHER DEATH ATTEMPTS TO MURDER LAURA DAVENANT.

I may learn a secret from him which may be of use to me, so why should I hesitate?"

With a firm hand she opened the gate which led from the garden into the road.

In another moment she and the Earl of Stonecliffe were side by side.

"Thank you, my dear madam; thank you for your kindness in granting my request."

"What is it your lordship has to say to me?"

"Simply this, that I have received information respecting a person whom I, in common with the whole world, have long believed to be dead."

"What have I to do with this?" asked Laura; but there was a shade of uneasiness in her tone.

The Earl of Stonecliffe did not make any immediate reply.

While they had been talking they had slowly paced along the now deserted road.

They were at some little distance from the inn.

Where they now stood a narrow lane joined the main road.

The earl, before answering, whistled shrilly.

Laura knew at once it was a signal.

She felt she had fallen into a trap.

She would have screamed for assistance, but she had not time.

Three rough, burly men sprang from the hedge, and seized her.

In a moment she was gagged, bound, and helpless.

"Yes," continued the nobleman, with a sardonic smile upon his handsome face, "yes; I have received intelligence that a person I elbieved to be dead has come to life. It is necessary for my peace and prosperity that that person should be kept out of the way, and as I never allow trifles to interfere with my comfort, I have taken steps accordingly. You understand me, Mrs. Davenant?"

Laura could not speak. She could only raise her hands with a supplicating gesture.

The earl gave a little, short laugh, and stroked his glossy black moustache with an air of satisfaction.

At a signal from him, the three men raised their burden from the ground, and bore her rapidly away down the lane.

A carriage was waiting in readiness.

One of the men mounted the box, the two others followed Laura into the interior, and seated themselves on either side of her.

"Drive quickly, or you will lose the train," said the earl.

The carriage drove off at a rapid rate, not taking the usual road—they were too wide awake for that—but making a circuit through unfrequented lanes.

The Earl of Stonecliffe watched till the vehicle disappeared round a corner.

His face assumed a smile of devilish satisfaction.

"Capital—capital !" he muttered ; " could not have happened better. I knew the bait would take. I was sure she could not resist the chance of hearing a secret about the Stonecliffe estates. Now, I am free—I can breathe once more. The only person who knows my secret is secure. Mother Death will not betray me."

The earl lit a cigar and walked rapidly across the fields, in the direction of his own house.

When Phil Davenant came to Easthorp House, for he went thither after leaving Admiral Rattlin's, he found the earl quietly seated in his study, in slippers and dressing gown.

His general appearance of sleepiness and laziness seemed to forbid the idea that he had left his home that evening.

He condoled with Phil.

Told him how sorry he was for him.

Expressed many wishes that he would soon find his wife.

Hinted she might have eloped, and at last sent Phil away without the slightest clue as to what had become of her he sought.

*   *   *   *   *

It was a cold, wild, stormy night.

The wind came sweeping across the Thames in sharp gusts, which made the chimney-pots of the waterside houses tremble.

The rain was driving through the streets, altogether making them as uncomfortable as they could well be.

It was a night upon which no one would venture out who could remain within doors.

Umbrellas were worse than useless, and any one venturing into the streets was certain to be wet to the skin before he knew where he was.

In this wind and pelting rain four figures were struggling along, down a narrow street which led to the river.

Three of them were men.

The fourth was of the opposite sex.

She they appeared to drag with them sorely against her will, and had any intelligent policeman seen the quartet he would have been perfectly justified in stopping them and making inquiries.

But the police knew better than to be visible on such a night, so the four advanced till they stood before a little dirty door of what appeared to be a riverside public-house.

Over their heads hung a half-obliterated sign, but by the wavering light of a gas-lamp Laura—for it was she—was enabled to decipher the words—"The Dodger's Delight."

One of her conductors knocked in a peculiar manner at the low door.

After some little delay it was opened by a most repulsive-looking hag, who stared in amazement at the group.

"Well, mother, we have come sooner than we were expected."

"Where is she ?"

"Here, mother."

Mother Death—for it was that worthy dame—took Laura by the shoulder, and turned her face upwards, so that the light of the gas-lamp fell full upon it.

"Humph !" said she ; " I shall have a hard job of it, I'm thinking. Come along, dear !" she continued, trying to speak in a softer tone, but failing miserably.

Laura had no choice but to follow, and Mother Death led her down the steps into the cellar with which we are already acquainted.

"Ha, ha, ha," laughed one of the ruffians, who had assisted in abducting her, " there goes another of Mother Death's lambs !"

CHAPTER LXII.

MOTHER DEATH'S DEN.

WHEN the door of the "Dodger's Delight" was opened, and Laura saw the hideous figure of Mother Death standing in the entrance, she shrank back in alarm, and it was only by force that her custodians got her within the walls of the public house.

With a frightful smile, which was meant to be pleasant, the old hag took one of Laura's cold hands in her skinny fingers, and led her down the stone steps, but not into the scene of debauchery in the cellar.

Instead of pushing open that swing-door, Mother Death took a large key from her pocket and unlocked a small side door, which gave admittance to what had doubtless once been the wine-cellar, but was now Mother Death's den.

The attempt made to furnish it was almost ludicrous.

Side by side with articles which indicated the most squalid poverty were others (spoils from various burglaries) of the most valuable and costly description.

It was a damp, dismal underground hole in itself, only lighted by a small grating in the roof.

The cell contained one bed, a tumble-down ramshackle affair enough, covered with a dirty, ragged patchwork quilt, and looking in its filth a far from tempting place to sleep in.

By the side of the bed, on a deal table which tottered on three legs, was a magnificent French clock which would have graced the most elegant drawing-room ; and tumbled in one corner of the cellar were silks and satins of the finest quality.

Mother Death, in accordance with the directions of the Earl of Stonecliffe, had endeavoured to make herself present a more enticing exterior than that she usually wore.

But she had failed utterly.

The dress which she wore, though of good material and fashionable make, was of no avail.

She looked like an ugly old scarecrow in its Sunday clothes.

The garments hung upon her sharp bones with less grace than if suspended on a peg.

The gorgeous cap which decked her head, and from beneath which stray wisps of dirty grey hair floated and straggled about her yellow face, made her look ten times more hideous than usual.

While sitting up in the cold, she had applied her lips pretty frequently to the brandy bottle.

Not that she was drunk.

No one had ever seen Mother Death what is generally called the worse for liquor.

She was of a spongy nature, and could lap up any given quantity of ardent spirit without its having any effect upon her.

True, her blear eyes sparkled a little more than was their wont, and her speech was somewhat thick, but in no other way did she betray that she had imbibed sufficient intoxicating liquor to lay half-a-dozen full grown men upon the floor.

This was the woman who half dragged half led poor Laura into her filthy den.

When they had both entered the cell, Mother Death's first act was to lock the door and return the key to her pocket.

This done, she seized a flaring candle and approached the shrinking girl, who, still gagged and bound, was completely helpless.

The old hag advanced the light to within a few inches of Laura's face, and honoured her with a strict scrutiny.

"Ha, ha !" she laughed, in a fiendish manner. "Ha, ha, my little lady, for all your proud looks I will break you ! You are quite safe here. You may call till you're hoarse, but no one will answer you ; you may batter the walls and the bars with those delicate white hands, but no one will heed ! Mother Death knows how to guard her lambs."

While she had been speaking these words, her hands had been busily engaged in unfastening the cords which bound Laura's wrists together.

This done, her next act was to remove the gag from her mouth.

"Where am I ? what does this all mean ?" inquired Laura, as soon as she recovered the use of her tongue.

"You are in my bed-room, my dear, and a very comfortable room it is, considering."

"Who are you?"

"They call me Mother Death. Don't you think I look my name?"

The hag as she said these words grinned a ghastly grin, which displayed her toothless gums, and Laura shuddered as she gazed upon the shrivelled skin, which seemed hardly to belong to a living being.

"Don't be frightened, my dear. I'm a harmless old woman enough."

"By what right have I been brought here?"

"Yes—yes—it's been raining all the evening," answered Mother Death, who wished to delay answering the question till she could think of a good lie, so suddenly feigned deafness.

"By whose authority have I been kidnapped?"

"Don't you know?"

"I can guess."

"Whose?"

"Is it the Earl of Stonecliffe?"

"The Earl ——"

"Yes."

"Oh, Lord! To think of the likes of me knowing anything about earls!"

"You do. I can see it in your face."

"To think o' that now. To think my old, parched-up, skinny features should be like those of a real live earl. Oh! Miss, you're chaffing."

Laura stamped her foot impatiently on the cold stones which formed the floor of the den.

"Don't go on like that, dear; you'll wear your boots out."

"What am I confined here for?"

Mother Death again lost her hearing, and began to croak out the tune (all in one note) of an old ballad.

Laura had worked herself to a high pitch of excitement.

She knew the hag was not deaf.

She knew she could answer her questions were she so disposed.

Laura caught sight of a short, sharp knife lying on a table. She seized it.

"Now, by Heaven, if you don't answer all the questions I ask you, I'll cut your throat!" and she flourished the weapon over the old woman's head.

"Help! Mur—!"

"Not another word!"

Laura's eyes glared so angrily that, for the time, she cowed Mother Death, who whined out—

"You wouldn't hurt an old woman—a poor old woman, who's never done you any harm—would you, dear?"

"Answer my questions!"

"I can't, dear, till you ask them."

"You know what it is I desire to find out."

"I don't, indeed."

"I want to discover if it were the Earl of Stonecliffe who ordered you to keep me prisoner. If it were he," and the whole expression of Laura's face altered to one of vengeful determination,—"if it were he, better that he had never seen the light of day than have committed this act!"

"Lor', how you frighten one!"

"Heaven knows I had enough cause to hate him before, but this has filled the cup to the brim; and as I live I swear he shall pay the penalty!"

Now it was certainly foolish of Laura to express herself thus violently, for Mother Death was eagerly watching her, and listening to every word; and two days afterwards the Earl of Stonecliffe received a strangely-folded letter, directed in a crabbed, stiff handwriting, informing him of the threats the prisoner had uttered, which letter was signed by Mother Death.

The old hag received in reply a short note.

So short was it that it was not necessary for her to turn over the first page.

So short that one would have thought she could have read it at a single glance.

Yet Mother Death pondered over it a long time.

She twisted it meditatively between her fingers.

As she did so, her brows contracted ominously, and her toothless gums worked and mumbled more than ever.

And this is what the letter said:—

"*The girl must be removed.*"

No more.

Not a single line more or less.

The woman to whom it was addressed knew only too well what it meant.

She knew from whom it came.

She knew to whom it referred.

It was a death-warrant.

Maybe it was not the first missive of similar purport that she had received.

Perchance the den in which Laura was kept prisoner had more than once resounded with the dying groans of some wretched victim.

The stones might have been stained with blood again and again.

The dirty pillow might have covered the face of some poor creature struggling in vain for breath.

Was it a presentiment of evil to come which caused these thoughts to take possession of Laura's mind?

She strove in vain to dispel them.

The gloomy ideas would return, and her heart sank within her as she saw the impossibility of escape.

The door was kept constantly locked.

The grating was high above her head.

She had nothing to do but to wait patiently to see what time would bring forth.

How the earl had discovered her secret she was at a loss to imagine; for, of course, she knew nothing of his having peeped through her bedroom window that night.

For three or four days after her forced confinement she had managed to retain the appearance she had assumed to mislead those who were likely to recognise her.

At the end of that time it became evident to her that it was impossible to maintain the disguise.

Accordingly she divested herself of the false hair, and washed the paint from her face.

To the great surprise of Mother Death her charge had altered from a middle-aged dark woman to a lively golden-haired girl.

It was like a trick in a pantomime, so complete was the transformation.

Without chronicling each day that passed in the gloomy den, we may state that Laura, though sad at her imprisonment and uneasy in the absence of all knowledge as to what the issue would be, had as yet experienced no ill-treatment or unkindness.

The old hag assumed a motherly tone and a benign leer whenever she addressed her; but for all that Laura had caught her more than once glaring at her in a fierce and vindictive manner.

The hideous uproar of the nocturnal orgies in the adjacent cellar sounded through the thick stone wall, and alarmed Laura not a little at first.

Soon she became more accustomed to it.

Luckily the drunken ribald songs and horrid blasphemy did not reach her ears in other form than confused noise.

Occasionally some word shouted forth would cause her to shudder; but the greater part of what took place so near to her was left to her imagination.

Not the least disagreeable part of her imprisonment was that Mother Death occupied the den at night.

The bed, in itself no tempting resting-place, seemed doubly disgusting when shared with the repulsive hag, and Laura could not bring herself to make the trial.

Instead, she nestled as best she was able in rugs and mats upon the cold stone floor, and shivered and dreamed away the night.

Her sleep, which came but in fits and starts, was ever interrupted by hideous dreams.

Dreams to which ordinary nightmare would have been bliss.

Dreams which caused her to start up affrighted from the ground with distended eyeballs and quivering limbs.

Dreams which bedewed her brow with a cold perspiration, for they were produced by an imagination heated and excited by vague dread and alarm.

Nor were her fears unfounded.

The most frightful of her dreams had its parallel in a waking reality.

She had sunk into an uneasy doze, in which, however, she seemed partially conscious of what was going on around her.

She heard Mother Death enter the cell, and knew she was mumbling and mouthing to herself as she undressed, preparatory to turning in for the night.

She heard this, and then came oblivion.

Suddenly she awoke.

What power it was induced her at that moment to unclose her eyes she knew not.

PUBLISHER'S NOTE

PP.132-133 ARE MISSING.

"Mrs. Davenant," said a voice with a strong north-country accent.

"Who calls me?" she asked, eagerly.

"Hush!"

"How do you know me?"

"It does not matter."

"Who are you?"

"A friend."

"A friend? Have I really a friend in the world?"

"You have, indeed; but pray do not speak so loud, or you will be overheard."

Laura lowered the tone of her voice.

"Can you help me?" she asked.

"I hope so."

"I am starving!"

"I feared it."

"Can you get me food?"

"I have some here."

"Give it me—quick—quick!"

The stranger let drop several slices of thick bread-and-butter, wrapped in the advertisement sheet of a penny paper.

Laura seized it eagerly.

So ravenous was she, that she could scarcely wait to remove the paper; and though the bread was stale, and the butter rank, she gnawed it more like a wild beast than an English lady.

Her appetite in some measure appeased, she whispered her thanks through the grating to her friend.

"Say nothing about it," he replied; "you have done much more than that for me."

"Impossible! When?"

"Do you not recognise me?"

"I cannot see you."

"My voice?"

"No."

"I am——"

"Who?"

"Hush! there comes Jerry Bight. If he finds me here, all chance of escape for you is gone. I will come again later, when every one is in bed."

With this hurried explanation Laura's visitor disappeared, or, more correctly speaking, the sound of his voice was no longer heard; and she, seating herself on Mother Death's bed, racked her brain in the vain endeavour to guess who there was in the world who would call himself her "friend."

For several hours she waited for him to come again.

At last she heard a light footstep on the stones, and immediately afterwards the same voice called her by name.

She responded eagerly.

"Come here!" said the stranger. "Get as close to the grating as you can, for I have much to tell you."

"Is there any chance of escape?"

"Yes."

"Thank you—thank you for saying that. Hope revives within me."

"But you must be cautious."

"Of course."

"The escape cannot be to-night."

"Why not?"

"It is impossible."

"Am I watched?"

"No."

"What is the object in keeping me here?"

"They wish to kill you."

"Kill me! How?"

"By starvation."

"Horrible!"

"It is, indeed."

"How do you know this?"

"I have played the spy. I have overheard a conversation which proves their diabolical design. Draw near, it is necessary for you to hear it."

"I am listening."

"Steel your nerves to listen to a horrible disclosure."

"Go on."

CHAPTER LXIV.

TREATING OF THE DANGERS OF YACHTING EXPEDITIONS AND GIVING A FULL AND TRUE ACCOUNT OF THE TOTAL WRECK OF THE "FIREFLY," AS WELL AS DESCRIBING THE STRANGE CAVERN IN WHICH FANNY WHITE TOOK REFUGE.

FOR many days the yacht sped merrily over the waters.

She was a pretty, gay, light little boat, but not particularly sea-worthy, as the party found to their cost.

Lord Delaine improved more and more upon further acquaintance, and the only drawback to general pleasure was the slight suspicion of jealousy which edged its way into the minds and hearts of each one of the party.

Fanny exerted her powers of charming to the utmost, and, it is needless to say, succeeded not only in quite gaining repossession of Master Jack, but also in binding Lord Delaine in the thraldom of love.

It must be confessed that this caused considerable annoyance to Letty Burton, who was thrown completely into the background; but there was no help for it, so she had to wear a smiling face, and make the best of it.

It was a cold night.

The sun had gone down, red, lowering and portentous.

The old sailor, who had actual command of the yacht, despite Lord Delaine's nominal captaincy, shook his head gravely, and shortened sail.

The party of four, unconscious of impending danger, retired to the principal cabin, and sought amusement in various games at cards to wile away the time till the hour for retiring to rest arrived.

Lord Delaine was dealing out the painted pasteboard, when a sudden knock at the cabin door, followed immediately by the entrance of old Bunting, the real commander of the *Firefly*, caused him to pause.

With a mysterious look the sailor beckoned the owner of the yacht from the cabin.

"Well, Bunting, what is it?"

"Beg pardon, my lord, but the weather's nasty."

"What do you mean?"

"Thick fog, my lord."

"Fog! Is that all?"

"No, my lord."

"Well, what else?"

"Stormy sunset, my lord."

"You think there is danger?"

"Well, you see, my lord, it's nasty being caught in a squall in a thick fog."

Lord Delaine went up upon deck to see for himself how matters looked.

Certainly Bunting had not exaggerated matters when he said it was "nasty."

The fog was so thick it was scarcely possible to see a yard ahead, and in addition a thick, blinding rain was falling.

"What had we better do, Bunting?"

"I don't see that we can do anything, my lord."

"Nonsense!"

"Well, my lord, every sail has been taken in, and we're just tossing about on the waves anyhow, like."

"Well!"

Bunting stroked his chin meditatively.

"What do you think?"

"I think if the wind keeps off we shall ride it out right enough."

"But if it doesn't?"

"Ah!" and again the old sailor rubbed his chin.

"What do you mean?"

"If the squall comes that I expect, my lord, I don't exactly see how we can help going ashore."

"Ashore? why, we're miles from land."

"Not so far as you think. For the last few hours we've been drifting a precious sight quicker than I like towards the Irish coast."

"And you think there is danger?"

"I do, my lord."

"What do you intend doing?"

"Looking out for the softest place on the shore to run her on to."

"Good heaven! you don't mean to say it's as bad as that?"

"I do, though."

"I must tell the ladies," cried Lord Delaine, excitedly, about to run back into the cabin.

"No, you mustn't," said Bunting, seizing his lordship's coat.

"Why not?"

"What's the good of frightening the poor things?"

"But they ought to know."

"Not a bit of it. They'd only come on deck crying and screaming, and getting in the way."

"That may be true."

"I know it's true. Now, you just do as I tell you, my lord. You go back and play with them cards as if there was nought the matter, and trust me to let you know if matters get worse."

Lord Delaine took the old sailor's advice, and neither of his guests had any idea that the alteration in his manner when he returned to them was owing to the knowledge that they all four stood a good chance of being drowned before twelve hours elapsed.

Fanny did not fail to chaff his lordship respecting his gloom; but the young nobleman, contrary to his usual custom, failed to reply, but continued mechanically dealing the cards, preserving a rigid silence.

After the lapse of an hour or more, Bunting again appeared in the cabin.

His whole manner betrayed unusual excitement, for he was a quiet, reserved, steady-going man, who showed emotion but rarely.

Lord Delaine fearing the worst, rushed out and followed the sailor to the deck.

He had hardly reached it when the squall struck the yacht, heeling her over till her gunwales were almost on the water.

With a shriek of terror Fanny and Letty rushed up, followed by Jack, who, although somewhat alarmed himself, strove to reassure them.

"Down, down—all of you, for your lives!" yelled Bunting, as a second gust, more violent than the first, came sweeping along.

Jack bundled the two girls down the ladder without standing upon ceremony.

Lord Delaine and the seamen caught hold of various ropes to prevent themselves being washed overboard, as a heavy sea struck the "Firefly," making her quiver all over and flooding the decks.

The strong wind had the effect of lifting the fog, and through a break in the thick atmosphere, those on deck saw they were driving rapidly towards a high black cliffed coast.

They felt nothing could save them.

The sight confirmed their worst fears.

Lord Delaine seized a hatchet, and called upon the men to do the same, and in a few moments the mainmast went overboard, with a thundering crash.

But the action was too late.

Had they known their danger and acted upon the knowledge sooner, it might have been beneficial.

As it was, it only slightly retarded their progress towards destruction.

There was no doubt about it.

No power on earth could save the fated boat from being dashed upon the black, frowning rocks, there to be ground to pieces.

And those on board?

It was a hideous fate to which to look forward. Still there was a chance of escape; but a small—very small one.

Everyone acting upon the impulse of the moment seized the article nearest him which he considered sufficiently buoyant to sustain him in the water.

Spars, life belts, casks, hencoops—all were brought into use.

Some of the most adventurous jumped at once into the boiling ocean, which curled and whitened over the stupendous cliffs.

But Death was their fate.

Either they were borne with such terrific violence against the ironbound coast that they were washed back bruised, stunned, and helpless, or else they sank in the deep waters, with a wild cry for help, to rise no more.

Wonderful to relate, both Fanny and Letty conducted themselves with the greatest courage, for although of course they were greatly alarmed, they forbore expressing their fears in useless shrieks and cries for help.

Jack's coolness served him well.

He bound both the ladies securely to two spars, for he knew their only chance of being saved was the mercy of the waves which might cast them ashore.

Lord Delaine had already fitted himself with a life-belt, and stood near the bow, determined that the moment the vessel struck he would leap overboard and make one grand struggle for life.

Everyone had long since abandoned the idea of attempting to save the "Firefly" from destruction.

It would be little short of a miracle if their lives were saved, so what did the yacht matter?

CRASH!

With a sudden shock which threw those who were standing off their balance, the pretty little yacht stuck firm and fast upon the rocks.

In an instant Lord Delaine was over the side, followed by about half the crew.

They were all seen madly buffeting with the waters for a few minutes.

Then a great green white-crested wave came curling into the little bay in which they had run ashore.

Curling high up above their heads and menacing them all with death.

Towering aloft, in the greatness of its might ridiculing the puny efforts of man to escape from the wrath of the elements.

With a mighty roar it dashed itself against the perpendicular black rocks, sending its spray and flakes of foam high up in air.

When the effect of this tremendous wave had subsided not a sign of those who two minutes before had leapt into the ocean was to be seen.

Hope whispered that they might have reached the land, but Despair ridiculed the idea.

"There is still a chance for us!" cried Jack, excitedly.

All on board stared at him in amazement.

"Yes," he continued, noticing their looks of incredulity; "I know perfectly well what I am talking about."

"How's it to be done?" asked Bunting.

"Those rocks are not far off. By means of a rope from them to the yacht every one might be got to land."

"Ha, ha!" laughed Bunting, contemptuously.

"What do you laugh at?"

"Ha, ha!"

"It's a good plan?"

"Oh, the plan is all right enough!"

"Well?"

"But you see——"

"What?"

"Whose going to carry it out?"

"I will!"

"You?"

"Yes!"

"What a reg'lar London lubber! A chap that doesn't know the difference between a marlingspike and a bowsprit!"

"Never mind that, I can swim."

"Don't make a fool of yourself, young man!"

"What the deuce do you mean?"

"No offence I hope, sir, which it wasn't intended; but what I mean to say is this, that unless you're a rare good hand in the water you'll make a body of yourself before five minutes go by."

"Oh, Jack! dearest Jack, don't risk your life!"

"I risk mine to save those of many others!"

"Jack, pray don't!" chimed in Lotty.

Our hero paid no attention to these remonstrances, but proceeded to divest himself of all superfluous clothing.

"You don't mean to say you really are going?" asked Bunting.

"Yes, I do."

"Well, you *are* a plucky card."

"Thank you for the compliment."

"What can I do for you, sir?"

"Keep firm hold on one end of this coil of rope. When I am safely ashore, I shall pull it once; when it is fastened securely, I will give three separate tugs at it, and then you will know all is ready, and that you may venture to cling to it as the means of preserving your life."

"Hurrah! You're a brave one."

With a parting kiss to Fanny, our hero jumped into the raging surf, with one end of the rope fastened round his waist.

It has already been stated that he was an expert in all athletic sports, still the strength of the waves rendered his muscular arms powerless.

Again and again he exerted all his energies to reach the shore, and each time the receding waves sucked him back with them.

His strength was well-nigh exhausted.

He felt that unless he could speedily accomplish his purpose he would have no power left to combat the watery element, and that he must be swept out to sea and be drowned.

His quick eye noted that one small place in the black rocks was filled with sand.

It was a picturesque little cove, where, under different circumstances, he might have longed to spend a bright summer afternoon with Fanny, but now he hailed it with delight, for he saw in it a further chance of saving his life, as well as that of her he held so dear.

He waited for a huge advancing wave, and then putting forth all his energies was borne on its crest completely into the tiny bay.

Once there, before the receding tide could suck him again into the open sea, he dug his hands and feet, with the power of despair, into the wet sand.

The back water well-nigh took him back with it, but clinging to the sand with the tenacity of one who struggles against death, he retained his hold, and before another wave came, he had scrambled to his feet and got from out its way. Breathless, sore, and bruised, he seated himself on a wet, slippery rock, to recover himself before he proceeded in his attempt to rescue the crew of the *Firefly*.

He gave one pull to the rope.

By so doing he announced he had reached the shore in safety to those still on board the yacht.

The signal was answered by a faint cheer.

Jack fancied he could distinguish Fanny's voice, and it nerved him to fresh efforts.

Stumbling and slipping, he clambered over the rocks till he found a good place to secure the rope.

He did not hurry in fastening it, for he knew the lives of many depended upon it, but took great care in making it as safe as possible.

At last it was done.

With a beating heart he announced the joyful intelligence to those on board by the preconcerted signal.

It was greeted with another cheer.

But that cheer died away in a dismal wail of despair.

Alas for all the poor fellows on board the *Firefly*. Just at the very moment when succour arrived and hope filled their hearts, the ill-fated vessel parted amidships, and a terrific sea swept over her.

One loud shriek!

One despairing cry went up to heaven.

Jack leant over the rock as far as he dared, and peered eagerly towards the wreck.

Not a living creature was to be seen, the sea had made a clear breach in the yacht, and with the exception of a few dark objects seen for the moment on the white crests of the waves, nothing was there to show that but three minutes before the shapeless mass of timber lying on the jagged black rock had been covered with human beings.

Jack was powerless to assist.

Even could he get down to the shore he could be of no service to those struggling.

An involuntary exclamation of despair broke from him as he saw his hopes of rescuing Fanny dashed to the ground.

He was alone, as far as he knew.

Alone upon a bleak, desolate shore, without clothes and without money.

To the best of his belief he alone of those who, a few hours before, had been full of health and life and happiness on board the *Firefly*, was in existence.

But were there no others saved?

Yes.

Fanny had by good luck, little short of a miracle, been cast by a wave high up upon the rocky shore, and lay there, stunned, bruised, bleeding, and motionless.

For many hours she lay there till the violence of the storm abated and the uproar of the elements subsided into a soft gentle rain.

The rain falling upon her upturned face revived her.

With a puzzled, bewildered expression she looked around, unable for the moment to remember what had passed.

Slowly the dreadful scene came back to her mind.

She remembered it all, and shuddered at the recollection.

When she came to look around her she saw the dangerous spot in which she was.

It was but a narrow ledge of slippery rock; above her towered the perpendicular cliffs, below her was a frightful precipice at the foot of which the waves dashed roaring and foaming, as if in anger at her escape.

How could she escape from her perilous position?

The ledge of rock was so very narrow and shelving that she dared not rise to her feet.

To ascend to the summit of the cliffs from where she was was an impossibility.

To descend to the sea was certain destruction.

As her only chance of escape, she crawled along the ledge upon her hands and knees, in the hope of coming to some place where the rocks would be less precipitous.

Slowly and carefully she made her way along, scrutinizing the solid wall for means to ascend.

But it was in vain.

Smooth, perpendicular, and slippery, she dared not make the attempt.

Had she done so, she must, without doubt, have been dashed to pieces.

A small cleft in the rock, scarcely wide enough to give admittance to a human being, attracted her attention.

It seemed to go in some distance, and Fanny, in the hope that there might be some other egress, entered.

She squeezed herself through the narrow opening, and found herself in a low, damp, dark passage, formed in the solid rock.

Carefully feeling her way, she crawled on.

She felt no alarm, for she hoped the passage might lead her to some place of security, and she continued her hazardous way with as great speed as circumstances would permit.

After awhile the passage became more lofty, and the rocks less damp to the touch.

At last she emerged from the passage.

She only knew the fact from finding that her hands no longer touched the wall on either side as they had hitherto.

Without some such guide, she feared to venture on further.

She paused and listened.

Afar off she heard the sound of trickling water.

She dared not go on.

In the course of time, her eyes became more accustomed to the darkness, and she could see the dim outline of the cavern in which she had taken refuge.

It was a solemn, grim-looking place, and to our heroine the rocks seemed to take strange, weird, fantastic forms.

Some made themselves into hideous distorted faces, which appeared to jeer and gibe at her—to mock her—to laugh at her.

Though naturally courageous, her heart somewhat failed her at this juncture; her body was enfeebled with her exertions, her mind was weakened from the same cause, and when the sound of horrid demoniacal laughter came borne towards her, she could stand it no longer.

With a wild shriek, she fell senseless.

CHAPTER LXV.

SOMETHING MORE ABOUT THE RED-HEADED POTBOY AT THE "DODGER'S DELIGHT."

LAURA, with beating heart, drew as close as possible to the grating.

She knew not what it could be that she was about to hear, but she dreaded the worst.

Looking up through the grating, she saw by the faint, flickering light of a far off lamp, an empty, vacant face, surmounted by a shock head of red hair, peering down at her.

The countenance was unknown to her.

She shuddered, and drew back in alarm.

What if it were only some trick of her gaolers?

What if it were an assassin?

With wonderful rapidity these ideas flashed through her brain.

"Who are you?" she asked.

"It doesn't matter."

"But it does. I will not come a step nearer unless you reveal to me your name, and how you came to know anything concerning me. Again—who are you?"

"I have already told you I am a friend."

"Your name?"

"Hush! Not so loud, or we shall be discovered."

"Tell me your name."

He whispered something, but in so low a tone that Laura failed to hear him.

FANNY WHITE ALARMED AT THE SIGHT OF THE HUNCHBACK.

"Speak louder."

"Philip Davenant!"

"Phil?"

"It is indeed I."

"How came you here?"

"Business brought me."

"Business?"

"Yes."

"What?"

"Your rescue."

"Do you really mean you were brave enough to venture here only for my sake?"

"I do."

"Heaven bless you!"

"I would do more than that for you."

"How can I ever repay you?"

"Your thanks and a kind smile are all I require."

"Tell me, how did you find me out?"

"It has been slow work."

"So I should think."

"Step by step I tracked you from Easthorpe to London—that was comparatively easy when once I got the clue—but looking for a person in the great metropolis is worse than the old simile of a needle in a bottle of hay."

"And you took all this trouble for me?"

"I did."

"Thank you—thank you a thousand times."

"Tush! It is nothing. It is not to talk of my own deeds that I have come here. I have something to tell you."

"What is it?"

"A diabolical plot has been formed by some villain who wishes to keep you out of the way."

"A plot?"

"Yes; a plot to deprive you of life."

Strong as Laura was, she was unable to repress a shudder at this confirmation of her own worst fears.

"Is there any—any immediate danger?" she faltered.

"Not to-night."

"When then?"

"To-morrow."

"Good heaven! what shall I do?"

"Do as I tell you."

"What is that?"

"Escape."

"It is impossible."

"No, it is not."

"What do you mean?"

"I mean that with my assistance, just ten minutes before the assassins enter your cell, you will leave it."

"But how?"

"Easily enough. I will remove this grating, and then, with the help of a rope, you will be able to reach the court-yard where I now am—after that it will be quite easy."

"But why not now? Cannot it be done to-night?"

"No."

"Why?"

"Because there are many about who would certainly discover us."

"What then?"

"The men who frequent this place are not likely to stick at any crime. There would be two murders instead of one."

"Horrible!"

"It is, indeed."

"You know this for a fact?"

"Yes. I got a situation here as potboy, hoping by that means to be of service to you. Two nights ago I accidentally overheard a discussion about you."

"About me?"

"Yes. As to what was the easiest and most silent, as well as the surest way of putting you to death."

"And the result? Tell me what they agreed upon," said Laura, with a shudder.

"Starvation."

"I feared it."

"You were to be kept locked up, without food or water, in the greatest agony, till death relieved you from your sufferings."

"And that is their fiendish plan to get me out of the way?"

"It was."

"What do you mean? Is it so no longer?"

"No."

"What then?"

"They have received from some source intelligence that the police intend searching the premises for stolen goods."

"Then they will liberate me?"

"Not so."

"Why not?"

"Because they dare not leave you behind to disclose any secrets you may have learnt with respect to this villanous place. You would only be an encumbrance to their flight—for Mr. Jerry Bight is obliged to be off to America in double quick time—so they have resolved that quicker means of putting you out of the way must be resorted to than the slow process of starvation."

"What means?"

"The knife."

"How did you learn this?"

"By listening. Five ruffians cast lots who should be the one to inflict the fatal wound. It fell on Jerry Bight, and ere this time to-morrow, unless you have made your escape, the deed will be done."

Laura covered her face with her hands.

"How can I ever thank you sufficiently?" said she, at length. "I owe everything to you."

"Do not thank me at all, but be ready to-morrow as soon as it is dark."

"Without doubt."

"That is well. Then good-night. In four and twenty hours' time you will again be free."

"Good-night."

Little wonder is there that Laura slept not that night. Her brain was too full of all she had heard to allow her much rest, and even when she did fall into an unquiet, fitful doze she started up repeatedly, dreaming that the assassins had altered the time and were coming sooner than they had at first arranged, to slay her.

With the first struggling rays of dawn which forced their way through the iron grating, she arose from her couch.

The day had come!

The day of such imminent danger to her.

Courageous and sanguine as she was by nature, she could not help every now and then giving way to gloomy fears.

Suppose the landlord were to discover that his pot-boy had turned traitor?

Where then would be her chance of deliverance?

"Surely," she thought, "the clocks must have stopped?"

Time never crept on so slowly as it did that day, while she sat waiting for the hour which, if all went well, was to restore her to freedom.

After a long, weary day the light began to diminish.

Who shall describe the inexpressible joy and delight with which Laura watched the shadows in her cell growing darker and darker, till at last the gloom of night fairly settled down.

With anxious mind and beating heart, she listened eagerly for the sound of Phil Davenant's footsteps.

But she listened in vain!

Once she heard, as she thought, some one at the door of her cell, and her heart sank within her, for she made no doubt but that the assassin had come to perpetrate his horrible crime.

But the lock remained unturned, and the door closed, so that after a time her hopes rose and again she watched beneath the grating.

She could not imagine what could detain Phil so long after the time he had appointed to be there.

At last, a low cautious whistle and a whispered inquiry as to whether she were quite ready, made her heart beat and flutter with the excitement, for she recognized the tones of the voice as belonging to him she called husband.

"Quite ready," she replied.

"Then be quick; there is not a moment to lose. The assassin is already on his way to your cell."

Laura needed no second bidding.

Phil busied himself in carefully removing the grating.

"Laura," he whispered, "you have yet time. Put the bolster into the bed, and cover it well over, and lay one of your caps upon the pillow. It may throw the villain off our scent."

Laura did as she was told, and arranged the things so well that in the dim evening light it looked unmistakeably as if some one were asleep there.

After some trouble, the grating was removed and the rope fixed.

Laura managed, by means of the rope, the ricketty furniture, and Phil Davenant's help to reach the ground.

With a deep sigh of relief, she looked down into the dirty, close little cell she had just left; and then, acting upon the impulse of the moment, stretched out her hand in gratitude to Phil, who raised it to his lips.

There was no time to be lost, and Phil, after hurrying his lovely charge over a brick wall, hailed a cab.

The pair got in, and were driven rapidly in a direction which Phil had whispered into the man's ear.

Thus Laura escaped almost miraculously from the clutches of the Earl of Stonecliffe; and Phil Davenant, whom she had sought to consider nothing but a paid machine to do her bidding, had risked his life to save hers.

＊　　　＊　　　＊　　　＊

Five minutes after Laura had left, the cell door was cautiously opened, and the face of Jerry Bight looked in.

Jerry did not like the job he had to accomplish, and had been priming himself with brandy.

Leaving the light outside, he stole to the bed-side, his tottering gait betraying, however, the state which he was in.

Arrived at the bed, he cautiously felt it with his coarse hand, till his fingers touched the bolster, which, by Phil's suggestion, occupied Laura's place.

Jerry Bight, without giving himself time for reflection, buried a large, sharp pointed carving-knife up to the handle in the mattrass!

An hour later, a telegraphic message flashed along the wires, addressed to the Earl of Stonecliffe.

It contained but the words—

"The deed is done!"

CHAPTER LXVI.

RESPECTING SOME DISCOVERIES MADE BY FANNY WHITE IN THE MYSTERIOUS CAVERN—SHOWING ALSO HOW SHE THOUGHT SHE WOULD DRESS HERSELF, AND WHAT A DREADFUL THING HAPPENED TO HER WHILE SO DOING.

WHEN Fanny recovered her senses she found herself still lying where she had fallen.

How long she had remained there she could form no notion.

It was pitch dark.

Around her reigned a silence as of the grave.

Unbroken—awfully impressive.

Almost seeming to crush her with its weight, and to press in her eyeballs, and lie heavy on her aching head.

She lay for a time motionless, listening intently, hoping to catch some sound, however faint.

But there was none.

Then she strove to recal her scattered senses, and think where she was.

Presently the recollection of the past recurred to her, and with it a necessity for immediate action.

But what must she do?

The pain which was caused by the violent throbbing of her aching head was well-nigh unendurable.

Her garments were all wringing wet, and clung to her form as a shroud covers a corpse.

Her limbs were stiff with cold.

All her joints ached.

Her teeth chattered convulsively.

She strove to rise to her feet, but her weakness was so great that she sank back again, and lay groaning in pain.

"Gracious God!" she thought to herself; "am I to die here, in this awful place? Is this to be my tomb?"

The idea was so terrible that it lent her strength—the strength of desperation.

She would make another effort.

Frantically she struggled.

She reached, after infinite difficulty, an upright posture.

Fortunately the rough wall of the cavern was close at hand.

When she staggered weakly forward she would have fallen again to the earth, but her outstretched hands came in contact with the rugged stone.

She leant against it, and supported herself for a while, though with the greatest difficulty.

Her knees gave way under her.

Her head bowed forward towards her breast.

It was as though its weight was too much for her slender neck to support.

She felt awfully ill; so ill that she conceived that nothing less than death was threatening her.

But after a time she somewhat recovered, and moved her way onwards feeling by the wall.

She wandered on and on.

The journey seemed, indeed, to be of such intolerable length that she doubted whether she would ever reach the end.

Sometimes she thought that she must have got into some vast chamber in this cavernous place, and was again and again making its circuit, feeling in vain for an outlet.

But then a moment's reflection sufficed to convince her that this could not be the case.

She had entered, and she must, therefore, find the way out.

It must be somewhere.

Warmed by this reflection she wandered onwards, creeping slowly and painfully towards the end—an end she little knew or dreamt of.

On, on—tediously, laboriously.

At times she was compelled to pause for breath.

At times she felt as though she must have sunk to the ground and died.

When she had entered the mysterious cavern there had been a faint light to guide her steps.

The light had, it is true, revealed the grotesque hideousness of the cavern walls, which had appeared to her excited imagination full of horrible faces, mouthing and jibing at her.

She saw nothing of this now, it is true, but surely this pitchy-darkness was still more frightful.

She had fancied at one time that she had heard a faint trickling sound, as of running water.

But now all was still.

"Oh, if I could only find my way out again!" she said to herself.

But there seemed little chance of this.

It was very evident that she had turned in the wrong direction to arrive at that result.

On the contrary, it appeared as though she had all this time been getting further and further into the heart of the cavern.

The reason for her arriving at this conclusion is very easily accounted for. The air had for some time grown closer, and the difficulty in breathing had steadily increased.

She paused at last and panted painfully.

She determined then to turn and retrace her steps.

But at the very moment when she was going to do so—groping with her hand upon the wall, it encountered some substance of a different nature to that which she had hitherto touched.

It appeared to be some very coarse canvas or sacking.

Leaning against it accidentally it gave way, and it was with a great effort that she saved herself from falling.

When, however, she had to some extent recovered from her surprise, she felt again at the canvas, and this time drawing it gently on one side saw a faint light upon the other side.

"Thank God, at last I have found the way out!" she thought.

But this notion was a most erroneous one.

On the contrary, as it proved, she had instead found the way in.

Very cautiously she advanced, after having drawn on one side the canvas, so as to admit of the passage of her body.

She helped herself along as before by the rough walls.

She was now in a narrow passage—so narrow that at times it scarcely admitted of her progress, and she was obliged to squeeze her way onwards.

The passage was a winding one, and turning a corner, after she had worked in vain for some time, to her astonishment she came suddenly upon a glare of light—a bright glare of light coming through the crevice of a half-closed door.

She started back at sight of it.

What could it mean?

Naturally enough she expected danger, though of what nature the danger was likely to prove, she could as yet form no idea, however faint.

But all was perfectly silent within, and she gathered courage.

Very cautiously and noiselessly she advanced.

She peeped into the room.

It was a strange place, but appeared to have no occupant.

She thrust her head into the room; then her body followed it by very slow degrees.

No—no one was there.

Being pretty sure of this fact, she drew a long breath and gazed around.

It was a large fire blazing upon a roughly-constructed hearth which illuminated the apartment.

A most extraordinary place it seemed, and one which required a lengthy survey before even its leading features could be readily grasped.

Looking round, however, Fanny saw that a curtain, which at first she had supposed covered some sort of window, was instead a part of the furniture of a quaintly-fashioned bedstead.

The discovery filled her with a sudden terror.

A dreadful thought occurred to her.

Suppose somebody was in the bed?

On tiptoe she approached.

Carefully she drew on one side the curtain.

No—no one was there.

This very much relieved her, and she began to think that, after all, why should she have any cause for alarm?

Who did this curious place belong to?

Very probably nobody of so ferocious a character that she need to fear their arrival.

She was not a very timid young lady, as the reader knows as well as I do by this time.

She, therefore, resolved to make herself at home.

It was not the first time, as the reader also knows, that she had so done at somebody else's expense.

"If I could only find a change of clothes."

Things happen almost as wonderfully sometimes in real life as they do in fairy tales.

As the thought was passing through her brain, her eye fell upon a large oaken chest.

She went straight to it and tried to raise the lid.

It yielded to her efforts, and she peeped inside.

A vast stock of all kinds of male apparel she there discovered.

"The very thing!" said she.

She felt quite as comfortable in the attire of the opposite sex as in that which properly belonged to her, and she was not very long in making up her mind to have a cheap outfit.

She therefore stirred up the fire to get as good a light as possible, and began to search the box.

In it she found all that she required.

A suit of clothes, such as a young gentleman might wear, she was somewhat surprised to see, but she did not pause to reflect deeply upon the subject, but pulled them out.

Yes.; there were a very elegant coat and waistcoat, and a pair of trousers of unexceptionable cut.

Also shoes and stockings, and a shirt of very fine fabric, which had evidently belonged to some wealthy person.

Finding all that was necessary for her equipment, Miss Fanny then leisurely divested herself of her own clothing.

Her garments were saturated with salt-water, and she found it a matter of no little difficulty to get rid of them.

There was, however, a sharp knife lying upon a table close at hand, and with this she very mercilessly slashed and ripped at her drenched clothes—cutting them bodily away.

She was truly in a most deplorable state.

Those beautiful little boots, which the love-sick Jack would have deemed it such a privilege to be allowed to unlace, they were nothing now but a squelching mass.

Those stockings, usually so white and spotless, and fitting so tightly to the well-shaped legs, hung now in bags and creases, and were woefully begrimed with mud.

But she was not long before she had disencumbered herself of all these ugly impediments, and stood in the ruddy glow and genial warmth, adorned only by her own loveliness.

A matchless loveliness was it, too.

A soft voluptuous form, with flesh of milky whiteness.

A faultless shape, yet plump and luscious as the fruit of a tropical clime.

Red pouting lips, and eyes which at times glistened with feverish desire, and anon seemed to languish in dreamy sensuousness.

A face and form to have maddened a saint.

But there was present no Peeping Tom to avail himself of the sight of the unrobed beauty, to conjure up in his depraved mind visions of unrighteous bliss.

She was alone and free from constraint.

The fire-light danced over her lovely form, flickering with lascivious dalliance around it.

She basked gratefully in the warmth, and a generous glow tingled through her.

While thus engaged her eyes lighted upon a flask on the table.

She took it up and found that its contents were wine.

A few mouthfuls served almost to completely restore her.

Her headache gradually left her.

The aching of her bones had almost gone.

She felt herself again.

The roses, too, slowly returned to her cheeks, and as she stood there like another Venus risen from the sea, so lovely a creature could scarcely be imagined, as this nude beauty with the rippling masses of golden hair.

It occurred though to Miss Fanny that it was high time she dressed herself—an idea which, by the way, my lady readers may probably think ought to have occurred much sooner; but, then, you know my heroine throughout has always been such a shocking slut.

She was a slut, there is no denying, and not more modest as a rule than she need to have been, but——

But she would not have relished the idea of any stranger finding her in the state in which she was.

The thought was rather startling when it flashed across her mind, and the circumstance which caused it so to do was a fancied noise.

She paused and listened.

Yes. She thought she heard a footstep.

"Good heavens!" cried Fanny; "what shall I do? and I can't find the way into these dreadful things."

CHAPTER LXVII.

SOME VERY EXTRAORDINARY DISCOVERIES INDEED—SOME RATHER LAUGHABLE, AND OTHERS VERY HORRIBLE.

FANNY struggled frantically with obstinate buttons which would not come undone, and others which would not be fastened up again.

Dressing in a hurry is a difficult matter under any circumstances.

When the house is very much on fire, for instance, and the bed-room floor is beginning to bulge downwards in the middle, like the limp parchment of an unsound drum.

Or when you are wakened up suddenly to go for a doctor.

Or when you have been bathing in the country and see a bull coming, or the furious farmer upon whose land you are trespassing.

Other cases may occur to the gentle reader from personal experience; there could scarcely be a time, however, when haste was more required than when poor Fanny feared that every moment some one would enter and find her—very much unprepared for their visit.

But by the time that she had frantically scrambled on her clothes she came to the conclusion, and not without some anger too, that she had been mistaken.

Nobody was coming.

She could have heard no footsteps.

She must have been mistaken.

"There will come somebody, though, I suppose," said she to herself. "I wonder who it will be?"

She also wondered how the proprietor would greet her.

"I wonder whether he will recognize his clothes?"

This idea suggested another.

She might as well get rid of the wet garments she had taken off.

She looked about for some place to stow them away.

It was a wonderful room this, full of queer nooks and corners, and she soon found one where she could cram the wet clothes out of sight.

Then she thought she would make a little tour of inspection.

She was very curious about this astonishing apartment and its contents.

Who could it belong to?

Probably some wreckers, she thought, by the look of the articles strewed about, which appeared as though in their time they had had many owners.

Such a wondrous collection she thought she had never seen before.

There were some curious old cabinets, and their shelves were crowded with curiosities, evidently collected from all quarters of the globe.

If it had been a shop in Wardour-street she could not have expected to find a more singular collection.

Sèvres glasses, Dresden china; wonderfully elaborate pieces of workmanship in gold and silver, necklaces, brooches, bracelets of strangely-shaped beads.

Among them, tiny idols, crucifixes, vessels for holding holy water. Chinese pictures of exquisite finish, but shamefully indecent design, calculated to raise the blush even to the cheeks of the most hardened and shameless. And resting on these vile productions, costly-bound bibles and prayer-books. A curious collection, indeed, without any order or arrangement; all tumbled together pell-mell, as though they were of no earthly value.

Fanny could not spend much time over these matters. She glanced at them all, however, upon the way, in a rapid fashion, intending if she ever had the chance to have a good look at them again upon some future occasion.

At the present time, however, she wanted to take a sort of bird's-eye view of the whole apartment, and take stock of its general contents.

She could do no more now.

Presently, in the course of her search she came to something, however, which was much more gratifying to her, at this moment, than would have been all the wealth of the Indies.

This was something to eat.

It is a sad thing to say of a young lady, perhaps you will be inclined to think, but it must nevertheless be confessed.

Miss Fanny then was a wonderful little gourmand.

It did not much matter what danger she passed through—in what peril she stood; she always got hungry at regular intervals.

She was, if I may be allowed a very vulgar observation, which, indeed, I should not dream of using if I did not know what a kind and indulgent reader I had to deal with, she was always ready for her "beans."

Having got pretty warm and comfortable, as far as clothes were concerned, she of course began to feel hungry.

She found a cupboard, as I have said, upon a shelf of which was half a cold chicken.

There was also a bottle, which when uncorked, was found to contain something extraordinarily choice in Burgundy.

"Tell you what, old chap," said Miss Fanny, aloud, addressing an imaginary host; "I don't know who you are, I am sure, but you know where you are to a week as far as your living is concerned."

There were no knives and forks to be found; but she got over this difficulty.

She had seen in one of the cabinets a beautiful silver-handled poniard, richly chased.

She fetched it now, unsheathed, and——

Began to cut up the chicken.

"Cheeky" is far too mild a term for such an awful young lady as this.

The enormity of her impudence struck Miss Fanny very forcibly when she had her pretty mouth full.

She, therefore, nearly choked herself.

Recovering, however, with a struggle, says she to herself—"Miss Fan, you're going it."

She "went it" again with renewed vigour.

Putting a most unreasonable quantity of fowl out of sight.

Ditto Burgundy.

Without mentioning some choice grapes, also stolen from the cupboard.

"Not bad," said Miss Fanny, wiping her mouth on a costly brocaded satin curtain; "whoever the old chap is who belongs to these diggings, I must confess that he is 'all there' as respects his victuals."

She had taken suddenly, you see, to be rather a slangy young lady.

The reason for this I am almost afraid to tell you.

But it must be done, I suppose, and so, were a thousand apologies——

The fact was, then, that Fanny had fasted too long and was too weak in the head to venture upon that Burgundy quite so freely.

The contents of the flask, too, which she had visited a while since were rather potent.

She had not noticed it.

The effects came before she was prepared for them.

They crept upon her stealthily.

She had no idea they were coming.

No idea they had come when they had.

Until at last.

At last poor Fanny became rather dizzy and confused.

She also became extremely reckless, and did not care very much to whom the cave belonged, or whose were the cold fowl and Burgundy of which she had been so freely partaking.

She took it into her head, however, to go another tour of inspection round the premises, after she had concluded her repast, and in turns she visited all the numerous cupboards and cabinets which the curious, cavern-like apartment into which she had made an entry contained.

There were also several chests, very strong and iron-bound, and made, it would seem, not only for the safe keeping of valuable property, but also to guard against bad weather.

They were, however, although they had strong and massive locks, all unfastened.

Fanny looked into them and turned over their contents.

All kinds of wearing apparel she found, of all sorts, and hues, and fashions.

One box was full of women's clothes.

She took more interest in these than any other—naturally.

She dragged them out, and examined them.

They were some of them of very costly fabric.

There were magnificent Indian shawls which, as well as she could judge, must have been worth full a hundred guineas each.

There were the most splendid silks; some made into dresses, some still in pieces.

There were all kinds of satins and brocades.

There were costly furs of great value.

There was a quantity of underclothing of the very best material—the finest quality.

There were even ladies' boots and shoes—some of the most exquisite workmanship.

Some were tiny little things fit only for fairies.

What Fanny thought rather singular though was, that nothing among this wonderful heterogeneous collection of apparel was new.

All had been worn—the shawls, the gowns, the mantles, the boots, the delicate satin slippers, the silk stockings, the soft underclothes still sweetly scented as though they yet encompassed blushing beauty.

As Fanny looked upon these things, thinking what a capital wardrobe she could make out of them, another thought occurred to her.

This not so pleasant a one.

Did these things belong to the dead?

It was an ugly reflection.

And yet not an unnatural one.

Was it not the most probable solution to the mystery of their presence here.

How otherwise could they have reached this strange place?

The owner of this underground abode was no doubt a wrecker.

He had collected all these things from time to time and hidden them.

Perhaps he was afraid to try and dispose of them afterwards.

Or——

No, that thought was too horrible.

Yet it might be!

Such things had occurred.

Was this cave inhabited by a band of robbers who murder travellers and concealed their garments here after they had disposed of their bodies upon the sands?

In either case it was upon the cast-off wearing apparel of the dead that she was looking now.

How horrible it seemed!

And to what endless conjectures did not the thought give rise, respecting the character and appearance of the once owners of these costly robes?

Young and lovely, perhaps were many of these now unsightly skeletons or rotting corpses, beneath the deep.

Ah! how little did they dream what might some day be their fate when they donned this gay apparel in thoughtless joy and happiness.

Flushed with the triumphs of youth and beauty.

Made only to love, or provoke desire, and now——

Now those soft voluptuous forms were black and decayed.

Those soft polished limbs devoid of flesh.

Those bright eyes dimmed and sightless.

Those swelling breasts of snowy whiteness shrunken away.

Their entire forms so full of bewitching grace and beauty gone to the crumbling dust from which they sprung.

Miss Fanny was not at most times inclined to be very sentimental.

Perhaps you may feel inclined to sneer at her having thus grown profoundly philosophical about a dead woman's pink silk stockings.

Perhaps it was rather absurd when you come to look at it.

She certainly was very serious, though, upon some account or other.

Perhaps it was that these delicate and fascinating parts of the female attire were somehow associated in her mind with the naughtiest episodes in her own shameful career.

Perhaps pink silk stockings have always been a gay and skittish article of wearing apparel, and the odds were greatly in favour of their wearer being more beautiful than wise.

Or perhaps, after all, it was more because the Burgundy had taken rather an unusual effect upon Miss Fanny's head.

I cannot explain the reason, I am sure.

After the profoundest consideration, I can only attribute it to—one thing or the other.

Two things at any rate were certain.

Miss Fanny was more than usually serious.

Miss Fanny was more than usually sleepy.

The thing I have most dread of, of all others, is being improbable.

I am always labouring under a great fear that I may describe some scene of rather an unusual character, and that you may think that I am exaggerating.

I am afraid now that you may think it outrageously improbable that Fanny, under the circumstances described, should dream of taking a nap.

But at any risk I mean to tell the truth, whether it be probable or not. I boldly declare that she did determine upon a nap,

She did not care a fillip of her pretty fingers what happened next, or to whom this mysterious cavernous apartment belonged.

She meant to lie down upon the bed and have forty winks.

"I will," said Miss Fan, with determination, and swearing the terrible oath with which Mr. Paul Bedford, as Norma, struck terror into the souls of the other vestal virgins, "by Jingo!"

She went and peeped into the singular bed which I have already described, and came to the conclusion that its interior was probably more comfortable than it looked.

At any rate she would try it.

There was a faint suspicion of mouldiness about the bed.

It almost led one to believe that the room was uninhabited.

But then that could not be, because of the bright fire which Fanny had found burning upon the hearth.

No; somebody must live there, and must have been there lately, or else who was it that had recently stirred the fire?

Fanny was too tired to enter deeply into this question.

She wanted to have a nap.

Surely no great harm would happen to her if she took one.

Besides, she would probably hear if any one came along the subterraneous passages.

Their approach would awaken her, and she would then have time to conceal herself somewhere.

She was rather too sleepy to think where.

She did not feel inclined to go deeply into the matter.

The bed looked tolerably clean; and as she was going only to be upon the outside, she thought it would do quite well enough for the purpose.

She stretched herself out, therefore, to her entire satisfaction, and drew to the curtains.

She intended just to sleep for about ten or twenty minutes.

She went off like a rock, and did not awake for at least a couple of hours.

Some noise in the room awoke her first.

It might have been somebody stirring the fire.

She raised herself upon her elbows, and listened.

There was a very curious kind of sound audible.

It was something like the blowing of a pig.

A grunting, wheezing noise, such as a wild animal might make snuffing the ground for food.

Nothing so very alarming, perhaps, in this sound, and yet it was extraordinary with what terror it filled the heart of the listener.

She stretched out her hand ever so gently to get hold of the bed-curtains.

She was eager, and yet dreaded to look out.

What was there?

What was she going to see?

It surely could not be anything so very dreadful. Why should it be?

She could give herself no satisfactory reason for her alarm, and yet her terror was to arrive.

It was with quite a struggle that at length she contrived to summon up a sufficient amount of courage to peep out.

When at length she did so, the sight that met her eyes transfixed her with horror.

Her eyes almost started from their sockets.

Her blood curdled in her veins.

Great drops of perspiration bedewed her brow.

Yes, indeed, the object which her eyes alighted upon was well calculated to fill her with alarm.

"Could it be human?" she asked herself at first.

It was apparently a male creature!

It had something of the shape of a man.

But, oh! how horribly distorted!

How ghastly horrible in its features!

How revoltingly misshapen in form!

It was meant for a man.

It wore men's clothes of a coarse and uncouth character.

But its features had nothing human in them.

Its nose was gone—eaten away by some frightful disease, most probably.

Its eyes were not in the position that people's eyes are usually placed.

It had a great, gaping gap of a mouth, like a slit cut with some blunt instrument, in the face.

It had horrible blubbery lips of a swollen bluish tint, which looked like putrid meat.

Great fangs—you could not call them teeth—were set here and there crossways, at all sorts of extraordinary angles indeed, in which it is not the custom for people's teeth to grow.

He was a humpback, and his livid face and red matted hair were thrust out far before his body when he walked.

One shoulder was much higher than the other.

One leg was much longer than the other.

His feet were different sizes, and his toes turned inwards so much, that when he sat down one foot lay over the other, and he had a habit of nursing his knees, as though he were perishing with cold.

His arms were as long as his legs, after the fashion of an ape.

Indeed he was more like a baboon than a man, and as he sat before the fire he grinned and chattered horribly to himself, just as a gorilla might have done in its native woods.

Fanny looked out between the curtains in silent terror.

She could scarcely believe her eyes, and rubbed them.

But yet she could not be mistaken.

She was not asleep.

This awful monster was a reality.

At the time that she first looked out it was stirring the fire, and the light of the flames fell full upon its hideous face.

Nothing so revolting as its noseless, half-sightless visage had she ever seen in her life before.

She could not draw back her head again.

She was perfectly paralysed with horror.

She lay as though she had been suddenly frozen stiff—motionless.

She griped the bed-curtain tightly in her hand.

The colour faded slowly away from her face, leaving it deadly white, as though the blood were running back from her heart.

Oh, how awfully horrible was this misshapen beast!

And had he turned upon her!

In that case she must have been discovered, for she could not have drawn back again in time to have escaped.

She seemed paralysed with horror, and for some time lost all command over herself.

Luckily for her, though, the creature did not look towards the bed, but having stirred the fire into a good blaze, sat down in front of it, nursed its knees, and made itself as comfortable as circumstances admitted of.

Fanny, when she could regain a command over herself, let fall the curtains and peeped through a little hole that she cut in them.

The hunchback thrust out his long, lean hands close to the fire.

Then he rubbed them one over the other, slowly blowing upon them.

After a time he rose from his seat and cast an inquiring glance round the room, as though in search of some missing object.

It appeared that it was the flask of spirits he was in search of, for when his eyes presently fell upon it, he made a snatch and took a long gulp at its contents.

Fanny turned deadly sick.

To think that she should have been innocently drinking out of the same bottle.

That her pouting lips had been applied to the same place that probably this beast's mouth had previously been brought in contact with.

But soon other things were going to occur at which she had more reason to feel disgusted.

Little did she dream as yet into what an awful den she had penetrated.

Little did she know the character of the hideous monster into whose lair she had fallen.

After he had taken two or three greedy gulps at the contents of the bottle, over which he snorted, and spluttered, and slobbered, in a way horrible to behold, he stared about him in a vague way, as though in search of some other object.

He then began to make up the fire.

He fetched from some place in the passage a quantity of faggots.

He piled them up upon the hearth and stirred them up.

They blazed fiercely, and roared up the hole which served as a chimney to this curious subterranean retreat.

He then raised from a dark corner, where he had placed

it, Fanny supposed, upon his first entrance into the cave, a sack, which he dragged before the fire.

It was three parts full of something or other.

Fanny eagerly peeped through the hole in the curtain, wondering what could be its contents.

The hunchback knelt down upon the floor, and began to unpack it.

He plunged his hands deeply down into the sack and began to claw out a variety of articles.

They appeared to be principally composed of female attire.

He pulled forth a black-silk dress, then a black silk quilted petticoat.

Then a quantity of underclothing.

Then a small parcel screwed up in a handkerchief.

This last he carefully unfastened.

He then disclosed to view several trinkets, which glittered brightly in the firelight.

There was a gold watch.

A long chain.

A pair of bracelets, and a brooch.

A variety of coins—gold and silver.

It would appear that these articles had belonged to some person in a good station of life.

"How had the hunchback become possessed of these?" Fanny wondered.

She puzzled her head awhile upon the subject, and could only arrive at one plausible conclusion.

This was that he was a wrecker.

He had found the owners of these clothes lying drowned upon the beach.

He had stripped and plundered the bodies.

It was indeed a horrible thought.

She shuddered when she reflected to what indignities her own corse might have been subjected had she been drowned and washed ashore.

For a moment she congratulated herself upon her escape.

But then the reflection that she had fallen alive into this villain's den was not a consoling one.

Might not he be tempted, when he found that she had discovered his secrets, to lay violent hands upon her?

She trembled as this idea flashed through her mind.

How lonely was the spot!

She was far removed from all hope of human aid.

Would such a scoundrel scruple about the perpetration of an outrage?

Her death?

Or worse!

It was truly a horrible position; the terrors of the situation in which she found herself placed almost deprived her of the power of reflection.

But as yet she was far from knowing the worst.

Far more horrible revelations were in store for her.

Revelations calculated to sicken her with terror.

To madden her with apprehensions of hellish cruelties to come.

Meanwhile the hunchback was busy with his sack.

He dragged out more of its contents.

A quantity of linen, upon which Fanny perceived, with feelings of unutterable horror, certain dark stains—the stains of blood.

Had, then, these clothes been taken from a murdered woman?

Had she been murdered and robbed by this ugly wretch who was now examining the spoil?

If the body had been washed up by the sea, the clothes would have been wet.

These were evidently quite dry.

The hunchback did not put them down to the fire, as, if they were wet, she would have thought that he would have done.

On the contrary, he rolled them in a bundle, and stuffed them into one of the boxes.

The blood-stained linen, however, he otherwise disposed of.

This he cut into shreds and flung upon the fire.

There it smoked for a few moments.

Then blazed fiercely.

Then flew up the chimney in a thousand sparks.

When he had done this, he plunged further down into the sack, and brought out something else.

Fanny opened her eyes in surprise and horror.

Opened them to the widest extent.

Her mouth fell open.

Her hair bristled upon her head.

Drops of perspiration burst out upon her face.

Gracious God! could she believe her eyes?

She must be dreaming.

It could not be; and yet, nevertheless, there could be no doubt of the dreadful truth.

The object was the dead body of an infant!

The hunchback lifted the child's corpse out of the sack, and laid it on the ground; then rising to his feet, stirred the fire into a fierce blaze.

Fanny clutched nervously at the bedpost to save herself from fainting.

But the sickening horror was yet to come.

CHAPTER LXVIII.

A SCENE OF HORROR.

FANNY, of course, supposed that the wretch's object was to burn the body.

Surely to be in the same room whilst such a fearful operation was in progress was fearful enough.

What could be worse?

The reader may well ask the question.

Yet a more dreadful sight than that was yet in store for the terrified girl!

When this misshapen brute had stirred the fire up into a blazing fury, he fetched out of one of the cupboards a piece of strong string.

This he tied round the body of the child, then fastened one end to a stout nail over the fire.

What was he going to do now?

Fanny watched his every movement with intense interest.

At first it was doubtful what was his object.

But the doubt was too soon dissipated by the horrible truth.

He was going to roast the child!

For what purpose?

Fanny shuddered as a faint idea of the truth occurred to her.

But as yet all was uncertainty.

She must wait.

She clutched the bedpost.

She held her breath.

At times she was compelled to keep a tight grip upon her throat.

Had she not done so, she felt that she could not have remained silent.

She must have shrieked aloud.

Shrieked aloud in frenzied horror at the unnatural spectacle.

Round and round before the fire the dead body of the infant revolved.

A stifling odour of scorched flesh pervaded the apartment.

Fanny was compelled to hold her nose.

She thought that nothing else would have prevented her vomiting.

She grasped her poniard tightly betwixt her fingers.

She more than once had half made up her mind to spring out upon the monster, and bury the cold steel in his heart.

But somehow she did not do so.

Something stronger than her will held her spell-bound upon the spot.

She could not, to have saved her life, have withdrawn from the awful sight.

She could not have torn herself away from the contemplation of this revolting scene.

A scene which filled her soul with loathing.

Horrible!

Oh, most horrible was it!

The monster by this time had done his cannibal cookery.

He was ready to commence his meal.

His hideous feast of blood!

Nor did he long delay.

While only half cooked he tore the body from the fire.

He began upon it like a ravenous wolf!

He dug his long, fang-like teeth into the flesh.

Into the tender infant flesh.

He snarled over it like a savage cur.

He worried it!

He gnawed it!

Jagged it!

Wrenched it piecemeal!

Whilst engaged in this disgusting repast, the face of the unnatural wretch was something awful to contemplate.

Blood besmeared, ensanguined, revolting in the extreme.

He had nought human left about him.

Fanny, as she gazed upon the filthy spectacle, almost expected that heaven's wrath would have descended upon his head.

That a thunder-bolt would have fallen upon the roof of this subterranean den of infamy.

That would have struck him down.

Struck him lifeless.

Brained the beast, yet stained with the life's blood of its innocent victim!

Suddenly in the midst of his ungodly repast, came an interruption.

The hunchback started into a listening posture.

He turned his head towards the door.

He placed his hand by the side of his ear.

Fanny also listened.

But her sense of hearing was not so acute.

She could hear nothing.

It was as certain, however, that the hunchback could detect some sound in the distance which alarmed him.

He placed his ear close to the ground, and listened intently.

Then, as it appeared, satisfied that previously he had not been mistaken, he started to his feet.

He rapidly thrust out of sight the remains of his feast.

Then catching up a pitcher of water, flung the greater portion of it upon the fire to deaden the flames.

Then he crept out of the door into the passage.

Fanny listened and waited in great anxiety.

Perhaps the wretch's place of concealment had been discovered.

It was going to be broken into.

She might be rescued.

She waited and listened, but as yet not the faintest sound reached her ears.

The hunchback very probably had much practice in watching for an attack from his enemies.

He heard their approach from afar off, and knew how to prepare for their arrival.

Whilst she waited the most profound silence ensued.

Then she fancied she heard a slight shuffling sound, as though of badly-shod feet being dragged along the ground.

It came nearer and nearer to the door.

Then there was the sound of a spring.

Then a suppressed shriek.

Then a desperate scuffle.

The sound of blows—of panting and buffeting.

Also of wild, cat-like cries, and fierce growlings.

The door was then flung open.

Then the hunchback came rolling into the room.

With him another person locked tightly in his embrace.

Those two were cuffing and punching one another with desperate ferocity.

They were boxing one another's ears.

Pulling one another's hair out by the roots.

Striking one another furiously in the face.

Kicking one another with all their might.

Trying to gouge one another.

Pinching, scratching, tearing, dragging, cuffing and kicking.

Two wild cats tied together by their tails, and hung over a clothes-line, could not have fought with more fiendish vindictiveness.

Fanny peeped through the hole in the bed-curtain upon this extraordinary scene, wondering what on earth could be the meaning of it.

The hunchback had almost extinguished the fire, and consequently she could but indistinctly discern the objects struggling on the ground.

She made out, however, that one was the hunchback.

In vain she strove to make out who the other was.

But presently she fancied she caught a glimpse of floating garments.

Could it be?

Yes.

No.

It was a woman!

Suddenly the fire blazed up brightly, lighting the whole apartment.

The conflict came to an abrupt termination.

The combatants sat up and looked at one another.

The expression of both denoted astonishment, real or feigned.

"Hullo!" cried the hunchback.

"Hullo!" cried the woman.

"It's you, is it?"

"Of course it is."

"Why didn't you say so, then?"

"Why didn't you ask?"

"Haven't you got a tongue in your head, you fool?"

"Haven't you?"

"Come now, let's have none of your sauce."

"Don't let's have none of yours."

"I'd pitch into you again for two twos."

"Try it."

"I will, if you don't shut up."

"Ugh!"

The woman gave a grunt of disgust, but made no other remark.

She picked herself up and rubbed her knees and elbows, both of which were somewhat bruised by the late scuffle.

"You savage brute!" she muttered, in an under tone; "you've knocked half the skin off me."

"I wish I'd knocked your ugly old head off," retorted the hunchback, savagely.

The woman, however, made no rejoinder.

She limped about the room, and presently found a candle.

Then, having struck a match against the wall, lit it.

Fanny was then able to take an observation of the newcomer's personal appearance.

A singular one it was too.

Fanny thought she never before had seen so melancholy an object.

She was dressed only in a miserable skirt, which clung about her long lean figure.

She was as thin as a lath.

So awfully thin indeed, that Fanny could scarcely believe such a fleshless frame could contain life.

She was no more than a skeleton.

A bag of bones.

A living anatomical study.

A thin skin only seemed to cover her lantern jaws.

Her eyes were deep sunk in their sockets; they were lustreless too, and had a fish-like look about them.

Her colourless lips barely covered her irregular and blackened teeth.

Her bare arms were nothing but long spike-like bones.

But the joints seemed large and swollen.

The elbow was like a great knob, such as you might fancy would have done well as the handle to a walking-stick.

She had enormous hands and feet.

Her knuckles were of unnatural dimensions.

The skin was tightly drawn over them.

Red and shining as though the friction of the bones had worn them thin.

As though they were about to burst forth bare and ghastly.

As the bones burst from the decaying flesh of a corpse left to rot upon the battle-field.

As for the rest of her body, she had no pretence to form or shape.

Her scanty clothing hung about her in bags.

You might as well have dressed up a broom-handle and expected symmetry.

The most horrible part about this blear-eyed old fragment of feminine humanity was, however, the baldness of her head.

Her scalp was white and hairless, and surrounded only by a fringe of ragged locks, extremely scanty even there.

She had bushy eyebrows, though, and bristles upon her chin.

Something like a ragged grey moustache ornamented her upper lip.

Her arms, too, were overgrown with hair, as though she were a man.

Why such a scandalous caricature of the softer sex had ever been allowed to disgrace petticoats, was a puzzle.

Fanny felt ill as she looked at her.

It certainly was a most trying scene for anybody's stomach—this which had been hitherto enacting in the hunchback's cave.

AN INTERESTING REHEARSAL.

Fanny looked wonderingly from one to the other.

Surely two such monsters were never before upon earth!

No wonder they had found one another out.

No wonder they lived together.

Most probably they were man and wife.

"I should rather have liked to have seen them making love," thought naughty Miss Fan.

She was, however, destined to see very little love-making upon this occasion.

Indeed neither of the amiable couple appeared to be upon very friendly terms.

They sat silently for some time upon opposite sides of the fire.

Each appeared to be busily engaged in inspecting their respective bruises.

Each, in a low tone of voice, was cursing the other.

At length a dialogue began.

The man glared evilly at his companion, and said—

"Well, scarecrow."

"Now, crookback," retorted the lady.

"What's brought you back again?"

"My legs."

"Call 'em legs? Ha! ha!"

"They're something like straight; that's moretl an yours are."

"I thought I'd got rid of you for good."

"You hoped so, I suppose?"

"I did so, I don't deceive you."

"Don't put yourself out of the way to be polite. You'd like to murder me, I'll bet a penny."

"I shall do so one day, perhaps, you old witch."

"Ah! I ain't afraid."

"P'raps not. I shall do it though, nevertheless."

"That's what you've often said."

"I'll do it now, you she devil, if you don't shut up. Hold your tongue, will you?"

"He! he! he!"

"You'd better not provoke me; I'm in no humour for it."

The woman appeared to think she had gone far enough too, for she became silent after a chuckle or two.

Presently the hunchback resumed.

"Did you do anything to-night?"

"Nothing."

"You haven't tried, I suppose?"

"Yes, I have."

"Where have you been?"

"To all the coach-offices."

"What was that for?"

"I thought I should have met with some young women who had come in to the town to try and find places."

"To be sure, we did once before."

"I went, too, to the agents, and asked whether they had any one upon their books."

"I don't like that; I think there's too much risk."

"I don't think there's more risk in that than the other way."

"What do you mean, then, in getting into conversation with the girls themselves?"

"Yes, that is the best way, I think."

"I don't, then. People have got to notice me too much as it is."

"How do you know?"

"I have overheard them talking, and I have been told."

"Who told you?"

"A girl I spoke to to-day."

"How was that?"

"I met her going for the beer, and got into conversation with her in the usual way."

"Well?"

"I asked her whether she was in service, and whether she would like to change her place."

"What did she say?"

"She said that depended upon circumstances."

"Well?"

"I told her, then, the old story—that my mistress was a lady of immense wealth, and had employed me to look for a maid-servant to travel with her abroad. She must be an orphan, or at least somebody whose friends would not interfere with her."

"To be sure."

"Well, then I stuffed her up with what a capital place it was, and what wages, and so on."

"Well?"

"I thought everything was going first-rate, but it wasn't, though."

"Why not?"

"Why, all at once she turns round upon me, and says—'I know you,' she says; 'you're the woman that spoke to the other girls.'"

"Damnation!"

"'The woman,' says she, 'that took the other girls away; and what's become of them?'"

"That was a poser."

"I didn't know what to answer, of course. She began making an awful to do; a crowd gathered round, and I was precious glad to make my escape."

"I'm afraid the game's done up in that line."

"The game's very nearly done up altogether."

"How so?"

"As I was coming by the police-court, I stopped to read the notices on the walls. There were two bills."

"What of?"

"Offering rewards."

"For the missing girls?"

"Yes, or the people who tempted them away."

"That's awkward."

"Very awkward, as you will think when you hear."

"Hear what?"

"Hear what was on the bills."

"What was?"

"A full description."

"Of whom?"

"Of me."

"Ha! ha! ha!"

"Now then, idiot."

"Hallo!"

"What are you grinning at?"

"I was thinking how you would like to be scragged."

"I sha'n't be scragged alone."

"You'd split on me, would you?"

"No occasion."

"What do you mean?"

"You're described too."

"It's a lie."

"Go and look yourself."

"Do you mean it?"

"You will know soon enough."

The hunchback left off grinning.

"The devil!" said he.

"They've described you to a nicety, and me too."

"The game's up, then."

"It is."

"Well, we could not expect it to go on for ever."

"No, we've done pretty well as it is."

"We've enticed away over a score of young women——"

"And robbed and murdered them without being discovered."

"Besides all the travellers we've been able to catch from time to time."

"And luckily not a soul made their escape."

"No; no one has lived to tell the story."

"Unless they were to dig the bodies up out of the lime-pit, they could prove nothing."

"They could prove nothing then, thanks to my idea of destroying the faces."

"No, we are safe so far."

"There is only one fear."

"And that is?"

"That they should discover this cave."

"Which isn't likely."

"Nobody has yet."

"No, nobody who has once entered here, except ourselves, has ever lived to give information."

Fanny listened to these monsters with increasing terror.

Anything so dreadful she could not have believed to have been within the limits of possibility.

And yet, had she been deeply versed in the annals of crime she would have known that such things were.

She would have known that crimes quite as horrible as any here described had taken place in France and England quite recently.

In spite of the vaunted omnipotence of the police.

And after the horrors of which she herself had been witness could she be surprised at anything else?

The hunchback and the female skeleton were for a time silent; both were busily employed with their evil thoughts.

Both were brooding over their hellish schemes for the concealment of past atrocities, and the perpetration of fresh.

"If they should once find their way in here, though," said the hunchback, breaking a lengthy silence, "we shall be ruined."

"They will find all the plunder, that is certain."

"Nothing will be more easy, then, than to identify some of the clothes belonging to the victims."

"Some of their trinkets and jewellery at any rate."

"There are portraits, too."

"There are names upon the clothes."

"Of course the whole affair would be blown at once."

"But we must not allow such a thing to take place."

"How can we help it if there are large rewards offered for us?"

"There is only one thing left."

"What is that?"

"Let us make our escape."

"What! leave the things?"

"No, only the most worthless. We might take the jewellery."

"And some of the best of the clothes?"

"Suppose we lose no time, then?"

"What, pack at once?"

"Let us get out the things ready to-night, and go away to-morrow."

"We must not move during the day."

"No, that wouldn't do."

"And I'm too tired to do anything now."

"The best plan will be to wait till to-morrow. We shall take all day to get the things ready."

"Then move away to-morrow night."

This conclusion having been arrived at, the two wretches dropped the subject.

"Have you had your supper?" the man asked.

The woman, instead of replying, began to sniff.

"You have, it seems."

"Ugh!"

"What have you been cooking?"

"Something I found out of doors. I didn't expect you, or I should have saved you some."

"I'm not hungry."

"What do you want, then?"

"Should like something to drink."

"There's some of that spirit we found on the sea captain."

"That'll do. Where is it?"

"In the cupboard."

The woman rose, and got out a bottle of curious shape.

Then looked for some glasses there; when found, she put them upon the table, and then looked about for water.

In this she was not so successful; for the hunchback had emptied the pitcher upon the fire some time ago, as the reader may remember.

The woman growled a good deal at the trouble of fetching more, and decided to do without it.

The hunchback, however, ordered her to fetch some.

"Fetch it yourself," said she.

"Do as you are bid," growled the hunchback.

"I shan't."

"If yer don't, I'll smash you."

This amiable dialogue terminated, however, in the woman obeying.

There was more reason than would have at first been supposed for this conduct on the part of the hunchback.

As a general rule, he was by no means addicted to any such weakness as mixing water with his grog.

His motive, however, soon became apparent.

Directly the door was closed, the hunchback rose from his seat, and rapidly unlocked a small box standing at the other end of the room.

From it he took a paper.

It contained some white powder.

He poured it into the glass which the woman had left upon the table.

Then hastily returned to his seat.

The woman, almost immediately afterwards, came back again.

When she placed the candle upon the table, however, he took it up, and pretended to be lighting his pipe.

It was too dark for her to see that there was any powder at the bottom of the glass.

She half-filled the tumbler, and tossed it off as though the liquor had been no stronger than tea.

This feat, however, brought on a violent fit of coughing.

The hunchback amiably chuckled.

"Serve you right," said he.

"Why?"

"For being so greedy. Is there any more spirit?"

"You can have it all for what I care."

"Don't you like it?"

"It's got a beastly taste."

"That's the beautiful smoky flavour."

"I don't like it, whatever it is?"

"It isn't meant to swallow in that way. You ought to sip it."

The woman made no reply.

She did not seem to be very well.

"What are you staring at, stupid?" asked the hunchback.

She was staring horribly at space.

Her eyes appeared to be starting out of her head.

She was swaying to and fro in her seat.

She clutched at the table edge.

"You are jolly company, you are," said the hunchback. "Sing us a song."

The woman clutched at her throat, and gasped for breath.

She opened her mouth and lolled out her tongue.

Her nostrils twitched convulsively.

Her face was deadly white, and seemed to glisten as stinking fish gleams in the dark.

The hunchback was not frightened, though.

He was too well acquainted with death to be scared at its most ghastly aspects.

Instead, the ruffian amused himself by gibes and jeers of a hideously brutal character.

"What makes you look so pretty?" he asked.

The woman tried to speak, but could not.

"See what comes of being greedy," said he.

The woman rose to her feet, stiff and rigid as though with agony.

Her lips were covered with white froth.

Her face was horribly convulsed.

Her thin claw-like fingers clutched frantically at empty air.

There was something so awful in the victim's aspect at this moment that the man, ruffian as he was, was for the moment silenced.

He drew back, and instinctively groped in his pocket for a weapon of defence.

The woman's eyes were fixed upon him.

They glittered like the eyes of a furious tigress.

Presently, with a violent effort, she cleared her throat, and then, in a half-choking tone, something between a howl and a screech, addressed him.

"Wretch! wretch!" she screamed; "you—you have poisoned me!"

"I have," replied the hunchback, with a savage curse; "I always said I would be the end of you."

"But not long to survive," she yelled.

Then concentrated all her energies for the effort and sprang upon him.

He was prepared for her coming, but the shock was so great that it dashed him to the ground.

She had the strength of a mad woman.

She held him down and buried her long claws in his cheeks, horribly lacerating them.

He struggled madly to free himself, but in vain.

She was like a savage beast, intent upon his death.

She held him down.

She strove to bury her teeth in his throat.

They rolled together upon the floor, and the fury tore handfulls of hair out of the ruffian's head, whose howls of pain were awful to listen to.

But gradually the poison began to get the mastery over her.

Her hold upon the hunchback relaxed.

He shook himself loose.

He flung his antagonist to the earth, and holding her powerless, groped in his pocket for his knife.

Once found, he dragged open the blade.

Then he twisted the fingers of his left hand in the hag's scanty grey locks.

He violently dragged back her head.

Her scraggy throat was thus laid bare.

With hellish rage he slashed and hacked at it.

The knife was very blunt.

It was with the greatest difficulty that he could effect his horrible purpose.

But he cut and slashed.

He hacked and hewed.

The crimson flood poured over the murderer's hands.

The hot blood splashed up into his face.

A devilish deed it was—unequalled for brutality.

Long after she was dead he still hacked at her, nor did he rest until he had severed her head from its gory trunk.

Then he rose from the ground, and laughed a low, diabolical laugh, such as might have come from a demon, rejoicing in the tortures of the damned.

"Do your worst!" he cried; "I always said that I would do for you. You threatened me, did you? Ha! ha! what are your threats worth now?"

He spurned the body from him with his foot as he uttered these words.

Then he took a deep gulp from the spirit bottle, and looked about him as though undecided what he should do next.

Fanny, whom horror had well-nigh deprived of her senses, watched him anxiously, hoping that a chance of escape would soon occur.

"If he is going?" she thought.

But such did not appear to be the hunchback's intention.

On the contrary, he presently employed himself in strongly barricading the door, after having locked and bolted it.

Then he took another long pull at the spirit-bottle.

Then dragged off his coat and approached the bed.

CHAPTER LXIX.

FANNY FALLS INTO THE POWER OF THE HUNCHBACK.

How can I describe the terror of the situation?

Hitherto, although her position had been a very critical one, there had been no great fear of discovery as long as she remained perfectly still.

The bed-curtains were thick and closely drawn, and they completely concealed her.

Of course there was always the danger of either the man or woman drawing them open, and so discovering her.

But neither had ever been near to the bed.

In the end one or the other would come, and then——

Then there was no hope for her.

Her only chance was to get through the curtains upon the other side, and hide under the bed.

She had been afraid of trying this, though.

She was afraid of making a noise.

If she had had her wits about her, she would have taken the opportunity of moving when the death-struggle was in progress.

But she had then been rooted motionless with horror.

Incapable of thought or action.

Now the critical moment had arrived.

She was lost.

No; there was yet a chance.

Not an instant, though, for hesitation.

She must move at once.

As the man came forward, she glided rapidly back.

As he opened the curtains on one side, the curtains upon the other closed upon her retreating form.

The inside of the bed, owing to the closely-drawn curtains, was very dark.

Her escape was unnoticed.

She crept down underneath as noiselessly as possible.

The rough movements of the hunchback above prevented any noise there she might make from being heard.

Then she lay still as death, waiting for him to go to sleep.

It was a weary task.

He rolled to and fro for some time, grunting and grumbling.

Presently he began to move.

"Thank goodness!" ejaculated Fanny.

And she began to creep from under the bed.

When her head was about twelve inches beyond the vallance, the hunchback awoke with a great snort.

Fanny drew back in terror.

In doing so she hit her head a sharp knock.

"Hallo!" cried the hunchback.

Fanny lay still quaking with fear.

"Who's there?" cried the hunchback.

But as you may suppose, Miss Fan did not volunteer any reply.

"Thought some one knocked," she heard the man say.

Then he growled and grumbled and grunted for awhile.

Then rolled over and began to snore again.

Fanny waited in a dreadfully cramped position.

She dare not move hand or foot for at least ten minutes.

It appeared to her to be like an age.

She waited anxiously.

She held her breath.

She ground her teeth to prevent herself crying out.

So intense was the irksomeness of this constrained silence.

At length she thought that she might venture.

Very cautiously she began to creep out.

Slowly—so slowly.

Barely an inch at a time.

She wriggled like a worm from beneath the bed.

The horrible hunchback still continued to snore.

She crawled upon her hands and knees.

In doing so, she placed her hand in something wet upon the ground,

When she came to look at it in the dim firelight, she shuddered violently.

It was blood!

The blood of the murdered victim!

Oh, horror!

"When would she be able to get out of this vile den?"

Slowly and cautiously she rose to her feet.

She was fearful lest every movement she made should arouse the slumbering monster.

As she gained an upright posture, he turned suddenly in the bed.

Fanny crouched in terror.

The hunchback lay silent, as though listening.

Fanny held her breath.

Had he heard her?

She dare not move head or foot.

Was he waiting for her to do so?

She could not hear him breathe.

And yet he might be sleeping.

What was she to do?

She could not bear to wait much longer.

And yet it was not safe to venture upon any movement.

Presently though, to her great relief, the brute began again to snore.

Then she cautiously crept towards the door.

The hunchback had lumbered up a quantity of furniture before it.

This she would have to move before she could open the door.

And then she would have to get possession of the key.

And where was that?

As well as she could recollect, she had seen him put it into his pocket.

How could she hope to get it?

Yet there was nothing for it but to try.

She therefore, with the greatest caution, set upon the work before her.

She found that after all it was not quite as difficult as she had supposed.

She very easily indeed contrived to move a cabinet, without shaking its contents or making any noise.

Then an arm-chair.

Then a box.

This last she knocked against the cabinet.

That made a rattle.

The hunchback started up.

"Who's there?" he asked.

Fanny crouched immediately, and was perfectly silent.

"Who's there?"

She made no reply.

"Who's there?"

No answer.

"Who's there?" he cried again.

She crouched motionless.

Scarcely breathing.

Her heart scarcely beating, so great was her fear.

The hunchback then raised himself upon his elbow.

Fanny could not pierce the obscurity which surrounded him.

She could not see him.

But she fancied she could guess what he was doing.

He was peering out into the room.

Which way was he looking?

Perhaps his eyes were turned in her direction.

He might be staring hard into the corner where she was hiding.

His eyes might be fixed upon her.

She almost fancied that she could see them.

She fancied that she could feel them—feel them scorching her sight.

Like live coals.

A horrible moment of suspense it was.

A horrible moment of terror.

Worse, far worse, than those other moments of terror which had preceded it—dreadful as ever they had been.

The hunchback remained motionless for a long while.

Scarcely knowing whether or not he had gone to sleep again, Fanny waited and listened.

At last, thinking that he must have dropped off again, she began to move.

But he heard her directly, and cried out—

"Wh-wh-who's there?"

His voice was agitated and husky.

He was evidently terrified.

Fanny was at a loss at first to account for the reason.

She would not have believed such a monster to be capable of fear.

But very soon the reason was apparent.

"Ag-gag-atha!" he stammered.

There was of course no answer.

Fanny wondered who he was calling to.

"Ag-gag-atha!" he repeated.

A deathlike silence followed.

"Are you n-not d-d-dead?" he asked, in a low, suppliating tone—a tone which was scarcely audible, so great was his fear. "Hav-vavn't I k-k-killed you?"

Now Fanny understood.

The wretch was addressing the dead woman.

He was evidently in an agony of fright.

She could hear the bed shaking.

He was trembling violently with fear.

She fancied she could hear his teeth chattering in his head.

"How he must be suffering," she thought.

And then another reflection as rapidly followed—

"Serve him right."

But a great idea now occurred to her.

Could she not practice upon his fears?

By so doing, she might effect her escape.

It was a chance—a chance worth trying.

"Is that you, Ag-gag-atha?" he asked again, in a faint voice.

Fanny replied with a hollow groan.

The bed shook awfully.

Fanny groaned again.

The bed shook.

The hunchback's teeth chattered.

"Spare me!" gasped the wretch.

Fanny was determined to go to extremities.

She crept along the floor upon her hands and knees.

The fire had burnt low.

It was so dark that it was not possible for her to be seen.

She had taken a desperate resolve.

She had mastered her repugnance.

She was bent upon a horrible act—an act which she would have shuddered at the bare thought of upon any other occasion.

But now she was desperate!

This was not a moment for squeamish scruples.

She had noticed where the murderer had flung the head of the woman.

She was now making for it—groping for it in the darkness.

Surely a more horrible search it would be difficult to imagine!

She groped her way on.

Her hands dabbled in blood.

But she heeded it not.

She reached the corner where it had been placed.

She stretched forth her hand.

It clutched the cold and clammy flesh.

She almost shrieked in horror.

She shivered from the crown of her head to the soles of her feet.

Her own flesh seemed to crawl upon her bones.

But she screwed up her courage.

She would not be scared out of her scheme of vengeance.

Why should she fear to touch this poor, harmless, lump of clay?

She, therefore, grasped the head by its scanty locks of hair.

By its blood-bespattered locks.

Its grey and gory tufts!

She carried it with its face turned from her.

She crawled towards the bed.

The hunchback must have heard her coming, for he lay perfectly motionless now.

His terror must have been fearful.

Her own excitement was so intense she could barely help uttering a wild cry.

But she restrained her feelings.

She crept towards him.

Nearer and nearer.

She was now close to the bed.

The darkness was profound, but she knew pretty well in what direction to go.

Nearer and nearer she approached.

The miserable, terror-stricken villain shivered with fright.

He heard the rustling noise.

He thought that the corpse was coming towards him.

He expected next moment to be clasped in a clammy embrace.

He writhed in anticipation.

But now she was upon him.

She had reached his side.

She thrust forward the head.

It came in contact with his face.

The corpse of his victim, as he supposed, was crawling, all mangled and bloody, into the bed.

He could bear no more than this.

He uttered a fearful yell.

A yell most horribly discordant.

A yell so terrific that never till her dying day did Fanny get rid of the recollection of its shuddering horror.

Then he lay motionless.

But now was the moment for obtaining possession of the key.

Fanny groped about in the hunchback's pockets.

He had swooned.

He was powerless.

She had soon found the key, for she had noticed particularly where he had placed it.

Once in her hand, she sprang from the bedside.

With one bound she reached the chamber door.

She groped about for the key-hole.

She fancied that, while so engaged, she heard a movement upon the bed.

Was he so soon returning to consciousness?

Did he suspect treachery?

She felt wildly for the lock.

She could not find it.

There certainly was a movement upon the bed.

He was rising.

In another moment he would be upon her.

"My God!" she muttered to herself, "I am lost!"

But no.

As he touched the ground she found the key-hole.

She thrust in the key.

Turned it.

Tore open the door.

Rushed wildly forth.

There was no doubt about it; the hunchback was upon her track.

She ran on in frantic haste.

She groped her way along.

She stretched forth her hands in advance.

By this means she avoided collision with the walls of the passages.

But only to a certain extent.

Many times she bumped and bruised herself cruelly.

But still she pursued her course.

Still she heard the sound of footsteps behind her.

They seemed to gain upon her.

She struggled on.

They came.

She redoubled her speed.

The footsteps came faster.

They were close to her now.

She fancied that she felt the hunchback's hot breath upon her.

She heard him panting.

He touched her.

Clutched her.

At the same moment she received a violent blow in the face.

A blow which struck her back senseless in the arms of her pursuer.

CHAPTER LXX.

THE ATTEMPTED OUTRAGE.

AND now surely Fanny's last moment had come!

There could be no escape now.

How long her insensibility endured, she could form no idea.

It seemed like a long, long weary night, full of horrible dreams.

When she at last awakened, she was lying upon the bed in the cavern.

A light was burning.

She looked about with shuddering fear.

The hunchback was crouching by the fireside.

She turned her eyes towards that part of the room where the body of the woman had last been lying.

But it was gone now.

She looked about in wonder.

The appearance of the room had considerably changed.

While she had been lying senseless, the hunchback, it would seem, had been busily employed in packing up some of the various articles of value with which it was so richly stocked.

But how was it that her life had been spared?

Was it any scruples about shedding more human blood which had deterred him from her murder?

She could not understand how it was.

Alas! too soon was she to know the horrible truth.

A truth so fearful that aught else would have been preferable.

Even death.

Death sudden and violent!

Some movement that she made caused the hunchback to look up.

He approached the bedside, and took a seat close to it.

"How are you now?" he asked.

But she made no reply for a moment.

It was with difficulty that she could sufficiently overcome the horror with which the sight of him inspired her to make any reply.

"You've been very ill?" he said.

And he spoke in a kind tone of voice.

"Have I?"

"Yes; very ill."

There was a pause then of some few minutes' duration.

"You didn't expect to see the light anymore, I suppose?" he said.

"No."

"You thought I should kill you?"

"Yes."

"You deserved it, at any rate."

"Why?"

"For coming here to pry into my secrets."

Fanny made no answer.

"What made you do it?" he asked.

She did not reply.

"Who prompted you?"

"No one!"

"How did you come here, then?"

"Alone."

"Who showed you the way, then?"

"No one."

"Where do you live?"

"In London."

"And how came you here?"

"I was wrecked upon the coast."

"And found the entrance to the cave?"

"Yes."

"And how long were you here before you ran away and I caught you?"

Fanny drew back with shivering horror from the wretch who thus questioned her.

"How long?" he repeated.

"I was here when you murdered your wife, wretch!" she cried, in a shrill tone, "I was here when—when——"

But she could not bring herself to repeat the nameless atrocity which she had been a witness of.

The hunchback broke into a hideous laugh.

"Since I had my supper?"

"Yes, monster!" she replied.

"And you were horrified!"

"I was."

"Bless you! that's nothing."

"Disgusting brute!"

"Ha! ha! ha! Ain't you surprised I didn't kill you?"

"You are going to do so, I suppose."

"Well, I don't know."

"Why not?"

"You are anxious to die, then?"

"No."

"You talk like it."

"I expect no mercy at your hands."

"But suppose I am merciful?"

"You merciful!"

"Suppose I spare your life on one condition?"

"One condition?"

"Yes; an easy one."

"What is it?"

"That you live here my prisoner."

"Death were better."

"Not so."

"I think it would be."

"You make a mistake."

"Indeed!"

"The death you should die at my hands would be more terrible than you can well imagine."

"I cannot dictate terms to you."

"Of course not, because you are in my power."

"I suppose I am."

"But, as I tell you, I do not intend to treat you badly."

He leered horribly as he said this.

Fanny looked at him in silent wonder; she thought he must be mad.

What else could he be?

Why did he want to spare her?

Presently the hunchback recommenced his questions.

"What brought you to this part of the world?"

"I came upon a pleasure excursion."

"With friends?"

"Yes."

"Were they drowned?"

"I think so; most of them."

"And what trade are you?"

"A—a—clerk."

"Oh!"

There was a long pause.

"And what is your name?"

"John Williams!"

"Oh!"

Another long pause.

Fanny looked at her companion in surprise.

As well as his horrible countenance was capable of expression, he appeared to be mirthfully inclined.

"Ha, ha, ha!" he cried at last.

Fanny stared in astonishment.

"John Williams, is it?" said he.

"Yes. Why?"

"Are women clerks, then, in London?"

"Wo—men!"

"Yes."

"Wh—what do you mean?"

"What do I mean! Do you suppose I'm a fool?"

"I—I——"

"Do you deny it?"

Fanny was silent. Indeed, the hunchback's words called her attention, for the first time, to the disordered condition of her attire.

In the struggle, the collar of her coat had been rudely torn open.

Her fair bosom was partly exposed.

A polished globe, white as ivory, was just visible, but half concealed by the shirt, which had been wrenched roughly open.

Upon the voluptuous outline of her fair form was the hideous monster now feasting his eyes.

The expression of libidinous satyr illuminated his revolting physiognomy.

Nothing so revolting could the terrified girl have believed to exist in human nature.

"I was awfully astonished when I found out it was a woman I had to deal with," said he, after a pause.

But Fanny drew from him with an expression of intense dislike.

Of overpowering disgust!

Loathing!

The hunchback continued in what he intended to be a conciliatory tone.

"Don't be frightened, my dear," he said; "I shan't murder you like I did the old woman, unless you act like a fool."

Fanny trembled.

"You know what a hideous old hag she was. How could I live with her any longer?"

Fanny crept further away from him.

"You, though, are different. You are so beautiful. I never saw anyone half as lovely as you are. I should not have believed it to be possible that there were such creatures. Why, I can understand men going mad with desire to possess such as you. I can understand them risking all they had on earth—of damning their souls to gain their end."

As he spoke he tried to take her hand in his; but she drew back from him in horror.

"If you will live with me I will spare your life," he said. "I have lots of money—thousands hidden away in these trunks. We will take it away with us. We will go to some quiet countryplace, where we can live alone—where my ugliness may not make me a laughing-stock of gaping fools, as it has always done. What do you say?"

"No, wretch!—a thousand times no!" cried the terrified girl.

"No?"

"I would rather die a score of deaths."

"You would?"

"Yes."

"Then listen to me," retorted the hunchback, with a snarl like that of a wild beast. "You shall be mine in spite of yourself. You are in my power; and, by heavens, you shall not escape!"

"What, monster! would you use force?"

"That would I; and when I have sated myself with wild delight, you shall die a horrible death! Ha, ha! we shall see which is to be the master."

As he spoke, the hunchback seized his victim in his arms, She struggled fiercely to resist him; but struggled vainly.

With furious eagerness he tore her apparel from her palpitating form.

Her bosom rose and fell like a tempestuous sea.

She panted for breath.

Her golden curls floated upon her bare breast and shoulders.

Her face, flushed with exertion, was, if possible, more beautiful than ever.

The hideous monster possessed the strength of a demon.

He strained her to his breast.

His eyes glared like burning coals.

He glued his horrible blue and swollen lips to hers, red and pouting.

He covered her lovely face and bare white bosom with passionate kisses.

She screamed and scratched and bit him like a fury; but her strength would not endure much longer.

She grew faint and weak.

She must soon fall.

The brutal miscreant would soon effect his hellish purpose.

But not yet.

For in her weakness, in her despair, came hope.

In her frantic struggles she felt something pushing her side.

It was the poinard she had forgotten.

She felt for it.

Seized it.

Made a blow at the hunchback's throat.

He saw the blow coming, and dived down his head to ward it from the spot at which she aimed.

But this movement caused her to cut him in the face.

A fearful slash it was!

And oh, horror! across the miscreant's eyes.

With a howl like that of some tortured beast of prey, he staggered back.

The blood poured from his face.

He fell screaming to the ground, and rolled about in his agony.

Fanny sprang from the bed, the dagger still in her hand.

Her first impulse was to stab him to the heart.

Had not the wretch deserved death at least a score of times?

But just when she was about to deal him the fatal blow, another thought occurred to her.

She caught sight of a rope lying upon the table.

With this she determined she would cord the ruffian, and so prevent his doing any harm.

But before she could do this, he had scrambled to his feet.

Howling like a wild beast, he staggered towards the fire, and got hold of the poker.

Brandishing this in the air, he made a rush at her.

But before he could reach her, he fell over a trunk and sprawled upon the ground.

In doing so he dropped the poker.

Fanny seized it.

She dealt him a blow upon the head.

Another and another.

The wretch lay quiet.

He was stunned.

And now thought Fanny how to escape.

She would delay no longer there.

She was rushing away at once from the fearful spot; but a moment's reflection caused her to alter her mind.

Was not there here boundless wealth?

Why should she not secure it?

Again her apparel was in such a state of disorder; she could never venture out in this condition.

She had soon made up her mind what to do.

First of all, with the rope, beforehand, she tied the hunchback securely, so as to prevent his interference.

Then she took stock of the room.

She found, greatly to her delight, that the murderer had saved her the trouble of packing.

He had made parcels of all the most valuable articles.

She found a couple of canvas bags, almost as much as she could lift.

One filled with gold.

The other with gems and jewels, all apparently of great value.

When she had looked at these things and determined how they were to be taken away, she searched in the chest of clothes, and brought out some articles of female clothing.

She dressed herself very carefully, for the hunchback showed no signs of returning animation.

She chose the most costly clothes she could find.

A splendid brocaded silk, an Indian shawl, some of the choicest underclothing.

She could not refrain from a shudder more than once as she thus dressed herself.

The thought of how these things had been obtained kept occurring to her.

What horrible death had they died?

What awful atrocities had been committed upon these poor defenceless creatures!

Had this hideous monster been ravisher as well as assassin?

What more likely?

And again a feeling of unutterable loathing and disgust crept over her when she thought of what might have been her own fate.

When she was ready to go she placed the canvas bags containing the articles of value into a carpet-bag which she found at the bottom of one of the trunks.

Carrying this with some considerable trouble, she took the candle in her other hand, and set out upon a voyage of discovery.

She wandered out into the passages.

It was a long and weary journey.

Even with a light, it was no easy matter to find the way.

The passages crossed and re-crossed one another.

It was most bewildering.

A perfect maze.

She was not, however, to be daunted.

She still pursued her way.

And at length, to her great joy, discovered a light.

It was the light of day.

She redoubled her speed.

She rushed eagerly towards it.

She reached it.

She passed out into the open air—the free air of heaven.

A gentle breeze fanned her feverish cheek.

She was free!

The poor girl fell upon her knees, and wept tears of joy and happiness.

"Thank God—thank God!" she uttered, fervently.

She never thought again to have left that awful cavern—to have escaped from her would-be murderer.

Suddenly, though, a thought struck her.

She must remain no longer here.

She was too near the cave.

She dragged along the bag as best she could.

It was very heavy.

She was obliged to carry it with both hands.

She was out upon the sea-coast—a wild and rugged shore.

No sign of human habitation.

Not a soul to be seen.

With great labour she carried along the bag.

With great difficulty she climbed the cliffs.

Then she wandered over a wide tract of deserted country.

Many hours was she thus occupied.

At length, as it was growing dusk, she reached a high road.

Along this she journeyed for a mile or so further.

Then suddenly she heard the sound of wheels behind her.

She turned round eagerly.

It was a stage-coach coming towards her.

She hailed it.

There was room inside.

She asked no questions respecting its destination.

She had not the vaguest idea where it was bound for—indeed, she hardly knew what county she was in.

She put her carpet-bag down beside her.

Lay her head upon it, and fell fast asleep.

CHAPTER LXXI.

SHEWS HOW THE REVEREND JACK PUDDING, OYLEY SWABB, AND EZEKIAH HERRINGBONE WENT TO GREAT PENDLETON, AND HOW THEY INTENDED TO GET UP A GRAND RELIGIOUS REVIVAL.

WHEN Fanny awoke, the stage coach was still travelling onwards at a rapid pace.

It was dark without, but a light was burning inside the coach.

When she opened her eyes, therefore, as she did not stir, she did not disturb her companions.

They were talking together in a low, earnest tone.

Perhaps it was the fact of their thus conversing which attracted her attention; otherwise, it is more than probable, she would have gone to sleep again without paying any attention to their talk.

But as it was, she fancied there must be something worth listening to.

She thought they must be talking secrets.

They say a woman can never keep a secret.

There is another thing equally sure—

That is, that a woman will never lose a chance of learning one.

The mere fact of its being anybody else's secret of course makes her doubly eager.

And when it is a compromising secret—a secret affecting another woman's honour—you may be sure she is eager enough to learn that.

Then as for keeping it.

But all you ladies know how you love one another.

What do we male creatures know, after all, of your inner mysteries?

It is only one or two dreadful rakes among us, who have seen and done the most shocking things, who have any experience.

The rest of us—miserable old bachelors and hen-pecked married men—what do we know? what can we know?

Absolutely nothing!

Bu all this time we are leaving Fanny, who is listening to—to something very singular, gentle reader, as presently you will see, if you will kindly lend me your attention.

Pretty Fanny, she had gone through a great deal.

She had seen some strange things during her short career upon town.

That little business in the cave was somewhat singular, you must allow.

But what was coming?

Ah! what was coming?

Perhaps not anything quite so horrid; but yet rather singular, I fancy you will admit, if you only follow her adventures.

Some strange mysteries were about to be revealed to her.

Some very strange mysteries about a certain class of society, which it is not the habit to turn into ridicule, but which nevertheless, in spite of any threats or intimidation, I mean to venture upon.

Those who kindly followed the fortunes of Master Charley Wag, a hero of mine who made a very successful *début* some time ago in society, and of pretty Mrs. Ruth, the female spy and betrayer, will allow, I think, that I have somewhat freely exposed religious hypocrites.

In Charley's life you had a show up of the "shepherds."

In Ruth's adventures you had some rather singular details respecting London nunneries.

I will say a few words more about shepherds here, and perhaps I may be able to tell you something new.

But as I previously observed, we must return to Fanny.

When Fan opened her eyes and ears, she saw her three fellow-passengers with their heads together.

Heard them whispering.

They were three clerical gents.

One was very fat, short-necked, and red-faced.

The other was a long, thin, ghastly-looking creature.

The third was inclined to be fat, and was goggle-eyed and rather pimply.

They all wore dirty white neckerchiefs.

They were all attired in seedy black.

Their coats were inclined to be greasy at the seams, as though they had worn them a long time.

They also stood badly in need of brushing.

All these reverend gents carried a dropsical umbrella.

All three had very bad hats.

All three smelt uncommonly strong of rum-and-water.

"Well," said the goggle-eyed one, "do you think it will wash?"

"Beautiful!" replied the fat man.

"'Ivenly!" said the long, thin one.

"There's lots of well-to-do people down this part, ain't there?"

"Oh, lot's; and all chapel people."

"That's the right sort."

"Oh, we shall make a tremendous haul."

"If we play our cards well."

"If we don't, it's our look out."

"Vell, I rayther think we shall do," said the fat man.

"Have you billed the place well?"

"Of course I've been down there every day, you know, tearing my lungs out, pretty well every Sunday."

"That's the best advertisement after all."

"If he roused them properly!"

"Roused 'em! I should think so. I told them to wait for Mr. Herringbone, too. Oh! they expect you, old chap, never fear."

"I'm glad they do," said the man, with a complacent grin. "I hope I shall be able to improve them."

"You let 'em have plenty of 'hell flames;'—that touches 'em up best."

"To be sure it does, Mr. Pudding," said the little fat man.

"And then you do a little comic business."

"And who can do it better?" asked Mr. Herringbone.

"Nobody," said the little man. "Shall you ever forget when he was preaching at the little 'Ebenezer,' and got astride of the banisters?"

"No; by Jingo! Jack; that was a great idea, though. By the way I forget how you brought it in."

"Well, it was this way," replied the Rev. Jack Pudding. "I was showing them how hard it was to go to heaven, and how easy to go to the other place. So I got out of the box, and going down the stairs, got astraddle of the banisters, and pulled myself up a little way. 'That's rayther a stiff job, dearly beloved brethren,' says I; 'but how jolly easy you can go down!' And then running up the stairs, I gets astride again, and comes down like a railway."

"Only the worst of it was that Jack slipped off the end, and went down a buster."

"That only heightened the effect," said the Rev. Jack Pudding.

"But it hurt you rather—didn't it?"

"You took some time wiping it off."

"They saw, at any rate, there was some bottom to your argument."

"But about our revival?"

"We must make a good thing of it."

"We will, I hope."

"We will give them some right down good twisters in the way of sermons."

"One or two miracles."

"A visitation or two."

"There's an old woman who's had a warning as it is."

"That's all right; we must egg on some others."

"When once one begins, all the rest do it."

"That's always the case."

"We must have some tea-meetings, of course."

"Of course; lots of hot water and sugar. It comes very cheap if you let them have it hot."

"Plenty of stick-jaw cake, too."

"To be sure; that doesn't cost much, and it draws people."

"By the way, Swabb," said the Rev. Jack, addressing the little fat man, "we must take care a lot of them don't bolt off after they've blown their kites out."

"What, without contributing?"

"That's what they did last time, some of them."

"They wont this time, though."

"No; I think we are rather more up to the back-door business now."

"We ought to be, at any rate."

"I tell you what, though; I wish we had got some novelty."

"Ah! but what?"

"That's the question."

"And who's to think of it?"

"If we only had something, though!"

"These revivals are growing rather stale."

"They'll be knocked on the head soon."

"That's very sure."

"I think there's just a chance for us, though."

"Before they're blown?"

"Yes."

"We must do our best."

"We will."

The three reverend gents then subsided into silence.

Mr. Pudding yawned.

Mr. Swabb followed suit.

Mr. Herringbone rubbed his eyes.

FANNY WHITE PREACHES A SERMON IN THE METHODIST CHAPEL.

"I'm awfully weary," said Mr. Pudding.

"I'm awfully hungry," said Mr. Herringbone.

"I wish we had some more rum," said Mr. Swabb.

"No chance of that, though, for some time to come."

"Not till we stop to change horses."

"We shan't do that any more, I think, till we reach our journey's end."

"Heigho!"

"Awful slow!"

"Disgusting!"

They travelled on again in silence for some time. Then said the Reverend Jack—

"How fast our friend there sleeps."

"Doesn't she?"

"I wonder who she is?"

"Some swell, I should say."

"I shouldn't think so, or she wouldn't have been walking."

"Was she?"

"Didn't you see where she hailed the coach?"

"Ah, to be sure!"

"Wonder what she looks like?"

"There's no telling through that veil."

"Nice voice, though."

"Should think she's pretty."

"Come, I say, Jack, take care."

"Perhaps she's one of the leading people at Peddlington."

"Perhaps so."

"I wish she was some lady of rank, and would patronise us."

"If she did, we could make a great draw."

"We could, indeed."

"Lord bless you! why it would be worth our whiles to pay any one to join in the swindle."

"The swag would be tremendous."

"I believe you."

They had talked themselves sleepy by this time.

One by one they began to nod.

Mr. Pudding was asleep first.

Mr. Swabb soon followed.

Mr. Herringbone was not very long after the other two.

Then Fanny began to ask herself what could be the meaning of the strangers' conversation she had heard.

Who were these persons?

Rogues, that was very certain.

What was the scheme they were concocting?

They were religious rogues.

Rascals who, under a false cloak of sanctity, traded upon the superstitious fears of the ignorant.

Mean-spirited knaves, capable of any dirty trick.

Wretches who would cheat the widow.

Rob the orphan.

And rejoice!

Rejoice at their own iniquity.

They were, too, so greasy, and dirty, and sodden in their mock sanctimoniousness.

Most pitiful wretches, truly.

Fanny's disgust with their appearance was only equalled by her disgust for their conversation.

"Oh, if I could only serve these wretches out."

This was the thought which entered her head.

And if she could do it she would.

But how?

How horribly that wretch Pudding did snore!

Swabb, too, snorted and choked away in a way which was positively frightful to listen to.

As for Herringbone, he slept with less noise.

But he also had an unpleasant way with him.

This was a habit of butting.

He kept administering himself head foremost to Mr. Swabb, upon the opposite seat.

Mr. Swabb objected to this, and pitched him back again.

Then he rolled over upon Mr. Pudding.

Mr. Pudding woke up and elbowed him.

Then Mr. Herringbone sat for a time bolt upright.

Then began to roll and pitch again as before.

But before very long the darkness without was relieved with certain specks of light, which Fanny with some difficulty made out to be lamps along the roadside.

Then she caught a glimpse of the gloomy outlines of houses.

Then there was an alteration in the noise made by the wheels.

The coach was going over a paved road.

There were houses, then streets, and squares, and crescents.

A large building, probably the town-hall.

Something which, at first sight, she took to be a statue, but which proved to be a pump.

Plenty of gaslights now.

Then a sudden halt and the shouting of the guard to the sleepy ostler at the inn.

A great deal more shouting directly, in chorus, and then a small crowd gathering round the coach-door, in which was a very sleepy waiter, and a sleepier chambermaid.

This latter came forward with her head wrapped up in a pocket-handkerchief, to guard against cold.

"Beds, gentlemen!" said she.

"Three," said Mr. Pudding.

"And the lady?" inquired the chambermaid.

"I also shall require an apartment," replied Fanny.

"Certainly, ma'am—this way, ma'am."

Fanny descended and followed the young woman into the hotel.

The chambermaid conducted her upstairs, and showed her a room which she could have.

Fanny objected to its size.

There was nothing better to be had.

In that case, then, she must put up with it, and get on as well as she could.

Would she have any supper?

No, nothing; she only wanted to go to sleep.

Wanted to go to sleep, indeed!

She thought she never, in all her life, had felt half as wearied.

She was almost dead with fatigue.

She could scarcely keep awake to undress herself.

She tore off her clothes and flung them carelessly down.

She, however, took particular notice of the fastening of the door.

Also looked under the bed.

Then having placed the candle in the washhand-basin, she got into bed, and had hardly placed her head upon the pillow before she fell asleep.

She had strange dreams.

She thought she was again in the cave.

She saw again the horrors which she had been a witness to.

Again she was pursued by the hideous hunchback.

Again she was struggling in the embraces of that amorous monster.

She awoke with a half shriek, but all was perfectly still.

When she slept again, all the leading events of her life seemed to pass, one after the other, in rapid succession, through her mind.

Her feats at school.

Her loves with Jack Rawlings.

The old house at Fulham and Lord Crokerton.

Her highway robberies.

The madhouse.

Her career as a ballet girl.

Again she awoke.

This time, however, it was broad daylight.

She did not feel inclined to spend any more time in bed.

She would get up.

There was a great noise and bustle in the street below.

Something curious was happening.

She got up and looked out of the window.

She little thought though, that she was going to take the part she eventually did in the revival which was agitating the town.

The High-street of Little Peddlington, ordinarily so quiet, wore upon this occasion a most animated appearance.

The pavement on either side was thronged.

There were indeed so many pedestrians that the road itself was full.

The peculiarity of the assemblage, however, appearing to Fanny to be that they were of a remarkably sanctified aspect.

There were a great number of the male kind, but they all wore sober clothes.

Most of them had on their Sunday suits, which were black and shiny, though as a general rule a good deal creased—a circumstance which indicated that they had been injudiciously folded, when put away into drawers.

The softer sex were, also, very serious indeed.

There was every variety of provincial female.

Some somewhat gaily attired, for godliness is not altogether opposed to smart ribbons in the creed of most ladies.

The greater part, however, wore dingy blacks and dowdy browns and shabby greys.

The greater part, also, wore good strong boots, which creaked loudly as they walked—a very sylph-like proceeding which, with a strong smell of hot pressed stuff, made these coy creatures charming company, no doubt, to the young men they kept company with.

Some of the ladies certainly had a large share of good looks.

Their greatest enemies must have allowed it—or ought to have done so.

Though I suppose women don't allow much beauty in their rivals—that is to say, not if they are beautiful.

And by the way I have often found that ladies are rapturous about unmistakeably plain friends.

There was every style here to-day in Little Peddlington.

There were the plumpy or fat, the scraggy or lean.

There were fine women, big enough for troopers.

There were young creatures, all grace and animation, whom Shylock would have been rather puzzled to have got his pound of flesh off.

There were red-haired maidens, with down-cast eyes, who I have no doubt were as naughty as they well could be, for all they looked so sly about it.

There were maidens with straw-coloured hair—a colour lately come into fashion with story-book writers; but most of these were unfortunately inclined to an unbecoming pinkness about the nose, and which you will find, if you take notice, is not an uncommon characteristic of "the woman with the yellow hair."

There were some very small maidens, but these made ever so much the most bustle in the throng, and took up more of the pavement than any of the big ones.

Certain maidens were there, too, who had been much too cruel upon mankind, and kept themselves perhaps a trifle too long in single blessedness, and they wore a vinegarish aspect, and were very severe indeed upon such of the other maidens who were inclined to be skittish.

There were a great many more women than men in the street Fanny saw.

She had often noticed the same thing at church, when she was in the habit of going to church, which she had not been very lately.

She therefore concluded that the crowd was owing to the great religious revival which she had heard the reverend gents in the mail-coach discussing.

There were a good many men also, of course; but nothing like so many men as women.

It is rather a sad reflection, too, but men are always backward where religion is concerned.

How is it?

Are they more unbelieving? haven't they time?

But this last idea is really too monstrous!

Nevertheless, it was one of Miss Fanny's ideas as she looked through the window in her nightcap.

"I dare say—in fact, I am certain—that most women go to church only because they've nothing else to do; and it's a sort of feeble excitement to them, poor creatures," said Fanny, with a laugh. "Sometimes they draw great houses where there's a handsome clergyman; but I shouldn't think that pretty parsons were popular with men. What would be, I wonder? Why, dash my buttons——"

Now, the reason why Miss White made use of this extremely unladylike expression, it was rather difficult to explain.

In the first place she wore no buttons, or at least an odd one or two on her petticoats; and the dashing of these would only have led to extremely unpleasant results.

Perhaps it was a saying which had become familiar to her when she donned male attire.

After all it doesn't matter.

She did say it anyhow.

"Dash my buttons," said Fanny, "I'll do it. I'll turn parson myself. It will be a novelty, at any rate. But how to set about it?"

That was a poser.

First thing, though, was to get dressed.

She lost little time over her toilet, although she managed to look very captivating at its conclusion.

Then she rang the bell.

It was answered by the chambermaid.

The same one Fanny had seen over night.

"Did you ring, miss?"

"Yes. What o'clock is it?"

"Just twelve, miss."

"So late?"

"We thought you were tired and would not disturb you."

"I am much obliged to you."

"Will you have breakfast, miss?"

"Yes—no. Where are those gentlemen who came with me last night?"

"Attending a meeting at the Little Ebenezer."

"Have they said when they would come back?"

"Yes, miss."

"When?"

"At one o'clock, to luncheon."

"Will they be alone, do you suppose?"

"I think so, miss; they have only ordered for three."

"What have they ordered?"

"I don't know, miss?"

"I want you to find out, then."

The girl stared.

"You needn't be astonished, and you needn't tell everybody in the house," said Fanny, "and perhaps you wont lose by it."

"I shouldn't think of mentioning anything, miss."

"I am sure of that, only don't."

"No, miss."

"Here's half a sovereign for you; now go and find out what they have ordered, and counter order it."

"Do what, miss?"

"Order whatever the gentlemen have ordered not to be cooked."

"But——"

"But what."

"If they should be angry."

"They wont be."

"Only I thought——"

"You needn't think anything about it; they are going to have luncheon with——"

"Have you asked them, miss?"

"I'm going to."

"But——"

"I told you I wouldn't have any buts. Go and do as I tell you."

The girl, without further argument, departed.

After a short delay she again entered.

"Well?" said Fanny.

"Chops and tomato-sauce."

"Very well. Have you got a good cook?"

"A very respectable person, miss."

"Bother his respectability. Has he got an idea beyond a savage?"

"Eh?"

"Can he make anything fit to eat?"

"He, miss? It's a she."

"A she, eh? Then I don't expect she can do very much; however, send her up here."

"Up here, miss."

"Yes."

"Certainly, miss."

"Go at once, then."

The servant left the room to do Miss White's bidding.

"That girl's a fool!" said Fanny; "but it's not uncommon in girls, either. I hate 'em."

Presently the cook came up.

She was very gracious and obliging. None the less so when Fanny had made her a little present.

"Cook," said she, "what can you let me have for luncheon?"

The cook considered awhile.

"It must be something very nice."

"Chops, miss."

"Something better."

"Eggs and bac——"

"Don't mention them. Have you any poultry?"

"Yes, miss."

"Can you cook an omelette?"

"I think so, miss."

"Well—well. Do whatever you can, but mind it must be something very nice indeed, and I shan't forget you for your trouble, if you please me."

The cook promised great things, though Fanny had no great hopes of the result.

She did not, however, say anything likely to discourage her, as she thought such a course would be an unwise one.

Fanny ordered a cup of tea and some bread and butter for her breakfast, and having been shown into a private sitting room, was at her own request supplied with writing materials.

Then, after some consideration, she sat down and wrote a note.

It was not exactly what you might call a ladylike handwriting, that of Miss Fanny.

That is to say, the tails of her y's were within limits, and her t's had not got loops to them.

It was not such a very legible hand, though, mind you.

Indeed it was decidedly indistinct.

There was a great deal of dash about it, let alone a smudge or two, and perhaps now and then a few difficulties in the way of spelling were more easily got over in a flourish than any other way.

However, that is neither here nor there. We are not going to talk about the style, but the contents of the letter which she indited.

It was addressed to one of the Right Reverend gents with whom she had travelled over night.

She recollected his name very well, because it was rather a peculiar one.

Had she forgotten, however, there was quite enough outside the window to recal the extraordinary cognomination to her mind.

Yes, right opposite to the hotel upon a dead wall was one of those enormous six-sheet posters, on which were these words—

TO-NIGHT! TO-NIGHT!! TO-NIGHT!!!

JACK PUDDING! JACK PUDDING! JACK PUDDING!

THE REVEREND HUMOROUS PREACHER,

FOR THIS NIGHT ONLY, AT AN ENORMOUS EXPENSE,

Has been engaged to Deliver an Oration at

THE GREAT AWAKENING MEETING,

AT THE LITTLE EBENEZER CHAPEL,

BACKSLIDER-STREET,

UPON

"THE LUSTS OF THE FLESH, AND THE LURES OF THE DEVIL;"

WITH

HORRIBLE DETAILS, AND A CLOG HORNPIPE.

Be in Time! Be in Time! Be in Time!

ADMISSION ONLY THREEPENCE.

Babies in arms not allowed to be awakened.

A very startling bill that was, certainly; but it was evidently just the sort of thing that was wanted.

Scores of people had congregated around it during the short time that Fanny had been looking out of the window.

Open-mouthed maidens had read it eagerly.

Wooden-headed rustics had scratched them (their own heads, I mean, not the open-mouthed maidens) and spelled through the astonishing announcement.

It would be difficult to say which were the greatest attraction, the "Horrible Details," or the "Clog Hornpipe."

But both combined were very sure of drawing a great chapel full of rustics.

But it was a question of the reverend gentleman's name that was occupying us.

It was, then, to the Reverend Jack that Fanny directed her letter, it ran as follows :—

"The Countess of Castlecounterpayne presents her compliments to the Reverend Mr. Pudding, and his reverend fellow-travellers, and requests the honour of their company to luncheon at one o'clock, when the Countess of Castlecounterpayne would esteem it a great favour if the reverend gentlemen would offer her some suggestions respecting the disposal of fifty pounds."

This was the letter. When it was written, Fanny gave it to the housemaid.

"I may remain here for a day or two," said Miss White. "Should anyone come to inquire for the Countess of Castlecounterpayne, it will be for me. I expect some of my servants may be here to-morrow or next day. I sincerely trust they may, for I am really lost without my attendants."

It was a wondrous sight to behold the way in which the servant-girl's face changed as Miss Fanny White thus addressed her.

I can hope to give you no idea of it, and unfortunately Mr. ROBERT PROWSE, whose clever pencil illustrates this work, has got another subject to manage.

She, however, grew more and more humble as she grew more and more confused.

Her style of addressing Miss Fanny underwent astonishing changes.

To begin with, it was "Yes, miss."

Then it got to "Yes, m-m-um."

Then to "Yes, me-lady."

Then to "Yes, your grace."

Lastly to "Yes, my lady—I beg your grace's pardon—I mean your ladyship—certainly—may it please you—I should say—exactly."

And the poor girl got herself into a terrible fix, and not only that.

The double knot which she seemed to have tied her tongue in appeared to have extended to her legs, for as she went out of the door they somehow got into confusion, and she sprawled upon the ground in a way which must have been extremely harassing to any modest virgin's feelings, even though it occurred before a person of her own sex.

For as that person was a countess, the poor little housemaid was horror-struck at the idea of having exhibited a reversed crinoline in so great a lady's presence.

Miss Fanny, however, was not too easily shocked.

She could see a good deal, I daresay, without—as the saying is—being struck blind.

She, therefore, kept her countenance as well as she could, whilst the young lady got the proper side up again.

The housemaid, for her part, was glad enough to get away.

She ran downstairs, and told the landlady who she had got in the house.

"The Countess of Castlecounterpayne !" cried the landlady in astonishment.

"A live countess," said the landlord.

"And such a lot of money !" said the housemaid.

"How do you know ?"

"I saw she had a purse full of gold."

"Bless me !"

"Yes; and such jewels !"

"You don't mean it ?"

"I do, though."

"I shouldn't have thought it."

"Oh, hundreds of pounds' worth !"

"Good gracious !"

"More than that, though !"

"Gracious goodness !"

"Oh, thousands and thousands !"

The news spread like wild-fire.

It was all over the hotel in a very short time.

It was all over the town very soon after.

People stared up at the windows of the hotel, and stood upon the other side of the way, endeavouring to catch a glimpse of the illustrious inmate.

Some of the other lodgers in the hotel crept on tip-toe upstairs, and peeped through the key-hole at the great lady.

It would have been rather embarrassing to Miss Fanny, I suppose, bold as she was, if she had known what was going on.

Luckily for her, though, she did not know; and so did not feel uncomfortable.

When the reverend gentlemen came home from the Ebenezer, the housemaid gave them the letter.

Great astonishment was depicted in the face of the Reverend Jack.

He opened his goggle-eyes to the utmost.

He opened his huge mouth.

"Hallo—what—which—where—I say, who sent this, young woman ?"

The housemaid told him.

The Reverend Jack scratched his head and re-read the letter.

When the girl had left the room, he said to his companions—

"Look here, Bill ! Read this !"

The reverend gent addressed, ran his eye over the contents of Fanny's note.

"Well !" said Mr. Pudding.

"Well !"

"Well !"

"Here's a go !"

"Queer thing, isn't it ?"

"Rather so."

"Just the thing we wanted."

"I believe you."

"Fifty pounds !—not bad, eh ?"

"There's more behind it, perhaps."

"Hundreds, most likely."

"But, I say——"

"Yes."

"Shall we go ?"

"Of course we must !"

"But then——"

"What ?"

"Do you think our togs are the correct thing ?"

"Oh, yes."

"Oughtn't we to have tail-coats ?"

"No; I don't think so."

"I hardly like it."

"Why not ?"

"Oh, I don't know. By the way, do you say 'My Lady' to a countess ?"

"Well—a—yes; I believe so. Shall we go up ?"

" Yes ; I think we'd better wash our hands first, though."

The reverend gents were in a great fluster.

It is all very well for the writers of the stories in half-penny and penny romances to talk of the aristocracy as though they were hand-and-glove with the upper ten-thousand.

Don't you believe them, though.

It is all very fine for these gentlemen at home in their attics to make so free ; but mind you, there is nothing that takes it out of a free-born Briton so much as talking to a lord.

If you want to see John Bull to a disadvantage—if you want to see a poor, truckling, cringing, lickspittling wretch, in short—then is your time.

And as it would be with your penny romance-writers (me among the rest, if you like ; for I don't care a button whether or not you believe that I am a man of property, and keep the best of carriage company), so it was with these reverend gents ; who, though they were on familiar terms with the Scriptures, none of them knew how to address a lady of title.

The shepherds had a consultation, and agreed that it would be best to send up and inquire whether the countess could receive them.

Fanny then sent down word that she could.

The reverend gents then, in a great flutter, trooped up stairs.

They found the lady ready to receive them, looking very beautiful.

Since she had sent the letter Fanny had been very busy.

She had sent for the best milliner in the town ; and although it was almost a public holiday, and scarcely a stroke of work was doing, she had little trouble in finding some one to do her bidding.

The reason was because it had got about that she was a countess.

Who would not serve a countess?

There was so much curiosity, too, respecting her.

It was a privilege to get a peep at her.

The milliner, therefore, came open-eared and open-mouthed.

She came, intending to be astonished.

She went away, though, more astonished than she expected to be.

Why? you ask.

Presently you will learn, perhaps ; but not until the proper time.

To return to the reverend gents, however. They came in, and found Miss Fanny looking very beautiful.

She rose, and smiled graciously.

They bowed with all the grace they could command.

Which was not much, by the way ; but that does not matter.

The Reverend Jack entered first.

He bowed, and brought down his head almost to the carpet.

In doing so, of course his coat-tails bobbed out.

He gave the next reverend therefore rather a severe bump in the waistcoat.

This reverend gasped for breath, and fell back upon the third.

They were all three treading upon one another's toes in the doorway, and rolling about like agitated ninepins.

Miss Fanny graciously requested them to be seated.

Then the three reverend gents sat upon the extreme edge of three separate chairs.

They all three looked extremely sheepish.

Miss Fanny put on the air of a condescending countess, or as near that as she could manage.

" I am truly grateful for this visit, gentlemen," said she.

" Not at all, thank you," replied the Reverend Jack, who had not any idea of what he was saying.

" I shall never cease to be grateful when I think of the chance that threw me into your company."

" But it was not chance ; it was the hand of Providence which guided my steps. Yes, my lady, we are all weak vessels," said the Reverend Jack, "and know not what is coming next."

" Luncheon is ready, my lady," said the housemaid, appearing at this point.

" Serve it," said Fanny.

The lunch was broughti n, and laid upon the table.

It certainly was a wonderful spread.

The very best wine, too.

The reverend gents sniffed savoury odour, and dug one another in the ribs.

Fanny bade them be seated, smiling graciously.

Five minutes afterwards all three shepherds were gorging like pigs.

They were a little bashful at first, but the waiter kept their glasses full.

They gained confidence as the bottles shrunk.

Presently the countess began to talk about business.

She asked how the awakening was getting on.

The Reverend Jack said that they hoped for a full chapel that evening. He was afraid, however, that it would not be the same next night.

" The vulgar mind requires novelty," said the countess.

" Indeed it does, my lady."

" Do you believe in the doctrine of the end justifying the means. ?"

" To a certain extent, my lady."

" I have been trying to think how I can help you."

" You are too good, my lady."

" If my name will be of any service."

" Can you ask, my lady ?"

" But I have thought of a plan of helping you more."

" Oh ! my lady."

" I mention fifty pounds."

The reverend gents looked eager.

" My bankers will send it down the day after to-morrow."

" Oh ! my lady."

" To-morrow night, if it will be of any service to you, I will preach a sermon."

" You, my lady ?"

" Here are five pounds which you will kindly spend in bills, and I think you had better lose no time in taking the necessary steps."

The reverend gents were wild with delight ; they had been in search of a novelty.

Here was one.

A tremendous novelty.

It was something uncommon to find a female preacher.

But to think that she should be a lady of title !

And so beautiful a lady.

When they left the room they talked it over.

" Do you think that she will be able to preach, Jack ?" asked one.

" I shouldn't think so."

" Well, then——"

" What does it matter when we've collared the money at the doors ? we shan't return it."

" Catch us doing that."

" Ah ! ah ! ah !"

" Oh ! oh ! oh !"

" He ! he ! he !"

They rushed frantically to the printer's to get the bills done.

That night they were finished and stuck upon the walls.

Next morning the town got up to find the announcement staring them in the face.

Meanwhile, however, the Reverend Jack's oration came off with great success.

There was a crowded chapel.

The horrible details thrilled through all the listeners' hearts.

The clog hornpipe caused roars of laughter.

Miss Fanny had a conspicuous place and attracted universal attention.

She looked very beautiful.

Everybody by this time knew who she was.

The Reverend Jack publicly thanked her for her liberality and announced that she would preach next night.

Miss Fanny was not very bashful, so she kept her countenance.

The flock, however, stared at her, open-mouthed, and there was a loud buzz of wonder.

" We shall pot some tin to-morrow," said the Reverend Jack, " mind if we don't."

And so they did, but they little thought what the next day would bring forth.

CHAPTER LXXII.

FANNY ASTONISHES THE NATIVES, BEWILDERS THE SHEPHERDS, AND DANCES A FANDANGO.

ALL day long the greatest excitement prevailed.

Everybody was talking of the coming event.

The reserved seats in the Little Ebenezer sold like wild-fire.

When the time came for the doors to open there was a terrific crowd which reached across the street.

It was a wonderful sight to see the flock jostling each other for the best places.

I don't suppose old women were ever half as "squodged" as they were that evening.

The young ladies didn't so much mind it, although they said they did.

As for the young men, you recollect what Jonas Chuzzlewit said, he liked to be squeezed by "gals."

To tell the truth, it is not unpleasant when they are what is called plumby or crumby. What do you think, my lady—I mean to say, gentlemen readers?

A great number of other people besides the usual flock, attended; indeed, there was scarcely an inch of room to spare in the chapel when the time came for the lady to begin her sermon.

All day long Miss Fanny had been rehearsing. She had written her discourse over night, and now she was quite prepared.

She came into the chapel, conducted by the Reverend Jack, who bowed her in.

She slowly ascended the steps to the pulpit.

There was a death-like silence.

A pin might have been heard to fall.

There was a pause, during which the countess slowly gazed around.

She slowly raised her hand.

She pointed to a particular young man in a near seat. Then suddenly asked—

"What brings you here? Is it to look at me? Is it to hear me? What do you want to see? What do you want to hear? I have nothing to say which you will think is worth listening to. Go away! go away! go away! —or—stop. The devil is waiting for you outside—not the devil you are accustomed to; he is artfully disguised this time; you will find him in a female shape; a beautiful woman with a swelling bust, red, pouting lips, the last thing out in bonnets, and one of 'Thomson's Prize Medal Crinolines.' But oh! beware of her, young gentleman with the auburn whiskers, and beautiful blue neck tie! Beware of her, for she is as great a devil as ever there was, and if you go her way you go to Hell."

Never before had the Little Ebenezers listened to such a wonderful address.

Never before had they heard such a delivery.

Never such wonderful acting.

The sermon thus began in a playful strain, but every now and then there came a startling climax, which electrified the listeners.

Gradually, though by slow degrees, the discourse got more and more thrilling.

Hell and damnation were dealt out freely.

The most fearful pictures of everlasting torment conjured up.

Then the most glowing descriptions of vice—descriptions in which the vice was perhaps depicted in rather too enticing a form, had not the awful consequences been immediately dragged before the eyes of the terrified hearers.

Gradually, as the countess proceeded, she warmed more and more with the subject.

She carried all before her, as she herself appeared to be carried away by the things of which she spoke.

Women sobbed, and shrieked, and fainted.

Smelling salts were in great request.

So were the shepherds, who did all in their power to revive such of the young ladies as were carried away by their feelings.

If they were not always successful, it certainly was not their fault.

After the discourse was concluded, the Reverend Jack Pudding went round to make a collection, and probably so much was never before taken in any Methodist chapel.

The discourse over, the countess returned to her hotel in triumph, after promising to preach again next night at the town-hall. And next night the crowd was truly terrific.

The admission had been raised, but yet more people came. Indeed, they came from all parts of the surrounding country to which the news had spread.

Fanny was listened to in wonder and received with deafening applause.

Such poetical language, such startling arguments, such warm and voluptuous imagery, and such savage denunciation, had never before been listened to by the worthy folks of that slow-going town.

The old women were struck dumb.

The young women were fiercely jealous.

Every man, young and old, was madly in love with the bewitching preacher.

When the evening came to an end, Miss Fanny invited the shepherds to her rooms, where a sumptuous supper was prepared for them.

She went to the hotel some time previous and prepared to receive them.

When they came she looked very lovely.

She had dressed herself in a wonderful robe, of a soft and clinging, half transparent character.

At the neck it was cut very low.

It exposed, in all their voluptuous splendour, the swelling globes of ivory whiteness which adorned her snow-white bosom.

To say that the rest of her fair person was concealed by the dress which covered it would, however, be gross exaggeration.

All the matchless symmetry of her form was fully developed.

Anything more luscious than her attire cannot be conceived.

The Greek dancing-girls would in vain have sought for a dress more calculated to inflame the passions of their masters, and excite a burning lust in the breasts of their depraved audience.

How can I hope to tell you what was the effect of her costume upon the three reverend gents.

They were all admirers of the ladies, as other shepherds have been before them.

They all went largely in for the good things which Miss Fanny had provided for them.

They all dipped their reverend red noses pretty deeply into the wine.

The result was that they all three grew rather excited.

They began by talking a great quantity of nonsense; they got on to acting very absurdly.

"Why should we ever separate?" asked Fanny. "Why not go round the world, showing to the best of our capability which is the path that should be chosen by the righteous?"

"Certainly," said the Reverend Jack, with a hiccup.

Then Fanny proposed that she should always remain with the reverend gentlemen; that she should pay all expenses, and that all they gained by her preaching should be saved, and spent in the building of a large chapel in London.

The reverend gentlemen desired nothing better, they said, and kicked one another under the table.

But the Reverend Jack Pudding suggested that a slight drawback existed, in the fact of the countess being a single woman.

If now she could only stoop from her high estate—if she could forget her noble birth, &c.

The other gents, however, cut Jack rather short when he was thus talking, and they would have got at loggerheads, had not the countess rung for coffee.

By the time this was served the three reverends were considerably the worse for liquor.

They had grown very incoherent, let alone amorous.

But the climax was to come.

After coffee the syren proposed a liquor—something which she said she had brought home from Spain.

The shepherds took small glasses round and thought it delicious.

They could never tell exactly how it all came about, though.

Somehow they were growing very confused.

Next morning they had a vague idea that the countess, arrayed like a ballet-girl, a sylph, a water-nymph, at any rate arrayed in the scantiest attire, had danced a Spanish fandango.

Oh! a delicious, maddening dance it was.

In which she flung her lovely shape into the most bewitching postures.

In which every art was employed to excite the imagination with pictures of riotous and lawless love.

But I need not try to describe what a fandango is like.

All travellers will tell you that it is the most shamefully indecent and disgraceful exhibition.

Oh! what—what a very wicked young woman that Miss White was!

And oh, what naughty shepherds!

When they awoke next morning with splitting headaches they asked after the countess.

There was great consternation in the hotel.

The countess had bolted!

She had not paid her bill.

She had robbed the reverend gents, too, of all the money that had been taken at the three nights' orations.

The Reverend Jack had had charge of it and he could not account for its disappearance.

Oh, young men and shepherds, beware of lady preachers who wear shockingly short frocks and dance fandangos.

The Reverend Jack was somewhat blamed at first though, until he could make a full explanation of his conduct.

One of the waiters of the hotel deposed to having met the worthy gentleman in the middle of the night wandering about in a hopeless state.

And I regret to say, in his shirt.

The housemaid had something to add.

She had heard suppressed screams.

The screams of a female in distress.

Whose screams were they?

That was the question.

The housemaid thought they were Fanny's, and consequently as she had no great love for that lady, lay in bed and chuckled.

However, the housemaid was mistaken.

They were not the cries of the countess.

Upon this occasion her most precious virtue was not in danger.

But in the next room to Fanny there slept an ancient spinster, aged threescore.

She unhappily left her door unlocked.

The Reverend Jack had drunk too much to be very certain of anything.

Alas! this poor fair one fell a victim to a fatal error.

Not an easy victim though, for she fought furiously in the ravisher's grasp.

She fought like half-a-dozen Lucretias rolled into one.

But the Reverend Jack on his side behaved like half-a-dozen Tarquins.

I drop the curtain upon the dreadful scene.

Let us not rudely intrude upon the spectacle of this despoiled maiden, weeping piteously over that which, let us suppose, was dearer to her than her life.

That which she had jealously guarded these threescore years.

CHAPTER LXXIII.

FANNY DISTRIBUTES TRACTS.

FIVE weeks after the events just related, all the newspapers were full of the account of a daring burglary which had been committed at one of the principal manufacturing towns in the north of England.

The persons concerned in this robbery were well-known offenders.

One was Jack Rawlings.

The other Harry Belvoir.

The former was caught, committed for trial, and sentenced to a long term of penal servitude.

Harry Belvoir escaped.

And Fanny? Had she deserted her old love? We shall see.

Allow me to present her to you under rather novel circumstances.

She is now called Miss Marianne Stanley, and she is a lady of independent means and lives in lodgings in the best part of the manufacturing town where the robbery has been committed.

It was the early part of an autumn, very clear, but rather cold.

In her parlour, in the dwelling above described, sat Miss Fanny—I mean to say Miss Stanley—by the side of her dining-table, upon which yet lay the remains of a costly dessert, and on which a large moderator-lamp burnt brightly.

A blazing fire before her cast a warm and ruddy glow around upon rich sofas, comfortable arm-chairs, and heavy damask curtains, which lent to the apartment an air of supreme comfort and luxuriousness.

The lamp-light fell upon the face and form of Fanny.

It revealed then a fuller perfection of beauty than when we first saw her at the pic-nic in our first chapter.

The bud had expanded into a glorious flower of womanhood.

As she sat there, dressed in a deep blue velvet robe, fitting tightly to her symmetrical person so as to show her voluptuous figure to the best advantage, she exhibited a picture of female loveliness rarely, if ever, equalled.

The well-turned features of her face bore upon them no traces of the wild life she had led, neither did they reveal anything of the storm raging within her bosom.

Her head reclined upon her milk-white hand.

Her fingers, covered with rich and sparkling gems, were half concealed by her golden curls.

She was pensively contemplating the fire.

Her face was calm as is the face of a loving and virtuous wife.

She might have been rejoicing in the possession of a cherished home; might have been glorying in her innocence. But, alas! we know that she could have no such consolation.

Calm and passionless as she seemed, her heart was in a feverish whirl.

She was fiercely and resolutely contemplating a bold scheme of action.

She was endeavouring to concoct some plan of delivery for her lover.

She sat thus for some time.

Then suddenly arose, and rang the bell.

She had made up her mind upon the course she was to pursue.

A plump maid-servant answered the summons.

"Emma," said Fanny, "do you know where that Mr. Sleekey, the Methodist minister, lives?"

Emma smiled.

"I know, I think, miss."

"Isn't he a tailor as well as a preacher?"

"Yes, miss."

"Go to his shop, then, at once, and tell him I should be glad to see him."

Emma retired with another broad grin; and, after a brief delay, returned with the Mr. Sleekey in question.

Mr. Sleekey was a tall and angular man.

He had a very spare person.

He had a very red nose.

His lips were rather sensual; and he had an eye which, for a minister, was a sly one.

As he entered the room, though he was as solemn as a judge, not the faintest smile illuminated his countenance.

Yet he looked a little sly for all that, and Miss Emma grinned broader than ever.

The reason was, that this sanctified tailor was known by the serving-maid to entertain a sneaking fondness for her mistress.

"Good evening, Mr. Sleekey."

"Good evening, miss," said the tailor.

As he spoke, the visitor's eye ran eagerly over the beautiful form before him, and fell again beneath her gaze to the carpet.

"I have sent for you," said Fanny.

"Certainly, miss," said the tailor.

"It is upon a very delicate matter I wish to see you."

"Indeed, miss."

"I may, though, I hope, trust to your honour not to reveal what may transpire between us."

"Certainly not, miss."

"Not to anybody."

"No, miss."

"Particularly not to your wife."

"Oh! certainly not to her, miss."

"I wish, then, that you should measure me for a suit of clothes."

"Measure you, miss?"

"For a suit of clerical clothes, such as the ministers of your church array themselves in on Sunday."

"What coat, waistcoat, and—and——"

"And trousers, to be sure. I don't want to be dressed like a Highlannder."

"No, no, miss, certainly."

"A complete suit, and to fit to a nicety."

"Oh, certainly, miss; but——"

"Well?"

"I am afraid that according to the law——"

"What now?"

"It is not allowable for one of your sex to assume our apparel."

"Never mind that," said Fanny. "I'll pay well."

And as she spoke she laid some shining sovereigns upon the table.

Mr. Sleekey eyed her and the money, and said—

"I have no objection, I am sure."

"Please to measure me."

Then Fanny drew herself up to her full height, and smiled blandly.

Mr. Sleekey produced his tape, and went to work; but he was in a great flutter. He was afraid of coming too near her.

"That's too loose," said she.

Then again.

"That's too tight."

"Will that do?"

"That's much better."

"Does that hurt you?"

"On the contrary."

"How low will you have the waistcoat?"

"So far. That will do."

"I've not got down the right number, I think," said Mr. Sleekey; "I must try the last measure again."

Indeed he was very nervous for some reason or other.

He trembled violently.

He twitched his tape over her person in a jerking sort of way, and his hands wandered in a bewildered way over her fair form.

His face was very much flushed, too, and his nose was redder than ever.

"That will do," said Fanny at last, thinking that the measurement had lasted quite long enough. "Let me have the clothes to-morrow night. Can you?"

"Oh, yes; I think so."

"How much will they be?"

The tailor paused a moment.

Then plumped down on his knees and covered her hands with burning kisses.

"Nothing to you, beautiful creature! I will make them for love if—if——"

But the words died from his lips when he saw the expression of the face of the woman before him.

There was something awfully threatening in it, which quite cooled his ardour.

"Are you mad?" asked Fanny. "Get up."

Then the tailor got up on his feet, and pocketing the money, beat a retreat, looking rather sheepish.

Two days afterwards, a very prim, methodistical young gentleman presented an order to inspect the county prison, signed by one of the visiting magistrates.

The jailor on the lock that day was not very fond of parsons, but as this one had a well-filled purse, he took to him more kindly than usual.

"Will you have any objection," said the young Methodist gentleman to the warder who conducted him round the prison, "to my distributing a few tracts among the prisoners?"

"What are they?" asked the warder.

"'Light in Darkness,' 'A Kiss for a Blow,' &c., &c.," said the Methodist gentleman, reading over the names.

The warder looked at them, and gave his assent.

Then he took the visitor upon a journey of inspection.

The young gentleman followed him through the prison, distributing his tracts, and talking so very sociably with his conductor, that the latter said he was the only parson he had ever known "as was not a humbug."

As the young gentleman walked along, though, if the other had eyed him narrowly, he would have been observed to peer anxiously around, as though in search for some well-known face.

He closely scanned each prisoner as he went.

But when the journey had almost come to an end a dark shade of disappointment passed over the Methodist gentleman's face.

"Where's the celebrated Rawlings?" he asked at last.

The jailor stopped before the door of a cell almost at the same moment.

"He is here," said the jailor. "He has been rather unruly, so we've had to lock him up alone. To-morrow, though, he will go back to the rest, if he behaves decently. Would you like to see him?"

"Yes; I feel some curiosity to look at him."

The door was opened, and there, sure enough, sat Jack Rawlings upon a hard bench, looking very pale and haggard.

As the door grated upon its hinges, Jack looked up.

He started when he saw the Methodist gentleman.

The Methodist gentleman laid his finger upon his lip for a moment, and winked his left eye.

Then Jack subsided into a careless attitude, and stared listlessly at his visitor.

"Here, my good man," said the young parson, "is a nice tract for you to read."

As he spoke, the Methodist handed him one.

Somehow it was rather thicker than usual, though.

Perhaps the Methodist thought that Rawlings required a stronger dose than the rest.

As for the jailor, he took no particular notice.

The cell was not very light and it was not very easy to detect that there was something between the leaves of the little work she had given him.

"Read it and benefit by its contents," said the Methodist gentleman, as he walked away, heaving a deep sigh.

"He's a bad 'un," said the jailor; "but his game is pretty well up."

"Was he not a companion of the notorious Fanny White?"

"Yes, he was, and an awful hussy she is, I'm told, but we'll warm her some day."

"Mind you keep a tight hold of her when you get her," said the Methodist gentleman.

"There is no fear of that," said the jailor.

The Methodist gentleman went straight home to Fanny's apartments, and changed his clerical suit for female attire.

"Dash my buttons!" said Fanny, as she lit a cigar, "only think of my coming the tract-distributing dodge. I wonder what I shall have to do next."

CHAPTER LXXIV.

THE BETRAYAL.

THE tract which Fanny had left her friend Jack, contained words of wisdom; it also contained three files and a gimlet.

Also a note which ran thus:—

"Dear, how are you?

"Work away with all your might.

"Here is a plan of the prison.

"Harry Belvoir will bribe the jailors so that he can communicate with you.

"Yours truly,
"FANNY."

Who shall say what was not Jack Rawlings's joy at the receipt of this letter?

It dissipated at once the gloom of his cell.

But to begin.

After some little consideration he determined to wait until he was taken out of solitary confinement.

In the course of two or three days he was put into another cell with a companion.

To this man he communicated the scheme.

One of the jailors also found an opportunity of whispering to him that he was his friend.

Jack rather mistrusted this individual, but he received a letter from Fanny to say that it is now all right.

Then they began their work.

The first night they managed to make an incision round the back of the door, which in the morning they concealed with putty, which the other prisoner had contrived to obtain.

Next night they set to work again.

Upon the same evening Fanny was waiting at her lodgings with great impatience, for she expected to receive tidings from her lover.

THE MARRIAGE OF FANNY WHITE WITH LORD CROKERTON.

Every moment she consulted her watch. Every sound in the street without, caused her to start and listen.

At last there came a knock at the door, and Harry Belvoir entered.

He kissed her hand gallantly and seated himself by the fire.

"Well!" said Fanny, "what is doing?"

"Everything progresses satisfactorily."

"How about the jailor?"

"I've squared him."

"Is he safe?"

"Safe as the bank."

"I hardly like trusting him!"

"You can, though; I am sure of him."

"And when do you think he will be free?" asked Fanny, eagerly.

"To-morrow."

"To-morrow?" she repeated, with joy.

Her eyes sparkled as she spoke, and she looked very beautiful.

Harry Belvoir thought so too, but said nothing.

He also thought what a pity it was she should love Jack and not him.

While they chatted over future prospects, they took supper together, and the wine circulated freely.

Fanny was in high spirits, and looked more beautiful than ever Belvoir thought.

From time to time he devoured her with a passionate gaze; but she was quite unconscious of his sentiments towards her.

She thought that their little flirtation had come to an end long ago.

"Good night," she said, at last. "To-morrow we shall all three meet."

"Not if I know it," said Belvoir, as he strolled homewards, smoking his cigar.

Belvoir was a villain. He had affected to join her in assisting Jack to escape, but he never intended that his rival should pass the prison-doors.

On the contrary, he desired that Rawlings should make the attempt, and be captured.

This would cause his term of imprisonment to be lengthened, Belvoir thought to himself, with a fiendish chuckle.

He had conceived a violent passion, too, for Fanny; and had vowed before Heaven that she should be his.

Surely enough he conducted the first part of his hellish scheme.

The hour arrived when Jack intended to attempt his escape.

A deathlike silence reigned throughout the prison.

Jack and his accomplice worked noiselessly.

They had cut a way through the door.

They raised the lock.

They drew back the bolts.

Then stealthily crept forth.

But upon the other side a sight awaited them which made their hearts sink within their breasts.

Three or four jailors were ready to receive them. Among them the man whom they had supposed to be their friend.

Fanny again sat waiting and listening.

She expected her lover to arrive.

In his place, however, at the appointed time, came instead Harry Belvoir.

Fanny sprang to her feet, and the eager smile died from her face.

"Where is he? where is he?"

"All is lost," replied Belvoir.

She uttered a shriek, and fell fainting to the ground.

Then he raised her in his arms, and strove to comfort her.

"Oh, no! I shall never see him again," she cried.

She raved and sobbed bitterly, and would not listen to him. But he still persisted.

He begged her to be calm; he begged her to be reasonable.

He entreated her to forget her grief, to make up her mind to the loss of her worthless lover.

Then he eagerly urged his own suit, and she heard at first in silent wonder.

Thinking, then, that she was willing, he grew more and more impassioned.

He devoured her lovely form with greedy, lustful gaze.

He took her in his arms and covered her tearful cheeks and rosy lips with burning kisses.

She struggled with all her strength; but she was weak in his strong grasp.

She strove to scream; but he glued his lips to hers, and stifled her cries.

Her efforts grew fainter.

She was well nigh suffocated by his embraces.

She wept and pleaded in vain. Her ruffianly assailant would not be repulsed; and his victim lay fainting at his mercy.

But when she recovered her consciousness, a crowd filled the room.

There, in handcuffs, stood Jack Rawlings, with flashing eyes and pale face.

Belvoir also was there, and in custody.

The police filled the room.

Fanny rose to her feet, and would have knelt to her lover; but he waved her off.

"Oh, Jack! Jack! I am not guilty," she said.

She learned afterwards that he had effected his escape, and arrived at the lodgings, alas! too late to save his sweetheart from her treacherous betrayer.

Neither would he, in spite of Fanny's passionate prayers and protestations, believe in her truth.

And thus they parted; and Jack Rawlings went back to jail.

Both he and Belvoir a fortnight afterwards were on board the convict-hulk at Woolwich.

CHAPTER LXXV.

IN WHICH EVERYBODY DOES SOMETHING EXTRAORDINARY.

OUR old friend, Lord Crokerton, since we saw him last has been growing very much older, although the time which has elapsed has not been very great.

As he grew older, his lordship grew childish; at least so his family said, and his relations, and the public generally.

He had never quite got over that thrashing Miss Fanny had given him at the lonely house in Fulham.

It had completely broken him up, as it seemed.

He took no part now in politics—no pleasure in anything but in the lowest and most shameful profligacy.

His house became notorious for the revolting orgies which were committed in it.

One day when he had arisen from his couch, and just passed out of the hands of his valet, who had been doing his best to botch up the dilapidated old nobleman's carcass, a visitor was announced.

The visitor was a beautiful woman.

The beautiful woman was Miss Fanny White.

She came there to consult him upon a subject of a peculiar nature. She had discovered the secret of Jack Rawlings' birth with the aid of Mother Death, who lay stricken down with paralysis in her vile den, and had sent for Fanny White.

She had learned that Jack Rawlings was the legitimate son of the late Earl of Stonecliffe.

She had come to consult Lord Crokerton, as he was a member of the Stonecliffe family, and to solicit his aid.

My Lord Crokerton, however, would back up no thieves and pickpockets, he said.

Fanny entreated, and my lord laughed.

She tried all her blandishments in vain.

He was eager enough to make love to her, but he would not listen to reason.

Then Fanny White registered a vow.

"I'll marry this old idiot," she said to herself; "and when I am a lady of title I can act for myself."

*   *   *   *   *

Every story must come to an end, and there are many ways of telling a story.

Some day, perhaps, you and I and Miss Fanny may find ourselves again together.

But in this book her story must speedily terminate.

I might fill another hundred pages in describing the wiles she practised upon poor old Crokerton; only I have neither time nor space.

She married him—that is enough.

He settled an enormous sum upon her before they were wed.

It was a very splendid affair. A public marriage—Fanny desired it.

The Bishop of London officiated, and all the newspapers gave a lengthy report of the ceremony.

His lordship looked very little like a bridegroom, though.

He looked more like a galvanized corpse than anything human.

He chatted and mumbled like an antiquated ape.

Fanny was very beautiful, and very loving.

The lady aristocracy turned up their noses at her.

She turned up her pretty little nose at them.

She drove the most beautiful pair of ponies in town.

She had an opera-box, and wore splendid diamonds.

It was said that she had a great many lovers, but I believe this is not the truth.

One day, down at Portsmouth, she saw Jack Rawlings working with the other convicts.

In time Lord Crokerton died, and then all his relations did their best to reduce Fanny to poverty.

They did not, however, succeed, and she still rode in her carriage, and laughed in her sleeve.

All at once she became pious; built a chapel, and patronized a fashionable clergyman—no other than her old flame, the Reverend Hugh Bell.

One day she was passing through the streets on foot, an unusual occurrence, and passed by a Punch-show.

At the sight of her, the dog Toby became wildly excited.

He sprang down, and ran towards her, wagging all the tail he had got, which was, by the way, precious little.

Her ladyship caught him up in her arms, and kissed him passionately.

"Filchit! Filchit! My own poor Filchit!"

The crowd laughed.

Fanny walked off in triumph, carrying her canine friend with her.

The Punch-show man was consoled for his loss by a sovereign.

About this time, Jack Rawlings got his ticket-of-leave, and came back to London.

With the instrumentality of her ladyship, he established his claim to the earldom of Stonecliffe.

Both the lord and the lady were a great scandal to all well-regulated minds.

They seemed to delight only in setting the world at defiance.

They spent money like water, and could afford to do it.

They were a good deal together, but—but they did not marry.

Theirs was a wild and varied life, and before they came to the end they had many ups and downs.

Well, and what else have I, here, to tell you?

That Manningtree, the poisoner, died by his own hand. The manner of his death was this.

When Jack Rawlings had dislodged him from his false position, his mind appeared to have been seriously impaired by the shock.

If he could have managed it, it is probable that Jack would have been counted among his many victims.

But Fanny White played her cards too well.

She was too artful for the wily villain.

He was outwitted by a woman.

How many other strong men have been, I should like to know, since the days of Adam!

Manningtree, at length foiled in his villanies, was obliged to hide his head.

He had lived in great extravagance and luxury since the old earl's death.

His debts were enormous.

Finding that there was no chance of his paying them, his creditors soon became importunate.

They stormed and raved.

They vowed vengeance of all kinds against him.

He was compelled to fly.

He disappeared quite suddenly from the scene, and many supposed that he had put an end to his existence.

But such was not the case.

He appeared to have no such idea.

On the contrary, wolf-like, he would have waged war against all mankind.

Murder, indeed, seemed to have become a perfect mania with him.

He fled precipitately before his pursuers.

He hid himself in obscurity.

He found a quiet lodging in a lonely suburb, where he thought he was not likely to be discovered.

Unfortunately for him, though, the place he had chosen was one where a stranger was a novelty, and, as he was of somewhat remarkable appearance, he soon became a celebrity.

People rushed to the windows to see him pass.

Little boys mobbed him in the street.

The gossips of the neighbourhood, who had little enough to talk about, were glad of a new subject.

"Oh, Mrs. Smith!"

"Oh, Mrs. Jones!"

"Have you seen him?"

"Seen who?"

"The strange gentleman."

"At No. 9?"

"Certainly."

"At Mrs. Stubbins's?"

"Exactly."

"Curious person, ain't he?"

"Very strange."

"Eccentric, I call it."

"Not far out, ma'am, perhaps, if we said mad."

"Well now, ma'am, I shouldn't at all wonder."

He said nothing, though, to his neighbours, the object of these remarks.

His landlady scarcely knew the sound of his remarks.

He was not very regular in his comings-in and goings-out.

Sometimes he would stay away from home for two or three days at a time.

Sometimes he would remain in the house for nearly a week without once crossing the threshold.

He was a good deal employed with chemical experiments. This the landlady did not approve of, as it burnt holes in the carpet.

It got about, after a time, that he was trying to find the philosopher's stone.

Then another rumour was started.

He was in league with evil spirits.

He had sold himself.

Sold himself to the devil.

This last had been ascertained to a dead certainty.

If they had only left him alone, though, he would have much cared what they said.

But that much they could not do.

They began to peep at him through the keyhole.

They caught him physicking the cat.

He had warning.

He left these lodgings, and took others more suited to his peculiarities, which here could pass unnoticed.

Then he plotted and planned without molestation.

He wanted all the money that remained to him in law.

He lost every action he engaged in.

At length he found himself, by the last fatal decision, a beggar.

People spoke in after times of the tall man, so ghastly in his pallor, who fixed his great eyes upon theirs with a wild, vacant stare.

He passed from the court into the street.

Through both he glided like a shadow.

People shrunk back as he approached.

No one knew him, but they dreaded the cold glare of his hollow eyes.

Sometimes he stared at them boldly.

Sometimes he shrank and cowered.

He walked rapidly.

He traversed the swarming city.

He took no heed of the noise and bustle.

He glared about him like a wild beast.

The mixture of bloodshot and glitter in his eyes was truly terrible.

On, on he went.

Gliding like a black spectre amid the plunging of horses and hoarse shouts of drivers.

A score of times the cry arose of "a man run over."

There were rushes to the spot.

But no.

He had escaped.

Thus he threaded the city.

He reached Whitechapel.

Thus he threaded labyrinths of crooked, noisome alleys.

On, on.

Whither was he bound?

He reached his home at last, in the neighbourhood of Bow.

He lived in a dark and gloomy house, into which he let himself with a key he carried.

The afternoon was calm and bright.

The wretched man looked out upon it.

There were singing birds.

The sun lay hot upon the green grass.

The sky was clear, deep blue.

Manningtree glared grimly at it through the dusky glass.

He appeared this afternoon paralysed and smitten down.

His lips quivered, and he muttered to himself.

A horrible change had come over his face during the last few hours.

The look of intelligence seemed to be deserting it.

The facial angles were weakened curiously.

The eyes were growing glassy.

The light in them was dim.

He was turning idiotic.

He stood there motionless, watching the sun; and till it sank and the night set in.

The darkness came silently around him.

After he had remained for a time in the gloom, he lit his candle, and went into a room which he had had fitted up as a laboratory.

Here were scores of bottles.

All kinds of curiously-shaped vessels—a variety of strange things.

He began his work.

He lit his fire.

He began his experiments.

For many hours, with glaring eyes, and hands which shook convulsively, he worked on.

A subtle vapour rose from the fire.

A stifling vapour, which made the light flicker and burn low.

He worked on.

But presently he placed his hand upon his brow.

He groaned.

He reeled.

His eyes filled with water.

His sight waned.

The vapour grew thicker.

Suddenly he gasped for breath and staggered.

Then he appeared to rally for a moment.

Pressing his hands before his eyes, he dashed from them the water which welled over their bloodshot orbs.

The vapour arose hot and choking.

He stooped over the fire.

He reeled, and tried to save himself.

The poison he had been manufacturing had done its work upon him.

He fell forward.

He clutched at air.

Next moment he had upset his furnace, and the live coals rolled about the room.

His garments were in a blaze; but he had not strength enough to extinguish the flames or call for help.

Fire! fire! fire!

The sky is blood-red.

Mobs ran pell-mell.

Fire! fire! fire!

The lurid reflection quivers in the firmament.

Fire! fire! fire!

There is a vast tramping of feet.

There is the galloping of horses.

The shouting of men.

Fire! fire! fire!

Columns of red-hot sparks.

Black smoke tinged by the flame.

The roar of the blaze is answered.

The shouts of the spectators.

The engines arrive.

But too late.

Red flame burst from the windows.

Tongues of fire flicker out from chimney-pots.

The house is a glaring furnace.

Then a fearful crash.

Then a roaring blaze.

Then an upward gust of sparks.

The roof has fallen in.

The poisoner's blackened corpse is burned in the ruins.

＊　　　＊　　　＊　　　＊　　　＊

And now what else have I to tell you?

That Laura and Phil were happily united.

That Belvoir never returned from transportation.

That all the good people were rewarded, and the wicked punished?

What else?

What is the good of my saying so-and-so, when you know as well as I do that it is all a pack of lies that I have been telling you from the very first.

But not very dull lies, I trust.

If I have amused you with my little story, that is all I can wish for.

I am not quite sure that Fanny ought not to have had a good whipping for her naughtiness.

But then she had her good qualities, you know, and she was very pretty.

I have the honour of wishing you, ladies and gentlemen, a very good day. Please to receive my best thanks for your kind attention.

I am very much obliged to you.

THE END.